# Across the Nightingale Floor

# Across the Nightingale Floor

## Lian Hearn

**Tales of the Otori • Book 1**

LARGE PRINT

This large print edition published in 2004 by
RB Large Print
A division of Recorded Books
A Haights Cross Communications Company
270 Skipjack Road
Prince Frederick, MD 20678

Published by arrangement with Penguin Books, Ltd.

The author gratefully acknowledges permission to quote from: *From the
Country of Eight Islands* by Hiroaki Sato, translated by Burton Watson.
Used by permission of Columbia University Press.

Publisher's Cataloging In Publication Data
(Prepared by Donohue Group, Inc.)

Hearn, Lian.
    Across the nightingale floor : tales of the Otori book 1 / Lian Hearn.

    p. (large print) ; cm.

ISBN: 1-4025-7642-0

1. Teenage boys—Fiction. 2. Orphans—Fiction. 3. Large type books.
4. Japan—Fiction. 5. Historical fiction. 6. Adventure fiction.
I. Title. II. Series: Hearn, Lian. Tales of the Otori ; bk. 1.

PR9619.3.H3725 A65 2004
823/.914
                Printed in the United States of America

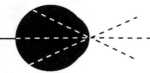

**This Large Print Book carries the
Seal of Approval of N.A.V.H.**

*To E.*

# AUTHOR'S NOTE

The three books that make up the *Tales of the Otori* are set in an imaginary country in a feudal period. Neither the setting nor the period is intended to correspond to any true historical era, though echoes of many Japanese customs and traditions will be found, and the landscape and seasons are those of Japan. Nightingale floors (*uguisubari*) are real inventions and were constructed around many residences and temples; the most famous examples can be seen in Kyoto at Nijo Castle and Chion'In. I have used Japanese names for places, but these have little connection with real places, apart from Hagi and Matsue, which are more or less in their true geographical positions. As for characters, they are all invented, apart from the artist Sesshu, who seemed impossible to replicate.

I hope I will be forgiven by purists for the liberties I have taken. My only excuse is that this is a work of the imagination.

The deer that weds

The autumn bush clover

They say

Sires a single fawn

And this fawn of mine

This lone boy

Sets off on a journey

Grass for his pillow

MANYOSHU VOL. 9,
NO. 1,790

# CHAPTER 1

My mother used to threaten to tear me into eight pieces if I knocked over the water bucket, or pretended not to hear her calling me to come home as the dusk thickened and the cicadas' shrilling increased. I would hear her voice, rough and fierce, echoing through the lonely valley. "Where's that wretched boy? I'll tear him apart when he gets back."

But when I did get back, muddy from sliding down the hillside, bruised from fighting, once bleeding great spouts of blood from a stone wound to the head (I still have the scar, like a silvered thumbnail), there would be the fire, and the smell of soup, and my mother's arms not tearing me apart but trying to hold me, clean my face, or straighten my hair, while I twisted like a lizard to get away from her. She was strong from endless hard work, and not old: She'd given birth to me before she was seventeen, and when she held me I could see we had the same skin, although in other ways we were not much alike, she having broad, placid features, while mine, I'd been told (for we had no mirrors in the remote mountain

1

village of Mino), were finer, like a hawk's. The wrestling usually ended with her winning, her prize being the hug I could not escape from. And her voice would whisper in my ears the words of blessing of the Hidden, while my stepfather grumbled mildly that she spoiled me, and the little girls, my half-sisters, jumped around us for their share of the hug and the blessing.

So I thought it was a manner of speaking. Mino was a peaceful place, too isolated to be touched by the savage battles of the clans. I had never imagined men and women could actually be torn into eight pieces, their strong, honey-colored limbs wrenched from their sockets and thrown down to the waiting dogs. Raised among the Hidden, with all their gentleness, I did not know men did such things to each other.

I turned fifteen and my mother began to lose our wrestling matches. I grew six inches in a year, and by the time I was sixteen I was taller than my stepfather. He grumbled more often, that I should settle down, stop roaming the mountain like a wild monkey, marry into one of the village families. I did not mind the idea of marriage to one of the girls I'd grown up with, and that summer I worked harder alongside him, ready to take my place among the men of the village. But every now and then I could not resist the lure of the mountain, and at the end of the day I slipped away, through the bamboo grove with its tall, smooth trunks and green slanting light, up the rocky path past the shrine of the mountain god, where the villagers left offerings of millet and oranges, into the forest of birch and cedar, where the cuckoo and the nightingale called enticingly, where I watched foxes and deer and heard the melancholy cry of kites overhead.

That evening I'd been right over the mountain to a place where the best mushrooms grew. I had a cloth full of them, the little white ones like threads, and the dark orange ones like fans. I was thinking how pleased my mother would be, and how the mushrooms would still my stepfather's scolding. I could already taste them on my tongue. As I ran through the bamboo and out into the rice fields where the red autumn lilies were already in flower, I thought I could smell cooking on the wind.

The village dogs were barking, as they often did at the end of the day. The smell grew stronger and turned acrid. I was not frightened, not then, but some premonition made my heart start to beat more quickly. There was a fire ahead of me.

Fires often broke out in the village: Almost everything we owned was made of wood or straw. But I could hear no shouting, no sounds of the buckets being passed from hand to hand, none of the usual cries and curses. The cicadas shrilled as loudly as ever; frogs were calling from the paddies. In the distance thunder echoed round the mountains. The air was heavy and humid.

I was sweating, but the sweat was turning cold

3

on my forehead. I jumped across the ditch of the last terraced field and looked down to where my home had always been. The house was gone.

I went closer. Flames still crept and licked at the blackened beams. There was no sign of my mother or my sisters. I tried to call out, but my tongue had suddenly become too big for my mouth, and the smoke was choking me and making my eyes stream. The whole village was on fire, but where was everyone?

Then the screaming began.

It came from the direction of the shrine, around which most of the houses clustered. It was like the sound of a dog howling in pain, except the dog could speak human words, scream them in agony. I thought I recognized the prayers of the Hidden, and all the hair stood up on my neck and arms. Slipping like a ghost between the burning houses, I went towards the sound.

The village was deserted. I could not imagine where everyone had gone. I told myself they had run away: My mother had taken my sisters to the safety of the forest. I would go and find them just as soon as I had found out who was screaming. But as I stepped out of the alley into the main street I saw two men lying on the ground. A soft evening rain was beginning to fall and they looked surprised, as though they had no idea why they were lying there in the rain. They would never get up again, and it did not matter that their clothes were getting wet.

One of them was my stepfather.

At that moment the world changed for me. A kind of fog rose before my eyes, and when it cleared nothing seemed real. I felt I had crossed over to the other world, the one that lies alongside our own, that we visit in dreams. My stepfather was wearing his best clothes. The indigo cloth was dark with rain and blood. I was sorry they were spoiled: He had been so proud of them.

I stepped past the bodies, through the gates and into the shrine. The rain was cool on my face. The screaming stopped abruptly.

Inside the grounds were men I did not know. They looked as if they were carrying out some ritual for a festival. They had cloths tied round their heads; they had taken off their jackets and their arms gleamed with sweat and rain. They were panting and grunting, grinning with white teeth, as though killing were as hard work as bringing in the rice harvest.

Water trickled from the cistern where you washed your hands and mouth to purify yourself on entering the shrine. Earlier, when the world was normal, someone must have lit incense in the great cauldron. The last of it drifted across the courtyard, masking the bitter smell of blood and death.

The man who had been torn apart lay on the wet stones. I could just make out the features on the severed head. It was Isao, the leader of the Hidden. His mouth was still open, frozen in a last contortion of pain.

The murderers had left their jackets in a neat pile against a pillar. I could see clearly the crest of the triple oak leaf. These were Tohan men, from the clan capital of Inuyama. I remembered a traveler who had passed through the village at the end of the seventh month. He'd stayed the night at our house, and when my mother had prayed before the meal, he had tried to silence her. "Don't you know that the Tohan hate the Hidden and plan to move against us? Lord Iida has vowed to wipe us out," he whispered. My parents had gone to Isao the next day to tell him, but no one had believed them. We were far from the capital, and the power struggles of the clans had never concerned us. In our village the Hidden lived alongside everyone else, looking the same, acting the same, except for our prayers. Why would anyone want to harm us? It seemed unthinkable.

And so it still seemed to me as I stood frozen by the cistern. The water trickled and trickled, and I wanted to take some and wipe the blood from Isao's face and gently close his mouth, but I could not move. I knew at any moment the men from the Tohan clan would turn, and their gaze would fall on me, and they would tear me apart. They would have neither pity nor mercy. They were already polluted by death, having killed a man within the shrine itself.

In the distance I could hear with actue clarity the drumming sound of a galloping horse. As the hoofbeats drew nearer I had the sense of forward memory that comes to you in dreams. I knew who I was going to see, framed between the shrine gates. I had never seen him before in my life, but my mother had held him up to us as a sort of ogre with which to frighten us into obedience: *Don't stray on the mountain, don't play by the river, or Iida will get you!* I recognized him at once. Iida Sadamu, lord of the Tohan.

The horse reared and whinnied at the smell of blood. Iida sat as still as if he were cast in iron. He was clad from head to foot in black armor, his helmet crowned with antlers. He wore a short black beard beneath his cruel mouth. His eyes were bright, like a man hunting deer.

Those bright eyes met mine. I knew at once two things about him: first, that he was afraid of nothing in heaven or on earth; second, that he loved to kill for the sake of killing. Now that he had seen me, there was no hope.

His sword was in his hand. The only thing that saved me was the horse's reluctance to pass beneath the gate. It reared again, prancing backwards. Iida shouted. The men already inside the shrine turned and saw me, crying out in their rough Tohan accents. I grabbed the last of the incense, hardly noticing as it seared my hand, and ran out through the gates. As the horse shied towards me I thrust the incense against its flank. It reared over me, its huge feet flailing past my cheeks. I heard the hiss of the sword descending through the air. I was aware of the Tohan all around me. It did not seem possible that they could miss me, but I felt as if I had split in two. I saw Iida's sword fall on me, yet I was untouched by it. I lunged at the horse again. It gave a snort of pain and a savage series of bucks. Iida, unbalanced by the sword thrust that had somehow missed its target, fell forward over its neck and slid heavily to the ground.

Horror gripped me, and in its wake panic. I had unhorsed the lord of the Tohan. There would be no limit to the torture and pain to atone for such an act. I should have thrown myself to the ground and demanded death. But I knew I did not want to die. Something stirred in my blood, telling me I would not die before Iida. I would see him dead first.

I knew nothing of the wars of the clans, nothing of their rigid codes and their feuds. I had spent my whole life among the Hidden, who are forbidden to kill and taught to forgive each other. But at that moment Revenge took me as a pupil. I recognized her at once and learned her lessons instantly. She was what I desired; she would save me from the feeling that I was a living ghost. In that split second I took her into my heart. I kicked out at the man closest to me, getting him between the legs, sank my teeth into a hand that grabbed my wrist, broke away from them, and ran towards the forest.

Three of them came after me. They were bigger than I was and could run faster, but I knew the ground, and darkness was falling. So was the rain, heavier now, making the steep tracks of the mountain slippery and treacherous. Two of the men kept calling out to me, telling me what they would take great pleasure in doing to me, swearing at me in words whose meaning I could only guess, but the third ran silently, and he was the one I was afraid of. The other two might turn back after a while, get back to their maize liquor or whatever foul brew the Tohan got drunk on, and claim to have lost me on the mountain, but this other one would never give up. He would pursue me forever until he had killed me.

As the track steepened near the waterfall the two noisy ones dropped back a bit, but the third quickened his pace as an animal will when it runs uphill. We passed by the shrine; a bird was pecking at the millet and it flew off with a flash of green and white in its wings. The track curved a little round the trunk of a huge cedar, and as I ran with stone legs and sobbing breath past the tree, someone rose out of its shadow and blocked the path in front of me.

I ran straight into him. He grunted as though I had winded him, but he held me immediately. He looked in my face and I saw something flicker in his eyes: surprise, recognition. Whatever it was, it made him grip me more tightly. There was no getting away this time. I heard the Tohan man stop, then the heavy footfalls of the other two coming up behind him.

"Excuse me, sir," said the man I feared, his voice steady. "You have apprehended the criminal we were chasing. Thank you."

The man holding me turned me round to face my pursuers. I wanted to cry out to him, to plead with him, but I knew it was no use. I could feel the soft fabric of his clothes, the smoothness of his hands. He was some sort of lord, no doubt, just like Iida. They were all of the same cut. He would do nothing to help me. I kept silent, thought of the prayers my mother had taught me, thought fleetingly of the bird.

"What has this criminal done?" the lord asked.

The man in front of me had a long face, like a wolf's. "Excuse me," he said again, less politely. "That is no concern of yours. It is purely the business of Iida Sadamu and the Tohan."

"Unnh!" the lord grunted. "Is that so? And who might you be to tell me what is and what is not my concern?"

"Just hand him over!" the wolf man snarled, all politeness gone. As he stepped forward, I knew suddenly that the lord was not going to hand me over. With one neat movement he twisted me behind his back and let go of me. I heard for the second time in my life the hiss of the warrior's sword as it is brought to life. The wolf man drew out a knife. The other two had poles. The lord raised the sword with both hands, sidestepped under one of the poles, lopped off the head of the man holding it, came back at the wolf man, and

10

took off the right arm, still holding the knife.

It happened in a moment, yet took an eternity. It happened in the last of the light, in the rain, but when I close my eyes I can still see every detail.

The headless body fell with a thud and a gush of blood, the head rolling down the slope. The third man dropped his stick and ran backwards, calling for help. The wolf man was on his knees, trying to stanch the blood from the stump at his elbow. He did not groan or speak.

The lord wiped the sword and returned it to its sheath in his belt. "Come on," he said to me.

I stood shaking, unable to move. This man had appeared from nowhere. He had killed in front of my eyes to save my life. I dropped to the ground before him, trying to find the words to thank him.

"Get up," he said. "The rest of them will be after us in a moment."

"I can't leave," I managed to say. "I must find my mother."

"Not now. Now is the time for us to run!" He pulled me to my feet, and began to hurry me up the slope. "What happened down there?"

"They burned the village and killed . . ." The memory of my stepfather came back to me and I could not go on.

"Hidden?"

"Yes," I whispered.

"It's happening all over the fief. Iida is stirring up hatred against them everywhere. I suppose you're one of them?"

"Yes." I was shivering. Although it was still late summer and the rain was warm, I had never felt so cold. "But that wasn't only why they were after me. I caused Lord Iida to fall from his horse."

To my amazement the lord began to snort with laughter. "That would have been worth seeing! But it places you doubly in danger. It's an insult he'll have to wipe out. Still, you are under my protection now. I won't let Iida take you from me."

"You saved my life," I said. "It belongs to you from this day on."

For some reason that made him laugh again. "We have a long walk, on empty stomachs and with wet garments. We must be over the range before daybreak, when they will come after us." He strode off at great speed, and I ran after him, willing my legs not to shake, my teeth not to chatter. I didn't even know his name, but I wanted him to be proud of me, never to regret that he had saved my life.

"I am Otori Shigeru," he said as we began the climb to the pass. "Of the Otori clan, from Hagi. But while I'm on the road I don't use that name, so don't you use it either."

Hagi was as distant as the moon to me, and although I had heard of the Otori, I knew nothing about them except that they had been defeated by the Tohan at a great battle ten years earlier on the plain of Yaegahara.

"What's your name, boy?"

"Tomasu."

"That's a common name among the Hidden. Better get rid of it." He said nothing for a while, and then spoke briefly out of the darkness. "You can be called Takeo."

And so between the waterfall and the top of the mountain I lost my name, became someone new, and joined my destiny with the Otori.

Dawn found us, cold and hungry, in the village of Hinode, famous for its hot springs. I was already farther from my own house than I had ever been in my life. All I knew of Hinode was what the boys in my village said: that the men were cheats and the women were as hot as the springs and would lie down with you for the price of a cup of wine. I didn't have the chance to find out if either was true. No one dared to cheat Lord Otori, and the only woman I saw was the innkeeper's wife who served our meals.

I was ashamed of how I looked, in the old clothes my mother had patched so often it was impossible to tell what color they'd been to start with, filthy, bloodstained. I couldn't believe that the lord expected me to sleep in the inn with him. I thought I would stay in the stables. But he seemed not to want to let me too often out of his sight. He told the woman to wash my clothes and sent me to the hot spring to scrub myself. When I came back, almost asleep from the effect of the hot water after the sleepless night, the morning meal was laid out in the room, and he was already eating. He gestured to me to join him. I knelt on the floor and said the prayers we always used before the first meal of the day.

"You can't do that," Lord Otori said through a mouthful of rice and pickles. "Not even alone. If you want to live, you have to forget that part of your life. It is over forever." He swallowed and took another mouthful. "There are better things to die for."

I suppose a true believer would have insisted on the prayers anyway. I wondered if that was what the dead men of my village would have done. I remembered the way their eyes had looked blank and surprised at the same time. I stopped praying. My appetite left me.

"Eat," the lord said, not unkindly. "I don't want to carry you all the way to Hagi."

I forced myself to eat a little so he would not despise me. Then he sent me to tell the woman to spread out the beds. I felt uncomfortable giving orders to her, not only because I thought she would laugh at me and ask me if I'd lost the use of my hands, but also because something was happening to my voice. I could feel it draining away from me, as though words were too weak to frame what my eyes had seen. Anyway, once she'd grasped what I meant, she bowed almost as low as she had to Lord Otori and bustled along to obey.

Lord Otori lay down and closed his eyes. He seemed to fall asleep immediately.

I thought I, too, would sleep at once, but my mind kept jumping around, shocked and exhausted. My burned hand was throbbing and I could hear everything around me with an unusual and slightly alarming clarity—every word that was spoken in the kitchens, every sound from the town. Over and over my thoughts kept returning to my mother and the little girls. I told myself I had not actually seen them dead. They had probably run away; they would be safe. Everyone liked my mother in our village. She would not have chosen death. Although she had been born into the Hidden, she was not a fanatic. She lit incense in the shrine and took offerings to the god of the mountain. Surely my mother, with her broad face, her rough hands, and her honey-colored skin, was not dead, was not lying somewhere under the sky, her sharp eyes empty and surprised, her daughters next to her!

My own eyes were not empty: They were shamefully full of tears. I buried my face in the mattress and tried to will the tears away. I could not keep my shoulders from shaking or my breath from coming in rough sobs. After a few moments I felt a hand on my shoulder and Lord Otori said quietly, "Death comes suddenly and life is fragile and brief. No one can alter this, either by prayers or spells. Children cry about it, but men and women do not cry. They have to endure."

His own voice broke on this last word. Lord Otori was as grief-stricken as I was. His face was

15

clenched but the tears still trickled from his eyes. I knew who I wept for, but I did not dare question him.

I must have fallen asleep, for I was dreaming I was at home, eating supper out of a bowl as familiar to me as my own hands. There was a black crab in the soup, and it jumped out of the bowl and ran away into the forest. I ran after it, and after a while I didn't know where I was. I tried to cry out "I'm lost!" but the crab had taken away my voice.

I woke to find Lord Otori shaking me.

"Get up!"

I could hear that it had stopped raining. The light told me it was the middle of the day. The room seemed close and sticky, the air heavy and still. The straw matting smelled slightly sour.

"I don't want Iida coming after me with a hundred warriors just because a boy made him fall off his horse," Lord Otori grumbled good-naturedly. "We must move on quickly."

I didn't say anything. My clothes, washed and dried, lay on the floor. I put them on silently.

"Though how you dared stand up to Sadamu when you're too scared to say a word to me . . ."

I wasn't exactly scared of him—more like in complete awe. It was as if one of God's angels, or one of the spirits of the forest, or a hero from the old days, had suddenly appeared in front of me and taken me under his protection. I could hardly have told you then what he looked like, for I did

16

not dare look at him directly. When I did sneak a glance at him, his face in repose was calm—not exactly stern, but expressionless. I did not then know the way it was transformed by his smile. He was perhaps thirty years old, or a little younger, well above medium height, broad-shouldered. His hands were light-skinned, almost white, well formed, and with long, restless fingers that seemed made to shape themselves around the sword's handle.

They did that now, lifting the sword from where it lay on the matting. The sight of it sent a shudder through me. I imagined it had known the intimate flesh, the lifeblood, of many men—had heard their last cries. It terrified and fascinated me.

"Jato," Lord Otori said, noticing my gaze. He laughed and patted the shabby black sheath. "In traveling clothes, like me. At home we both dress more elegantly!"

*Jato*, I repeated under my breath. The snake sword, which had saved my life by taking life.

We left the inn and resumed our journey past the sulfur-smelling hot springs of Hinode and up another mountain. The rice paddies gave way to bamboo groves, just like the ones around my village; then came chestnuts, maples, and cedars. The forest steamed from the warmth of the sun, although it was so dense that little sunlight penetrated to us below. Twice, snakes slithered out of our path, one the little black adder and another, larger one the color of tea. It seemed to roll like

17

a hoop, and it leaped into the undergrowth as though it knew Jato might lop off its head. Cicadas sang stridently, and the min-min moaned with head-splitting monotony.

We went at a brisk pace despite the heat. Sometimes Lord Otori would outstride me and I would toil up the track as if utterly alone, hearing only his footsteps ahead, and then come upon him at the top of the pass, gazing out over the view of mountains, and beyond them more mountains stretching away, and everywhere the impenetrable forest.

He seemed to know his way through this wild country. We walked for long days and slept only a few hours at night, sometimes in a solitary farmhouse, sometimes in a deserted mountain hut. Apart from the places we stopped at, we met few people on this lonely road: a woodcutter, two girls collecting mushrooms who ran away at the sight of us, a monk on a journey to a distant temple. After a few days we crossed the spine of the country. We still had steep hills to climb, but we descended more frequently. The sea became visible, a distant glint at first, then a broad silky expanse with islands jutting up like drowned mountains. I had never seen it before, and I couldn't stop looking at it. Sometimes it seemed like a high wall about to topple across the land.

My hand healed slowly, leaving a silver scar across my right palm.

The villages became larger, until we finally

stopped for the night in what could only be called a town. It was on the high road between Inuyama and the coast and had many inns and eating places. We were still in Tohan territory, and the triple oak leaf was everywhere, making me afraid to go out in the streets, yet I felt the people at the inn recognized Lord Otori in some way. The usual respect people paid to him was tinged by something deeper, some old loyalty that had to be kept hidden. They treated me with affection, even though I did not speak to them. I had not spoken for days, not even to Lord Otori. It did not seem to bother him much. He was a silent man himself, wrapped up in his own thoughts, but every now and then I would sneak a look at him and find him studying me with an expression on his face that might have been pity. He would seem to be about to speak, then he'd grunt and mutter, "Never mind, never mind, things can't be helped."

The servants were full of gossip, and I liked listening to them. They were deeply interested in a woman who had arrived the night before and was staying another night. She was traveling alone to Inuyama, apparently to meet Lord Iida himself, with servants, naturally, but no husband or brother or father. She was very beautiful though quite old, thirty at least, very nice, kind, and polite to everyone but—traveling alone! What a mystery! The cook claimed to know that she was recently widowed and was going to join her son in the capital, but the chief maid said that was nonsense, the woman had never had children, never been married, and then the horse boy, who was stuffing his face with his supper, said he had heard from the palanquin bearers that she had had two children, a boy who died and a girl who was a hostage in Inuyama.

The maids sighed and murmured that even wealth and high birth could not protect you from fate, and the horse boy said, "At least the girl lives, for they are Maruyama, and they inherit through the female line."

This news brought a stir of surprise and understanding and renewed curiosity about Lady Maruyama, who held her land in her own right, the only domain to be handed down to daughters, not to sons.

"No wonder she dares to travel alone," the cook said.

Carried away by his success, the horse boy went on, "But Lord Iida finds this offensive. He seeks to take over her territory, either by force or, they say, by marriage."

The cook gave him a clip round the ear. "Watch your words! You never know who's listening!"

"We were Otori once, and will be again," the boy muttered.

The chief maid saw me hanging about in the doorway and beckoned to me to come in. "Where are you traveling to? You must have come a long way!"

I smiled and shook my head. One of the maids,

passing on her way to the guest rooms, patted me on the arm and said, "He doesn't talk. Shame, isn't it?"

"What happened?" the cook said. "Someone throw dust in your mouth like the Ainu dog?"

They were teasing me, not unkindly, when the maid came back, followed by a man I gathered was one of the Maruyama servants, wearing on his jacket the crest of the mountain enclosed in a circle. To my surprise he addressed me in polite language. "My lady wishes to talk to you."

I wasn't sure if I should go with him, but he had the face of an honest man, and I was curious to see the mysterious woman for myself. I followed him along the passageway and through the court-yard. He stepped onto the veranda and knelt at the door to the room. He spoke briefly, then turned to me and beckoned to me to step up.

I snatched a rapid glance at her and then fell to my knees and bowed my head to the floor. I was sure I was in the presence of a princess. Her hair reached the ground in one long sweep of black silkiness. Her skin was as pale as snow. She wore robes of deepening shades of cream, ivory, and dove gray embroidered with red and pink peonies. She had a stillness about her that made me think first of the deep pools of the mountain and then, suddenly, of the tempered steel of Jato, the snake sword.

"They tell me you don't talk," she said, her voice as quiet and clear as water.

I felt the compassion of her gaze, and the blood rushed to my face.

"You can talk to me," she went on. Reaching forward, she took my hand and with her finger drew the sign of the Hidden on my palm. It sent a shock through me, like the sting of a nettle. I could not help pulling my hand away.

"Tell me what you saw," she said, her voice no less gentle but insistent. When I didn't reply she whispered, "It was Iida Sadamu, wasn't it?"

I looked at her almost involuntarily. She was smiling, but without mirth.

"And you are from the Hidden," she added.

Lord Otori had warned me against giving myself away. I thought I had buried my old self, along with my name, Tomasu. But in front of this woman I was helpless. I was about to nod my head, when I heard Lord Otori's footsteps cross the courtyard. I realized that I recognized him by his tread, and I knew that a woman followed him, as well as the man who had spoken to me. And then I realized that if I paid attention, I could hear everything in the inn around me. I heard the horse boy get up and leave the kitchen. I heard the gossip of the maids, and knew each one from her voice. This acuteness of hearing, which had been growing slowly ever since I'd ceased to speak, now came over me with a flood of sound. It was almost unbearable, as if I had the worst of fevers. I wondered if the woman in front of me was a sorceress who had bewitched me. I did not dare lie to her, but I could not speak.

I was saved by the woman coming into the room. She knelt before Lady Maruyama and said quietly, "His lordship is looking for the boy."

"Ask him to come in," the lady replied. "And, Sachie, would you kindly bring the tea utensils?"

Lord Otori stepped into the room, and he and Lady Maruyama exchanged deep bows of respect. They spoke politely to each other like strangers, and she did not use his name, yet I had the feeling they knew each other well. There was a tension between them that I would understand later, but which then only made me more ill at ease.

"The maids told me about the boy who travels with you," she said. "I wished to see him for myself."

"Yes, I am taking him to Hagi. He is the only survivor of a massacre. I did not want to leave him to Sadamu." He did not seem inclined to say anything else, but after a while he added, "I have given him the name of Takeo."

She smiled at this—a real smile. "I'm glad," she said. "He has a certain look about him."

"Do you think so? I thought it too."

Sachie came back with a tray, a teakettle, and a bowl. I could see them clearly as she placed them on the matting, at the same level as my eyes. The bowl's glaze held the green of the forest, the blue of the sky.

"One day you will come to Maruyama to my grandmother's tea-house," the lady said. "There we can do the ceremony as it should be performed. But for now we will have to make do as best we can."

She poured the hot water, and a bittersweet smell wafted up from the bowl. "Sit up, Takeo," she said.

She was whisking the tea into a green foam. She passed the bowl to Lord Otori. He took it in both hands, turned it three times, drank from it, wiped the lip with his thumb, and handed it with a bow back to her. She filled it again and passed it to me. I carefully did everything the lord had done, lifted it to my lips, and drank the frothy liquid. Its taste was bitter, but it was clearing to the head. It steadied me a little. We never had anything like this in Mino: Our tea was made from twigs and mountain herbs.

I wiped the place I had drunk from and handed the bowl back to Lady Maruyama, bowing clumsily. I was afraid Lord Otori would notice and be ashamed of me, but when I glanced at him his eyes were fixed on the lady.

She then drank herself. The three of us sat in silence. There was a feeling in the room of something sacred, as though we had just taken part in the ritual meal of the Hidden. A wave of longing swept over me for my home, my family, my old life, but although my eyes grew hot, I did not allow myself to weep. I would learn to endure.

On my palm I could still feel the trace of Lady Maruyama's fingers.

★   ★   ★

The inn was far larger and more luxurious than any of the other places we had stayed during our swift journey through the mountains, and the food we ate that night was unlike anything I had ever tasted. We had eel in a spicy sauce, and sweet fish from the local streams, many servings of rice, whiter than anything in Mino, where if we ate rice three times a year we were lucky. I drank rice wine for the first time. Lord Otori was in high spirits— "floating," as my mother used to say—his silence and grief dispelled, and the wine worked its cheerful magic on me too.

When we had finished eating he told me to go to bed: He was going to walk outside a while to clear his head. The maids came and prepared the room. I lay down and listened to the sounds of the night. The eel, or the wine, had made me restless and I could hear too much. Every distant noise made me start awake. I could hear the dogs of the town bark from time to time, one starting, the others joining in. After a while I felt I could recognize each one's distinctive voice. I thought about dogs, how they sleep with their ears twitching and how only some noises disturb them. I would have to learn to be like them or I would never sleep again.

When I heard the temple bells toll at midnight, I got up and went to the privy. The sound of my own piss was like a waterfall. I poured water over my hands from the cistern in the courtyard and stood for a moment, listening.

It was a still, mild night, coming up to the full moon of the eighth month. The inn was silent: Everyone was in bed and asleep. Frogs were croaking from the river and the rice fields, and once or twice I heard an owl hoot. As I stepped quietly onto the veranda I heard Lord Otori's voice. For a moment I thought he must have returned to the room and was speaking to me, but a woman's voice answered him. It was Lady Maruyama.

I knew I should not listen. It was a whispered conversation that no one could hear but me. I went into the room, slid the door shut, and lay down on the mattress, willing myself to fall asleep. But my ears had a longing for sound that I could not deny, and every word dropped clearly into them.

They spoke of their love for each other, their few meetings, their plans for the future. Much of what they said was guarded and brief, and much of it I did not understand then. I learned that Lady Maruyama was on her way to the capital to see her daughter, and that she feared Iida would again insist on marriage. His own wife was unwell and not expected to live. The only son she had borne him, also sickly, was a disappointment to him.

"You will marry no one but me," he whispered, and she replied, "It is my only desire. You know it." He then swore to her he would never take a wife, nor lie with any woman, unless it were she,

26

and he spoke of some strategy he had, but did not spell it out. I heard my own name and conceived that it involved me in some way. I realized there was a long-existing enmity between him and Iida that went all the way back to the battle of Yaegahara.

"We will die on the same day," he said. "I cannot live in a world that does not include you."

Then the whispering turned to other sounds, those of passion between a man and a woman. I put my fingers in my ears. I knew about desire, had satisfied my own with the other boys of my village, or with girls in the brothel, but I knew nothing of love. Whatever I heard, I vowed to myself I would never speak of it. I would keep these secrets as close as the Hidden keep theirs. I was thankful I had no voice.

I did not see the lady again. We left early the next morning, an hour or so after sunrise. It was already warm; monks were sprinkling water in the temple cloisters and the air smelled of dust. The maids at the inn had brought us tea, rice, and soup before we left, one of them stifling a yawn as she set the dishes before me, and then apologizing to me and laughing. It was the girl who had patted me on the arm the day before, and when we left she came out to cry, "Good luck, little lord! Good journey! Don't forget us here!"

I wished I was staying another night. The lord laughed at it, teasing me and saying he would have to protect me from the girls in Hagi. He could hardly have slept the previous night, yet his high spirits were still evident. He strode along the highway with more energy than usual. I thought we would take the post road to Yamagata, but instead we went through the town, following a river smaller than the wide one that flowed alongside the main road. We crossed it where it ran fast and narrow between boulders, and headed once more up the side of a mountain.

We had brought food with us from the inn for the day's walk, for once we were beyond the small villages along the river, we saw no one. It was a narrow, lonely path, and a steep climb. When we reached the top we stopped and ate. It was late afternoon, and the sun sent slanting shadows across the plain below us. Beyond it, towards the East, lay range after range of mountains turning indigo and steel-gray.

"That is where the capital is," Lord Otori said, following my gaze.

I thought he meant Inuyama, and I was puzzled.

He saw it and went on, "No, the real capital, of the whole country—where the Emperor lives. Way beyond the farthest mountain range. Inuyama lies to the southeast." He pointed back in the direction we had come. "It's because we are so far from the capital, and the Emperor is so weak, that war lords like Iida can do as they please." His mood was turning somber again. "And below us is the scene of the Otori's worst defeat, where my father was killed. That is Yaegahara. The Otori were betrayed by the Noguchi, who changed sides and joined Iida. More than ten thousand died." He looked at me and said, "I know what it is like to see those closest to you slaughtered. I was not much older than you are now."

I stared out at the empty plain. I could not imagine what a battle was like. I thought of the blood of ten thousand men soaking into the earth of Yaegahara. In the moist haze the sun was turning red, as if it had drawn up the blood from the land. Kites wheeled below us, calling mournfully.

"I did not want to go to Yamagata," Lord Otori said as we began to descend the path. "Partly because I am too well known there, and for other reasons. One day I will tell them to you. But it means we will have to sleep outside tonight, grass for our pillow, for there is no town near enough to stay in. We will cross the fief border by a secret route I know, and then we will be in Otori territory, safely out of reach of Sadamu."

I did not want to spend the night on the lonely plain. I was afraid of ten thousand ghosts, and of the ogres and goblins that dwelled in the forest around it. The murmur of a stream sounded to me like the voice of the water spirit, and every time a fox barked or an owl hooted I came awake, my pulse racing. At one stage the earth itself shook, in a slight tremor, making the trees rustle and dislodging stones somewhere in the distance. I thought I could hear the voices of the dead, calling for revenge, and I tried to pray, but all I

29

could feel was a vast emptiness. The secret god, whom the Hidden worship, had been dispersed with my family. Away from them, I had no contact with him.

Next to me Lord Otori slept as peacefully as if he had been in the guest room of the inn. Yet, I knew that, even more than I was, he would have been aware of the demands of the dead. I thought with trepidation about the world I was entering— a world that I knew nothing about, the world of the clans, with their strict rules and harsh codes. I was entering it on the whim of this lord, whose sword had beheaded a man in front of my eyes, who as good as owned me. I shivered in the damp night air.

We rose before dawn and, as the sky was turning gray, crossed the river that marked the boundary to the Otori domain.

After Yaegahara the Otori, who had formerly ruled the whole of the Middle Country, were pushed back by the Tohan into a narrow strip of land between the last range of mountains and the northern sea. On the main post road the barrier was guarded by Iida's men, but in this wild isolated country there were many places where it was possible to slip across the border, and most of the peasants and farmers still considered themselves Otori and had no love for the Tohan. Lord Otori told me all this as we walked that day, the sea now always on our right-hand side. He also told me about the countryside, pointed out the farming methods used, the dikes built for irrigation, the nets the fishermen wove, the way they extracted salt from the sea. He was interested in everything and knew about everything. Gradually the path became a road and grew busier. Now there were farmers going to market at the next village, carrying yams and greens, eggs and dried mushrooms, lotus root and bamboo. We stopped at the market and bought new straw sandals, for ours were falling to pieces.

That night, when we came to the inn, everyone there knew Lord Otori. They ran out to greet him with exclamations of delight, and flattened themselves to the ground in front of him. The best rooms were prepared, and at the evening meal course after course of delicious food appeared. He seemed to change before my eyes. Of course I had known he was of high birth, of the warrior class, but I still had no idea exactly who he was or what part he played in the hierarchy of the clan. However, it was dawning on me that it must be exalted. I became even more shy in his presence. I felt that everyone was looking at me sideways, wondering what I was doing, longing to send me packing with a cuff on the ear.

The next morning he was wearing clothes befitting his station; horses were waiting for us, and four or five retainers. They grinned at each other a bit when they saw I knew nothing about horses, and they seemed surprised when Lord Otori told one of them to take me on the back of his horse,

31

although of course none of them dared say anything. On the journey they tried to talk to me— they asked me where I'd come from and what my name was—but when they found I was mute, they decided I was stupid, and deaf too. They talked loudly to me in simple words, using sign language.

I didn't care much for jogging along on the back of the horse. The only horse I'd ever been close to was Iida's, and I thought all horses might bear me a grudge for the pain I'd caused that one. And I kept wondering what I would do when we got to Hagi. I imagined I would be some kind of servant, in the garden or the stables. But it turned out Lord Otori had other plans for me.

On the afternoon of the third day since the night we had spent on the edge of Yaegahara, we came to the city of Hagi, the castle town of the Otori. It was built on an island flanked by two rivers and the sea. From a spit of land to the town itself ran the longest stone bridge I had ever seen. It had four arches, through which the ebbing tide raced, and walls of perfectly fitted stone. I thought it must have been made by sorcery, and when the horses stepped onto it I couldn't help closing my eyes. The roar of the river was like thunder in my ears, but beneath it I could hear something else— a kind of low keening that made me shiver.

At the center of the bridge Lord Otori called to me. I slipped from the horse's back and went to where he had halted. A large boulder had been set into the parapet. It was engraved with characters.

"Can you read, Takeo?"

I shook my head.

"Bad luck for you. You will have to learn!" He laughed. "And I think your teacher will make you suffer! You'll be sorry you left your wild life in the mountains."

He read aloud to me: "'The Otori clan welcomes the just and the loyal. Let the unjust and the disloyal beware.'" Beneath the characters was the crest of the heron.

I walked alongside his horse to the end of the bridge. "They buried the stonemason alive beneath the boulder," Lord Otori remarked offhandedly, "so he would never build another bridge to rival this one, and so he could guard his work forever. You can hear his ghost at night talking to the river."

Not only at night. It chilled me, thinking of the sad ghost imprisoned within the beautiful thing he had made, but then we were in the town itself, and the sounds of the living drowned out the dead.

Hagi was the first city I had ever been in, and it seemed vast and overwhelmingly confusing. My head rang with sounds: cries of street sellers, the clack of looms from within the narrow houses, the sharp blows of stonemasons, the snarling bite of saws, and many that I'd never heard before and could not identify. One street was full of potters, and the smell of the clay and the kiln hit my nostrils. I'd never heard a potter's wheel before, or the roar of the furnace. And lying beneath all the other sounds were the chatter, cries, curses, and laughter of human beings, just as beneath the smells lay the ever-present stench of their waste.

Above the houses loomed the castle, built with its back to the sea. For a moment I thought that was where we were heading, and my heart sank, so grim and foreboding did it look, but we turned to the east, following the Nishigawa river to where it joined the Higashigawa. To our left lay an area of winding streets and canals where tiled-roofed walls surrounded many large houses, just visible through the trees.

The sun had disappeared behind dark clouds, and the air smelled of rain. The horses quickened their step, knowing they were nearly home. At the end of the street a wide gate stood open. The guards had come out from the guardhouse next to it and dropped to their knees, heads bowed, as we went past.

Lord Otori's horse lowered its head and rubbed it roughly against me. It whinnied and another horse answered from the stables. I held the bridle, and the lord dismounted. The retainers took the horses and led them away.

He strode through the garden toward the house. I stood for a moment, hesitant, not knowing whether to follow him or go with the men, but he turned and called my name, beckoning to me.

The garden was full of trees and bushes that grew, not like the wild trees of the mountain, dense and pressed together, but each in its own place, sedate and well trained. And yet, every now and then I thought I caught a glimpse of the mountain as if it had been captured and brought here in miniature.

It was full of sound, too—the sound of water flowing over rocks, trickling from pipes. We stopped to wash our hands at the cistern, and the water ran away tinkling like a bell, as though it were enchanted.

The house servants were already waiting on the veranda to greet their master. I was surprised there were so few, but I learned later that Lord Otori lived in great simplicity. There were three young girls, an older woman, and a man of about fifty years. After the bows the girls withdrew and the two old people gazed at me in barely disguised amazement.

"He is so like . . . !" the woman whispered.

"Uncanny!" the man agreed, shaking his head.

Lord Otori was smiling as he stepped out of his sandals and entered the house. "I met him in the dark! I had no idea till the following morning. It's just a passing likeness."

"No, far more than that," the old woman said, leading me inside. "He is the very image." The man followed, gazing at me with lips pressed together as though he had just bitten on a pickled plum—as though he foresaw nothing but trouble would spring from my introduction into the house.

"Anyway, I've called him Takeo," the lord said over his shoulder. "Heat the bath and find clothes for him."

The old man grunted in surprise.

"Takeo!" the woman exclaimed. "But what's your real name?"

When I said nothing, just shrugged and smiled, the man snapped, "He's a half-wit!"

"No, he can talk perfectly well," Lord Otori returned impatiently. "I've heard him talk. But he saw some terrible things that silenced him. When the shock has faded he'll speak again."

"Of course he will," said the old woman, smiling and nodding at me. "You come with Chiyo. I'll look after you."

"Forgive me, Lord Shigeru," the old man said stubbornly—I guessed these two had known the lord since he was a child, and had brought him up—"but what are your plans for the boy? Is he to be found work in the kitchen or the garden? Is he to be apprenticed? Has he any skills?"

"I intend to adopt him," Lord Otori replied. "You can start the procedures tomorrow, Ichiro."

There was a long moment of silence. Ichiro looked stunned, but he could not have been more flabbergasted than I was. Chiyo seemed to be trying not to smile. Then they both spoke together. She murmured an apology and let the old man speak first.

"It's very unexpected," he said huffily. "Did you plan this before you left on your journey?"

"No, it happened by chance. You know my grief after my brother's death and how I've sought relief in travel. I found this boy, and since then somehow every day the grief seems more bearable."

Chiyo clasped her hands together. "Fate sent him to you. As soon as I set eyes on you, I knew you were changed—healed in some way. Of course no one can ever replace Lord Takeshi. . . .."

Takeshi! So Lord Otori had given me a name like that of his dead brother. And he would adopt me into the family. The Hidden speak of being reborn through water. I had been reborn through the sword.

"Lord Shigeru, you are making a terrible mistake," Ichiro said bluntly. "The boy is a nobody, a commoner. . . . What will the clan think? Your uncles will never allow it. Even to make the request is an insult."

"Look at him," Lord Otori said. "Whoever his parents were, someone in his past was not a commoner. Anyway, I rescued him from the Tohan. Iida wanted him killed. Since I saved his life, he belongs to me, and so I must adopt him. To be safe from the Tohan he must have the protection of the clan. I killed a man for him, possibly two."

"A high price. Let's hope it goes no higher," Ichiro snapped. "What had he done to attract Iida's attention?"

"He was in the wrong place at the wrong time, nothing more. There's no need to go into his history. He can be a distant relative of my mother's. Make something up."

"The Tohan have been persecuting the Hidden,"

Ichiro said astutely. "Tell me he's not one of them."

"If he was, he is no longer," Lord Otori replied with a sigh. "All that is in the past. It's no use arguing, Ichiro. I have given my word to protect this boy, and nothing will make me change my mind. Besides, I have grown fond of him."

"No good will come of it," Ichiro said.

The old man and the younger one stared at each other for a moment. Lord Otori made an impatient movement with his hand, and Ichiro lowered his eyes and bowed reluctantly. I thought how useful it would be to be a lord—to know that you would always get your own way in the end.

There was a sudden gust of wind, the shutters creaked, and with the sound the world became unreal for me again. It was as if a voice spoke inside my head: *This is what you are to become.* I wanted desperately to turn back time to the day before I went mushrooming on the mountain—back to my old life with my mother and my people. But I knew my childhood lay behind me, done with, out of reach forever. I had to become a man and endure whatever was sent me.

With these noble thoughts in my mind I followed Chiyo to the bathhouse. She obviously had no idea of the decision I'd come to: She treated me like a child, making me take off my clothes and scrubbing me all over before leaving me to soak in the scalding water. Later, she came back with a light cotton robe and told me to put it on. I did exactly as I was told. What else could I do? She rubbed my hair with a towel, and combed it back, tying it in a top knot.

"We'll get this cut," she muttered, and ran her hand over my face. "You don't have much beard yet. I wonder how old you are? Sixteen?"

I nodded. She shook her head and sighed. "Lord Shigeru wants you to eat with him," she said, and then added quietly, "I hope you will not bring him more grief."

I guessed Ichiro had been sharing his misgivings with her.

I followed her back to the house, trying to take in every aspect of it. It was almost dark by now; lamps in iron stands shed an orange glow in the corners of the rooms, but did not give enough light for me to see much. Chiyo led me to a staircase in the corner of the main living room. I had never seen one before: We had ladders in Mino, but no one had a proper staircase like this. The wood was dark, with a high polish—oak, I thought—and each step made its own tiny sound as I trod on it. Again, it seemed to me to be a work of magic, and I thought I could hear the voice of its creator within it.

The room was empty, the screens overlooking the garden wide open. It was just beginning to rain. Chiyo bowed to me—not very deeply, I noticed—and went back down the staircase. I listened to her footsteps and heard her speak to the maids in the kitchen.

I thought the room was the most beautiful I had ever been in. Since then I've known my share of castles, palaces, nobles' residences, but nothing can compare with the way the upstairs room in Lord Otori's house looked that evening late in the eight-month with the rain falling gently on the garden outside. At the back of the room one huge pole, the trunk of a single cedar, rose from floor to ceiling, polished to reveal the knots and the grain of the wood. The beams were of cedar, too, their soft reddish brown contrasting with the creamy white walls. The matting was already fading to soft gold, the edges joined by broad strips of indigo material with the Otori heron woven into them in white.

A scroll hung in the alcove with a painting of a small bird on it. It looked like the green-and-white-winged flycatcher from my forest. It was so real that I half expected it to fly away. It amazed me that a great painter would have known so well the humble birds of the mountain.

I heard footsteps below and sat down quickly on the floor, my feet tucked neatly beneath me. Through the open windows I could see a great gray and white heron standing in one of the garden pools. Its beak jabbed into the water and came up holding some little wriggling creature. The heron lifted itself elegantly upwards and flew away over the wall.

Lord Otori came into the room, followed by two of the girls carrying trays of food. He looked at me and nodded. I bowed to the floor. It occurred to me that he, Otori Shigeru, was the heron and I was the little wriggling thing he had scooped up, plunging down the mountain into my world and swooping away again.

The rain fell more heavily, and the house and garden began to sing with water. It overflowed from the gutters and ran down the chains and into the stream that leaped from pool to pool, every waterfall making a different sound. The house sang to me, and I fell in love with it. I wanted to belong to it. I would do anything for it, and anything its owner wanted me to do.

When we had finished the meal and the trays had been removed, we sat by the open window as night drew in. In the last of the light, Lord Otori pointed towards the end of the garden. The stream that cascaded through it swept under a low opening in the tiled roof wall into the river beyond. The river gave a deep, constant roar and its gray-green waters filled the opening like a painted screen.

"It's good to come home," he said quietly. "But just as the river is always at the door, so is the world always outside. And it is in the world that we have to live."

# CHAPTER 2

The same year Otori Shigeru rescued the boy who was to become Otori Takeo at Mino, certain events took place in a castle a long way to the south. The castle had been given to Noguchi Masayoshi by Iida Sadamu for his part in the battle of Yaegahara. Iida, having defeated his traditional enemies, the Otori, and forced their surrender on favorable terms to himself, now turned his attention to the third great clan of the Three Countries, the Seishuu, whose domains covered most of the south and west. The Seishuu preferred to make peace through alliances rather than war, and these were sealed with hostages, both from great domains, like the Maruyama, and smaller ones, like their close relatives, the Shirakawa.

Lord Shirakawa's eldest daughter, Kaede, went to Noguchi Castle as a hostage when she had just changed her sash of childhood for a girl's, and she had now lived there for half her life—long enough to think of a thousand things she detested about it. At night, when she was too tired to sleep and did not dare even toss and turn in case one of the

42

older girls reached over and slapped her, she made lists of them inside her head. She had learned early to keep her thoughts to herself. At least no one could reach inside and slap her mind, although she knew more than one of them longed to. Which was why they slapped her so often on her body or face.

She clung with a child's single-mindedness to the faint memories she had of the home she had left when she was seven. She had not seen her mother or her younger sisters since the day her father had escorted her to the castle.

Her father had returned three times since then, only to find she was housed with the servants, not with the Noguchi children, as would have been suitable for the daughter of a warrior family. His humiliation was complete: He was unable even to protest, although she, unnaturally observant even at that age, had seen the shock and fury in his eyes. The first two times they had been allowed to speak in private for a few moments. Her clearest memory was of him holding her by the shoulders and saying in an intense voice, "If only you had been born a boy!" The third time he was permitted only to look at her. After that he had not come again, and she had had no word from her home.

She understood his reasons perfectly. By the time she was twelve, through a mixture of keeping her eyes and ears open and engaging the few people sympathetic to her in seemingly innocent conversation, she knew her own position: She was a hostage, a pawn in the struggles between the clans. Her life was worth nothing to the lords who virtually owned her, except in what she added to their bargaining power. Her father was the lord of the strategically important domain of Shirakawa; her mother was closely related to the Maruyama. Since her father had no sons, he would adopt as his heir whoever Kaede was married to. The Noguchi, by possessing her, also possessed his loyalty, his alliance, and his inheritance.

She no longer even considered the great things—fear, homesickness, loneliness—but the sense that the Noguchi did not even value her as a hostage headed her list of things she hated, as she hated the way the girls teased her for being left-handed and clumsy, the stench of the guards' room by the gate, the steep stairs that were so hard to climb when you were carrying things . . . And she was always carrying things: bowls of cold water, kettles of hot water, food for the always-ravenous men to cram into their mouths, things they had forgotten or were too lazy to fetch for themselves. She hated the castle itself, the massive stones of the foundations, the dark oppressiveness of the upper rooms, where the twisted roof beams seemed to echo her feelings, wanted to break free of the distortion they were trapped in and fly back to the forest they came from.

And the men. How she hated them. The older she grew, the more they harassed her. The maids her age competed for their attentions. They flattered and cosseted the men, putting on childish voices, pretending to be delicate, even simple-minded, to gain the protection of one soldier or another. Kaede did not blame them for it—she had come to believe that all women should use every weapon they had to protect themselves in the battle that life seemed to be—but she would not stoop to that. She could not. Her only value, her only escape from the castle, lay in marriage to someone of her own class. If she threw that chance away, she was as good as dead.

She knew she should not have to endure it. She should go to someone and complain. Of course it was unthinkable to approach Lord Noguchi, but maybe she could ask to speak to the lady. On second thought, even to be allowed access to her seemed unlikely. The truth was, there was no one to turn to. She would have to protect herself. But the men were so strong. She was tall for a girl—too tall, the other girls said maliciously—and not weak—the hard work saw to that—but once or twice a man had grabbed her in play and held her just with one hand, and she had not been able to escape. The memory made her shiver with fear.

And every month it became harder to avoid their attentions. Late in the eighth month of her fifteenth year a typhoon in the West brought days of heavy rain. Kaede hated the rain, the way it made everything smell of mold and dampness, and she hated the way her skimpy robes clung to her when they were wet, showing the curve of her back and thighs, making the men call after her even more.

"Hey, Kaede, little sister!" a guard shouted to her as she ran through the rain from the kitchen, past the second turreted gate. "Don't go so fast! I've got an errand for you! Tell Captain Arai to come down, will you? His lordship wants him to check out a new horse."

The rain was pouring like a river from the crenellations, from the tiles, from the gutters, from the dolphins that topped every roof as a protection against fire. The whole castle spouted water. Within seconds she was soaked, her sandals saturated, making her slip and stumble on the cobbled steps. But she obeyed without too much bitterness; for, of everyone in the castle, Arai was the only person she did not hate. He always spoke nicely to her, he didn't tease or harass her, and she knew his lands lay alongside her father's and he spoke with the same slight accent of the West.

"Hey, Kaede!" The guard leered as she entered the main keep. "You're always running everywhere! Stop and chat!"

When she ignored him and started up the stairs, he shouted after her, "They say you're really a boy! Come here and show me you're not a boy!"

"Fool!" she muttered, her legs aching as she began the second flight of stairs.

The guards on the top floor were playing some kind of gambling game with a knife. Arai got to his feet as soon as he saw her and greeted her by name.

"Lady Shirakawa." He was a big man, with an impressive presence and intelligent eyes. She gave him the message. He thanked her, looking for a moment as though he would say something more to her, but seemed to change his mind. He went hastily down the stairs.

She lingered, gazing out of the windows. The wind from the mountains blew in, raw and damp. The view was almost completely blotted out by clouds, but below her was the Noguchi residence, where, she thought resentfully, she should by rights be living, not running around in the rain at everyone's beck and call.

"If you're going to dawdle, Lady Shirakawa, come and sit down with us," one of the guards said, coming up behind her and patting her on the backside.

"Get your hands off me!" she said angrily.

The men laughed. She feared their mood: They were bored and tense, fed up with the rain, the constant watching and waiting, the lack of action.

"Ah, the captain forgot his knife," one of them said. "Kaede, run down after him."

She took the knife, feeling its weight and balance in her left hand.

"She looks dangerous!" the men joked. "Don't cut yourself, little sister!"

She ran down the stairs, but Arai had already left the keep. She heard his voice in the yard and was about to call to him, but before she could get outside, the man who had spoken to her earlier stepped out of the guardroom. She stopped dead, hiding the knife behind her back. He stood right in front of her, too close, blocking the dim gray light from outside.

"Come on, Kaede, show me you're not a boy!"

He grabbed her by the right hand and pulled her close to him, pushing one leg between hers, forcing her thighs apart. She felt the hard bulge of his sex against her, and with her left hand, almost without thinking, she jabbed the knife into his neck.

He cried out instantly and let go of her, clasping his hands to his neck and staring at her with amazed eyes. He was not badly hurt, but the wound was bleeding freely. She could not believe what she had done. *I am dead*, she thought. As the man began to shout for help, Arai came back through the doorway. He took in the scene at a glance, grabbed the knife from Kaede, and without hesitation slit the guard's throat. The man fell, gurgling, to the ground.

Arai pulled Kaede outside. The rain sluiced over them. He whispered, "He tried to rape you. I came back and killed him. Anything else and we are both dead."

She nodded. He had left his weapon behind, she had stabbed a guard: both unforgivable offences. Arai's swift action had removed the only witness. She thought she would be shocked at the man's death and at her part in it, but she found she was only glad. *So may they all die*, she thought, *the Noguchi, the Tohan, the whole clan.*

48

"I will speak to his lordship on your behalf, Lady Shirakawa," Arai said, making her start with surprise. "He should not leave you unprotected." He added, almost to himself, "A man of honor would not do that."

He gave a great shout up the stairwell for the guards, then said to Kaede, "Don't forget, I saved your life. More than your life!"

She looked at him directly. "Don't forget, it was your knife," she returned.

He gave a wry smile of forced respect. "We are in each other's hands, then."

"What about them?" she said, hearing the thud of steps on the stairs. "They know I left with the knife."

"They will not betray me," he replied. "I can trust them."

"I trust no one," she whispered.

"You must trust me," he said.

Later that day Kaede was told she was to move to the Noguchi family residence. As she wrapped her few belongings into her carrying cloth, she stroked the faded pattern, with its crests of the white river for her family and the setting sun of the Seishuu. She was bitterly ashamed of how little she owned. The events of the day kept going through her mind: the feel of the knife in the forbidden left hand, the grip of the man, his lust, the way he had died. And Arai's words: *A man of honor would not do that!* He should not have spoken of his lord like that. He would never have dared to, not even to her, if he did not already have rebellion in his mind. Why had he treated her so well, not only at that vital moment, but previously? Was he, too, seeking allies? He was already a powerful and popular man; now she saw that he might have greater ambitions. He was capable of acting in an instant, seizing opportunities.

She weighed all these things carefully, knowing that even the smallest of them added to her holding in the currency of power.

All day the other girls avoided her, talking together in huddled groups, falling silent when she passed them. Two had red eyes; perhaps the dead man had been a favorite or a lover. No one showed her any sympathy. Their resentment made her hate them more. Most of them had homes in the town or nearby villages: They had parents and families they could turn to. They were not hostages. And he, the dead guard, had grabbed her, had tried to force her. Anyone who loved such a man was an idiot.

A servant girl she had never seen before came to fetch her, addressing her as Lady Shirakawa and bowing respectfully to her. Kaede followed her down the steep cobbled steps that led from the castle to the residence, through the bailey, under the huge gate, where the guards turned their faces away from her in anger, and into the gardens that surrounded Lord Noguchi's house.

She had often seen the gardens from the castle, but this was the first time she had walked in them since she was seven years old. They went to the back of the large house, and Kaede was shown into a small room.

"Please wait here for a few minutes, lady."

After the girl had gone, Kaede knelt on the floor. The room was of good proportions, even though it was not large, and the doors stood open onto a tiny garden. The rain had stopped and the sun was shining fitfully, turning the dripping garden into a mass of shimmering light. She gazed at the stone lantern, the little twisted pine, the cistern of clear water. Crickets were singing in the branches; a frog croaked briefly. The peace and the silence melted something in her heart, and she suddenly felt near tears.

She fought them back, fixing her mind on how much she hated the Noguchi. She slipped her arms inside her sleeves and felt the bruises. She hated them all the more for living in this beautiful place, while she, of the Shirakawa family, had been housed with servants.

The internal door behind her slid open, and a woman's voice said, "Lord Noguchi wishes to speak with you, lady."

"Then you must help me get ready," she said. She could not bear to go into his presence looking as she did, her hair undressed, her clothes old and dirty.

The woman stepped into the room, and Kaede turned to look at her. She was old, and although her face was smooth and her hair still black, her hands were wrinkled and gnarled like a monkey's paws. She studied Kaede with a look of surprise on her face. Then, without speaking, she unpacked the bundle, taking out a slightly cleaner robe, a comb, and hairpins.

"Where are my lady's other clothes?"

"I came here when I was seven," Kaede said angrily. "Don't you think I might have grown since then? My mother sent better things for me, but I was not allowed to keep them!"

The woman clicked her tongue. "It's lucky that my lady's beauty is such that she has no need of adornment."

"What are you talking about?" Kaede said, for she had no idea what she looked like.

"I'll dress your hair now. And find you clean footwear. I am Junko. Lady Noguchi has sent me to wait on you. I'll speak to her later about clothes."

Junko left the room and came back with two girls carrying a bowl of water, clean socks, and a small carved box. Junko washed Kaede's face, hands and feet, and combed out her long black hair. The maids murmured as if in amazement.

"What is it? What do they mean?" Kaede said nervously.

Junko opened the box and took out a round mirror. Its back was beautifully carved with flowers and birds. She held it so Kaede could see her reflection. It was the first time she had looked in a mirror. Her own face silenced her.

The women's attentions and admiration restored

her confidence a little, but it began to seep away again as she followed Junko into the main part of the residence. She had only seen Lord Noguchi from a distance since her father's last visit. She had never liked him, and now she realized she was afraid of the meeting.

Junko fell to her knees, slid open the door to the audience room, and prostrated herself. Kaede stepped into the room and did the same. The matting was cool beneath her forehead and smelled of summer grass.

Lord Noguchi was speaking to someone in the room and took no notice of her whatsoever. He seemed to be discussing his rice allowances: how late the farmers were in handing them over. It was nearly the next harvest, and he was still owed part of the last crop. Every now and then the person he was addressing would humbly put in a placatory comment—the adverse weather, last year's earthquake, the imminent typhoon season, the devotion of the farmers, the loyalty of the retainers—at which the lord would grunt, fall silent for a full minute or more, and then start complaining all over again.

Finally he fell silent for one last time. The secretary coughed once or twice. Lord Noguchi barked a command, and the secretary backed on his knees towards the door.

He passed close to Kaede, but she did not dare raise her head.

"And call Arai," Lord Noguchi said, as if it were an afterthought.

Now he will speak to me, Kaede thought, but he said nothing, and she remained where she was, motionless.

The minutes passed. She heard a man enter the room and saw Arai prostrate himself next to her. Lord Noguchi did not acknowledge him either. He clapped his hands, and several men came quickly into the room. Kaede felt them step by her, one after another. Glancing at them sideways, she could see they were senior retainers. Some wore the Noguchi crest on their robes, and some the triple oak leaf of the Tohan. She felt they would have happily stepped on her, as if she were a cockroach, and she vowed to herself that she would never let the Tohan or the Noguchi crush her.

The warriors settled themselves heavily on the matting.

"Lady Shirakawa," Lord Noguchi said at last. "Please sit up."

As she did so, she felt the eyes of every man in the room on her. An intensity that she did not understand came into the atmosphere.

"Cousin," the lord said, a note of surprise in his voice, "I hope you are well."

"Thanks to your care, I am," she replied using the polite phrase, although the words burned her tongue like poison. She felt her terrible vulnerability here, the only woman, hardly more than a child, among men of power and brutality. She snatched a quick glance at the lord from below her lashes. His face looked petulant to her, lacking either strength or intelligence, showing the spitefulness she already knew he possessed.

"There was an unfortunate incident this morning," Lord Noguchi said. The hush in the room deepened. "Arai has told me what happened. I want to hear your version."

Kaede touched her head to the ground, her movements slow, her thoughts racing. She had Arai in her power at that moment. And Lord Noguchi had not called him captain, as he should have done. He had given him no title, shown him no courtesy. Did he already have suspicions about his loyalty? Did he already know the true version of events? Had one of the guards already betrayed Arai? If she defended him, was she just falling into a trap set for them both?

Arai was the only person in the castle who had treated her well. She was not going to betray him now. She sat up and spoke with downcast eyes but in a steady voice. "I went to the upper guard room to give a message to Lord Arai. I followed him down the stairs: He was wanted in the stables. The guard on the gate detained me with some pretext. When I went to him he seized me." She let the sleeves fall back from her arm. The bruises had already begun to show, the purple-red imprint of a man's fingers on her pale skin. "I cried out. Lord Arai heard me, came back, and rescued me." She bowed again, conscious of her own grace. "I

55

owe him and my lord a debt for my protection." She stayed, her head on the floor.

"Unnh," Lord Noguchi grunted. There was another long silence. Insects droned in the afternoon heat. Sweat glistened on the brows of the men sitting motionless. Kaede could smell their rank animal odor, and she felt sweat trickle between her breasts. She was intensely aware of her real danger. If one of the guards had spoken of the knife left behind, the girl who took it and walked down the stairs with it in her hand . . . she willed the thoughts away, afraid the men who studied her so closely would be able to read them clearly.

Eventually Lord Noguchi spoke, casually, even amiably. "How was the horse, Captain Arai?"

Arai raised his head to speak. His voice was perfectly calm. "Very young, but fine looking. Of excellent stock and easy to tame."

There was a ripple of amusement. Kaede felt they were laughing at her, and the blood rose in her cheeks.

"You have many talents, Captain," Noguchi said. "I am sorry to deprive myself of them, but I think your country estate, your wife and son, may need your attention for a while, a year or two. . . ."

"Lord Noguchi." Arai bowed, his face showing nothing.

*What a fool Noguchi is*, Kaede thought. *I'd make sure Arai stayed right here where I could keep an eye on him. Send him away and he'll be in open revolt before a year has passed.*

Arai backed out, not looking even once towards Kaede. *Noguchi's probably planning to have him murdered on the road*, she thought gloomily. *I'll never see him again.*

With Arai's departure the atmosphere lightened a little. Lord Noguchi coughed and cleared his throat. The warriors shifted position, easing their legs and backs. Kaede could feel their eyes still on her. The bruises on her arms, the man's death had aroused them. They were no different from him.

The door behind her slid open, and the servant who had brought her from the castle came in with bowls of tea. She served each of the men and seemed to be about to leave when Lord Noguchi barked at her. She bowed, flustered, and set a cup in front of Kaede.

Kaede sat up and drank, eyes lowered, her mouth so dry she could barely swallow. Arai's punishment was exile; what would hers be?

"Lady Shirakawa, you have been with us for many years. You have been part of our household."

"You have honored me, lord," she replied.

"But I think that pleasure is to be ours no longer. I have lost two men on your account. I'm not sure I can afford to keep you with me!" He chuckled, and the men in the room laughed in echo.

*He's sending me home!* The false hope fluttered in her heart.

"You obviously are old enough to be married. I think the sooner the better. We will arrange a suitable marriage for you. I am writing to inform your parents who I have in mind. You will live with my wife until the day of your marriage."

She bowed again, but before she did so, she caught the glance that flickered between Noguchi and one of the older men in the room. *It will be to him*, she thought, *or a man like him, old, depraved, brutal.* The idea of marriage to anyone appalled her. Even the thought that she would be better treated living in the Noguchi household could not raise her spirits.

Junko escorted her back to the room and then led her to the bath-house. It was early evening and Kaede was numb with exhaustion. Junko washed her and scrubbed her back and limbs with rice bran.

"Tomorrow I will wash your hair," she promised. "It's too long and thick to wash tonight. It will never dry in time, and then you will take a chill."

"Maybe I will die from it," Kaede said. "It would be the best thing."

"Never say that," Junko scolded her, helping her into the tub to soak in the hot water. "You have a great life ahead of you. You are so beautiful! You will be married, have children."

She brought her mouth close to Kaede's ear and whispered, "The captain thanks you for keeping faith with him. I am to look after you on his behalf."

*What can women do in this world of men?* Kaede thought. *What protection do we have? Can anyone look after me?*

She remembered her own face in the mirror, and longed to look at it again.

# CHAPTER 3

The heron came to the garden every afternoon, floating like a gray ghost over the wall, folding itself improbably, and standing thigh deep in the pool, as still as a statue of Jizo. The red and gold carp that Lord Otori took pleasure in feeding were too large for it, but it held its position motionless for long minutes at a time, until some hapless creature forgot it was there and dared to move in the water. Then the heron struck, faster than eye could follow, and, with the little wriggling thing in its beak, reassembled itself for flight. The first few wing beats were as loud as the sudden clacking of a fan, but after that it departed as silently as it had come.

The days were still very hot, with the languorous heat of autumn, which you long to be over and cling on to at the same time, knowing this fiercest heat, hardest to bear, will also be the year's last.

I had been in Lord Otori's house for a month. In Hagi the rice harvest was over, the straw drying in the fields and on frames around the farmhouses. The red autumn lilies were fading. Persimmons turned gold on the trees, while the leaves became brittle, and spiny chestnut shells lay in the lanes and alleys, spilling out their glossy fruit. The autumn full moon came and went. Chiyo put chestnuts, tangerines, and rice cakes in the garden shrine, and I wondered if anyone was doing the same in my village.

The servant girls gathered the last of the wild-flowers, bush clover, wild pinks, and autumn wort, standing them in buckets outside the kitchen and the privy, their fragrance masking the smells of food and waste, the cycles of human life.

My state of half-being, my speechlessness, persisted. I suppose I was in mourning. The Otori household was, too, not only for Lord Otori's brother but also for his mother, who had died in the summer from the plague. Chiyo related the story of the family to me. Shigeru, the oldest son, had been with his father at the battle of Yaegahara and had strongly opposed the surrender to the Tohan. The terms of the surrender had forbidden him inheriting from his father the leadership of the clan. Instead his uncles, Shoichi and Masahiro, were appointed by Iida.

"Iida Sadamu hates Shigeru more than any man alive," Chiyo said. "He is jealous of him and fears him."

Shigeru was a thorn in the side of his uncles as well, as the legal heir to the clan. He had ostensibly withdrawn from the political stage and had devoted himself to his land, trying out new methods, experimenting with different crops. He had married young, but his wife had died two years later in childbirth, the baby dying with her.

His life seemed to me to be filled with suffering, yet he gave no sign of it, and if I had not learned all this from Chiyo I would not have known of it. I spent most of the day with him, following him around like a dog, always at his side, except when I was studying with Ichiro.

They were days of waiting. Ichiro tried to teach me to read and write, my general lack of skill and retentiveness enraging him, while he reluctantly pursued the idea of adoption. The clan were opposed: Lord Shigeru should marry again, he was still young, it was too soon after his mother's death. The objections seemed to be endless. I could not help feeling that Ichiro agreed with most of them, and they seemed perfectly valid to me too. I tried my hardest to learn, because I did not want to disappoint the lord, but I had no real belief or trust in my situation.

Usually in the late afternoon Lord Shigeru would send for me, and we would sit by the window and look at the garden. He did not say much, but he would study me when he thought I was not looking. I felt he was waiting for something: for me to speak, for me to give some sign—but of what I did not know. It made me anxious, and the anxiety made me more sure that I was disappointing him and even less able to learn. One afternoon Ichiro came to the upper room to complain again about me. He had been exasperated to the point of beating me earlier that day. I was sulking in the corner, nursing my bruises, tracing with my finger on the matting the shapes of the characters I'd learned that day, in a desperate attempt to try to retain them.

"You made a mistake," Ichiro said. "No one will think the worse of you if you admit it. The circumstances of your brother's death explain it. Send the boy back to where he came from, and get on with your life."

*And let me get on with mine*, I felt he was saying. He never let me forget the sacrifices he was making in trying to educate me.

"You can't recreate Lord Takeshi," he added, softening his tone a little. "He was the result of years of education and training—and the best blood to begin with."

I was afraid Ichiro would get his way. Lord Shigeru was as bound to him and Chiyo by the ties and obligations of duty as they were to him. I'd thought he had all the power in the household, but in fact Ichiro had his own power, and knew how to wield it. And in the opposite direction, his uncles had power over Lord Shigeru. He had to obey the dictates of the clan. There was no reason for him to keep me, and he would never be allowed to adopt me.

"Watch the heron, Ichiro," Lord Shigeru said. "You see his patience, you see how long he stands without moving to get what he needs. I have the same patience, and it's far from exhausted."

63

Ichiro's lips were pressed tight together in his favorite sour-plum expression. At that moment the heron stabbed and left, clacking its wings.

I could hear the squeaking that heralded the evening arrival of the bats. I lifted my head to see two of them swoop into the garden. While Ichiro continued to grumble, and the lord to answer him briefly, never losing his temper, I listened to the noises of the approaching night. Every day my hearing grew sharper. I was becoming used to it, learning to filter out whatever I did not need to listen to, giving no sign that I could hear every-thing that went on in the house. No one knew that I could hear all their secrets.

Now I heard the hiss of hot water as the bath was prepared, the clatter of dishes from the kitchen, the sliding sigh of the cook's knife, the tread of a girl in soft socks on the boards outside, the stamp and whinny of a horse in the stables, the cry of the female cat, feeding four kittens and always famished, a dog barking two streets away, the clack of clogs over the wooden bridges of the canals, children singing, the temple bells from Tokoji and Daishoin. I knew the song of the house, day and night, in sunshine and under the rain. This evening I realized I was always listening for something more. I was waiting too. For what? Every night before I fell asleep my mind replayed the scene on the mountain, the severed head, the wolf man clutching the stump of his arm. I saw again Iida Sadamu on the ground, and the bodies

64

of my stepfather and Isao. Was I waiting for Iida and the wolf man to catch up with me? Or for my chance of revenge?

From time to time I still tried to pray in the manner of the Hidden, and that night I prayed to be shown the path I should take. I could not sleep. The air was heavy and still, the moon, a week past full, hidden behind thick banks of cloud. The insects of the night were noisy and restless. I could hear the suck of the gecko's feet as it crossed the ceiling hunting them. Ichiro and Lord Shigeru were both sound asleep, Ichiro snoring. I did not want to leave the house I'd come to love so much, but I seemed to be bringing nothing but trouble to it. Perhaps it would be better for everyone if I just vanished in the night.

Without any real plan to go—What would I do? How would I live?—I began to wonder if I could get out of the house without setting the dogs barking and arousing the guards. That was when I started consciously listening for the dogs. Usually I heard them bark on and off throughout the night, but I'd learned to distinguish their barks and to ignore them mostly. I set my ears for them but heard nothing. Then I started listening for the guards: the sound of a foot on stone, the clink of steel, a whispered conversation. Nothing. Sounds that should have been there were missing from the night's familiar web.

Now I was wide-awake, straining my ears to hear above the water from the garden. The stream and river were low: There had been no rain since the turn of the moon.

There came the slightest of sounds, hardly more than a tremor, between the window and the ground.

For a moment I thought it was the earth shaking, as it so often did in the Middle Country. Another tiny tremble followed, then another.

Someone was climbing up the side of the house.

My first instinct was to yell out, but cunning took over. To shout would raise the household, but it would also alert the intruder. I rose from the mattress and crept silently to Lord Shigeru's side. My feet knew the floor, knew every creak the old house would make. I knelt beside him and, as though I had never lost the power of speech, whispered in his ear, "Lord Otori, someone is outside."

He woke instantly, stared at me for a moment, then reached for the sword and knife that lay beside him. I gestured to the window. The faint tremor came again, just the slightest shifting of weight against the side of the house.

Lord Shigeru passed the knife to me and stepped to the wall. He smiled at me and pointed, and I moved to the other side of the window. We waited for the assassin to climb in.

Step by step he came up the wall, stealthy and unhurried, as if he had all the time in the world, confident that there was nothing to betray him. We waited for him with the same patience, almost

66

as if we were boys playing a game in a barn.

Except the end was no game. He paused on the sill to take out the garrote he planned to use on us, and then stepped inside. Lord Shigeru took him in a stranglehold. Slippery as an eel, the intruder wriggled backwards. I leaped at him, but before I could say *knife*, let alone use it, the three of us fell into the garden like a flurry of fighting cats.

The man fell first, across the stream, striking his head on a boulder. Lord Shigeru landed on his feet. My fall was broken by one of the shrubs. Winded, I dropped the knife. I scrabbled to pick it up, but it was not needed. The intruder groaned, tried to rise, but slipped back into the water. His body dammed the stream; it deepened around him, then with a sudden babble flowed over him. Lord Shigeru pulled him from the water, striking him in the face and shouting at him, "Who? Who paid you? Where are you from?"

The man merely groaned again, his breath coming in loud, rasping snores.

"Get a light," Lord Shigeru said to me. I thought the household would be awake by now, but the skirmish had happened so quickly and silently that they all slept on. Dripping water and leaves, I ran to the maids' room.

"Chiyo!" I called. "Bring lights, wake the men!"

"Who's that?" she replied sleepily, not knowing my voice.

"It's me, Takeo! Wake up! Someone tried to kill Lord Shigeru!"

I took a light that still burned in one of the candle stands and carried it back to the garden.

The man had slipped further into unconsciousness. Lord Shigeru stood staring down at him. I held the light over him. The intruder was dressed in black, with no crest or marking on his clothes. He was of medium height and build, his hair cut short. There was nothing to distinguish him.

Behind us we heard the clamor of the household coming awake, screams as two guards were discovered garroted, three dogs poisoned.

Ichiro came out, pale and shaking. "Who would dare do this?" he said. "In your own house, in the heart of Hagi? It's an insult to the whole clan!"

"Unless the clan ordered it," Lord Shigeru replied quietly.

"It's more likely to be Iida," Ichiro said. He saw the knife in my hand and took it from me. He slashed the black cloth from neck to waist, exposing the man's back. There was a hideous scar from an old sword wound across the shoulder blade, and the backbone was tattooed in a delicate pattern. It flickered like a snake in the lamplight.

"He's a hired assassin," Lord Shigeru said, "from the Tribe. He could have been paid by anyone."

"Then it must be Iida! He must know you have the boy! Now will you get rid of him?"

"If it hadn't been for the boy, the assassin would have succeeded," the lord replied. "It was he who woke me in time. . . . He spoke to me," he cried as realization dawned. "He spoke in my ear and woke me up!"

Ichiro was not particularly impressed by this. "Has it occurred to you that he might have been the target, not you?"

"Lord Otori," I said, my voice thick and husky from weeks of disuse. "I've brought nothing but danger to you. Let me go, send me away." But even as I spoke, I knew he would not. I had saved his life now, as he had saved mine, and the bond between us was stronger than ever.

Ichiro was nodding in agreement, but Chiyo spoke up: "Forgive me, Lord Shigeru. I know it's nothing to do with me and that I'm just a foolish old woman. But it's not true that Takeo has brought you nothing but danger. Before you returned with him, you were half crazed with sorrow. Now you are recovered. He has brought joy and hope as well as danger. And who dares enjoy one and escape the other?"

"How should I of all people not know this?" Lord Shigeru replied. "There is some destiny that binds our lives together. I cannot fight that, Ichiro."

"Maybe his brains will have returned with his tongue," Ichiro said scathingly.

The assassin died without regaining consciousness. It turned out he'd had a poison pellet in his mouth and had crushed it as he fell. No one knew his identity, though there were plenty of rumors. The dead guards were buried in a solemn ceremony, and mourned, and the dogs were mourned by me, at least. I wondered what pact they had made, what fealty they had sworn, to be caught up in the feuds of men, and to pay with their lives. I did not voice these thoughts: There were plenty more dogs. New ones were acquired and trained to take food from one man only, so they could not be poisoned. There were any number of men, too, for that matter. Lord Shigeru lived simply, with few armed retainers, but it seemed many among the Otori clan would have happily come to serve him—enough to form an army, if he'd so desired.

The attack did not seem to have alarmed or depressed him in any way. If anything, he was invigorated by it, his delight in the pleasures of life sharpened by his escape from death. He floated, as he had done after the meeting with Lady Maruyama. He was delighted by my newly recovered speech and by the sharpness of my hearing.

Maybe Ichiro was right, or maybe his own attitude towards me softened. Whatever the reason, from the night of the assassination attempt on, learning became easier. Slowly the characters began to unlock their meaning and retain their place in my brain. I even began to enjoy them, the different shapes that flowed like water, or perched solid and squat like black crows in winter. I wouldn't admit it to Ichiro, but drawing them gave me a deep pleasure.

Ichiro was an acknowledged master, well known for the beauty of his writing and the depth of his learning. He was really far too good a teacher for me. I did not have the mind of a natural student. But what we both discovered was that I could mimic. I could present a passable copy of a student, just as I could copy the way he'd draw from the shoulder, not the wrist, with boldness and concentration. I knew I was just mimicking him, but the results were adequate.

The same thing happened when Lord Shigeru taught me the use of the sword. I was strong and agile enough, probably more than average for my height, but I had missed the boyhood years when the sons of warriors practice endlessly at sword, bow, and horsemanship. I knew I would never make them up.

Riding came easily enough. I watched Lord Shigeru and the other men, and realized it was mainly a matter of balance. I simply copied what I saw them do and the horse responded. I realized, too, that the horse was shyer and more nervous than I was. To the horse I had to act like a lord, hide my own feelings for his sake, and pretend I was perfectly in control and knew exactly what was going on. Then the horse would relax beneath me and be happy.

I was given a pale gray horse with a black mane and tail, called Raku, and we got on well together. I did not take to archery at all, but in using the sword again I copied what I saw Lord Shigeru do, and the results were passable. I was given a long sword of my own, and wore it in the sash of my new clothes as any warrior's son would. But despite the sword and the clothes I knew I was only an imitation warrior.

So the weeks went by. The household accepted that Lord Otori intended to adopt me, and little by little their attitude towards me changed. They spoiled, teased, and scolded me in equal measures. Between the studying and training I had little spare time and I was not supposed to go out alone, but I still had my restless love of roaming, and whenever I could I slipped away and explored the city of Hagi. I liked to go down to the port, where the castle in the west and the old volcano crater in the east held the bay like a cup in their two hands. I'd stare out to sea and think of all the fabled lands that lay beyond the horizon and envy the sailors and fishermen.

There was one boat that I always looked for. A boy about my own age worked on it. I knew he was called Terada Fumio. His father was from a low-rank warrior family who had taken up trade and fishing rather than die of starvation. Chiyo knew all about them, and I got this information at first from her. I admired Fumio enormously. He had actually been to the mainland. He knew the sea and the rivers in all their moods. At that time I could not even swim. At first we just nodded at each other, but as the weeks went by we became friends. I'd go aboard and we'd sit and eat persimmons, spitting the pips into the water, and talk about the things boys talk about. Sooner or later we would get on to the Otori lords; the Terada hated them for their arrogance and greed. They suffered from the ever-increasing taxes that the castle imposed, and from the restrictions placed on trade. When we talked about these things it was in whispers, on the seaward side of the boat, for the castle, it was said, had spies everywhere.

I was hurrying home late one afternoon after one of these excursions. Ichiro had been called to settle an account with a merchant. I'd waited for ten minutes and then decided he was not coming back and made my escape. It was well into the tenth month. The air was cool and filled with the smell of burning rice straw. The smoke hung over the fields between the river and the mountains, turning the landscape silver and gold. Fumio had been teaching me to swim, and my hair was wet, making me shiver a little. I was thinking about hot water and wondering if I could get something to eat from Chiyo before the evening meal, and whether Ichiro would be in a bad enough temper to beat me, and at the same time I was listening, as I always did, for the moment when I would begin to hear the distinct song of the house from the street.

I thought I heard something else, something that made me stop and look twice at the corner of the wall, just before our gate. I did not think there was anyone there, then almost in the same instant

I saw there was someone, a man squatting on his heels in the shadow of the tile roof.

I was only a few yards from him, on the opposite side of the street. I knew he'd seen me. After a few moments he stood up slowly as if waiting for me to approach him.

He was the most ordinary-looking person I'd ever seen, average height and build, hair going a little gray, face pale rather than brown, with unmemorable features, the sort that you can never be sure of recognizing again. Even as I studied him, trying to work him out, his features seemed to change shape before my eyes. And yet, beneath the very ordinariness lay something extraordinary, something deft and quick that slipped away when I tried to pinpoint it.

He was wearing faded blue-gray clothes and carrying no visible weapon. He did not look like a workman, a merchant, or a warrior. I could not place him in any way, but some inner sense warned me that he was very dangerous.

At the same time there was something about him that fascinated me. I could not pass by without acknowledging him. But I stayed on the far side of the street, and was already judging how far it was to the gate, the guards, and the dogs.

He gave me a nod and a smile, almost of approval. "Good day, young lord!" he called, in a voice that held mockery just below the surface. "You're right not to trust me. I've heard you're

74

clever like that. But I'll never harm you, I promise you."

I felt his speech was as slippery as his appearance, and I did not count his promise for much.

"I want to talk to you," he said, "and to Shigeru too."

I was astonished to hear him speak of the lord in that familiar way. "What do you have to say to me?"

"I can't shout it to you from here," he replied with a laugh. "Walk with me to the gate and I'll tell you."

"You can walk to the gate on that side of the road and I'll walk on this side," I said, watching his hands to catch the first movement towards a hidden weapon. "Then I'll speak to Lord Otori and he can decide if you are to meet him or not."

The man smiled to himself and shrugged, and we walked separately to the gate, he as calmly as if he were taking an evening stroll, me as jumpy as a cat before a storm. When we got to the gate and the guards greeted us, he seemed to have grown older and more faded. He looked like such a harmless old man, I was almost ashamed of my mistrust.

"You're in trouble, Takeo," one of the men said. "Master Ichiro has been looking for you for an hour!"

"Hey, Grandpa," the other called to the old man. "What are you after, a bowl of noodles or something?"

Indeed, the old man did look as if he needed a square meal. He waited humbly, saying nothing, just outside the gate sill.

"Where'd you pick him up, Takeo? You're too softhearted, that's your trouble! Get rid of him!"

"I said I would tell Lord Otori he was here, and I will," I replied. "But watch his every movement, and whatever you do, don't let him into the garden."

I turned to the stranger to say "Wait here" and caught a flash of something from him. He was dangerous, all right, but it was almost as if he were letting me see a side of him that he kept hidden from the guards. I wondered if I should leave him with them. Still, there were two of them armed to the teeth. They should be able to deal with one old man.

I tore through the garden, kicked off my sandals, and climbed the stairs in a couple of bounds. Lord Shigeru was sitting in the upstairs room, gazing out over the garden.

"Takeo," he said, "I've been thinking, a tea room over the garden would be perfect."

"Lord . . ." I began, then was transfixed by a movement in the garden below. I thought it was the heron, it stood so still and gray, then I saw it was the man I had left at the gate.

"What?" Lord Shigeru said, seeing my face.

I was gripped by terror that the assassination attempt was to be repeated. "There's a stranger in the garden," I cried. "Watch him!" My next

76

fear was for the guards. I ran back down the stairs and out of the house. My heart was pounding as I came to the gate. The dogs were all right. They stirred when they heard me, tails wagging. I shouted; the men came out, astonished.

"What's wrong, Takeo?"

"You let him in!" I said in a fury. "The old man, he's in the garden."

"No, he's out there in the street where you left him."

My eyes followed the man's gesture, and for a moment I, too, was fooled. I *did* see him, sitting outside in the shade of the roofed wall, humble, patient, harmless. Then my vision cleared. The street was empty.

"You fools!" I said. "Didn't I tell you he was dangerous? Didn't I tell you on no account to let him in? What useless idiots are you, and you call yourselves men of the Otori clan? Go back to your farms and guard your hens, and may the foxes eat every one of them!"

They gaped at me. I don't think any one in the household had ever heard me speak so many words at once. My rage was greater because I felt responsible for them. But they had to obey me. I could only protect them if they obeyed me.

"You are lucky to be alive," I said, drawing my sword from my belt and racing back to find the intruder.

He was gone from the garden, and I was beginning to wonder if I'd seen another mirage, when

I heard voices from the upstairs room. Lord Shigeru called my name. He did not sound in any danger—more as if he were laughing. When I went into the room and bowed, the man was sitting next to him as if they were old friends, and they were both chuckling away. The stranger no longer looked so ancient. I could see he was a few years older than Lord Shigeru, and his face now was open and warm.

"He wouldn't walk on the same side of the street, eh?" the lord said.

"That's right, and he made me sit outside and wait." They both roared with laughter and slapped the matting with open palms. "By the way, Shigeru, you should train your guards better. Takeo was right to be angry with them."

"He was right all along," Lord Shigeru said, a note of pride in his voice.

"He's one in a thousand—the sort that's born, not made. He has to be from the Tribe. Sit up, Takeo, let me look at you."

I lifted my head from the floor and sat back on my heels. My face was burning. I felt the man had tricked me after all. He said nothing, just studied me quietly.

Lord Shigeru said, "This is Muto Kenji, an old friend of mine."

"Lord Muto," I said, polite but cold, determined not to let my feelings show.

"You don't have to call me lord," Kenji said. "I am not a lord, though I number a few among my

78

friends." He leaned towards me. "Show me your hands."

He took each hand in turn, looking at the back and then at the palm.

"We think him like Takeshi," Lord Shigeru said.

"Unnh. He has a look of the Otori about him." Kenji moved back to his original position and gazed over the garden. The last of the color had leached from it. Only the maples still glowed red. "The news of your loss saddened me," he said.

"I thought I no longer wanted to live," Lord Shigeru replied. "But the weeks pass and I find that I do. I am not made for despair."

"No, indeed," Kenji agreed, with affection. They both looked out through the open windows. The air was chill with autumn, a gust of wind shook the maples, and leaves fell into the stream, turning darker red in the water before they were swept into the river.

I thought longingly of the hot bath, and shivered.

Kenji broke the silence. "Why is this boy who looks like Takeshi, but is obviously from the Tribe, living in your household, Shigeru?"

"Why have you come all this way to ask me?" he replied, smiling slightly.

"I don't mind telling you. News on the wind was that someone heard an intruder climbing into your house. As a result, one of the most dangerous assassins in the Three Countries is dead."

"We have tried to keep it secret," Lord Shigeru said.

"It's our business to find out such secrets. What was Shintaro doing in your house?"

"Presumably he came to kill me," Lord Shigeru replied. "So it was Shintaro. I had my suspicions, but we had no proof." After a moment he added, "Someone must truly desire my death. Was he hired by Iida?"

"He had worked for the Tohan for some time. But I don't think Iida would have you assassinated in secret. By all accounts he would rather watch the event with his own eyes. Who else wants you dead?"

"I can think of one or two," the lord answered.

"It was hard to believe Shintaro failed," Kenji went on. "We had to find out who the boy was. Where did you find him?"

"What do you hear on the wind?" Lord Shigeru countered, still smiling.

"The official story, of course: that he's a distant relative of your mother's; from the superstitious, that you took leave of your senses and believe he's your brother returned to you; from the cynical, that he's your son, got with some peasant woman in the East."

Lord Shigeru laughed. "I am not even twice his age. I would have had to have fathered him at twelve. He is not my son."

"No, obviously, and despite his looks, I don't believe he's a relative or a revenant. Anyway, he has to be from the Tribe. Where did you find him?"

One of the maids, Haruka, came and lit the lamps, and immediately a large blue-green moon moth blundered into the room and flapped towards the flame. I stood and took it in my hand, felt its powdery wings beat against my palm, and released it into the night, sliding the screens closed before I sat again.

Lord Shigeru made no reply to Kenji, and then Haruka returned with tea. Kenji did not seem angry or frustrated. He admired the tea bowls, which were of the simple, pink-hued local ware, and drank without saying any more, but watching me all the time.

Finally he asked me a direct question. "Tell me, Takeo, when you were a child, did you pull the shells off living snails, or tear the claws from crabs?"

I didn't understand the question. "Maybe," I said, pretending to drink, even though my bowl was empty.

"Did you?"

"No."

"Why not?"

"My mother told me it was cruel."

"I thought so." His voice had taken on a note of sadness, as though he pitied me. "No wonder you've been trying to fend me off, Shigeru. I felt a softness in the boy, an aversion to cruelty. He was raised among the Hidden."

"Is it so obvious?" Lord Shigeru said.

"Only to me." Kenji sat cross-legged, eyes narrowed, one arm resting on his knee. "I think I know who he is."

Lord Shigeru sighed, and his face became still and wary. "Then, you had better tell us."

"He has all the signs of being Kikuta: the long fingers, the straight line across the palm, the acute hearing. It comes on suddenly, around puberty, sometimes accompanied by loss of speech, usually temporary, sometimes permanent. . . ."

"You're making this up!" I said, unable to keep silent any longer. In fact, a sort of horror was creeping over me. I knew nothing of the Tribe, except that the assassin had been one of them, but I felt as if Muto Kenji were opening a dark door before me that I dreaded entering.

Lord Shigeru shook his head. "Let him speak. It is of great importance."

Kenji leaned forward and spoke directly to me. "I am going to tell you about your father."

Lord Shigeru said dryly, "You had better start with the Tribe. Takeo does not know what you mean when you say he is obviously Kikuta."

"Is that so?" Kenji raised one eyebrow. "Well, I suppose if he was brought up by the Hidden, I shouldn't be surprised. I'll begin at the beginning. The five families of the Tribe have always existed. They were there before the lords and the clans. They go back to a time when magic was greater than strength of arms, and the gods still walked the earth. When the clans sprang up, and men

82

formed allegiances based on might, the Tribe did not join any of them. To preserve their gifts, they took to the roads and became travelers, actors and acrobats, peddlers and magicians."

"They may have done so in the beginning," Lord Shigeru interrupted. "But many also became merchants, amassing considerable wealth and influence." He said to me, "Kenji himself runs a very successful business in soybean products as well as money lending."

"Times have become corrupt," Kenji said. "As the priests tell us, we are in the last days of the law. I was talking about an earlier age. These days it's true, we are involved in business. From time to time we may serve one or other of the clans and take its crest, or work for those who have befriended us, like Lord Otori Shigeru. But whatever we have become, we preserve the talents from the past, which once all men had but have now forgotten."

"You were in two places at once," I said. "The guards saw you outside, while I saw you in the garden."

Kenji bowed ironically to me. "We can split ourselves and leave the second self behind. We can become invisible and move faster than the eye can follow. Acuteness of vision and hearing are other traits. The Tribe has retained these abilities through dedication and hard training. And they are abilities that others in this warring country find useful, and pay highly for. Most members of the Tribe become spies or assassins at some stage in their life."

I was concentrating on trying not to shiver. My blood seemed to have drained out of me. I remembered how I had seemed to split in half beneath Iida's sword. And all the sounds of the house, the garden, and the city beyond rang with increasing intensity in my ears.

"Kikuta Isamu, who I believe was your father, was no exception. His parents were cousins and he combined the strongest gifts of the Kikuta. By the time he was thirty, he was a flawless assassin. No one knows how many he killed; most of the deaths seemed natural and were never attributed to him. Even by the standards of the Kikuta he was secretive. He was a master of poisons, in particular certain mountain plants that kill while leaving no trace.

"He was in the mountains of the East—you know the district I mean—seeking new plants. The men in the village where he was lodging were Hidden. It seems they told him about the secret god, the command not to kill, the judgment that awaits in the afterlife: You know it all, I don't need to tell you. In those remote mountains, far from the feuds of the clans, Isamu had been taking stock of his life. Perhaps he was filled with remorse. Perhaps the dead called out to him. Anyway, he renounced his life with the Tribe and became one of the Hidden."

"And was executed?" Lord Shigeru spoke out of the gloom.

"Well, he broke the fundamental rules of the Tribe. We don't like being renounced like that, especially not by someone with such great talents. That sort of ability is all too rare these days. But to tell the truth, I don't know what exactly happened to him. I didn't even know he had had a child. Takeo, or whatever his real name is, must have been born after his father's death."

"Who killed him?" I said, my mouth dry.

"Who knows? There were many who wanted to, and one of them did. Of course, no one could have got near him if he had not taken a vow never to kill again."

There was a long silence. Apart from a small pool of light from the glowing lamp, it was almost completely dark in the room. I could not see their faces, though I was sure Kenji could see mine.

"Did your mother never tell you this?" he asked eventually.

I shook my head. There is so much that the Hidden don't tell, so much they keep secret even from each other. What isn't known can't be revealed under torture. If you don't know your brother's secrets, you cannot betray him.

Kenji laughed. "Admit it, Shigeru, you had no idea who you were bringing into your household. Not even the Tribe knew of his existence—a boy with all the latent talent of the Kikuta!"

Lord Shigeru did not reply, but as he leaned forward into the lamplight I could see he was smiling, cheerful and openhearted. I thought what a contrast there was between the two men: the lord so open, Kenji so devious and tricky.

"I need to know how this came about. I'm not talking idly with you, Shigeru. I need to know." Kenji's voice was insistent.

I could hear Chiyo fussing on the stairs. Lord Shigeru said, "We must bathe and eat. After the meal we'll talk again."

*He will not want me in his house, now that he knows I am the son of an assassin.* This was the first thought that came to me as I sat in the hot water, after the older men had bathed. I could hear their voices from the upper room. They were drinking wine now and reminiscing idly about the past. Then I thought about the father I had never known, and felt a deep sadness that he had not been able to escape his background. He had wanted to give up the killing, but it would not give him up. It had reached out its long arms and found him, as far away as Mino, just as, years later, Iida had sought out the Hidden there. I looked at my own long fingers. Was that what they were designed for? To kill?

Whatever I had inherited from him, I was also my mother's child. I was woven from two strands that could hardly be less alike, and both called to me through blood, muscle, and bone. I remembered, too, my fury at the guards. I knew I had been acting then as their lord. Was this to be a third strand in my life, or would I be sent away now that Lord Shigeru knew who I was?

86

The thoughts became too painful, too difficult to unravel, and anyway, Chiyo was calling to me to come and eat. The water had warmed me at last, and I was hungry.

Ichiro had joined Lord Shigeru and Kenji, and the trays were already set out before them. They were discussing trivial things when I arrived: the weather, the design of the garden, my poor learning skills and generally bad behavior. Ichiro was still displeased with me for disappearing that afternoon. It seemed like weeks ago that I had swum in the freezing autumn river with Fumio.

The food was even better than usual, but only Ichiro enjoyed it. Kenji ate fast, the lord hardly touched anything. I was alternately hungry and nauseated, both dreading and longing for the end of the meal. Ichiro ate so much and so slowly that I thought he would never be through. Twice we seemed to be finished when he took "Just another tiny mouthful." At last he patted his stomach and belched quietly. He was about to embark on another long gardening discussion, but Lord Shigeru made a sign to him. With a few parting comments and a couple more jokes to Kenji about me, he withdrew. Haruka and Chiyo came to clear away the dishes. When they had left, their footsteps and voices fading away to the kitchen, Kenji sat forward, his hand held out, palm open, towards Lord Shigeru.

"Well?" he said.

I wished I could follow the women. I didn't want

to be sitting here while these men decided my fate. For that was what it would come to, I was sure. Kenji must have come to claim me in some way for the Tribe. And Lord Shigeru would surely be only too happy now to let me go.

"I don't know why this information is so important to you, Kenji," Lord Shigeru said. "I find it hard to believe that you don't know it all already. If I tell you, I trust it will go no further. Even in this house no one knows but Ichiro and Chiyo.

"You were right when you said I did not know whom I had brought into my house. It all happened by chance. It was late in the afternoon, I had strayed somewhat out of my path and was hoping to find lodging for the night in the village that I later discovered was called Mino. I had been traveling alone for some weeks after Takeshi's death."

"You were seeking revenge?" Kenji asked quietly.

"You know how things are between Iida and myself—how they have been since Yaegahara. But I could hardly have hoped to come upon him in that isolated place. It was purely the strangest of coincidences that we two, the most bitter enemies, should have been there on the same day. Certainly if I had met Iida there, I would have sought to kill him. But this boy ran into me on the path instead."

He briefly told of the massacre, Iida's fall from the horse, the men pursuing me.

"It happened on the spur of the moment. The

men threatened me. They were armed. I defended myself."

"Did they know who you were?"

"Probably not. I was in traveling clothes, unmarked; it was getting dark, raining."

"But you knew they were Tohan?"

"They told me Iida was after the boy. That was enough to make me want to protect him."

Kenji said, as though changing the subject, "I've heard Iida is seeking a formal alliance with the Otori."

"It's true. My uncles are in favor of making peace, although the clan itself is divided."

"If Iida learns you have the boy, the alliance will never go forward."

"There is no need to tell me things I already know," the lord said with the first flash of anger.

"Lord Otori," Kenji said in his ironic way, and bowed.

For a few moments no one spoke. Then Kenji sighed. "Well, the fates decide our lives, no matter what we think we are planning. Whoever sent Shintaro against you, the result is the same. Within a week the Tribe knew of Takeo's existence. I have to tell you that we have an interest in this boy, which we will not relinquish."

I said, my voice sounding thin in my own ears, "Lord Otori saved my life and I will not leave him."

He reached out and patted me on the shoulder as a father might. "I'm not giving him up," he said to Kenji.

"We want above all to keep him alive," Kenji replied. "While it seems safe, he can stay here. There is one other concern, though. The Tohan you met on the mountain: Presumably you killed them?"

"One at least," Lord Shigeru replied, "possibly two."

"One," Kenji corrected him.

Lord Shigeru raised his eyebrows. "You know all the answers already. Why do you bother asking?"

"I need to fill in certain gaps, and know how much you know."

"One, two—what does it matter?"

"The man who lost his arm survived. His name is Ando; he's long been one of Iida's closest men."

I remembered the wolfish man who had pursued me up the path, and could not help shivering.

"He did not know who you were, and does not yet know where Takeo is. But he is looking for you both. With Iida's permission, he has devoted himself to the quest for revenge."

"I look forward to our next meeting," Lord Shigeru replied.

Kenji stood and paced around the room. When he sat down, his face was open and smiling, as though we had done nothing all evening save exchange jokes and talk about gardens.

"It's good," he said. "Now that I know exactly what danger Takeo is in, I can set about protecting him and teaching him to protect himself." Then he did something that astonished me: He bowed to the floor before me and said, "While I am alive, you will be safe. I swear it to you." I thought he was being ironic, but some disguise slipped from his face, and for a moment I saw the true man beneath. I might have seen Jato come alive. Then the cover slipped back, and Kenji was joking again. "But you have to do exactly what I tell you!"

He grinned at me. "I gather Ichiro finds you too much. He shouldn't be bothered by cubs like you at his age. I will take over your education. I will be your teacher."

He drew his robe around him with a fussy movement and pursed his lips, instantly becoming the gentle old man I had left outside the gate. "That is, if Lord Otori will graciously permit it."

"I don't seem to have any choice," Lord Shigeru said, and poured more wine, smiling his open-hearted smile.

My eyes flicked from one face to the other. Again I was struck by the contrast between them. I thought I saw in Kenji's eyes a look that was not quite scorn, but close to it. Now that I know the ways of the Tribe so intimately, I know their weakness is arrogance. They become infatuated with their own amazing skills, and underestimate those of their antagonists. But at that moment Kenji's look just angered me.

Shortly after that, the maids came to spread out the beds and put out the lamps. For a long time I lay sleepless, listening to the sounds of the night.

The evening's revelations marched slowly through my mind, scattered, re-formed, and marched past again. My life no longer belonged to me. But for Lord Shigeru I would be dead now. If he had not run into me by accident, as he said, on the mountain path . . .

Was it really by accident? Everyone, even Kenji, accepted his version: It had all happened on the spur of the moment, the running boy, the threatening men, the fight . . .

I relived it all in my mind. And I seemed to recall a moment when the path ahead was clear. There was a huge tree, a cedar, and someone stepped out from behind it and seized me—not by accident, but deliberately. I thought of Lord Shigeru and how little I really knew about him. Everyone took him at face value: impulsive, warmhearted, generous. I believed him to be all these things, but I couldn't help wondering what lay beneath. *I'm not giving him up,* he had said. But why would he want to adopt one of the Tribe, the son of an assassin? I thought of the heron, and how patiently it waited before it struck.

The sky was lightening and the roosters were crowing before I slept.

The guards had a lot of fun at my expense when Muto Kenji was installed as my teacher.

"Watch out for the old man, Takeo! He's pretty dangerous. He might stab you with the brush!"

It was a joke they never seemed to tire of. I

learned to say nothing. Better they should think me an idiot than that they should know and spread abroad the old man's real identity. It was an early lesson for me. The less people think of you, the more they will reveal to you or in your presence. I began to wonder how many blank-faced, seemingly dull-witted but trustworthy servants or retainers were really from the Tribe, carrying out their work of intrigue, subterfuge, and sudden death.

Kenji initiated me into the arts of the Tribe, but I still had lessons from Ichiro in the ways of the clans. The warrior class was the complete opposite of the Tribe. They set great store by the admiration and respect of the world, and their reputation and standing in it. I had to learn their history and etiquette, courtesies and language. I studied the archives of the Otori, going back for centuries, all the way to their half-mythical origins in the Emperor's family, until my head was reeling with names and genealogies.

The days shortened, the nights grew colder. The first frosts rimed the garden. Soon the snow would shut off the mountain passes, winter storms would close the port, and Hagi would be isolated until spring. The house had a different song now, muffled, soft, and sleeping.

Something had unlocked a mad hunger in me for learning. Kenji said it was the character of the Tribe surfacing after years of neglect. It embraced everything, from the most complex characters in writing to the demands of swordplay. These I learned wholeheartedly, but I had a more divided response to Kenji's lessons. I did not find them difficult—they came all too naturally to me—but there was something about them that repelled me, something within me that resisted becoming what he wanted me to be.

"It's a game," he told me many times. "Play it like a game." But it was a game whose end was death. Kenji had been right in his reading of my character. I had been brought up to abhor murder, and I had a deep reluctance to take life.

He studied that aspect of me. It made him uneasy. He and Lord Shigeru often talked about ways to make me tougher.

"He has all the talents, save that one," Kenji said one evening in frustration. "And that lack makes all his talents a danger to him."

"You never know," Shigeru replied. "When the situation arises, it is amazing how the sword leaps in the hand, almost as though it has a will of its own."

"You were born that way, Shigeru, and all your training has reinforced it. My belief is that Takeo will hesitate in that moment."

"Unnh," the lord grunted, moving closer to the brazier and pulling his coat around him. Snow had been falling all day. It lay piled in the garden, each tree coated, each lantern wearing a thick white cap. The sky had cleared and frost made the snow sparkle. Our breath hung in the air as we spoke.

Nobody else was awake, just the three of us, huddled round the brazier, warming our hands on cups of hot wine. It made me bold enough to ask, "Lord Otori must have killed many men?"

"I don't know that I've kept a count," he replied. "But apart from Yaegahara, probably not so very many. I have never killed an unarmed man, or killed for pleasure, as some are corrupted into. Better you should stay the way you are than come to that."

I wanted to ask, *Would you use an assassin to get revenge?* But I did not dare. It was true that I disliked cruelty and shrank from the idea of killing. But every day I learned more about Shigeru's desire for revenge. It seemed to seep from him into me, where it fed my own desire. That night I slid open the screens in the early hours of the morning and looked out over the garden. The waning moon and a single star lay close together in the sky, so low that they looked as if they were eavesdropping on the sleeping town. The air was knife-cold.

*I could kill*, I thought. *I could kill Iida.* And then: *I will kill him. I will learn how.*

A few days after that, I surprised Kenji and myself. His ability to be in two places at once still fooled me. I'd see the old man in his faded robe, sitting, watching me while I practiced some sleight of hand or backwards tumble, and then his voice would call me from outside the building. But this time, I felt or heard his breath, jumped towards him, caught him round the neck, and had him on the ground before I even thought, *Where is he?*

And to my amazement my hands went of their own accord to the spot on the artery in the neck where pressure brings death.

I had him there for only a moment. I let go and we stared at each other.

"Well," he said. "That's more like it!"

I looked at my long-fingered, clever hands as if they belonged to a stranger.

My hands did other things I had not known they could do. When I was practicing writing with Ichiro, my right hand would suddenly sketch a few strokes, and there would be one of my mountain birds about to fly off the paper, or the face of someone I did not know I remembered. Ichiro cuffed me round the head for it, but the drawings pleased him, and he showed them to Lord Shigeru.

He was delighted, and so was Kenji.

"It's a Kikuta trait," Kenji boasted, as proud as if he'd invented it himself. "Very useful. It gives Takeo a role to play, a perfect disguise. He's an artist: He can sketch in all sorts of places and no one will wonder what he can hear."

Lord Shigeru was equally practical. "Draw the one-armed man," he commanded.

The wolfish face seemed to jump of its own accord from the brush. Lord Shigeru stared at it. "I'll know him again," he muttered.

A drawing master was arranged, and through

96

the winter days my new character evolved. By the time the snow melted, Tomasu, the half-wild boy who roamed the mountain and read only its animals and plants, was gone forever. I had become Takeo, quiet, outwardly gentle, an artist, somewhat bookish, a disguise that hid the ears and eyes that missed nothing, and the heart that was learning the lessons of revenge.

I did not know if this Takeo was real or just a construction created to serve the purposes of the Tribe, and the Otori.

# CHAPTER 4

The bamboo grass had turned white-edged and the maples had put on their brocade robes. Junko brought Kaede old garments from Lady Noguchi, carefully unpicking them and resewing them with the faded parts turned inwards. As the days grew colder she was thankful that she was no longer in the castle, running through the courtyards and up and down steps as snow fell on frozen snow. Her work became more leisurely: She spent her days with the Noguchi women, engaged in sewing and household crafts, listening to stories and making up poems, learning to write in women's script. But she was far from happy.

Lady Noguchi found fault with everything about her: She was repelled by her left-handedness, she compared her looks unfavorably to her daughters', she deplored her height and her thinness. She declared herself shocked by Kaede's lack of education in almost everything, never admitting that this might be her fault.

In private, Junko praised Kaede's pale skin, delicate limbs, and thick hair, and Kaede, gazing in the mirror whenever she could, thought that maybe she was beautiful. She knew men looked at her with desire, even here in the lord's residence, but she feared all men. Since the guard's assault on her, their nearness made her skin crawl. She dreaded the idea of marriage. Whenever a guest came to the house, she was afraid he might be her future husband. If she had to come into his presence with tea or wine, her heart raced and her hands shook, until Lady Noguchi decided she was too clumsy to wait on guests and must be confined to the women's quarters.

She grew bored and anxious. She quarreled with Lady Noguchi's daughters, scolded the maids over trifles, and was even irritable with Junko.

"The girl must be married," Lady Noguchi declared, and to Kaede's horror a marriage was swiftly arranged with one of Lord Noguchi's retainers. Betrothal gifts were exchanged, and she recognized the man from her audience with the lord. Not only was he old—three times her age, married twice before, and physically repulsive to her—but she knew her own worth. The marriage was an insult to her and her family. She was being thrown away. She wept for nights and could not eat.

A week before the wedding, messengers came in the night, rousing the residence. Lady Noguchi summoned Kaede in rage.

"You are very unlucky, Lady Shirakawa. I think you must be cursed. Your betrothed husband is dead."

The man, celebrating the coming end to his widowhood, had been drinking with friends, had had a sudden seizure, and had fallen stone dead into the wine cups.

Kaede was sick with relief, but the second mortality was also held to be her fault. Two men had now died on her account, and the rumor began to spread that whoever desired her courted death.

She hoped it might put everyone off marrying her, but one evening, when the third month was drawing to a close and the trees were putting out bright new leaves, Junko whispered to her, "One of the Otori clan has been offered as my lady's husband."

They were embroidering, and Kaede lost the swaying rhythm of the stitching and jabbed herself with the needle, so hard that she drew blood. Junko quickly pulled the silk away before she stained it.

"Who is he?" she asked, putting her finger to her mouth and tasting the salt of her own blood.

"I don't know exactly. But Lord Iida himself is in favor, and the Tohan keen to seal the alliance with the Otori. Then they will control the whole of the Middle Country."

"How old is he?" Kaede forced herself to ask next.

"It's not clear yet, lady. But age does not matter in a husband."

Kaede took up the embroidery again: white

cranes and blue turtles on a deep pink background—a wedding robe. "I wish it would never be finished!"

"Be happy, Lady Kaede. You will be leaving here. The Otori live in Hagi, by the sea. It's an honorable match for you."

"Marriage frightens me," Kaede said.

"Everyone's frightened of what they don't know! But women come to enjoy it; you'll see." Junko chuckled to herself.

Kaede remembered the hands of the guard, his strength, his desire, and felt revulsion rise in her. Her own hands, usually deft and quick, slowed. Junko scolded her, but not unkindly, and for the rest of the day treated her with great gentleness.

A few days later she was summoned to Lord Noguchi. She had heard the tramp of horses' feet and the shouts of strange men as guests arrived, but had as usual kept out of the way. It was with trepidation that she entered the audience room, but to her surprise and joy, her father was seated in a place of honor, at Lord Noguchi's side.

As she bowed to the ground she saw the delight leap into his face. She was proud that he saw her in a more honorable position now. She vowed she would never do anything to bring him sorrow or dishonor.

When she was told to sit up, she tried to take a discreet look at him. His hair was thinner and grayer, his face more lined. She longed for news of her mother and sisters; she hoped she would be granted some time alone with him.

"Lady Shirakawa," Lord Noguchi began. "We have received an offer for you in marriage, and your father has come to give his consent."

Kaede bowed low again, murmuring, "Lord Noguchi."

"It is a great honor for you. It will seal the alliance between the Tohan and the Otori, and unite three ancient families. Lord Iida himself will attend your wedding: Indeed, he wants it to take place in Inuyama. Since your mother is not well, a relative of your family, Lady Maruyama, is going to escort you to Tsuwano. Your husband is to be Otori Shigeru, a nephew of the Otori lords. He and his retainers will meet you in Tsuwano. I don't think any other arrangements need to be made. It's all very satisfactory."

Kaede's eyes had flown to her father's face when she heard her mother was not well. She hardly took in Lord Noguchi's subsequent words. Later she realized that the whole affair had been arranged with the least possible inconvenience and expense to himself: some robes for travel and to be married in, possibly a maid to accompany her. Truly he had come out of the whole exchange well.

He was joking now about the dead guard. The color rose in Kaede's face. Her father's eyes were cast down.

*I'm glad be lost a man over me,* she thought savagely. *May be lose a hundred more.*

Her father was to return home the following day, his wife's illness preventing a longer stay. In his expansive mood, Lord Noguchi urged him to spend time with his daughter. Kaede led her father to the small room overlooking the garden. The air was warm, heavy with the scents of spring. A bush warbler called from the pine tree. Junko served them tea. Her courtesy and attentiveness lightened her father's mood.

"I am glad you have one friend here, Kaede," he murmured.

"What is the news of my mother?" she said, anxiously.

"I wish it were better. I fear the rainy season will weaken her further. But this marriage has lifted her spirits. The Otori are a great family, and Lord Shigeru, it seems, a fine man. His reputation is good. He is well liked and respected. It's all we could have hoped for you—more than we could have hoped."

"Then I am happy with it," she said, lying to please him.

He gazed out at the cherry blossoms, each tree heavy, dreaming in its own beauty. "Kaede, the matter of the dead guard . . ."

"It was not my fault," she said hastily. "Captain Arai acted to protect me. All the fault was with the dead man."

He sighed. "They are saying that you are dangerous to men—that Lord Otori should beware. Nothing must happen to prevent this wedding. Do you understand me, Kaede? If it does not go ahead—if the fault can be laid on you—we are all as good as dead."

Kaede bowed, her heart heavy. Her father was like a stranger to her.

"It's been a burden on you to carry the safety of our family for all these years. Your mother and your sisters miss you. I myself would have had things differently, if I could choose over again. Maybe if I had taken part in the battle of Yaegahara, had not waited to see who would emerge the victor but had joined Iida from the start . . . but it's all past now, and cannot be brought back. In his way Lord Noguchi has kept his side of the bargain. You are alive; you are to make a good marriage. I know you will not fail us now."

"Father," she said as a small breeze blew suddenly through the garden, and the pink and white petals drifted like snow to the ground.

The next day her father left. Kaede watched him ride away with his retainers. They had been with her family since before her own birth, and she remembered some of them by name: her father's closest friend, Shoji, and young Amano, who was only a few years older than she was. After they had left through the castle gate, the horses' hooves crushing the cherry blossoms that carpeted the shallow cobbled steps, she ran to the bailey to watch them disappear along the banks of the river. Finally the dust settled, the town dogs quieted, and they were gone.

The next time she saw her father she would be a married woman, making the formal return to her parents' home.

Kaede went back to the residence, scowling to keep her tears at bay. Her spirits were not improved by hearing a stranger's voice. Someone was chatting away to Junko. It was the sort of chat that she most despised, in a little-girl voice with a high-pitched giggle. She could just imagine the girl, tiny, with round cheeks like a doll, a small-stepped walk like a bird's, and a head that was always bobbing and bowing.

When she hurried into the room, Junko and the strange girl were working on her clothes, making the last adjustments, folding and stitching. The Noguchi were losing no time in getting rid of her. Bamboo baskets and paulownia wood boxes stood ready to be packed. The sight of them upset Kaede further.

"What is this person doing here?" she demanded irritably.

The girl flattened herself to the floor, overdoing it, as Kaede had known she would.

"This is Shizuka," Junko said. "She is to travel with Lady Kaede to Inuyama."

"I don't want her," Kaede replied. "I want you to come with me."

"Lady, it's not possible for me to leave. Lady Noguchi would never permit it."

"Then tell her to send someone else."

Shizuka, still facedown on the ground, gave what

sounded like a sob. Kaede, sure that it was feigned, was unmoved.

"You are upset, lady. The news of the marriage, your father's departure . . ." Junko tried to placate her. "She's a good girl, very pretty, very clever. Sit up, Shizuka: Let Lady Shirakawa look at you."

The girl raised herself but did not look directly at Kaede. From her downcast eyes, tears trickled. She sniffed once or twice. "Lady, please don't send me away. I'll do anything for you. I swear, you'll never have anyone look after you better than me. I'll carry you in the rain, I'll let you warm your feet on me in the cold." Her tears seemed to have dried and she was smiling again.

"You didn't warn me how beautiful Lady Shirakawa is," she said to Junko. "No wonder men die for her!"

"Don't say that!" Kaede cried. She walked angrily to the doorway. Two gardeners were cleaning leaves off the moss, one by one. "I'm tired of having it said of me."

"It will always be said," Junko remarked. "It is part of the lady's life now."

"I wish men would die for me," Shizuka laughed. "But they just seem to fall in and out of love with me as easily as I do with them!"

Kaede did not turn around. The girl shuffled on her knees to the boxes and began folding the garments again, singing softly as she did it. Her voice was clear and true. It was an old ballad about the little village in the pine forest, the girl, the young man. Kaede thought she recalled it from her childhood. It brought clearly into her mind the fact that her childhood was over, that she was to marry a stranger, that she would never know love. Maybe people in villages could fall in love, but for someone in her position it was not even to be considered.

She strode across the room and, kneeling next to Shizuka, took the garment roughly from her. "If you're going to do it, do it properly!"

"Yes, lady." Shizuka flattened herself again, crushing the robes around her. "Thank you, lady, you'll never regret it!"

As she sat up again she murmured, "People say Lord Arai takes a great interest in Lady Shirakawa. They talk of his regard for her honor."

"Do you know Arai?" Kaede said sharply.

"I am from his town, lady. From Kumamoto."

Junko was smiling broadly. "I can say good-bye with a calm mind if I know you have Shizuka to look after you."

So Shizuka became part of Kaede's life, irritating and amusing her in equal measures. She loved gossip, spread rumors without the least concern, was always disappearing into the kitchens, the stables, the castle, and coming back bursting with stories. She was popular with everyone and had no fear of men. As far as Kaede could see, they were more afraid of her, in awe of her teasing words and sharp tongue. On the surface she appeared slapdash, but her care of

Kaede was meticulous. She massaged away her headaches, brought ointments made of herbs and beeswax to soften her creamy skin, plucked her eyebrows into a more gentle shape. Kaede came to rely on her, and eventually to trust her. Despite herself, Shizuka made her laugh, and she brought her for the first time into contact with the outside world, from which Kaede had been isolated.

So Kaede learned of the uneasy relationships between the clans, the many bitter grudges left after Yaegahara, the alliances Iida was trying to form with the Otori and the Seishuu, the constant to-and-fro of men vying for position and preparing once again for war. She also learned of the Hidden, Iida's persecution of them, and his demands that his allies should do the same.

She had never heard of such people and thought at first that Shizuka was making them up. Then one evening Shizuka, uncharacteristically subdued, whispered to her that men and women had been found in a small village and brought to Noguchi in basket cages. They were to be hung from the castle walls until they died of hunger and thirst. The crows pecked at them while they were still alive.

"Why? What crime did they commit?" she questioned.

"They say there is a secret god, who sees everything and who they cannot offend or deny. They would rather die."

Kaede shivered. "Why does Lord Iida hate them so?"

Shizuka glanced over her shoulder, even though they were alone in the room. "They say the secret god will punish Iida in the afterlife."

"But Iida is the most powerful lord in the Three Countries. He can do what he wants. They have no right to judge him." The idea that a lord's actions should be judged by ordinary village people was ludicrous to Kaede.

"The Hidden believe that their god sees everyone as equal. There are no lords in their god's eyes. Only those who believe in him and those who do not."

Kaede frowned. No wonder Iida wanted to stamp them out. She would have asked more but Shizuka changed the subject.

"Lady Maruyama is expected any day now. Then we will begin our journey."

"It will be good to leave this place of death," Kaede said.

"Death is everywhere." Shizuka took the comb and with long, even strokes ran it through Kaede's hair. "Lady Maruyama is a close relative of yours. Did you meet her when you were a child?"

"If I did I don't remember it. She is my mother's cousin, I believe, but I know very little about her. Have you met her?"

"I have seen her," Shizuka said with a laugh. "People like me don't really meet people like her!"

"Tell me about her," Kaede said.

"As you know, she owns a large domain in the southwest. Her husband and her son are both dead, and her daughter, who would inherit, is a hostage in Inuyama. It is well known that the lady is no friend to the Tohan, despite her husband being of that clan. Her stepdaughter is married to Iida's cousin. There were rumors that after her husband's death, his family had her son poisoned. First Iida offered his brother to her in marriage, but she refused him. Now they say he himself wants to marry her."

"Surely he is married already, and has a son," Kaede interrupted.

"None of Lady Iida's other children has survived beyond childhood, and her health is very poor. It might fail at any time."

*In other words, he might murder her*, Kaede thought, but did not dare say it.

"Anyway," Shizuka went on, "Lady Maruyama will never marry him, so they say, and she will not allow her daughter to either."

"She makes her own decisions about who she will marry? She sounds like a powerful woman."

"Maruyama is the last of the great domains to be inherited through the female line," Shizuka explained. "This gives her more power than other women. And then, she has other powers that seem almost magic. She bewitches people to get her own way."

"Do you believe such things?"

"How else can you explain her survival? Her late

husband's family, Lord Iida, and most of the Tohan would crush her, but she survives, despite having lost her son to them and seeing them hold her daughter."

Kaede felt her heart twist in sympathy. "Why do women have to suffer this way? Why don't we have the freedom men have?"

"It's the way the world is," Shizuka replied. "Men are stronger and not held back by feelings of tenderness or mercy. Women fall in love with them, but they do not return that love."

"I will never fall in love," Kaede said.

"Better not to," Shizuka agreed, and laughed. She prepared the beds, and they lay down to sleep. Kaede thought for a long time about the lady who held power like a man, the lady who had lost a son and as good as lost a daughter. She thought of the girl, hostage in the Iida stronghold at Inuyama, and pitied her.

Lady Noguchi's reception room was decorated in the mainland style, the doors and screens painted with scenes of mountains and pine trees. Kaede disliked all the pictures, finding them heavy, their gold leaf flamboyant and ostentatious, save the one farthest to the left. This was of two pheasants, so lifelike that they looked as if they might suddenly take flight. Their eyes were bright, their heads cocked. They listened to the conversation in the room with more animation than most of the women who knelt before Lady Noguchi.

On the lady's right sat the visitor, Lady Maruyama. Lady Noguchi made a sign to Kaede to approach a little closer. She bent to the floor and listened to the two-tongued words being spoken above her head.

"Of course we are distraught at losing Lady Kaede: She has been like our own daughter. And we hesitate to burden Lady Maruyama. We ask only that Kaede be allowed to accompany you as far as Tsuwano. There the Otori lords will meet her."

"Lady Shirakawa is to be married into the Otori family?" Kaede liked the low, gentle voice she heard. She raised her head very slightly so she could see the lady's small hands folded in her lap.

"Yes, to Lord Otori Shigeru," Lady Noguchi purred. "It is a great honor. Of course, my husband is very close to Lord Iida, who himself desires the match."

Kaede saw the hands clench until the blood drained from them. After a pause, so long it was almost impolite, Lady Maruyama said, "Lord Otori Shigeru? Lady Shirakawa is fortunate indeed."

"The lady has met him? I have never had that pleasure."

"I know Lord Otori very slightly," Lady Maruyama replied. "Sit up, Lady Shirakawa, let me see your face."

Kaede raised her head.

"You are so young!" the older woman exclaimed.

112

"I am fifteen, lady."

"Only a little older than my daughter." Lady Maruyama's voice was thin and faint. Kaede dared look in the dark eyes, with their perfect shape. The pupils were dilated as if in shock, and the lady's face was whiter than any powder could have made it. Then she seemed to regain some control over herself. A smile came to her lips, though it did not reach her eyes.

*What have I done to her?* Kaede thought in confusion. She had felt instinctively drawn to her. She thought Shizuka was right: Lady Maruyama could get anyone to do anything for her. Her beauty was faded, it was true, but somehow the faint lines round the eyes and mouth simply added to the character and strength of the face. Now the coldness of her expression wounded Kaede deeply.

*She doesn't like me*, the girl thought, with an overwhelming sense of disappointment.

# CHAPTER 5

The snow melted and the house and garden began to sing with water again. I had been in Hagi for six months. I had learned to read, write, and draw. I had learned to kill in many different ways, although I was yet to put any one of them into practice. I felt I could hear the intentions of men's hearts, and I'd learned other useful skills, though these were not so much taught to me by Kenji, as drawn up out of me. I could be in two places at once, and take on invisibility, and could silence dogs with a look that dropped them immediately into sleep. This last trick I discovered on my own, and kept it from Kenji, for he taught me deviousness along with everything else.

I used these skills whenever I grew tired of the confines of the house, and its relentless routine of study, practice, and obedience to my two severe teachers. I found it all too easy to distract the guards, put the dogs to sleep, and slip through the gate without anyone seeing me. Even Ichiro and Kenji more than once were convinced I was sitting somewhere quietly in the house with ink and brush, when I was out with Fumio, exploring the back alleys around the port, swimming in the river, listening to the sailors and the fishermen, breathing in the heady mix of salt air, hemp ropes and nets, and seafood in all its forms, raw, steamed, grilled, made into little dumplings or hearty stews that made our stomachs growl with hunger. I caught the different accents, from the West, from the islands, even from the mainland, and listened to conversations no one knew could be overheard, learning always about the lives of the people, their fears and their desires.

Sometimes I went out on my own, crossing the river either by the fish weir or swimming. I explored the lands on the far side, going deep into the mountains where farmers had their secret fields, tucked away among the trees, unseen and therefore untaxed. I saw the new green leaves burgeon in the coppices, and heard the chestnut groves come alive with buzzing insects seeking the pollen on their golden catkins. I heard the farmers buzz like insects, too, grumbling endlessly about the Otori lords, the ever-increasing burden of taxes. And time and again Lord Shigeru's name came up, and I learned of the bitterness held by more than half the population that it was his uncles, and not he, in the castle. This was treason, spoken of only at night or deep in the forest, when no one could overhear except me, and I said nothing about it to anyone.

Spring burst on the landscape; the air was warm, the whole earth alive. I was filled with a restlessness

I did not understand. I was looking for something, but had no idea what it was. Kenji took me to the pleasure district, and I slept with girls there, not telling him I had already visited the same places with Fumio, and finding only a brief release from my longing. The girls filled me with pity as much as lust. They reminded me of the girls I'd grown up with in Mino. They came in all likelihood from similar families, sold into prostitution by their starving parents. Some of them were barely out of childhood, and I searched their faces, looking for my sisters' features. Shame often crept over me, but I did not stay away.

The spring festivals came, packing the shrines and the streets with people. Drums shouted every night, the drummers' faces and arms glistening with sweat in the lantern light, possessed beyond exhaustion. I could not resist the fever of the celebrations, the frenzied ecstasy of the crowds. One night I'd been out with Fumio, following the god's statue as it was carried through the streets by a throng of struggling, excited men. I had just said good-bye to him, when I was shoved into someone, almost stepping on him. He turned towards me and I recognized him: It was the traveler who had stayed at our house and tried to warn us of Iida's persecution. A short squat man, with an ugly, shrewd face, he was a kind of peddler who sometimes came to Mino. Before I could turn away I saw the flash of recognition in his eyes, and saw pity spring there too.

He shouted to make himself heard above the yelling crowd. "Tomasu!"

I shook my head, making my face and eyes blank, but he was insistent. He tried to pull me out of the crowd into a passageway. "Tomasu, it's you, isn't it—the boy from Mino?"

"You're mistaken," I said. "I know no one called Tomasu."

"Everyone thought you were dead!"

"I don't know what you're talking about," I laughed, as if at a great joke, and tried to push my way back into the crowd. He grabbed my arm to detain me and as he opened his mouth I knew what he was going to say.

"Your mother's dead. They killed her. They killed them all. You're the only one left! How did you get away?" He tried to pull my face close to his. I could smell his breath, his sweat.

"You're drunk, old man!" I said. "My mother is alive and well in Hofu, last I heard." I pushed him off and reached for my knife. "I am of the Otori clan." I let anger replace my laughter.

He backed away. "Forgive me, lord. It was a mistake. I see now you are not who I thought you were." He was a little drunk, but fear was fast sobering him.

Through my mind flashed several thoughts at once, the most pressing being that now I would have to kill this man, this harmless peddler who had tried to warn my family. I saw exactly how it would be done: I would lead him deeper into the

117

passageway, take him off balance, slip the knife into the artery in the neck, slash upwards, then let him fall, lie like a drunk, and bleed to death. Even if anyone saw me, no one would dare apprehend me.

The crowd surged past us; the knife was in my hand. He dropped to the ground, his head in the dirt, pleading incoherently for his life.

*I cannot kill him,* I thought, and then: *There is no need to kill him. He's decided I'm not Tomasu, and even if he has his doubts, he will never dare voice them to anyone. He is one of the Hidden, after all.*

I backed away and let the crowd carry me as far as the gates of the shrine. Then I slipped through the throng to the path that ran along the bank of the river. Here it was dark, deserted, but I could still hear the shouts of the excited crowd, the chants of the priests, and the dull tolling of the temple bell. The river lapped and sucked at the boats, the docks, the reeds. I remembered the first night I spent in Lord Shigeru's house. *The river is always at the door. The world is always outside. And it is in the world that we must live.*

The dogs, sleepy and docile, followed me with their eyes as I went through the gate, but the guards did not notice. Sometimes on these occasions I would creep into the guardroom and take them by surprise, but this night I had no stomach for jokes. I thought bitterly how slow and unobservant they were, how easy it would be for another member of the Tribe to enter, as the assassin had done. Then I was filled with revulsion for this world of stealth, duplicity, and intrigue that I was so skilled in. I longed to be Tomasu again, running down the mountain to my mother's house.

The corners of my eyes were burning. The garden was full of the scents and sounds of spring. In the moonlight the early blossoms gleamed with a fragile whiteness. Their purity pierced my heart. How was it possible for the world to be so beautiful and so cruel at the same time?

Lamps on the veranda flickered and guttered in the warm breeze. Kenji was sitting in the shadows. He called to me, "Lord Shigeru has been scolding Ichiro for losing you. I told him, 'You can gentle a fox but you'll never turn it into a house dog!'" He saw my face as I came into the light. "What happened?"

"My mother is dead." *Only children cry. Men and women endure.* Within my heart the child Tomasu was crying, but Takeo was dry-eyed.

Kenji drew me closer and whispered, "Who told you?"

"Someone I knew from Mino was at the shrine."

"He recognized you?"

"He thought he did. I persuaded him he was wrong. But while he still thought I was Tomasu, he told me of my mother's death."

"I'm sorry for it," Kenji said perfunctorily. "You killed him, I hope."

I didn't reply. I didn't need to. He knew almost as soon as he'd formed the question. He thwacked

119

me on the back in exasperation, as Ichiro did when I missed a stroke in a character. "You're a fool, Takeo!"

"He was unarmed, harmless. He knew my family."

"It's just as I feared. You let pity stay your hand. Don't you know the man whose life you spare will always hate you? All you did was convince him you are Tomasu."

"Why should he die because of my destiny? What benefit would his death bring? None!"

"It's the disasters his life, his living tongue, may bring that concern me," Kenji replied, and went inside to tell Lord Shigeru.

I was in disgrace in the household and forbidden to wander alone in the town. Kenji kept a closer eye on me, and I found it almost impossible to evade him. It didn't keep me from trying. As always, an obstacle only had to be set before me for me to seek to overcome it. I infuriated him by my lack of obedience, but my skills grew even more acute, and I came to have more and more confidence in them.

Lord Shigeru spoke to me of my mother's death after Kenji had told him of my failure as an assassin. "You wept for her the first night we met. There must be no sign of grief now. You don't know who is watching you."

So the grief remained unexpressed, in my heart. At night I silently repeated the prayers of the

Hidden for my mother's soul, and for my sisters'. But I did not say the prayers of forgiveness she had taught me. I had no intention of loving my enemies. I let my grief feed my desire for revenge.

That night was also the last time I saw Fumio. When I managed to evade Kenji and get to the port again, the Terada ships had vanished. I learned from the other fishermen that they had left one night, finally driven into exile by high taxes and unfair regulations. The rumors were that they had fled to Oshima, where the family originally hailed from. With that remote island as a base, they would almost certainly turn to piracy.

Around this time, before the plum rains began, Lord Shigeru became very interested in construction and proceeded with his plans to build a tea room on one end of the house. I went with him to choose the wood, the cedar trunks that would support floor and roof, the slabs of cypress for the walls. The smell of sawn wood reminded me of the mountains, and the carpenters had the characteristics of the men of my village, being mostly taciturn but given to sudden outbursts of laughter over their unfathomable jokes. I found myself slipping back into my old patterns of speech, using words from the village I had not used for months. Sometimes my slang even made them chuckle.

Lord Shigeru was intrigued by all the stages of building, from seeing the trees felled in the forest to the preparation of the planks and the different methods of laying floors. We made many visits to the lumberyard, accompanied by the master carpenter, Shiro, a man who seemed to be fashioned from the same material as the wood he loved so much, brother to the cedar and the cypress. He spoke of the character and spirit of each type of wood, and what it brings from the forest into the house.

"Each wood has its own sound," he said. "Every house has its own song."

I had thought only I knew how a house can sing. I'd been listening to Lord Shigeru's house for months now, had heard its song quiet into winter music, had listened to its beams and walls as it pressed closer to the ground under the weight of snow, froze and thawed and shrank and stretched. Now it sang again of water.

Shiro was watching me as though he knew my thoughts.

"I've heard Lord Iida has ordered a floor to be made that sings like a nightingale," he said. "But who needs to make a floor sing like a bird when it already has its own song?"

"What's the purpose of such a floor?" Lord Shigeru asked, seemingly idly.

"He's afraid of assassination. It's one more piece of protection. No one can cross the floor without it starting to chirp."

"How is it made?"

The old man took a piece of half-made flooring and explained how the joists were placed so the boards squeaked. "They have them, I'm told, in the capital. Most people want a silent floor. They'd reject a noisy one, make you lay it again. But Iida can't sleep at night. He's afraid someone will creep in on him—and now he lies awake, afraid his floor will sing!" He chuckled to himself.

"Could you make such a floor?" Lord Shigeru inquired.

Shiro grinned at me. "I can make a floor so quiet, even Takeo can't hear it. I reckon I can make one that would sing."

"Takeo will help you," the lord announced. "He needs to know exactly how it is constructed."

I did not dare ask why then. I already had a fair idea, but I did not want to put it into words. The discussion moved on to the tea room, and while Shiro directed its building, he made a small singing floor, a boardwalk that replaced the verandas of the house, and I watched every board laid, every joist and every peg.

Chiyo complained that the squeaking gave her a headache, and that it sounded more like mice than any bird. But eventually the household grew used to it, and the noises became part of the everyday song of the house.

The floor amused Kenji to no end: He thought it would keep me inside. Lord Shigeru said no more about why I had to know how the floor was made, but I imagine he knew the pull it would have on me. I listened to it all day long. I knew exactly who was walking on it by their tread. I could predict the next note of the floor's song.

I tried to walk on it without awakening the birds. It was hard—Shiro had done his job well—but not impossible. I had watched the floor being made. I knew there was nothing enchanted about it. It was just a matter of time before I mastered it. With the almost fanatical patience that I knew now was a trait of the Tribe, I practiced crossing the floor.

The rains began. One night the air was so hot and humid, I could not sleep. I went to get a drink from the cistern and then stood in the doorway, looking at the floor stretching away from me. I knew I was going to cross it without waking anyone.

I moved swiftly, my feet knowing where to step and with how much pressure. The birds remained silent. I felt the deep pleasure, no kin to elation, that acquiring the skills of the Tribe brings, until I heard the sound of breathing, and turned to see Lord Shigeru watching me.

"You heard me," I said, disappointed.

"No, I was already awake. Can you do it again?"

I stayed crouched where I was for a moment, retreating into myself in the way of the Tribe, letting everything drain from me except my awareness of the noises of the night. Then I ran back across the nightingale floor. The birds slept on.

I thought about Iida lying awake in Inuyama, listening for the singing birds. I imagined myself creeping across the floor towards him, completely silent, completely undetected.

If Lord Shigeru was thinking the same thing, he did not mention it. All he said now was, "I'm disappointed in Shiro. I thought his floor would outwit you."

Neither of us said, *But will Iida's?* Nevertheless the question lay between us, in the heavy night air of the sixth month.

The teahouse was also finished, and we often shared tea there in the evenings, reminding me of the first time I had tasted the expensive green brew prepared by Lady Maruyama. I felt Lord Shigeru had built it with her in mind, but he never mentioned it. At the door of the tea room grew a twin-trunked camellia; maybe it was this symbol of married love that started everyone talking about the desirability of marriage. Ichiro in particular urged the lord to set about finding another wife. "Your mother's death, and Takeshi's, have been an excuse for some time. But you have been unmarried for nearly ten years now, and have no children. It's unheard of!"

The servants gossiped about it, forgetting that I could hear them clearly from every part of the house. The general opinion among them was in fact close to the truth, although they did not really believe it themselves. They decided Lord Shigeru must be in love with some unsuitable or unobtainable woman. They must have sworn fidelity to each other, the girls sighed, since to their regret he had never invited any of them to share his bed.

The older women, more realistic, pointed out that these things might occur in songs but had no bearing on the everyday life of the warrior class. "Maybe he prefers boys," Haruka, the boldest of the girls, replied, adding in a fit of giggles. "Ask Takeo!" Whereupon Chiyo said preferring boys was one thing, and marriage was another. The two had nothing to do with each other.

Lord Shigeru evaded all these questions of marriage, saying he was more concerned with the process of my adoption. For months nothing had been heard from the clan, except that the subject was still under deliberation. The Otori had more pressing concerns to attend to. Iida had started his summer campaign in the East, and fief after fief had either joined the Tohan or been conquered and annihilated. Soon he would turn his attention again to the Middle Country. The Otori had grown used to peace. Lord Shigeru's uncles were disinclined to confront Iida and plunge the fief into war again. Yet, the idea of submitting to the Tohan rankled with most of the clan.

Hagi was rife with rumors, and tense. Kenji was uneasy. He watched me all the time, and the constant supervision made me irritable.

"There are more Tohan spies in town every week," he said. "Sooner or later one of them is going to recognize Takeo. Let me take him away."

"Once he is legally adopted and under the protection of the clan, Iida will think twice about touching him," Lord Shigeru replied.

"I think you underestimate him. He will dare anything."

"Maybe in the East. But not in the Middle Country."

They often argued about it, Kenji pressing the lord to let me go away with him, Lord Shigeru evading him, refusing to take the danger seriously, holding that once I was adopted I would be safer in Hagi than anywhere.

I caught Kenji's mood. I was on guard all the time, always alert, always watching. The only time I found peace was when I was absorbed in learning new skills. I became obsessive about honing my talents.

Finally the message came at the end of the seventh month: Lord Shigeru was to bring me to the castle the next day, where his uncles would receive me and a decision would be given.

Chiyo scrubbed me, washed and trimmed my hair, and brought out clothes that were new but subdued in color. Ichiro went over and over all the etiquette and the courtesies, the language I should use, how low I should bow. "Don't let us down," he hissed at me as we left. "After all he has done for you, don't let Lord Shigeru down."

Kenji did not come with us but said he would follow us as far as the castle gate. "Just keep your ears open," he told me—as if it were possible for me to do anything else.

I was on Raku, the pale gray horse with the black mane and tail. Lord Shigeru rode ahead of me on his black horse, Kyu, with five or six retainers. As we approached the castle I was seized by panic. Its power as it loomed ahead of us, its complete dominance over the town, unnerved me. What was I doing, pretending to be a lord, a warrior? The Otori lords would take one look at me and see me for what I was: the son of a peasant woman and an assassin. Worse, I felt horribly exposed, riding through the crowded street. I imagined that everyone was looking at me.

Raku felt the panic and tensed. A sudden movement in the crowd made him shy slightly. Without thinking, I let my breathing slow and softened my body. He quieted immediately. But his action had spun us around, and as I turned his head back I caught sight of a man in the street. I only saw his face for a moment, but I knew him at once. I saw the empty sleeve on his right-hand side. I had drawn his likeness for Lord Shigeru and Kenji. It was the man who had pursued me up the mountain path, whose right arm Jato had sliced through.

He did not appear to be watching me, and I had no way of knowing if he had recognized me. I drew the horse back and rode on. I don't believe I gave the slightest sign I had noticed him. The entire episode lasted no more than a minute.

Strangely, it calmed me. *This is real*, I thought. *Not a game. Maybe I am pretending to be something I'm not, but if I fail in it, it means death.* And then I thought, *I am Kikuta. I am of the Tribe. I am a match for anyone.*

As we crossed the moat I spotted Kenji in the crowd, an old man in a faded robe. Then the main gates were opened to us, and we rode through into the first courtyard.

Here we dismounted. The men stayed with the horses, and Lord Shigeru and I were met by an elderly man, the steward, who took us to the residence.

It was an imposing and gracious building on the seaward side of the castle, protected by a smaller bailey. A moat surrounded it all the way to the seawall, and inside the moat was a large, beautifully designed garden. A small, densely wooded hill rose behind the castle; above the trees rose the curved roof of a shrine.

The sun had come out briefly, and the stones steamed in the heat. I could feel the sweat forming on my forehead and in my armpits. I could hear the sea hissing at the rocks below the wall. I wished I were swimming in it.

We took off our sandals, and maids came with cool water to wash our feet. The steward led us into the house. It seemed to go on forever, room after room stretching away, each one lavishly and expensively decorated. Finally we came to an antechamber where he asked us to wait for a little while. We sat on the floor for what seemed like an hour at least. At first I was outraged—at the insult to Lord Shigeru, at the extravagant luxury of the house, which I knew came from the taxes imposed on the farmers. I wanted to tell Lord

Shigeru about my sighting of Iida's man in Hagi, but I did not dare speak. He seemed engrossed in the painting on the doors: a gray heron stood in a teal-green river, gazing at a pink and gold mountain.

Finally I remembered Kenji's advice and spent the rest of the time listening to the house. It did not sing of the river, like Lord Shigeru's, but had a deeper and graver note, underpinned by the constant surge of the sea. I counted how many different footsteps I could hear, and decided there were fifty-three people in the household. I could hear three children in the garden, playing with two puppies. I heard the ladies talking about a boat trip they were hoping to make if the weather held.

Then from deep inside the house I heard two men talking quietly. I heard Shigeru's name mentioned. I realized I was listening to his uncles uttering things they would let no one but each other hear.

"The main thing is to get Shigeru to agree to the marriage," said one. His was the older voice, I thought, stronger and more opinionated. I frowned, wondering what he meant. Hadn't we come to discuss adoption?

"He's always resisted marrying again," said the other, slightly deferential, presumably younger. "And to marry to seal the Tohan alliance, when he has always opposed it . . . It may simply bring him out in the open."

"We are at a very dangerous time," the older man said. "News came yesterday about the situation in the West. It seems the Seishuu are preparing to challenge Iida. Arai, the lord of Kumamoto, considers himself offended by the Noguchi, and is raising an army to fight them and the Tohan before winter."

"Is Shigeru in contact with him? It could give him the opportunity he needs. . . ."

"You don't need to spell it out," his brother replied. "I'm only too aware of Shigeru's popularity with the clan. If he is in alliance with Arai, together they could take on Iida."

"Unless we . . . shall we say, *disarm* him."

"The marriage would answer very well. It would take Shigeru to Inuyama, where he'll be under Iida's eye for a while. And the lady in question, Shirakawa Kaede, has a certain very useful reputation."

"You're not suggesting . . . ?"

"Two men have already died in connection with her. It would be regrettable if Shigeru were the third, but hardly our fault."

The younger man laughed quietly in a way that made me want to kill him. I breathed deeply, trying to calm my fury.

"What if he continues to refuse to marry?" he asked.

"We make it a condition of this adoption whim of his. I can't see how it will do us any harm."

"I've been trying to trace the boy," the younger

man said, his voice taking on the pedantic tone of an archivist. "I don't see how he can be related to Shigeru's late mother. There is no sign of him in the genealogies."

"I suppose he is illegitimate," the older man said. "I've heard he looks like Takeshi."

"Yes, his looks make it hard to argue against any Otori blood, but if we were to adopt all our illegitimate children . . ."

"Ordinarily of course it would be out of the question. But just now . . ."

"I agree."

I heard the floor creak slightly as they stood.

"One last thing," the older brother said. "You assured me Shintaro would not fail. What went wrong?"

"I've been trying to find out. Apparently this boy heard him and woke Shigeru. Shintaro took poison."

"He heard him? Is he also from the Tribe?"

"It's possible. A Muto Kenji turned up at Shigeru's last year: Some kind of tutor is the official story, but I don't think he is giving the usual kind of instruction." Again the younger brother laughed, making my flesh crawl. But I also felt a deep scorn for them. They had been told of my acute hearing, yet they did not imagine it could apply to them, here in their own house.

The slight tremor of their footsteps moved from the inner room, where this secret conversation had been taking place, into the room behind the painted doors.

A few moments later the elderly man came back, slid the doors open gently, and indicated that we should enter the audience chamber. The two lords sat side by side on low chairs. Several men knelt along each side of the room. Lord Shigeru immediately bowed to the ground, and I did the same, but not before I had taken a quick look at these two brothers, against whom my heart was already bitter in the extreme.

The older one, Lord Otori Shoichi, was tall but not particularly muscular. His face was lean and gaunt; he wore a small mustache and beard, and his hair was already going gray. The younger one, Masahiro, was shorter and squatter. He held himself very erect, as small men do. He had no beard; his face was sallow in color, and spotted with several large black moles. His hair was still black, but thin. In both of them, the distinctive Otori features, the prominent cheekbones and curved nose, were marred by the defects of character that made them both cruel and weak.

"Lord Shigeru—nephew—you are very welcome," Shoichi said graciously.

Lord Shigeru sat up, but I remained with my forehead on the floor.

"You have been much in our thoughts," Masahiro said. "We have been very concerned for you. Your brother's passing away, coming so soon after your mother's death and your own illness, has been a heavy burden to you."

The words sounded kindly, but I knew they were spoken by the second tongue.

"I thank you for your concern," Shigeru replied, "but you must allow me to correct you in one thing. My brother did not pass away. He was murdered."

He said it without emotion, as if simply stating a fact. No one in the room made any reaction. A deep silence followed.

Lord Shoichi broke it by saying, with feigned cheerfulness, "And this is your young charge? He is also welcome. What is his name?"

"We call him Takeo," Shigeru replied.

"Apparently he has very sharp hearing?" Masahiro leaned forward a little.

"Nothing out of the ordinary," Shigeru said. "We all have sharp hearing when we are young."

"Sit up, young man," Masahiro said to me. When I did so, he studied my face for a few moments and then asked, "Who is in the garden?"

I furrowed my brow as if the idea of counting them had only just occurred to me. "Two children and a dog," I hazarded. "A gardener by the wall?"

"And how many people in the household would you estimate?"

I shrugged slightly, then thought it was very impolite and tried to turn it into a bow. "Upwards of forty-five? Forgive me, Lord Otori, I have no great talents."

"How many are there, brother?" Lord Shoichi asked.

"Fifty-three, I believe."

"Impressive," the older brother said, but I heard his sigh of relief.

I bowed to the floor again and, feeling safer there, stayed low.

"We have delayed in this matter of adoption for so long, Shigeru, because of our uncertainty as to your state of mind. Grief seemed to have made you very unstable."

"There is no uncertainty in my mind," Shigeru replied. "I have no living children, and now that Takeshi is dead, I have no heir. I have obligations to this boy, and he to me, that must be fulfilled. He is already accepted by my household and has made his home with us. I ask that this situation be formalized and that he be adopted into the Otori clan."

"What does the boy say?"

"Speak, Takeo," Lord Shigeru prompted me.

I sat up, swallowing hard, suddenly overwhelmed by a deep emotion. I thought of the horse, shying as my heart shied now. "I owe my life to Lord Otori. He owes me nothing. The honor he is bestowing is far too great for me, but if it is his—and your lordships'—will. I accept with all my heart. I will serve the Otori clan faithfully all my life."

"Then it may be so," Lord Shoichi said.

"The documents are prepared," Lord Masahiro added. "We will sign them immediately."

"My uncles are very gracious and kind," Shigeru said. "I thank you."

"There is another matter, Shigeru, in which we seek your cooperation."

I had dropped to the floor again. My heart lurched in my throat. I wanted to warn him in some way, but of course I could not speak.

"You are aware of our negotiations with the Tohan. We feel alliance is preferable to war. We know your opinion. You are still young enough to be rash. . . ."

"At nearly thirty years, I can no longer be called young." Again Shigeru stated this fact calmly, as though there could be no arguing with it. "And I have no desire for war for its own sake. It is not the alliance that I object to as such: It is the current nature and conduct of the Tohan."

His uncles made no response to this remark, but the atmosphere in the room chilled a little. Shigeru also said nothing more. He had made his view-point clear enough—too clear for his uncles' liking. Lord Masahiro made a sign to the steward, who clapped his hands quietly, and a few moments later tea appeared, brought by a maid who might have been invisible. The three Otori lords drank. I was not offered any.

"Well, the alliance is to go forward," Lord Shoichi said eventually. "Lord Iida has proposed that it be sealed by a marriage between the clans. His closest ally, Lord Noguchi, has a ward. Lady Shirakawa Kaede is her name."

Shigeru was admiring the teacup, holding it out in one hand. He placed it carefully on the matting in front of him and sat without moving a muscle.

"It is our desire that Lady Shirakawa become your wife," Lord Masahiro said.

"Forgive me, Uncle, but I have no desire to marry again. I have had no thoughts of marriage."

"Luckily you have relatives who will think of it for you. This marriage is greatly desired by Lord Iida. In fact, the alliance depends on it."

Lord Shigeru bowed. There was another long silence. I could hear footsteps coming from far away, the slow, deliberate tread of two people, one carrying something. The door behind us slid open and a man stepped past me and dropped to his knees. Behind him came a servant carrying a lacquer writing table, with ink block and brush and red vermilion paste for the seals.

"Ah, the adoption papers!" Lord Shoichi said genially. "Bring them to us."

The secretary advanced on his knees and the table was set before the lords. The secretary then read the agreement aloud. The language was flowery but the content was simple enough: I was entitled to bear the name of Otori and to receive all the privileges of a son of the household. In the event of children being born to a subsequent marriage, my rights would be equal to theirs, but not greater. In return I agreed to act as a son to Lord Shigeru, to accept his authority, and to swear allegiance to the Otori clan. If he died with no other legal heir, I would inherit his property.

The lords took up the seals.

"The marriage will be held in the ninth month," Masahiro said, "when the Festival of the Dead is over. Lord Iida wishes it to take place in Inuyama itself. The Noguchi are sending Lady Shirakawa to Tsuwano. You will meet her there and escort her to the capital."

The seals seemed to my eyes to hang in the air, suspended by a supernatural power. There was still time for me to speak out, to refuse to be adopted on such terms, to warn Lord Shigeru of the trap that had been set for him. But I said nothing. Events had moved beyond human control. Now we were in the hands of destiny.

"Shall we affix the seal, Shigeru?" Masahiro said with infinite politeness.

Lord Shigeru did not hesitate for a moment. "Please do so," he said. "I accept the marriage, and I am happy to be able to please you."

So the seals were affixed, and I became a member of the Otori clan and Lord Shigeru's adopted son. But as the seals of the clan were pressed to the documents, we both knew that they sealed his own fate.

By the time we returned to the house, the news of my adoption had been borne on the wind ahead of us, and everything had been prepared for celebration. Lord Shigeru and I both had reasons to be less than wholehearted, but he seemed to put whatever misgivings he had about marriage aside and to be genuinely delighted. So was the whole household. I realized that I had truly become one of them over the months I had been with them. I was hugged, caressed, fussed over, and plied with red rice and Chiyo's special good-luck tea, made from salted plum and seaweed, until my face ached with smiling and the tears I had not shed from grief filled my eyes for joy.

Lord Shigeru had become even more worthy of my love and loyalty. His uncles' treachery towards him had outraged me on his behalf, and I was terrified about the plot they had now laid against him. Then there was the question of the one-armed man. Throughout the evening I felt Kenji's eyes on me: I knew he was waiting to hear what I had learned, and I was longing to tell him and Lord Shigeru. But by the time the beds were spread out and the servants had retired, it was past midnight, and I was reluctant to break the joyful mood with bad tidings. I would have gone to bed saying nothing, but Kenji, the only one of us who was truly sober, stopped me when I went to douse the lamp, saying, "First you must tell us what you heard and saw."

"Let it wait till morning," I said.

I saw the darkness that had lain behind Shigeru's gaze deepen. I felt an immense sadness come over me, sobering me completely. He said, "I suppose we must learn the worst."

"What made the horse shy?" Kenji asked.

"My own nervousness. But as he shied I saw the one-armed man."

"Ando. I saw him too. I did not know if you had, you gave no sign of it."

"Did he recognize Takeo?" Lord Shigeru asked immediately.

"He looked carefully at both of you for an instant and then pretended to have no further interest. But just the fact that he is here suggests he had heard something." He looked at me and went on, "Your peddler must have talked!"

"I am glad the adoption is legal now," Shigeru said. "It gives you a certain amount of protection."

I knew I had to tell him of the conversation I had overheard, but I was finding it hard even to speak of their baseness. "Forgive me, Lord Otori," I began. "I heard your uncles speaking privately."

"While you were counting—or miscounting—the household, I suppose," he replied dryly. "They were discussing the marriage?"

"Who is to be married?" Kenji said.

"I seem to have been contracted into a marriage to seal the alliance with the Tohan," Shigeru replied. "The lady in question is a ward of Lord Noguchi; Shirakawa is her name."

Kenji raised his eyebrows but did not speak. Shigeru went on, "My uncles made it clear that Takeo's adoption depended on this marriage." He stared into the darkness and said quietly, "I am

140

caught between two obligations. I cannot fulfill both, but I cannot break either."

"Takeo should tell us what the Otori lords said," Kenji murmured.

I found it easier to speak to him. "The marriage is a trap. It is to send Lord Shigeru away from Hagi, where his popularity and opposition to the Tohan alliance may split the clan. Someone called Arai is challenging Iida in the West. If the Otori were to join him, Iida would be caught between them." My voice trailed away, and I turned to Shigeru. "Lord Otori knows all this?"

"I am in contact with Arai," he said. "Go on."

"Lady Shirakawa has the reputation of bringing death to men. Your uncles plan to . . ."

"Murder me?" His voice was matter-of-fact.

"I should not have to report so shameful a thing," I muttered, my face burning. "It was they who paid Shintaro."

Outside, the cicadas shrilled. I could feel sweat forming on my forehead, it was so close and still, a dark night with no moon or stars. The smell of the river was rank and muddy, an ancient smell, as ancient as treachery.

"I knew I was no favorite with them," Shigeru said. "But to send Shintaro against me! They must think I am really dangerous." He clapped me on the shoulder. "I have a lot to thank Takeo for. I am glad he will be with me in Inuyama."

"You're joking," Kenji exclaimed. "You cannot take Takeo there!"

"It seems I must go, and I feel safer if he is with me. Anyway, he is my son now. He must accompany me."

"Just try and leave me behind!" I put in.

"So you intend to marry Shirakawa Kaede?" Kenji said.

"Do you know her, Kenji?"

"I know of her. Who doesn't? She's barely fifteen and quite beautiful, they say."

"In that case, I'm sorry I can't marry her." Shigeru's voice was light, almost joking. "But it will do no harm if everyone thinks I will, for a while at least. It will divert Iida's attention, and will give us a few more weeks."

"What prevents you from marrying again?" Kenji said. "You spoke just now of the two obligations you are caught between. Since you agreed to the marriage in order that the adoption should go ahead, I understand that Takeo stands first with you. You're not secretly married already, are you?"

"As good as," Shigeru admitted after a pause. "There is someone else involved."

"Will you tell me who?"

"I have kept it secret for so long, I'm not sure I can," Shigeru replied. "Takeo can tell you, if he knows."

Kenji turned to me. I swallowed and whispered, "Lady Maruyama?"

Shigeru smiled. "How long have you known?"

"Since the night we met the lady at the inn in Chigawa."

Kenji, for the first time since I'd known him, looked really startled. "The woman Iida burns for, and wants to marry? How long has it been going on for?"

"You won't believe me," Shigeru replied.

"A year? Two?"

"Since I was twenty."

"That must be nearly ten years!" Kenji seemed as impressed by the fact that he had known nothing about the affair as by the news itself. "Yet another reason for you to hate Iida." He shook his head in amazement.

"It is more than love," Shigeru said quietly. "We are allies as well. Between them, she and Arai control the Seishuu and the southwest. If the Otori join them, we can defeat Iida." He paused and then went on, "If the Tohan take over the Otori domain, we will see the same cruelty and persecution that I rescued Takeo from in Mino. I cannot stand by and watch Iida impose his will on my people, see my country devastated, my villages burned. My uncles—Iida himself—know that I would never submit to that. So they mean to remove me from the scene. Iida has invited me into his lair, where he almost certainly intends to have me killed. I intend to use this to my advantage. What better way, after all, to get into Inuyama?"

Kenji stared at him, frowning. I could see Shigeru's openhearted smile in the lamplight. There was something irresistible about him. His courage made my own heart catch fire. I understood why people loved him.

"These are things that do not concern the Tribe," Kenji said finally.

"I've been frank with you; I trust that all this will go no further. Lady Maruyama's daughter is a hostage with Iida. Apart from that, more than your secrecy, I would be grateful for your help."

"I would never betray you, Shigeru, but sometimes, as you yourself said, we find ourselves with divided loyalties. I cannot pretend to you that I am not of the Tribe. Takeo is Kikuta. Sooner or later the Kikuta will claim him. There is nothing I can do about that."

"It's up to Takeo to make that choice when the time comes," Shigeru said.

"I have sworn allegiance to the Otori clan," I said. "I will never leave you, and I will do anything you ask of me."

For I was already seeing myself in Inuyama, where Lord Iida Sadamu lurked behind his nightingale floor.

# CHAPTER 6

Kaede left Noguchi castle with no regrets and few hopes for the future, but since she had hardly been beyond its walls in the eight years she had been a hostage with the Noguchi, and since she was only fifteen, she could not help but be entranced by everything she saw. For the first few miles she and Lady Maruyama were carried in palanquins by teams of porters, but the swaying motion made her feel sick, and at the first rest stop she insisted on getting out and walking with Shizuka. It was high summer; the sun was strong. Shizuka tied a shady hat on her head, and also held up a parasol over her.

"Lady Shirakawa must not appear before her husband as brown as I am," she giggled.

They traveled until midday, rested for a while at an inn, and then went on for another few miles before evening. By the time they stopped, Kaede's mind was reeling with all she had seen: the brilliant green of the rice fields, as smooth and luxuriant as the pelt of an animal; the white splashing rivers that raced beside the road; the mountains that rose before them, range after range, clad in

145

their rich summer green, interwoven with the crimson of wild azaleas. And the people on the road, of every sort and description: warriors in armor, bearing swords and riding spirited horses; farmers carrying all manner of things that she'd never seen before; oxcarts and packhorses, beggars and peddlers.

She was not supposed to stare at them, and they were supposed to bow to the ground as the procession went past, but she sneaked as many looks at them as they did at her.

They were accompanied by Lady Maruyama's retainers; the chief among them, a man named Sugita, treated the lady with the easy familiarity of an uncle. Kaede found that she liked him.

"I liked to walk when I was your age," Lady Maruyama said as they ate the evening meal together. "I still prefer it, to be truthful, but I also fear the sun."

She gazed at Kaede's unlined skin. She had been kind to her all day, but Kaede could not forget her first impression, that the older woman did not like her and that in some way she had offended her.

"You do not ride?" she asked. She had been envying the men on their horses: They seemed so powerful and free.

"Sometimes I ride," Lady Maruyama replied. "But when I am a poor defenseless woman traveling through Tohan land, I allow myself to be carried in the palanquin."

146

Kaede looked questioningly at her. "Yet, Lady Maruyama is said to be powerful," she murmured.

"I must hide my power among men," she replied, "or they will not hesitate to crush me."

"I have not been on a horse since I was a child," Kaede admitted.

"But all warriors' daughters should be taught to ride!" Lady Maruyama exclaimed. "Did the Noguchi not do so?"

"They taught me nothing," Kaede said with bitterness.

"No use of the sword and knife? No archery?"

"I did not know women learned such things."

"In the West they do." There was a short silence. Kaede, hungry for once, took a little more rice.

"Did the Noguchi treat you well?" the lady asked.

"In the beginning, no, not at all." Kaede felt herself torn between her usual guarded response to anyone who questioned her, and a strong desire to confide in this woman, who was of the same class as she was and who was her equal. They were alone in the room, apart from Shizuka and Lady Maruyama's woman, Sachie, who both sat so still Kaede was hardly aware of them. "After the incident with the guard, I was moved to the residence."

"Before that?"

"I lived with the servant girls in the castle."

"How shameful," Lady Maruyama said, her own voice bitter now. "How do the Noguchi dare?

When you are Shirakawa . . ." She looked down and said, "I fear for my own daughter, who is held hostage by Lord Iida."

"It was not so bad when I was a child," Kaede said. "The servants pitied me. But when the springtime began, and I was neither child nor woman, no one protected me. Until a man had to die . . ."

To her own astonishment, her voice faltered. A sudden rush of emotion made her eyes fill with tears. The memory came flooding back to her: the man's hands, the hard bulge of his sex against her, the knife in her hand, the blood, his death before her eyes.

"Forgive me," she whispered.

Lady Maruyama reached across the space between them and took her hand. "Poor child," she said, stroking Kaede's fingers. "All the poor children, all the poor daughters. If only I could free you all."

Kaede wanted nothing more than to sob her heart out. She struggled to regain control. "After that, they moved me to the residence. I was given my own maid, first Junko, then Shizuka. Life was much better there. I was to be married to an old man. He died, and I was glad. But then people began to say that to know me, to desire me, brings death."

She heard the other woman's sharp intake of breath. For a moment neither of them spoke.

"I do not want to cause any man's death," Kaede

said in a low voice. "I fear marriage. I do not want Lord Otori to die because of me."

When Lady Maruyama replied, her voice was thin. "You must not say such things, or even think them."

Kaede looked at her. Her face, white in the lamplight, seemed filled with a sudden apprehension.

"I am very tired," the lady went on. "Forgive me if I do not talk more tonight. We have many days on the road together, after all." She called to Sachie. The food trays were removed and the beds spread out.

Shizuka accompanied Kaede to the privy and washed her hands when she had finished there.

"What did I say to offend her?" Kaede whispered. "I don't understand her: One moment she is friendly, the next she stares at me as if I were poison to her."

"You're imagining things," Shizuka said lightly. "Lady Maruyama is very fond of you. Apart from anything else, after her daughter, you are her closest female relative."

"Am I?" Kaede replied and, when Shizuka nodded emphatically, asked, "Is that so important?"

"If anything happened to them, it is you who would inherit Maruyama. No one's told you this, because the Tohan still hope to acquire the domain. It's one of the reasons why Iida insisted you should go to the Noguchi as a hostage."

When Kaede said nothing, Shizuka went on,

"My lady is even more important than she thought she was!"

"Don't tease me! I feel lost in this world. I feel as if I know nothing!"

Kaede went to bed, her mind swirling. She was aware of Lady Maruyama's restlessness through the night as well, and the next morning the lady's beautiful face looked tired and drawn. But she spoke to Kaede kindly and, when they set out, arranged for a gentle brown horse to be provided for her. Sugita lifted her onto its back, and at first one of the men walked at its head, leading it. She remembered the ponies she had ridden as a child and the ability began to come back. Shizuka would not let her ride for the whole day, saying her muscles would ache too much and she would be too tired, but she loved the feeling of being on the horse's back, and could not wait to mount again. The rhythm of its gait calmed her a little and helped her to organize her thoughts. Mostly she was appalled at her lack of education and her ignorance of the world she was entering. She was a pawn on the board of the great game the warlords were playing, but she longed to be more than that, to understand the moves of the game and to play it herself.

Two things happened to disturb her further. One afternoon they had paused for a rest at an unusual time, at a crossroads, when they were joined by a small group of horsemen riding from the southwest, almost as if by some prearranged appointment.

Shizuka ran to greet them in her usual way, eager to know where they were from and what gossip they might bring. Kaede, watching idly, saw her speak to one of the men. He leaned low from the saddle to tell her something; she nodded with deep seriousness and then gave the horse a slap on its flank. It jumped forward. There was a shout of laughter from the men, followed by Shizuka's high-pitched giggle, but in that moment Kaede felt she saw something new in the girl who had become her servant, an intensity that puzzled her.

For the rest of the day Shizuka was her usual self, exclaiming over the beauties of the countryside, picking bunches of wildflowers, exchanging greetings with everyone she met, but at the lodging place that night Kaede came into the room to find Shizuka talking earnestly to Lady Maruyama, not like a servant, but sitting knee to knee with her, as an equal.

Their talk immediately turned to the weather and the next day's arrangements, but Kaede felt a sense of betrayal. Shizuka had said to her, *People like me don't really meet people like her.* But there was obviously some relationship between them that she had known nothing about. It made her suspicious and a little jealous. She had come to depend on Shizuka and did not want to share her with others.

The heat grew more intense and travel more uncomfortable. One day the earth shook several times, adding to Kaede's unease. She slept badly, troubled as much by suspicions as by fleas and other night insects. She longed for the journey to end, and yet, she dreaded arriving. Every day she decided she would question Shizuka, but every night something held her back. Lady Maruyama continued to treat her with kindness, but Kaede did not trust her, and she responded cautiously and with reserve. Then she felt ungracious and childish. Her appetite disappeared again.

Shizuka scolded her at night in the bath. "All your bones stick out, lady. You must eat! What will your husband think?"

"Don't start talking about my husband!" Kaede said hurriedly. "I don't care what he thinks. Maybe he will hate the sight of me and leave me alone!"

And then she was ashamed again for the childishness of the words.

They came at last to the mountain town of Tsuwano, riding through the narrow pass at the end of the day, the ranges already black against the setting sun. The breeze moved through the terraced rice fields like a wave through water, lotus plants raised their huge jade-green leaves, and around the fields wildflowers blossomed in a riot of color. The last rays of the sun turned the white walls of the town to pink and gold.

"This looks like a happy place!" Kaede could not help exclaiming.

Lady Maruyama, riding just ahead of her, turned in the saddle. "We are no longer in Tohan country. This is the beginning of the Otori fief," she said.

"Here we will wait for Lord Shigeru."

The next morning Shizuka brought strange clothes instead of Kaede's usual robes.

"You are to start learning the sword, lady," she announced, showing Kaede how to put them on. She looked at her with approval. "Apart from the hair, Lady Kaede could pass for a boy," she said, lifting the heavy weight of hair away from Kaede's face and tying it back with a leather cord.

Kaede ran her hands over her own body. The clothes were of rough, dark-dyed hemp, and fitted her loosely. They were like nothing she had ever worn. They hid her shape and made her feel free. "Who says I am to learn?"

"Lady Maruyama. We will be here several days, maybe a week, before the Otori arrive. She wants you to be occupied, and not fretting."

"She is very kind," Kaede replied. "Who will teach me?"

Shizuka giggled and did not answer. She took Kaede across the street from their lodgings to a long, low building with a wooden floor. Here they removed their sandals and put on split-toed boots. Shizuka handed Kaede a mask to protect her face, and took down two long wooden poles from a rack on the wall.

"Did the lady ever learn to fight with these?"

"As a child, of course," Kaede replied. "Almost as soon as I could walk."

"Then you will remember this." Shizuka handed one pole to Kaede and, holding the other firmly in both hands, executed a fluid series of movements, the pole flashing through the air faster than the eye could follow.

"Not like that!" Kaede admitted, astonished. She would have thought Shizuka hardly able to lift the pole, let alone wield it with such power and skill.

Shizuka giggled again, changing under Kaede's eyes from concentrated warrior to scatterbrained servant. "Lady Kaede will find it all comes back! Let's begin."

Kaede felt cold, despite the warmth of the summer morning. "You are the teacher?"

"Oh, I only know a little, lady. You probably know just as much. I don't suppose there's anything I can teach you."

But even though Kaede found that she did remember the movements, and had a certain natural ability and the advantage of height, Shizuka's skill far surpassed anything she could do. At the end of the morning she was exhausted, dripping with sweat and seething with emotion. Shizuka, who as a servant did everything in her power to please Kaede, was completely ruthless as a teacher. Every stroke had to be perfectly executed: Time after time, when Kaede thought she was finally finding the rhythm, Shizuka would stop her and politely point out that her balance was on the wrong foot, or that she had left herself open to sudden death, had they been fighting with the sword. Finally she signaled that they should finish, placed the poles back in the rack, took off the face masks, and wiped Kaede's face with a towel.

"It was good," she said. "Lady Kaede has great skill. We will soon make up for the years that were lost."

The physical activity, the shock of discovering Shizuka's skill, the warmth of the morning, the unfamiliar clothes, all combined to break down Kaede's self-control. She seized the towel and buried her face in it as sobs racked her.

"Lady," Shizuka whispered, "lady, don't cry. You have nothing to fear."

"Who are you really?" Kaede cried. "Why are you pretending to be what you are not? You told me you did not know Lady Maruyama!"

"I wish I could tell you everything, but I cannot yet. But my role here is to protect you. Arai sent me for that purpose."

"You know Arai too? All you said before was that you were from his town."

"Yes, but we are closer than that. He has the deepest regard for you, feeling himself to be in your debt. When Lord Noguchi exiled him, his anger was extreme. He felt himself insulted by Noguchi's distrust as well as his treatment of you. When he heard you were to be sent to Inuyama to be married, he made arrangements for me to accompany you."

"Why? Will I be in danger there?"

"Inuyama is a dangerous place. Even more so now, when the Three Countries are on the brink of war. Once the Otori alliance is settled by your marriage, Iida will fight the Seishuu in the West."

In the bare room, sunlight slanted through the dust raised by their feet. From beyond the lattice windows Kaede could hear the flow of water in the canals, the cries of street sellers, the laughter of children. That world seemed so simple and open, with none of the dark secrets that lay beneath her own.

"I am just a pawn on the board," she said bitterly. "You will sacrifice me as swiftly as the Tohan would."

"No, Arai and I are your servants, lady. He has sworn to protect you, and I obey him." She smiled, her face suddenly vivid with passion.

*They are lovers,* Kaede thought, and felt again a pang of jealousy that she had to share Shizuka with anyone else. She wanted to ask, *What about Lady Maruyama? What is her part in this game? And the man I am to marry?* But she feared the answer.

"It's too hot to do more today," Shizuka said, taking the towel from Kaede and wiping her eyes. "Tomorrow I'll teach you how to use the knife."

As they stood she added, "Don't treat me any differently. I am just your servant, nothing more."

"I should apologize for the times I treated you badly," Kaede said awkwardly.

"You never did!" Shizuka laughed. "If anything, you were far too lenient. The Noguchi may have taught you nothing useful, but at least you did not learn cruelty from them."

156

"I learned embroidery," Kaede said, "but you can't kill anyone with a needle."

"You can," Shizuka said offhandedly. "I'll show you one day."

For a week they waited in the mountain town for the Otori to arrive. The weather grew heavier and more sultry. Storm clouds gathered every night around the mountain peaks, and in the distance lightning flickered, yet it did not rain. Every day Kaede learned to fight with the sword and the knife, starting at daybreak, before the worst of the heat, and training for three hours at a stretch, the sweat pouring off her face and body.

Finally, one day at the end of the morning, as they were rinsing their faces with cold water, above the usual sounds of the streets came the tramp of horses, the barking of dogs.

Shizuka beckoned Kaede to the window. "Look! They are here! The Otori are here."

Kaede peered through the lattice. The group of horsemen approached at a trot. Most of them wore helmets and armor, but on one side rode a bareheaded boy not much older than herself. She saw the curve of his cheekbone, the silky gleam of his hair.

"Is that Lord Shigeru?"

"No," Shizuka laughed. "Lord Shigeru rides in front. The young man is his ward, Lord Takeo."

She emphasized the word *lord* in an ironic way that Kaede would recall later, but at the time she hardly noticed, for the boy, as if he had heard his name spoken, turned his head and looked towards her.

His eyes suggested depths of emotion, his mouth was sensitive, and she saw in his features both energy and sadness. It kindled something in her, a sort of curiosity mixed with longing, a feeling she did not recognize.

The men rode on. When the boy disappeared from sight she felt she had lost a part of herself. She followed Shizuka back to the inn like a sleep-walker. By the time they got there, she was trembling as if with fever. Shizuka, completely misunderstanding, tried to reassure her.

"Lord Otori is a kind man, lady. You mustn't be afraid. No one will harm you."

Kaede said nothing, not daring to open her mouth, for the only word she wanted to speak was his name. *Takeo.*

Shizuka tried to get her to eat—first soup to warm her, then cold noodles to cool her—but she could swallow nothing. Shizuka made her lie down. Kaede shivered beneath the quilt, her eyes bright, her skin dry, her body as unpredictable to her as a snake.

Thunder crackled in the mountains and the air swam with moisture.

Alarmed, Shizuka sent for Lady Maruyama. When she came into the room an old man followed her.

"Uncle!" Shizuka greeted him with a cry of delight.

"What happened?" Lady Maruyama said, kneeling beside Kaede and placing her hand on her forehead. "She is burning; she must have taken a chill."

"We were training," Shizuka explained. "We saw the Otori arrive, and she seemed to be struck by a sudden fever."

"Can you give her something, Kenji?" Lady Maruyama asked.

"She dreads the marriage," Shizuka said quietly.

"I can cure a fever, but that I cannot cure," the old man said. "I'll have them brew some herbs. The tea will calm her."

Kaede lay perfectly still with her eyes closed. She could hear them clearly, but they seemed to speak from another world, one that she had been plucked out of the moment her eyes met Takeo's. She roused herself to drink the tea, Shizuka holding her head as if she were a child, and then she drifted into a shallow sleep. She was woken by thunder rolling through the valley. The storm had finally broken and rain was pelting down, ringing off the tiles and sluicing the cobbles. She had been dreaming vividly, but the moment she opened her eyes the dream vanished, leaving her only with the lucid knowledge that what she felt was love.

She was astonished, then elated, then dismayed. At first she thought she would die if she saw him, then that she would die if she didn't. She berated herself: How could she have fallen

159

in love with the ward of the man she was to marry? And then she thought: What marriage? She could not marry Lord Otori. She would marry no one but Takeo. And then she found herself laughing at her own stupidity. As if anyone married for love. *I've been overtaken by disaster*, she thought at one moment, and at the next, *How can this feeling be a disaster?*

When Shizuka returned she insisted that she had recovered. Indeed, the fever had abated, replaced by an intensity that made her eyes glow and her skin gleam.

"You are more beautiful than ever!" Shizuka exclaimed as she bathed and dressed her, putting on the robes that had been prepared for her betrothal, for her first meeting with her future husband.

Lady Maruyama greeted her with concern, asking after her health, and was relieved to find she was recovered. But Kaede was aware of the older woman's nervousness as she followed her to the best room in the inn, which had been prepared for Lord Otori.

She could hear the men talking as the servants slid the doors open, but they fell silent at the sight of her. She bowed to the floor, conscious of their gaze, not daring to look at any of them. She could feel every pulse in her body as her heart began to race.

"This is Lady Shirakawa Kaede," Lady Maruyama said. Her voice was cold, Kaede thought, and again wondered what she had done to offend the lady so much.

"Lady Kaede, I present you to Lord Otori Shigeru," Lady Maruyama went on, her voice now so faint it could hardly be heard.

Kaede sat up. "Lord Otori," she murmured, and raised her eyes to the face of the man she was to marry.

"Lady Shirakawa," he replied with great politeness. "We heard you were unwell. You are recovered?"

"Thank you, I am quite well." She liked his face, seeing kindness in his gaze. *He deserves his reputation*, she thought. *But how can I marry him?* She felt color rise in her cheeks.

"Those herbs never fail," said the man sitting on his left. She recognized the voice of the old man who had had the tea made for her, the man Shizuka called Uncle. "Lady Shirakawa has the reputation of great beauty, but her reputation hardly does her justice."

Lady Maruyama said, "You flatter her, Kenji. If a girl is not beautiful at fifteen, she never will be."

Kaede felt herself flush even more.

"We have brought gifts for you," Lord Otori said. "They pale beside your beauty, but please accept them as a token of my deepest regard and the devotion of the Otori clan. Takeo."

She thought he spoke the words with indifference, even coldness, and imagined he would always feel that way towards her.

161

The boy rose and brought forward a lacquered tray. On it were packages wrapped in pale pink silk crepe, bearing the crest of the Otori. Kneeling before Kaede, he presented it to her.

She bowed in thanks.

"This is Lord Otori's ward and adopted son," Lady Maruyama said. "Lord Otori Takeo."

She did not dare look at his face. She allowed herself instead to gaze on his hands. They were long-fingered, supple, and beautifully shaped. The skin was a color between honey and tea, the nails tinged faintly lilac. She sensed the stillness within him, as if he were listening, always listening.

"Lord Takeo," she whispered.

He was not yet a man like the men she feared and hated. He was her age; his hair and skin had the same texture of youth. The intense curiosity she had felt before returned. She longed to know everything about him. Why had Lord Otori adopted him? Who was he really? What had happened to make him so sad? And why did she think he could hear her heart's thoughts?

"Lady Shirakawa." His voice was low, with a touch of the East in it.

She had to look at him. She raised her eyes and met his gaze. He stared at her, almost puzzled, and she felt something leap between them, as though somehow they had touched across the space that separated them.

The rain had eased a little earlier, but now it began again, with a drumming roar that all but drowned their voices. The wind rose, too, making the lamp flames dance and the shadows loom on the walls.

*May I stay here forever*, Kaede thought.

Lady Maruyama said sharply. "He has met you, but you have not been introduced: This is Muto Kenji, an old friend of Lord Otori, and Lord Takeo's teacher. He will help Shizuka in your instruction."

"Sir," she acknowledged him, glancing at him from under her eyelashes. He was staring at her in outright admiration, shaking his head slightly as if in disbelief. *He seems like a nice old man*, Kaede thought, and then: *But he is not so old after all!* His face seemed to slip and change in front of her eyes.

She felt the floor beneath her move with the very slightest of tremors. No one spoke, but from outside someone shouted in surprise. Then there was only the wind and the rain again.

A chill came over her. She must let none of her feelings show. Nothing was as it seemed.

# CHAPTER 7

After my formal adoption into the clan, I began to see more of the young men of my own age from warrior families. Ichiro was much sought after as a teacher, and since he was already instructing me in history, religion, and the classics, he agreed to take on other pupils as well. Among these was Miyoshi Gemba, who, with his older brother, Kahei, was to become one of my closest allies and friends. Gemba was a year older than me. Kahei was already in his twenties, and too old for Ichiro's instruction, but he helped teach the younger men the arts of war.

For these I now joined the men of the clan in the great hall opposite the castle, where we fought with poles and studied other martial arts. On its sheltered southern side was a wide field for horsemanship and archery. I was no better with the bow than I'd ever been, but I could acquit myself well enough with the pole and the sword. Every morning, after two hours of writing practice with Ichiro, I would ride with a couple of men through the winding streets of the castle town and spend four or five hours in relentless training.

In the late afternoons I returned to Ichiro with his other pupils, and we struggled to keep our eyes open while he tried to teach us the principles of Kung Tzu and the history of the Eight Islands. The summer solstice passed, and the Festival of the Weaver Star, and the days of the great heat began. The plum rains had ended, but it remained very humid, and heavy storms threatened. The farmers gloomily predicted a worse than usual typhoon season.

My lessons with Kenji also continued, but at night. He stayed away from the clan hall, and warned me against revealing my Tribe skills.

"The warriors think it's sorcery," he said. "They'll despise you for it."

We went out on many nights, and I learned to move invisibly through the sleeping town. We had a strange relationship. I did not trust him at all in daylight. I'd been adopted by the Otori, and I'd given my heart to them. I did not want to be reminded that I was an outsider, even a freak. But it was different at night. Kenji's skills were unparalleled. He wanted to share them with me, and I was mad with hunger to learn them—partly for their own sake, because they fulfilled some dark need that was born into me, and partly because I knew how much I had to learn if I was ever to achieve what Lord Shigeru wanted me to do. Although he had not yet spoken of it to me, I could think of no other reason why he had rescued me from Mino. I was the son of an assassin, a member of the Tribe, now his adopted son. I was going with him to Inuyama. What other purpose could there be but to kill Iida?

Most of the boys accepted me, for Shigeru's sake, and I realized what a high regard they and their fathers had for him. But the sons of Masahiro and Shoichi gave me a hard time, especially Masahiro's oldest son, Yoshitomi. I grew to hate them as much as I hated their fathers, and I despised them, too, for their arrogance and blindness. We often fought with the poles. I knew their intentions towards me were murderous. Once Yoshitomi would have killed me if I had not in an instant used my second self to distract him. He never forgave me for it and often whispered insults to me: *Sorcerer. Cheat.* I was actually less afraid of him killing me than of having to kill him in self-defense or by accident. No doubt it improved my swordsmanship, but I was relieved when the time for our departure came and no blood had been shed.

It was not a good time for traveling, being in the hottest days of summer, but we had to be in Inuyama before the Festival of the Dead began. We did not take the direct highway through Yamagata, but went south to Tsuwano, now the outpost town of the Otori fief, on the road to the West, where we would meet the bridal party and where the betrothal would take place. From there we would cross into Tohan territory and pick up the post road at Yamagata.

Our journey to Tsuwano was uneventful and enjoyable despite the heat. I was away from Ichiro's teaching and from the pressures of training. It was like a holiday, riding in Shigeru and Kenji's company, and for a few days we all seemed to put aside our misgivings of what lay ahead. The rain held off, though lightning flickered round the ranges all night, turning the clouds indigo, and the full summer foliage of the forests surrounded us in a sea of green.

We rode into Tsuwano at midday, having risen at sunrise for the last leg of the journey. I was sorry to arrive, knowing it meant the end of the innocent pleasures of our lighthearted travel. I could not have imagined what was going to take their place. Tsuwano sang of water, its streets lined with canals teeming with fat golden and red carp. We were not far from the inn when suddenly, above the water and the sounds of the bustling town, I clearly heard my own name spoken by a woman. The voice came from a long, low building with white walls and lattice windows, some kind of fighting hall. I knew there were two women inside but I could not see them, and I wondered briefly why they were there, and why one of them should have said my name.

When we came to the inn I heard the same woman talking in the courtyard. I realized she was Lady Shirakawa's maid, and we learned the lady was unwell. Kenji went to her and came back wanting to describe her beauty at length, but the storm broke, and I was afraid the thunder would make the horses restive, so I hurried off to the stables without listening to him. I did not want to hear of her beauty. If I thought about her at all, it was with dislike, for the part she was to play in the trap set for Shigeru.

After a while Kenji caught up with me in the stables, and brought the maid with him. She looked like a pretty, good-natured, scatter-brained girl, but even before she grinned at me in a less than respectful way and addressed me as "Cousin!" I'd picked her as a member of the Tribe.

She held her hands up against mine. "I am also Kikuta, on my mother's side. But Muto on my father's. Kenji is my uncle."

Our hands had the same long-fingered shape and the same line straight across the palm. "That's the only trait I inherited," she said ruefully. "The rest of me is pure Muto."

Like Kenji, she had the power to change her appearance so that you were never sure you recognized her. At first I thought she was very young; in fact she was almost thirty and had two sons.

"Lady Kaede is a little better," she told Kenji. "Your tea made her sleep, and now she insists on getting up."

"You worked her too hard," Kenji said, grinning. "What were you thinking of, in this heat?" To me he added, "Shizuka is teaching Lady Shriakawa the sword. She can teach you too. We'll be here for days in this rain."

He turned back to her. "Maybe you can teach him ruthlessness," he said. "It's all he lacks."

"It's hard to teach," Shizuka replied. "You either have it, or not."

"She has it," Kenji told me. "Stay on her right side!"

I didn't reply. I was a little irritated that Kenji should point out my weakness to Shizuka as soon as we met her. We stood under the eaves of the stable yard, the rain drumming on the cobbles before us, the horses stamping behind.

"Are these fevers a common thing?" Kenji asked.

"Not really. This is the first of its kind. But she is not strong. She hardly eats; she sleeps badly. She frets over the marriage and over her family. Her mother is dying, and she has not seen her since she was seven."

"You have become fond of her," Kenji said, smiling.

"Yes, I have, although I only came to her because Arai asked me to."

"I've never seen a more beautiful girl," Kenji admitted.

"Uncle! You are really smitten by her!"

"I must be getting old," he said. "I find myself moved by her plight. However things work out, she will be the loser."

A huge clap of thunder broke over our heads. The horses bucked and plunged on their lines. I ran to quiet them. Shizuka returned to the inn and Kenji went in search of the bathhouse. I did not see them again until evening.

Later, bathed and dressed in formal robes, I attended on Lord Shigeru for the first meeting with his future wife. We had brought gifts, and I unpacked them from the boxes, together with the lacquerware that we carried with us. A betrothal should be a happy occasion, I suppose, although I had never been to one before. Maybe for the bride it is always a time of apprehension. This one seemed to me to be fraught with tension and full of bad omens.

Lady Maruyama greeted us as if we were no more than slight acquaintances, but her eyes hardly left Shigeru's face. I thought she had aged since I'd met her in Chigawa. She was no less beautiful, but suffering had etched her face with its fine lines. Both she and Shigeru seemed cold, to each other and to everyone else, especially to Lady Shirakawa.

Her beauty silenced us. Despite Kenji's enthusiasm earlier, I was quite unprepared for it. I thought then that I understood Lady Maruyama's suffering: At least part of it had to be jealousy. How could any man refuse the possession of such beauty? No one could blame Shigeru if he accepted it: He would be fulfilling his duty to his uncles and the demands of the alliance. But the marriage would deprive Lady Maruyama of not only the man she had loved for years but also her strongest ally.

The undercurrents in the room made me uncomfortable and awkward. I saw the pain Lady Maruyama's coldness caused Kaede, saw the flush rise in her cheeks making her skin lovelier than ever. I could hear her heartbeat and her rapid breath. She did not look at any of us, but kept her eyes cast down. I thought, *She is so young, and terrified.* Then she raised her eyes and looked at me for a moment. I felt she was like a person drowning in the river, and if I reached out my hand I would save her.

"So, Shigeru, you have to choose between the most powerful woman in the Three Countries and the most beautiful," Kenji said later while we were sitting up talking, and after many flasks of wine had been shared. Since the rain seemed likely to keep us in Tsuwano for some days, there was no need to go to bed early in order to rise before dawn. "I should have been born a lord."

"You have a wife, if only you stayed with her," Shigeru replied.

"My wife is a good cook, but she has a wicked tongue, she's fat, and she hates traveling," Kenji grumbled. I said nothing, but laughed to myself, already knowing how Kenji profited from his wife's absence: in the pleasure quarter.

Kenji continued to joke, with, I thought, some deeper purpose of sounding Shigeru out, but the lord replied to him in the same vein, as if he truly were celebrating his betrothal. I went to sleep, fuddled by the wine, to the sound of rain pelting on the roof, cascading down the gutters and over the cobbles. The canals ran to the brim; in the distance I could hear the song of the river grow to a shout as it tumbled down the mountain.

I woke in the middle of the night and was immediately aware that Shigeru was no longer in the room. When I listened I could hear his voice, talking to Lady Maruyama, so low that no one could hear it but me. I had heard them speak like that nearly a year before, in another inn room. I was both appalled at the risk they were taking and amazed at the strength of the love that sustained them through such infrequent meetings.

*He will never marry Shirakawa Kaede*, I thought, but did not know if this realization delighted me or alarmed me.

I was filled with unease and lay awake till dawn. It was a gray, wet dawn, too, with no sign of any break in the weather. A typhoon, earlier than usual, had swept across the western part of the country, bringing downpours, floods, broken bridges, impassable roads. Everything was damp and smelled of mold. Two of the horses had hot, swollen hocks, and a groom had been kicked in the chest. I ordered poultices for the horses and arranged for an apothecary to see the man. I was eating a late breakfast when Kenji came to remind me about sword practice. It was the last thing I felt like doing.

"What else do you plan to do all day," he

demanded, "sit around and drink tea? Shizuka can teach you a lot. We might as well make the most of being stuck here."

So I obediently finished eating and followed my teacher, running through the rain to the fighting school. I could hear the thump and clash of the sticks from outside. Inside, two young men were fighting. After a moment I realized one was not a boy but Shizuka: She was more skillful than her opponent, but the other, taller and with greater determination, was making it quite a good match. At our appearance, though, Shizuka easily got beneath the guard. It wasn't until the other took off the mask that I realized it was Kaede.

"Oh," she said angrily, wiping her face on her sleeve, "they distracted me."

"Nothing must distract you, lady," Shizuka said. "It's your main weakness. You lack concentration. There must be nothing but you, your foe, and the swords."

She turned to greet us. "Good morning, Uncle! Good morning, Cousin!"

We returned the greeting and bowed more respectfully to Kaede. Then there was a short silence. I was feeling awkward: I had never seen women in a fighting hall before—never seen them dressed in practice clothes. Their presence unnerved me. I thought there was probably some-thing unseemly about it. I should not be here with Shigeru's betrothed wife.

"We should come back another time," I said,

"when you have finished."

"No, I want you to fight with Shizuka," Kenji said. "Lady Shirakawa can hardly return to the inn alone. It will profit her to watch."

"It would be good for the lady to practice against a man," Shizuka said, "since if it comes to battle, she will not be able to choose her opponents."

I glanced at Kaede and saw her eyes widen slightly, but she said nothing.

"Well, she should be able to beat Takeo," Kenji said sourly. I thought he must have a headache from the wine, and indeed, I myself felt a little the worse for wear.

Kaede sat on the floor, cross-legged like a man. She untied the ties that held back her hair and it fell around her, reaching the ground. I tried not to look at her.

Shizuka gave me a pole and took up her first stance.

We sparred a bit, neither of us giving anything away. I'd never fought with a woman before, and I was reluctant to go all out in case I hurt her. Then, to my surprise, when I feinted one way she was already there, and a twisting upwards blow sent the pole out of my hands. If I'd been fighting Masahiro's son, I'd have been dead.

"Cousin," she said reprovingly. "Don't insult me, please."

I tried harder after that, but she was skillful and amazingly strong. It was only after the second bout that I began to get the upper hand, and then only

174

after her instruction. She conceded the fourth bout, saying, "I have already fought all morning with Lady Kaede. You are fresh, Cousin, as well as being half my age."

"A little more than half, I think!" I panted. Sweat was pouring off me. I took a towel from Kenji and wiped myself down.

Kaede said, "Why do you call Lord Takeo 'Cousin'?"

"Believe it or not, we are related, on my mother's side," Shizuka said. "Lord Takeo was not born an Otori, but adopted."

Kaede looked seriously at the three of us. "There is a likeness between you. It's hard to place exactly. But there is something mysterious, as though none of you is what you seem to be."

"The world being what it is, that is wisdom, lady," Kenji said, rather piously, I thought. I imagined he did not want Kaede to know the true nature of our relationship: that we were all from the Tribe. I did not want her to know either. I much preferred her to think of me as one of the Otori.

Shizuka took up the cords and tied back Kaede's hair. "Now you should try against Takeo."

"No," I said immediately. "I should go now. I have to see to the horses. I must see if Lord Otori needs me."

Kaede stood. I was aware of her trembling slightly, and acutely aware of her scent, a flowery fragrance with her sweat beneath it.

"Just one bout," Kenji said. "It can't do any harm."

Shizuka went to put on Kaede's mask, but she waved her away.

"If I am to fight men, I must fight without a mask," she said.

I took up the pole reluctantly. The rain was pouring down even more heavily. The room was dim, the light greenish. We seemed to be in a world within a world, isolated from the real one, bewitched.

It started like an ordinary practice bout, both of us trying to unsettle the other, but I was afraid of hitting her face, and her eyes never left mine. We were both tentative, embarking on something utterly strange to us whose rules we did not know. Then, at some point I was hardly aware of, the fight turned into a kind of dance. Step, strike, parry, step. Kaede's breath came more strongly, echoed by mine, until we were breathing in unison, and her eyes became brighter and her face more glowing, each blow became stronger, and the rhythm of our steps fiercer. For a while I would dominate, then she, but neither of us could get the upper hand. Did either of us want to?

Finally, almost by mistake, I got around her guard and, to avoid hitting her face, let the pole fall to the ground. Immediately, Kaede lowered her own pole and said, "I concede."

"You did well," Shizuka said, "but I think Takeo could have tried a little harder."

I stood and stared at Kaede, open-mouthed like an idiot. I thought, *If I don't hold her in my arms now, I will die.*

Kenji handed me a towel and gave me a rough push in the chest. "Takeo . . ." he started to say.

"What?" I said stupidly.

"Just don't complicate things!"

Shizuka said, as sharply as if she were warning of danger, "Lady Kaede!"

"What?" Kaede said, her eyes still fixed on my face.

"I think we've done enough for one day," Shizuka said. "Let's return to your room."

Kaede smiled at me, suddenly unguarded. "Lord Takeo," she said.

"Lady Shirakawa." I bowed to her, trying to be formal, but utterly unable to keep myself from smiling back at her.

"Well, that's torn it," Kenji muttered.

"What do you expect, it's their age!" Shizuka replied. "They'll get over it."

As Shizuka led Kaede from the hall, calling to the servants who were waiting outside to bring umbrellas, it dawned on me what they were talking about. They were right in one thing, and wrong in another. Kaede and I had been scorched by desire for each other, more than desire, love, but we would never get over it.

For a week the torrents of rain kept us penned up in the mountain town. Kaede and I did not train together again. I wished we had never done

177

so: It had been a moment of madness, I had never wanted it, and now I was tormented by the results. I listened for her all day long, I could hear her voice, her step, and at night—when only a thin wall separated us—her breathing. I could tell how she slept (restlessly) and when she woke (often). We spent time together—we were forced to by the smallness of the inn, by being in the same traveling party, by being expected to be with Lord Shigeru and Lady Maruyama—but we had no opportunity to speak to each other. We were both, I think, equally terrified of giving our feelings away. We hardly dared look at each other, but occasionally our eyes would meet, and the fire leaped between us again.

I went lean and hollow-eyed with desire, made worse by lack of sleep, for I reverted to my old Hagi ways and went exploring at night. Shigeru did not know, for I left while he was with Lady Maruyama, and Kenji either did not or pretended not to notice. I felt I was becoming as insubstantial as a ghost. By day I studied and drew; by night I went in search of other people's lives, moving through the small town like a shadow. Often the thought came to me that I would never have a life of my own, but would always belong to the Otori or to the Tribe.

I watched merchants calculating the loss the water damage would bring them. I watched the townspeople drink and gamble in bars and let prostitutes lead them away by the arm. I watched parents sleep, their children between them. I climbed walls and drainpipes, walked over roofs and along fences. Once I swam the moat, climbed the castle walls and gate, and watched the guards, so close I could smell them. It amazed me that they did not see or hear me. I listened to people talking, awake and in their sleep, heard their protestations, their curses and their prayers.

I went back to the inn before dawn, drenched to the skin, took off my wet clothes, and slipped naked and shivering beneath the quilts. I dozed and listened to the place waking around me. First the cocks crowed, then the crows began cawing; servants woke and fetched water; clogs clattered over the wooden bridges; Raku and the other horses whinnied from the stables. I waited for the moment when I would hear Kaede's voice.

The rain poured down for three days and then began to lessen. Many people came to the inn to speak to Shigeru. I listened to the careful conversations and tried to discern who was loyal to him and who would be only too eager to join in his betrayal. We went to the castle to present gifts to Lord Kitano, and I saw in daylight the walls and gate I had climbed at night.

He greeted us with courtesy and expressed his sympathy for Takeshi's death. It seemed to be on his conscience, for he returned to the subject more than once. He was of an age with the Otori lords and had sons the same age as Shigeru. They did not attend the meeting. One was said to be away,

179

the other unwell. Apologies were expressed, which I knew were lies.

"They lived in Hagi when they were boys," Shigeru told me later. "We trained and studied together. They came many times to my parents' house and were as close as brothers to Takeshi and myself." He was silent for a moment, then went on: "Well, that was many years ago. Times change and we must all change with them."

But I could not be so resigned. I felt bitterly that the closer we came to Tohan territory, the more isolated he was becoming.

It was early evening. We had bathed and were waiting for the meal. Kenji had gone to the public bathhouse, where a girl had taken his fancy, he said. The room gave on to a small garden. The rain had lessened to a drizzle and the doors were wide open. There was a strong smell of sodden earth and wet leaves.

"It will clear tomorrow," Shigeru said. "We will be able to ride on, but we will not get to Inuyama before the festival. We will be forced to stay in Yamagata, I think." He smiled entirely mirthlessly and said, "I shall be able to commemorate my brother's death in the place where he died. But I cannot let anyone know my feelings. I must pretend to have put aside all thought of revenge."

"Why go into Tohan territory?" I asked. "It's not too late to turn back. If it's my adoption that binds you to the marriage, I could go away with Kenji. It's what he wants."

"Certainly not!" he replied. "I've given my word to these arrangements and set my seal on them. I have plunged into the river now and must go where the current takes me. I would sooner Iida killed me than despised me." He looked around the room, listening. "Are we completely alone? Can you hear anyone?"

I could hear the usual evening sounds of the inn: the soft tread of maids as they carried food and water; from the kitchen, the sound of the cook's knife chopping; water boiling; the muttered conversation of the guards in the passageway and the courtyard. I could hear no other breath but our own.

"We are alone."

"Come closer. Once we are among the Tohan, we will have no chance to talk. There are many things I need to tell you before . . ." He grinned at me, a real smile this time. ". . . before whatever happens in Inuyama!

"I've thought about sending you away. Kenji desires it for your safety, and of course his fears are justified. I must go to Inuyama, come what may. However, I am asking an almost impossible service from you, far beyond any obligation you may have to me, and I feel I must give you a choice. Before we ride into Tohan territory, after you have heard what I have to say, if you wish to leave with Kenji and join the Tribe, you are free to do so."

I was saved from answering by a faint sound

from the passageway. "Someone is coming to the door." We were both silent.

A few moments later the maids entered with trays of food. When they had left again, we began to eat. The food was sparse, because of the rain— some sort of soused fish, rice, devil's tongue and pickled cucumbers—but I don't think either of us tasted it.

"You may wonder what my hatred of Iida is based on," Shigeru said. "I have always had a personal dislike for him, for his cruelty and double-dealing. After Yaegahara and my father's death, when my uncles took over the leadership of the clan, many people thought I should have taken my own life. That would have been the honorable thing to do—and, for them, a convenient solution to my irritating presence. But as the Tohan moved into what had been Otori land, and I saw the devastating effect of their rule on the common people, I decided a more worthwhile response would be to live and seek revenge. I believe the test of government is the contentment of the people. If the ruler is just, the land receives the blessings of Heaven. In Tohan lands the people are starving, debt-ridden, harassed all the time by Iida's officials. The Hidden are tortured and murdered—crucified, suspended upside down over pits of waste, hung in baskets for the crows to feed on. Farmers have to expose their newborn children and sell their daughters because they have nothing to feed them with."

He took a piece of fish and ate it fastidiously, his face impassive.

"Iida became the most powerful ruler in the Three Countries. Power brings its own legitimacy. Most people believe any lord has the right to do as he pleases in his own clan and his own country. It's what I, too, was brought up to believe in. But he threatened my land, my father's land, and I was not going see it handed over to him without a fight.

"This had been in my mind for many years. I took on a personality for myself that is only partly my own. They call me Shigeru the Farmer. I devoted myself to improving my land and talked of nothing but the seasons, crops, and irrigation. These matters interest me anyway, but they also gave me the excuse to travel widely through the fief and learn many things I would not otherwise have known.

"I avoided Tohan lands, apart from yearly visits to Terayama, where my father and many of my ancestors are buried. The temple was ceded to the Tohan, along with the city of Yamagata after Yaegahara. But then the Tohan cruelty touched me personally, and my patience began to wear thin.

"Last year, just after the Festival of the Weaver Star, my mother fell ill with a fever. It was particularly virulent: She was dead within a week. Three other members of the household died, including her maid. I also became sick. For four weeks I hovered between life and death, delirious, knowing nothing. I was not expected to recover, and when I did, I wished I had died, for it was then that I learned my brother had been killed in the first week of my illness.

"It was high summer. He was already buried. No one could tell me what had happened. There seemed to be no witnesses. He had recently taken a new lover, but the girl had disappeared too. We heard only that a Tsuwano merchant had recognized his body in the streets of Yamagata and had arranged burial at Terayama. In desperation I wrote to Muto Kenji, whom I had known since Yaegahara, thinking the Tribe might have some information. Two weeks later a man came to my house late at night, bearing a letter of introduction with Kenji's seal. I would have taken him for a groom or a foot soldier; he confided in me that his name was Kuroda, which I knew can be a Tribe name.

"The girl Takeshi had fallen for was a singer, and they had gone together to Tsuwano for the Star Festival. That much I knew already, for as soon as my mother fell sick, I'd sent word to him not to return to Hagi. I'd meant for him to stay in Tsuwano, but it seems the girl wished to go on to Yamagata, where she had relatives, and Takeshi went with her. Kuroda told me that there were comments made in an inn—insults to the Otori, to myself. A fight broke out. Takeshi was an excellent swordsman. He killed two men and wounded several others, who ran away. He went back to the girl's relatives' house. Tohan men returned in the middle of the night and set fire to the house. Everyone in it burned to death or was stabbed as they tried to escape the flames."

I closed my eyes briefly, thinking I could hear their screams.

"Yes, it was like Mino," Shigeru said bitterly. "The Tohan claimed the family were Hidden, though it seems almost certain they were not. My brother was in traveling clothes. No one knew his identity. His body lay in the street for two days."

He sighed deeply. "There should have been outrage. Clans have gone to war over less. At the very least, Iida should have apologized, punished his men, and made some restitution. But Kuroda reported to me that when Iida heard the news, his words were 'One less of those Otori upstarts to worry about. Too bad it wasn't the brother.' Even the men who committed the act were astonished, Kuroda said. They had not known who Takeshi was. When they found out, they expected their lives to be forfeit.

"But Iida did nothing, nor did my uncles. I told them in private what Kuroda had told me. They chose not to believe me. They reminded me of the rashness of Takeshi's behavior in the past, the fights he had been involved in, the risks he took. They forbade me from speaking publicly about the matter, reminding me that I was still far from well and suggesting I should go away for a while, make a trip to the eastern mountains, try the hot springs, pray at the shrines.

"I decided I would go away, but not for the purposes they suggested."

"You came to find me in Mino," I whispered.

He did not answer me at once. It was dark outside now, but there was a faint glow from the sky. The clouds were breaking up, and between them the moon appeared and disappeared. For the first time I could make out the outline of the mountains and the pine trees, black against the night sky.

"Tell the servants to bring lights," Shigeru said, and I went to the door to call the maids. They came and removed the trays, brought tea, and lit the lamps in the stands. When they had left once more, we drank the tea in silence. The bowls were a dark blue glaze. Shigeru turned his in his hand and then upended it to read the potter's name. "It's not as pleasing to my mind as the earth colors of Hagi," he said, "but beautiful nonetheless."

"May I ask you a question?" I said, and then fell silent again, not sure if I wanted to know the answer.

"Go on," he prompted.

"You have allowed people to believe we met by accident, but I felt you knew where to find me. You were looking for me."

He nodded. "Yes, I knew who you were as soon as I saw you on the path. I had come to Mino with the express purpose of finding you."

"Because my father was an assassin?"

"That was the main reason, but not the only one."

I felt as if there were not enough air in the room for me to draw the breath I needed. I did not bother with whatever other reasons Lord Shigeru might have had. I needed to concentrate on the main one.

"But how did you know, when I myself did not know—when the Tribe did not know?"

He said, his voice lower than ever, "Since Yaegahara, I have had time to learn many things. I was just a boy then, a typical warrior's son, with no ideas beyond the sword and my family's honor. I met Muto Kenji there, and in the months afterwards he opened my eyes to the power that lay beneath the warrior class's rule. I discovered something about the networks of the Tribe, and I saw how they controlled the warlords and the clans. Kenji became a friend, and through him I met many other Tribe members. They interested me. I probably know more about them than any other outsider. But I've kept this knowledge to myself, never telling anyone else. Ichiro knows a little, and now you do too."

I thought of the heron's beak plunging down into the water.

"Kenji was wrong, the first night he came to Hagi. I knew very well who I was bringing into my household. I had not realized, though, that your talents would be so great." He smiled at me, the openhearted smile that transformed his face. "That was an unexpected reward."

Now I seemed to have lost the power of speech again. I knew we had to broach the subject of Shigeru's purpose in seeking me out and saving my life, but I could not bring myself to speak so baldly of such things. I felt the darkness of my Tribe nature rise within me. I said nothing and waited.

Shigeru said, "I knew I would have no rest under Heaven while my brother's murderers lived. I held their lord responsible for their actions. And in the meantime, circumstances had changed. Arai's falling out with Noguchi meant the Seishuu were again interested in an alliance with the Otori against Iida. Everything seemed to point to one conclusion: that the time had come to assassinate him."

Once I heard the words, a slow excitement began to burn within me. I remembered the moment in my village when I decided I was not going to die but live and seek revenge—the night in Hagi, under the winter moon, when I had known I had the ability and the will to kill Iida. I felt the stirrings of deep pride that Lord Shigeru had sought me out for this purpose. All the threads of my life seemed to lead towards it.

"My life is yours," I said. "I will do whatever you want."

"I'm asking you to do something extremely dangerous, almost impossible. If you choose not to do it, you may leave with Kenji tomorrow. All debts between us are canceled. No one will think the less of you."

"Please don't insult me," I said, and made him laugh.

I heard steps in the yard and a voice on the veranda. "Kenji is back."

A few moments later he came into the room, followed by a maid bringing fresh tea. He looked us over while she poured it and, once she had left, said, "You look like conspirators. What have you been plotting?"

"Our visit to Inuyama," Shigeru replied. "I have told Takeo my intentions. He is coming with me of his own free will."

Kenji's expression changed. "To his death," he muttered.

"Maybe not," I said lightly. "I am not boasting, but if anyone can get near Lord Iida, it will be me."

"You're just a boy," my teacher snorted. "I've told Lord Shigeru this already. He knows all my objections to this rash plan. Now I'll tell you. Do you really think you'll be able to kill Iida? He's survived more assassination attempts than I've had girls. You are yet to kill anyone! Added to which, there's every chance that you'll be recognized either in the capital or along the way. I believe your peddler did talk about you to someone. It was no accident that Ando turned up in Hagi. He came to check out the rumor and saw you with

189

Shigeru. It's my guess Iida already knows who and where you are. You're likely to be arrested as soon as you enter Tohan territory."

"Not if he is with me, one of the Otori coming to make a friendly alliance," the lord said. "Anyway, I've told him that he's free to go away with you. It's by his own choice that he comes with me."

I thought I detected a note of pride in his voice. I said to Kenji, "There is no question of me leaving. I must go to Inuyama. And anyway, I have scores of my own to settle."

He sighed sharply. "Then I suppose I'll have to go with you."

"The weather has cleared. We can move on tomorrow," Shigeru said.

"There's one other thing I must tell you, Shigeru. You astonished me by keeping your affair with Lady Maruyama hidden for so long. I heard something in the bathhouse, a joke, that makes me believe it is no longer a secret."

"What did you hear?"

"One man, having his back scrubbed, remarked to the girl that Lord Otori was in town with his future wife, and she replied, 'His current wife as well.' Many laughed as if they got her meaning, and went on to speak of Lady Maruyama, and Iida's desire for her. Of course, we are still in Otori country; they have nothing but admiration for you, and they like this rumor. It enhances the Otori reputation and is like a knife in the ribs for the

Tohan. All the more reason for it to be repeated until it reaches Iida's ears."

I could see Shigeru's face in the lamplight. There was a curious expression on it. I thought I could read pride there as well as regret.

"Iida may kill me," he said, "but he cannot change the fact that she prefers me over him."

"You are in love with death, like all your class," Kenji said, a depth of anger in his voice that I had never heard before.

"I have no fear of death," Shigeru replied. "But it is wrong to say I am in love with it. Quite the opposite: I think I've proved how much I love life. But it is better to die than to live with shame, and that is the point I have come to now."

I could hear footsteps approaching. I turned my head like a dog, and both men fell silent. There was a tap on the door and it slid open. Sachie knelt in the entrance. Shigeru immediately rose and went to her. She whispered something and went quietly away. He turned to us and said, "Lady Maruyama wishes to discuss tomorrow's travel arrangements. I will go to her room for a while."

Kenji said nothing, but bowed his head slightly.

"It may be our last time together," Shigeru said softly, and stepped into the passage, sliding the door closed behind him.

"I should have got to you first, Takeo," Kenji grumbled. "Then you would never have become a lord, never been tied to Shigeru by bonds of loyalty. You would be Tribe through and through.

You wouldn't think twice about taking off with me now, tonight."

"If Lord Otori had not got to me first, I would be dead!" I replied fiercely. "Where was the Tribe when the Tohan were murdering my people and burning my home? He saved my life then. That's why I cannot leave him. I never will. Never ask me again!"

Kenji's eyes went opaque. "Lord Takeo," he said ironically.

The maids came to spread the beds, and we did not speak again.

The following morning the roads out of Tsuwano were crowded. Many travelers were taking advantage of the finer weather to resume their journey. The sky was a clear deep blue and the sun drew moisture from the earth until it steamed. The stone bridge across the river was undamaged, but the water ran wild and high, throwing tree branches, planks of wood, dead animals and other corpses, possibly, against the piers. I was thinking fleetingly of the first time I'd crossed the bridge at Hagi when I saw a drowned heron floating in the water, its gray and white feathers waterlogged, all its gracefulness crumpled and broken. The sight of it chilled me. I thought it a terrible omen.

The horses were rested and stepped out eagerly. If Shigeru was less eager, if he shared my forebodings, he gave no sign of it. His face was calm, his eyes bright. He seemed to glow with energy and life. It made my heart twist to look at him—made me feel his life and his future all lay in my assassin hands. I looked at my hands as they lay against Raku's pale gray neck and black mane and wondered if they would let me down.

I saw Kaede only briefly, as she stepped into the palanquin outside the inn. She did not look at me. Lady Maruyama acknowledged our presence with a slight bow but did not speak. Her face was pale, her eyes dark-ringed, but she was composed and calm.

It was a slow, laborious journey. Tsuwano had been protected from the wost of the storm behind its mountain barriers, but as we descended into the valley the full extent of the damage became clear. Houses and bridges had been washed away, trees uprooted, fields flooded. The village people watched us, sullen or with open anger, as we rode through the midst of their suffering, and added to it by commandeering their hay to feed our horses, their boats to carry us across the swollen rivers. We were already days overdue and had to press on at whatever cost.

It took us three days to reach the fief border, twice as long as expected. An escort had been sent to meet us here: one of Iida's chief retainers, Abe, with a group of thirty Tohan men, outnumbering the twenty Otori Lord Shigeru rode with. Sugita and the other Maruyama men had returned to their own domain after our meeting in Tsuwano.

Abe and his men had been waiting a week and

were impatient and irritable. They did not want to spend the time that the Festival of the Dead required in Yamagata. There was little love lost between the two clans; the atmosphere became tense and strained. The Tohan men were arrogant and swaggering. We Otori were made to feel that we were inferior, coming as supplicants, not equals. My blood boiled on Shigeru's behalf, but he seemed unmoved, remaining as courteous as usual, and only slightly less cheerful.

I was as silent as in the days when I could not speak. I listened for snatches of conversation that would reveal, like straws, the direction of the wind. But in Tohan country, people were taciturn and close. They knew spies were everywhere and walls had ears. Even when the Tohan men got drunk at night, they did so silently, unlike the noisy, cheerful fashion of the Otori.

I had not been so close to the triple oak leaf since the day of the massacre at Mino. I kept my eyes down and my face averted, afraid I would see or be recognized by one of the men who had burned my village and murdered my family. I used my disguise as an artist, frequently taking out my brushes and ink stone. I went away from my true nature, becoming a gentle, sensitive, shy person who hardly spoke and who faded into the background. The only person I addressed was my teacher. Kenji had become as diffident and unobtrusive as I had. Occasionally we conversed in hushed tones about calligraphy or the mainland style of painting. The Tohan men despised and discounted us.

Our stay in Tsuwano became like the memory of a dream to me. Had the sword fight really taken place? Had Kaede and I been caught and scorched by love? I hardly saw her for the next few days. The ladies lodged in separate houses and took their meals apart. It was not hard to act, as I told myself I must, as if she did not exist, but if I heard her voice my heart raced, and at night her image burned behind my eyes. Had I been bewitched?

The first night Abe ignored me, but on the second, after the evening meal, when wine had made him belligerent, he stared at me for a long time before remarking to Shigeru, "This boy—some relative, I suppose?"

"The son of a distant cousin of my mother," Shigeru replied. "He's the second oldest of a large family, all orphans now. My mother had always wanted to adopt him, and after her death I carried out her intention."

"And landed yourself with a milksop," Abe laughed.

"Well, sadly, maybe," Shigeru agreed. "But he has other talents that are useful. He is quick at calculating, and writing, and has some skill as an artist." His tone was patient, disappointed, as though I were an unwelcome burden to him, but I knew each comment like this served only to build up my character. I sat with eyes cast down, saying nothing.

Abe poured himself more wine and drank, eyeing me over the bowl's rim. His eyes were small and deep-set in a pockmarked, heavy-featured face. "Not much use in these times!"

"Surely we can expect peace, now that our two clans are moving towards alliance," Shigeru said quietly. "There may be a new flowering of the arts."

"Peace with the Otori maybe. They'll cave in without a fight. But now the Seishuu are causing trouble, stirred up by that traitor, Arai."

"Arai?" Shigeru questioned.

"A former vassal of Noguchi. From Kumamoto. His lands lie alongside your bride's family's. He's been raising fighting men all year. He'll have to be crushed before winter." Abe drank again. An expression of malicious humor crept into his face, making the mouth curve more cruelly. "Arai killed the man who allegedly tried to violate Lady Shirakawa, then took offence when Noguchi exiled him." His head swung towards me with the drunk's second sight. "I'll bet you've never killed a man, have you, boy?"

"No, Lord Abe," I replied. He laughed. I could sense the bully in him, close to the surface. I did not want to provoke him.

"How about you, old man?" He turned towards Kenji, who in his role of insignificant teacher had been drinking wine with delight. He seemed half intoxicated, but in fact was far less drunk than Abe.

"Although the sages teach us that the noble man

196

may—indeed, should—avenge death," he said in a high-pitched, pious voice, "I have never had cause to take such extreme action. On the other hand, the Enlightened One teaches his followers to refrain from taking the life of any sentient being, which is why I partake only of vegetables." He drank with appreciation and refilled his bowl. "Luckily wine, brewed from rice, is included in that category."

"Don't you have any warriors in Hagi, that you travel with such companions?" Abe scoffed.

"I am supposed to be going to my wedding," Shigeru returned mildly. "Should I be more prepared for battle?"

"A man should always be prepared for battle," Abe replied, "especially when his bride has the reputation yours has. You're aware of it, I suppose?" He shook his massive head. "It would be like eating puffer fish. One bite might kill you. Doesn't it alarm you?"

"Should it?" Shigeru poured more wine and drank.

"Well, she's exquisite, I admit. It would be worth it!"

"Lady Shirakawa will be no danger to me," Shigeru said, and led Abe on to speak of his exploits during Iida's campaigns in the East. I listened to his boasting and tried to discern his weaknesses. I had already decided I was going to kill him.

\* \* \*

The next day we came to Yamagata. It had been badly hit by the storm, with many dead and a huge loss of crops. Nearly as big as Hagi, it had been the second city in the Otori fief, until it had been handed over to the Tohan. The castle had been rebuilt and given to one of Iida's vassals. But most of the townspeople still considered themselves Otori, and Lord Shigeru's presence was one more reason for unrest. Abe had hoped to be in Inuyama before the Festival of the Dead began, and was angry at being stuck in Yamagata. It was considered inauspicious to travel, except to temples and shrines, until the Festival was over.

Shigeru was plunged into sadness, being for the first time at the place of Takeshi's death. "Every Tohan man I see, I ask myself: Were you one of them?" he confided in me late that night. "And I imagine they ask themselves why they are still unpunished, and despise me for letting them live. I feel like cutting them all down!"

I had never heard him express anything other than patience. "Then we would never get to Iida," I replied. "Every insult the Tohan heap on us will be avenged then."

"Your scholarly self is becoming very wise, Takeo," he said, his voice a little lighter. "Wise and self-controlled."

The next day he went with Abe to the castle to be received by the local lord. He came back sadder and more disturbed than ever. "The Tohan seek to avert unrest by blaming the Hidden for the

198

disasters of the storms," he told me briefly. "A handful of wretched merchants and farmers were denounced and arrested. Some died under torture. Four are suspended from the castle walls. They've been there for three days."

"They're still alive?" I whispered, my skin crawling.

"They may last a week or more," Shigeru said. "In the meantime, the crows eat their living flesh."

Once I knew they were there, I could not stop hearing them: at times a quiet groaning, at other times a thin screaming, accompanied in daylight by the constant cawing and flapping of the crows. I heard it all that night and the following day, and then it was the first night of the Festival of the Dead.

The Tohan imposed a curfew on their towns, but the festival followed older traditions, and the curfew was lifted until midnight. As night fell we left the inn and joined the crowds of people going first to the temples and then to the river. All the stone lanterns that lined the approaches to the shrines were lit, and candles were set on the tombstones, the flickering lights throwing strange shadows that made bodies gaunt and faces skull-like. The throng moved steadily and silently as though the dead themselves had emerged from the earth. It was easy to get lost in it, easy to slip away from our watchful guards.

It was a warm, still night. I went with Shigeru to the riverbank, and we set lighted candles adrift in fragile little boats laden with offerings for the dead. The temple bells were tolling, and chanting and singing drifted across the slow, brown water. We watched the lights float away on the current, hoping the dead would be comforted and would leave the living in peace.

Except that I had no peace in my heart. I thought of my mother, my stepfather and my sisters, my long-dead father, the people of Mino. Lord Shigeru no doubt thought of his father, his brother. It seemed their ghosts would not leave us until they were avenged. All around us, people were setting their lit boats afloat, weeping and crying, and making my heart twist with useless sorrow that the world was how it was. The teaching of the Hidden, such as I remembered, came into my mind, but then I remembered that all those who had taught it to me were dead.

The candle flames burned for a long time, growing smaller and smaller, until they looked like fireflies, and then like sparks, and then like the phantom lights you see when you gaze too long on flames. The moon was full, with the orange tinge of late summer. I dreaded going back to the inn, to the stuffy room where I would toss and turn all night and listen to the Hidden dying against the castle wall.

Bonfires had been lit along the riverbank, and now people began to dance, the haunting dance that welcomes the dead, lets them depart, and comforts the living. Drums were beating and music playing. It lifted my spirits a little and I got to my feet to watch. In the shadows of the willow trees I saw Kaede.

She was standing with Lady Maruyama, Sachie, and Shizuka. Shigeru stood up and strolled towards them. Lady Maruyama approached him, and they greeted each other in cool, formal language, exchanging sympathy for the dead and commenting on the journey. They turned, as was perfectly natural, to stand side by side and watch the dancing. But I felt I could hear the longing beneath their tone, and see it in their stance, and I was afraid for them. I knew they could dissemble—they had done so for years—but now they were entering a desperate endgame, and I feared they would throw away caution before the final move.

Kaede was now alone on the bank, apart from Shizuka. I seemed to arrive at her side without volition, as though I had been picked up by spirits and put down next to her. I managed to greet her politely but diffidently, thinking that if Abe spotted me, he would simply think I was suffering from calf-love for Shigeru's betrothed. I said something about the heat, but Kaede was trembling as though she were cold. We stood in silence for a few moments, then she asked in a low voice, "Who are you mourning, Lord Takeo?"

"My mother, my father." After a pause I went on, "There are so many dead."

"My mother is dying," she said. "I hoped I would

see her again, but we have been so delayed on this journey, I fear I will be too late. I was seven years old when I was sent as a hostage. I have not seen my mother or my sisters for over half my life."

"And your father?"

"He is also a stranger to me."

"Will he be at your . . . ?" To my surprise my throat dried up, and I found I could not speak the word.

"My marriage?" she said, bitterly. "No, he will not be there." Her eyes had been fixed on the light-filled river. Now she looked past me at the dancers, at the crowd watching them.

"They love each other," she said, as though speaking to herself. "That's why she hates me."

I knew I should not be there, I should not be talking to her, but I could not make myself move away. I tried to maintain my gentle, diffident, well-behaved character. "Marriages are made for reasons of duty and alliance. That does not mean they have to be unhappy. Lord Otori is a good man."

"I am tired of hearing that. I know he is a good man. I am only saying, he will never love me." I knew her eyes were on my face. "But I know," she went on, "that love is not for our class."

I was the one who was trembling now. I raised my head, and my eyes met hers.

"So why do I feel it?" she whispered.

I did not dare say anything. The words I wanted to say swelled up huge in my mouth. I could taste their sweetness and their power. Again I thought I would die if I did not possess her.

The drums pounded. The bonfires blazed. Shizuka spoke out of the darkness. "It's growing late, Lady Shirakawa."

"I am coming," Kaede said. "Good night, Lord Takeo."

I allowed myself one thing, to speak her name, as she had spoken mine. "Lady Kaede."

In the moment before she turned away, I saw her face come alight, brighter than the flames, brighter than the moon on the water.

# CHAPTER 8

We followed the women slowly back to the town, and then went to our separate lodging houses. Somewhere on the way the Tohan guards caught up with us, and we had their escort to the inn door. They stayed outside and one of our own Otori men kept watch in the passageway.

"Tomorrow we will ride to Terayama," Shigeru said as we prepared for bed. "I must visit Takeshi's grave and pay my respects to the abbot, who was an old friend of my father's. I have some gifts for him from Hagi."

We had brought with us many gifts. The pack-horses had been laden with them, along with our own baggage, clothes for the wedding, food for the journey. I did not think anything more of the wooden box that we would carry to Terayama, or what it might contain. I was restless with other longings, other concerns.

The room was as stuffy as I'd feared. I could not sleep. I heard the temple bells toll at midnight, and then all sounds faded away under the curfew, apart from the pitiful groans of the dying from the castle walls.

In the end I got up. I had no real plan in my head. I was just driven into action by sleeplessness. Both Kenji and Shigeru were asleep, and I could tell that the guard outside was dozing. I took the watertight box in which Kenji kept capsules of poison, and tied it inside my undergarment. I dressed in dark traveling clothes and took the short sword, thin garrotes, a pair of grapples, and a rope from their hiding place within the wooden chests. Each of these movements took a long time, as I had to execute them in complete silence, but time is different for the Tribe, slowing down or speeding up as we will it to. I was in no hurry, and I knew the two men in the room would not wake.

The guard stirred as I stepped past him. I went to the privy to relieve myself, and sent my second self back past him into the room. I waited in the shadows until he dozed again, then went invisible, scaled the roof from the inner courtyard, and dropped down into the street.

I could hear the Tohan guards at the gate of the inn, and I knew there would be patrols in the streets. With one part of my mind I was aware that what I was doing was dangerous to the point of madness, but I could not help myself. Partly I wanted to test the skills Kenji had taught me before we got to Inuyama, but mostly I just wanted to silence the groans from the castle so that I could go to sleep.

I worked my way through the narrow streets, zigzagging towards the castle. A few houses still had lights behind the shutters, but most were already in darkness. I caught snatches of conversation as I went past: a man comforting a weeping woman, a child babbling as if in fever, a lullaby, a drunken argument. I came out onto the main road that led straight to the moat and the bridge. A canal ran alongside it, stocked against siege with carp. Mostly they slept, their scales shining faintly in the moonlight. Every now and then one would wake with a sudden flip and splash. I wondered if they dreamed.

I went from doorway to doorway, ears alert all the time for the tread of feet, the clink of steel. I was not particularly worried about the patrols: I knew I would hear them long before they heard me, and above that, I had the skills of invisibility and the second self. By the time I reached the end of the street and saw the waters of the moat under the moonlight, I had stopped thinking much at all, beyond a satisfaction deep within me that I was Kikuta and doing what I was born to do. Only the Tribe know this feeling.

On the town side of the moat there was a clump of willow trees, their heavy summer foliage falling right to the water. For defensive purposes they should have been cleared: Maybe some resident of the castle, the lord's wife or mother, loved their beauty. Under the moonlight their branches looked frozen. There was no wind at all. I slipped between them, crouched down, and looked at the castle for a long time.

It was bigger than the castles at either Tsuwano or Hagi, but the construction was similar. I could see the faint outline of the baskets against the white walls of the keep behind the second south gate. I had to swim the moat, scale the stone wall, get over the first gate and across the south bailey, climb the second gate and the keep, and climb down to the baskets from above.

I heard footsteps and shrank into the earth. A troop of guards was approaching the bridge. Another patrol came from the castle, and they exchanged a few words.

"Any problems?"

"Just the usual curfew breakers."

"Terrible stink!"

"It'll be worse tomorrow. Hotter."

One group went into the town; the other walked over the bridge and up the steps to the gate. I heard the shout that challenged them, and their reply. The gate creaked as it was unbarred and opened. I heard it slam shut and the footsteps fade away.

From my position under the willows I could smell the stagnant waters of the moat, and beneath that another stench: of human corruption, of living bodies rotting slowly.

At the water's edge were flowering grasses and a few late irises. Frogs croaked and crickets shrilled. The warm air of the night caressed my face. Two swans, unbelievably white, drifted into the path of the moon.

I filled my lungs with air and slipped into the water, swimming close to the bottom and aiming slightly downstream so that I surfaced under the shadow of the bridge. The huge stones of the moat wall gave natural footholds; my main concern here was being seen against the pale stone. I could not maintain invisibility for more than a couple of minutes at a time. Time that had gone so slowly before now speeded up. I moved fast, going up the wall like a monkey. At the first gate I heard voices, the guards coming back from their circular patrol. I flattened myself against a drainpipe, went invisible, and used the sound of their steps to mask the grapple as I threw it up over the massive overhang of the wall.

I swung myself up and, staying on the tiled roof, ran around to the south bailey. The baskets with the dying men in them were almost directly over my head. One was calling over and over for water, one moaned wordlessly, and one was repeating the name of the secret god in a rapid monotone that made the hairs on the back of my neck stand up. The fourth was completely silent. The smell of blood, piss, and shit was terrible. I tried to close my nostrils to it, and my ears to the sounds. I looked at my hands in the moonlight.

I had to cross above the gatehouse. I could hear the guards within it, making tea and chatting. As the kettle clinked on the iron chain, I used the grapples to climb the keep to the parapet that the baskets were slung from.

They were suspended by ropes, about forty feet above the ground, each one just large enough to hold a man forced down on his knees, head bent forward, arms tied behind his back. The ropes seemed strong enough to bear my weight, but when I tested one from the parapet, the basket lurched and the man within cried out sharply in fear. It seemed to shatter the night. I froze. He sobbed for a few minutes, then whispered again, "Water! Water!"

There was no answering sound apart from a dog barking far in the distance. The moon was close to the mountains, about to disappear behind them. The town lay sleeping, calm.

When the moon had set, I checked the hold of the grapple on the parapet, took out the poison capsules, and held them in my mouth. Then I climbed down the wall, using my own rope and feeling for each foothold on the stone.

At the first basket I took off my headband, still wet from the river, and could just reach through the weave to hold it to the man's face. I heard him suck and say something incoherent.

"I can't save you," I whispered, "but I have poison. It will give you a quick death."

He pressed his face to the mesh and opened his mouth for it.

The next man could not hear me, but I could reach the carotid artery where his head was slumped against the side of the basket, and so I silenced his groans with no pain to him.

I then had to climb again to the parapet to reposition my rope, for I could not reach the other baskets. My arms were aching, and I was all too aware of the flagstones of the yard below. When I reached the third man, the one who had been praying, he was alert, watching me with dark eyes. I murmured one of the prayers of the Hidden and held out the poison capsule.

He said, "It is forbidden."

"Let any sin be on me," I whispered. "You are innocent. You will be forgiven."

As I pushed the capsule into his mouth, with his tongue he traced the sign of the Hidden against my palm. I heard him pray, and then he went silent forever.

I could feel no pulse at the throat of the fourth, and thought he was already dead, but just to be sure I used the garrote, tightening it around his neck and holding it while I counted the minutes away under my breath.

I heard the first cock crow. As I climbed back to the parapet the silence of the night was profound. I had stilled the groans and the screams. I thought the contrasting quiet was sure to wake the guards. I could hear my own pulse beat crashing like a drum.

I went back the way I had come, not using the grapple, but dropping from the walls to the ground, moving even faster than before. Another cock crowed and a third answered. The town would soon be waking. Sweat was pouring from me, and the waters of the moat felt icy. My breath barely held for the swim back, and I surfaced well short of the willow trees, startling the swans. I breathed and dived again.

I came up on the bank and headed for the willows, meaning to sit there for a few moments to get my breath back. The sky was lightening. I was exhausted. I could feel my concentration and focus slipping. I could hardly believe what I had done.

To my horror I heard someone already there. It was not a soldier but some outcaste, I thought, a leather worker perhaps, judging by the smell of the tannery that clung to him. Before I could recover my strength enough to go invisible, he saw me, and in that flash of a look I realized he knew what I had done.

*Now I shall have to kill again,* I thought, sickened that this time it would not be release but murder. I could smell blood and death on my own hands. I decided to let him live, left my second self beneath the tree, and in an instant was on the other side of the street.

I listened for a moment, and heard the man speak to my image before it faded.

"Sir," he said hesitantly, "forgive me. I've been listening to my brother suffer for three days. Thank you. May the secret one be with you and bless you."

Then my second self vanished and he cried out in shock and amazement. "An angel!"

I could hear his rough breathing, almost sobbing, as I ran from doorway to doorway. I hoped the patrols did not catch up with him, hoped he would not speak of what he had seen, trusted that he was one of the Hidden, who take their secrets to the grave.

The wall around the inn was low enough to leap up. I went back to the privy and the cistern, where I spat out the remaining capsules, and washed my face and hands as if I had just risen. The guard was half awake when I passed him. He mumbled, "Is it day already?"

"An hour away, still," I replied.

"You look pale, Lord Takeo. Have you been unwell?"

"A touch of the gripes, that's all."

"This damn Tohan food," he muttered, and we both laughed.

"Will you have some tea?" he asked. "I'll wake the maids."

"Later. I'll try and sleep for a while."

I slid the door open and stepped into the room. The darkness was just giving way to gray. I could tell by his breathing that Kenji was awake.

"Where've you been?" he whispered.

"In the privy. I didn't feel well."

"Since midnight?" he said, incredulous.

I was pulling off my wet clothes and hiding the weapons under the mattress at the same time.

212

"Not that long. You were asleep."

He reached out and felt my undergarment. "This is soaking! Have you been in the river?"

"I told you, I didn't feel well. Maybe I couldn't get to the privy in time."

Kenji thwacked me hard on the shoulder, and I heard Shigeru wake.

"What is it?" he whispered.

"Takeo's been out all night. I was worried about him."

"I couldn't sleep," I said. "I just went out for a while. I've done it before, in Hagi and Tsuwano."

"I know you have," Kenji said. "But that was Otori country. It's a lot more dangerous here."

"Well, I'm back now." I slipped under the quilt and pulled it over my head, and almost immediately fell into a sleep as deep and dreamless as death.

When I woke, it was to the sound of the crows. I had only slept for about three hours, but I felt rested and peaceful. I did not think about the previous night. Indeed, I had no clear memory of it, as though I had acted in a trance. It was one of those rare days of late summer when the sky is a clear light blue and the air soft and warm, with no stickiness. A maid came into the room with a tray of food and tea and, after bowing to the floor and pouring the tea, said quietly, "Lord Otori is waiting for you in the stables. He asks you to join him as soon as possible. And your teacher wishes you to bring drawing materials."

I nodded, my mouth full.

She said, "I will dry your clothes for you."

"Get them later," I told her, not wanting her to find the weapons, and when she left I jumped up, got dressed, and hid the grapples and the garrote in the false bottom of the traveling chest where Kenji had packed them. I took up the pouch with my brushes, and the lacquer box that contained the ink stone, and wrapped them in a carrying cloth. I put my sword in my belt, thought myself into being Takeo, the studious artist, and went out to the stable yard.

As I passed the kitchen I heard one of the maids whisper, "They all died in the night. People are saying an angel of Death came. . . ."

I walked on, my eyes lowered, adjusting my gait so that I seemed a little clumsy. The ladies were already on horseback. Shigeru stood in conversation with Abe, who I realized was to accompany us. A young Tohan man stood beside them, holding two horses. A groom held Shigeru's Kyu and my Raku.

"Come along, come along," Abe exclaimed when he saw me. "We can't wait all day while you laze in bed."

"Apologize to Lord Abe," Shigeru said with a sigh.

"I am very sorry; there is no excuse at all," I babbled, bowing low to Abe and to the ladies, trying not to look at Kaede. "I was studying late."

Then I turned to Kenji and said deferentially, "I have brought the drawing materials, sir."

214

"Yes, good," he replied. "You will see some fine works at Terayama, and may even copy them if we have time."

Shigeru and Abe mounted, and the groom brought Raku to me. My horse was pleased to see me: He dropped his nose to my shoulder and nuzzled me. I let the movement push me off balance, so that I stumbled slightly. I went to Raku's right side and pretended to find mounting somewhat of a problem.

"Let's hope his drawing skills are greater than his horsemanship," Abe said derisively.

"Unfortunately, they are nothing out of the ordinary." I did not think Kenji's annoyance with me was feigned.

I made no reply to either of them, just contented myself with studying Abe's thick neck as he rode in front of me, imagining how it would feel to tighten the garrote around it or to slide a knife into his solid flesh.

These dark thoughts occupied me until we were over the bridge and out of the town. Then the beauty of the day began to work its magic on me. The land was healing itself after the ravages of the storm. Morning-glory flowers had opened, brilliant blue, even where the vines were torn down in the mud. Kingfishers flashed across the river, and egrets and herons stood in the shallows. A dozen different dragonflies hovered about us, and orange-brown and yellow butterflies flew up from around the horses' feet.

On the flat land of the river plain we rode between bright green rice fields, the plants flattened by the storm but already pushing themselves upright again. Everywhere people were hard at work; even they seemed cheerful despite the storm's destruction all around them. They reminded me of the people of my village, their indomitable spirit in the face of disaster, their unshakable belief that no matter what might befall them, life was basically good and the world benign. I wondered how many more years of Tohan rule would it take to gouge that belief from their hearts.

The paddy fields gave way to terraced vegetable gardens, and then, as the path became steeper, to bamboo groves, closing around us with their dim, silver-green light. The bamboo in its turn gave way to pines and cedars, the thick needles underfoot muffling the horses' tread.

Around us stretched the impenetrable forest. Occasionally we passed pilgrims on the path, making the arduous journey to the holy mountain. We rode in single file, so conversation was difficult. I knew Kenji was longing to question me about the previous night, but I did not want to talk about it or even to think about it.

After nearly three hours we came to the small cluster of buildings around the outer gate of the temple. There was a lodging house here for visitors. The horses were taken away to be fed and watered, and we ate the midday meal, simple vegetable dishes prepared by the monks.

"I am a little tired," Lady Maruyama said when we had finished eating. "Lord Abe, will you stay here with Lady Shirakawa and myself while we rest for a while?"

He could not refuse, though he seemed reluctant to let Shigeru out of his sight.

Shigeru gave the wooden box to me, asking me to carry it up the hill, and I also took my own pack of brushes and ink. The young Tohan man came with us, scowling a little, as though he distrusted the whole excursion, but it must have seemed harmless enough, even to the suspicious. Shigeru could hardly pass by so close to Terayama without visiting his brother's grave, especially a year after his death and at the time of the Festival of the Dead.

We began to climb the steep stone steps. The temple was built on the side of the mountain, next to a shrine of great antiquity. The trees in the sacred grove must have been four or five hundred years old, their huge trunks rising up into the canopy, their gnarled roots clinging to the mossy ground like forest spirits. In the distance I could hear monks chanting and the boom of gongs and bells, and beneath these sounds the voice of the forest, the min-min, the splash of the waterfall, the wind in the cedars, birds calling. My high spirits at the beauty of the day gave way to another, deeper feeling; a sense of awe and expectancy, as if some great and wonderful secret were about to be revealed to me.

217

We came finally to the second gate, which led into another cluster of buildings where pilgrims and other visitors stayed. Here we were asked to wait and given tea to drink. After a few moments two priests approached us. One was an old man, rather short and frail with age, but with bright eyes and an expression of great serenity. The other was much younger, stern-faced and muscular.

"You are very welcome here, Lord Otori," the old man said, making the Tohan man's face darken even more. "It was with great sorrow that we buried Lord Takeshi. You have come, of course, to visit the grave."

"Stay here with Muto Kenji," Shigeru said to the soldier, and he and I followed the old priest to the graveyard, where the tombstones stood in rows beneath the huge trees. Someone was burning wood, and the smoke drifted beneath the trunks, making blue rays out of the sunlight.

The three of us knelt in silence. After a few moments the younger priest came with candles and incense and passed them to Shigeru, who placed them before the stone. The sweet fragrance floated around us. The lamps burned steadily, since there was no wind, but their flames could hardly be seen in the brightness of the sun. Shigeru also took two objects from his sleeve—a black stone like the ones from the seashore around Hagi, and a straw horse such as a child might play with— and placed these on the grave.

I remembered the tears he had shed the first

night I had met him. Now I understood his grief, but neither of us wept.

After a while the priest rose, touching Shigeru on the shoulder, and we followed him to the main building of this remote country temple. It was made of wood, cypress and cedar, which had faded over time to silver-gray. It did not look large, but its central hall was perfectly proportioned, giving a sense of space and tranquillity, leading the gaze inwards to where the golden statue of the Enlightened One seemed to hover among the candle flames as if in Paradise.

We loosened our sandals and stepped up into the hall. Again the young monk brought incense, and we placed it at the golden feet of the statue. Kneeling to one side of us, he began to chant one of the sutras for the dead.

It was dim inside, and my eyes were dazzled by the candles, but I could hear the breathing of others within the temple, beyond the altar, and as my vision adjusted to the darkness I could see the shapes of monks sitting in silent meditation. I realized the hall was much bigger than I had at first thought, and there were many monks here, possibly hundreds.

Even though I was raised among the Hidden, my mother took me to the shrines and temples of our district, and I knew a little of the teachings of the Enlightened One. I thought now, as I had often thought before, that people when they pray look and sound the same. The peace of this place pierced my soul. What was I doing here, a killer, my heart bent on revenge?

When the ceremony was over we went back to join Kenji, who seemed to be deep in a one-sided discussion with the Tohan man about art and religion.

"We have a gift for the lord abbot," Shigeru said, picking up the box, which I had left with Kenji.

A twinkle appeared in the priest's eye. "I will take you to him."

"And the young men would like to see the paintings," Kenji said.

"Makoto will show them. Follow me, please, Lord Otori."

The Tohan man looked taken aback as Shigeru disappeared behind the altar with the old priest. He made as if to follow them, but Makoto seemed to block his path, without touching or threatening him.

"This way, young man!"

With a deliberate tread he somehow herded the three of us out of the temple and along a boardwalk to a smaller hall.

"The great painter Sesshu lived in this temple for ten years," he told us. "He designed the gardens and painted landscapes, animals, and birds. These wooden screens are his work."

"That is what it is to be an artist," Kenji said in his querulous teacher's voice.

"Yes, master," I replied. I did not have to pretend to be humble: I was genuinely awed by the work before our eyes. The black horse, the white cranes, seemed to have been caught and frozen in an instant of time by the consummate skill of the artist. You felt that at any moment the spell would be broken, the horse would stamp and rear, the cranes would see us and launch themselves into the sky. The painter had achieved what we would all like to do: capture time and make it stand still.

The screen closest to the door seemed to be bare. I peered at it, thinking the colors must have faded. Makoto said, "There were birds on it, but the legend goes that they were so lifelike, they flew away."

"You see how much you have to learn," Kenji told me. I thought he was rather overdoing it, but the Tohan man gave me a scornful glance and, after a cursory look at the paintings, went outside and sat down under a tree.

I took out the ink stone, and Makoto brought me some water. I prepared the ink and unfolded a roll of paper. I wanted to trace the master's hand and see if he could transfer, across the chasm of the years, what he had seen, into my brush.

Outside, the afternoon heat increased, shimmering, intensified by the crickets' shrilling. The trees cast great pools of inky shade. Inside the hall it was cooler, dim. Time slowed. I heard the Tohan man's breathing even as he fell asleep.

"The gardens are also Sesshu's work," Makoto said, and he and Kenji sat themselves down on the matting, their backs towards the paintings and me, looking out onto the rocks and trees. In the distance a waterfall murmured, and I could hear two wood doves cooing. From time to time Kenji made a comment or asked a question about the garden, and Makoto replied. Their conversation grew more desultory, until they also seemed to be dozing.

Left alone with my brush and paper, and the incomparable paintings, I felt the same focus and concentration steal over me that I'd felt the previous night, taking me into the same half-trancelike state. It saddened me a little that the skills of the Tribe should be so similar to the skills of art. A strong desire seized me to stay in this place for ten years like the great Sesshu, and draw and paint every day until my paintings came to life and flew away.

I made copies of the horse and the cranes, copies that did not satisfy me at all, and then I painted the little bird from my mountain as I had seen it flying off at my approach, with a flash of white in its wings.

I was absorbed by the work. From far away I could hear Shigeru's voice, speaking to the old priest. I was not really listening: I assumed he was seeking some spiritual counsel from the old man, a private matter. But the words dropped into my hearing, and it slowly dawned on me that their talk was of something quite different: burdensome new taxes, curtailment of freedom, Iida's desire to destroy the temples, several thousand monks in remote monasteries, all trained as warriors and desiring to overthrow the Tohan and restore the lands to the Otori.

I grinned ruefully to myself. My concept of the temple as a place of peace, a sanctuary from war, was somewhat misplaced. The priests and the monks were as belligerent as we were, as bent on revenge.

I did one more copy of the horse, and felt happier with it. I had caught something of its fiery power. I felt that Sesshu's spirit had indeed touched me across time, and maybe had reminded me that when illusions are shattered by truth, talent is set free.

Then I heard another sound from far below that set my heart racing: Kaede's voice. The women and Abe were climbing the steps to the second gate.

I called quietly to Kenji, "The others are coming."

Makoto got swiftly to his feet and padded silently away. A few moments later the old priest and Lord Shigeru stepped into the hall, where I was putting the finishing strokes to the copy of the horse.

"Ah, Sesshu spoke to you!" the old priest said, smiling.

I gave the picture to Shigeru. He was sitting looking at it when the ladies and Abe joined us. The Tohan man woke and tried to pretend he had not been asleep. The talk was all of paintings and gardens. Lady Maruyama continued to pay special attention to Abe, asking his opinion and flattering him until even he became interested in the subject.

Kaede looked at the sketch of the bird. "May I have this?" she asked.

"If it pleases you, Lady Shirakawa," I replied. "I'm afraid it is very poor."

"It does please me," she said in a low voice. "It makes me think of freedom."

The ink had dried rapidly in the heat. I rolled the paper and gave it to her, my fingers grazing hers for a moment. It was the first time we had touched. Neither of us said any more. The heat seemed more intense, the crickets more insistent. A wave of fatigue swept over me. I was dizzy with lack of sleep and emotion. My fingers had lost their assurance and trembled as I packed away the painting things.

"Let us walk in the garden," Shigeru said, and took the ladies outside. I felt the old priest's gaze on me.

"Come back to us," he said, "when all this is over. There will always be a place for you here."

I thought of all the turmoil and changes the temple had seen, the battles that raged around it. It seemed so tranquil: The trees stood as they had for hundreds of years, the Enlightened One sat among the candles with his serene smile. Yet, even in this place of peace men were planning war. I could never withdraw into painting and planning gardens until Iida was dead.

"Will it ever be over?" I replied.

"Everything that has a beginning has an ending," he said.

I bowed to the ground before him, and he placed his palms together in a blessing.

Makoto walked out into the garden with me. He was looking at me quizzically. "How much do you hear?" he said quietly.

I looked around. The Tohan men were with Shigeru at the top of the steps. "Can you hear what they are saying?"

He measured the space with his eye. "Only if they shout it."

"I hear every word. I can hear them in the eating house below. I can tell you how many people are gathered there."

It struck me then that it sounded like a multitude.

Makoto gave a short laugh, amazement mixed with appreciation. "Like a dog?"

"Yes, like a dog," I replied.

"Useful to your masters."

His words stayed with me. I was useful to my masters, to Lord Shigeru, to Kenji, to the Tribe. I had been born with dark talents I did not ask for, yet I could not resist honing and testing them, and they had brought me to the place I was now. Without them I would surely be dead. With them I was drawn every day further into this world of lies, secrecy, and revenge. I wondered how much of this Makoto would understand, and wished I could share my thoughts with him. I felt an instinctive liking for him—more than liking: trust. But the shadows were lengthening; it was nearly the hour of the Rooster. We had to leave to get back to Yamagata before nightfall. There was no time to talk.

When we descended the steps there was indeed a huge crowd of people gathered outside the lodging house.

"Are they here for the Festival?" I said to Makoto.

"Partly," he said, and then in an aside so no one else could hear him: "But mainly because they have heard Lord Otori is here. They haven't forgotten the way things were before Yaegahara. Nor have we here. . . .

"Farewell," he said as I mounted Raku. "We'll meet again."

On the mountain path, on the road, it was the same. Many people were out, and they all seemed to want to take a look with their own eyes at Lord Shigeru. There was something eerie about it, the silent people dropping to the ground as we rode past, then getting to their feet to stare after us, their faces somber, their eyes burning.

The Tohan men were furious, but there was nothing they could do. They rode some way ahead of me, but I could hear their whispered conversation as clearly as if they poured the words into my ears.

"What did Shigeru do at the temple?" Abe asked.

"Prayed, spoke to the priest. We were shown the works by Sesshu; the boy did some painting."

"I don't care what the boy did! Was Shigeru alone with the priest?"

"Only for a few minutes," the younger man lied.

Abe's horse plunged forward. He must have jerked on the bridle in anger.

"He's not plotting anything," the young man said airily. "It's all just what it seems. He's on his way to be married. I don't see why you're so worried. The three of them are harmless. Fools—cowards, even—but harmless."

"You're the fool if you think that," Abe growled. "Shigeru is a lot more dangerous than he seems. He's no coward, for a start. He has patience. And no one else in the Three Countries has this effect on the people!"

They rode in silence for a while, then Abe muttered, "Just one sign of treachery and we have him."

The words floated back to me through the perfect summer evening. By the time we reached the river it was dusk, a blue twilight lit by fireflies among the rushes. On the bank the bonfires were already blazing for the second night of the festival. The previous night had been grief-filled and subdued. Tonight the atmosphere was wilder, with an undercurrent of ferment and violence. The streets were crowded, the throng thickest along the edge of the moat. People were standing staring at the first gate of the castle.

As we rode past we could see the four heads

displayed above the gate. The baskets had already been removed from the walls.

"They died quickly," Shigeru said to me. "They were lucky."

I did not reply. I was watching Lady Maruyama. She took one quick look at the heads and then turned away, her face pale but composed. I wondered what she was thinking, if she was praying.

The crowd tumbled and surged like a sorrowful beast at the slaughterhouse, alarmed by the stench of blood and death.

"Don't linger," Kenji said. "I'm going to listen to a little gossip here and there. I'll meet you back at the inn. Stay indoors." He called to one of the grooms, slid from his horse, gave the reins to the man, and disappeared into the crowd.

As we turned into the straight street I had run down the night before, a contingent of Tohan men rode towards us with drawn swords.

"Lord Abe!" called one of them. "We are to clear the streets. The town is in turmoil. Get your guests inside and put guards on the gates."

"What set this off?" Abe demanded.

"The criminals all died in the night. Some man claims an angel came and delivered them!"

"Lord Otori's presence is not helping the situation," Abe said bitterly as he urged us towards the inn. "We'll ride on tomorrow."

"The festival is not over," Shigeru remarked. "Travel on the third day will only bring bad luck."

"That can't be helped! The alternative could be worse." He had drawn his sword and now it whistled through the air as he slashed at the crowd. "Get down!" he yelled.

Alarmed by the noise, Raku plunged forward, and I found myself riding knee to knee with Kaede. The horses swung their heads towards each other, taking courage from each other's presence. They trotted the length of the street in perfect stride.

She said, looking forward, in a voice so quiet that no one but I could hear it above the turmoil around us: "I wish we could be alone together. There are so many things I want to know about you. I don't even know who you really are. Why do you pretend to be less than you are? Why do you hide your deftness?"

I would have gladly ridden alongside her like that forever, but the street was too short, and I was afraid to answer her. I pushed my horse forward, as if indifferent to her, but my heart was pounding at her words. It was all I wanted: to be alone with her, to reveal my hidden self, to let go of all the secrets and deceptions, to lie with her, skin against skin.

Would it ever be possible? Only if Iida died.

When we came to the inn I went to oversee the care of the horses. The Otori men who had stayed behind greeted me with relief. They had been anxious for our safety.

"The town's alight," one said. "One false move

and there'll be fighting on the streets."

"What have you heard?" I asked.

"Those Hidden the bastards were torturing. Someone got to them and killed them. Unbelievable! Then some man figures he saw an angel!"

"They know Lord Otori is here," another added. "They still consider themselves Otori. I reckon they've had enough of the Tohan."

"We could take this town if we had a hundred men," the first muttered.

"Don't say these things, even to yourselves, even to me," I warned them. "We don't have a hundred men. We are at the mercy of the Tohan. We are supposed to be the instruments of an alliance: We must be seen to be such. Lord Shigeru's life depends on it."

They went on grumbling while they unsaddled the horses and fed them. I could feel the fire starting to burn in them, the desire to wipe out old insults and settle old scores.

"If any one of you draws a sword against the Tohan, his life is forfeit to me!" I said angrily.

They were not deeply impressed. They might know more about me than Abe and his men, but still, to them I was just young Takeo, a bit studious, fond of painting, not bad with the sword stick now, but always too gentle, too soft. The idea that I would actually kill one of them made them grin.

I feared their recklessness. If fighting broke out I had no doubt that the Tohan would seize the chance to charge Shigeru with treachery. Nothing must happen now that would prevent us getting unsuspected to Inuyama.

By the time I left the stables my head was aching fiercely. I felt as if it had been weeks since I'd slept. I went to the bathhouse. The girl who had brought me tea that morning and had said she would dry my clothes was there. She scrubbed my back and massaged my temples, and would certainly have done more for me if I had not been so tired and my mind so full of Kaede. She left me soaking in the hot water, but as she withdrew she whispered, "The work was well done."

I'd been dozing off but her words made me snap awake. "What work?" I asked, but she was already gone. Uneasy, I got out of the tub and returned to the room, the headache still a dull pain across my forehead.

Kenji was back. I could hear him and Shigeru speaking in low voices. They broke off when I entered the room, both staring at me. I could see from their faces that they knew.

Kenji said, "How?"

I listened. The inn was quiet, the Tohan still out on the streets. I whispered, "Two with poison, one with the garrote, one with my hands."

He shook his head. "It's hard to believe. Within the castle walls? Alone?"

I said, "I can't remember much about it. I thought you would be angry with me."

"I *am* angry," he replied. "More than angry—

furious. Of all the idiotic things to do. We should be burying you tonight, by all rights."

I braced myself for one of his blows. Instead he embraced me. "I must be getting fond of you," he said. "I don't want to lose you."

"I would not have thought it possible," Shigeru said. It seemed he could not help smiling. "Our plan may succeed after all!"

"People in the street are saying it must be Shintaro," Kenji remarked, "though no one knows who paid him or why."

"Shintaro is dead," I said.

"Well, not many people know that. Anyway, the general opinion is that this assassin is some sort of heavenly spirit."

"A man saw me, the brother of one of the dead. He saw my second self, and when it faded he thought it was an angel."

"As far as I can find out, he has no idea of your identity. It was dark, he did not see you clearly. He truly thought it was an angel."

"But why did you do it, Takeo?" Shigeru asked. "Why take such a risk now?"

Again, I could hardly remember. "I don't know, I couldn't sleep. . . ."

"It's that softness he has," Kenji said. "It drives him to act from compassion, even when he kills."

"There's a girl here," I said. "She knows something. She took my wet clothes this morning, and just now she said—"

"She's one of us," Kenji interrupted me, and as

soon as he said it I realized I'd known that she was from the Tribe. "Of course, the Tribe suspected at once. They know how Shintaro died. They know you are here with Lord Shigeru. No one can believe you did it without being detected, but they also know there is no one else who could have done it."

"Can it be kept a secret, though?" Shigeru asked.

"No one's going to give Takeo away to the Tohan, if that's what you mean. And they don't seem to suspect anything. Your acting's improving," he told me. "Even I believed you were no more than a well-meaning bumbler today."

Shigeru smiled again. Kenji went on, his voice unnaturally casual, "The only thing is, Shigeru, I know your plans; I know Takeo has agreed to serve you in their execution. But after this episode, I don't believe the Tribe will allow Takeo to remain with you much longer. They are now certain to claim him."

"Another week is all we need," Shigeru whispered.

I felt the darkness rise like ink in my veins. I raised my eyes and looked Shigeru full in the face—something I still rarely dared to do. We smiled at each other, never closer than when we were agreed on assassination.

From the streets outside came sporadic shouts, cries, the pad of running men, the tramp of horses, the crackling of fires, rising to wailing and screaming. The Tohan were clearing the streets, imposing the curfew. After a while the noise abated and the quiet of the summer evening returned. The moon had risen, drenching the town in light. I heard horses come into the inn yard, and Abe's voice. A few moments later there was a soft tap on the door, and maids came in with trays of food. One of them was the girl who had spoken to me earlier. She stayed to serve us after the others had left, saying quietly to Kenji, "Lord Abe has returned, sir. There will be extra guards outside the rooms tonight. Lord Otori's men are to be replaced by Tohan."

"They won't like that," I said, recalling the men's unrest.

"It seems provocative," Shigeru murmured. "Are we under some suspicion?"

"Lord Abe is angry and alarmed by the level of violence in the town," the girl replied. "He says it is to protect you."

"Would you ask Lord Abe to be good enough to wait on me?"

The girl bowed and left. We ate, mostly in silence. Towards the end of the meal Shigeru began to speak of Sesshu and his paintings. He took out the scroll of the horse and unrolled it. "It's quite pleasing," he said. "A faithful copy, yet something of yourself in it. You could become quite an artist. . ."

He did not go on, but I was thinking the same thought: *in a different world, in a different life, in a country not governed by war. . . .*

"The garden is very beautiful," Kenji observed. "Although it is small, to my mind it is more exquisite than the larger examples of Sesshu's work."

"I agree," Shigeru said. "Of course, the setting at Terayama is incomparable."

I could hear Abe's heavy tread approaching. As the door slid open I was saying humbly, "Can you explain the placement of the rocks to me, sir?"

"Lord Abe," Shigeru said, "please come in." He called to the girl: "Bring fresh tea and wine."

Abe bowed somewhat perfunctorily and settled himself on the cushions. "I will not stay long: I have not yet eaten, and we must be on the road at first light."

"We were speaking of Sesshu," Shigeru said. The wine was brought and he poured a cup for Abe.

"A great artist," Abe agreed, drinking deeply. "I regret that in these troubled times, the artist is less important than the warrior." He threw a scornful look at me that convinced me my disguise was still safe. "The town is quiet now, but the situation is still grave. I feel my men will offer you greater protection."

"The warrior is indispensable," Shigeru said. "Which is why I prefer to have my own men around me."

In the silence that followed I saw clearly the difference between them. Abe was no more than a glorified baron. Shigeru was heir to an ancient clan. Despite his reluctance, Abe had to defer to him.

He pushed his lower lip out. "If that is Lord Otori's wish . . ." he conceded finally.

"It is." Shigeru smiled slightly and poured more wine.

After Abe had left, the lord said, "Takeo, watch with the guards tonight. Impress on them that if there are any disturbances, I won't hesitate to hand them over to Abe for punishment. I fear a premature uprising. We are so close now to our aim."

It was an aim that I clung to single-mindedly. I gave no further thought to Kenji's statement that the Tribe would claim me. I concentrated solely on Iida Sadamu, in his lair in Inuyama. I would get to him across the nightingale floor. And I would kill him. Even the thought of Kaede only served to intensify my resolve. I didn't need to be an Ichiro to work out that if Iida died before Kaede's marriage, she would be set free to marry me.

# CHAPTER 9

We were roused early in the morning and were on the road a little after daybreak. The clearness of the day before had disappeared; the air was heavy and sticky. Clouds had formed in the night and rain threatened.

People had been forbidden to gather in the streets, and the Tohan enforced the ruling with their swords, cutting down a night-soil collector who dared to stop and stare at our procession and beating to death an old woman who did not get out of the way in time.

It was inauspicious enough to be traveling on the third day of the Festival of the Dead. These acts of cruelty and bloodshed seemed added ill omens for our journey.

The ladies were carried in palanquins, so I saw nothing of Kaede until we stopped for the mid-day meal. I did not speak to her, but I was shocked by her appearance. She was so pale, her skin seemed transparent, and her eyes were dark-ringed. My heart twisted. The more frail she became, it seemed the more hopelessly I loved her.

Shigeru spoke to Shizuka about her, concerned by her pallor. She replied that the movement of the palanquin did not agree with Kaede—it was nothing more than that—but her eyes flickered towards me and I thought I understood their message.

We were a silent group, each wrapped up in our own thoughts. The men were tense and irritable. The heat was oppressive. Only Shigeru seemed at ease, his conversation as light and carefree as if he were truly going to celebrate a longed-for wedding. I knew the Tohan despised him for it, but I thought it one of the greatest displays of courage I had seen.

The farther east we went, the less damage from the storms we encountered. The roads improved as we approached the capital, and each day we covered more miles. On the afternoon of the fifth day we arrived at Inuyama.

Iida had made this eastern city his capital after his success at Yaegahara, and had begun building the massive castle then. It dominated the town with its black walls and white crenellations, its roofs that looked as if they had been flung up into the sky like cloths. As we rode towards it I found myself studying the fortifications, measuring the height of the gates and the walls, looking for footholds. . . . *Here I will go invisible, bere I will need grapples. . . .*

I had not imagined the town would be so large, that there would be so many warriors on guard in the castle and housed around it.

238

Abe reined his horse back so he was alongside me. I'd become a favorite butt for his jokes and bullying humor. "This is what power looks like, boy. You get it by being a warrior. Makes your work with the brush look pretty feeble, eh?"

I didn't mind what Abe thought of me, as long as he never suspected the truth. "It's the most impressive place I've ever seen, Lord Abe. I wish I could study it closely, its architecture, its works of art."

"I'm sure that can be arranged," he said, ready enough to be patronizing now that he was safely back in his own city.

"Sesshu's name still lives among us," I remarked, "while the warriors of his age have all been forgotten."

He burst out laughing. "But you're no Sesshu, are you?"

His contempt made the blood rise to his face, but I meekly agreed with him. He knew nothing about me: It was the only comfort I had.

We were escorted to a residence close to the castle moat. It was spacious and beautiful. All the appearances suggested that Iida was committed to the marriage and to the alliance with the Otori. Certainly no fault could be found with the attention and honor paid to Shigeru. The ladies were carried to the castle itself, where they would stay at Iida's own residence, with the women of his household. Lady Maruyama's daughter lived there.

I did not see Kaede's face, but as she was carried away she let her hand appear briefly through the curtain of the palanquin. In it she held the scroll I had given her, the painting of my little mountain bird that she said made her think of freedom.

A soft evening rain was beginning to fall, blurring the outlines of the castle, glistening on the tiles and the cobblestones. Two geese flew overhead with a steady beating of wings. As they disappeared from sight I could still hear their mournful cry.

Abe returned later to the residence with wedding gifts and effusive messages of welcome from Lord Iida. I reminded him of his promise to show me the castle, pestering him and putting up with his banter, until he agreed to arrange it for the following day.

Kenji and I went with him in the morning, and I dutifully listened and sketched while first Abe and then, when he grew bored, one of his retainers took us around the castle. My hand drew trees, gardens, and views, while eye and brain absorbed the layout of the castle, the distance from the main gate to the second gate (the Diamond Gate, they called it), from the Diamond Gate to the inner bailey, from the inner bailey to the residence. The river flowed along the eastern side; all four sides were moated. And while I drew I listened, placed the guards, both seen and hidden, and counted them.

The castle was full of people: warriors and foot

soldiers, blacksmiths, fletchers and armorers, grooms, cooks, maids, servants of all kinds. I wondered where they all went at night, and if it ever became quiet.

The retainer was more talkative than Abe, keen to boast about Iida, and naively impressed by my drawing. I sketched him quickly and gave him the scroll. In those days few portraits were made, and he held it as if it were a magic talisman. After that he showed us more than he should have, including the hidden chambers where guards were always stationed, the false windows of the watchtowers, and the route the patrols took throughout the night.

Kenji said very little, beyond criticizing my drawing and correcting a brush stroke now and then. I wondered if he was planning to come with me when I went into the castle at night. One moment I thought I could do nothing without his help; the next I knew I wanted to be alone.

We came finally to the central keep and were taken inside, introduced to the captain of the guard, and allowed to climb the steep wooden steps to the highest floor. The massive pillars that held up the main tower were at least seventy feet in height. I imagined them as trees in the forest, how vast their canopy would be, how dense and dark their shade. The cross beams still held the twists they had grown with, as though they longed to spring upwards and be living trees again. I felt the castle's power as though it were a sentient being drawn up against me.

From the top platform, under the curious eyes of the midday guards, we could see out over the whole city. To the north rose the mountains I had crossed with Shigeru, and beyond them the plain of Yaegahara. To the southeast lay my birthplace, Mino. The air was misty and still, with hardly a breath of wind. Despite the heavy stone walls and the cool, dark wood, it was stiflingly hot. The guards' faces shone with sweat, their armor heavy and uncomfortable.

The southern windows of the main keep looked down onto the second, lower keep, which Iida had transformed into his residence. It was built above a huge fortification wall that rose almost directly from the moat. Beyond the moat, on the eastern side, was a strip of marshland, about a hundred yards or so in width, and then the river, flowing deep and strong, swollen by the storms. Above the fortification wall ran a row of small windows, but the doors of the residence were all on the western side. Gracefully sloping roofs covered the verandas and gave onto a small garden, surrounded by the walls of the second bailey. It would have been hidden from the eye at ground level, but here we could peer down into it as eagles might.

On the opposite side the northwest bailey housed the kitchens and other offices.

My eyes kept going from one side of Iida's palace to the other. The western side was so beautiful, almost gentle, the eastern side brutal in its austerity and power, and the brutality was increased by the iron rings set in the walls below the lookout windows. These, the guards told us, were used to hang Iida's enemies from, the victims' suffering deepening and enhancing his enjoyment of his power and splendor.

As we descended the steps again I could hear them mocking us, making the jokes I'd learned the Tohan always made at Otori expense: that they prefer boys to girls in bed, they'd rather eat a good meal than have a decent fight, that they were seriously weakened by their addiction to hot springs, which they always pissed in. Their raucous laughter floated after us. Embarrassed, our companion muttered an apology.

Assuring him we had taken no offense, I stood for a moment in the gateway of the inner bailey, ostensibly smitten by the beauty of the morning-glory flowers that straggled over the stone walls of the kitchens. I could hear all the usual kitchen sounds: the hiss of boiling water, the clatter of steel knives, a steady pounding as someone made rice cakes, the shouts of the cooks and the servant girls' high-pitched chatter. But beneath all that, from the other direction, from within the garden wall, there was something else reaching into my ears.

After a moment I realized what it was: the tread of people coming and going across Iida's nightingale floor.

"Can you hear that strange noise?" I said innocently to Kenji.

He frowned. "What can it be?"

Our companion laughed. "That's the nightingale floor."

"The nightingale floor?" we questioned together.

"It's a floor that sings. Nothing can cross it, not even a cat, without the floor chirping like a bird."

"It sounds like magic," I said.

"Maybe it is," the man replied, laughing at my credulity. "Whatever it is, his lordship sleeps better at night for its protection."

"What a marvelous thing! I'd love to see it," I said.

The man, still smiling, obligingly led us round the bailey to the southern side where the gate to the garden stood open. The gate was not high, but it had a massive overhang, and the steps through it were set on a steep angle so that they could be defended by one man. We looked through the gate to the building beyond. The wooden shutters were all open. I could see the massive gleaming floor that ran the whole length of the building.

A procession of maids bringing trays of food, for it was almost midday, stepped out of their sandals and onto the floor. I listened to its song, and my heart failed me. I recalled running so lightly and silently across the floor around the house in Hagi. This floor was four times its size, its song infinitely more complex. There would be no opportunity to practice. I would have one chance alone to outwit it.

I stayed as long as I plausibly could, exclaiming

and admiring while trying to map every sound, and from time to time, remembering that Kaede was somewhere within that building, straining my ears in vain to hear her voice.

Eventually Kenji said, "Come along, come along! My stomach is empty. Lord Takeo will be able to see the floor again tomorrow when he accompanies Lord Otori."

"Do we come to the castle again tomorrow?"

"Lord Otori will wait on Lord Iida in the afternoon," Kenji said. "I suppose Lord Takeo will accompany him."

"How thrilling," I replied, but my heart was as heavy as stone at the prospect.

When we returned to our lodging house, Lord Shigeru was looking at wedding robes. They were spread out over the matting, sumptuous, brightly colored, embroidered with all the symbols of good fortune and longevity: plum blossoms, white cranes, turtles.

"My uncles have sent these for me," he said. "What do you think of their graciousness, Takeo?"

"It is extreme," I replied, sickened by their duplicity.

"Which should I wear, in your opinion?" He took up the plum-blossom robe and the man who had brought the garments helped him put it on.

"That one is fine," Kenji said. "Now let's eat."

Lord Shigeru, however, lingered for a moment, passing his hands over the fine fabric, admiring the delicate intricacy of the embroidery. He did not speak, but I thought I saw something in his face: regret, perhaps, for the wedding that would never take place, and maybe, when I recall it now, premonition of his own fate.

"I will wear this one," he said, taking it off and handing it to the man.

"It is indeed becoming," the man murmured. "But few men are as handsome as Lord Otori."

Shigeru smiled his openhearted smile but made no other response, nor did he speak much during the meal. We were all silent, too tense to speak of trivial matters, and too aware of possible spies to speak of anything else.

I was tired but restless. The afternoon heat kept me inside. Although the doors were all opened wide onto the garden, not a breath of air came into the rooms. I dozed, trying to recall the song of the nightingale floor. The sounds of the garden, the insects' droning, the waterfall's splash, washed over me, half waking me, making me think I was back in the house in Hagi.

Towards evening, rain began to fall again and it became a little cooler. Kenji and Shigeru were engrossed in a game of Go, Kenji being the black player. I must have fallen completely asleep, for I was awakened by a tap on the door and heard one of the maids tell Kenji a messenger had come for him.

He nodded, made his move, and got up to leave the room. Shigeru watched him go, then studied the board, as though absorbed only in the problems of the game. I stood, too, and looked at the layout of the pieces. I had watched the two of them play many times, and always Shigeru proved the stronger player, but this time I could tell the white pieces were under threat.

I went to the cistern and splashed water on my face and hands. Then, feeling trapped and suffocated inside, I crossed the courtyard to the main door of the lodging house and stepped out into the street.

Kenji stood on the opposite side of the road, talking to a young man who was dressed in the running clothes of a messenger. Before I could catch what they were saying, he spotted me, clapped the young man on the shoulder, and bade him farewell. He crossed the street towards me, dissembling, looking like my harmless old teacher. But he would not look me in the eye, and in the moment before he'd seen me I felt that the true Muto Kenji had been revealed, as it had been once before: the man beneath all the disguises, as ruthless as Jato.

They continued to play Go until late into the night. I could not bear to watch the slow annihilation of the white player, but I could not sleep, either, my mind full of what lay ahead of me, and plagued, too, by suspicions of Kenji. The next morning he went out early, and while he was away Shizuka came, bringing wedding gifts from Lady Maruyama. Concealed in the wrapping were two small scrolls. One was a letter, which Shizuka passed to Lord Shigeru.

He read it, his face closed and lined with fatigue. He did not tell us what was in it, but folded it and put it in the sleeve of his robe. He took the other scroll and, after glancing at it, passed it to me. The words were cryptic, but after a few moments I grasped their meaning. It was a description of the interior of the residence, and clearly showed where Iida slept.

"Better to burn them, Lord Otori," Shizuka whispered.

"I will. What other news?"

"May I come closer?" she asked, and spoke into his ear so quietly that only he and I could hear. "Arai is sweeping through the southwest. He has defeated the Noguchi and is within reach of Inuyama."

"Iida knows this?"

"If not, he soon will. He has more spies than we do."

"And Terayama? Have you heard from there?"

"They are confident they can take Yamagata without a struggle, once Iida—"

Shigeru held up a hand, but she had already stopped speaking.

"Tonight, then," he said briefly.

"Lord Otori." Shizuka bowed.

"Is Lady Shirakawa well?" he said in a normal voice, moving away from her.

"I wish she were better," Shizuka replied quietly. "She does not eat or sleep."

My heart had stopped beating for a moment

when Shigeru had said *tonight*. Then it had taken on a rapid but measured rate, sending the blood powering through my veins. I looked once more at the plan in my hand, writing its message into my brain. The thought of Kaede, her pale face, the fragile bones of her wrists, the black mass of her hair, made my heart falter again. I stood up and went to the door to hide my emotion.

"I deeply regret the harm I am doing her," Shigeru said.

"She fears to bring harm to you," Shizuka replied, and added in a low voice, "among all her other fears. I must return to her. I am afraid to leave her alone."

"What do you mean?" I exclaimed, making them both look at me.

Shizuka hesitated. "She often speaks of death," she said finally.

I wanted to send some message to Kaede. I wanted to run to the castle and pluck her out of it—take her away somewhere where we would be safe. But I knew there was no such place, and never would be, until all this was over. . . .

I also wanted to ask Shizuka about Kenji—what he was up to, what the Tribe had in mind—but maids came bringing the midday meal, and there was no further opportunity to speak in private before she left.

We spoke briefly of the arrangements for the afternoon's visit while we ate. Afterwards, Shigeru wrote letters while I studied my sketches of the castle. I was aware of his gaze often on me, and felt there were many things he still wished to say to me, but he did not say them. I sat quietly on the floor, looking out onto the garden, letting my breathing slow, retreating into the dark silent self that dwelled within me, setting it loose so that it took over every muscle, sinew, and nerve. My hearing seemed sharper than ever. I could hear the whole town, its cacophony of human and animal life, joy, desire, pain, grief. I longed for silence, to be free of it all. I longed for night to come.

Kenji returned, saying nothing of where he had been. He watched silently as we dressed ourselves in formal robes with the Otori crest on the back. He spoke once to suggest that it might be wiser for me not to go to the castle, but Shigeru pointed out I would draw more attention to myself if I stayed behind. He did not add that I needed to see the castle one more time. I was also aware that I needed to see Iida again. The only image I had of him was of the terrifying figure I had seen in Mino a year ago: the black armor, the antlered helmet, the sword that had so nearly ended my life. So huge and powerful had this image become in my mind that to see him in the flesh, out of armor, was a shock.

We rode with all twenty of the Otori men. They waited in the first bailey with the horses while Shigeru and I went on with Abe. As we stepped out of our sandals onto the nightingale floor, I held my breath, listening for the birdsong beneath my feet. The residence was dazzlingly decorated in the modern style, the paintings so exquisite that they almost distracted me from my dark purpose. They were not quiet and restrained, like the Sesshus at Terayama, but gilded and flamboyant, full of life and power. In the antechamber, where we waited for over half an hour, the doors and screens were decorated with cranes in snowy willow trees. Shigeru admired them, and under Abe's sardonic eye we spoke in low voices of painting and of the artist.

"To my mind, these are far superior to Sesshu," the Tohan lord said. "The colors are richer and brighter, and the scale is more ambitious."

Shigeru murmured something that was neither agreement nor disagreement. I said nothing. A few moments later an elderly man came in, bowed to the floor, and spoke to Abe. "Lord Iida is ready to receive his guests."

We rose and stepped out again onto the nightingale floor, following Abe to the Great Hall. Here Lord Shigeru knelt at the entrance, and I imitated him. Abe gestured to us to step inside, where we knelt again, bowing right to the ground. I caught a glimpse of Iida Sadamu sitting at the far end of the hall on a raised platform, his cream and gold robes spread out around him, a red and gold fan in his right hand, a small black formal hat on his head. He was smaller than I remembered but no less imposing. He seemed eight or ten years older

251

than Shigeru and was about a head shorter. His features were ordinary, apart from the fine shaped eyes that betrayed his fierce intelligence. He was not a handsome man, but he had a powerful, compelling presence. My old terror leaped fully awake inside me.

There were about twenty retainers in the room, all prostrate on the floor. Only Iida and the little page boy on his left sat upright. There was a long silence. It was approaching the hour of the Monkey. There were no doors open, and the heat was oppressive. Beneath the perfumed robes lay the rank smell of male sweat. Out of the corner of my eye I could see the lines of concealed closets, and from them I heard the breathing of the hidden guards, the faint creak as they shifted position. My mouth was dry.

Lord Iida spoke at last. "Welcome, Lord Otori. This is a happy occasion: a marriage, an alliance."

His voice was rough and perfunctory, making the polite forms of speech sound incongruous in his mouth.

Shigeru raised his head and sat unhurriedly. He replied equally formally, conveyed greetings from his uncles and the entire Otori clan. "I am happy that I may be of service to two great houses."

It was a subtle reminder to Iida that they were of equal rank, by birth and blood.

Iida smiled entirely mirthlessly and replied, "Yes, we must have peace between us. We do not want to see a repeat of Yaegahara."

Shigeru inclined his head. "What is past is past."

I was still on the floor, but I could see his face in profile. His gaze was clear and straightforward, his features steady and cheerful. No one would guess that he was anything other than what he appeared: a young bridegroom, grateful for the favor of an older lord.

They spoke for a while, exchanging pleasantries. Then tea was brought and served to the two of them.

"The young man is your adopted son, I hear," Iida said as the tea was poured. "He may drink with us."

I had to sit up then, although I would have preferred not to. I bowed again to Iida and shuffled forward on my knees, willing my fingers not to tremble as I took the bowl. I could feel his gaze on me, but I did not dare meet his eyes, so I had no way of knowing if he recognized me as the boy who had burned his horse's flank and landed him on the ground in Mino.

I studied the tea bowl. Its glaze was a gleaming iron gray, filled with red lights, such as I had never seen before.

"He is a distant cousin of my late mother's," Lord Shigeru was explaining. "It was her desire that he be adopted into our family, and after her death I carried out her wishes."

"His name?" Iida's eyes did not leave my face as he drank noisily from his bowl.

"He has taken the name of Otori," Shigeru replied. "We call him Takeo."

He did not say *after my brother*, but I felt Takeshi's name hang in the air, as though his ghost had drifted into the hall.

Iida grunted. Despite the heat in the room, the atmosphere became chillier and more dangerous. I knew Shigeru was aware of it. I felt his body tense, though his face was still smiling. Beneath the pleasantries lay years of mutual dislike, compounded by the legacy of Yaegahara, Iida's jealousy, and Shigeru's grief and his desire for revenge.

I tried to become Takeo, the studious artist, introverted and clumsy, gazing in confusion at the ground.

"He has been with you how long?"

"About a year," Shigeru replied.

"There is a certain family resemblance," Iida said. "Ando, would you not agree?"

He was addressing one of the retainers who knelt sideways to us. The man raised his head and looked at me. Our eyes met, and I knew him at once. I recognized the long, wolfish face with its high, pale brow and deep-set eyes. His right side was hidden from me, but I did not need to see it to know that his right arm was missing, lopped off by Jato in Otori Shigeru's hand.

"A very strong resemblance," the man, Ando, said. "I thought that the first time I saw the young lord." He paused, and then added: "In Hagi."

I bowed humbly to him. "Forgive me, Lord

Ando, I did not think we had had the pleasure of meeting."

"No, we did not meet," he agreed. "I merely saw you with Lord Otori, and thought how much you resembled . . . the family."

"He is, after all, a relative," Shigeru said, sounding not in the least perturbed by these cat-and-mouse exchanges. I was no longer in any doubt. Iida and Ando knew exactly who I was. They knew it was Shigeru who had rescued me. I fully expected them to order our arrest immediately, or to have the guards kill us where we sat, among the tea utensils.

Shigeru moved very slightly, and I knew he was prepared to leap to his feet, sword in hand, if it came to that. But he would not throw away the months of preparation lightly. The tension mounted in the room as the silence deepened.

Iida's lips curved in a smile. I could sense the pleasure he took in the situation. He would not go for the kill yet: He would toy with us a little longer. There was nowhere we could escape to, deep in Tohan territory, constantly under watch, with only twenty men. I had no doubt he planned to eliminate both of us, but he was going to savor the delight of having his old enemy in his power.

He moved on to discuss the wedding. Beneath the cursory politeness I could hear contempt and jealousy. "Lady Shirakawa has been a ward of Lord Noguchi, my oldest and most trusted ally."

He said nothing of Noguchi's defeat by Arai.

Had he not heard of it, or did he think we did not yet know?

"Lord Iida does me great honor," Shigeru replied.

"Well, it was time we made peace with the Otori." Iida paused for a while and then said, "She's a beautiful girl. Her reputation has been unfortunate. I hope this does not alarm you."

There was the slightest ripple from the retainers—not quite laughter, just an easing of facial muscles into knowing smiles.

"I believe her reputation is unwarranted," Shigeru replied evenly. "And while I am here as Lord Iida's guest, I am in no way alarmed."

Iida's smile had faded and he was scowling. I guessed he was eaten up by jealousy. Politeness and his own self-esteem should have prevented him from what he said next, but they did not. "There are rumors about you," he said bluntly.

Shigeru raised his eyebrows, saying nothing.

"A long-standing attachment, a secret marriage," Iida began to bluster.

"Lord Iida astonishes me," Shigeru replied coolly. "I am not young. It is natural I should have known many women."

Iida regained control of himself and grunted a reply, but his eyes burned with malevolence. We were dismissed with perfunctory courtesy, Iida saying no more than "I look forward to our meeting in three days' time, at the marriage ceremony."

When we rejoined the men, they were tense and

bad-tempered, having had to put up with the taunts and threats of the Tohan. Neither Shigeru nor I said anything as we rode down the stepped street and through the first gate. I was absorbed in memorizing as much as I could of the castle layout, and my heart was smoldering with hatred and rage against Iida. I would kill him, for revenge for the past, for his insolent treatment of Lord Otori—and because if I did not kill him that night, he would kill us both.

The sun was a watery orb in the west as we rode back to the lodging house, where Kenji awaited us. There was a slight smell of burning in the room. He had destroyed the messages from Lady Maruyama while we were away. He studied our faces.

"Takeo was recognized?" he said.

Shigeru was taking off the formal robes. "I need a bath," he said, and smiled as if releasing himself a little from the iron self-control he had been exerting. "Can we speak freely, Takeo?"

From the kitchens came the sounds of the servants preparing the evening meal. Steps crossed the walkway from time to time, but the garden was empty. I could hear the guards at the main gate. I heard a girl approach them with bowls of rice and soup.

"If we whisper," I replied.

"We must speak quickly. Come close, Kenji. Yes, he was recognized. Iida is full of suspicions and fears. He will strike at any moment."

257

Kenji said, "I'll take him away at once. I can hide him within the city."

"No!" I said. "Tonight I go to the castle."

"It will be our only chance," Shigeru whispered. "We must strike first."

Kenji looked at each of us. He sighed deeply. "Then I will come with you."

"You've been a good friend to me," Shigeru said quietly. "You do not have to risk your life."

"It's not for you, Shigeru. It's to keep an eye on Takeo," Kenji replied. To me he said, "You'd better look at the walls and the moat again, before curfew. I'll walk down with you. Bring your drawing materials. There will be an interesting play of light on the water."

I gathered my things together and we left. But at the door, just before he stepped outside, Kenji surprised me by turning again to Shigeru and bowing deeply. "Lord Otori," he said. I thought he was being ironic; only later did I realize it was a farewell.

I made no farewells beyond the usual bow, which Shigeru acknowledged. The evening light from the garden was behind him and I could not see his face.

The cloud cover had thickened. It was damp but not raining, a little cooler now the sun had set, but still heavy and muggy. The streets were filled with people taking advantage of the hour between sunset and curfew. They kept bumping into me, making me anxious and uneasy. I saw spies and assassins everywhere. The meeting with Iida had unnerved me, turning me once again into Tomasu, into the terrified boy who had fled from the ruins of Mino. Did I really think I could climb into Inuyama Castle and assassinate the powerful lord I had just seen, who knew I was one of the Hidden, the only one from my village to escape him before? I might pretend to be Lord Otori Takeo, or Kikuta—one of the Tribe—but the truth was, I was neither. I was one of the Hidden, one of the hunted.

We walked westwards, along the southern side of the castle. As it grew dark I was thankful that there would be no moon and no stars. Torches flared from the castle gate, and the shops were lit by candles and oil lamps. There was a smell of sesame and soy, rice wine and grilling fish. Despite everything, I was hungry. I thought to stop and buy something, but Kenji suggested going a little farther. The street became darker and emptier. I could hear some wheeled vehicle rumbling over cobblestones, and then the sounds of a flute. There was something unspeakably eerie about it. The hairs on the back of my neck stood up in warning.

"Let's go back," I said, and at that moment a small procession emerged from an alley in front of us. I took them for street performers of some sort. An old man wheeled a cart with decorations and pictures on it. A girl was playing the flute, but she let it fall when she saw us. Two young men came out of the shadows holding tops, one spinning, one flying. In the half-light they seemed magical, possessed by spirits. I stopped. Kenji stood right behind me. Another girl stepped towards us, saying, "Come and look, lord."

I recognized her voice, but it was a couple of moments before I placed her. Then I jumped backwards, evading Kenji and leaving my second self by the cart. It was the girl from the inn at Yamagata, the girl of whom Kenji had said, "She's one of us."

To my surprise one of the young men followed me, taking no notice of my image. I went invisible, but he guessed where I was. I knew for certain then. These were Tribe, come to claim me, as Kenji had said, had known they would. I dropped to the ground, rolled, slid beneath the cart, but my teacher was on the other side. I tried to bite his hand, but his other one came up to my jaw, forcing it away. I kicked him instead, went limp in his grasp, tried to slide through his fingers, but all the tricks I knew he had taught me.

"Be quiet, Takeo," he hissed. "Stop struggling. No one's going to hurt you."

"All right," I said, and went still. He loosened his grip and in that moment I got away from him. I pulled my knife from my sash. But the five of them were fighting in earnest now. One of the young men feinted at me, making me back up to the cart. I slashed out at him and felt the knife

260

strike bone. Then I cut one of the girls. The other had gone invisible, and I felt her drop like a monkey from the top of the cart, her legs around my shoulders, one hand over my mouth, the other at my neck. I knew of course the place she was going for, and twisted violently, losing my balance. The man I'd cut got my wrist, and I felt it bend backwards until I lost my grip on the knife. The girl and I fell together to the ground. Her hands were still at my throat.

Just before I lost consciousness I clearly saw Shigeru sitting in the room, waiting for us to return. I tried to scream in outrage at the enormity of the betrayal, but my mouth was covered, and even my ears could hear nothing.

# CHAPTER 10

It was early evening, on the third day after her
arrival at Inuyama. Since the moment the
swaying palanquin had carried her into the
castle, Kaede's spirits had fallen lower and lower.
Even more than Noguchi, Inuyama was oppressive and full of terror. The women of the household were subdued and grief-stricken, still
mourning their lady, Iida's wife, who had died in
the early summer. Kaede had only seen their lord
briefly, but it was impossible not to be aware of
his presence. He dominated the residence, and
everyone moved in fear of his moods and rages.
No one spoke openly. Congratulations were
mouthed to her by women with tired voices and
empty eyes, and they prepared her wedding robes
with listless hands. She felt doom settle over her.

Lady Maruyama, after her initial joy at seeing
her daughter, was preoccupied and tense. Several
times she seemed inclined to take Kaede into her
confidence, but they were rarely alone for long.
Kaede spent the hours trying to recall all the
events of the journey, trying to make some sense
out of the undercurrents that swirled around her,

but she realized she knew nothing. Nothing was as it seemed, and she could trust no one—not even Shizuka, despite what the girl had told her. For her family's sake she must steel herself to go through with the marriage to Lord Otori: She had no reason to suspect that the marriage would not go ahead as planned, and yet, she did not believe in it. It seemed as remote as the moon. But if she did not marry—if another man died on her account—there would be no way out for her but her own death.

She tried to face it with courage, but to herself she could not pretend: She was fifteen years old, she did not want to die, she wanted to live and to be with Takeo.

The stifling day was slowly drawing to an end, the watery sun casting an eerie reddish light over the town. Kaede was weary and restless, longing to divest herself of the layers of robes she wore, longing for the coolness and dark of night, yet dreading the next day, and the next.

"The Otori lords came to the castle today, didn't they?" she said, trying to keep the emotion out of her voice.

"Yes, Lord Iida received them." Shizuka hesitated. Kaede felt her eyes on her, and was aware of her pity. Shizuka said quietly, "Lady . . ." She went no further.

"What is it?"

Shizuka began to speak brightly of wedding clothes as two maids passed by outside, their feet making the floor sing. When the sound had died away, Kaede asked, "What were you about to say?"

"You remember I told you that you could kill someone with a needle? I'm going to show you how. You never know, you might need it."

She took out what looked like an ordinary needle, but when Kaede held it she realized it was stronger and heavier, a miniature weapon. Shizuka demonstrated how to drive it into the eye or into the neck.

"Now hide it in the hem of your sleeve. Be careful, don't stick yourself with it."

Kaede shuddered, half-appalled, half-fascinated. "I don't know if I could do it."

"You stabbed a man in rage," Shizuka said.

"You know that?"

"Arai told me. In rage or fear, humans don't know what they are capable of. Keep your knife with you at all times. I wish we had swords, but they are too hard to conceal. The best thing, if it comes to a fight, is to kill a man as soon as possible and take his sword."

"What's going to happen?" Kaede whispered.

"I wish I could tell you everything, but it's too dangerous for you. I just want you to be prepared."

Kaede opened her mouth to question her further, but Shizuka murmured, "You must be silent: Ask me nothing and say nothing to anyone. The less you know, the safer you are."

Kaede had been given a small room at the end of the residence, next to the larger room where the Iida women were, with Lady Maruyama and her daughter. Both rooms opened onto the garden that lay along the southern side of the residence, and she could hear the splash of water and the slight movement of the trees. All night Kaede was aware of Shizuka's wakefulness. Once she sat and saw the girl cross-legged in the doorway, barely visible against the starless sky. Owls hooted in the dark hours, and at dawn from the river came the cries of waterfowl. It began to rain.

She dozed off listening to them, and was woken by the strident calls of crows. The rain had stopped and it was already hot. Shizuka was dressed. When she saw Kaede was awake, she knelt beside her and whispered, "Lady, I have to try to speak to Lord Otori. Will you please get up and write a letter to him, a poem or something? I need a pretext to visit him again."

"What's happened?" Kaede said, alarmed by the girl's drawn face.

"I don't know. Last night I was expecting something. . . . It didn't happen. I have to go and find out why."

In a louder voice she said, "I will prepare ink, but my lady must not be so impatient. You have all day to write suitable poems."

"What shall I write?" Kaede whispered. "I don't know how to write poetry. I never learned."

"It doesn't matter, something about married love, mandarin ducks, the clematis and the wall."

Kaede could almost have believed Shizuka was

joking, except that the girl's demeanor was deathly serious.

"Help me dress," she said imperiously. "Yes, I know it is early, but stop complaining. I must write at once to Lord Otori."

Shizuka smiled encouragingly at her, forcing her mouth in her pale face.

She wrote something, she hardly knew what, and in the loudest voice possible told Shizuka to hurry to the Otori lodging house with it. Shizuka went with a show of reluctance, and Kaede heard her complain quietly to the guards, heard their laughter in response.

She called for the maids to bring her tea and, when she had drunk it, sat gazing out onto the garden, trying to calm her fears, trying to be as courageous as Shizuka. Every now and then her fingers went to the needle in her sleeve, or to the smooth, cool handle of the knife inside her robe. She thought of how Lady Maruyama and Shizuka had taught her to fight. What were they anticipating? She had felt herself a pawn in the game being played around her, but at least they had tried to prepare her, and they had given her weapons.

Shizuka was back within the hour, bringing a letter in return from Lord Otori, a poem written with lightness and skill.

Kaede gazed at it. "What does it mean?"

"It's just an excuse. He had to write something in return."

"Is Lord Otori well?" she asked formally.

"Yes, indeed, and waiting with all his heart for you."

"Tell me the truth," Kaede whispered. She looked at Shizuka's face, saw the hesitation in her eyes. "Lord Takeo—he's dead?"

"We don't know." Shizuka sighed deeply. "I must tell you. He has disappeared with Kenji. Lord Otori believes the Tribe has taken him."

"What does that mean?" She felt the tea she had drunk earlier move in her stomach, and thought for a moment she would vomit.

"Let us walk in the garden while it's still cool," Shizuka said calmly.

Kaede stood and thought she would faint. She felt drops of sweat form, cold and clammy, on her brow. Shizuka held her under the elbow and led her onto the veranda, knelt in front of her, and helped her feet into her sandals.

As they walked slowly down the path among the trees and shrubs, the babble of water from the stream covered their voices. Shizuka whispered quickly and urgently into Kaede's ear.

"Last night there was to be an attempt on Iida's life. Arai is barely thirty miles away with a huge army. The warrior monks at Terayama are poised to take the town of Yamagata. The Tohan could be overthrown."

"What does it have to do with Lord Takeo?"

"He was to be the assassin. He was to climb into the castle last night. But the Tribe took him."

"Takeo? The assassin?" Kaede felt like laughing at such an unlikely idea. Then she remembered the darkness that he retreated to, how he always hid his deftness. She realized she hardly knew what lay beneath the surface, yet she had known that there was something more. She took a deep breath, trying to steady herself.

"Who are the Tribe?"

"Takeo's father was of the Tribe, and he was born with unusual talents."

"Like yours," Kaede said flatly. "And your uncle's."

"Far greater than either of us," Shizuka said. "But you are right: We are also from the Tribe."

"You are a spy? An assassin? Is that why you pretend to be my servant?"

"I don't pretend to be your friend," Shizuka replied swiftly. "I've told you before that you can trust me. Indeed, Arai himself entrusted you to my care."

"How can I believe that when I have been told so many lies?" Kaede said, and felt the corners of her eyes grow hot.

"I am telling you the truth now," Shizuka said, somber.

Kaede felt the faintness of shock sweep over her and then recede a little, leaving her calm and lucid. "My marriage to Lord Otori—was that arranged to give him a reason to come to Inuyama?"

"Not by him. On his part the marriage was made a condition of Takeo's adoption. But once he had agreed to it, he saw it would give him a reason to bring Takeo into the Tohan stronghold." Shizuka paused and then said very quietly, "Iida and the Otori lords may use the marriage to you as a cover for Shigeru's death. This is partly why I was sent to you: to protect you both."

"My reputation will always be useful," she said bitterly, made all too aware of the power men had over her, and how they used it, regardless. The faintness came over her again.

"You must sit for a while," Shizuka said. The shrubs had given way to a more open garden with a view over the moat and the river to the mountains beyond. A pavilion had been built across the stream, placed to catch every faint trace of breeze. They made their way to it, stepping carefully across the rocks. Cushions had been prepared on the floor, and here they sat down. The flowing water gave a sense of coolness, and kingfishers and swallows swooped through the pavilion with sudden flashes of color. In the pools beyond, lotus flowers lifted their purple-pink blooms, and a few deep-blue irises still flowered at the water's edge, their petals almost the same color as the cushions.

"What does it mean, to be taken by the Tribe?" Kaede asked, her fingers restlessly rubbing the fabric beneath her.

"The family Takeo belongs to, the Kikuta, thought the assassination attempt would fail. They did not want to lose him, so they stepped in to prevent it. My uncle played a role in this."

"And you?"

"No, I was of the opinion that the attempt should be made. I thought Takeo had every chance of succeeding, and no revolt against the Tohan will happen while Iida lives."

*I can't believe I'm hearing this*, Kaede thought. *I am caught up in such treachery. She speaks of Iida's murder as lightly as if he were a peasant or an outcaste. If anyone heard us, we would be tortured to death.* Despite the growing heat, she shivered.

"What will they do with him?"

"He will become one of them, and his life will become a secret to us and everyone."

*So I will never see him again*, she thought.

They heard voices coming from the path, and a few moments later Lady Maruyama, her daughter, Mariko, and her companion, Sachie, came across the stream and sat down with them. Lady Maruyama looked as pale as Shizuka had earlier, and her manner was in some indefinable way changed. She had lost some of her rigid self-control. She sent Mariko and Sachie a little way off to play with the shuttle-cock toy the girl had brought with her.

Kaede made an effort to converse normally. "Lady Mariko is a lovely girl."

"She has no great beauty, but she is intelligent and kind," her mother replied. "She takes more after her father. Maybe she is lucky. Even beauty is dangerous for a woman. Better not to be desired by men." She smiled bitterly, and then whispered to Shizuka, "We have very little time. I hope I can trust Lady Shirakawa."

"I will say nothing to give you away," Kaede said in a low voice.

"Shizuka, tell me what happened."

"Takeo was taken by the Tribe. That is all Lord Shigeru knows."

"I never thought Kenji would betray him. It must have been a bitter blow."

"He said it was always a desperate gamble. He blames no one. His main concern now is your safety. Yours and the child's."

Kaede's first thought was that Shizuka meant the daughter, Mariko, but she saw the slight flush in Lady Maruyama's face. She pressed her lips together, saying nothing.

"What should we do? Should we try to flee?" Lady Maruyama was twisting the sleeve of her robe with white fingers.

"You must do nothing that would arouse Iida's suspicions."

"Shigeru will not flee?" The lady's voice was reed thin.

"I suggested it, but he says he will not. He is too closely watched, and besides, he feels he can only survive by showing no fear. He must act as though he has perfect trust in the Tohan and the proposed alliance."

"He will go through with the marriage?" Her voice rose.

"He will act as though that is his intention,"

Shizuka said carefully. "We must also act the same, if we want to save his life."

"Iida has sent messages to me pressing me to accept him," Lady Maruyama said. "I have always refused him for Shigeru's sake." She stared, distraught, into Shizuka's face.

"Lady," Shizuka said, "don't speak of these things. Be patient, be brave. All we can do is wait. We must pretend nothing out of the ordinary has happened, and we must prepare for Lady Kaede's wedding."

"They will use it as a pretext to kill him," Lady Maruyama said. "She is so beautiful and so deadly."

"I don't want to cause any man's death," Kaede cried, "least of all Lord Otori's." Her eyes filled with tears suddenly, and she looked away.

"What a shame you cannot marry Lord Iida and bring death to *him!*" Lady Maruyama exclaimed.

Kaede flinched as though she had been slapped.

"Forgive me," Lady Maruyama whispered. "I am not myself. I have hardly slept. I am mad with fear— for him, for my daughter, for myself, for our child. You do not deserve my rudeness. You have been caught up in our affairs through no fault of your own. I hope you will not think too badly of me."

She took Kaede's hand and pressed it. "If my daughter and I die, you are my heir. I entrust my land and my people to you. Take care of them well." She looked away, across the river, her eyes bright with tears. "If it is the only way to save his life, he must marry you. But then they will kill him anyway."

At the end of the garden, steps had been cut in the fortification wall down to the moat, where two pleasure boats lay moored. There was a gate across the steps, which Kaede guessed would be closed at nightfall, but which now stood open. The moat and the river could be seen through it. Two guards sat lazily by the wall, looking stupefied by the heat.

"It will be cool today out on the water," Lady Maruyama said. "The boatmen might be bought. . . ."

"I would not advise it, lady," Shizuka said urgently. "If you try to escape, you will arouse Iida's suspicions. Our best chance is to placate him until Arai is closer."

"Arai will not approach Inuyama while Iida lives," Lady Maruyama said. "He will not commit himself to a siege. We have always considered this castle impregnable. It can only fall from within."

She glanced again from the water to the keep. "It traps us," she said. "It holds us in its grip. Yet, I must get away."

"Don't attempt anything rash," Shizuka pleaded.

Mariko came back, complaining it was too hot to play. She was followed by Sachie.

"I will take her inside," Lady Maruyama said. "She has lessons, after all. . . ." Her voice tailed away, and tears sprang in her eyes again. "My poor child," she said. "My poor children." She clasped her hands across her belly.

273

"Come, lady," Sachie said. "You must lie down."

Kaede felt tears of sympathy in her own eyes. The stones of the keep and the walls around her seemed to press in on her. The crickets' shrill was intense and brain-numbing; the heat seemed to reverberate from the ground. Lady Maruyama was right, she thought: They were all trapped, and there was no way of escaping.

"Do you wish to return to the house?" Shizuka asked her.

"Let's stay here a little longer." It occurred to Kaede that there was one more thing she had to talk about. "Shizuka, you seem able to come and go. The guards trust you."

Shizuka nodded. "I have some of the skills of the Tribe in this respect."

"Out of all of the women here, you are the only one who could escape." Kaede hesitated, not sure how to phrase what she felt she must say. Finally she said abruptly, "If you want to leave, you must go. I do not want you to stay on my account." Then she bit her lip and looked swiftly away, for she did not see how she would survive without the girl she had come to depend on.

"We are safest if none of us tries to leave," Shizuka whispered. "But apart from that, it is out of the question. Unless you order me to go, I will never leave you. Our lives are bound together now." She added, as if to herself, "It is not only men who have honor."

"Lord Arai sent you to me," Kaede said, "and

274

you tell me you are from the Tribe, who asserted their power over Lord Takeo. Are you really free to make such decisions? Do you have the choice of honor?"

"For someone who was taught nothing, Lady Shirakawa knows a great deal," Shizuka said, smiling, and for a moment Kaede felt her heart lighten.

She stayed by the water most of the day, eating only a little. The ladies of the household came to join her for a few hours, and they spoke of the beauty of the garden and the wedding arrangements. One of them had been to Hagi, and she described the city with admiration, telling Kaede some of the legends of the Otori clan, whispering of their ancient feud with the Tohan. They all expressed their joy that Kaede was to put an end to this feud, and told her how delighted Lord Iida was with the alliance.

Not knowing how to reply, and aware of the treachery beneath the wedding plans, Kaede sought refuge in shyness, smiled until her face ached, but hardly spoke.

She glanced away and saw Lord Iida in person crossing the garden, in the direction of the pavilion, accompanied by three or four of his retainers.

The ladies immediately fell silent. Kaede called to Shizuka, "I think I will go inside. My head aches."

"I will comb out your hair and massage your

head," Shizuka said, and indeed the weight of her hair seemed intolerable to Kaede. Her body felt sticky and chafed beneath the robes. She longed for coolness, for night.

However, as they moved away from the pavilion, Lord Abe left the group of men and strode towards them. Shizuka immediately dropped to her knees, and Kaede bowed to him, though not as deeply.

"Lady Shirakawa," he said, "Lord Iida wishes to speak to you."

Trying to hide her reluctance, she returned to the pavilion, where Iida was already seated on the cushions. The women had withdrawn and were engaged in looking at the river.

Kaede knelt on the wooden floor, lowering her head to the ground, aware of his deep eyes, pools of molten iron, sweeping over her.

"You may sit up," he said briefly. His voice was rough and the polite forms sat uneasily on his tongue. She felt the gaze of his men, the heavy silence that had become familiar to her, the mixture of lust and admiration.

"Shigeru is a lucky man," Iida said, and she heard both threat and malice in the men's laughter. She thought he would speak to her about the wedding or about her father, who had already sent messages to say he could not attend, due to his wife's illness. His next words surprised her.

"I believe Arai is an old acquaintance of yours?"

"I knew him when he served Lord Noguchi," she replied carefully.

"It was on your account that Noguchi exiled him," Iida said. "Noguchi made a grave mistake, and he's paid for it severely. Now it seems I'm going to have to deal with Arai on my own doorstep." He sighed deeply. "Your marriage to Lord Otori comes at a very good time."

Kaede thought, *I am an ignorant girl, brought up by the Noguchi, loyal and stupid. I know nothing of the intrigues of the clans.*

She made her face doll-like, her voice childish. "I only want to do what Lord Iida and my father want for me."

"You heard nothing on your journey of Arai's movements? Shigeru did not discuss them at any time?"

"I have heard nothing from Lord Arai since he left Lord Noguchi," she replied.

"Yet, they say he was quite a champion of yours."

She dared to look up at him through her eyelashes. "I cannot be held responsible for the way men feel about me, lord."

Their eyes met for a moment. His look was penetrating, predatory. She felt he also desired her, like all the others, piqued and tantalized by the idea that involvement with her brought death.

Revulsion rose in her throat. She thought of the needle concealed in her sleeve, imagined sliding it into his flesh.

"No," he agreed, "nor can we blame any man for admiring you." He spoke over his shoulder to Abe: "You were right. She is exquisite." It was as if he spoke of an inanimate piece of art. "You were going inside? Don't let me detain you. I believe your health is delicate."

"Lord Iida." She bowed to the ground again and shuffled backwards to the edge of the pavilion. Shizuka helped her to her feet and they walked away.

Neither of them spoke until they were back in the room. Then Kaede whispered, "He knows everything."

"No," Shizuka said, taking up the comb and beginning to work on Kaede's hair. "He is not sure. He has no proof of anything. You did well." Her fingers massaged Kaede's scalp and temples. Some of the tension began to ease. Kaede leaned back against her. "I would like to go to Hagi. Will you come with me?"

"If that comes to pass, you won't need me," Shizuka replied, smiling.

"I think I will always need you," Kaede said. A wistful note crept into her voice. "Maybe I would be happy with Lord Shigeru. If I hadn't met Takeo, if he did not love—"

"Shush, shush," Shizuka sighed, her fingers working and stroking.

"We might have had children," Kaede went on, her voice dreamy and slow. "None of that is going to happen now, yet I must pretend it will."

"We are on the brink of war," Shizuka whispered. "We do not know what will happen in the next few days, let alone the future."

"Where would Lord Takeo be now? Do you know?"

"If he is still in the capital, in one of the secret houses of the Tribe. But they may have already moved him out of the fief."

"Will I ever see him again?" Kaede said, but she didn't expect an answer, nor did Shizuka give one. Her fingers worked on. Beyond the open doors, the garden shimmered in the heat, the crickets more strident than ever.

Slowly the day faded and the shadows began to lengthen.

# CHAPTER 11

I was unconscious for a few moments only. When I came round I was in the dark, and guessed at once I was inside the cart. There were at least two people inside with me. One, I could tell from his breathing, was Kenji, the other, from her perfume, one of the girls. They were pinioning me, one arm each.

I felt terribly sick, as though I'd been hit on the head. The movement of the cart didn't help.

"I'm going to vomit," I said, and Kenji let go of one arm. The sickness half-rose in my throat as I sat up. I realized the girl had let go of my other arm. I forgot about vomiting in my desperate desire to escape. I threw myself, arms across my head, at the hinged opening of the cart.

It was firmly fastened from the outside. I felt the skin on one hand tear against a nail. Kenji and the girl grabbed me, forcing me down as I struggled and thrashed. Someone outside called out, a sharp angry warning.

Kenji swore at me. "Shut up! Lie still! If the Tohan find you now, you're dead!"

But I had gone beyond reason. When I was a

boy I used to bring wild animals home, fox cubs, stoats, baby rabbits. I could never tame them. All they wanted, blindly, irrationally, was to escape. I thought of that blind rush now. Nothing mattered to me except that Shigeru should not believe I had betrayed him. I would never stay with the Tribe. They would never be able to keep me.

"Shut him up," Kenji whispered to the girl as he struggled to hold me still, and under her hands the world went sickening and black again.

The next time I came around I truly believed I was dead and in the underworld. I could not see or hear. It was pitch-dark and everything had gone completely silent. Then feeling began to return. I hurt too much all over to be dead. My throat was raw, one hand throbbed, the other wrist ached where it had been bent backwards. I tried to sit up, but I was tied up in some way, loosely with soft bindings, just enough to restrain me. I turned my head, shaking it. There was a blindfold across my eyes, but it was being deafened that seemed the worst thing. After a few moments I realized that my ears had been plugged with something. I felt a surge of relief that I had not lost my hearing.

A hand against my face made me jump. The blindfold was removed and I saw Kenji kneeling beside me. An oil lamp burned on the floor next to him, lighting his face. I thought fleetingly how dangerous he was. Once he had sworn to protect me with his life. The last thing I wanted now was his protection.

His mouth moved as he spoke.

"I can't hear anything," I said. "Take the plugs out."

He did so, and my world returned to me. I stayed without speaking for a few moments, placing myself in it again. I could hear the river in the distance: So I was still in Inuyama. The house I was in was silent, everyone sleeping except guards. I could hear them whispering inside the gate. I guessed it was late at night, and at that moment heard the midnight bell from a distant temple.

I should have been inside the castle now.

"I'm sorry we hurt you," Kenji said. "You didn't need to struggle so much."

I could feel the bitter rage about to erupt inside me again. I tried to control it. "Where am I?"

"In one of the Tribe houses. We'll move you out of the capital in a day or two."

His calm, matter-of-fact voice infuriated me further. "You said you would never betray him, the night of my adoption. Do you remember?"

Kenji sighed. "We both spoke that night of conflicting obligations. Shigeru knows I serve the Tribe first. I warned him then, and often since, that the Tribe has a prior claim to you, and that sooner or later it would make it."

"Why now?" I said bitterly. "You could have left me for one more night."

"Maybe I personally would have given you that chance. But the incident at Yamagata pushed things beyond my control. Anyway, you would be dead by now, and no use to anyone."

"I could have killed Iida first," I muttered.

"That outcome was considered," Kenji said, "and judged not to be in the best interests of the Tribe."

"I suppose most of you work for him?"

"We work for whoever pays us best. We like a stable society. Open warfare makes it hard to operate. Iida's rule is harsh but stable. It suits us."

"You were deceiving Shigeru all the time, then?"

"As no doubt he has often deceived me." Kenji was silent for a good minute, and then went on, "Shigeru was doomed from the start. Too many powerful people want to get rid of him. He has played well to survive this far."

A chill came over me. "He must not die," I whispered.

"Iida will certainly seize on some pretext to kill him," Kenji said mildly. "He has become far too dangerous to be allowed to live. Quite apart from the fact that he offended Iida personally—the affair with Lady Maruyama, your adoption—the scenes at Yamagata alarmed the Tohan profoundly." The lamp flickered and smoked. Kenji added quietly, "The problem with Shigeru is, people love him."

"We can't abandon him! Let me go back to him."

"It's not my decision," Kenji replied. "Even if it were, I could not do it now. Iida knows you are from the Hidden. He would hand you over to Ando as he promised. Shigeru, no doubt, will have a warrior's death, swift, honorable. You would be tortured: You know what they do."

I was silent. My head ached, and an unbearable sense of failure was creeping over me. Everything in me had been aimed like a spear at one target. Now the hand that had held me had been removed and I had fallen, useless, to the earth.

"Give up, Takeo," Kenji said, watching my face. "It's over."

I nodded slowly. I might as well pretend to agree. "I'm terribly thirsty."

"I'll make some tea. It will help you sleep. Do you want anything to eat?"

"No. Can you untie me?"

"Not tonight," Kenji replied.

I thought about that while I was drifting in and out of sleep, trying to find a comfortable position to lie in with my hands and feet tied. I decided it meant Kenji thought I could escape, once I was untied, and if my teacher thought I could, then it was probably true. It was the only comforting thought I had, and it did not console me for long.

Towards dawn it began raining. I listened to the gutters filling, the eaves dripping. Then the cocks began to crow and the town woke. I heard the servants stirring in the house, smelled smoke as fires were lit in the kitchen. I listened to the voices and the footsteps, and counted them, mapping the layout of the house, where it stood in the street, what was on either side. From the smells and the sounds as work began I guessed I was hidden within a brewery, one of the big merchant houses on the edge of the castle town. The room I was in had no exterior windows. It was as narrow as an eel's bed and remained dark even long after sunrise.

The wedding was to be held the day after tomorrow. Would Shigeru survive till then? And if he was murdered before, what would happen to Kaede? My thoughts tormented me. How would Shigeru spend these next two days? What was he doing now? What was he thinking of me? The idea that he might imagine I had run away of my own free will was agony to me. And what would be the opinion of the Otori men? They would despise me.

I called to Kenji that I needed to use the privy. He untied my feet and took me there. We stepped out of the small room into a larger one, and then downstairs into the rear courtyard. A maid came with a bowl of water and helped me wash my hands. There was a lot of blood on me, more than seemed likely from the one cut from the nail. I must have done some damage with my knife to someone. I wondered where the knife was now.

When we went back into the secret room Kenji left my feet untied.

"What happens next?" I asked.

"Try and sleep longer. Nothing will happen today."

"Sleep! I feel as if I will never sleep again!"

Kenji studied me for a moment and then said briefly, "It will all pass."

If my hands had been free, I would have killed him. I leaped at him as I was, swinging my bound hands to catch him in the side. I took him by surprise, and we both went flying, but he turned beneath me as quick as a snake and pinioned me to the ground. If I was enraged, so now was he. I'd seen him exasperated with me before, but now he was furious. He struck me twice across the face, real blows that shook my teeth and left me dizzy.

"Give up!" he shouted. "I'll beat you into it if I have to. Is that what you want?"

"Yes!" I shouted back. "Go ahead and kill me. It's the only way you'll keep me here!"

I arched my back and rolled sideways, getting rid of his weight, trying to kick and bite. He struck me again, but I got away from him and, swearing at him in rage, flung myself against him.

I heard rapid steps outside, and the doors slid open. The girl from Yamagata and one of the young men ran into the room. The three of them subdued me eventually, but I was more than half-mad with fury, and it took a while before they could tie my feet again.

Kenji was seething with anger. The girl and the young man looked from me to him and back again. "Master," the girl said, "leave him with us. We'll watch him for a while. You need some rest." Clearly they were astonished and shocked by his loss of control.

We had been together for months as master and pupil. He had taught me almost everything I knew.

I had obeyed him without question, had put up with his nagging, his sarcasm, and his chastisements. I had put aside my initial suspicions and had come to trust him. All that was shattered as far as I was concerned, and would never be restored.

Now he knelt in front of me, seized my head, and forced me to look at him. "I'm trying to save your life!" he shouted. "Can't you get that into your thick skull?"

I spat at him and braced myself for another blow, but the young man restrained him.

"Go, master," he urged him.

Kenji let go of me and stood up. "What stubborn, crazy blood did you get from your mother?" he demanded. When he reached the door he turned and said, "Watch him all the time. Don't untie him."

When he had gone I wanted to scream and sob like a child in a tantrum. Tears of rage and despair pricked my eyelids. I lay back on the mattress, face turned towards the wall.

The girl left the room shortly after and came back with cold water and a cloth. She made me sit up and wiped my face. My lip was split, and I could feel the bruising around one eye and across the cheekbone. Her gentleness made me feel she had a certain sympathy towards me, though she said nothing.

The young man watched without speaking, either.

Later she brought tea and some food. I drank the tea but refused to eat anything.

"Where's my knife?" I said.

"We have it," she replied.

"Did I cut you?"

"No, that was Keiko. Both she and Akio were wounded on the hand, but not too badly."

"I wish I had killed you all."

"I know," she replied. "No one can say that you didn't fight. But you had five members of the Tribe against you. There is no shame."

Shame, however, was what I felt seeping through me as though it stained my white bones black.

The long day passed, oppressive and slow. The evening bell had just rung from the temple at the end of the street when Keiko came to the door and spoke in a whisper to my two guards. I could hear what she said perfectly well, though out of habit I pretended not to. Someone had come to see me, someone called Kikuta.

A few minutes later a lean man of medium height stepped into the room, followed by Kenji. There was a similarity between them, the same shifting look that made them unremarkable. This man's skin was darker, closer to my own in color. His hair was still black, although he must have been nearly forty years old.

He stood and looked at me for a few moments, then crossed the room, knelt beside me, and, as Kenji had the first time he met me, took my hands and turned them palms up.

"Why is he tied up?" he said. His voice was unremarkable, too, though the intonation was northern.

"He tries to escape, master," the girl said. "He is calmer now, but he has been very wild."

"Why do you want to escape?" he asked me. "You are finally where you belong."

"I don't belong here," I replied. "Before I had even heard of the Tribe, I swore allegiance to Lord Otori. I am legally adopted into the Otori clan."

"Unnh," he grunted. "The Otori call you Takeo, I hear. What is your real name?"

I did not reply.

"He was raised among the Hidden," Kenji said quietly. "The name he was given at birth was Tomasu."

Kikuta hissed through his teeth. "That's best forgotten," he said. "Takeo will do for the time being, though it's never been a Tribe name. Do you know who I am?"

"No," I said, though I had a very good idea.

"No, *master*." The young guard couldn't help the whispered reproof.

Kikuta smiled. "Did you not teach him manners, Kenji?"

"Courtesy is for those who deserve it," I said.

"You will learn that I do deserve it. I am the head of your family, Kikuta Kotaro, first cousin to your father."

"I never knew my father, and I have never used his name."

"But you are stamped with Kikuta traits: the sharpness of hearing, artistic ability, all the other talents we know you have in abundance, as well as the line on your palms. These are things you can't deny."

From away in the distance came a faint sound, a tap at the front door of the shop below. I heard someone slide the door open and speak, an unimportant conversation about wine. Kikuta's head had also turned slightly. I felt something: the beginnings of recognition.

"Do you hear everything?" I said.

"Not as much as you. It fades with age. But pretty well everything."

"At Terayama, the young man there, the monk, said, 'Like a dog.'" A bitter note crept into my voice. "'Useful to your masters,' he said. Is that why you kidnapped me, because I will be useful to you?"

"It's not a question of being useful," he said. "It's a matter of being born into the Tribe. This is where you belong. You would still belong if you had no talents at all, and if you had all the talents in the world, but were not born into the Tribe, you could never belong and we would have no interest in you. As it is, your father was Kikuta: You are Kikuta."

"I have no choice?"

He smiled again. "It's not something you choose, any more than you chose to have sharp hearing."

This man was calming me in some way as I had

calmed horses: by understanding my nature. I had never met anyone before who knew what it was like to be Kikuta. I could feel it exerting an attraction on me.

"Suppose I accept that; what will you do with me?"

"Find you somewhere safe, in another province, away from the Tohan, while you finish your training."

"I don't want any more training. I am done with teachers!"

"Muto Kenji was sent to Hagi because of his long-standing friendship with Shigeru. He has taught you a lot, but Kikuta should be taught by Kikuta."

I was no longer listening. "Friendship? He deceived and betrayed him!"

Kikuta's voice went quiet. "You have great skills, Takeo, and no one's doubting your courage or your heart. It's just your head that needs sorting out. You have to learn to control your emotions."

"So I can betray old friends as easily as Muto Kenji?" The brief moment of calm had passed. I could feel the rage about to erupt again. I wanted to surrender to it, because it was only rage that wiped out shame. The two young people stepped forward, ready to restrain me, but Kikuta waved them back. He himself took my bound hands and held them firmly.

"Look at me," he said.

Despite myself, my eyes met his. I could feel myself drowning in the whirlpool of my emotions, and only his eyes kept me from going under. Slowly the rage abated. A tremendous weariness took its place. I could not fight the sleep that rolled towards me like clouds over the mountain. Kikuta's eyes held me until my own eyes closed, and the mist swallowed me up.

When I woke, it was daylight, the sun slanting into the room beyond the secret one and throwing a dim orange light into where I lay. I couldn't believe it was afternoon again: I must have slept for nearly a whole day. The girl was sitting on the floor a little way from me. I realized the door had just closed; the sound had wakened me. The other guard must have just stepped out.

"What's your name?" I said. My voice was croaky, my throat still sore.

"Yuki."

"And him?"

"Akio."

He was the one she'd said I'd wounded. "What did that man do to me?"

"The Kikuta master? He just put you to sleep. It's something Kikuta can do."

I remembered the dogs in Hagi. Something Kikuta can do. . . .

"What hour is it?" I said.

"First half of the Rooster."

"Is there any news?"

"Of Lord Otori? Nothing." She came a little closer and whispered, "Do you want me to take a message to him?"

I stared at her. "Can you?"

"I've worked as a maid at the place he is lodged in, as I did at Yamagata." She gave me a look full of meaning. "I can try and speak to him tonight or tomorrow morning."

"Tell him I did not leave voluntarily. Ask him to forgive me. . . ." There was far too much to try to put into words. I broke off. "Why would you do this for me?"

She shook her head, smiled, and indicated we should say no more. Akio returned to the room. One of his hands was bandaged, and he treated me coldly.

Later they untied my feet and took me to the bath, undressed me, and helped me into the hot water. I was moving like a cripple and every muscle in my body ached.

"It's what you do to yourself when you go mad with rage," Yuki said. "You have no idea how much you can hurt yourself with your own strength."

"That's why you have to learn self-control," Akio added. "Otherwise you are only a danger to others as well as yourself."

When they took me back to the room he said, "You broke every rule of the Tribe with your disobedience. Let this be a punishment to you."

I realized it was not only resentment for my wounding him: He disliked me and was jealous too. I didn't care one way or the other. My head ached fiercely, and although the rage had left me, it had been replaced with the deepest sorrow.

My guards seemed to accept that some sort of truce had been reached, and left me untied. I was in no condition to go anywhere. I could hardly walk, let alone climb out of windows and scale roofs. I ate a little, the first food I had taken in two days. Yuki and Akio left, their places taken by Keiko and the other young man, whose name was Yoshinori. Keiko's hands were also bandaged. They both seemed as hostile towards me as Akio. We did not talk at all.

I thought of Shigeru and prayed that Yuki would be able to speak to him. Then I found myself praying in the manner of the Hidden, the words coming unbidden onto my tongue. I had absorbed them, after all, with my mother's milk. Like a child I whispered them to myself, and maybe they brought me comfort, for after a while I slept again, deeply.

The sleep refreshed me. When I woke, it was morning; my body had recovered a little and I could move without pain. Yuki was back, and when she saw I was awake, she dispatched Akio on some errand. She seemed older than the others, and had some authority over them.

She told me immediately what I longed to hear. "I went to the lodging house last night and managed to speak to Lord Otori. He was greatly relieved to hear you are unharmed. His main fear was that you had been captured or murdered by the Tohan. He wrote to you yesterday, in the vain hope you might be able to retrieve the letter someday."

"You have it?"

She nodded. "He gave me something else for you. I hid it in the closet."

She slid open the door to the closet where the bedding was stored, and from beneath a pile of quilts took out a long bundle. I recognized the cloth: It was an old traveling robe of Shigeru's, maybe the very one he had been wearing when he had saved my life in Mino. She put it in my hands and I held it up to my face. There was something rigid wrapped up inside it. I knew immediately what it was. I unfolded the robe and lifted Jato out.

I thought I would die of grief. Tears fell then: I could not prevent them.

Yuki said gently, "They are to go unarmed to the castle for the wedding. He did not want the sword to be lost if he did not return."

"He will not return," I said, the tears streaming like a river.

Yuki took the sword from me and rewrapped it, stowing it away again in the closet.

"Why did you do this for me?" I said. "Surely you are disobeying the Tribe?"

"I am from Yamagata," she replied. "I was there when Takeshi was murdered. The family who died with him—I grew up with their daughter. You saw what it was like in Yamagata, how much the people love Shigeru. I am one of them. And I believe Kenji, the Muto master, has wronged both of you." There was a note of challenge in her voice that sounded almost like an outraged—and disobedient—child. I did not want to question her further. I was just immensely grateful for what she had done for me.

"Give me the letter," I said after a while.

He had been taught by Ichiro and his handwriting was everything mine should have been but wasn't, bold and flowing: *Takeo, I am most happy that you are safe. There is nothing to forgive. I know that you would not betray me, and I always knew that the Tribe would try to take you. Think of me tomorrow.*

The main letter followed. . . .

Takeo, for whatever reasons, we could not follow through with our gamble. I have many regrets, but am spared the sorrow of sending you to your death. I believe you to be with the Tribe; your destiny is therefore out of my hands. However, you are my adopted son and my only legal heir. I hope one day you will be able to take up your Otori inheritance. If I die at Iida's hands, I charge you to avenge my death, but not to mourn it, for I believe I will achieve more in death than in life. Be patient. I also ask that you will look after Lady Shirakawa.

Some bond from a former life must have decreed the strength of our feelings. I am glad we met at Mino. I embrace you.

Your adopted father, Shigeru.

It was set with his seal.

"The Otori men believe you and the Muto master to have been murdered," Yuki said. "No one believes you would have left voluntarily. I thought you would like to know."

I thought of them all, the men who had teased and spoiled me, taught me and put up with me, been proud of me, and still thought the best of me. They were going to certain death, but I envied them, for they would die with Shigeru, while I was condemned to live, starting with that terrible day.

Every sound from outside made me start. At one time, soon after midday, I thought I heard far in the distance the clash of swords and the screams of men, but no one came to tell me anything. An oppressive and unnatural silence settled over the town.

My only consolation was the thought of Jato, lying hidden within arm's reach. Many times I was on the point of seizing the sword and fighting my way out of the house, but Shigeru's last message to me had been to be patient. Rage had given way to grief, but now, as my tears dried, grief gave way to determination. I would not throw away my life unless I took Iida with me.

Around the hour of the Monkey I heard a voice in the shop below. My heart stopped, for I knew it was news of some sort. Keiko and Yoshinori were with me, but after about ten minutes Yuki came and told them they were to go.

She knelt beside me and put her hand on my arm. "Muto Shizuka has sent a message from the castle. The masters are coming to speak to you."

"Is he dead?"

"No, worse: He is captured. They will tell you."

"He is to kill himself?"

Yuki hesitated. She spoke swiftly without looking at me. "Iida has accused him of harboring a member of the Hidden—of being one of them himself. Ando has a personal feud against him and is demanding punishment. Lord Otori has been stripped of the privileges of the warrior class and is to be treated as a common criminal."

"Iida would not dare," I said.

"He has already done it."

I heard footsteps approaching from the outer room as outrage and shock sent energy flooding through me. I leaped at the closet and pulled out the sword, drawing it in the same movement from the sheath. I felt it cleave to my hands. I raised it above my head.

Kenji and Kikuta stepped into the room. They went very still when they saw Jato in my hands. Kikuta reached inside his robe for a knife, but Kenji did not move.

"I am not going to attack you," I said, "though you deserve to die. But I will kill myself. . . ."

Kenji rolled his eyes upwards. Kikuta said mildly, "We hope you won't have to resort to that." Then after a moment he hissed and went on almost impatiently, "Sit down, Takeo. You've made your point."

We all lowered ourselves onto the floor. I placed the sword on the matting next to me.

"I see Jato found you," Kenji said. "I should have expected that."

"I brought it, master," Yuki said.

"No, the sword used you. So it goes from hand to hand. I should know: It used me to find Shigeru after Yaegahara."

"Where is Shizuka?" I said.

"Still in the castle. She did not come herself. Just to send a message was very dangerous, but she wanted us to know what happened, and asked what we intended to do about it."

"Tell me."

"Lady Maruyama tried to flee from the castle yesterday with her daughter." Kikuta's voice was level and dispassionate. "She bribed some boatmen to take her across the river. They were betrayed and intercepted. All three women threw themselves into the water. The lady and her daughter drowned, but the servant, Sachie, was rescued. Better for her that she had drowned, for she was then tortured until she revealed the relationship with Shigeru, the alliance with Arai, and the lady's connection with the Hidden."

"The pretense that the wedding would take place was maintained until Shigeru was inside the castle," Kenji said. "Then the Otori men were cut down, and he was accused of treason." He paused for a moment and then continued quietly. "He is already strung from the castle wall."

"Crucified?" I whispered.

"Hung by the arms."

I closed my eyes briefly, imagining the pain, the dislocation of the shoulders, the slow suffocation, the terrible humiliation.

"'A warrior's death, swift and honorable'?" I said, in accusation, to Kenji.

He did not reply. His face, usually so mobile, was still, his pale skin, white.

I put my hand out and touched Jato. I said to Kikuta, "I have a proposition to put to the Tribe. I believe you work for whoever pays you most. I will buy my services from you with something you seem to value—that is, my life and my obedience. Let me go tonight and bring him down. In return I will give up the name of Otori and join the Tribe. If you don't agree, I will end my life here. I will never leave this room."

The two masters exchanged a glance. Kenji nodded imperceptibly. Kikuta said, "I have to accept that the situation has changed, and we seem to have come to a stalemate." There was a sudden flurry in the street, feet running and shouts. We both listened in an identical Kikuta way. The sounds faded, and he went on, "I accept your proposal. You have my permission to go into the castle tonight."

"I will go with him," Yuki said, "and I'll prepare everything we may need."

"If the Muto master agrees."

"I agree," Kenji said. "I will come too."

"You don't need to," I said.

"All the same, I'm coming with you."

"Do we know where Atai is?" I asked.

Kenji said, "Even if he were to march all night, he would not be here before daybreak."

"But he is on his way?"

"Shizuka believes he will not move against the castle. His only hope is to provoke Iida into fighting him on the border."

"And Terayama?"

"They will erupt when they hear of this outrage," Yuki said. "The town of Yamagata too."

"No revolt will succeed while Iida lives, and anyway, these wider concerns are not ours," Kikuta interrupted with a flash of anger. "You may bring Shigeru's body down; our agreement covers nothing more."

I said nothing. *While Iida lives . . .*

It was raining again, the gentle sound enveloping the town, washing tiles and cobbles, freshening the stale air.

"What of Lady Shirakawa?" I said.

"Shizuka says she is in shock, but calm. No suspicion seems to be attached to her, apart from the blame that goes with her unfortunate reputation. People say she is cursed, but she is not suspected of being part of the conspiracy. Sachie, the servant, was weaker than the Tohan thought, and she escaped their torture into death before, it seems, incriminating Shizuka."

"Did she reveal anything about me?"

Kenji sighed, "She knew nothing, except that you were from the Hidden and rescued by Shigeru, which Iida knew already. He and Ando think Shigeru adopted you purely to insult them, and that you fled when you were recognized. They do not suspect your Tribe identity, and they do not know of your skills."

That was one advantage. Another was the weather and the night. The rain lessened to a drizzling mist; the cloud cover was dense and low, completely obscuring moon and stars. And the third was the change that had come over me. Something inside me that had been half-formed before had set into its intended shape. My outburst of mad rage, followed by the profound Kikuta sleep, had burned away the dross from my nature and left a core of steel. I recognized in myself the glimpses I'd had of Kenji's true self, as if Jato had come to life.

The three of us went through the equipment and clothing. After that I spent an hour exercising. My muscles were still stiff, though less sore. My right wrist bothered me the most. When I'd raised Jato before, the pain had shot back to the elbow. In the end Yuki strapped it up for me with a leather wrist guard.

Towards the second half of the hour of the Dog, we ate lightly and then sat in silence, slowing breathing and heartbeat. We darkened the room to improve our night vision. An early curfew had been imposed, and after the horsemen had patrolled the streets, driving people inside, the streets were quiet. Around us the house sang its evening song: dishes being cleared away, dogs fed, guards settling down for the night watch. I could hear the tread of maids as they went to spread out the bedding, the click of the abacus from the front room as someone did the day's accounts. Gradually the song dwindled to a few constant notes: the deep breathing of the sleeping, occasional snores, once the cry of a man at the moment of physical passion. These mundane human sounds touched my soul. I found myself thinking of my father, of his longing to live an ordinary human life. Had he cried out like that when I was conceived?

After a while Kenji told Yuki to leave us alone for a few minutes and came to sit beside me. He said in a low voice, "The accusation of being connected with the Hidden—how far does that go?"

"He never mentioned it to me, other than to change my name from Tomasu and warn me against praying."

"The rumor is that he would not deny it; he refused to defile the images." Kenji's voice was puzzled, almost irritated.

"The first time I met Lady Maruyama, she traced the sign of the Hidden on my hand," I said slowly.

"He kept so much concealed from me," Kenji said. "I thought I knew him!"

"Did he know of the lady's death?"

"Apparently Iida told him with delight."

I thought about this for a few moments. I knew Shigeru would have refused to deny the beliefs Lady Maruyama held so deeply. Whether he believed them or not, he would never submit to Iida's bullying. And now he was keeping the promise he had made to her in Chigawa. He would marry no other woman and he would not live without her.

"I couldn't know Iida would treat him like this," Kenji said. I felt he was trying to excuse himself in some way, but the betrayal was too great for me to forgive. I was glad he was coming with me, and thankful for his skills, but after this night I never wanted to see him again.

"Let's go and bring him down," I said. I got up and called quietly to Yuki. She came back into the room and the three of us put on the dark night attire of the Tribe, covering our faces and hands so no inch of skin showed. We took garrotes, ropes and grapples, long and short knives, and poison capsules that would give us a swift death.

I took up Jato. Kenji said, "Leave it here. You can't climb with a long sword." I ignored him. I knew what I would need it for.

The house I'd been hidden in was well to the west of the castle town, among the merchants' houses south of the river. The area was crisscrossed with many narrow alleys and laneways, making it easy to move through unseen. At the end of the street we passed the temple, where lights still burned as the priests prepared for the midnight rituals. A cat sat beside a stone lantern. It did not stir as we slipped by.

We were approaching the river when I heard the chink of steel and the tramp of feet. Kenji went invisible in a gateway. Yuki and I leaped silently onto the roof of the wall and merged into the tiles.

The patrol consisted of a man on horseback and six foot soldiers. Two of them carried flaming torches. They progressed along the road that ran beside the river, lighting each alleyway and peering down it. They made a great deal of noise, and so did not alarm me at all.

The tiles against my face were damp and slippery. The mild drizzle continued, muffling sound.

The rain would be falling on Shigeru's face. . . .

I dropped from the wall, and we went on towards the river.

A small canal ran alongside the alley. Yuki led us into it where it disappeared into a drain beneath the road. We crawled through it, disturbing the sleeping fish, and emerged where it flowed into the river, the water masking our footsteps. The dark bulk of the castle loomed in front of us. The cloud cover was so low that I could barely make out the highest towers. Between us and the fortification wall lay first the river, then the moat.

"Where is he?" I whispered to Kenji.

"On the east side, below Iida's palace. Where we saw the iron rings."

Bile rose in my throat. Fighting it back, I said, "Guards?"

"In the corridor immediately above, stationary. On the ground below, patrols."

As I had done at Yamagata, I sat and looked at the castle for a long time. None of us spoke. I could feel the dark Kikuta self rising, flowing into vein and muscle. So would I flow into the castle, and force it to give up what it held.

I took Jato from my belt and laid it on the bank, hiding it in the long grass. "Wait there," I said silently. "I will bring your master to you."

We slipped one by one into the river and swam beneath the surface to the far bank. I could hear the first patrol in the gardens beyond the moat. We lay in the reeds until it had passed, then ran over the narrow strip of marshland and swam in the same way across the moat.

The first fortification wall rose straight from the moat. At the top was a small tiled wall that ran all the way round the garden in front of the residence and the narrow strip of land behind, between the residence walls and the fortification wall. Kenji dropped onto the ground to watch for patrols while Yuki and I crept along the tiled roof to the southeast corner. Twice we heard Kenji's warning cricket's chirp and went invisible on top of the wall while the patrols passed below us.

I knelt and looked upwards. Above me was the row of windows of the corridor at the back of the residence. They were all closed and barred, save one, closest to the iron rings from which Shigeru was suspended, a rope around each wrist. His head hung forward on his chest, and I thought he was already dead, but then I saw that his feet were braced slightly against the wall, taking some of the weight from his arms. I could hear the slow rasp of his breath. He was still alive.

The nightingale floor sang. I flattened myself back onto the tiles. I heard someone lean from the window above, and then a cry of pain from Shigeru as the rope was jerked and his feet slipped.

"Dance, Shigeru, it's your wedding day!" the guard jeered.

I could feel the slow burn of rage. Yuki laid one hand on my arm, but I was not going to erupt. My rage was cold now, and all the more powerful.

We waited there for a long time. No more patrols passed below. Had Kenji silenced them all? The lamp in the window flickered and smoked. Someone came there every ten minutes or so. Each time the suffering man at the end of the ropes found a foothold, one of the guards came and shook him loose. Each time the cry of pain was weaker, and it took him longer to recover.

The window remained open. I whispered to Yuki. "We must climb up. If you can kill them as they come back, I'll take the rope. Cut the wrist ropes when you hear the deer bark. I'll lower him down."

"I'll meet you at the canal," she mouthed.

Immediately after the next visit from the torturers, we dropped to the ground, crossed the narrow strip of land, and began to scale the residence wall. Yuki climbed in through the window while I, clinging to the ledge beneath it, took the rope from my waist and lashed it to one of the iron rings.

The nightingales sang. Invisible, I froze against the wall. I heard someone lean out above me, heard the slightest gasp, the thud of feet kicking helplessly against the garrote, then silence.

Yuki whispered, "Go!"

I began to climb down the wall towards Shigeru, the rope paying out as I went. I had nearly reached him when I heard the cricket chirp. Again I went invisible, praying the mist would hide the extra rope. I heard the patrol pass below me. There was a sound from the moat, a sudden splash. Their attention was distracted by it. One of the men went towards the edge of the wall, holding his torch out over the water. The light shone dully off a white wall of mist.

"Just a water rat," he called. The men disappeared and I heard their footsteps fade slowly away.

Now time speeded up. I knew another guard would soon appear above me. How much longer could Yuki kill them off one by one? The walls were slippery, the rope even more so. I slithered down the last few feet until I was level with Shigeru.

His eyes were closed, but he either heard or felt my presence. He opened them, whispered my name without surprise, and gave the ghost of his openhearted smile, breaking my heart again.

I said, "This will hurt. Don't make a sound."

He closed his eyes again and braced his feet against the wall.

I tied him to me as firmly as I could and barked like a deer to Yuki. She slashed the ropes that held Shigeru. He gasped despite himself as his arms were freed. The extra weight dislodged me from the slippery surface of the wall, and we both fell towards the ground as I prayed that my rope would hold. It brought us up short but with a terrible jolt, with about four feet to spare.

Kenji stepped out of the darkness and together we untied Shigeru and carried him to the wall.

Kenji threw the grapples up and we managed to drag him over. Then we tied the rope to him again and Kenji lowered him down the wall while I climbed down alongside, trying to ease him a little.

We could not stop at the bottom, but had to swim him straightaway across the moat, covering his face with a black hood. Without the mist we would have been immediately discovered, for we could not take him underwater. Then we carried him across the last strip of castle land to the riverbank. By this time he was barely conscious, sweating from pain, his lips raw where he had bitten them to prevent himself from crying out. Both shoulders were dislocated, as I had expected, and he was coughing up blood from some internal injury.

It was raining more heavily. A real deer barked as we startled it, and it bounded away, but there was no sound from the castle. We took Shigeru into the river and swam gently and slowly to the opposite bank. I was blessing the rain, for it masked us, muffling every sound, but it also meant that when I looked back at the castle, I could see no sign of Yuki.

When we reached the bank we laid him down in the long summer grass. Kenji knelt beside him and took off the hood, wiping the water from his face.

"Forgive me, Shigeru," he said.

Shigeru smiled but did not speak. Summoning up his strength, he whispered my name.

"I'm here."

"Do you have Jato?"

"Yes, Lord Shigeru."

"Use it now. Take my head to Terayama and bury me next to Takeshi." He paused as a fresh spasm of pain swept over him and then said, "And bring Iida's head to me there."

As Kenji helped him to kneel he said quietly, "Takeo has never failed me." I drew Jato from the scabbard. Shigeru stretched out his neck and murmured a few words: the prayers the Hidden use at the moment of death, followed by the name of the Enlightened One. I prayed, too, that I would not fail him now. It was darker than when Jato in his hand had saved my life.

I lifted the sword, felt the dull ache in my wrist,

and asked Shigeru's forgiveness. The snake sword leaped and bit and, in its last act of service to its master, released him into the next world.

The silence of the night was utter. The gushing blood seemed monstrously loud. We took the head, bathed it in the river, and wrapped it in the hood, both dry-eyed, beyond grief or remorse.

There was a movement below the surface of the water, and seconds later Yuki surfaced like an otter. With her acute night vision she took in the scene, knelt by the body, and prayed briefly. I lifted the head—how heavy it was!—and put it in her hands.

"Take it to Terayama," I said. "I will meet you there."

She nodded, and I saw the slight flash of her teeth as she smiled.

"We must all leave now," Kenji hissed. "It was well done, but it's finished."

"First I must give his body to the river." I could not bear to leave it unburied on the bank. I took stones from the mouth of the canal and tied them into the loincloth that was his only garment. The others helped me carry him into the water.

I swam out to the deepest part of the river and let go, feeling the tug and drift as the body sank. Blood rose to the surface, dark against the white mist, but the river carried it away.

I thought of the house in Hagi where the river was always at the door and of the heron that came to the garden every evening. Now Otori Shigeru was dead. My tears flowed, and the river carried them away as well.

But for me the night's work was not finished. I swam back to the bank and picked up Jato. There was hardly a trace of blood on the blade. I wiped it and put it back in the scabbard. I knew Kenji was right—it would hamper my climbing—but I needed Jato now. I did not say a word to Kenji, and nothing to Yuki beyond "I'll see you in Terayama."

Kenji whispered, "Takeo," but without conviction. He must have known nothing would stop me. He embraced Yuki swiftly. It was only then that I realized that she was of course his daughter. He followed me back into the river.

# CHAPTER 12

Kaede waited for night to come. She knew there was no other choice but to kill herself. She thought about dying with the same intensity she brought to everything. Her family's honor had depened on the marriage—so her father had told her. Now in the confusion and turmoil that had surrounded her all day, she clung to the conviction that the only way to protect her family's name was to act with honor herself.

It was early evening on what should have been her wedding day. She was still dressed in the robes that the Tohan ladies had prepared for her. They were more sumptuous and elegant than anything she had ever worn, and inside them she felt as tiny and fragile as a doll. The women's eyes had been red with weeping for the death of Lady Maruyama, but Kaede had been told nothing about this until after the massacre of the Otori men. Then one horror after another was revealed to her, until she thought she would go mad from outrage and grief.

The residence with its elegant rooms, its treasures of art, its beautiful gardens, had become a place of violence and torture. Outside its walls, across the nightingale floor, hung the man she was supposed to have married. All afternoon she had heard the guards, their taunts and their foul laughter. Her heart swelled to breaking point, and she wept constantly. Sometimes she heard her own name mentioned, and knew that her reputation had grown worse. She felt she had caused Lord Otori's downfall. She wept for him, for his utter humiliation at Iida's hands. She wept for her parents and the shame she was bringing on them.

Just when she thought she had cried her eyes dry, the tears welled and streamed down her face again. Lady Maruyama, Mariko, Sachie . . . they were all gone, swept away by the current of Tohan violence. All the people she cared about were either dead or vanished.

And she wept for herself because she was fifteen years old and her life was over before it had begun. She mourned the husband she would never know, the children she would never bear, the future that the knife would put an end to. Her only consolation ws the painting Takeo had given her. She held it in her hand and gazed on it constantly. Soon she would be free, like the little bird of the mountain.

Shizuka went to the kitchens for a while to ask for some food to be brought, joining in the guards' jokes with apparent heartlessness as she went past. When she returned the mask fell away. Her face was drawn with grief.

"Lady," she said, her bright voice belying her true feelings, "I must comb your hair. It's all over the place. And you must change your clothes."

She helped Kaede undress and called to the maids to take the heavy wedding robes away.

"I will put on my night robe now," Kaede said. "I will see no one else today."

Clad in the light cotton garment, she sat on the floor by the open window. It was raining gently and a little cooler. The garden dripped with moisture as though it, too, were in deepest mourning.

Shizuka knelt behind her, taking up the heavy weight of her hair and running her fingers through it. She breathed into Kaede's ear, "I sent a message to the Muto residence in the city. I have just heard back from them. Takeo was hidden there, as I thought. They are going to permit him to retrieve Lord Otori's body."

"Lord Otori is dead?"

"No, not yet." Shizuka's voice trailed away. She was shaking with emotion. "The outrage," she murmured, "the shame. He cannot be left there. Takeo must come for him."

Kaede said, "Then he, too, will die today."

"My messenger is also going to try to reach Arai," Shizuka whispered. "But I do not know if he can arrive in time to help us."

"I never believed any one could challenge the Tohan," Kaede said. "Lord Iida is invincible. His cruelty gives him power." She gazed out of the window at the falling rain, the gray mist that

315

enshrouded the mountains. "Why have men made such a harsh world?" she said in a low voice.

A string of wild geese flew overhead, calling mournfully. In the distance beyond the walls a deer barked.

Kaede put her hand to her head. Her hair was wet with Shizuka's tears. "When will Takeo come?"

"If he does, late at night." There was a long pause and then Shizuka said, "It is a hopeless venture."

Kaede did not reply. *I will wait for him*, she promised herself. *I will see him once more.*

She felt the cool handle of the knife inside her robe. Shizuka noticed the movement, drew her close, and embraced her. "Don't be afraid. Whatever you do, I will stay with you. I will follow you into the next world."

They held each other for a long time. Exhausted by emotion, Kaede slipped into the stage of bewilderment that accompanies grief. She felt as if she were dreaming and had entered another world, one in which she lay in Takeo's arms, without fear. *Only he can save me,* she found herself thinking. *Only he can bring me back to life.*

Later she told Shizuka she would like to bathe, and asked her to pluck her brow and eyebrows and scrub her feet and legs smooth. She ate a little and then sat in outwardly composed silence, meditating on what she had been taught as a child, remembering the serene face of the Enlightened One at Terayama.

"Have compassion on me," she prayed. "Help me to have courage."

The maids came to spread the beds. Kaede was getting ready to lie down and had placed the knife underneath the mattress. It was well into the hour of the Rat, and the residence had fallen silent, apart from the distant laughter of the guards, when they heard footsteps making the floor chirp. There was a tap on the door. Shizuka went to it and immediately dropped to the ground. Kaede heard Lord Abe's voice.

*He has come to arrest Shizuka,* she thought in terror.

Shizuka said, "It's very late, lord. Lady Shirakawa is exhausted," but Abe's voice was insistent. His footsteps retreated. Shizuka turned to Kaede and just had time to whisper, "Lord Iida wishes to visit you," before the floor sang again.

Iida stepped into the room, followed by Abe and the one-armed man, whose name she'd learned was Ando.

Kaede took one look at their faces, flushed with wine and with the triumph of their revenge. She dropped to the floor, her head pressed against the matting, her heart racing.

Iida settled himself down cross-legged. "Sit up, Lady Shirakawa."

She raised her head unwillingly and looked at him. He was casually dressed in nightclothes, but wore his sword in his sash. The two men who knelt behind him were also armed. They now sat up,

317

too, studying Kaede with insulting curiosity.

"Forgive me for this late intrusion," Iida said, "but I felt the day should not end without me expressing my regrets for your unfortunate situation." He smiled at her, showing his big teeth, and said over his shoulder to Shizuka, "Leave."

Kaede's eyes widened and her breath came sharply, but she did not dare turn her head to look at Shizuka. She heard the door slide closed and guessed the girl would be somewhere close, on the other side. She sat without moving, eyes cast down, waiting for Iida to continue.

"Your marriage, which I thought was to form an alliance with the Otori, seems to have been the excuse for vipers to try to bite me. I think I have exterminated the nest, however." His eyes were fixed on her face. "You spent several weeks on the road with Otori Shigeru and Maruyama Nakomi. Did you never suspect they were plotting against me?"

"I knew nothing, lord," she said, and added quietly, "If there was a plot, it could only succeed with my ignorance."

"Unnh," he grunted, and after a long pause said, "Where is the young man?"

She had not thought her heart could beat more quickly, but it did, pounding in her temples and making her faint. "Which young man, Lord Iida?"

"The so-called adopted son. Takeo."

"I know nothing of him," she replied, as if puzzled. "Why should I?"

"What kind of a man would you say he was?"

"He was young, very quiet. He seemed bookish; he liked to paint and draw." She forced herself to smile. "He was clumsy and . . . perhaps not very brave."

"That was Lord Abe's reading. We know now that he was one of the Hidden. He escaped execution a year ago. Why would Shigeru not only harbor but adopt a criminal like that, except to affront and insult me?"

Kaede could not answer. The webs of intrigue seemed unfathomable to her.

"Lord Abe believes the young man fled when Ando recognized him. It seems he is a coward. We'll pick him up sooner or later and I'll string him up next to his adopted father." Iida's eyes flickered over her, but she made no response. "Then my revenge on Shigeru will be complete." His teeth gleamed as he grinned. "However, a more pressing question is: What is to become of you. Come closer."

Kaede bowed and moved forward. Her heartbeat had slowed—indeed, seemed almost to have stopped. Time slowed too. The night became more silent. The rain was a gentle hiss. A cricket chirped.

Iida leaned forward and studied her. The lamplight fell on his face, and when she raised her eyes she saw his predatory features slacken with desire.

"I am torn, Lady Shirakawa. You are irretrievably tainted by these events, yet your father has been loyal to me, and I feel a certain responsibility towards you. What am I to do?"

"My only desire is to die," she replied. "Allow me to do so honorably. My father will be satisfied with that."

"Then there is the question of the Maruyama inheritance," he said. "I've thought of marrying you myself. That would deal with the problem of what happens to the domain, and would put an end to these rumors about your dangerous effect on men."

"The honor would be too great for me," she replied.

He smiled and ran one long fingernail across his front teeth. "I know you have two sisters. I may marry the older one. All in all, I think it is preferable if you take your own life."

"Lord Iida." She bowed to the ground.

"She's quite a wonderful girl, isn't she?" Iida said over his shoulder to the men behind him. "Beautiful, intelligent, brave. And all to be wasted."

She sat upright again, her face turned away from him, determined to show nothing to him.

"I suppose you are a virgin." He put out a hand and touched her hair. She realized he was far more drunk than he had appeared. She could smell the wine on his breath as he leaned towards her. To her fury, the touch made her tremble. He saw it and laughed. "It would be a tragedy to die a virgin. You should know at least one night of love."

Kaede stared at him in disbelief. She saw then all his depravity, how far he had descended into the pit of lust and cruelty. His great power had made him arrogant and corrupt. She felt as if she were in a dream, in which she could see what was going to happen but was powerless to prevent it. She could not believe his intentions.

He took her head in both hands and bent over her. She turned her face away, and his lips brushed her neck.

"No," she said. "No, lord. Do not shame me. Let me just die!"

"There is no shame in pleasing me," he said.

"I beseech you, not before these men," she cried, going limp as if she were surrendering to him. Her hair fell forward, covering her.

"Leave us," he said to them curtly. "Let no one disturb me before dawn."

She heard the two men leave, heard Shizuka speak to them, wanted to cry out, but did not dare. Iida knelt beside her, picked her up, and carried her to the mattress. He untied her girdle and her robe fell open. Removing his sword and loosening his own garments, he lay beside her. Her skin was crawling with fear and revulsion.

"We have all night," he said, the last words he spoke. The feel of his body pressing against her brought back vividly the guard at Noguchi Castle. His mouth on hers drove her nearly mad with disgust. She threw her arms back over her head, and he grunted in appreciation as her body arched against his. With her left hand she found the needle in her right sleeve. As he lowered himself onto her she drove the needle into his eye. He gave a cry, indistinguishable from a moan of passion. Pulling the knife from beneath the mattress with her right hand, she thrust it upwards. His own weight as he fell forward took it into his heart.

# CHAPTER 13

I was soaked from the river and from the rain, water clinging to my hair and eyelashes, dripping like the rushes, like bamboo and willow. And although it left no mark on my dark clothes, I was soaked, too, with blood. The mist had thickened even more. Kenji and I moved in a phantom world, insubstantial and invisible. I found myself wondering if I had died without knowing it and had come back as an angel of revenge. When the night's work was done I would fade back into the netherworld. And all the time grief was starting up its terrible chanting in my heart, but I could not listen to it yet.

We came out of the moat and climbed the wall. I felt the weight of Jato against my flank. It was as if I carried Shigeru with me. I felt as if his ghost had entered me and had engraved itself on my bones. From the top of the garden wall I heard the steps of a patrol. Their voices were anxious; they suspected intruders, and when they saw the ropes that Yuki had cut, they stopped, exclaiming in surprise, and peering upwards to the iron rings where Shigeru had hung.

We took two each. They died in four strokes, before they could look down again. Shigeru had been right. The sword leaped in my hand as if it had a will of its own, or as if his own hand wielded it. No compassion or softness of mine hindered it.

The window above us was still open, and the lamp still burned faintly. The palace seemed quiet, wrapped in the sleep of the Hour of the Ox. As we climbed inside we fell over the bodies of the guards Yuki had killed earlier. Kenji gave a faint approving sound. I went to the door between the corridor and the guardroom. I knew four such small rooms lay along the corridor. The first one was open and led into the antechamber where I had waited with Shigeru and we had looked at the paintings of the cranes. The other three were hidden behind the walls of Iida's apartments.

The nightingale floor ran around the whole residence and through the middle, dividing the men's apartments from the women's. It lay before me, gleaming slightly in the lamp light, silent.

I crouched in the shadows. From far away, almost at the end of the building, I could hear voices: two men at least, and a woman.

Shizuka.

After a few moments I realized the men were Abe and Ando; as for guards, I wasn't sure how many: perhaps two with the lords and ten or so others hidden in the secret compartments. I placed the voices in the end room, Iida's own. Presumably the lords were waiting for him there—but where was he and why was Shizuka with them?

Her voice was light, almost flirtatious, theirs tired, yawning, a little drunk.

"I'll fetch more wine," I heard her say.

"Yes, it looks like it's going to be a long night," Abe replied.

"One's last night on earth is always too short," Shizuka replied, a catch in her voice.

"It needn't be your last night, if you make the right move," Abe said, a heavy note of admiration creeping into his voice. "You're an attractive woman, and you know your way around. I'll make sure you're looked after."

"Lord Abe!" Shizuka laughed quietly. "Can I trust you?"

"Get some more wine and I'll show you how much."

I heard the floor sing as she stepped out of the room onto it. Heavier steps followed her, and Ando said, "I'm going to watch Shigeru dance again. I've waited a year for this."

As they moved through the middle of the residence I ran along the floor around the side and crouched by the door of the antechamber. The floor had stayed silent beneath my feet. Shizuka went past me, and Kenji gave his cricket chirp. She melted into the shadows.

Ando stepped into the antechamber and went to the guardroom. He called angrily to them to wake up, and then Kenji had him in a grip of iron.

I went in, pulling off my hood, holding the lamp up so that he could see my face.

"Do you see me?" I whispered. "Do you know me? I am the boy from Mino. This is for my people. And for Lord Otori."

His eyes were filled with disbelief and fury. I would not use Jato on him. I took the garrote and killed him with that, while Kenji held him and Shizuka watched.

I whispered to her, "Where is Iida?"

She said, "With Kaede. In the farthest room on the women's side. I'll keep Abe quiet while you go around. He is alone with her. If there's any trouble here, I'll deal with it with Kenji."

I hardly took in her words. I'd thought my blood was cold, but now it turned to ice. I breathed deeply, let the Kikuta blackness rise in me and take me over completely, and ran out onto the nightingale floor.

Rain hissed gently in the garden beyond. Frogs croaked from the pools and the marshland. The women breathed deeply in sleep. I smelled the scent of flowers, the cypress wood of the bath-house, the acrid stench from the privies. I floated across the floor as weightless as a ghost. Behind me the castle loomed, in front of me flowed the river. Iida was waiting for me.

In the last small room at the end of the residence, a lamp burned. The wooden shutters were open but the paper ones closed, and against the orange glow of the lamp I could see the shadow of a woman sitting motionless, her hair falling around her.

With Jato ready, I pulled the screen open and leaped into the room.

Kaede, sword in hand, was on her feet in a moment. She was covered in blood.

Iida lay slumped on the mattress, facedown. Kaede said, "It's best to kill a man and take his sword. That's what Shizuka said."

Her eyes were dilated with shock, and she was trembling. There was something almost supernatural about the scene: the girl, so young and frail; the man, massive and powerful, even in death; the hiss of the rain; the stillness of the night. . . .

I put Jato down. She lowered Iida's sword and stepped towards me. "Takeo," she said, as if awakening from a dream. "He tried to . . . I killed him. . . ."

Then she was in my arms. I held her until she stopped shaking.

"You're soaking wet," she whispered. "Aren't you cold?"

I had not been, but now I was, shivering almost as much as she was. Iida was dead, but I had not killed him. I felt cheated of my revenge, but I could not argue with fate, which had dealt with him through Kaede's hands. I was both disappointed and mad with relief. And I was holding Kaede, as I had longed to for weeks.

When I think about what happened next, I can

only plead that we were bewitched, as we had been since Tsuwano. Kaede said, "I expected to die tonight."

"I think we will," I said.

"But we will be together," she breathed against my ear. "No one will come here before dawn."

Her voice, her touch, set me aching with love and desire for her.

"Do you want me?" she said.

"You know I do." We fell to our knees, still holding each other.

"You aren't afraid of me? Of what happens to men because of me?"

"No. You will never be dangerous to me. Are you afraid?"

"No," she said, with a kind of wonder in her voice. "I want to be with you before we die." Her mouth found mine. She undid her girdle and her robe fell open. I pulled my wet clothes off and felt against me the skin I had longed for. Our bodies rushed towards each other with the urgency and madness of youth.

I would have been happy to die afterwards, but like the river, life dragged us forward. It seemed an eternity had passed, but it could have been no more than fifteen minutes, for I heard the floor sing and heard Shizuka return to Abe. In the room next to us a woman said something in her sleep, following it with a bitter laugh that set the hairs upright on my neck.

"What's Ando doing?" Abe said.

"He fell asleep," Shizuka replied, giggling. "He can't hold his wine like Lord Abe."

The liquid gurgled from flask to bowl. I heard Abe swallow. I touched my lips to Kaede's eyelids and hair. "I must go back to Kenji," I whispered. "I can't leave him and Shizuka unprotected."

"Why don't we just die together now," she said, "while we are happy?"

"He came on my account," I replied. "If I can save his life, I must."

"I'll come with you." She stood swiftly and retied her robe, taking up the sword again. The lamp was guttering, almost extinguished. In the distance I heard the first cock crow from the town.

"No. Stay here while I go back for Kenji. We'll meet you here and escape through the garden. Can you swim?"

She shook her head. "I never learned. But there are boats on the moat. Perhaps we can take one of them."

I pulled on my wet clothes again, shuddering at their clamminess against my skin. When I took up Jato, I felt the ache in my wrist. One of the blows of the night must have jarred it again. I knew I had to take Iida's head now, so I told Kaede to stretch out his neck by his hair. She did so, flinching a little.

"This is for Shigeru," I whispered as Jato sliced through his neck. He had already bled profusely, so there was no great gush of blood. I cut his robe and wrapped the head in it. It was as heavy as

Shigeru's had been when I handed it to Yuki. I could not believe it was still the same night. I left the head on the floor, embraced Kaede one last time, and went back the way I had come.

Kenji was still in the guardroom, and I could hear Shizuka chuckling with Abe. He whispered, "The next patrol is due any minute. They're going to find the bodies."

"It's done," I said. "Iida is dead."

"Then let's go."

"I have to deal with Abe."

"Leave him to Shizuka."

"And we have to take Kaede with us."

He peered at me in the gloom. "Lady Shirakawa? Are you mad?"

Very likely I was. I did not answer him. Instead, I stepped heavily and deliberately onto the nightingale floor.

It cried out immediately. Abe called, "Who's there?"

He rushed out of the room, his robe loose, sword in his hand. Behind him came two guards, one of them holding a torch. In its light Abe saw me, and recognized me. His expression was first astonished, then scornful. He strode towards me, making the floor sing loudly. Behind him Shizuka leaped at one of the guards and cut his throat. The other turned in amazement, dropping the torch as he drew his sword.

Abe was shouting for help. He came towards me like a madman, the great sword in his hand. He

330

cut at me and I parried it, but his strength was huge, and my arm weakened by pain. I ducked under his second blow and went invisible briefly. I was taken aback by his ferocity and skill.

Kenji was alongside me, but now the rest of the guards came pouring from their hiding places. Shizuka dealt with two of them; Kenji left his second self below the sword of one, and then knifed him in the back. My attention was totally taken up with Abe, who was driving me down the nightingale floor towards the end of the building. The women had woken and ran out screaming, distracting Abe as they fled past him and giving me a moment to recover my breath. I knew we could deal with the guards, once I had got Abe out of the way. But at the same time I knew he was vastly more skillful and experienced than I was.

He was driving me into the corner of the building, where there was no room to evade him. I went invisible again, but he knew there was nowhere for me to go. Whether I was invisible or not, his sword could still cut me in two.

Then, when it seemed he had me, he faltered and his mouth fell open. He gazed over my shoulder, a look of horror on his face.

I did not follow his look, but in that moment of inattention drove Jato downwards. The sword fell from my hands as my right arm gave. Abe lurched forward, his brains bursting from the great split in his skull. I ducked out of the way and turned to see Kaede standing in the doorway, the lamp behind her. In one hand she held Iida's sword, in the other his head.

Side by side we fought our way back across the nightingale floor. Every stroke made me wince in pain. Without Kaede at my right side, I would have died then.

Everything was turning blurred and indistinct before my eyes. I thought the mist from the river had penetrated the residence, but then I heard crackling and smelled smoke. The torch the guard had dropped had set the wooden screens on fire.

There were cries of fear and shock. The women and servants were running from the fire, out of the residence and into the castle, while guards from the castle were trying to get through the narrow gate into the residence. In the confusion and the smoke, the four of us fought our way into the garden.

By now the residence was fully ablaze. No one knew where Iida was or if he was alive or dead. No one knew who had made this attack on the supposedly impregnable castle. Was it men or demons? Shigeru had been spirited away. Was it by men or angels?

The rain had eased, but the mist grew thicker as dawn approached. Shizuka led us through the garden to the gate and the steps down to the moat. The guards here had already started on their way up towards the residence. Distracted and confused as they were, they hardly put up a fight. We unbarred the gate easily from the inside and stepped into one of the boats, casting off the rope.

The moat was connected to the river through the marshland we had crossed earlier. Behind us the castle stood out stark against the flames. Ash floated towards us, falling on our hair. The river was surging, and the waves rocked the wooden pleasure boat as the current carried us into it. It was hardly more than a punt, and I feared if the water grew any wilder it would capsize. Ahead of us the piles of the bridge suddenly appeared. For a moment I thought we would be flung against them, but the boat dived through, nose first, and the river carried us on, past the town.

None of us said much. We were all breathing hard, charged with the near confrontation with death, subdued maybe by the memory of those we had sent on into the next world, but deeply, achingly glad we were not among them. At least, that was how I felt.

I went to the stern of the boat and took the oar, but the current was too strong to make any headway. We had to go where it took us. The mist turned white as dawn came, but we could see no more through it than when it had been dark. Apart from the glow of the flames from the castle, everything else had disappeared.

I was aware of a strange noise, however, above the song of the river. It was like a great humming, as though a huge swarm of insects were descending on the city.

"Can you hear that?" I said to Shizuka.

She was frowning. "What is it?"

"I don't know."

The sun brightened, burning off the haze. The hum and throb from the bank increased, until the sound resolved itself into something I suddenly recognized: the tramp of feet of thousands of men and horses, the jingle of harness, the clash of steel. Colors flashed at us through the torn shreds of mist; the crests and banners of the Western clans.

"Arai is here!" Shizuka cried.

There are chronicles enough of the fall of Inuyama, and I took no further part in it, so there is no need for me to describe it here.

I had not expected to live beyond that night. I had no idea what to do next. I had given my life to the Tribe, that much was clear to me, but I still had duties to perform for Shigeru.

Kaede knew nothing of my bargain with the Kikuta. If I were Otori, Shigeru's heir, it would be my duty to marry her, and indeed there was nothing I wanted more. If I were to become Kikuta, Lady Shirakawa would be as unobtainable as the moon. What had happened between us now seemed like a dream. If I thought about it, I felt I should be ashamed of what I had done, and so like a coward I put it out of my mind.

We went first to the Muto residence where I had been hidden, changed our clothes, grabbed a little food. Shizuka went immediately to speak to Arai, leaving Kaede in the charge of the women of the house.

I did not want to speak to Kenji, or anyone. I wanted to get to Terayama, bury Shigeru, and place Iida's head on the grave. I knew I had to do this quickly, before the Kikuta controlled me fully. I was aware that I had already disobeyed the master of my family by returning to the castle. Even though I had not killed Iida myself, everyone would assume I had, against the express wishes of the Tribe. I could not deny it without causing immense harm to Kaede. I did not intend to disobey forever. I just needed a little more time.

It was easy enough to slip out of the house during the confusion of that day. I went to the lodging house where I had stayed with Shigeru. The owners had fled before Arai's army, taking most of their possessions with them, but many of our things were still in the rooms, including the sketches I had done at Terayama, and the writing box on which Shigeru had written his final letter to me. I looked at them with sorrow. Grief's clamor was growing louder and louder inside me, demanding my attention. It seemed I could feel Shigeru's presence in the room, see him sitting in the open doorway as night fell and I did not return.

I did not take much: a change of clothes, a little money, and my horse, Raku, from the stables. Shigeru's black, Kyu, had disappeared, as had most of the Otori horses, but Raku was still there, restive and uneasy as the smell of fire drifted over the town. He was relieved to see me. I saddled him up, tied the basket that held Iida's head to the saddle bow, and rode out of the city, joining the throngs of people on the highway who were fleeing from the approaching armies.

I went swiftly, sleeping only a little at night. The weather had cleared, and the air was crisp with a hint of autumn. Each day the mountains rose clear-edged against a brilliant blue sky. Some of the trees were already showing golden leaves. Bush clover and arrowroot were beginning to flower. It was probably beautiful, but I saw no beauty in anything. I knew I had to reflect on what I would do, but I could not bear to look at what I had done. I was in that stage of grief where I could not bear to go forward. I only wanted to go back, back to the house in Hagi, back in time to when Shigeru was alive, before we left for Inuyama.

On the afternoon of the fourth day, when I had just passed Kushimoto, I became aware that the travelers on the road were now streaming towards me. I called to a farmer leading a packhorse, "What's up ahead?"

"Monks! Warriors!" he shouted back. "Yamagata has fallen to them. The Tohan are fleeing. They say Lord Iida is dead!"

I grinned, wondering what he would do if he saw the grisly baggage on my saddle. I was in traveling clothes, unmarked with any crest. No one knew who I was, and I did not know that my name had already become famous.

Before long I heard the sound of men at arms on the road ahead, and I took Raku into the forest. I did not want to lose him or get embroiled in petty fights with the retreating Tohan. They were moving fast, obviously hoping to reach Inuyama before the monks caught up with them, but I felt they would be held up at the pass at Kushimoto and would probably have to make a stand there.

They straggled past for most of the rest of the day, while I worked my way northward through the forest, avoiding them as often as I could, though twice I had to use Jato to defend myself and my horse. My wrist still bothered me, and as the sun set I became more uneasy—not for my own safety, but that my mission would not be accomplished. It seemed too dangerous to try to sleep. The moon was bright, and I rode all night beneath its light, Raku moving on with his easy stride, one ear forward, one back.

Dawn came and I saw in the distance the shape of the mountains that surrounded Terayama. I would be there before the end of the day. I saw a pool below the road, and stopped to let Raku drink. The sun rose, and in its warmth I became suddenly sleepy. I tied the horse to a tree and took the saddle for a pillow, lay down, and fell immediately asleep.

I was woken by the earth shaking beneath me. I lay for a moment, looking at the dappled light that fell on the pool, listening to the trickle of the water and the tread of hundreds of feet approaching

337

along the road. I stood, meaning to take Raku deeper into the forest to hide him, but when I looked up I saw that the army was not the last of the Tohan. The men wore armor and carried weapons, but the banners were of the Otori, and of the temple at Terayama. Those that did not wear helmets had shaven heads, and in the front rank I recognized the young man who had shown us the paintings.

"Makoto!" I called to him, climbing the bank towards him. He turned to me, and a look of joy and astonishment crossed his face.

"Lord Otori? Is it really you? We feared you would be dead too. We are riding to avenge Lord Shigeru."

"I am on my way to Terayama," I said. "I am taking Iida's head to him, as he commanded me."

His eyes widened a little. "Iida is already dead?"

"Yes, and Inuyama has fallen to Arai. You'll catch up with the Tohan at Kushimoto."

"Won't you ride with us?"

I stared at him. His words made no sense to me. My work was almost done. I had to finish my last duty to Shigeru, and then I would disappear into the secret world of the Tribe. But of course there was no way Makoto could know of the choices I had made.

"Are you all right?" he asked. "You're not wounded?"

I shook my head. "I have to place the head on Shigeru's grave."

Makoto's eyes gleamed. "Show it to us!"

I brought the basket and opened it. The smell was strengthening and flies had gathered on the blood. The skin was a waxy gray color, the eyes dull and bloodshot.

Makoto took it by the topknot, leaped onto a boulder by the side of the road, and held it up to the monks gathered around. "Now see what Lord Otori has done!" he shouted, and the men shouted back a great hurrah. A wave of emotion swept through them. I heard my name repeated over and over again as, one by one at first, and then as if with a single mind, they knelt in the dust before me, bowing to the ground.

Kenji was right: People had loved Shigeru—the monks, the farmers, most of the Otori clan—and because I had carried out the revenge, that love was transferred to me.

It seemed to add to my burdens. I did not want this adulation. I did not deserve it, and I was in no position to live up to it. I bade farewell to the monks, wished them success, and rode on, the head back in its basket.

They did not want me to go alone, and so Makoto came with me. He told me how Yuki had arrived at Terayama with Shigeru's head, and they were preparing the burial rites. She must have traveled day and night to get there so soon, and I thought of her with enormous gratitude.

By evening we were in the temple. Led by the old priest, the monks who remained there were chanting the sutras for Shigeru, and the stone had already been erected over the place where the head was buried. I knelt by it and placed his enemy's head before him. The moon was half-full. In its ethereal light the rocks in the Sesshu garden looked like men praying. The sound of the waterfall seemed louder than by day. Beneath it I could hear the cedars sighing as the night breeze stirred them. Crickets shrilled and frogs were croaking from the pools below the cascade. I heard the beating of wings, and saw the shy hawk owl swoop through the graveyard. Soon it would migrate again; soon summer would be over.

I thought it was a beautiful place for his spirit to rest in. I stayed by the grave for a long time, tears flowing silently. He had told me that only children cry. Men endure, he said, but what seemed unthinkable to me was that I should be the man who would take his place. I was haunted by the conviction that I should not have dealt the deathblow. I had beheaded him with his own sword. I was not his heir: I was his murderer.

I thought longingly of the house in Hagi, with its song of the river and the world. I wanted it to sing that song to my children. I wanted them to grow up beneath its gentle shelter. I daydreamed that Kaede would prepare tea in the room Shigeru built, and our children would try to outwit the nightingale floor. In the evenings we would watch the heron come to the garden, its great gray shape standing patiently in the stream.

In the depths of the garden someone was playing the flute. Its liquid notes pierced my heart. I did not think I would ever recover from my grief.

The days passed, and I could not leave the temple. I knew I must make a decision and leave, but each day I put it off. I was aware that the old priest and Makoto were concerned for me, but they left me alone, apart from looking after me in practical ways, reminding me to eat, to bathe, to sleep.

Every day people came to pray at Shigeru's grave. At first a trickle, then a flood, of returning soldiers, monks, farmers, and peasants filed reverently past the tombstone, prostrating themselves before it, their faces wet with tears. Shigeru had been right: He was even more powerful, and more beloved, in death than in life.

"He will become a god," the old priest predicted. "He will join the others in the shrine."

Night after night I dreamed of Shigeru as I had last seen him, his features streaked with water and blood, and when I woke, my heart pounding with horror, I heard the flute. I began to look forward to the mournful notes as I lay sleepless. I found its music both painful and consoling.

The moon waned; the nights were darker. We heard of the victory at Kushimoto from the returning monks. Life at the temple began to return to normal, the old rituals closing like water over the heads of the dead. Then word came that Lord Arai, who was now master of most of the

Three Countries, was coming to Terayama to pay his respects to Shigeru's grave.

That night, when I heard the flute music, I went to talk to the player. It was, as I had half suspected, Makoto. I was deeply touched that he should have been watching over me, accompanying me in my sorrow.

He was sitting by the pool, where sometimes in the day I had seen him feed the golden carp. He finished the phrase and laid the flute down.

"You will have to come to a decision once Arai is here," he said. "What will you do?"

I sat down next to him. The dew was falling, and the stones were wet. "What should I do?"

"You are Shigeru's heir. You must take up his inheritance." He paused, then said, "But it is not that simple, is it? There is something else that calls you."

"It doesn't exactly call me. It commands me. I am under an obligation. . . . It's hard to explain it to anyone."

"Try me," he said.

"You know I have acute hearing. Like a dog, you once said."

"I shouldn't have said that. It hurt you. Forgive me."

"No, you were right. 'Useful to your masters,' you said. Well, I am useful to my masters, and they are not the Otori."

"The Tribe?"

"You know of them?"

342

"Only a little," he said. "Our abbot mentioned them."

There was a moment when I thought he was going to say something else, that he was waiting for me to ask a question. But I did not know the right question to ask then, and I was too absorbed in my own thoughts, and my own need to explain them.

"My father was of the Tribe, and the talents I have come from him. They have claimed me, as they believe they have the right. I made a bargain with them that they would allow me to rescue Lord Shigeru, and in return I would join them."

"What right do they have to demand that of you, when you are Shigeru's legal heir?" he asked, indignant.

"If I try to escape from them, they will kill me," I replied. "They believe they have that right, and as I made the bargain, I believe it too. My life is theirs."

"You must have made the agreement under duress," he said. "No one will expect you to keep it. You are Otori Takeo. I don't think you realize how famous you have become, how much your name means."

"I killed him," I said, and to my shame felt the tears begin to flow again. "I can never forgive myself. I can't take on his name and his life. He died at my hands."

"You gave him an honorable death," Makoto whispered, taking my hands in his. "You fulfilled

343

every duty a son should to his father. Everywhere you are admired and praised for it. And to kill Iida too. It is the stuff of legends."

"I have not fulfilled every duty," I replied. "His uncles plotted his death with Iida, and they go unpunished. And he charged me to take care of Lady Shirakawa, who has suffered terribly through no fault of her own."

"That would not be too much of a burden," he said, eyeing me ironically, and I felt the blood rise in my face. "I noticed your hands touching," he said, and after a pause: "I notice everything about you."

"I want to fulfil his wishes, yet I feel unworthy. And anyway, I am bound by my oath to the Tribe."

"That could be broken, if you wanted."

Maybe Makoto was right. On the other hand, maybe the Tribe would not let me live. And besides, I could not hide it from myself: Something in me was drawn to them. I kept recalling how I'd felt Kikuta had understood my nature, and how that nature had responded to the dark skills of the Tribe. I was all too aware of the deep divisions within me. I wanted to open my heart to Makoto, but to do so would mean telling him everything, and I could not talk about being born into the Hidden to a monk who was a follower of the Enlightened One. I thought of how I had now broken all the commandments. I had killed many times.

While we spoke in whispers in the darkened garden, the silence broken only by the sudden splash of a fish or the distant hooting of owls, the feeling between us had grown more intense. Now Makoto drew me into his embrace and held me closely. "Whatever you choose, you must let go of your grief," he said. "You did the best you could. Shigeru would have been proud of you. Now you have to forgive, and be proud of, yourself."

His affectionate words, his touch, made the tears flow again. Beneath his hands I felt my body come back to life. He drew me back from the abyss and made me desire to live again. Afterwards, I slept deeply, and did not dream.

Arai came with a few retainers and twenty or so men, leaving the bulk of his army to maintain the peace in the East. He meant to ride on and settle the borders before winter came. He had never been patient; now he was driven. He was younger than Shigeru, about twenty-six, in the prime of manhood, a big man with a quick temper and an iron will. I did not want him as an enemy, and he made no secret of the fact that he wanted me as an ally and would support me against the Otori lords. Moreover, he had already decided that I should marry Kaede.

He had brought her with him, as custom dictated she should visit Shigeru's grave. He thought we should both stay at the temple while arrangements were made for the marriage. Shizuka of course accompanied her and found an opportunity to speak privately to me.

"I knew we'd find you here," she said. "The Kikuta have been furious, but my uncle persuaded them to give you a little more leeway. Your time's running out, though."

"I am ready to go to them," I replied.

"They will come for you tonight."

"Does Lady Shirakawa know?"

"I have tried to warn her, and I have tried to warn Arai." Shizuka's voice was heavy with frustration.

For Arai had very different plans. "You are Shigeru's legal heir," he said as we sat in the guest room of the temple, after he had paid his respects to the grave. "It's entirely fitting that you marry Lady Shirakawa. We will secure Maruyama for her, and then turn our attention to the Otori next spring. I need an ally in Hagi." He was scrutinizing my face. "I don't mind telling you, your reputation makes you a desirable one."

"Lord Arai is too generous," I replied. "However, there are other considerations that may prevent me from complying with your wishes."

"Don't be a fool," he said shortly. "I believe my wishes and yours mesh very well together."

My mind had gone empty: My thoughts had all taken flight like Sesshu's birds. I knew Shizuka would be listening from outside. Arai had been Shigeru's ally; he had protected Kaede; now he had conquered most of the Three Countries. If I owed anyone allegiance, it was to him. I did not think I could just disappear without giving him some explanation.

"Anything I achieved was with the help of the Tribe," I said slowly.

A flicker of anger crossed his face, but he did not speak.

"I made a pact with them, and to keep my side of it, I must give up the Otori name and go with them."

"Who are the Tribe?" he exploded. "Everywhere I turn I run into them. They are like rats in the grain store. Even those closest to me . . . !"

"We could not have defeated Iida without their help," I said.

He shook his large head and sighed. "I don't want to hear this nonsense. You were adopted by Shigeru, you are Otori, you will marry Lady Shirakawa. That is my command."

"Lord Arai." I bowed to the ground, fully aware that I could not obey him.

After visiting the grave, Kaede had returned to the women's guest house and I had no chance to speak to her. I longed to see her but also feared it. I was afraid of her power over me, and mine over her. I was afraid of hurting her and, worse, of not daring to hurt her. That night, sleepless, I went again and sat in the garden, longing for silence but always listening. I knew I would go with Kikuta when he came for me that night, but I could not rid my mind of the image and memory of Kaede, the sight of her next to Iida's body, the feel of her skin against mine, her frailty as I entered her. The idea of never feeling that again was so painful, it took the breath from my lungs.

I heard the soft tread of a woman's feet. Shizuka placed her hand, so like mine in shape and design, on my shoulder and whispered, "Lady Shirakawa wishes to see you."

"I must not," I replied.

"They will be here before dawn," Shizuka said. "I have told her they will never relinquish their claim on you. In fact, because of your disobedience in Inuyama, the master has already decided that if you do not go with them tonight, you will die. She wants to say good-bye."

I followed her. Kaede was sitting at the far end of the veranda, her figure lit dimly by the setting moon. I thought I would recognize her outline anywhere, the shape of her head, the set of her shoulders, the characteristic movement as she turned her face towards me.

The moonlight glinted on her eyes, making them like pools of black mountain water when the snow covers the land and the world is all white and gray. I dropped on my knees before her. The silvery wood smelled of the forest and the shrine, of sap and incense.

"Shizuka says you must leave me, that we cannot be married." Her voice was low and bewildered.

"The Tribe will not allow me to lead that life. I am not—can never now be—a lord of the Otori clan."

"But Arai will protect you. It's what he wants. Nothing need stand in our way."

"I made a deal with the man who is the master of my family," I said. "My life is his from now on."

In that moment, in the silence of the night, I thought of my father, who had tried to escape his blood destiny and had been murdered for it. I did not think my sadness could be any deeper, but this thought dredged out a new level.

Kaede said, "In eight years as a hostage I never asked anyone for anything. Iida Sadamu ordered me to kill myself: I did not plead with him. He was going to rape me: I did not beg for mercy. But I am asking you now: Don't leave me. I am begging you to marry me. I will never ask anyone for anything again."

She threw herself to the ground before me, her hair and her robe touching the floor with a silky hiss. I could smell her perfume. Her hair was so close, it brushed my hands.

"I'm afraid," she whispered. "I'm afraid of myself. I am only safe with you."

It was even more painful than I had anticipated. And what made it worse was the knowledge that if we could just lie together, skin against skin, all pain would cease.

"The Tribe will kill me," I said finally.

"There are worse things than death! If they kill you, I will kill myself and follow you." She took my hands in hers and leaned towards me. Her eyes were burning, her hands dry and hot, the bones as fragile as a bird's. I could feel the blood racing beneath the skin. "If we can't live together we should die together."

Her voice was urgent and excited. The night air seemed suddenly chill. In songs and romances, couples died together for love. I remembered Kenji's words to Shigeru: *You are in love with death, like all your class.* Kaede was of the same class and background, but I was not. I did not want to die. I was not yet eighteen years old.

My silence was enough answer for her. Her eyes searched my face. "I will never love anyone but you," she said.

It seemed we had hardly ever looked directly at each other. Our glances had always been stolen and indirect. Now that we were parting, we could gaze into each other's eyes, beyond modesty or shame. I could feel her pain and her despair. I wanted to ease her suffering, but I could not do what she asked. Out of my confusion, as I held her hands and stared deeply into her eyes, some power came. Her gaze intensified as if she were drowning. Then she sighed and her eyes closed. Her body swayed. Shizuka leaped forward from the shadows and caught her as she fell. Together we lowered her carefully to the floor. She was deeply asleep, as I had been under Kikuta's eyes in the hidden room.

I shivered, suddenly terribly cold.

"You should not have done that," Shizuka whispered.

I knew my cousin was right. "I did not mean

to," I said. "I've never done it to a human being before. Only to dogs."

She slapped me on the arm. "Go to the Kikuta. Go and learn to control your skills. Maybe you'll grow up there."

"Will she be all right?"

"I don't know about these Kikuta things," Shizuka said.

"I slept for twenty-four hours."

"Presumably, whoever put you to sleep knew what they were doing," she retorted.

From far away down the mountain path I could hear people approaching: two men walking quietly, but not quietly enough for me.

"They're coming," I said.

Shizuka knelt beside Kaede and lifted her with her easy strength. "Good-bye, Cousin," she said, her voice still angry.

"Shizuka . . ." I began as she walked towards the room. She stopped for a moment but did not turn.

"My horse, Raku—will you see Lady Shirakawa takes him?" I had nothing else to give her.

Shizuka nodded and moved away into the shadows, out of my sight. I heard the door slide, her tread on the matting, the faint creak of the floor as she laid Kaede down.

I went back to my room and gathered together my belongings. I owned nothing, really: the letter from Shigeru, my knife, and Jato. Then I went to the temple, where Makoto knelt in meditation. I

351

touched him on the shoulder, and he rose and came outside with me.

"I'm leaving," I whispered. "Don't tell anyone before morning."

"You could stay here."

"It's not possible."

"Come back then when you can. We can hide you here. There are so many secret places in the mountains. No one would ever find you."

"Maybe I'll need that one day," I replied. "I want you to keep my sword for me."

He took Jato. "Now I know you'll be back." He put out his hand and traced the outline of my mouth, the edge of bone beneath my cheek, the nape of my neck.

I was light-headed with lack of sleep, with grief and desire. I wanted to lie down and be held by someone, but the footsteps were crossing the gravel now.

"Who's there?" Makoto turned, the sword ready in his hand. "Shall I rouse the temple?"

"No! These are the people I must go with. Lord Arai must not know."

The two of them, my former teacher Muto Kenji and the Kikuta master, waited in the moonlight. They were in traveling clothes, unremarkable, rather impoverished, two brothers perhaps, scholars or unsuccessful merchants. You had to know them as I did to see the alert stance, the hard line of muscle that spoke of their great physical strength, the ears and eyes that missed nothing, the supreme intelligence that made warlords like Iida and Arai seem brutal and clumsy.

I dropped to the ground before the Kikuta master and bowed my head to the dust.

"Stand up, Takeo," he said, and to my surprise both he and Kenji embraced me.

Makoto clasped my hands. "Farewell. I know we'll meet again. Our lives are bound together."

"Show me Lord Shigeru's grave," Kikuta said to me gently, in the way I remembered: as one who understood my true nature.

*But for you he would not be in it,* I thought, but I did not speak it. In the peace of the night I began to accept that it was Shigeru's fate to die the way he did, just as it was his fate now to become a god, a hero to many people, who would come here to the shrine to pray to him, to seek his help, for hundreds of years to come, as long as Terayama stood—maybe forever.

We stood with bowed heads before the newly carved stone. Who knows what Kenji and Kikuta said in their hearts? I asked Shigeru's forgiveness, thanked him again for saving my life in Mino, and bade him farewell. I thought I heard his voice and saw his openhearted smile.

The wind stirred the ancient cedars; the night insects kept up their insistent music. It would always be like this, I thought, summer after summer, winter after winter, the moon sinking towards the west, giving the night back to the stars, and they, in an hour or two, surrendering it to the brightness of the sun.

The sun would pass above the mountains, pulling the shadows of the cedars after it, until it descended again below the rim of the hills. So the world went, and humankind lived on it as best they could, between the darkness and the light.

# ACKNOWLEDGMENTS

The main characters, Takeo and Kaede, came into my head on my first trip to Japan in 1993. Many people have helped me research and realize their story. I would like to thank the Asialink Foundation, who awarded me a fellowship in 1999 to spend three months in Japan, the Australia Council, the Department of Trade and Foreign Affairs and the Australian Embassy in Tokyo, and ArtsSA, the South Australian Government Arts Department. In Japan I was sponsored by Yamaguchi Prefecture's Akiyoshidai International Arts Village whose staff gave me invaluable help in exploring the landscape and the history of Western Honshuu. I would particularly like to thank Mr. Kori Yoshinori, Ms. Matsunaga Yayoi, and Ms. Matsubara Manami. I am especially grateful to Mrs. Tokorigi Masako for showing me the Sesshu paintings and gardens and to her husband, Miki, for information on horses in the medieval period.

Spending time in Japan with two theater companies gave me many insights—deepest thanks to Kazenoko in Tokyo and Kyushuu and Gekidan

Urinko in Nagoya, and to Ms. Kimura Miyo, a wonderful traveling companion, who accompanied me to Kanazawa and the Nakasendo and who has answered many questions for me about language and literature.

I thank Mr. Mogi Masaru and Mrs. Mogi Akiko for their help with research, their suggestions for names, and, above all, their ongoing friendship.

In Australia I would like to thank my two Japanese teachers, Mrs. Thuy Coombes and Mrs. Etsuko Wilson, Simon Higgins, who made some invaluable suggestions, my agent, Jenny Darling, my son Matt, my first reader on all three books, and the rest of my family for not only putting up with but sharing my obsessions.

I would also like to acknowledge the insights and expert knowledge of the samurai history archive on the World Wide Web and members of the discussion forum.

Calligraphy was drawn for me by Ms. Sugiyama Kazuko and Etsuko Wilson. I am immensely grateful to them.

# chemical
## COMPOUNDS

# chemical COMPOUNDS

NEIL SCHLAGER, JAYNE WEISBLATT, AND
DAVID E. NEWTON, *EDITORS*

Charles B. Montney, *Project Editor*

VOLUME **1**

1,3-BUTADIENE–
ETHYL ACETATE

**U·X·L**
*An imprint of Thomson Gale,*
*a part of The Thomson Corporation*

THOMSON
™
GALE

Detroit • New York • San Francisco • San Diego • New Haven, Conn. • Waterville, Maine • London • Munich

# Chemical Compounds

Neil Schlager, Jayne Weisblatt, and David E. Newton, Editors

**Project Editor**
Charles B. Montney

**Editorial**
Luann Brennan, Kathleen J. Edgar, Jennifer Greve, Madeline S. Harris, Melissa Sue Hill, Debra M. Kirby, Kristine Krapp, Elizabeth Manar, Kim McGrath, Paul Lewon, Heather Price, Lemma Shomali

**Indexing Services**
Barbara Koch

**Imaging and Multimedia**
Randy Bassett, Michael Logusz

**Product Design**
Kate Scheible

**Composition**
Evi Seoud, Mary Beth Trimper

**Manufacturing**
Wendy Blurton, Dorothy Maki

**LIBRARY OF CONGRESS CATALOGING-IN-PUBLICATION DATA**

Weisblatt, Jayne.
  Chemical compounds / Jayne Weisblatt ; Charles B. Montney, project editor.
    v. cm.
  Includes bibliographical references and indexes.
  Contents: v. 1. Acetaminophen through Dimethyl ketone -- v. 2. Ethyl acetate through Polypropylene -- v. 3. Polysiloxane through Zinc oxide.
  ISBN 1-4144-0150-7 (set : alk. paper) -- ISBN 1-4144-0451-4 (v. 1 : alk. paper) -- ISBN 1-4144-0452-2 (v. 2 : alk. paper) -- ISBN 1-4144-0453-0 (v. 3 : alk. paper)
  1. Chemicals. 2. Organic compounds. 3. Inorganic compounds. I. Montney, Charles B., 1962- II. Title.
  QD471.W45 2006
  540--dc22
                                                      2005023636

This title is also available as an e-book
ISBN 1-4144-0467-0
Contact your Thomson Gale sales representative for ordering information.

Printed in China
10 9 8 7 6 5 4 3 2 1

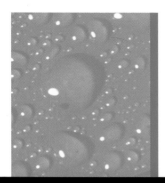

# contents

**volume I**

*Reader's Guide* . . . . . . . . . . . . . . . . . . . xiii

*Timeline of the Development of*

*Chemical Compounds* . . . . . . . . . . . . . .xxi

*Words to Know* . . . . . . . . . . . . . . . .xxxvii

1,3-Butadiene . . . . . . . . . . . . . . . . . . . . I

2,2′-Dichlorodiethyl Sulfide . . . . . . . . . . 5

2-(4-Isobutylphenyl)propionic Acid . . . . . 9

2,4,6-Trinitrotoluene . . . . . . . . . . . . 15

Acetaminophen . . . . . . . . . . . . . . . . 19

Acetic acid . . . . . . . . . . . . . . . . . . 23

Acetylene . . . . . . . . . . . . . . . . . . . 27

Acetylsalicylic acid . . . . . . . . . . . . . . 31

Alpha-Tocopherol . . . . . . . . . . . . . . 37

Aluminum Fluoride . . . . . . . . . . . . . . 41

Aluminum Hydroxide . . . . . . . . . . . . 45

Aluminum Oxide . . . . . . . . . . . . . . . 49

Aluminum Potassium Sulfate . . . . . . . . 53

Ammonia . . . . . . . . . . . . . . . . . . . 57

Ammonium Chloride . . . . . . . . . . . . . 63

Ammonium Hydroxide . . . . . . . . . . . . 69

Ammonium Nitrate . . . . . . . . . . . . . . 73

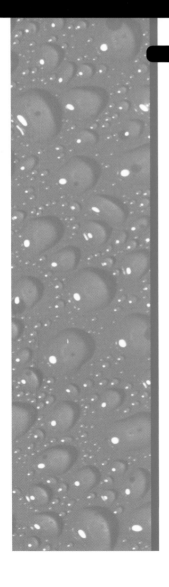

Contents

Ammonium Sulfate . . . . . . . . . . . . . . . . 77

Amoxicillin . . . . . . . . . . . . . . . . . . . 81

Amyl Acetate . . . . . . . . . . . . . . . . . . 85

Amyl Nitrite . . . . . . . . . . . . . . . . . . 89

Ascorbic Acid . . . . . . . . . . . . . . . . . 93

Benzene . . . . . . . . . . . . . . . . . . . . 99

Benzoic Acid . . . . . . . . . . . . . . . . . 105

Beta-Carotene . . . . . . . . . . . . . . . . . 109

Boric Acid . . . . . . . . . . . . . . . . . . . 115

Butane . . . . . . . . . . . . . . . . . . . . . 119

Butyl Acetate . . . . . . . . . . . . . . . . . 125

Butyl Mercaptan . . . . . . . . . . . . . . . . 129

Butylated Hydroxyanisole and Butylated
    Hydroxytoluene . . . . . . . . . . . . . . 133

Caffeine . . . . . . . . . . . . . . . . . . . . 137

Calcium Carbonate . . . . . . . . . . . . . . 143

Calcium Hydroxide . . . . . . . . . . . . . . 147

Calcium Oxide . . . . . . . . . . . . . . . . . 151

Calcium Phosphate . . . . . . . . . . . . . . 155

Calcium Silicate . . . . . . . . . . . . . . . . 161

Calcium Sulfate . . . . . . . . . . . . . . . . 165

Camphor . . . . . . . . . . . . . . . . . . . . 171

Carbon Dioxide . . . . . . . . . . . . . . . . 177

Carbon Monoxide . . . . . . . . . . . . . . . 183

Carbon Tetrachloride . . . . . . . . . . . . . 189

Cellulose . . . . . . . . . . . . . . . . . . . . 195

Cellulose Nitrate . . . . . . . . . . . . . . . . 201

Cellulose Xanthate . . . . . . . . . . . . . . . 207

Chloroform . . . . . . . . . . . . . . . . . . . 211

Chlorophyll . . . . . . . . . . . . . . . . . . . 217

Cholesterol . . . . . . . . . . . . . . . . . . . 223

Cinnamaldehyde . . . . . . . . . . . . . . . . 229

Citric Acid . . . . . . . . . . . . . . . . . . . 233

Collagen . . . . . . . . . . . . . . . . . . . . 239

Copper(I) Oxide . . . . . . . . . . . . . . 243

Copper(II) Oxide . . . . . . . . . . . . . . 247

Copper(II) Sulfate . . . . . . . . . . . . . .251

Cumene . . . . . . . . . . . . . . 255

Cyanoacrylate . . . . . . . . . . . . . . 259

Cyanocobalamin . . . . . . . . . . . . . . 265

Denatonium Benzoate . . . . . . . . . . . . . .271

Dichlorodifluoromethane . . . . . . . . . . . . . . 277

Dichlorodiphenyltrichloroethane . . . . . . . . . . 283

Dimethyl Ketone . . . . . . . . . . . . . . 289

Ethyl Acetate . . . . . . . . . . . . . . 293

*Compounds by Formula* . . . . . . . . . . . . . .liii

*Compounds by Element* . . . . . . . . . . . . . lix

*Compounds by Type* . . . . . . . . . . . . . .lxv

*For Further Information* . . . . . . . . . . . . . lxix

*Index* . . . . . . . . . . . . . . lxxix

**volume 2** *Reader's Guide* . . . . . . . . . . . . . . . . . xiii

*Timeline of the Development of*

   *Chemical Compounds* . . . . . . . . . . . . . .xxi

*Words to Know* . . . . . . . . . . . . .xxxvii

Ethyl Alcohol . . . . . . . . . . . . . . 297

Ethylbenzene . . . . . . . . . . . . . . 303

Ethylene . . . . . . . . . . . . . . 307

Ethylene Glycol . . . . . . . . . . . . . .313

Ethylene Oxide . . . . . . . . . . . . . .317

Folic Acid . . . . . . . . . . . . . .321

Formaldehyde . . . . . . . . . . . . . . 325

Fructose . . . . . . . . . . . . . . 329

Gamma-1,2,3,4,5,6-Hexachlorocyclohexane . . . 333

Gelatin . . . . . . . . . . . . . . 337

Glucose . . . . . . . . . . . . . . 343

# Contents

Glycerol . . . . . . . . . . . . . . . . . 349

Hexane . . . . . . . . . . . . . . . . . . 353

Hydrogen Chloride . . . . . . . . . . . . 357

Hydrogen Peroxide . . . . . . . . . . . . 363

Iron(II) Oxide . . . . . . . . . . . . . . 367

Iron(III) Oxide . . . . . . . . . . . . . . 371

Isoamyl Acetate . . . . . . . . . . . . . 377

Isoprene . . . . . . . . . . . . . . . . . 381

Isopropyl Alcohol . . . . . . . . . . . . . 387

Lactic Acid . . . . . . . . . . . . . . . . 391

Lactose . . . . . . . . . . . . . . . . . . 397

L-Aspartyl-L-Phenylalanine Methyl Ester . . . . 401

Luminol . . . . . . . . . . . . . . . . . 407

Magnesium Chloride . . . . . . . . . . . . 411

Magnesium Hydroxide . . . . . . . . . . . 415

Magnesium Oxide . . . . . . . . . . . . . 419

Magnesium Silicate Hydroxide . . . . . . . 423

Magnesium Sulfate . . . . . . . . . . . . 429

Menthol . . . . . . . . . . . . . . . . . 435

Mercury(II) Sulfide . . . . . . . . . . . . 439

Methane . . . . . . . . . . . . . . . . . 443

Methyl Alcohol . . . . . . . . . . . . . . 449

Methyl Mercaptan . . . . . . . . . . . . . 455

Methyl-t-butyl Ether . . . . . . . . . . . . 459

Monosodium Glutamate . . . . . . . . . . 465

N,N-Diethyl-3-Methylbenzamide . . . . . . . 469

Naphthalene . . . . . . . . . . . . . . . 473

Naproxen . . . . . . . . . . . . . . . . . 477

Niacin . . . . . . . . . . . . . . . . . . 483

Nicotine . . . . . . . . . . . . . . . . . 487

Nitric Acid . . . . . . . . . . . . . . . . 493

Nitric Oxide . . . . . . . . . . . . . . . 497

Nitrogen Dioxide . . . . . . . . . . . . . 503

Nitroglycerin . . . . . . . . . . . . . . . 507

Nitrous Oxide . . . . . . . . . . . . . . . . . .513

Nylon 6 and Nylon 66 . . . . . . . . . . . . . .519

Oxalic Acid . . . . . . . . . . . . . . . . . . 525

Pectin . . . . . . . . . . . . . . . . . . . . .531

Penicillin . . . . . . . . . . . . . . . . . . 535

Perchlorates . . . . . . . . . . . . . . . . . .541

Petrolatum . . . . . . . . . . . . . . . . . . 547

Petroleum . . . . . . . . . . . . . . . . . . . 553

Phenol . . . . . . . . . . . . . . . . . . . . 559

Phosphoric Acid . . . . . . . . . . . . . . . . 565

Poly(Styrene-Butadiene-Styrene) . . . . . . . .571

Polycarbonates . . . . . . . . . . . . . . . . 575

Polyethylene . . . . . . . . . . . . . . . . . 579

Polymethyl Methacrylate . . . . . . . . . . . . 583

Polypropylene . . . . . . . . . . . . . . . . . 587

Polysiloxane . . . . . . . . . . . . . . . . . .591

*Compounds by Formula* . . . . . . . . . . . . .liii

*Compounds by Element* . . . . . . . . . . . . . lix

*Compounds by Type* . . . . . . . . . . . . . .lxv

*For Further Information* . . . . . . . . . . . lxix

*Index* . . . . . . . . . . . . . . . . . . . . lxxix

**volume 3** *Reader's Guide* . . . . . . . . . . . . . . . . . xiii

*Timeline of the Development of*

*Chemical Compounds* . . . . . . . . . . . . .xxi

*Words to Know* . . . . . . . . . . . . . . . .xxxvii

Polystyrene . . . . . . . . . . . . . . . . . . 597

Polytetrafluoroethylene . . . . . . . . . . . . 603

Polyurethane . . . . . . . . . . . . . . . . . 609

Polyvinyl Chloride . . . . . . . . . . . . . . .615

Potassium Bicarbonate . . . . . . . . . . . . .621

Potassium Bisulfate . . . . . . . . . . . . . . 625

Contents

Potassium Bitartrate . . . . . . . . . . . . . . . 629

Potassium Carbonate . . . . . . . . . . . . . . 633

Potassium Chloride . . . . . . . . . . . . . . . . 639

Potassium Fluoride . . . . . . . . . . . . . . . . 643

Potassium Hydroxide . . . . . . . . . . . . . . 647

Potassium Iodide . . . . . . . . . . . . . . . . . .651

Potassium Nitrate . . . . . . . . . . . . . . . . . 655

Potassium Sulfate . . . . . . . . . . . . . . . . . 659

Propane . . . . . . . . . . . . . . . . . . . . . . . . 663

Propylene . . . . . . . . . . . . . . . . . . . . . . . 669

Pyridoxine . . . . . . . . . . . . . . . . . . . . . . 673

Retinol . . . . . . . . . . . . . . . . . . . . . . . . . 677

Riboflavin . . . . . . . . . . . . . . . . . . . . . . . 683

Saccharin . . . . . . . . . . . . . . . . . . . . . . . 689

Silicon Dioxide . . . . . . . . . . . . . . . . . . 695

Silver Iodide . . . . . . . . . . . . . . . . . . . . .701

Silver Nitrate . . . . . . . . . . . . . . . . . . . . 705

Silver(I) Oxide . . . . . . . . . . . . . . . . . . . 711

Silver(I) Sulfide . . . . . . . . . . . . . . . . . . 715

Sodium Acetate . . . . . . . . . . . . . . . . . .719

Sodium Bicarbonate . . . . . . . . . . . . . . 723

Sodium Carbonate . . . . . . . . . . . . . . . . 729

Sodium Chloride . . . . . . . . . . . . . . . . . 735

Sodium Cyclamate . . . . . . . . . . . . . . . .741

Sodium Fluoride . . . . . . . . . . . . . . . . . 747

Sodium Hydroxide . . . . . . . . . . . . . . . 753

Sodium Hypochlorite . . . . . . . . . . . . . 759

Sodium Perborate . . . . . . . . . . . . . . . . 765

Sodium Phosphate . . . . . . . . . . . . . . . 769

Sodium Polyacrylate . . . . . . . . . . . . . . 773

Sodium Silicate . . . . . . . . . . . . . . . . . . 779

Sodium Sulfite . . . . . . . . . . . . . . . . . . . 785

Sodium Tetraborate . . . . . . . . . . . . . . . 789

Sodium Thiosulfate . . . . . . . . . . . . . . . 795

Stannous Fluoride . . . . . . . . . . . . . . . 799

Styrene . . . . . . . . . . . . . . . . . . . 803

Sucrose . . . . . . . . . . . . . . . . . . . 807

Sucrose Polyester . . . . . . . . . . . . . . .813

Sulfur Dioxide . . . . . . . . . . . . . . . .819

Sulfuric Acid . . . . . . . . . . . . . . . . 825

Tannic Acid . . . . . . . . . . . . . . . . . .831

Testosterone . . . . . . . . . . . . . . . . 837

Theobromine . . . . . . . . . . . . . . . . 843

Thiamine . . . . . . . . . . . . . . . . . . 847

Toluene . . . . . . . . . . . . . . . . . . . 853

Triclocarban . . . . . . . . . . . . . . . . . 859

Triclosan . . . . . . . . . . . . . . . . . . 863

Urea . . . . . . . . . . . . . . . . . . . . 867

Vanillin . . . . . . . . . . . . . . . . . . . 873

Water . . . . . . . . . . . . . . . . . . . . 879

Zinc Oxide . . . . . . . . . . . . . . . . . . 885

*Compounds by Formula* . . . . . . . . . . . .liii

*Compounds by Element* . . . . . . . . . . . . lix

*Compounds by Type* . . . . . . . . . . . . .lxv

*For Further Information* . . . . . . . . . . . lxix

*Index* . . . . . . . . . . . . . . . . . . . lxxix

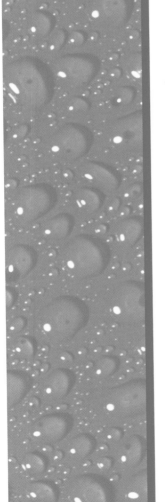

# reader's guide

Water; sugar; nylon; vitamin C. These substances are all very different from each other. But they all share one property in common: They are all chemical compounds. A chemical compound consists of two or more chemical elements, joined to each other by a force known as a chemical bond.

This book describes 180 chemical compounds, some familiar to almost everyone, and some less commonly known. Each description includes some basic chemical and physical information about the compound, such as its chemical formula, other names by which the compound is known, and the molecular weight, melting point, freezing point, and solubility of the compound. Here are some things to know about each of these properties:

Other Names: Many chemical compounds have more than one name. Compounds that have been known for many centuries often have common names that may still be used in industry, the arts, or some other field. For example, muriatic acid is a very old name for the compound now called hydrochloric acid. The name remains in common use today. Marine acid and spirit of salt are other ancient names for hydrochloric acid, but they are seldom used in the modern world. All compounds have systematic names, names based on a set of rules devised by the International Union of Pure and Applied Chemistry (IUPAC). For example, the systematic name for the poisonous gas whose common name is mustard gas is 2,2'-dichlorodiethyl sulfide. When chemists talk about chemical compounds, they usually use only the official IUPAC name for a compound since that name leaves no doubt as to the substance about which they are talking. In some cases, a compound may have more than one official name, depending on the set of rules used in the naming process. For example, 1,1′-thiobis[2-chloroethane] is also an acceptable name for mustard gas. The "Other Names" section of each entry lists both the systematic (IUPAC) and common names for a compound.

Many compounds also have another kind of name, a brand name or trade name given to them by their manufacturers. For example, some trade names for the pain killer acetaminophen are Panadol™, Tylenol™, Aceta™, Genapap™, Tempra™, and Depacin™. The symbol next to each name means that the name is registered to the company that makes the compound. Trades names may be mentioned in the Overview or Uses sections of the entry for each compound.

Chemical Formula: A chemical formula is a set of symbols that tells the elements present in a compound and the relative numbers of each element. For example, the chemical formula for the compound carbon dioxide is $CO_2$. That formula tells that for every one carbon atom (C) in carbon dioxide there are two atoms of oxygen (O).

Chemists use different kinds of formulas to describe a compound. The simplest formula is a molecular formula. A molecular formula like $CO_2$ tells the kind and relative number of elements present in the compound. Another kind of formula is a structural formula. A structural formula provides one additional piece of information: The arrangement of elements in a compound. The structural formula for methanol (wood alcohol), for example, is $CH_3OH$. That formula shows that methanol consists of a carbon atom (C) to which are attached three hydrogen (H) atoms ($CH_3$). The carbon atom is also joined to an oxygen atom (O) which, in turn, is attached to a hydrogen atom (H).

Structural formulas can be written in a variety of ways. Another way to draw the structural formula for methanol, for example, is to show where individual bonds between atoms branch off other atoms in different directions. These structural formulas can be seen on the first page of nearly all entries in *Chemical Compounds*. In a third type of structural formula, the ball-and-stick formula, each element is represented by a ball of some size, shape, and/or color. The chemical bond that holds them together is represented by sticks. This can be represented on paper in a drawing that simulates a three-dimensional model, by computer software, or actually in three dimensions from a kit with balls and sticks.

All three kinds of structural formulas are given for each compound described in this book. The only exception is some very large compounds known as polymers that contain many hundreds or thousands of atoms. In such cases, the formulas given shown only one small segment of the compound.

Compound Type: Millions of chemical compounds exist. To make the study of these compounds easier, chemists divide them into a number of categories. Nearly all compounds can be classified as either organic or inorganic. Organic compounds contain the element carbon; inorganic compounds do not. A few important exceptions to that rule exist, as indicated in the description of such compounds.

Both organic and inorganic compounds can be further divided into more limited categories, sometimes called families of compounds. Some families of organic compounds are the hydrocarbons (made of carbon and hydrogen only), alcohols (containing the -OH group), and carboxylic acids (containing the -COOH groups). Many interesting and important organic compounds belong to the polymer family. Polymers consist of very large molecules in which a single small unit (called the monomer) is repeated hundreds or thousands of times over. Some polymers are made from two or, rarely, three monomers joined to each other in long chains.

Most inorganic compounds can be classified into one of four major groups. Those groups are the acids (all of which contain at least one hydrogen (H) atom), bases (which all have a hydroxide (OH) group), oxides (which all have an oxygen (O)), and salts (which include almost everything else). A few organic and inorganic compounds described in this book do not easily fit into any of these families. They are classified simply as organic or inorganic.

Molecular Weight: The molecular weight of a compound is equal to the weight of all the elements of which it is made. The molecular weight of carbon dioxide ($CO_2$), for example, is equal to the atomic weight of carbon (12) plus two times the atomic weight of oxygen (2 x 16 = 32), or 44. Chemists have been studying atomic weights and molecular weights for a long time, and the molecular weights of most compounds are now known with a high degree of certainty. The molecular weights expressed in this book are taken from the *Handbook of Chemistry and Physics*, 86th edition, published in 2005. The Handbook is one of the oldest, most widely used, and most highly regarded reference books in chemistry.

Melting Point and Boiling Point: The melting point of a compound is the temperature at which it changes from a solid to a liquid. Its boiling point is the temperature at which it changes from a liquid to a gas. Most organic compounds have precise melting points and/or, sometimes, precise boiling points. This fact is used to identify organic compounds. Suppose a chemist finds that a certain unknown compound melts at exactly 16.5°C. Reference books show that only a small number of compounds melt at exactly that temperature (one of which is capryllic acid, responsible for the distinctive odor of some goats). This information helps the chemist identify the unknown compound.

Inorganic compounds usually do not have such precise melting points. In fact, they may melt over a range of temperatures (from 50°C to 55°C, for example) or sublime without melting. Sublimation is the process by which a substance changes from a solid to gas without going through the liquid phase. Other inorganic compounds decompose, or break apart, when heated and do not have a true melting point.

Researchers often find different melting points and boiling points for the same compound, depending on the reference book they use. The reason for this discrepancy is that many scientists have measured the melting points and boiling points of compounds. Those scientists do not always get the same result. So, it is difficult to know what the "true" or "most correct" value is for these properties. In this book, the melting points and boiling points stated are taken from the *Handbook of Chemistry and Physics*.

Some compounds, for a variety of reasons, have no specific melting or boiling point. The term "not applicable" is used to indicate this fact.

Solubility: The solubility of a compound is its tendency to dissolve in some (usually) liquid, such as water, alcohol, or acetone. Solubility is an important property because most chemical reactions occur only when the reactants (the substances reacting with each other) are dissolved. The most common solvent for inorganic compounds is water. The most common solvents for organic compounds are the so-called organic solvents, which include alcohol, ether, acetone, and benzene. The solubility section in the entry for each compound lists the solvents in which it will dissolve well (listed as "soluble"), to a slight extent ("slightly soluble"), or not at all ("insoluble").

Overview: The overview provides a general introduction to the compound, with a pronunciation of its name, a brief history of its discovery and/or use, and other general information.

How It Is Made: This section explains how the compound is extracted from the earth or from natural materials and/or how it is made synthetically (artificially). Some production methods are difficult to describe because they include reactants (beginning compounds) with difficult chemical names not familiar to most people with little or no background in chemistry. Readers with a special interest in the synthesis (artificial production) of these compounds should consult their local librarian or a chemistry teacher at a local high school or college for references that contain more information on the process in question. The For Further Information section may also contain this information.

Interesting Facts This section contains facts and tidbits of information about compounds that may not be essential to a chemist, an inventor, or some other scientific specialist, but may be of interest to the general reader.

Common Uses and Potential Hazards Chemical compounds are often of greatest interest because of the way they can be used in medicine, industry, or some other practical application. This section lists the most important uses of each compound described in the book.

All chemical compounds pose some risk to humans. One might think that water, sugar, and salt are the safest compounds in the world. But, of course, one can drown in water, become seriously overweight by eating too much sugar, and develop heart problems by using too much salt. The risk posed by a chemical compound really depends on a number of factors, one of the most important of which is the amount of the compound to which one is exposed. The safest rule to follow in dealing with chemical compounds is that they are ALL dangerous under some circumstances. One should always avoid spilling any chemical compound on the skin, inhaling its fumes, or swallowing any of the compound. If an accident of this kind occurs, one should seek professional medical advice immediately. This book is not a substitute for prompt first aid properly applied.

Having said all that, some compounds do pose more serious health threats than others, and some individuals are at greater risks than others. Those special health risks are mentioned toward the end of the "Common Uses and Potential Hazards" section of each entry.

For Further Information As the name suggests, this section provides ideas for books, articles, and Internet sources that provide additional information on the chemical compound listed.

## ADDED FEATURES

*Chemical Compounds* contains several features to help answer questions related to compounds, their properties, and their uses.

- The book contains three appendixes: a list by formula, list by element contained in compounds, and list by type of compound.

- Each entry contains up to two illustrations to show the relationship of the atoms in a compound to each other, one a black and white structural formula, and one a color ball-and-stick model of a molecule or portion of a molecule of the compound.

- A chronology and timeline in each volume locates significant dates in the development of chemical compounds with other historical events.

- "For Further Information," a list of useful books, periodicals, and websites, provides links to further learning opportunities.

- The comprehensive index, which appears in each volume, quickly points readers to compounds, people, and events mentioned throughout *Chemical Compounds*.

## ACKNOWLEDGMENTS

In compiling this reference, the editors have been fortunate in being able to rely upon the expertise and contributions of the following educators who served as advisors:

Ruth Mormon, Media Specialist, The Meadows School, Las Vegas, Nevada

Cathy Chauvette, Sherwood Regional Library, Alexandria, Virginia

Jan Sarratt, John E. Ewing Middle School, Gaffney, South Carolina

Rachel Badanowski, Southfield High School, Southfield, Michigan

The editors would also like to thank the artists of Publishers Resource Group, under the lead of Farley Pedini, for their fast and accurate work and grace under pressure.

## COMMENTS AND SUGGESTIONS

We welcome your comments on *Chemical Compounds.* Please write: Editors, *Chemical Compounds*, U•X•L, 27500 Drake Rd., Farmington Hills, MI 48331; call toll-free 1-800-877-4253; fax, 248-699-8097; or send e-mail via http://www.gale.com.

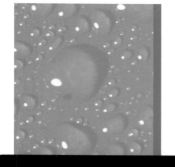

# timeline of the development of chemical compounds

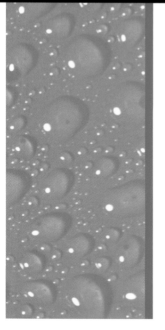

C. 3000 BCE • Egyptians develop a method for converting gypsum to plaster of Paris, which is then used as mortar to join blocks in buildings.

C. 2700 BCE • Chinese documents mention sodium chloride and the consumption of tea.

C. 1550 BCE • The analgesic properties of willow tree bark, from which salicylic acid comes, are described in Egyptian scrolls.

C. 1000 BCE • Ancient Egyptians use dried peppermint leaves.

800 BCE • Chinese and Arabic civilizations use borax for making glass and in jewelry work.

510 BCE • Persian emperor Darius makes the first recorded reference to sugar when he refers to the sugar cane growing on the banks of the Indus River.

184 BCE • Roman writer Cato the Elder describes a method of producing calcium oxide.

c. 1st century CE • Roman philosopher Pliny the Elder writes about a substance he calls hammoniacus sal, which appears to have been ammonium chloride.

1st century CE • The first recipes calling for the use of pectin to make jams and jellies are recorded.

c. 575 CE • The cultivation of the coffee tree begins in Africa.

659 • Cinnamaldehyde is described in the famous Chinese medical text, the *Tang Materia Medica.*

8th century • Arabian chemist Abu Musa Jabir ibn Hayyan, also known as Geber, writes about his work with several compounds, such as sodium chloride, sulfuric acid, nitric acid, citric acid, and acetic acid.

1242 • English natural philosopher Roger Bacon describes a method for making gunpowder.

Late 1200s • First mention of camphor by a Westerner occurs in the writings of Marco Polo.

| | | 8TH CENTURY | C. 6 BCE | 622 |
|---|---|---|---|---|
| | | BCE | Jesus of | Mohammed's |
| 4000 BCE | | First recorded | Nazareth | flight from |
| Iron Age begins | | Olympic Games. | is born. | Mecca to Medina. |
| in Egypt. | | | | |

| 4000 BCE | 3000 BCE | 2000 BCE | 1000 BCE | 1 CE | 500 |
|---|---|---|---|---|---|

1300s • Potassium sulfate becomes known to alchemists.

1500s • Spanish explorers bring vanilla to Europe from South and Central America, where it had already been used to flavor food.

1603 • Flemish chemist Jan Baptista van Helmont isolates a new gas produced during the combustion of wood, which is eventually called carbon dioxide.

1608 • Potash is one of the first chemicals to be exported by American colonists, with shipments leaving Jamestown, Virginia.

1610 • French alchemist Jean Béguin prepares acetone.

1620 • Flemish physician and alchemist Jan Baptista van Helmont first discovers nitric oxide.

1625 • German chemist Johann Rudolf Glauber is believed to have been the first to produce hydrogen chloride in a reasonably pure form. Later he is first to make ammonium nitrate artificially.

1695 • The term *Epsom salts* is introduced by British naturalist Nehemiah Grew, who names the compound after the spring waters near Epsom, England, from which it was often extracted.

1096–1099
First Crusade

1215
Magna Carta
accepted by King
John of England.

1492
Christopher
Columbus sails
to the Americas.

1620
Pilgrims land at
Plymouth, Mass.

| 1000 | 1200 | 1400 | 1500 | 1600 | 1700 |

1700 • German chemist Georg Ernst Stahl extracts acetic acid from vinegar by distillation.

1702 • German chemist Wilhelm Homberg is believed to be the first person to prepare boric acid in Europe.

1720s • German chemist Johann Schulze makes discoveries that lead to using silver nitrate in printing and photography.

1746 • The first commercially successful method for making sulfuric acid is developed.

1747 • German chemist Andreas Sigismund Marggraf isolates a sweet substance from raisins that comes to be known as glucose.

1753 • James Lind reports that citrus fruits are the most effective means of preventing scurvy.

1769 • Oxalic acid is first isolated by German chemist Johann Christian Wiegleb.

1770s • British chemist Joseph Priestly does pioneering work with the compounds carbon dioxide, carbon monoxide, hydrogen chloride, and nitrous oxide, among others.

1770s • Swedish chemist Karl Wilhelm Scheele discovers and works with phosphoric acid, glycerol, lactic acid, and potassium bitartrate.

1726
Czar Peter the Great
of Russia dies.

1754
French and Indian
War begins in
North America.

| 1700 | 1710 | 1720 | 1730 | 1740 | 1750 |

1773 • French chemist Hilaire Marin Rouelle identifies urea as a component of urine.

Late 1700s • Commercial production of sodium bicarbonate as baking soda begins.

1776 • Carbon monoxide is first prepared synthetically by French chemist Joseph Marie François de Lassone, although he mistakenly identifies it as hydrogen.

1790 • The first patent ever issued in the United States is awarded to Samuel Hopkins for a new and better way of making pearl ash.

1794 • Ethylene is first prepared by a group of Dutch chemists.

Early 1800s • Silver iodide is first used in photography by French experimenter Louis Daguerre.

1817–1821 • French chemists Joseph Bienaimé Caventou and Pierre Joseph Pelletier successfully extract caffeine, quinine, strychnine, brucine, chinchonine, and chlorophyll from a variety of plants.

1817 • Irish pharmacist Sir James Murray uses magnesium hydroxide in water to treat stomach and other ailments. The compound is eventually called milk of magnesia.

1776
The U.S. Declaration
of Independence is
signed.

1789
French Revolution

1793
Cotton gin is
invented by
Eli Whitney.

1811–1812
Three severe
earthquakes
occur near New
Madrid, Missouri.

1812.
War of 1812
begins.

| 1760 | 1770 | 1780 | 1790 | 1800 | 1810 |

1818 • Hydrogen peroxide is discovered by French chemist Louis Jacques Thénard.

1819 • French naturalist Henri Braconnot discovers cellulose.

1825 • British chemist and physicist Michael Faraday discovers "bicarburet of hydrogen," which is later called benzene.

1830 • Peregrine Phillips, a British vinegar merchant from England, develops the contact process for making sulfuric acid. In the early 21st century it is still the most common way to make sulfuric acid.

1831 • Chloroform is discovered almost simultaneously by American, French, and German chemists. Its use as an anesthetic is discovered in 1847.

1831 • Beta-carotene is first isolated by German chemist Heinrich Wilhelm Ferdinand Wackenroder.

1834 • Cellulose is first isolated and analyzed by French botanist Anselme Payen.

1835 • Polyvinyl chloride is first discovered accidentally by French physicist and chemist Henry Victor Regnault. PVC is rediscovered (again accidentally) in 1926.

1819
U.S. acquires
Florida from
Spain.

1820
The Missouri
Compromise
is enacted.

1823
U.S. president
James Monroe
proclaims the
Monroe Doctrine.

1831
Cyrus McCormick's
reaper is introduced.

1810          1820          1830

1836 • British chemist Edmund Davy discovers acetylene.

1838 • French chemist Pierre Joseph Pelletier discovers toluene.

1839 • German-born French chemist Henri Victor Regnault first prepares carbon tetrachloride.

1839 • German druggist Eduard Simon discovers styrene in petroleum.

1845 • Swiss-German chemist Christian Friedrich Schönbein discovers cellulose nitrate.

1846 • Americans Austin Church and John Dwight form a company to make and sell sodium bicarbonate. The product will become known as Arm & Hammer® baking soda.

Mid 1800s • Hydrogen peroxide is first used commercially—primarily to bleach hats.

1850s • Oil is first discovered in the United States in western Pennsylvania.

1846
Mexican-
American
War begins.

1847
Gold
discovered
in California.

1850
Levi Strauss
manufactures
his first pair
of jeans.

1858
Lincoln debates
Douglas in Illinois
senate campaign.

1840                    1850                    1860

1853 • French chemist Charles Frederick Gerhardt develops a method for reacting salicylic acid (the active ingredient in salicin) with acetic acid to make the first primitive form of aspirin.

1859 • Ethylene glycol and ethylene oxide are first prepared by French chemist Charles Adolphe Wurtz.

1860s • Swedish chemist Alfred Nobel develops a process for manufacturing nitroglycerin on a large scale.

1863 • TNT is discovered by German chemist Joseph Wilbrand, although the compound is not recognized as an explosive until nearly 30 years later.

1865 • The use of carbolic acid as an antiseptic is first suggested by Sir Joseph Lister.

1865 • German botanist Julius von Sachs demonstrates that chlorophyll is responsible for photosynthetic reactions that take place within the cells of leaves.

1870 • American chemist Robert Augustus Chesebrough extracts and purifies petrolatum from petroleum and begins manufacturing it, eventually using the name Vaseline™.

1873 • German chemist Harmon Northrop Morse rediscovers and synthesizes acetaminophen. It had been discovered originally in 1852, but at the time it was ignored.

| 1861 American Civil War starts. | 1866 Mendel discovers laws of heredity. | 1869 Dmitri Mendeleev formulates the periodic law. | 1876 Alexander Graham Bell patents the telephone. | 1884 Worldwide system of standard time is adopted. |

1860         1870         1880

1879 • Saccharin, the first artificial sweetener discovered, is synthesized accidentally by Johns Hopkins researchers Constantine Fahlberg and Ira Remsen.

1879 • Riboflavin is first observed by British chemist Alexander Wynter Blyth.

1883 • Copper(I) oxide is the first substance found to have semiconducting properties.

1886 • American chemist Charles Martin Hall invents a method for making aluminum metal from aluminum oxide, which drastically cuts the price of aluminum.

1889 • French physiologist Charles E. Brown-Séquard performs early experiments on the effects of testosterone.

1890s • Commercial production of perchlorates begins.

1890s-early 1900s • British chemists Charles Frederick Cross, Edward John Bevan, and Clayton Beadle identify the compound now known as cellulose. They also develop rayon.

Late 1890s • Artificial methods of the production of pure vanillin are developed.

1901 • The effects of fluorides in preventing tooth decay are first observed.

1888
George Eastman
introduces the
Kodak camera.

1896
Henry Ford
assembles the
first motor car.

1901
The first Nobel
prizes are awarded.

1890

1900

1910

1904 • German physicist Wilhelm Hallwachs discovers that a combination of copper metal and copper(I) oxide displays the photoelectric effect.

1910 • The first plant for the manufacture of rayon in the United States is built. By 1925 rayon becomes more popular than silk.

1910 • Japanese scientist Suzuki Umetaro discovers thiamine.

1912 • Nicotinic acid is first isolated by Polish-American biochemist Casimir Funk.

1914–1917 • Ethylene glycol is manufactured for use in World War I in explosives and as a solvent.

1914–1918 • A shortage of sugar during World War I leads to the reintroduction of saccharin to sweeten food. Saccharin production would boom again during World War II.

Late 1910s • Mustard gas is first used in war. Later it is found to be effective in treating cancer in experimental animals.

1922 • Vitamin E is discovered by two scientists at the University of California at Berkeley.

---

1905
Einstein formulates the theory of relativity.

1912
The *Titanic* sinks on her maiden voyage.

1914–1918
World War I

1919
First man-made nuclear reaction occurs.

1922
Soviet Union comes into existance.

1910                    1915                    1920

1928 • Polymethylmethacrylate (PMMA) is first synthesized in the laboratories of the German chemical firm Röhm and Haas.

1928 • Scottish bacteriologist Alexander Fleming accidentally discovers penicillin.

1930 • DuPont begins manufacturing dichlorodifluoro-methane under the name Freon®.

1930 • A polymer based on styrene is produced by researchers at the German chemical firm I. G. Farben. Polystyrene comes to the United States in 1937.

1930s • Properties and methods of synthesizing many vita-mins, such as riboflavin, thiamine, niacin, ascorbic acid, pyridoxine, alpha-tocopherol, and retinol, are developed.

Early 1930s • SBS is first developed by German chemists Walter Bock and Eduard Tschunkur.

1933 • British chemists Reginald Gibson and Eric Fawcett accidentally re-discover polyethylene, which was first discovered in 1889.

1935 • Nylon is invented by Wallace Carothers. It is used in consumer products within three years.

1935 • German chemist Adolf Friedrich Johann Butenandt synthesizes testosterone.

1927
Charles Lindbergh
flies solo across the
Atlantic Ocean.

1929
The Great
Depression
begins

1925                                          1930                                          1935

1937 • German forensic scientist Walter Specht discovers that blood can act as the catalyst needed to produce chemiluminescence with luminol, a compound discovered in the late 1800s.

1937 • Plexiglas® (made from polymethylmethacrylate) is exhibited at the World's Trade Fair in Paris.

1937 • The basic process for making polyurethanes is first developed by German chemist Otto Bayer.

1937 • The cyclamate family of compounds is discovered by Michael Sveda, a graduate student at the University of Illinois.

1938 • Polytetrafluoroethylene is invented by Roy J. Plunkett by accident at DuPont's Jackson Laboratory.

1939 • Swiss chemist Paul Hermann Müller finds that DDT is very effective as an insecticide, which makes it useful in preventing infectious diseases such as malaria.

1939-1945 • During World War II, the U.S. military finds a number of uses for nylon, polyurethanes, polystyrene, percholorates, and silica gel.

Early 1940s • Penicillin is first produced for human use and is valuable in saving the lives of soldiers wounded in World War II.

| 1939 World War II begins. | 1941 First regular television broadcasts begin. | 1942 Irving Berlin writes song "White Christmas." | 1945 U.S. drops two atomic bombs on Japan. | 1946 First "baby boomers" are born. |

| 1935 | 1940 | 1945 |

1940s • A research chemist at the General Electric Company, E. G. Rochow, finds an efficient way of making organosiloxanes in large quantities.

1941 • Folic acid is isolated and identified by American researcher Henry K. Mitchell.

1941 • The first polyurethane adhesive, for the joining of rubber and glass, is made.

1942 • American researchers Harry Coover and Fred Joiner discover cyanoacrylate.

1946 • DEET is patented by the U.S. Army for use on military personnel working in insect-infested areas. It is made available to the public in 1957.

1947 • On April 16, an ammonium nitrate explosion in Texas City, Texas, becomes the worst industrial accident in U.S.

1950s • Earliest reports surface about athletes using testosterone to enhance their sports performance.

1950s • A stretchable material made of polyurethane, called spandex, is introduced.

1951 • Phillips Petroleum Company begins selling polypropylene under the trade name of Marlex®.

1953 • Polycarbonate, polyethylene, and synthetic rubber are developed.

| 1950 Korean War begins. | 1953 Molecular structure of DNA is discovered. | 1955 Jonas Salk invents the polio vaccine. | 1958 First satellite broadcasts occur. |

1950         1955         1960

1955 • Proctor & Gamble releases the first toothpaste containing stannous fluoride, Crest®.

Mid 1950s • Wham-O creates the hula-hoop—a ring of plastic that is made with low-grade polyethylene.

1956 • British chemist Dorothy Hodgkin determines the chemical structure of cyanocobalamin.

1958 • Scientist W. Barnes of the chemical firm T. & H. Smith in Edinburgh, Scotland, discovers denatonium benzoate.

Early 1960s • Ibuprofen is developed by researchers at the Boots Company, a British drug manufacturer.

1960s • Triclosan becomes a common ingredient in soaps and other cleaning projects.

1960s • MTBE is first synthesized by researchers at the Atlantic Richfield Corporation as an additive designed to increase the fuel efficiency of gasoline.

1962 • Amoxicillin is discovered by researchers at the Beecham pharmaceutical laboratories.

1965 • Aspartame is discovered accidentally by James M. Schlatter.

1963
U.S. President
John F. Kennedy
is assassinated.

1975
Vietnam War
ends.

1950          1960          1970

1980s • A ceramic form of copper(I) oxide is found to have superconducting properties at temperatures higher than previously known superconductors.

1980s • Polycarbonate bottles begin to replace the more cumbersome and breakable glass bottles.

1987 • Procter & Gamble seeks FDA approval of sucrose polyester. Ten years pass before the FDA grants that approval.

1994 • The U.S. Food and Drug Administration approves the sale of naproxen as an over-the-counter medication.

1995 • On April 19, American citizens Timothy McVeigh and Terry Nichols use a truckload of ammonium nitrate and other materials to blow up the Alfred P. Murrah Federal Building in Oklahoma City, Oklahoma.

Early 2000s • Some 350,000 propane-powered vehicles exist in the United States and about 4 million are used worldwide.

2004 • The leading chemical compound manufactured in the United States is sulfuric acid, with 37,515,000 metric tons (41,266,000 short tons) produced. Next is ethylene, with about 26.7 million metric tons (29.4 million short tons) produced.

| 1981 First personal computers become available. | 1989 The oil tanker *Exxon Valdez* sinks off Alaska. | 1991 Soviet Union is dissolved. | 2001 World Trade Center in New York City is destroyed. |

| 1980 | 1990 | 2000 | 2006 |

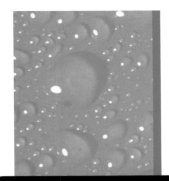
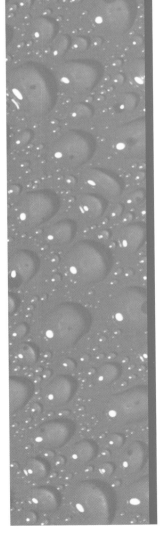

# words to know

 **A**

**ACETYL** The organic group of acetic acid.

**ADHESIVE** A substance used to bond two surfaces together.

**ALCHEMY** An ancient field of study from which the modern science of chemistry evolved.

**ALKALI** A chemical base that can combine with an acid to produce a salt.

**ALKALINE** A substance that has a pH higher than 7.

**ALKALOID** An organic base that contains the element nitrogen.

**ALKANE** A type of hydrocarbon that has no double bonds because it contains the maximum possible number of hydrogen

**ALKENE** A kind of hydrocarbon with at least one double bond between carbons.

**ALKYL GROUP** A chemical group containing hydrogen and carbon atoms.

ALLOTROPE A form of an element that is different from its typical form, with a different chemical bond structure between atoms.

AMIDE An organic compound that includes the CON group bound to hydrogen.

AMINO ACID An organic compound that contains at least one carboxyl group (-COOH) and one amino group (-NH$_2$). They are the building blocks of which proteins are made.

ANALGESIC A substance the relieves pain.

ANHYDROUS Free from water and especially water that is chemically combined in a crystalline substance.

ANION A negatively charged ion.

ANODE The electrode in a battery in which electrons are lost (oxidized).

AROMATIC COMPOUND A compound whose chemical structure is based on that of benzene (C$_6$H$_6$).

BIODEGRADABLE Something that can be easily broken down by the action of bacteria.

BLOCK COPOLYMER A polymer composed of two or more different polymers, each of which clumps in blocks of identical molecules.

BORATE A salt that contains boron.

BRINE Salt water; water with a large amount of salt dissolved in it, such as seawater or water used to pickle vegetables.

BYPRODUCT A product that is made while making something else.

**CARBOHYDRATES** Organic compounds composed of carbon, oxygen, and hydrogen, which are used by the body as food.

**CARBOXYL GROUPS** Groups of atoms consisting of a carbon atom double bonded to an oxygen atom and single bonded to a hydroxyl (-OH) group (-COOH).

**CARCINOGEN** A substance that causes cancer in humans or other animals.

**CATALYST** A material that increases the rate of a chemical reaction without undergoing any change in its own chemical structure.

**CATHODE** The electrode in a battery through which electrons enter the fuel cell.

**CATION** A positively charged ion.

**CAUSTIC** Capable of burning or eating away, usually by the action of chemical reactions.

**CENTRIFUGE** A device that separates substances that have different densities by using centrifugal force.

**CHELATE** A chemical compound that is in the form of a ring. It usually contains one metal ion attached to a minimum of two nonmetal ions by coordinate bonds.

**CHEMILUMINESCENCE** Light produced by a chemical reaction.

**CHIRAL** A molecule with different left-handed and right-handed forms; not mirror symmetric.

**CHLOROFLUOROCARBONS (CFCS)** A family of chemicals made up of carbon, chlorine, and fluorine. CFCs were used as a refrigerant and propellant before they were banned for fear that they were destroying the ozone layer.

CHROMATOGRAPHY A process by which a mixture of substances passes through a column consisting of some material that causes the individual components in the mixture to separate from each other.

COAGULATE To make a liquid become a semisolid.

COENZYME A chemical compound that works along with an enzyme to increase the rate at which chemical reactions take place.

COMPOUND A substance formed of two or more elements that are chemically combined.

COPOLYMER A polymer made from more than one type of monomer.

COVALENT COMPOUND A compound in which the atoms are bonded to each other by sharing electrons.

CROSS-LINKED Polymer chains that are linked together to create a chemical bond.

CRYOGENICS The study of substances at very low temperatures, using substances such as liquefied hydrogen or liquefied helium.

DECOMPOSE To break a substance down into its most basic elements.

DENATURED To be made not fit for drinking.

DERIVATIVE Something gotten or received from another source.

DESICCANT Chemical agent that absorbs or adsorbs moisture.

DIATOMIC Composed of two atoms.

DISACCHARIDE A compound formed by the joining of two sugar molecules.

DISPERSANT A substance that keeps another substance from clumping together or becoming lumpy.

DISTILLATION A process of separating liquid by heating it and then condensing its vapor.

ELASTOMER A polymer known for its flexibility and elastic qualities; a type of rubber.

ELECTRODE A conductor through which an electric current flows.

ELECTROLYSIS A process in which an electric current is used to bring about chemical changes.

ELECTROLYTE A substance which, when dissolved in water, will conduct an electric current.

EMULSIFIER A substance that combines two other substances together that do not usually mix together and ensures they are spread evenly.

ESTER A compound formed by the reaction between an acid and an alcohol.

EXOTHERMIC Accompanied by the freeing of heat.

FAT An ester formed in the reaction between glycerol $(C_3H_5(OH)_3)$ and a fatty acid, an organic acid with more than eight carbon atoms.

FERROUS Containing or made from iron.

FLOCCULANT A type of polymer, or large man-made particle, that is created by a repetitive chain of atoms.

FLUOROCARBON A chemical compound that contains carbon and fluorine, such as chlorofluorocarbon.

FOSSIL FUEL A fuel, such as petroleum, natural gas, or coal, formed from the compression of plant and animal matter underground millions of years ago.

FREE RADICAL An atom or group of atoms with a single unpaired electron that can damage healthy cells in the body.

G/MOL Grams per mole: a measure of molar mass that indicates the amount of the compound that is found in a mole of the compound. The molecular weight (also known as relative molecular mass) is the same number as the molar mass, but the g/mol unit is not used.

GLOBAL WARMING The increase in the average global temperature.

GLUCONEOGENESIS The production of glucose from non-carbohydrate sources, such as proteins and fats.

GLYCOGEN A carbohydrate that is stored in the liver and muscles, which breaks down into glucose.

GREENHOUSE EFFECT The increase of the average global temperature due to the trapping of heat in the atmosphere.

HARD WATER Water with a high mineral content that does not lather easily.

HELIX A spiral; a common shape for protein molecules.

HORMONE A chemical that delivers messages from one cell or organ to another.

HYDRATE A chemical compound formed when one or more molecules of water is added physically to the molecule of some other substance.

HYDROCARBON A chemical compound consisting of only carbon and hydrogen, such as fossil fuels.

HYDROGENATION A chemical reaction of a substance with molecular hydrogen, usually in the presence of a catalyst.

HYDROLYSIS The process by which a compound reacts with water to form two new compounds.

INCOMPLETE COMBUSTION Combustion that occurs in such a way that fuel is not completely oxidized.

INERT A substance that is chemically inactive.

INORGANIC Relating to or obtained from nonliving things.

ION An atom or molecule with an electrical charge, either positive or negative.

IONIC BOND A force that attracts and holds positive and negative ions together.

IONIC COMPOUND A compound that is composed of positive and negative ions, so that the total charge of the positive ions is balanced by the total charge of the negative ions.

ISOMER Two or more forms of a chemical compound with the same molecular formula, but different structural formulas and different chemical and physical properties.

ISOTOPE A form of an element with the usual number of protons in the nucleus but more or less than the usual number of electrons.

KREBS CYCLE A series of chemical reactions in the body that form part of the pathway by which cells break down carbohydrates, fats, and proteins for energy. Also called the citric acid cycle.

LATENT Lying hidden or undeveloped.

LEACH Passing a liquid through something else in order to dissolve minerals from it.

LEWIS ACID An acid that can accept two electrons and form a coordinate covalent bond.

LIPID An organic compound that is insoluble in water, but soluble in most organic solvents, such as alcohol, ether, and acetone.

MEGATON A unit of explosive force equal to one million metric tons of TNT.

METABOLISM All of the chemical reactions that occur in cells by which fats, carbohydrates, and other compounds are broken down to produce energy and the compounds needed to build new cells and tissues.

METALLURGY The science of working with metals and ores.

METHYLXANTHINE A family of chemicals including caffeine, theobromine, and theophylline, many of which are stimulants.

MINERALOGIST A scientist who studies minerals.

MISCIBLE Able to be mixed; especially applies to the mixing of one liquid with another.

MIXTURE A collection of two or more elements or compounds with no definite composition.

MONOMER A single molecule that can be strung together with like molecules to form a polymer.

MONOSACCHARIDE A simple sugar, made up of three to nine carbon atoms.

MORDANT A substance used in dyeing and printing that reacts chemically with both a dye and the material being dyed to help hold the dye permanently to the material.

NARCOTIC An addictive drug that relieves pain and causes drowsiness.

NEUROTRANSMITTER A chemical that relays signals along neurons.

NEUTRALIZE To make a substance neutral that is neither acidic or alkaline.

NITRATING AGENT A substance that turns other substances into nitrates, which are compounds containing $NO_3$.

NSAID Non-steroidal anti-inflammatory drug, a drug that can stop pain and prevent inflammation and fever but that is not a steroid and does not have the same side effects as steroids.

ORGANIC Relating to or obtained from living things. In chemistry, refers to compounds made of carbon combined with other elements.

OXIDANT A substance that causes oxidation of a compound by removing electrodes from the compound. Also known as oxidizing agent.

OXIDATION STATE The sum of negative and positive charges, which indirectly indicates the number of electrons accepted or donated in the bond between elements.

OXIDIZE To combine a substance with oxygen, or to remove hydrogen from a molecule using oxygen, or to remove electrons from a molecule.

PARTICULATE MATTER Tiny particles of pollutants suspended in the air.

PETROCHEMICALS Chemical compounds that form in rocks, such as petroleum and coal.

PH (POTENTIAL HYDROGEN) The acidity or alkalinity of a substance based on its concentration of hydrogen ions.

PHOSPHATE A compound that is a salt of phosphoric acid, which consists of phosphorus, oxygen, sometimes hydrogen, and another element or ion.

PHOTOELECTRIC EFFECT The emission of electrons by a substance, especially metal, when light falls on its surface.

PHOTOSYNTHESIS The process by which green plants and some other organisms using the energy in sunlight to convert carbon dioxide and water into carbohydrates and oxygen.

PHOTOVOLTAIC EFFECT A type of photoelectric effect where light is converted to electrical voltage by a substance.

PLASTICIZER A substance added to plastics to make them stronger and more flexible.

POLYAMIDE A polymer, such as nylon, containing recurrent amide groups linking segments of the polymer chain.

POLYMER A substance composed of very large molecules built up by linking small molecules over and over again.

POLYSACCHARIDE A very large molecule made of many thousands of simple sugar molecules joined to each other in long, complex chains.

PRECIPITATE A solid material that settles out of a solution, often as the result of a chemical reaction.

PRECURSOR A compound that gives rise to some other compound in a series of reactions.

PROPRIETARY Manufactured, sold, or known only by the owner of the item's patent.

PROSTAGLANDINS A group of potent hormone-like substances that are produced in various tissues of the body. Prostaglandins help with a wide range of physiological functions, such as control of blood pressure, contraction of smooth muscles, and modulation of inflammation.

PROTEIN A large, complex compound made of long chains of amino acids. Proteins have a number of essential functions in living organisms.

QUARRY An open pit, often big, that is used to obtain stone.

REAGENT A substance that is employed to react, measure, or detect with another substance.

REDUCTION A chemical reaction in which oxygen is removed from a substance or electrons are added to a substance.

REFRACTORY A material with a high melting point, resistant to melting, often used to line the interior of industrial furnaces.

RESIN A solid or semi-solid organic material that is used to make lacquers, adhesives, plastics, and many other clear substances.

SALT An ionic compound where the anion is derived from an acid.

SEMICONDUCTOR A material that has an electrical conductance between that of an insulator and a conductor. When charged with electricity or light, semiconductors change their state from nonconductive to conductive or vice versa.

SEQUESTERING AGENT A substance that binds to metals in water to prevent them from combining with other components in the water and forming compounds that could stain (sequestering agents are sometimes used in cleaning products). Also called a "chelating agent."

SILICATE A salt in which the anion contains both oxygen and silicon.

SOLUBLE Capable of being dissolved in a liquid such as water.

SOLUTION A mixture whose properties and uniform throughout the mixture sample.

SOLVENT A substance that is able to dissolve one or more other substances.

SUBLIME To go from solid to gaseous form without passing through a liquid phase.

SUPERCONDUCTIVITY A state in which a material loses all electrical resistance: once established, an electrical current will flow forever.

SUPERCOOLED WATER Water that remains in liquid form, even though its temperature is below 0°C.

SUSPENSION A mixture of two substances that do not dissolve in each other.

SYNTHESIZE To produce a chemical by combining simpler chemicals.

TERATOGENIC Causing birth defects; comes from the Greek word "teratogenesis," meaning "monster-making."

THERMAL Involving the use of heat.

TOXIC Poisonous or acting like a poison.

TOXIN A poison, usually produced by microorganisms or by plants or animals.

TRAP A reservoir or area within Earth's crust made of non-porous rock that can contain liquids or gases, such as water, petroleum, and natural gas.

ULTRAVIOLET LIGHT Light that is shorter in wavelength than visible light and can fade paint finishes, fabrics, and other exposed surfaces.

VASODILATOR A chemical that makes blood vessels widen, reducing blood pressure.

VISCOUS Having a syrupy quality causing a material to flow slowly.

VITRIFICATION The process by which something is changed into glass or a glassy substance, usually by heat.

VOLATILE Able to turn to vapor easily at a relatively low temperature.

WATER OF HYDRATION Water that has combined with a compound by some physical means.

OTHER NAMES:
Biethylene; bivinyl; divinyl; erythrene; vinylethylene

FORMULA:
CH$_2$=CHCH=CH$_2$

ELEMENTS:
Carbon, hydrogen

COMPOUND TYPE:
Alkene (unsaturated hydrocarbon)

STATE:
Gas

MOLECULAR WEIGHT:
54.09 g/mol

MELTING POINT:
−108.91°C
(−164.04°F)

BOILING POINT:
−4.41°C (−24.1°F)

SOLUBILITY:
Insoluble in water; soluble in alcohol, ether, and benzene

KEY FACTS

# 1,3-Butadiene

## OVERVIEW

1,3-butadiene (one-three-byoo-tah-DYE-een) is a colorless gas with a mild, slightly sweet odor. It occurs naturally in petroleum, from which it is extracted at refineries. The compound was first discovered in petroleum in 1886 by the English chemist Henry E. Armstrong (1848-1937) and his colleague A. K. Miller (no dates available). This discovery apparently had no practical application until 1910 when the Russian chemist Sergei Lebedev (1874-1934) developed a method for polymerizing butadiene to make a rubber-like substance. Even then, Lebedev's invention, called polybutadiene, was primarily a laboratory curiosity. There was relatively little demand for rubber products that could not be met by the vast supplies of natural rubber from Southeast Asia.

That situation began to change in the 1920s and 1930s. The demand for rubber products in automobiles and other motor vehicles, especially tires, grew rapidly as car and truck production increased rapidly year after year. At the same

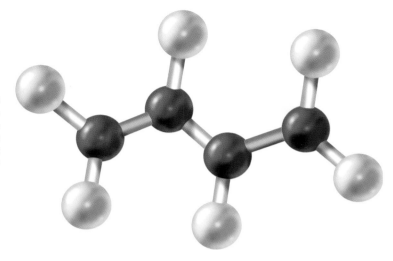

time, manufacturers began to worry about losing their supply of natural rubber from traditional suppliers in Java, Malaysia, Sumatra, and other parts of Asia. As a result, chemists in Europe and the United States began to look for synthetic substitutes for natural rubber. Lebedev's discovery provided one solution to this problem, and butadiene-based synthetic rubber products were soon flowing from manufacturing plants.

## HOW IT IS MADE

Butadiene is made by three processes in the United States. The first two of those processes begin with four-carbon compounds called butane ($CH_3CH_2CH_2CH_3$) and butene ($CH_2=CHCH_2CH_3$ and $CH_3CH=CHCH_3$). These compounds are treated in one of two ways so as to add one more double bond to the molecules, resulting in the formation of 1,3-butadiene ($CH_2=CHCH=CH_2$). The third and most common process is known as steam cracking. Steam cracking is a process by which large petroleum molecules are exposed to very hot steam, causing them to break apart into smaller molecules. Steam cracking is the method by which ethylene, the most important organic chemical produced in the United States, is made. 1,3-butadiene is a by-product of this process, and is separated from the major product, ethylene, after cracking is complete.

## Interesting Facts

- In 2004, U.S. manufacturers produced 2.2 million metric tons (2.4 million short tons) of 1,3-butadiene, ranking it number 22 among all chemicals produced in the United States.

### COMMON USES AND POTENTIAL HAZARDS

Virtually all of the 1,3-butadiene produced is used in the manufacture of polymers. Polybutadiene itself is too soft for most industrial rubber uses. So it is sometimes mixed with other polymers to make products with a variety of desirable qualities. Or it is polymerized with other monomers to make specialized copolymers. One of the most popular of the mixed polymers is polystyrene-polybutadiene. The second polymer in this mixture, polystyrene, is a polymer of the compound styrene ($C_6H_5CH{=}CH_2$). Some other uses of 1,3-butadiene include:

- Raw material in the manufacture of fungicides such as Captan and Captofol;

- Manufacture of latex adhesives;

- Production of domestic products, such as the backing on nylon carpet, appliance and electrical equipment, and luggage;

- Manufacture of industrial products, such as piping and conduits.

1,3-butadiene has a variety of harmful effects on humans, including irritation of the respiratory system, fatigue, drowsiness, headache, vertigo, loss of consciousness, respiratory paralysis, and death. The compound is also thought to be a carcinogen. Only people who work directly with the compound, however, are likely to experience such effects, and only then in unusual situations. The average person is likely to have no contact with the compound.

## Words to Know

**CARCINOGEN** A substance that causes cancer in humans or other animals.

**COPOLYMER** A polymer made with two different monomers.

**POLYMER** A compound consisting of very large molecules made of one or two small repeated units called monomers.

**POLYMERIZING** The process by which polymers are made.

FOR FURTHER INFORMATION

"1,3-Butadiene." National Safety Council.
http://www.nsc.org/library/chemical/13-Butad.htm (accessed September 14, 2005).

"1,3-Butadiene Health Effects." Occupational Safety & Health Administration.
http://www.osha.gov/SLTC/butadiene/healtheffects.html (accessed September 14, 2005).

Johnson, Peter S. *Rubber Processing: An Introduction.* Cincinatti, OH: Hanser Gardner Publications, 2001.

"ToxFAQs for 1,3-Butadiene." Agency for Toxic Substances and Disease Registry.
http://www.atsdr.cdc.gov/tfacts28.html (accessed September 14, 2005).

*See Also* Styrene

OTHER NAMES:
Mustard gas; see
Overview for more
names

FORMULA:
$(CH_2CH_2Cl)_2S$

ELEMENTS:
Carbon, hydrogen,
chlorine, sulfur

COMPOUND TYPE:
Organic sulfide

STATE:
Liquid

MOLECULAR WEIGHT:
159.09 g/mol

MELTING POINT:
13 to 14°C (55 to 57°F)

BOILING POINT:
217°C (423°F)

SOLUBILITY:
Insoluble in water;
soluble in alcohol,
ether, acetone,
benzene, and other
organic solvents;
soluble in fats

KEY FACTS

# 2,2′-Dichlorodiethyl Sulfide

## OVERVIEW

2,2′-dichlorodiethyl sulfide (two-two-prime-di-KLO-ro-di-ETH-el sul-fyd) is more commonly known as mustard gas. It is also known as bis-(2-chloroethyl) sulfide; sulfur mustard; yprite; and 1,1′-thiobis[2-chloroethane]. The compound occurs as a yellowish liquid that, in a pure form, has no odor. Small amounts of impurities give it the distinctive odor of mustard, from which it gets its common name. It may also smell like garlic or horseradish because of impurities.

Mustard gas was discovered by the English physicist Frederick Guthrie (1833–1886) in 1860. While working with the compound, Guthrie spilled mustard gas on his skin and found that it produced a painful red blister. That property has led to the primary use of mustard gas, as a chemical agent used in warfare. When sprayed on a person, the compound can blister the skin, burn the eyes, and irritate the lungs. In large doses, it can kill a person. Mustard gas was first used as a chemical weapon on July 12, 1917 by the German army in an attack on Canadian soldiers at Ypres,

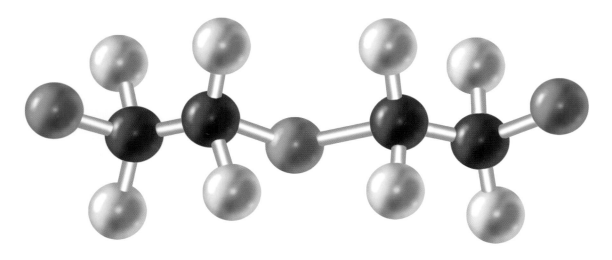

Belgium. An estimated 20,000 troops were killed in the attack. By the end of World War I, an estimated 120,000 British troops had died as a result of mustard gas attacks.

The damage caused by mustard gas was due at least in part because troops had no means of protecting themselves against the compound. It was able to penetrate virtually any type of protective clothing then available. The damage caused by mustard gas is so horrible that most nations have agreed not to use it in wars. One exception may have occurred during the Iraq-Iran war of 1980-1988, when the Iraqis sprayed Iranian troops with a gas very much like mustard gas in 1984. Later, in 1987 and 1988, Iraq's ruler Saddam Hussein also used mustard gas against Kurdish people living in northern Iraq.

## HOW IT IS MADE

The usual method for making mustard gas in the United States is called the Levenstein process. In this process, ethylene gas ($CH_2=CH_2$) is bubbled through sulfur chloride ($S_2Cl_2$), a yellowish-red oil with a very strong odor. In Germany and other nations, the compound is made by treating the organic compound 2,2'-dihydroxyethyl sulfide with hydrochloric acid.

## COMMON USES AND POTENTIAL HAZARDS

Virtually the only use for mustard gas is as a chemical agent in warfare. But, interestingly enough, the compound

## Interesting Facts

- Another name for mustard gas, yprite, comes from the Belgian city Ypres (pronounced "EE-pr"), where the compound was first use as a military weapon.

- The use of mustard gas was outlawed by the Chemical Weapons Convention, adopted in 1993. The United States starting destroying its stockpile of mustard gas even earlier, in 1985, and is now thought to have none of the chemical agent left.

- Mustard gas was not used during World War II. The compound was, nonetheless, responsible for the deaths of more than 100 U.S. men. On December 2, 1943, a German attack on the harbor of Bari, Italy, resulted in the sinking of about two dozen ships. Some of those ships were carrying mustard gas. When they sank, they released the gas into the surrounding water, where survivors inhaled and swallowed the poisonous compound.

has been used in one other very different way: in the treatment of cancer. The husband and wife medical team of E.B. and H.D. Krumbhaar discovered in 1919 that mustard gas was effective in treating cancer in experimental animals. (They called the compound by its then-popular name, yellow cross gas.) The compound was one of the first chemicals to be used in the treatment of cancer. Researchers continued to study the cancer-fighting properties of mustard gas for more than twenty years, but the compound has never been widely used for that purpose.

The effects of exposure to mustard gas vary over time. At first, a person who has inhaled the gas may become nauseated, experience itchy and sore eyes, and begin vomiting. His or her skin turns red and blisters may develop. Exposure to large amounts of the gas may result in permanent damage to the eyes and respiratory system resulting, in the worst cases, in coma and death. People exposed to mustard gas who survive may later develop mouth, lung, or stomach cancer.

FOR FURTHER INFORMATION

"Molecule of the Month: Mustard Gas." Bristol University. http://www.chm.bris.ac.uk/motm/mustard/mustard.htm (accessed on September 13, 2005).

"Mustard Gas." International Progamme on Chemical Safety. http://www.inchem.org/documents/pims/chemical/mustardg. htm (accessed on September 13, 2005).

Strobel, Warren P. "Saddam's Lingering Atrocity." U.S. News & World Report (November 27, 2000): 52.

"ToxFAQs for Sulfur Mustard." Agency for Toxic Substances and Disease Registry. http://www.atsdr.cdc.gov/tfacts49.html (accessed on September 13, 2005).

**OTHER NAMES:**
Ibuprofen; see Overview for more names

**FORMULA:**
$C_{13}H_{18}O_2$

**ELEMENTS:**
Carbon, hydrogen, oxygen

**COMPOUND TYPE:**
Organic acid

**STATE:**
Solid

**MOLECULAR WEIGHT:**
206.28 g/mol

**MELTING POINT:**
76°C (169°F)

**BOILING POINT:**
Not applicable; decomposes above melting point

**SOLUBILITY:**
Slightly soluble in water; soluble in most organic solvents

# 2-(4-Isobutylphenyl)-propionic Acid

## OVERVIEW

2-(4-Isobutylphenyl)propionic acid (two four eye-so-BYOO-tuhl-PHEEN-uhl PRO-pi-on-ik AS-id) is a colorless crystalline solid widely used as an analgesic and anti-inflammatory medication. It is most commonly known as ibuprofen, but is also known as α-methyl-4-(2-methylpropyl)benzeneacetic acid and 4-isobutyl-@alpha;-methylphenylacetic acid. It is also sold under a variety of trade names, including Aches-n-Pain®, Advil®, Andran®, Antagil®, Antarene®, Excedrin IB®, Genpril®, Ibuprin®, Medipren®, Midol®, Motrin®, Nuprin®, PediaProfen®, Rufen®, and Vicoprofen®.

Ibuprofen was developed by researchers at the Boots Company, a British drug manufacturer, in the early 1960s. Those researchers had found that the anti-inflammatory property of aspirin was due to the presence of a carboxylic acid (-COOH) group in the compound. They searched for other carboxylic acids that might have similar properties and, after testing more than 600 compounds, discovered that ibuprofen met that criterion. It was twice as effective as

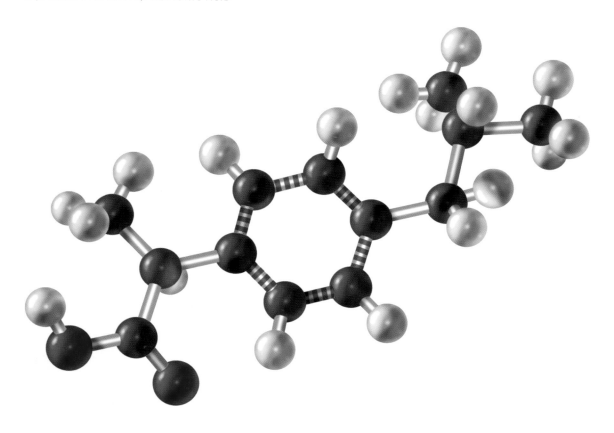

*2-(4-isobutylphenyl) propionic acid.* Red atoms are oxygen; white atoms are hydrogen; and black atoms are carbon. Gray sticks indicate double bonds. Striped sticks indicate a benzene ring.
PUBLISHERS RESOURCE GROUP

acetylsalicylic acid (aspirin), the standard against which they were testing their products. They initially called their discovery "Brufen."

In 1974, Boots licensed the Upjohn Company in the United States to begin making a commercial version of Brufen. Upjohn called its product Motrin and marketed the compound primarily to people with arthritis. It soon became a popular drug with both doctors and patients, who found they were able to control the pain of arthritis with a non-addictive product that was easier on the stomach than aspirin.

Boots also entered the U.S. market several years later, selling ibuprofen under the trade name of Rufen. A number of other drug companies were eager to begin marketing their version of ibuprofen, and when the U.S. Food and Drug Administration approved ibuprofen for over-the-counter

## Interesting Facts

Some evidence suggests that taking ibuprofen for two years or more may reduce the risk of developing Alzheimer's disease.

sales, they were ready. Whitehall Laboratories introduced Advil and Upjohn and Bristol-Meyers jointly released Nuprin. After Boots' patent ran out in 1985, several other drug manufacturers began producing their own versions of the popular pain-killing and anti-inflammatory product.

### HOW IT IS MADE

The original method for making ibuprofen developed by Boots researchers begins with 2-methylpropylbenzene, a compound with a four-carbon methylpropyl group attached to a benzene ring. 2-methylpropybenzene is a readily available product with a molecular structure quite similar to that of ibuprofen. Then, in a series of six steps, various groups of atoms are added, removed, or transposed to produce the 2-(4-isobutylphenyl)propionic acid molecule.

Other methods for preparing ibuprofen have also been developed. One of the most recent procedures has been invented by green chemists. Green chemists are chemists who look for methods of making chemical compounds that are less wasteful of raw materials, more sensitive to environmental concerns, and less hazardous to human health. The green chemistry method of making ibuprofen also begins with 2-methylpropylbenzene, but uses different catalysts and fewer steps to produce ibuprofen. Overall, the green method of making ibuprofen is twice as efficient (half as much waste products) as the original Boots method.

### COMMON USES AND POTENTIAL HAZARDS

Ibuprofen is a nonsteroidal anti-inflammatory drug, or NSAID. The term nonsteroidal indicates that ibuprofen is not a steroid, a common class of drugs used to reduce

## Words to Know

**ANALGESIC** a substance the relieves pain.

**CATALYST** a material that increases the rate of a chemical reaction without undergoing any change in its own chemical structure.

**GREEN CHEMISTRY** the practice of making chemical compounds that are less wasteful of raw materials, more sensitive to environmental concerns, and less hazardous to human health.

inflammation and swelling. Scientists believe that ibuprofen works by inhibiting the enzyme cyclooxygenase (COX), which converts arachidonic acid to prostaglandins. Arachidonic acid is a naturally occurring fatty acid that is used to build a number of important biochemical compounds, including the prostaglandins. The prostaglandins are involved in the transmission of pain impulses throughout the nervous system. If the COX enzyme is prevented from functioning, arachidonic acid can not be converted into prostaglandins, and pain messages will not be transmitted.

Ibuprofen is especially effective in treating certain kinds of pain and inflammation, including those associated with menstrual cramps, various kinds of arthritis, headaches and migraines, pain from injuries and surgery, and discomfort associated with influenza and gout.

The major risk associated with use of ibuprofen is stomach irritation. The inventors of ibuprofen had hoped to find a substance that causes less stomach irritation than aspirin. Ibuprofen does seem to cause fewer gastrointestinal problems than does aspirin. Nevertheless, it can still cause severe problems in some patients, especially those who take large doses. Common complaints from the use of ibuprofen include nausea, stomach pain, and diarrhea. Patients who are especially sensitive or who take high doses of ibuprofen for long periods may experience damage to the stomach lining.

As with any drug, some patients should avoid taking ibuprofen entirely. These include individuals with heart or kidney problems, people who are taking so-called "blood thinners," pregnant women during the last three months of pregnancy, people with asthma, and people who are allergic to aspirin.

FOR FURTHER INFORMATION

"Ibuprofen." Chemical Land 21.
    http://www.chemicalland21.com/arokorhi/lifescience/phar/
    IBUPROFEN.htm (accessed on November 3, 2005).

"Ibuprofen—Oral." MedicineNet.com.
    http://www.medicinenet.com/ibuprofen-oral/article.htm
    (accessed on November 3, 2005).

Rainsford, K. D., ed. *Ibuprofen: A Critical Bibliographic Review.*
    Bethesda, MD: CCR Press, 1999.

*See Also* Acetylsalicylic Acid

NO$_2$

H$_3$C

NO$_2$  NO$_2$

# 2,4,6-Trinitrotoluene

## OVERVIEW

2,4,6-trinitrotoluene (two four six try-nye-troh-TOL-yoo-een), or TNT, is a yellow odorless solid that occurs in the form of crystalline needles. Its major use is in the manufacture of explosives. It may be used alone or in combination with other explosive chemicals. Although not as powerful as some other explosives, it has the advantage of being relatively insensitive to shock. Workers can handle the explosive without fear that it will suddenly explode if dropped or jarred. In fact, a blasting cap or detonator is needed to cause TNT to explode. Blasting caps and detonators are very sensitive explosives that can be attached to less sensitive explosives like TNT. Any small shock to the blasting cap or detonator will cause it to explode. That explosion, in turn, causes the less sensitive explosive, such as TNT, to blow up.

TNT was discovered by the German chemist Joseph Wilbrand (1811–1894) in 1863, although the compound was not recognized as an explosive until almost thirty years later. The compound was first produced commercially in Germany

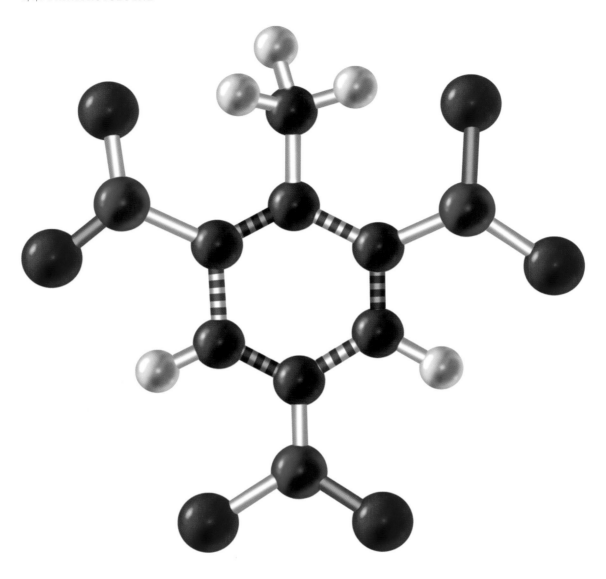

*2,4,6-Trinitrotoluene.* Red atoms are oxygen; white atoms are hydrogen; black atoms are carbon; and blue atoms are nitrogen. Gray sticks indicate double bonds. Striped sticks indicate a benzene ring.
PUBLISHERS RESOURCE GROUP

in 1901 and first used by Germany and its enemies during World War I. The explosive became so popular during the war that production of TNT could not keep up with demand by armies on both sides of the conflict.

## HOW IT IS MADE

The method developed by Wilbrand for manufacturing TNT is simple, efficient, and inexpensive, and remains the

## Interesting Facts

- During World War I (1914–1918), people who made explosives for the military (usually women and girls) were sometimes called "canary girls." Their name came from the fact that their skin turned yellow when exposed to solid TNT. Women with red hair also found their hair turning an orangish or ginger color because of exposure to TNT.

- TNT has become the standard for explosive power in the world today. When someone talks about a "15 kiloton bomb" they are referring to a bomb with the explosive equivalent of 15 thousand ("kilo") tons of TNT. Nuclear weapons commonly have explosive powers rated in the kiloton or megaton (million tons of TNT) range.

primary process by which TNT is produced today. Wilbrand made TNT by adding nitric acid ($HNO_3$) and sulfuric acid ($H_2SO_4$) to toluene ($C_6H_5CH_3$).

## COMMON USES AND POTENTIAL HAZARDS

By far the most common use of TNT is in the manufacture of explosives. Until the discovery of nuclear energy in the 1940s, TNT was the most powerful explosive known to humans. Today, TNT is often combined with other explosives to make even more powerful bombs. Some examples include the following:

- Torpex, a mixture of TNT, wax and aluminum used in underwater explosives, such as those found in torpedoes. Torpex is about 50 percent more powerful than pure TNT;

- Pentolite, a combination of TNT and pentaerythritol tetranitrate (PETN) used primarily in blasting caps and detonators;

- Military dynamite, which contains the explosive RDX, TNT, motor oil, and cornstarch, is less powerful than pure dynamite, but much safer to handle;

# Words to Know

**CARCINOGEN** A chemical that causes cancer in humans or other animals.

- Amatol, a combination of TNT and ammonium nitrate, is often substituted for TNT in ordnance (weapons);

- Minol, a variation of amatol that includes 20 percent aluminum to increase its explosive power; and

- Baratol, a mixture of TNT and barium nitrate that explodes more slowly than pure TNT.

In addition to its primary use in explosives, 2,4,6-trinitrotoluene is also used to produce a very attractive yellow tint in the manufacture of dyes and photographic chemicals.

2,4,6-trinitrotoluene is a hazardous chemical that can produce both short- and long-term health effects, such as respiratory problems, skin irritation, anemia, and lung damage. Some research shows the compound may be carcinogenic in laboratory animals, but not in humans. Since most people are never exposed to TNT, these hazards are primarily of concern to men and women engaged in the manufacture or use of TNT.

### FOR FURTHER INFORMATION

Cooper, P. W., and S. R. Kurowski. *Introduction to the Technology of Explosives.* New York: Wiley-VCH, 1997.

"Public Health Statement for 2,4,6-Trinitrotoluene." Agency for Toxic Substances and Disease Registry. http://www.atsdr.cdc.gov/toxprofiles/phs81.html (accessed September 15, 2005).

$$CH_3 - C(=O) - N(H) - C_6H_4 - OH$$

# Acetaminophen

## OVERVIEW

Acetaminophen (uh-SEE-toe-Min-oh-fen) is one of the most commonly used analgesics in the world. It is also known as p-Acetylaminophenol; p-acetamidophenol; N-acetyl-p-aminophenol; p-hydroxyacetanilide; and paracetamol. It is an ingredient in more than 100 commercial products including Abensanil®, Acamol®, Acetagesic®, Alpinyl®, Alvedon®, Anaflon®, Anelix®, Anhiba®, Calpol®, Datril®, Dirox®, Doliprane®, Dymadon®, Enelfa®, Eneril®, Exdol®, Febrilix®, Febrolin®, Fendon®, Finimal®, Hedex®, Homoolan®, Lonarid®, Multin®, Panadol®, Phendon®, Tylenol®, Valdol®, and Valgesic®. Acetaminophen is often combined with other ingredients in medications such as cold and flu products, cough suppressants, and allergy medications in order to treat more than one symptom at a time.

Acetaminophen was first discovered in 1852 by the French chemist Charles Frederic Gerhardt, who also discovered aspirin a year later. His results were largely ignored, however, until a German chemist, Harmon Northrop Morse

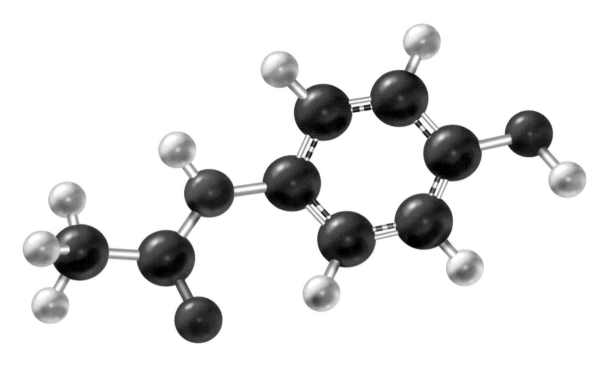

*Acetaminophen.* Red atoms are oxygen; white atoms are hydrogen; black atoms are carbon; and blue atom is nitrogen. Gray sticks indicate double bonds. PUBLISHERS RESOURCE GROUP

(1848–1920) re-discovered and synthesized the compound in 1873. Even then, the medicinal qualities of the compound were not appreciated for another twenty years, and the compound was not even prescribed or used by doctors until 1949. Since that time, however, it has become extremely popular, exceeded only by aspirin as the most popular analgesic sold in the world.

## HOW IT IS MADE

Acetaminophen is made in a straight-forward reaction between p-aminophenol [$C_6H_4(OH)(NH_2)$] and acetic anhydride [$(CH_3CO)_2O$]. As its formula shows, the p-aminophenol provides the basic structure from which acetaminophen is formed, with the acetic anhydride adding the -$CH_3CO$ group of atoms needed to complete the compound.

## COMMON USES AND POTENTIAL HAZARDS

In addition to its use as a pain reliever, acetaminophen has a number of industrial uses, including:

## Interesting Facts

Ancient Romans boiled fermented wine (vinegar) in lead pots to make a sweet syrup called sapa. The acetic acid in the vinegar dissolved a small amount of lead from which the pots were made, producing lead acetate ($Pb[C_2H_3O_2]$). When they used sapa as a sweetening agent in their foods, the Romans ingested the lead acetate which, over long periods of time, caused the lead poisoning from which so many of them died.

Researchers are constantly looking for new, more efficient, more environmentally-friendly methods for making acetic acid. In 2003, for example, chemists at the University of Southern California reported on a new method for making acetic acid directly from methane gas ($CH_4$) using a catalyst of palladium and sulfuric acid. Other researchers are looking for ways to oxidize the waste gases produced from industrial processes to acetic acid.

## COMMON USES AND POTENTIAL HAZARDS

Acetic acid is probably best known to most people as vinegar. In this form, it is used as a condiment and a food preservative. The greatest volume of acetic acid is used, however, in a variety of chemical processes, especially the manufacture of plastic materials such as polyvinyl acetate (PVA), polyethylene terephthalate (PET), and cellulose acetate. A more recent use of acetic acid is in the manufacture of calcium magnesium acetate (CMA), a deicer. Traditionally, roads, highways, and airport runways have been treated with calcium chloride ($CaCl_2$) or some other salt to remove snow and ice. These compounds have serious environmental effects, however, and researchers have long been looking for alternatives that are as effective in removing snow and ice, but less harmful to the environment. CMA has been the most promising of these alternatives, and its production has produced a growing demand for acetic acid. Some other applications of acetic acid include:

* As a cleaning agent;

* In the manufacture of photographic materials;

## Words to Know

**ALCHEMY** An ancient field of study from which the modern science of chemistry evolved.

**CATALYST** A material that increases the rate of a chemical reaction without undergoing any change in its own chemical structure.

**DISTILLATION** A process of separating two or more substances by boiling the mixture of which they are composed and condensing the vapors produced at different temperatures.

- For the production of a variety of organic compounds, such as those used in the manufacture of packaging materials, paints, adhesives and artificial fibers;
- As a fumigant (pesticide) to preserve fruits and grains;
- In the printing of textiles; and
- As an acidifier to improve the flow of oil from wells.

Dilute acetic acid in the form of vinegar is harmless and has been consumed by humans for centuries. Prolonged contact with the skin or eyes may, however, produce irritation of tissues and should be avoided. Concentrated forms of acetic acid pose more serious health risks, such as irritation of the gastrointestinal system, respiratory system, and eyes. Most people do not come into contact with the concentrated acid, and safety precautions are of importance only to individuals who handle the material in their work.

### FOR FURTHER INFORMATION

"Acetic Acid." Chemical of the Week. http://scifun.chem.wisc.edu/chemweek/AceticAcid/AceticAcid.html (accessed on September 16, 2005).

"Acetic Acid and CMA." https://netfiles.uiuc.edu/mcheryan/www/cma.htm (accessed on September 16, 2005).

"Acetic Acid and Derivatives." *Kirk-Othmer Encyclopedia of Chemical Technology*, 4th ed. Vol. 1. New York: John Wiley & Sons, 1991, pp. 121-175.

*See Also* Amyl acetate; butyl acetate; ethyl acetate; isoamyl acetate

$$H \text{——} C \equiv C \text{——} H$$

# Acetylene

## OVERVIEW

Acetylene (uh-SET-ill-ene) is the simplest hydrocarbon, consisting of two carbon atoms joined to each other by a triple bond with their associated hydrogen atoms. It occurs as a colorless gas with a sweet odor when pure, but an unpleasant odor due to the presence of phosphine ($PH_3$) and/or arsine ($AsH_3$), with which it is often contaminated. Acetylene is a highly flammable gas that is also somewhat explosive. This property accounts for one of its most important uses, in torches that burn at very high temperatures.

Acetylene was discovered by the British chemist Edmund Davy (1785-1857) in 1836. Davy obtained the gas accidentally when he combined water with potassium carbide ($KCH_2$) while attempting to make potassium metal. He noted that the gas burned with a bright flame and thought it might be used as a source of illumination. That application was impractical, however, because of the high cost of potassium carbide. When the German chemist Frederich Wöhler (1800-1882) discovered the far less expensive calcium carbide

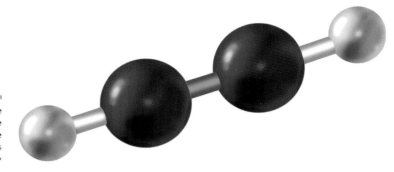

*Acetyline.* White atoms are hydrogen and black atoms are carbon. Gray sticks indicate double bonds. PUBLISHERS RESOURCE GROUP

($CaC_2$) in 1862, however, that problem was solved, and the demand for acetylene in lamps and other applications grew rapidly.

## HOW IT IS MADE

The original method of making acetylene by the action of water on calcium carbide was abandoned when more efficient methods of synthesis became available. One of those methods, known as the Wulff process, involves the cracking of hydrocarbons from petroleum. In this process, liquid petroleum, which consists of many different kinds of hydrocarbons, is heated with very hot steam, causing the hydrocarbons to break apart ("crack") into smaller compounds. Acetylene is one of these compounds.

A later improvement on this procedure was developed by the German chemist Walter Reppe (1892–1969), sometimes called the Father of Acetylene Chemistry. Since Reppe worked at that time for the BASF chemical corporation, the process is also known as the BASF process of making acetylene. In this procedure, hydrocarbons from petroleum are treated with an oxidizing agent that causes them to break apart to form smaller compounds, one of which, again, is acetylene.

## COMMON USES AND POTENTIAL HAZARDS

By far the most important use of acetylene is in the manufacture of other chemicals, such as vinyl chloride, vinylidene chloride, vinyl acetate, acrylonitrile, trichloroethylene

## Interesting Facts

Acetylene was used as a source of illumination beginning in the early 1900s. In one type of acetylene lamp, water was allowed to drop on a solid chunk of calcium carbide at a controlled rate. The acetylene produced then passed into an ignition chamber, where it burned with a brilliant white light. Acetylene lamps were used in a variety of settings, such as the source of light for bicycles and early motor cars and as a source of illumination for miners. Some small towns even used acetylene lamps as their major source of town lighting. Acetylene lamps continue to be a popular collectors item among antique dealers today.

and perchloroethylene, and the family of plastics known as the acrylates. (The name vinyl refers to the remnant of an acetylene molecule after one hydrogen atom has been removed: $-CH_2=CH-$.) About 20 percent of all the acetylene produced is used for torches that produce very hot flames. In one such torch, the oxyacetylene torch, acetylene gas and oxygen are mixed and ignited at the tip of the torch. The combination of gases burns at a temperature of 3,000°C to 3,500°C (5,500°F to 6,300°F). Oxyacetylene torches are used to cut through metal and to weld two metals to each other. They can be used in very cold climates and even under water.

Acetylene is both very flammable and explosive. Anyone who works with the compound or uses it in any form should know how to use the device that contains the gas. Acetylene also has the somewhat unusual chemical property of reacting with certain metals, such as copper and silver, to form highly explosive compounds known as acetylides. Lamps, torches, and other devices built to hold and dispense acetylene can not contain any of these metals. High concentrations of the gas also pose a health hazard to humans. It is classified as an asphyxiant, a gas that can produce disorientation, unconsciousness, and death when inhaled to excess.

## Words to Know

**OXIDATION** A chemical reaction in which oxygen reacts with some other substance or, alternatively, in which some substances loses electrons to another substance, the oxidizing agent.

**SYNTHESIS** A chemical reaction in which some desired chemical product is made from simple beginning chemicals, or reactants.

### FOR FURTHER INFORMATION

"Acetylene—Properties, Purity and Packaging."
http://www.c-f-c.com/specgas_products/acetylene.htm
(accessed on September 16, 2005).

"The Environmental Impact of Acetylene Compared to Impact of Propane-Chemtane 2." Chemtane.
http://www.chemtane2.com/environmental/cva_env_impact.
html (accessed on September 16, 2005).

O'Hara, Kelly. "Chemistry Hall of Fame—1997—Acetylene." York University.
http://www.chem.yorku.ca/hall_of_fame/essays97/acetylene/
acetylen.htm (accessed on September 16, 2005).

"Oxy-acetylene Welding and Cutting." ESAB.
http://www.esabna.com/EUWeb/OXY_handbook/589oxy2_1.
htm (accessed on September 16, 2005).

*See Also* Polyvinyl chloride

K E Y   F A C T S

# Acetylsalicylic Acid

## OVERVIEW

Acetylsalicylic acid (uh-SEE-till-sal-in-SILL-ik As-id, or uh-se-TEEL-sal-ih-SEEL-ik AS-id), more commonly known as aspirin, is the world's most commonly used therapeutic drug. By one estimate, about 137 million aspirin tablets are taken every day throughout the world. The drug is also known by other names including: *o*-acetoxybenzoic acid; 2-(acetyloxy)-benzoic acid; 2-carboxyphenyl acetate; and benzoic acid, 2-hydroxyacetate, in addition to about ten other systematic names and many common names.

The analgesic properties of willow tree bark, from which salicylic acid comes, have been known for well over 3,500 years. They were first described in Egyptian scrolls dating to about 1550 BCE and were later recommended by a number of ancient authorities, including the famous Greek physician Hippocrates (c. 460-370 BCE), the Roman encyclopedist Aulus Cornelius Celsus (c. 10 BCE-date of death unknown), the Roman philosopher Pliny the Elder (23 CE-CE), and the Greek physician Pedanius Dioscorides (40-90 CE).

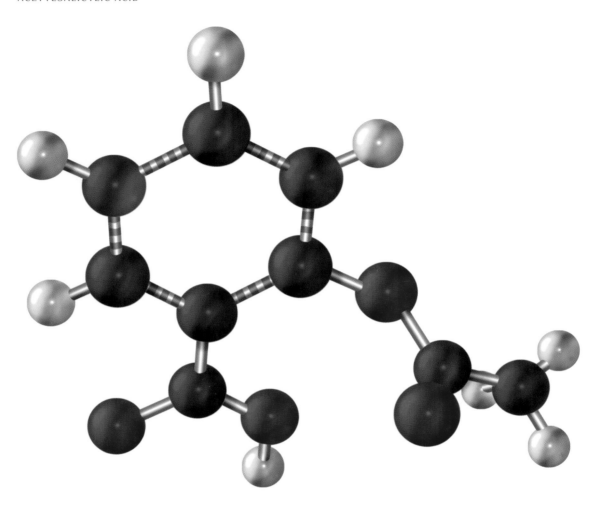

*Acetylsalicylic acid.* Red atoms are oxygen; white atoms are hydrogen; and black atoms are carbon. Striped sticks indicate a benzene ring. PUBLISHERS RESOURCE GROUP

In the period from 1828 to 1829, the active ingredient in willow bark was first isolated by three individuals, the German pharmacist Johann Büchner (dates not available), the French chemist Henri Leroux (dates not available), and the the Italian chemist, Raffaele Piria (1815-1865). Büchner gave the name salicin to the bitter-tasting yellow crystals extracted from willow bark after the Latin name for the willow tree, Salix. In 1853, the French chemist Charles Frederick Gerhardt (1816-1857) developed a method for reacting salicylic acid (the active ingredient in salicin) with acetic acid to make the first primitive form of aspirin.

## Interesting Facts

- The name aspirin comes from a very old name for salicylic acid, spiraeic acid.

- After Hofmann's discovery, Bayer received a registered trademark for the name aspirin, meaning that no other company could use the name for acetylsalicylic acid. When Germany was defeated in World War I (1914-1918), Allied forces seized the Bayer company's property and possessions and made the name available to all drug manufacturers.

For many years the way aspirin works in the body was not understood. Scientists now know that the compound's helpful effects come from its action on prostaglandins. Prostaglandins are hormone-like substances released by cells that are injured. They cause the body to release other substances that sensitize nerve endings to pain and start the healing process. Aspirin blocks prostaglandin production, thus relieving the sensation of pain and the inflammation that are the body's response to injury. Aspirin reduces fever by acting on the region of the brain that regulates body temperature and heart rate. Prostaglandins block the body's natural system for producing heat so that by blocking the release of prostaglandins, aspirin allows the regulation of body temperature to continue as usual. Aspirin's protection against heart attack and stroke occur because of its effect on one special type of prostaglandin, known as thromboxane A2. Thromboxane A2 promotes the accumulation of cells that takes place when a blood clot forms. By blocking or slowing down the production of thromboxane A2, aspirin prevents the formation of blood clots and, hence, the probability of heart attack and stroke.

### HOW IT IS MADE

The modern method for making aspirin was developed in 1897 by the German chemist Felix Hoffman (1868-1946), an employee of the German chemical manufacturer Bayer AG Chemical Works. In this procedure, phenol ($C_6H_5OH$) is treated with sodium hydroxide and carbon dioxide to make salicylic

## Words to Know

**ANALGESIC** A substance that relieves pain.    **THERAPEUTIC** Having healing properties.

acid. The salicylic acid is then reacted with acetic acid ($CH_3COOH$) to make acetylsalicylic acid, or aspirin. The preparation of aspirin by this procedure is quite simple and is often assigned to students in beginning high school and college chemistry classes. Aspirin tablets themselves include only acetylsalicylic acid, to which is added a small amount of water, starch and lubricant that act as a binder to hold the tablet together.

## COMMON USES AND POTENTIAL HAZARDS

The exclusive use of aspirin is as a medicine. It has three important properties as a drug. It relieves pain, reduces inflammation, and reduces fever. In addition to its effectiveness in treating these medical symptoms, it is inexpensive and available in a variety of forms, including chewable tablets, extended-release formulations, effervescent tablets, and even in chewing gums. Aspirin is often prescribed in low, daily doses as a preventative measure for individuals at risk for heart attack and stroke.

While aspirin has many medical benefits, it is not without risk for some individuals. Some people are allergic to the compound and can not tolerate even a low dose. Such individuals experience a number of symptoms if they ingest high doses of aspirin, symptoms that include ringing in the ears, nausea, vomiting, dizziness, confusion, hallucinations, coma, seizures, rapid breathing, fever, and, in the most severe cases, death. Aspirin use is not recommended in children under the age of twelve who show symptoms of viral infections because it can lead to an extremely rare but deadly complication known as Reye's syndrome.

### FOR FURTHER INFORMATION

Arnst, Catherine. "A Preemptive Strike against Cancer." *Business Week* (June 7, 2004): 48.

"Aspirin." Plant-Derived Drugs.
http://phytomedical.com/Plant/Aspirin.asp (accessed on September 17, 2005).

Jeffreys, Diarmuid. *Aspirin: The Remarkable Story of a Wonder Drug.* New York: Bloomsbury, 2004.

"Molecule of the Month: Aspirin."
http://www.bris.ac.uk/Depts/Chemistry/MOTM/
aspirin/aspirin.htm (accessed on September 17, 2005).

*See Also* Acetaminophen

OTHER NAMES:
See Overview.

FORMULA:
$C_{29}H_{50}O$

ELEMENTS:
Carbon, hydrogen,
oxygen

COMPOUND TYPE:
Organic

STATE:
Liquid

MOLECULAR WEIGHT:
430.69 g/mol

MELTING POINT:
2.5°C to 3.5°C (36°F to
38°F)

BOILING POINT:
350°C (660°F;
decomposes)

SOLUBILITY:
Insoluble in water;
soluble in alcohol,
ether, acetone, oils,
and most organic
solvents

KEY FACTS

# Alpha-Tocopherol

## OVERVIEW

Alpha-tocopherol (AL-fa toe-KOF-er-ol) is also known as 2,5,7,8-tetramethyl-2-(4,8,12-trimethyltridecyl)chroman-6-ol and 3,4-Dihydro-2,5,7,8-tetramethyl-2-(4,8,12-trimethyltridecyl)-2H-1-benzopyran-6-ol, as well as by many other systematic names. It is one of a family of compounds, the tocopherols, that makes up vitamin E. Other members of the family include the beta ($\beta$), gamma ($\gamma$), delta ($\delta$), and epsilon ($\epsilon$) tocopherols. All tocopherols share the same basic molecular structure, differing only in slightly different arrangements of methyl ($CH_3$-) and hydroxyl (OH-) groups. In terms of biological activity, $\alpha$-tocopherol is the most important member of the tocopherol family. The tocopherols are all pale yellow, viscous oils found in a variety of plants, including almonds, mustard greens, green and red peppers, spinach, and sunflower seeds. The most important source for the vitamin is wheat germ.

Vitamin E was discovered in 1922 by two scientists at the University of California at Berkeley, Herbert McLean Evans

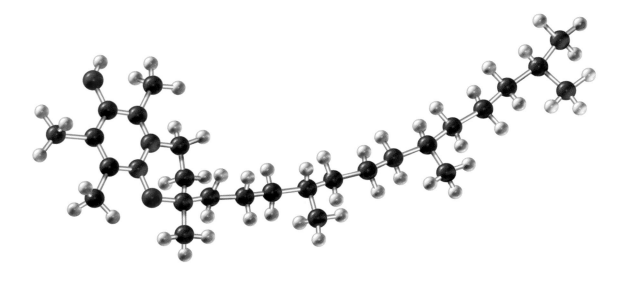

*Alpha-tocopheryl.* Red atoms are oxygen; white atoms are hydrogen; and black atoms are carbon. PUBLISHERS RESOURCE GROUP

(1882-1971) and Katherine Scott Bishop (1889-1976). Evans and Bishop found that rats whose diet was deficient in a-tocopherol did not reproduce normally. Scientists are now aware that the primary function of vitamin D in the human body is as an antioxidant. An antioxidant is a substance that reacts with and prevents the harmful effects of chemical strictures known as free radicals. A free radical is an atom or group of atoms with a single unpaired electron, making the atom or atoms unusually reactive. Free radicals are thought to be a primary cause of cell damage leading to cardiovascular disease, cancer, and aging.

Vitamin E was first produced synthetically (artificially) in 1938 by Swiss chemist Paul Karrer (1889-1971), who had been awarded the Nobel Prize in chemistry a year earlier for his studies of vitamin A, vitamin $B_2$, and other important biological compounds.

## HOW IT IS MADE

A variety of methods is now available for the synthesis (artificial production) of the tocopherols. In the most commonly used procedure, 2,3,5-trimethylhydroquinone is reacted with isophytol over one of many possible catalysts. A small amount of the vitamin is still obtained from natural sources, usually as the by-product in the treatment of one of its natural sources.

## Interesting Facts

As a general rule, vitamins and minerals are equally potent (effective) whether they come from natural sources or synthetic procedures. Vitamin E is an exception to that general rule. Synthetic forms of the vitamin are generally less potent than natural forms. The reason for this fact is that natural vitamin E exists in only one stereoisomeric form. Stereoisomers are two or more forms of a compound with the same kind and number of atoms. But the atoms in stereoisomers have somewhat different orientations in space. These slight differences in geometric shape are responsible for slight differences in biological activity. Natural vitamin E consists of only one stereoisomer, which is very active biologically. Synthetic vitamin E consists of two stereoisomers, only one of which (the one that occurs in natural vitamin E) is biologically active. So synthetic vitamin E tends to be about half as active biologically as natural vitamin E.

## COMMON USES AND POTENTIAL HAZARDS

Vitamin E deficiency disorders are rare in humans. The vast majority of people get all the vitamin E they need in their daily diets. Three groups of people may, however, require vitamin E supplements. The first group consists of individuals who are unable to absorb fat in their diets, so that the vitamin E they ingest is immediately eliminated from their bodies. The second group consists of a small fraction of people who have genetic disorders that make it impossible for them to utilize α-tocopherol. The third group of individuals consist of premature and very young babies. All babies are born deficient in vitamin E, but they normally overcome that deficiency in the first few weeks of their lives. Premature babies and some babies born at term may experience a variety of health problems as a result of vitamin E deficiency. Lack of normal reflexes, inability to orient itself, muscle weekness, and loss of balance are typical symptoms of vitamin E deficiency in babies. Deficiency problems for individuals in all three groups can be overcome by taking supplementary vitamin E.

## Words to Know

**CARCINOGEN** A chemical that causes cancer in humans or other animals.

**VISCOUS** Describes a syrupy liquid that flows slowly.

In addition to its use as a vitamin supplement for normal individuals and those at risk for vitamin E deficiency, the tocopherols have a few other uses:

- In the curing of meat to block the action of nitrosa-mines, a group of compound that occurs naturally in meats and may be carcinogenic;

- As an additive to animal feed to replace vitamins lost during feed processing; and

- As a food additive in vegetable oils and shortening to prevent oxidation (spoilage).

### FOR FURTHER INFORMATION

Challem, Jack, and Melissa Diane Smith. *Basic Health Publications User's Guide to Vitamin E: Don't Be a Dummy: Become an Expert on What Vitamin E Can Do for Your Health.* North Bergen, NJ: Basic Health Publications, 2002.

Packer, Lester, and Carol Colman. *The Antioxidant Miracle: Put Lipoic Acid, Pycogenol, and Vitamins E and C to Work for You.* New York: Wiley, 1999.

"Vitamin E." National Institutes of Health, Office of Dietary Supplements. http://ods.od.nih.gov/factsheets/vitamine.asp (accessed on September 17, 2005).

"Vitamin E (tocopherol)." Vitamin and Health Supplements Guide. http://www.vitamins-supplements.org/vitamin-E.php (accessed on September 17, 2005).

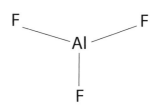

OTHER NAMES:
Aluminum trifluoride

FORMULA:
AlF$_3$

ELEMENTS:
Aluminum, fluorine

COMPOUND TYPE:
Inorganic salt

STATE:
Solid

MOLECULAR WEIGHT:
83.98 g/mol

MELTING POINT:
1291°C (2356°F; begins
to sublime above
1250°C [2280°F])

BOILING POINT:
Not applicable

SOLUBILITY:
Slightly soluble in
cold water, soluble in
hot water; insoluble
in alcohol, acetone,
and most organic
solvents

KEY FACTS

# Aluminum Fluoride

## OVERVIEW

Aluminum fluoride (uh-LOO-min-um FLOR-ide) is a highly stable compound that occurs as a white crystalline solid. It resists the action of even strong solvents, such as hot concentrated sulfuric acid. The compound often occurs as a hydrate containing one or more molecules of water of hydration. The most common of these hydrates has the chemical formula AlF$_3$·3.5H$_2$O, meaning that for every two molecules of aluminum fluoride in a crystal, there are seven molecules of water. The major uses of aluminum fluoride are in a variety of applications in the chemical industry.

## HOW IT IS MADE

Three methods are available for the preparation of aluminum fluoride commercially. In the first method, alumina trihydrate (aluminum hydroxide; Al(OH)$_3$) is treated with hydrofluoric acid (HF). A second method of preparation is almost identical except that it takes place in the dry state

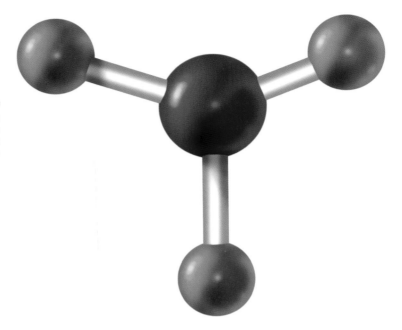

between dry alumina trihydrate and gaseous hydrogen fluoride. The third method involves the addition of fluorosilicic acid ($H_2SiF_6$) to alumina trihdrate. The last of these methods is commercially attractive because fluorosilicic acid is obtained inexpensively as a by-product in the production of fertilizers and phosphoric acid.

## COMMON USES AND POTENTIAL HAZARDS

The primary use of aluminum fluoride is in the production of aluminum metal. In that process, aluminum is extracted from one of its compounds (usually aluminum oxide) by passing an electric current through the molten (melted) compound. The addition of aluminum fluoride to the raw materials used in the process reduces the temperature at which the reaction occurs and improves the conductivity of the molten compound.

Some other uses of aluminum fluoride include:

- As a catalyst in the synthesis of organic compounds;
- To suppress the process of fermentation in the wine- and beer-making industries;

## Interesting Facts

Controversy exists about the health hazards of aluminum fluoride. On the one hand, the compound would appear to pose a relatively minor risk when ingested because it is so insoluble in water and other solvents. If it does not dissolve in the body, it can not get into the blood stream. On the other hand, it can cause health problems if inhaled or deposited on the skin. Opponents of water fluoridation argue that aluminum fluoride is sufficiently toxic to humans that it should not be added to public water supplies.

- In the manufacture of ceramics and glass; and

- As a flux in the preparation of glazes, enamels and in metallurgical processes.

Most authorities agree that aluminum fluoride does not pose a health hazard when ingested in moderate amounts because of its low solubility. The compound may pose a threat if inhaled or deposited on the skin, however. In modest amounts, it may produce skin and eye irritations that range from moderate to severe; irritation of the nose, throat, and lungs, that may include nosebleeds; and asthma-like

## Words to Know

**FLUX** A material that lowers the melting point of another substance or mixture of substances or that is used in cleaning a metal.

**HYDRATE** A chemical compound formed when one or more molecules of water is added physically to the molecule of some other substance.

**SYNTHESIS** A chemical reaction in which some desired chemical product is made from simple beginning chemicals, or reactants.

**WATER OF HYDRATION** Water that has combined with a compound by some physical means.

symptoms with coughing, shortness of breath, and tightness in the chest. Long-term exposure may result in weakness of the bones and stiffening of the joints.

### FOR FURTHER INFORMATION

"Aluminum Fluoride." ChemExper Chemical Directory. http://www.chemexper.com/chemicals/supplier/cas/ 7784-18-1.html (accessed on September 18, 2005).

"Aluminum Fluoride." Chemical Land 21. http://www.chemicalland21.com/industrialchem/inorganic/ ALUMINUM%20FLUORIDE.htm (accessed on September 18, 2005).

"Aluminum Fluoride." Solvay Chemicals. http://www.solvaychemicals.us/pdf/Inorganic_Fluorides/ ALF.pdf (accessed on September 18, 2005).

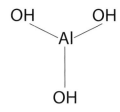

K E Y   F A C T S

# Aluminum Hydroxide

## OVERVIEW

Aluminum hydroxide (uh-LOO-min-um hi-DROK-side) is also known as alumina hydrate, aluminum hydrate, aluminum trihydrate, hydrated alumina, hydrated aluminum oxide, and aluminum white. It is a white crystalline powder that occurs in nature as the mineral gibbsite, one of the three minerals (along with boehmite, diaspore) that makes up bauxite. Bauxite is a rocky material from which the metal aluminum is extracted commercially. Aluminum hydroxide is perhaps best known to the average person as an ingredient in antacids, compounds for the treatment of upset stomach, acid indigestion, and related symptoms. It is found in products such as Maalox®, Mylanta®, and Gelusil®. A closely related chemical compound, aluminum hydroxychloride (Al$_2$Cl(OH)$_5$) is the active ingredient in most deodorants and anti-perspirants.

## HOW IT IS MADE

Most aluminum hydroxide is produced by treating bauxite with a hot, concentrated solution of sodium hydroxide

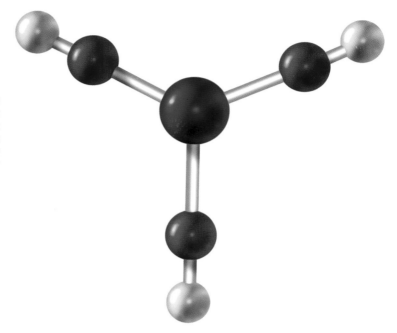

*Aluminum hydroxide.* Red atoms are oxygen; white atoms are hydrogen; and turquoise atom is aluminum. PUBLISHERS RESOURCE GROUP

(NaOH). As the solution cools, aluminum hydroxide settles out of the reaction mixture as a gelatinous (jelly-like) precipitate, which can then be dried and saved as a white powder. The aluminum hydroxide can also be precipitated by passing carbon dioxide gas through the solution.

## COMMON USES AND POTENTIAL HAZARDS

Aluminum hydroxide is an effective antacid because it is, chemically, a base. As such, it reacts with stomach acid (hydrochloric acid; HCl), to reduce the symptoms of heartburn, upset stomach, acid indigestion, and gastritis, an inflammation of the stomach lining. The compound can also be used to treat peptic ulcers on a long-term basis. A peptic ulcer is an open sore in the lining of the stomach or the first part of the small intestine.

Aluminum hydroxide also has a number of industrial applications, such as:

- A raw material for the preparation of other aluminum compounds;

- An additive for cosmetics, paper, plastics, and rubber to give the final product more bulk;

## Interesting Facts

Aluminum hydroxide is one of the most common adjuvants used in vaccines today. An adjuvant is a substance added to a vaccine to increase the efficiency with which it prevents disease. The mechanisms by which adjuvants such as aluminum hydroxide achieve this objective are not always known.

- In abrasives designed for use with plastics and brass;
- An additive for glass products that adds strength and resistance to attack by chemicals and weathering and to heat shock;
- As the world's most popular flame retardant.

Studies have not shown that aluminum hydroxide poses health risks of any kind to human beings.

### FOR FURTHER INFORMATION

"Aluminum Hydroxide." Chemical Land 21. http://www.chemicalland21.com/industrialchem/inorganic/aloh3.htm (accessed on September 18, 2005).

"Aluminum Hydroxide." Drugs.com. http://www.drugs.com/MTM/aluminum_hydroxide.html (accessed on September 18, 2005).

## Words to Know

**ADJUVANT** A substance added to a vaccine to increase the efficiency with which it prevents disease.

**ANTACID** A medicine used for the treatment of upset stomach, acid indigestion, and related symptoms.

**PRECIPITATE** A solid material that settles out of a solution, often as the result of a chemical reaction.

"Aluminum Hydroxide Resources." drugs@mongabay.com. http://names.mongabay.com/drugs/ingredients/ ALUMINUM_HYDROXIDE.html (accessed on September 18, 2005).

Malakoff, David. "Public Health: Aluminum Is Put on Trial as a Vaccine Booster." *Science* (May 26, 2000): 1323.

*See Also* Aluminum oxide

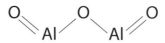

# Aluminum Oxide

## OVERVIEW

Aluminum oxide (uh-LOO-min-um OK-side) is white crystal-line powder that occurs in nature in a variety of minerals, including boehmite, bayerite, corundum, diaspore, and gibbsite. Corundum is second hardest naturally occurring mineral. Only diamond is harder. Aluminum oxide occurs in a variety of chemical forms in a variety of gemstones, including chrysoberyl, ruby, sapphire, and spinel. The color of these gemstones is a result of impurities, such as chromium (in the case of ruby) and iron and titanium (in the case of sapphire). The colors may also vary depending on the kind and amount of each impurity.

Aluminum oxide's commercial uses depend not only on its hardness, but also on its high melting point and its low electrical conductivity. The compound is also non-combustible and resistant to attack by most solvents and other chemical agents.

## HOW IT IS MADE

Aluminum oxide is produced by washing the rocky material bauxite with a hot solution of sodium hydroxide (NaOH).

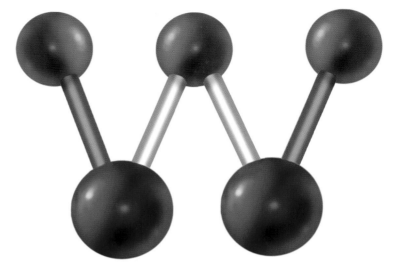

The aluminum hydroxide ($Al(OH_3)$) that is produced in this reaction is then heated to drive off water, producing aluminum oxide. Wastes from coal mining operation are also treated to extract the aluminum sulfate ($Al_2(SO_4)_3$) they contain. The aluminum sulfate is converted to aluminum hydroxide which, again, is heated to produce aluminum oxide.

## COMMON USES AND POTENTIAL HAZARDS

The primary use of aluminum oxide is the manufacture of aluminum metal. When an electric current is passed through molten (melted) aluminum oxide, the compound breaks down to form aluminum metal and oxygen gas. The method is called the Hall process after the American chemist Charles Martin Hall who invented it.

Aluminum oxide is also widely used as an abrasive. An abrasive is a very hard material used to grind, polish, sand, scour, scrub, smooth or polish some other material. Among the products that include aluminum oxide as an abrasive are emery boards, sandpaper, grinding and polishing wheels and belts, lens grinding devices, and gem polishing wheels.

The high melting point of aluminum oxide also makes it a good refractory product. A refractory material is one that does not melt easily, making it suitable for lining the inside

## Interesting Facts

- The hardness of materials is measured on the Mohs scale, named after the German mineralogist Frederick Mohs (1773–1839), who suggested the system. The scale runs from 1 (the softest known natural material, talc) to 10 (the hardest known natural material, diamond). Corundum has a hardness of 8.8 on the Mohs scale.

- The invention of a method for making aluminum metal from aluminum oxide by the 23-year-old American chemist Charles Martin Hall (1863–1914) in 1886 resulted in a reduction in the price of aluminum metal from about twelve dollars a pound to less than a dollar a pound.

of furnaces or the manufacture of glass and ceramic materials that will not melt when exposed to very high temperatures. Some other uses of aluminum oxide include:

- In finely-divided form, as the packing material in chromatographic columns. Chromatography is a process by which individual components of a mixture are separated from each other by passing them through a tube filled with some absorbent material (such as aluminum oxide).

- As a catalyst in many industrial chemical reactions;

- In the paper-making process, as a filler that adds body to the final product;

- For the production of artificial gemstones;

- As a food additives, where it acts as a dispersant, a substance that keeps a product from clumping together in a package; and

- As the internal coating on frosted light bulbs.

The U.S. Occupational Safety and Health Administration (OSHA) classifies aluminum oxide as a *nuisance dust* in the workplace. A nuisance dust is one for which no serious harmful effects have been identified as long as its release is kept under control. It may, however, cause unpleasant

## Words to Know

**CATALYST** A material that increases the rate of a chemical reaction without undergoing any change in its own chemical structure

**CHROMATOGRAPHY** A process by which a mixture of substances passes through a column consisting of some material that causes the individual components in the mixture to separate from each other.

**DISPERSANT** A substance that keeps another substance from clumping together or becoming lumpy.

**REFRACTORY** Does not melt easily; able to withstand high temperatures.

**SOLVENT** A substance that is able to dissolve one or more other substances.

symptoms, such as irritation of the skin, eyes, and lungs if present in unusually large amounts. The simplest treatment for problems related to nuisance dusts is to move away from the contaminated area where an adequate supply of fresh air is available.

### FOR FURTHER INFORMATION

"Aluminum Oxide, $Al_2O_3$." Accuratus. http://www.accuratus.com/alumox.html (accessed on September 19, 2005).

Frost, Randall. "Abrasives." *Gale Encyclopedia of Science.* Edited by K. Lee Lerner and Brenda Wilmoth Lerner. 3rd ed. Vol. 1. Detroit, Mich.: Gale, 2004.

"The Mineral Corundum." Amethyst Galleries. http://mineral.galleries.com/minerals/oxides/corundum/corundum.htm (accessed on September 19, 2005).

Misra, Chanakya. *Industrial Alumina Chemicals.* Washington, D.C.: American Chemical Society, 1986.

*See Also* Aluminum hydroxide

$$O^- \quad S \quad O$$
$$O^- \quad \quad O$$

$$K^+ \quad \overset{O}{\underset{-O}{S}} \overset{O}{\underset{O}{}} \quad Al^{3+}$$

# Aluminum Potassium Sulfate

OTHER NAMES:
See Overview.

FORMULA:
$KAl(SO_4)_2$

ELEMENTS:
Potassium, aluminum,
sulfur, oxygen

COMPOUND TYPE:
Inorganic salt

STATE:
Solid

MOLECULAR WEIGHT:
258.20 g/mol

MELTING POINT:
92.5°C (198°F; loses
water of hydration
beginning at 64.5°C
(148°F)

BOILING POINT:
200°C (392°F; loses all
water of hydration)

SOLUBILITY:
Soluble in cold water;
very soluble in hot
water; insoluble in
alcohol, ether,
acetone, and other
organic solvents

KEY FACTS

## OVERVIEW

Aluminum potassium sulfate (uh-LOO-min-um po-TASS-see-um sul-fate) is also known as aluminum potassium sulfate dodecahydrate, potash alum, potassium alum, and kalinite. It normally occurs in the form of the dodecahydrate, meaning that each molecule of the compound is associated with twelve molecules of water. The formula of the hydrate is $KAl(SO_4)_2 \cdot 12H_2O$. In this form, it occurs as white odorless crystals. The compound gradually loses its water of hydration when heated, giving up the first nine molecules of water at 64.5°C (148°F), and the remaining three molecules of water at about 200°C (392°F).

Aluminum potassium sulfate belongs to a family of compounds known collectively as the alums. The term *alum* refers to a double salt that consists of aluminum, the sulfate group ($SO_4$), and one other metal. The presence of two metals, aluminum plus one other metal, accounts for the name double salt. Other common alums are aluminum ammonium sulfate and aluminum sodium sulfate.

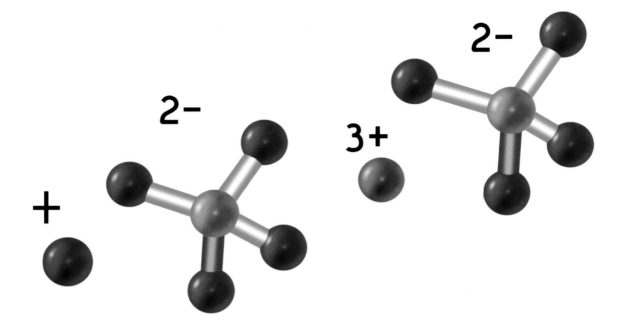

*Aluminum potassium sulfate.*
Red atoms are oxygen; yellow
atoms are sulfur; turquoise
atom is potassium; and orange
atom is aluminum. Gray sticks
indicate double bonds.

The alums were known as far back as ancient Egypt and China, where they were used as deodorants. Alums are effective for this purpose because they are astringents, substances that cause tissues to shrink or contract, thus reducing the tendency of sweat glands to produce perspiration. As astringents, alums were also used in the field of medicine to treat wounds and prevent bleeding. Until the nineteenth century, however, chemists did not recognize that the substance they knew as alum was actually a variety of different compounds.

## HOW IT IS MADE

Aluminum potassium sulfate occurs naturally in the form of the minerals alunite and kalinite. Where these minerals are available, the compound can be mined and purified to obtain potash alum. Where the minerals are not available, the compound can be produced synthetically by combining aqueous aluminum sulfate with aqueous potassium sulfate. The two compounds react with each other in solution to form the double salt, aluminum potassium sulfate, which can then be extracted by allowing the solutions to evaporate, during which the desired compound crystallizes out.

## Interesting Facts

- During the fifteenth century, the Vatican achieved control of the alum industry in Europe. When King Henry VIII of England quarreled with Pope Clemens VII a century later over his desire to marry a second time, the pope cut off supplies of alum to Great Britain. Since alum was an essential product in the dyeing of clothes, the English clothing industry rapidly fell into dire circumstances.

## COMMON USES AND POTENTIAL HAZARDS

One of aluminum potassium sulfate's major uses is in the dyeing of fibers and fabrics, where it is employed as a mordant. A mordant is a substance that reacts with a dye, helping it attach more permanently to a fiber or fabric. Aluminum potassium sulfate has also been used in the paper-making industry for many centuries, where it has a variety of applications. For example, it can be used to give paper a tough, shiny surface or to increase the intensity of inks, paints, and dyes used on the paper. Some water treatment plants also use aluminum potassium sulfate in their purification systems. The compound is added to water, where it combines with colloidal particles suspended in water to form larger clumps, which then settle out of the water. Other uses of aluminum potassium sulfate include:

- As a food additive, used to control the acidity of the product;
- In the manufacture of matches;
- For the waterproofing of fabrics;
- In the tanning of leather;
- In the manufacture of deodorants;
- To add hardness and toughness to cement;
- In the production of fireworks;

## Words to Know

**AQUEOUS SOLUTION** A solution that consists of some material dissolved in water.

**ASTRINGENT** A material triggers a loss of water from tissue, thereby causing the tissues to shrink and contract.

**COLLOID** A mixture consisting of tiny particles suspended, but not dissolved, in water.

**DOUBLE SALT** A salt that includes aluminum and one other metal, such as potassium.

**MORDANT** A substance that reacts with a dye so that it attaches to a fiber or fabric more easily.

• As an astringent in medical treatments; and

• In the preparation of other compounds of aluminum in the chemical industry.

FOR FURTHER INFORMATION

"Aluminum Potassium Sulfate Resources." http://names.mongabay.com/drugs/ingredients/ALUMINUM_ POTASSIUM_SULFATE.html (accessed on September 18, 2005).

Hart-Davis, Adam. "Thomas Challoner and His Astonishing Alum Industry." ExNet. http://www2.exnet.com/1995/12/18/science/ science.html#LINKS-BACK (accessed on September 18, 2005).

"Material Safety Data Sheet: Aluminum Potassium Sulfate Dode-cahydrate." Department of Chemistry, Iowa State University. http://avogadro.chem.iastate.edu/MSDS/AlKSO4.htm (accessed on September 18, 2005).

"Potassium Aluminum Sulfate." *Gale Encyclopedia of Science.* Edited by K. Lee Lerner and Brenda Wilmoth Lerner. 3rd ed. Vol. 5. Detroit, Mich.: Gale, 2004.

*See Also* Potassium Sulfate

OTHER NAMES:
None

FORMULA:
$NH_3$

ELEMENTS:
Nitrogen, hydrogen

COMPOUND TYPE:
Inorganic base

STATE:
Gas

MOLECULAR WEIGHT:
17.03 g/mol

MELTING POINT:
−77.7°C (−108°F)

BOILING POINT:
−33.35°C (−28.03°F)

SOLUBILITY:
Very soluble in cold
water; soluble in
alcohol, ether, and
many organic solvents

KEY FACTS

# Ammonia

## OVERVIEW

Ammonia (uh-MOH-nyah) is a colorless gas with a strong, suffocating odor. It was present in the primordial (original) atmosphere of the Earth. Scientists believe that it may have been the source of nitrogen for the earliest forms of life. Ammonia was the first chemical compound to be found in interstellar space, the space between stars. It is a major component of the atmosphere of many planets in our solar system.

Early chemists learned to produce ammonia from animal parts, such as the horns of deer. But it was the English chemist and physicist Joseph Priestley (1733-1804) who first collected and studied the pure gas. In 1785, the French chemist Claude-Louis Berthollet (1748-1822) determined the correct chemical formula for the gas, $NH_3$.

In 2004, American companies produced 10,762,000 metric tons (11,863,000 short tons) of ammonia, making it the tenth highest-volume chemical made in the United States. Only ten years earlier, it had ranked number 5 on

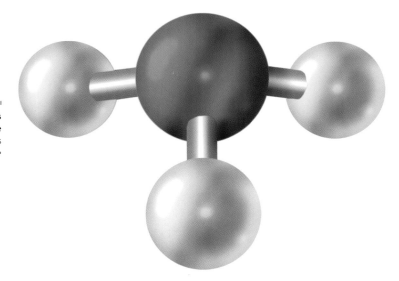

the list of all chemicals produced by volume. About 90 percent of all the ammonia used in the United States goes to the production of fertilizers.

## HOW IT IS MADE

Ammonia is produced naturally by the action of certain types of bacteria on nitrogen found in the atmosphere. It is also formed during the decay of dead organisms.

Until the end of the nineteenth century, ammonia was produced commercially by the cyanamide process. Calcium carbide ($CaC_2$), nitrogen gas ($N_2$), and steam were reacted with each other to produce ammonia.

In the early 1900s, the German chemist Fritz Haber (1868-1934) developed a method for making ammonia directly from its elements, nitrogen and hydrogen. The two gases are combined with each other at high temperature (400°C to 650°C; 750°F to 1200°F) and pressure (200 to 400 atmospheres; 3,000 to 6,000 pounds per square inch) over a catalyst made of finely-divided iron. Haber's process was later refined and improved by German chemical engineer Carl Bosch (1874-1940). Haber and Bosch both won Nobel Prizes in chemistry for their work on the production of ammonia. The Haber-Bosch process remains the most common form of ammonia production in many countries, including the United

## Interesting Facts

- Ammonia's name comes from an ancient Egyptian practice conducted at the temple of the sun god Amon (or Ammon) near Karnak. Camel dung burned at the temple gave off a strong odor (ammonia) and left behind a white crystalline substance on the ground. The white substance was given the name of sal ammoniac, or salt of Amon, and the gas itself later became known as ammonia.

- The Haber-Bosch process was developed largely because of Germany's need for explosives in World War I. Ammonia gas is converted to nitric acid, which, in turn, is used in making sodium and potassium nitrate, major components of explosives. Fritz Haber believed that it was his patriotic duty to contribute to the German war effort in whatever way he could, which led to his development of a new method for making ammonia.

States. Small amounts of ammonia are also produced during the process by which soft coal is converted to coke.

Ammonia is a natural product of metabolism in all animals. When proteins break down, the nitrogen they contain is converted, in part, to ammonia. The ammonia is then converted to urea, which is excreted in the urine.

### COMMON USES AND POTENTIAL HAZARDS

Ammonia is used in a variety of forms as a fertilizer. It can be liquified or dissolved in water and sprayed on land, or it can be converted into any one of a number of compounds, such as ammonium nitrate, ammonium phosphate, or ammonium sulfate. In these forms, it is spread as dry granules on the land. Urea, made from ammonia and carbon dioxide, is also used as a feed supplement for cattle. Plants and animals use the nitrogen in ammonia and its compounds to synthesize new proteins that contribute to their growth and development.

The next largest use of ammonia is in the synthesis of nitric acid ($HNO_3$). In a process developed by the German chemist Wilhelm Ostwald (1853-1932), ammonia, oxygen, and water are reacted together in a series of steps that results in the formation of nitric acid. Nitric acid, the thirteenth most important chemical in the United States in terms of productions, has a number of important uses, including the manufacture of explosives. Like the Haber-Bosch process, the Ostwald process contributed to the success experienced by Germany during World War I.

In addition to its use in the manufacture of fertilizers and explosives, smaller amounts of ammonia are used:

- As a refrigerant;
- In the manufacture of plastics;
- As a raw material in the manufacture of other nitrogen-containing chemicals;
- In the production of dyes;
- As a rocket fuel;
- For the neutralization of acids during the refining of petroleum;
- In order to produce specialized types of steel; and
- As a nutrient in yeast cultures in food processing operations.

Both gaseous and liquid ammonia pose moderate health hazards to those who come into contact with them. For example, farmers who handle liquid ammonia risk the possibility of painful blistering of the skin or damage to the mucous membranes if they come into contact with the ferilizer. Ammonia fumes can irritate the mouth, nose, and throat, causing coughing and gagging responses. Higher levels of exposure may irritate the lungs, resulting in shortness of breath and producing headaches, nausea, and vomiting. Very high exposures can cause a buildup of fluid in the lungs that can result in death. Since ammonia is a common ingredient of many household products, everyone should be aware of its health risks, although the threat posed by such products is, in fact, very small.

# Words to Know

**CATALYST** A material that increases the rate of a chemical reaction without undergoing any change in its own chemical structure.

**METABOLISM** The process including all of the chemical reactions that occur in cells by which fats, carbohydrates, and other compounds are broken down to produce energy and the compounds needed to build new cells and tissues.

**MUCOUS MEMBRANES** Tissues that line the moist inner lining of the digestive, respiratory, urinary and reproductive systems.

**SYNTHESIS** A chemical reaction in which some desired chemical product is made from simple beginning chemicals, or reactants.

FOR FURTHER INFORMATION

"Ammonia." Masterliness.
http://www.masterliness.com/a/Ammonia.htm
(accessed on September 19, 2005).

Buechel, K. H., et al. Industrial Inorganic Chemistry. New York: VCH, 2000, pp. 29-43.

"The Facts about Ammonia." New York State Department of Health.
http://www.health.state.ny.us/nysdoh/bt/chemical_terrorism/docs/ammonia_general.pdf
(accessed on September 19, 2005).

"Toxicological Profile for Ammonia." Agency for Toxic Substances and Disease Registry.
http://www.atsdr.cdc.gov/toxprofiles/tp126.html
(accessed on September 19, 2005).

"Uses and Production of Ammonia (Haber Process)." Ausetute.
http://www.ausetute.com.au/haberpro.html
(accessed on September 19, 2005).

*See Also* Ammonium Chloride; Ammonium Hydroxide; Ammonium Nitrate; Ammonium Sulfate; Nitric Acid; Potassium Nitrate; Urea

$$Cl^- \qquad H \overset{\displaystyle +}{\underset{\displaystyle H}{\overset{\displaystyle |}{N}}} \overset{\displaystyle H}{\underset{\displaystyle H}{}}$$

OTHER NAMES:
Ammonium muriate;
sal ammoniac;
salmiac

FORMULA:
NH₄Cl

ELEMENTS:
Nitrogen, hydrogen,
chlorine

COMPOUND TYPE:
Inorganic salt

STATE:
Solid

MOLECULAR WEIGHT:
53.49 g/mol

MELTING POINT:
340°C (640°F;
sublimes at melting
point)

BOILING POINT:
Not applicable

SOLUBILITY:
Soluble in water;
slightly soluble in
alcohol; insoluble in
most organic solvents

KEY FACTS

# Ammonium Chloride

## OVERVIEW

Ammonium chloride (uh-MOH-ni-um KLOR-ide) occurs as odorless white crystals with a cool, salt-like taste. The compound is of interest to historians of chemistry as being one of the first chemicals mentioned by ancient scholars and the first compound of ammonia to have been discovered. For example, the Roman philosopher Pliny the Elder (23-79 CE) wrote about a substance he called hammoniacus sal that appears to have been ammonium chloride. The problem is that various authorities used the term *sal ammoniac* for a variety of materials that were clearly different from each other. No one really knew the compound's actual chemical composition until 1700, when it was discovered by the French botanist Joseph Tournefort (1656-1708). In any case, *sal ammoniac* was an important raw material in early industrial operations, including primarily dyeing and metallurgical operations.

*Sal ammoniac* is also the name of the mineral form of ammonium chloride. The mineral occurs only rarely in

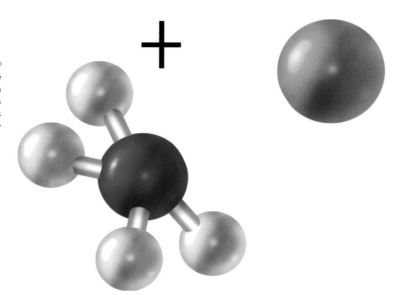

nature, and only then in arid (dry) regions. Since ammonium chloride is quite soluble in water, it remains on the ground only in places where there is little rain. One such location is around the vents of active volcanoes. The compound is formed in these regions when hydrogen chloride (HCl) in volcanic gases and ammonia ($NH_3$) produced by the decay of plants and animals react with each other to form ammonium chloride, which then settles out onto the ground.

## HOW IT IS MADE

One straightforward method of making ammonium chloride is by combining an aqueous solution of some compound of ammonia, usually ammonium sulfate ($[NH_4]_2SO_4$), with hydrochloric acid (HCl) and collecting the ammonium chloride that forms by evaporation. Commercially, the compound is obtained as a by-product of the so-called ammonia-soda process for making sodium carbonate ($Na_2SO_4$). In this process, invented by the Belgian chemist Ernest Solvay (1838-1922) in 1861, ammonia, sodium chloride (NaCl), and carbon dioxide ($CO_2$) are combined with each other in a series of reactions to make

## Interesting Facts

- Sal ammoniac was an important substance in the study of alchemy. The goals and methods of alchemy changed considerably over the period from about the twelfth century to about the sixteenth century and were somewhat different from culture to culture. For example, one Islamic alchemist, Abu Bakr Mohammed ar-Razi (865–925) classified sal ammoniac as one of the fundamental spirits of matter, along with mercury, sulfur, and arsenic.

sodium carbonate, a very important commercial product. Ammonium chloride is also formed during the reactions and is removed as a by-product.

### COMMON USES AND POTENTIAL HAZARDS

Ammonium chloride has a wide variety of commercial uses. One of the best known uses is in dry cell batteries. Dry cell batteries consist of three parts: the anode (the metal bottom of the battery), the cathode (the metal knob at the top of the battery), and the electrolyte (a moist solid material that makes up the body of the battery). Electrons produced in a chemical reaction within the battery flow out of the cathode, through an external circuit (the device to which the battery is attached), back into the battery through the anode, and back to the cathode through the electrolyte. The electrolyte in a dry cell battery consists of a pasty mixture of ammonium chloride with water.

Some other uses of ammonium chloride include:

- As a mordant in dyeing and printing operations;

- As a flux for soldering;

- For the production of other ammonium compounds, especially those used as fertilizers;

- In the manufacture of certain types of polymers, especially the family known as the urea-formaldehyde resins;

## Words to Know

**ALCHEMY** An ancient field of study from which the modern science of chemistry evolved.

**AQUEOUS SOLUTION** A solution that consists of some material dissolved in water.

**ELECTROPLATING** Process by which a thin layer of one metal is deposited on top of a second metal by passing an electric current through a solution of the first metal.

**FLUX** A material that lowers the melting point of another substance or mixture of substances or that is used in cleaning a metal.

**MORDANT** A substance used in dyeing and printing that reacts chemically with both a dye and the material being dyed to help hold the dye permanently to the material.

**POLYMER** A compound consisting of very large molecules made of one or two small repeated units called monomers.

• For the electroplating of metals; and

• As an additive to a licorice-type candy popular in some parts of the world, to which it gives a characteristic salty taste.

Exposure to ammonium chloride may carry certain health risks. When inhaled or deposited on the skin, it may cause irritation of the tissues that may require treatment. The compound is potentially toxic if swallowed. These potential problems are generally of concern primarily to people who work with the compound directly, as in the industries mentioned above. Anyone who is exposed to ammonium chloride should see medical attention immediately.

### FOR FURTHER INFORMATION

"Ammonium Chloride: Helping to Provide Portable Electricity." The Science Center.
http://www.science-education.org/classroom_activities/chlorine_compound/ammonium_chloride.html (accessed on September 19, 2005).

"Ammonium Chloride, Technical." Zaclon Incorporated.
http://www.zaclon.com/pdf/amchltec_datasheet.pdf (accessed on September 19, 2005).

"Material Safety Data Sheet: Ammonium Chloride." Department of Chemistry, Iowa State University. http://avogadro.chem.iastate.edu/MSDS/NH4Cl.htm (accessed on September 19, 2005).

Patnaik, Praydot. *Handbook of Inorganic Chemicals.* New York: McGraw-Hill, 2003.

*See Also* Ammonia; Ammonium Hydroxide; Sodium Carbonate; Urea

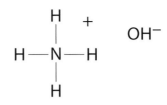

OTHER NAMES:
Ammonia solution,
aqua ammonia,
ammonium hydrate,
spirits of hartshorn

FORMULA:
NH₄OH

ELEMENTS:
Nitrogen, hydrogen,
oxygen

COMPOUND TYPE:
Inorganic base

STATE:
Aqueous solution
(exists only in
solution)

MOLECULAR WEIGHT:
35.05 g/mol

MELTING POINT:
Not applicable

BOILING POINT:
Not applicable

SOLUBILITY:
Not applicable

# Ammonium Hydroxide

## OVERVIEW

Ammonium hydroxide (uh-MOH-ni-um hye-DROK-side) is a clear, colorless aqueous solution consisting of ammonia gas dissolved in water. The compound does not exist in any other state. Ammonium hydroxide has a strong pungent, suffocating odor caused by the release of ammonia gas from the solution. Most solutions of ammonium hydroxide range in concentration from less than one percent to about 35 percent ammonia. For most commercial purposes the lowest concentration is about 10 percent ammonia in water.

## HOW IT IS MADE

Ammonium hydroxide is prepared by passing ammonia gas (NH₃) into water. Once prepared, ammonium hydroxide solutions tend to be very stable.

## COMMON USES AND POTENTIAL HAZARDS

The uses of ammonium hydroxide are closely related to those of ammonia gas from which it is made. The advantage

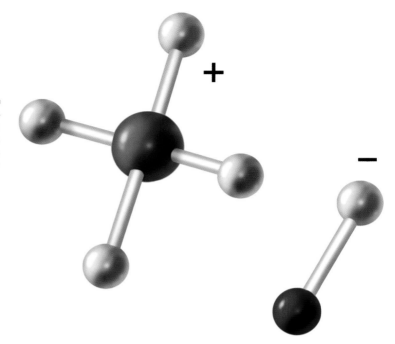

*Ammonium hydroxide.* White atoms are hydrogen; red atom is oxygen; and blue atom is nitrogen. PUBLISHERS RESOURCE GROUP

of using ammonium hydroxide over ammonia is that the reactant (the ammonia) may be more easily controlled when dissolved in water than when available as a gas.

Some uses of ammonium hydroxide include:

- As a cleaning agent in a variety of industrial and commercial products, such as household ammonia, where the concentration of the solution is generally in the range of 3 to 10 percent;

- In the manufacture of rayon and other textiles;

- As a refrigerant;

- As a food additive to maintain the proper level of acidity in the food;

- In the production of soaps and detergents, pharmaceuticals, ceramics, explosives, and inks; and

- In the fireproofing of wood.

Health hazards posed by ammonium hydroxide are a consequence of the ammonia present in the solution. When exposed to the air, such solutions tend to release some ammonia gas, which users may breathe in. The gas may then

## Words to Know

**AQUEOUS SOLUTION** A solution that consists of some material dissolved in water.

**PUNGENT** Intensely sharp or biting.

cause irritation of the eyes, nose, and throat that, for weak solutions, is generally unpleasant but not dangerous. Exposure to higher concentrations of ammonia released from ammonium hydroxide may result in more serious health problems, such as severe burning of the eyes, nose, and throat and permanent damage to these parts of the body, including blindness, lung disease, and death. One of the most dangerous hazards posed by ammonium hydroxide occurs when it is mixed with substances containing chlorine, such as bleaching products. That combination may result in large amounts of heat and toxic gases that can cause serious injuries and even death.

### FOR FURTHER INFORMATION

"Ammonia: Public Health Statement." Agency for Toxic Substances and Disease Registry.
http://www.atsdr.cdc.gov/toxprofiles/tp126-c1.pdf (accessed on September 19, 2005).

"Ammonium Hydroxide." Industrial Resources Group, Ltd.
http://www.indresgroup.com/aqua.htm (accessed on September 19, 2005).

"Ammonium Hydroxide." Medline Plus Medical Encyclopedia.
http://www.nlm.nih.gov/medlineplus/ency/article/002491.htm (accessed on September 19, 2005).

*See Also* Ammonia

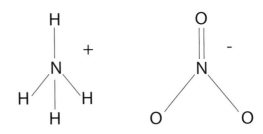

OTHER NAMES:
German saltpeter;
Norway saltpeter;
nitric acid,
ammonium salt

FORMULA:
$NH_4NO_3$

ELEMENTS:
Nitrogen, hydrogen,
oxygen

COMPOUND TYPE:
Inorganic salt

STATE:
Solid

MOLECULAR WEIGHT:
80.04 g/mol

MELTING POINT:
169.6°C (337.3°F)

BOILING POINT:
211°C (412°F);
decomposes at its
boiling point

SOLUBILITY:
Very soluble in water,
soluble in alcohol and
acetone

KEY FACTS

# Ammonium Nitrate

## OVERVIEW

Ammonium nitrate (uh-MOH-ni-um NYE-trate) is a white crystalline substance first made artificially in 1659 by the German chemist Johann Rudolf Glauber (1604–1670). The compound does not occur in nature because it is so soluble that it is washed out of the soil by rain and surface water. Ammonium nitrate is stable at lower temperatures, but tends to decompose explosively when heated to temperatures above 200°C (390°F). Its two most important uses today are in fertilizers and explosives. In 2004, it ranked fourteenth among all chemicals manufactured in the United States. Just over six million metric tons (6.6 million short tons) of the compound were produced in 2004.

## HOW IT IS MADE

Ammonium nitrate is made commercially by passing ammonia gas ($NH_3$) and a water solution of nitric acid ($HNO_3$) through a pipe. The ammonia combines with the

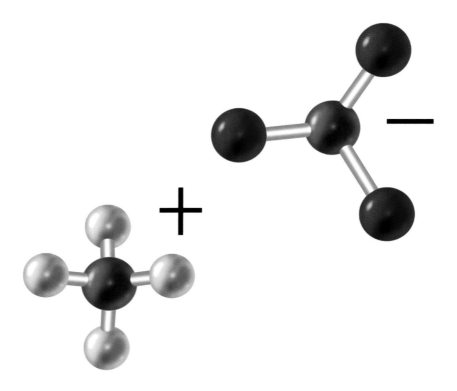

*Ammonium nitrate.* Red atoms are oxygen; white atoms are hydrogen; and blue atoms are nitrogen. PUBLISHERS RESOURCE GROUP

nitric acid to form ammonium nitrate. The formula for this reaction can be written as $NH_3 + HNO_3 \rightarrow NH_4NO_3$.

Large amounts of heat are released during the reaction, so the pipe and supporting equipment must be very strong. The solution of ammonium nitrate in water is allowed to evaporate, leaving behind pure white crystals of the compound.

## COMMON USES AND POTENTIAL HAZARDS

The primary use of ammonium nitrate is the manufacture of fertilizers. In 2005, about 2 million metric tons (2.2 million short tons) of ammonium nitrate fertilizer was used in the United States. The compound is added to soil to provide the nitrogen that plants need to grow. It may be used by itself or in combination with another nitrogen-rich compound, urea, in a mixture known as UAN.

Ammonium nitrate is also an important component of some explosives. It provides the oxygen needed to cause some other material to catch fire and burn very rapidly,

## Interesting Facts

The German alchemist Andreas Libau (c.1540-1616), better known by his Latinized name of Libavius, wrote what is widely regarded as the first textbook on chemistry in 1597. In that book, *Alchemia*, he described a method for making ammonium sulfate, probably the first mention of the compound in modern sources.

- In the tanning of leather;
- As a fireproofing agent for fabrics and paper;
- In the manufacture of viscose rayon;
- As an additive to cattle feed
- As a nutrient in bacterial cultures;
- In the processing of certain metals, such as chromium and gold; and
- In the manufacture of polymers used in the production of chipboard.

### FOR FURTHER INFORMATION

"Ammonium Sulfate." Hazardous Substances Data Bank. http://toxnet.nlm.nih.gov/cgi-bin/sis/search/ r?dbs+hsdb:@term+@na+Ammonium+Sulfate (accessed on September 20, 2005).

## Words to Know

**ALCHEMY** Ancient field of study from which the modern science of chemistry evolved.

**POLYMER** A compound consisting of very large molecules made of one or two small repeated units called monomers.

"Ammonium Sulfate Advantage: FAQs." Honeywell. http://www.sulfn.com/main/pages/faqs.asp (accessed on July 22, 2005).

"Ammonium Sulfate Industrial Grade." BASF. http://www.basf.de/en/produkte/chemikalien/anorganika/ammonium/ammoniumsulfat_industrial.htm?id=Voo-YYuHV7-Ro7bsf1Gb (accessed on September 20, 2005).

Bariyanga, Joseph. "Fertilizer." *Chemistry: Foundations and Applications.* Edited by J. J. Lagowski. Vol. 2. New York: Macmillan Reference USA, 2004.

*See Also* Ammonia; Sulfuric Acid

OTHER NAMES:
See Overview.

FORMULA:
$C_{16}H_{19}N_3O_5S$

ELEMENTS:
Carbon, hydrogen,
nitrogen, oxygen,
sulfur

COMPOUND TYPE:
Organic
(pharmaceutical)

STATE:
Solid

MOLECULAR WEIGHT:
365.40 g/mol

MELTING POINT:
No data available

BOILING POINT:
No data available

SOLUBILITY:
Soluble in water and
alcohol; insoluble in
most organic solvents

K E Y   F A C T S

# Amoxicillin

## OVERVIEW

Amoxicillin (uh-MOX-uh-sill-in) is also known as D-(-)-alpha-amino-p-hydroxybenzyl penicillin and (2S,5R,6R)-6-[(R)-(-)-2-amino-2-(phydroxyphenyl)acetamido]-3,3-dimethyl-7-oxo-4-thia-1-azabicyclo[3.2.0]heptane-2-carboxylic acid. It is an off-white crystalline antibiotic, a substance that inhibits the growth of microorganisms. It is generally available in the form of the trihydrate (having three molecules of water for each molecule of amoxicillin) with the formula $C_{16}H_{19}N_3O_5S \cdot 3H_2O$. Amoxicillin is effective against a number of disease-causing bacteria, including *streptococci*, the bacterium that cause strep throat, and most strains of *pneumo cocci*, the bacterium that cause pneumonia, *gonococci*, the bacterium that cause gonorrhea, and *meningococci*, the bacterium that cause meningitis. Amoxicillin works by blocking the formation of bacteria cell walls. Without cell walls, the bacteria die.

Amoxicillin belongs to a group of semisynthetically produced antibiotics called the aminopenicillins. The term

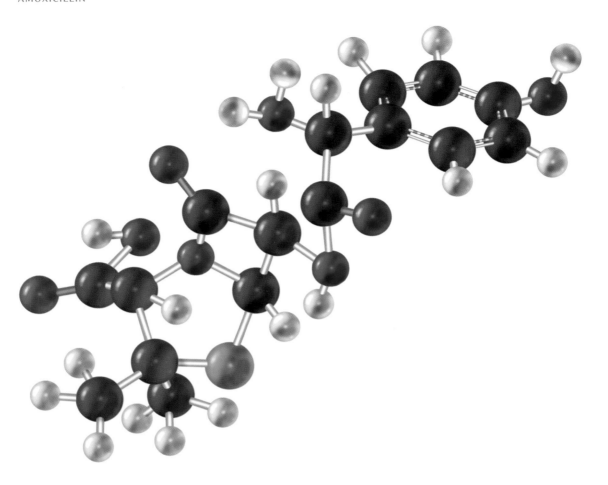

*Amoxicillin.* Red atoms are oxygen; white atoms are hydrogen; black atoms are carbon; blue atoms are nitrogen; and green atom is sulfur. Gray sticks are double bonds; striped sticks show a benzene ring. PUBLISHERS RESOURCE GROUP

semisynthetic means that some stages in the preparation of the compound make use of naturally-occurring organisms, such as bacteria or yeast, and some stages involve chemical synthesis. Preparation of the aminopenicillins begins with the antibiotic penicillin itself, usually made by one of the molds in the *Penicillium* family, such as *Penicillium chrysogenum* or *Penicillium notatum.* The penicillin molecule is then modified by the addition of a hydroxyl, methyl, or some other group. Other semisynthetic antibiotics related to amoxicillin and penicillin are ampicillin, benzylpenicillin (penicillin G), and phenoxymethylpenicillin (penicillin V).

Scottish bacteriologist Alexander Fleming (1881–1955) discovered penicillin in 1928. The antibiotic was first produced for human use in the early 1940s. Over time, researchers

## Interesting Facts

- The original U.S. patent on amoxicillin granted to Beecham Laboratories in 1965 has expired, allowing other pharmaceutical manufacturers to make the drug. This fact accounts for the more than three dozen trade names under which it is sold.

discovered ways of changing the chemical structure of penicillin to create semisynthetic versions. The new antibiotics they created were more effective than penicillin against a wider range of bacteria, often with fewer side-effects. Amoxicillin was discovered by researchers at the Beecham pharmaceutical laboratories in 1962 and marketed about a decade later under the trade name of Amoxil®. The drug is now available under a number of trade names, including Larotid®, Trimox®, Wymox®, Polymox®, and Augmentin®.

### HOW IT IS MADE

The preparation of amoxicillin involves a complex series of reactions that begins with penicillin produced by molds or other microorganisms. A variety of chemical reagents is then used to replace one hydrogen atom in the penicillin molecule by the $CH(NH_2)C_6H_4OH$ group that converts penicillin into amoxicillin.

### COMMON USES AND POTENTIAL HAZARDS

Amoxicillin is available only by prescription and is used against a variety of disease-causing bacteria, such as the cocci bacteria listed above, as well as *Bordetella pertussis*, the bacterium that causes whooping cough, *Salmonella typhi*, the bacterium that causes typhoid, and *Vibrio cholerae*, the bacterium that causes cholera.

The safety of amoxicillin has been extensively tested in trials with both experimental animals and humans. It poses no risk to the vast majority of people. As with all drugs,

## Words to Know

**ANAPHYLAXIS** A serious allegic reaction to a substance that may include respiratory symptoms, fainting, swelling and itching.

**REAGENT** A substance used in a chemical reaction.

**SEMISYNTHETIC** A compound that is prepared in such a way that some stages in the preparation use naturally-occurring organisms, such as bacteria or yeast, and some stages involve chemical synthesis.

**SYNTHESIS** A chemical reaction in which some desired chemical product is made from simple beginning chemicals, or reactants.

however, some individuals may experience adverse reactions to the use of amoxicillin. These reactions include fever, skin rash, joint pain, or swollen glands. More serious reactions can include nausea, diarrhea, or anaphylaxis, a potentially fatal allergic reaction. Adverse reactions are most likely to occur among people who have asthma, kidney disease, leukemia, intestinal problems, chronic illness, or a known allergy to other penicillin drugs.

### FOR FURTHER INFORMATION

"Amoxicillin." Drugs.com. http://www.drugs.com/amoxicillin.html (accessed on September 20, 2005).

"Amoxicilin." Medline Plus. http://www.nlm.nih.gov/medlineplus/druginfo/medmaster/a685001.html (accessed on December 6, 2005).

"Amoxicillin." University of Maryland Medical Center. http://www.umm.edu/altmed/ConsDrugs/Amoxicillincd.html (accessed on September 20, 2005).

"Amoxil® Prescribing Information." GlaxoSmithKline. http://us.gsk.com/products/assets/us_amoxil.pdf (accessed on September 20, 2005).

*See Also* Penicillin

$$H_3C - C(=O) - O - CH_2 - CH_2 - CH_2 - CH_2 - CH_3$$

OTHER NAMES:
Pentyl acetate; acetic
acid, amyl ester

FORMULA:
$CH_3COOC_5H_{11}$

ELEMENTS:
Carbon, hydrogen,
oxygen

COMPOUND TYPE:
Ester (organic)

STATE:
Liquid

MOLECULAR WEIGHT:
130.18 g/mol

MELTING POINT:
−70.8°C (−95.4°F)

BOILING POINT:
149.2°C (300.6°F)

SOLUBILITY:
Slightly soluble in
water; soluble in
alcohol, ether, and
most organic solvents

# Amyl Acetate

## OVERVIEW

Amyl acetate (A-mil AS-uh-tate) is a colorless liquid with a distinctive banana-like flavor and odor. Three major isomers of amyl acetate exist: normal (*n*-amyl), secondary (*sec*-amyl), and isoamyl (3-methyl-1-butyl) acetate. Isomers are two or more forms of a chemical compound with the same molecular formula, but different structural formulas and different chemical and physical properties. As an example, the boiling points of the three isomers of amyl acetate are 149.2°C (300.6°F), 142.0°C (287.6°F), and 140.0°C (284.0°F), respectively. Although the amyl acetates are probably best known as flavoring agents because of their distinctive banana-like flavor, they all have a number of interesting industrial applications also.

## HOW IT IS MADE

The amyl acetates are made industrially in essentially the same way they are made in a high school or college chemistry

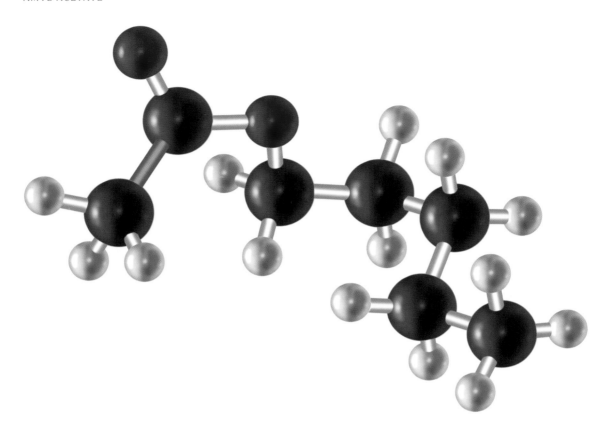

laboratory. Acetic acid ($HC_2H_3O_2$) is added to amyl alcohol ($C_5H_{11}OH$) with a small amount of concentrated sulfuric acid ($H_2SO_4$) as a catalyst. The specific amyl acetate produced depends on the specific amyl alcohol used in the reaction. The product is separated from the reaction mixture by boiling the liquid mixture.

## COMMON USES AND POTENTIAL HAZARDS

Amyl acetate is used as a flavoring agent in the United States and several other countries. It is often blended with other esters to produce flavors that are more fruity and rounded. The compound is also used to flavor products such as chewing gum.

Some applications of amyl acetate depend on its distinctive banana-like odor. The compound may be used, for example, to cover up the unpleasant odors present in certain products,

## Interesting Facts

Amyl acetate is the primary component of banana oil and pear oil.

such as shoe polish. Amyl acetate is also used as a warning odor in devices through which gases flow, such as respirators. A warning odor is a distinctive smell that allows users to be aware that a leak exists in a product carrying a gas that has no odor of its own.

Among the many industrial applications of amyl acetate are the following:

- As a solvent for paints and lacquers;
- As an ingredient in fingernail polishes;
- In the production of penicillin; and
- In the manufacture of photographic film, printed and dyed fabrics, and phosphors used in fluorescent lamps.

Amyl acetate is thought to pose a moderate to low health risk. It may cause respiratory problems if inhaled or damage to the skin and eyes if spilled on the body. The most serious safety risk it poses is its flammability. It catches fire easily and burns rapidly, with a moderate risk of exploding under certain circumstances.

### FOR FURTHER INFORMATION

"Amyl Acetate." CAMEO: Conservation and Art Material Encyclopedia Online.
http://www.mfa.org/_cameo/frontend/material_description.asp?name=amyl+acetate&language;=1 (accessed on September 21, 2005).

"n-amyl acetate." CHEMINFO.
http://intox.org/databank/documents/chemical/amylacet/cie455.htm (accessed on September 20, 2005).

"n-amyl acetate." New Jersey Department of Health and Senior Services.
http://www.state.nj.us/health/eoh/rtkweb/1321.pdf (accessed on September 21, 2005).

## Words to Know

**CATALYST** A material that increases the rate of a chemical reaction without undergoing any change in its own chemical structure

**ESTER** An organic compound formed in the reaction between an organic acid and an alcohol.

**ISOMER** Two or more forms of a chemical compounds with the same molecular formula, but different structural formulas and different chemical and physical properties

**PHOSPHOR** A chemical that gives off light when exposed to an electrical current.

"sec-amyl acetate." CHEMINFO.
http://intox.org/databank/documents/chemical/amylacet/cie468.htm (accessed on September 20, 2005).

"sec-amyl acetate." New Jersey Department of Health and Senior Services.
http://www.state.nj.us/health/eoh/rtkweb/1643.pdf (accessed on September 21, 2005).

*See Also* Acetic Acid; Cellulose Nitrate; Penicillin

$$H_3C - \overset{\overset{\displaystyle H}{|}}{\underset{\underset{\displaystyle H}{|}}{C}} - \overset{\overset{\displaystyle H}{|}}{\underset{\underset{\displaystyle H}{|}}{C}} - \overset{\overset{\displaystyle H}{|}}{\underset{\underset{\displaystyle H}{|}}{C}} - \overset{\overset{\displaystyle H}{|}}{\underset{\underset{\displaystyle H}{|}}{C}} - \overset{\displaystyle O}{}  N = O$$

OTHER NAMES:
Pentyl nitrite

FORMULA:
$C_5H_{11}NO_2$ or
$(CH_3)_2CHCH_2CH_2NO_2$

ELEMENTS:
Carbon, hydrogen,
nitrogen, oxygen

COMPOUND TYPE:
Ester (organic)

STATE:
Liquid

MOLECULAR WEIGHT:
117.15 g/mol

MELTING POINT:
Not available

BOILING POINT:
n-amyl nitrite: 104.5°C
(220°F); isoamyl
nitrite: 99.2°C (210°F)

SOLUBILITY:
Almost insoluble in
water; soluble in
alcohol

KEY FACTS

# Amyl Nitrite

## OVERVIEW

Amyl nitrite (A-mil NYE-trite) commonly occurs in two isomeric forms: n-amyl nitrite and isoamyl nitrite (3-methylamyl nitrite or 3-methylpentyl nitrite). In common usage, the term amyl nitrite most commonly refers to the isoamyl form. Both isomers occur as yellowish liquids with a distinctive sweet odor and a pungent taste. They are unstable and break down when exposed to air, light, or water. Both isomers are probably best known as vasodilators, substances that cause blood vessels to relax and expand, allowing an increased flow of blood through the body. Because of its widespread use as a hazardous recreational drug, isoamyl nitrite has been banned, except for specified medical uses.

## HOW IT IS MADE

Isoamyl nitrite is prepared in a straightforward synthesis in the reaction between isoamyl alcohol $(CH_3)_2CHCH_2CH_2OH$) and nitrous acid ($HNO_2$). The usual method of preparation is

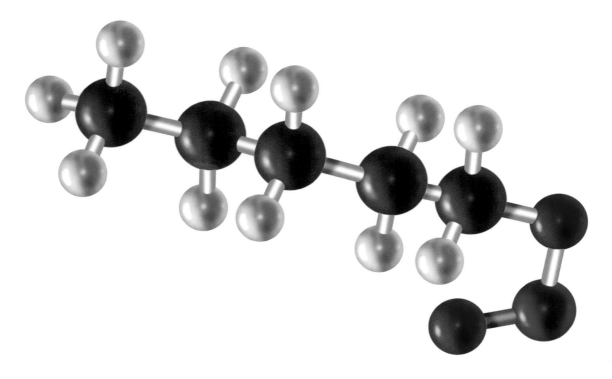

to combine starch with concentrated nitric acid ($HNO_3$) to form gaseous nitrous acid. The nitrous acid is then passed through warm isoamyl alcohol. The compound can also be produced by distilling a mixture of potassium nitrite ($KNO_2$), isoamyl alcohol, and sulfuric acid ($H_2SO_4$).

## COMMON USES AND POTENTIAL HAZARDS

The amyl nitrites are used in medicine for the treatment of pain due to angina, chest pain that occurs because of the constriction of blood vessels. The compounds cause the blood vessels to relax, expand, and ease the flow of blood, with a resulting decrease in chest pain. They are also used by emergency medical providers to treat poisoning by hydrogen cyanide and hydrogen sulfide gas. The amyl nitrites are converted in the body to a compound called methemoglobin, which binds to hydrogen cyanide and hydrogen sulfide, reducing their toxic effects.

U.S. law permits the sale of amyl nitrites as additives to perfumes and for other odorizing purposes. For example, they may be sold as room deodorizers, to eliminate the

## Interesting Facts

- Although isoamyl nitrite has legitimate industrial and medical uses, it is probably best known as a recreational drug called "poppers." The name comes from a popping sound that occurs when a bottle of the liquid is opened. The health consequences of using poppers are such that the U.S. government passed a ban on the sale of poppers in 1991, except for certain specific purposes. The ban has not eliminated the use of isoamyl nitrite as a recreational drug, since people can still buy the compound for one of its permitted uses.

unpleasant smells that may accumulate in a space. Some people who purchase these room deodorizers or perfumes actually use them as recreational drugs.

An important industrial application of the amyl nitrites is in the production of diazonium compounds. Diazonium compounds contain a characteristic -N=N- grouping and constitute an important family of dyes.

The health risks associated with the use of the amyl nitrites arise because they act as vasodilators. As blood vessels expand and blood flow increases after inhalation of amyl nitrites, blood rushes to the head, and a person may become dizzy and light-headed. These symptoms may provide a "rush"

## Words to Know

**DISTILLATION** A process of separating two or more substances by boiling the mixture of which they are composed and condensing the vapors produced at different temperatures.

**ISOMERS** Two or more forms of a chemical compound with the same molecular formula, but different structural formulas and different chemical and physical properties.

**VASODILATOR** Drug that causes blood vessels to relax and expand.

of excitement that makes them desirable to some people as stimulants. But prolonged use may result in more serious health problems, including headache, nausea, loss of balance, shortness of breath, and rapid heartbeat. For individuals with heart problems, such conditions can lead to heart failure and death.

FOR FURTHER INFORMATION

"Amyl Nitrite." WholeHealthMD.com. http://www.wholehealthmd.com/refshelf/drugs_view/ 1,1524,35,00.html (accessed on December 7, 2005).

"Amyl Nitrite (Systemic)." Medline Plus. http://www.nlm.nih.gov/medlineplus/druginfo/uspdi/ 202034.html (accessed on December 7, 2005).

Gahlinger, Paul M. *Illegal Drugs: A Complete Guide to Their History.* Salt Lake City, UT: Sagebrush Press, 2001.

"Isoamyl nitrite." International Programme on Chemical Safety. http://www.inchem.org/documents/icsc/icsc/eics1012.htm (accessed on December 7, 2005).

**OTHER NAMES:**
L-ascorbic acid;
vitamin C

**FORMULA:**
$C_6H_8O_6$

**ELEMENTS:**
Carbon, hydrogen,
oxygen

**COMPOUND TYPE:**
Organic acid

**STATE:**
Solid

**MOLECULAR WEIGHT:**
176.12 g/mol

**MELTING POINT:**
191°C (376°F);
decomposes

**BOILING POINT:**
Not applicable

**SOLUBILITY:**
Soluble in water and
alcohol; insoluble in
ether, benzene, and
chloroform

K E Y   F A C T S

# Ascorbic Acid

## OVERVIEW

Ascorbic acid (as-KOR-bik AS-id), or vitamin C, is one of the most important dietary vitamins for humans because it plays a crucial role in building collagen, the protein that serves as a support structure for the body. It is a water-soluble vitamin, which means that the body excretes any excess vitamin C in the urine and cannot store a surplus. For that reason, humans must consume vitamin C in their daily diets. Vitamin C is found in many fruits and vegetables and most kinds of fresh meat. Citrus fruits, such as oranges and lemons, are especially rich in the compound.

Humans have known about the consequences of vitamin C deficiency for centuries. People traveling long distances on land or by sea often came down with an illness called scurvy. The same illness struck people living in their own homes during long winters. The disease was characterized by pain and weakness in the joints, fatigue, bleeding gums, tooth loss, slow healing of wounds, and bruising. These symptoms were caused as the body's connective tissue broke down

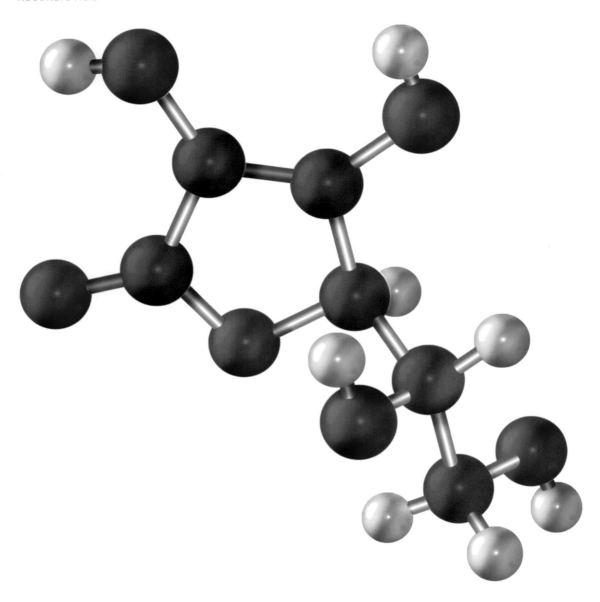

*Ascorbic acid.* Red atoms are oxygen; white atoms are hydrogen; and black atoms are carbon. Gray sticks are double bonds. PUBLISHERS RESOURCE GROUP

and small blood vessels ruptured. These symptoms began to disappear as fresh foods became more available. If they did not get enough fresh food in their diets, people could die of scurvy.

Scurvy was common enough that many people searched for its cause and cure. Sailors were especially vulnerable to the disease, and the first recorded investigations involving vitamin C were done by seafaring men. In 1536, French explorer Jacques Cartier (1491-1557) cured his sailors of scurvy by following the advice of Indians in Newfoundland, feeding them extract of pine needles. Scottish physician James Lind (1716-1794) began investigating the disease in 1747. He read many historical accounts of the diseases and combined that information with his own observations to deduce that scurvy occurred only among people with very limited diets. He went on a ten-week sea voyage and fed the solders various foods to see which ones were best at curing scurvy. Citrus fruits proved to be most effective in preventing the disease, a result that Lind reported in 1753. Captain James Cook (1728-1779) led expeditions to the South Seas in the late 1700s and kept his crew healthy by feeding them sauerkraut. In 1795 the British navy began serving its sailors a daily portion of lime juice, and two things happened: British sailors stopped getting scurvy, and people began calling sailors "limeys."

Many people refused to believe that scurvy was caused by a dietary deficiency, suggesting that it was instead the result of eating bad food or lack of exercise. In 1907, Norwegian biochemists Alex Holst (1861-1931) and Theodore Frohlich conducted a study in which guinea pigs were fed an experimental diet that caused them to develop scurvy. The link between the vitamin and the disease was firmly established by this research. Ascorbic acid was first isolated independently by the Hungarian-American biochemist Albert Szent-Györgi (1893-1986) and the American biochemist Charles Glen King (1896-1988) in 1932. It was synthesized a year later by the English chemist Sir Walter Norman Haworth (1883-1950) and the Polish-Swiss chemist Tadeusz Reichstein (1897-1996), again working independently of each other.

## HOW IT IS MADE

Plants and most animals (humans and guinea pigs being two exceptions) synthesize vitamin C in their cells through a series of reactions in which the sugar galactose is eventually converted to ascorbic acid. For many years, the compound has been made commercially by a process known as the Reichstein process, named after its inventor Tadeusz Reichstein. This process begins with ordinary glucose, which is converted to another sugar, sorbitol, which is then fermented to obtain

## Interesting Facts

- The vitamin C produced by plants and by synthetic methods are chemically identical and have identical effects in the human body.

- American chemist Linus Pauling (1901-1994) believed that very large doses of vitamin C could prevent and cure the common cold and other flu-like diseases. Because of his reputation (he won two Nobel Prizes, one in chemistry, as well as the Peace Prize), his viewpoint was highly respected. He was not, however, able to prove his theory to the satisfaction of his scientific colleagues.

yet another sugar, sorbose. The sorbose is then converted step-by-step into a series of other products, the last of which is ascorbic acid.

Chemists have long been searching for an alternative to the Reichstein process because it uses so much energy and produces by-products that are hazardous to the environment. In the 1960s, Chinese scientists developed a method that involves only two steps in the synthesis of ascorbic acid, and in the early 2000s, Scottish scientists were attempting to develop a method that involved only a single step using fermentation. Currently, however, the Reichstein process remains the most popular method for making the compound.

### COMMON USES AND POTENTIAL HAZARDS

The best known use of vitamin C is as a nutritional supplement, taken to ensure that one receives his or her daily minimum requirement of the vitamin. The recommended daily allowance (RDA) of vitamin C for adults is 60 milligrams per day. Anyone who eats a well-balanced diet that includes citrus fruits, tomatoes, and green leafy vegetables probably does not need to take a vitamin supplement. However, the amount of vitamin C one normally receives from a supplement is unlikely to cause any harm.

## Words to Know

**REDUCTION** Chemical reaction in which oxygen is removed from a substance or electrons are added to a substance.

**SYNTHESIS** Chemical reaction in which some desired chemical product is made from simple beginning chemicals, or reactants.

In addition to its nutritional uses, ascorbic acid has a number of other industrial applications, including:

- As a food preservative;
- As a reducing agent in chemical processes;
- As a preservative in foods;
- As a color fixing agent in meats, helping meats keep their bright red appearance;
- As an additive to bread dough, where it helps increase the activity of yeast used in the dough; and
- As a treatment for abscission in citrus plants, the tendency for a plant to lose its leaves, flowers, and fruits.

### FOR FURTHER INFORMATION

"Ascorbic Acid." International Programme on Chemical Safety. http://www.inchem.org/documents/icsc/icsc/eics0379.htm (accessed on September 21, 2005).

Carpenter, Kenneth J. *The History of Scurvy and Vitamin C.* Cambridge, UK: Cambridge University Press, 1986.

"L-Ascorbic Acid." University of Texas at Austin College of Engineering Department of Biomedical Engineering. http://www.engr.utexas.edu/bme/ugrad/UGLab/resources/ MSDS/ascorbic%20acid.pdf (accessed on September 21, 2005).

Mead, Clifford, and Thomas Hager, eds. *Linus Pauling: Scientist and Peacemaker.* Portland, OR: Oregon State University Press, 2001.

*See Also* Collagen; Glucose

H

H C H
C C

C C
H C C H

C

H

# Benzene

OTHER NAMES:
Benzol;
cyclohexatriene

FORMULA:
$C_6H_6$

ELEMENTS:
Carbon, hydrogen

COMPOUND TYPE:
Aromatic hydro-
carbon (organic)

STATE:
Liquid

MOLECULAR WEIGHT:
78.11 g/mol

MELTING POINT:
5.49°C (41.9°F)

BOILING POINT:
80.09°C (176.2°F)

SOLUBILITY:
Slightly soluble in
water; soluble in
alcohol, ether, and
acetone

KEY FACTS

OVERVIEW

Benzene (BEN-zeen) is a clear, colorless liquid with an aromatic (fragrant) odor. It occurs in coal and petroleum, from which it is extracted for commercial use. Benzene is very flammable, burning with a smoking flame. The compound was discovered in 1825 by the English chemist and physicist Michael Faraday (1791-1867), who gave the compound the name of bicarburet of hydrogen. It was given its modern name of benzene (benzin, at the time) by the German chemist Eilhardt Mitscherlich (1794-1863).

The chemical structure of benzene remained one of the great mysteries in chemistry for nearly half a century. The compound's formula, $C_6H_6$, suggests that it contains three double bonds. A double bond consists of four electrons that hold two atoms in close proximity to each other in a molecule. Yet benzene has none of the chemical properties common to double-bonded substances. The solution to this problem was suggested in 1865 by the German chemist Friedrich August Kekulé (1829-1896). Kekulé suggested that the six

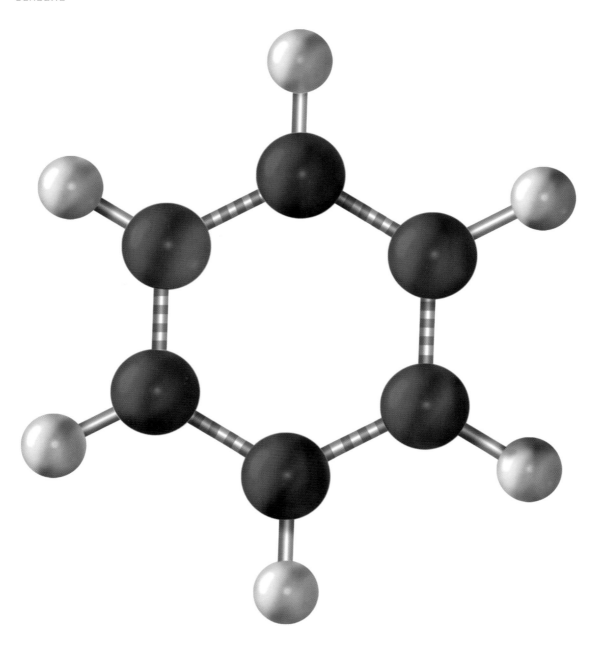

*Benzene.* White atoms are hydrogen and black atoms are carbon. Striped sticks indicate a benzene ring. PUBLISHERS RESOURCE GROUP

carbon atoms in the benzene molecule are arranged in a ring, with one hydrogen atom attached to each carbon. The ring itself consists of three double bonds and three single bonds, alternating with each other in the ring. The fact that the double bonds in benzene do not act like double bonds in other compounds was explained by the German chemist Johannes Thiele (1860-1935), who suggested that the bonds in benzene shift back and forth between single and double bonds so rapidly that they are not able to behave like typical double bonds. Chemists now use a variety of chemical formulas for representing the character of chemical bonds in benzene.

Benzene is a very popular raw material for a variety of industrial chemical reactions. In 2004, U.S. manufacturers produced 8.8 million metric tons (9.7 million short tons) of benzene, placing it in twelfth place among all chemicals made in the United States that year.

## HOW IT IS MADE

At one time, benzene was obtained from coal tar, the thick gooey liquid left over after soft coal is converted to coke. This method has now been largely replaced by a variety of methods that use crude oil or refined petroleum as a raw material. In the most popular of these methods, toluene ($C_6H_5CH_3$) from petroleum is heated over a catalyst of platinum metal and aluminum oxide ($Al_2O_3$). The toluene loses its methyl group ($-CH_3$), leaving benzene as the primary product. Other methods are available for changing the molecular structure of hydrocarbons found in petroleum and converting them to benzene.

## COMMON USES AND POTENTIAL HAZARDS

By far the most important use of benzene is as a raw material in the synthesis of other organic compounds. More than 90 percent of the benzene produced in the United States is used to make ethylbenzene (55 percent), cumene (24 percent), and cyclohexane (12 percent). The first two compounds rank fifteenth and twentieth, respectively, among all chemicals produced in the United States each year. Another five percent of benzene production goes to the synthesis of a large variety of other organic compounds, including nitrobenzene, chlorobenzene, and maleic anhydride, a raw material for the manufacture of plastics. Smaller amounts of benzene are used as a solvent for

## Interesting Facts

- Kekulé's discovery of the formula for benzene is one of the most interesting in the history of chemistry. The story is told that he worked so hard on the problem that he often dreamed about the compound at night. One evening, he dreamed of a snake with a tail in its mouth. Kekulé immediately awoke, went to his work table, and drew a structure for the benzene molecule inspired by the snake: a molecule in the shape of a ring made of carbon atoms.

cleaning purposes, in chemical reactions, and as a gasoline additive.

As with most chemicals, benzene can enter the body in one of three ways: through the skin, the nose, or the throat. People who handle or work with benzene in their workplaces are at greatest risk of exposure to benzene and should take precautions in working with the material. Because of its serious health hazards, benzene is no longer included in most materials with which the average person comes into contact. On those occasions when a person does come into contact with benzene, first aid and medical attention should be sought for treatment of the exposure.

The health effects of exposure to liquid benzene or benzene fumes depends on the amount of benzene taken into the body. The most common symptoms of benzene exposure include irritation of the mucous membranes, convulsions, depression, and restlessness. At greater doses, a person may experience respiratory failure, followed by death. Even at low concentrations, benzene can cause long-term effects for people who are regularly in contact with the compound. The most important of these effects are carcinogenic. Benzene is known to cause damage to bone marrow, resulting in a form of cancer of the blood known as leukemia.

## Words to Know

**CARCINOGEN** A chemical that causes cancer in humans or other animals.

**CATALYST** A material that increases the rate of a chemical reaction without undergoing any change in its own chemical structure.

**MUCOUS MEMBRANES** Tissues that line the moist inner lining of the digestive,

respiratory, urinary, and reproductive systems.

**SYNTHESIS** A chemical reaction in which some desired chemical product is made from simple beginning chemicals, or reactants.

### FOR FURTHER INFORMATION

"Chronic Toxicity Summary: Benzene." California Office of Health Hazard Assessment. http://www.oehha.org/air/chronic_rels/pdf/71432.pdf (accessed on September 21, 2005).

Newton, David E. "Benzene." In *Gale Encyclopedia of Science.* Edited by K. Lee Lerner and Brenda Wilmoth Lerner. 3rd ed., vol. 1. Detroit: Gale, 2004.

"Spectrum Chemical Fact Sheet: Benzene." Spectrum Laboratories. http://www.speclab.com/compound/c71432.htm (accessed on September 21, 2005).

"Toxicity Summary for Benzene." The Risk Assessment Information System. http://risk.lsd.ornl.gov/tox/profiles/benzene.shtml (accessed on September 21, 2005).

"Toxicological Profile for Benzene." Agency for Toxic Substances and Disease Registry. http://www.atsdr.cdc.gov/toxprofiles/tp3.html (accessed on September 21, 2005).

*See Also* Benzoic Acid; Styrene

# Benzoic Acid

## OVERVIEW

Benzoic acid (ben-ZO-ik AS-id) is the simplest of the aromatic carboxylic acids, a family of organic compounds containing the carboxyl (-COOH) group. It occurs in the form of white crystalline needles or thin plates. Many naturally occurring plants contain benzoic acid, including most types of berries and the natural product called gum benzoin, a plant common to the islands of Java, Sumatra, and Borneo. Gum benzoin may contain up to 20 percent benzoic acid. Benzoic acid is also excreted by most animals (except fowl) in the form of a related compound called hippuric acid ($C_6H_5CONHCH_2COOH$).

## HOW IT IS MADE

Some benzoic acid is prepared from gum benzoin and other natural compounds containing high concentrations of the compound. Three methods are available for making benzoic acid commercially. In one method, toluene ($C_6H_5CH_3$) is

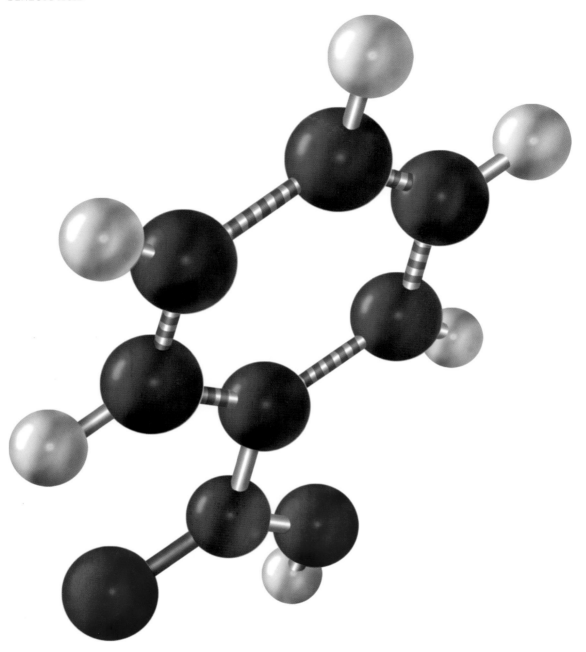

*Benzoic acid.* Red atoms are oxygen; white atoms are hydrogen; and black atoms are carbon.

oxidized at high temperature and pressure over a cobalt catalyst. In a second procedure, phthalic anhydride $(C_6H_4(CO)_2O)$ is heated to remove carbon dioxide, with the formation of benzoic acid. In the third method, toluene is first converted to benzotrichloride ($C_6H_5Cl_3$), which is then hydrolyzed to obtain benzoic acid.

## COMMON USES AND POTENTIAL HAZARDS

More than half of all the benzoic acid produced in the United States is used in the manufacture of various polymeric products, primarily the family of plastics known as the polyvinyl acetates (PVAs). The PVAs, in turn, are used as adhesives, caulks, sealants, and coatings for paper, film, and plastic foil. About a quarter of all benzoic acid is converted to its sodium and potassium salts, sodium benzoate ($C_6H_5COONa$) and potassium benzoate ($C_6H_5COOK$), for use as food preservatives. Sodium benzoate and potassium benzoate are now the most widely used food preservatives in the world. They are added to a host of products, such as soft drinks and fruit juices, jams and jellies, baked goods, and salad dressings. They are also added to a number of non-food products such as mouthwashes, toothpastes, cosmetic creams, and deodorants.

Other uses of benzoic acid include:

• As an additive to antifreezes, where is acts to prevent corrosion of engine parts;

• As a seasoning agent in the processing of tobacco products;

• As a stabilizing agent in the processing of photographs; and

• For the treatment of fungal infections.

Benzoic acid and its sodium and potassium salts pose moderate health hazards to people who work directly with them. They may cause skin, nose, and eye problems if inhaled or deposited on the body. In the form of finely divided dust, they may also pose a fire or explosive risk. Most people do not encounter any of these compounds in a form in which they pose a health risk. All three compounds are considered safe by the U.S. Food and Drug Administration as food additives provided their concentration in foods does not exceed 0.1 percent. Other nations have set a safe level for the three compounds as food additives as high as 1.25 percent.

# Words to Know

**CATALYST** A material that increases the rate of a chemical reaction without undergoing any change in its own chemical structure.

**HYDROLYSIS** The process by which a compound reacts with water to form two new compounds.

**POLYMER** A compound consisting of very large molecules made of one or two small repeated units called monomers.

## FOR FURTHER INFORMATION

"Benzoic Acid." Chemical Land 21.
http://www.chemicalland21.com/arokorhi/industrialchem/organic/BENZOIC%20ACID.htm (accessed on September 22, 2005).

"Benzoic Acid and Sodium Benzoate." International Programme on Chemical Safety.
http://www.inchem.org/documents/cicads/cicad26.htm (accessed on September 22, 2005).

"Benzoic Acid (CASRN 65-85-0)." U.S. Environmental Protection Agency.
http://www.epa.gov/iris/subst/0355.htm (accessed on September 22, 2005).

*See Also* Denatonium Benzoate

# Beta-Carotene

## OVERVIEW

Beta-carotene (β-carotene; BAY-tuh KARE-oh-teen) belongs to a family of organic compounds called the carotenoids. The carotenoids are all brightly pigmented (colored) compounds found in a number of plants, bacteria, algae, and fungi. Beta-carotene is responsible for the yellowish to orange color of pumpkins, apricots, sweet potatoes, nectarines, and, most notably, carrots. The compound also occurs in spinach and broccoli, but in such small concentrations that the green chlorophyl present masks the orange color of beta-carotene. In its pure form, beta-carotene occurs as purple crystals shaped like thin leaflets.

In plants, algae, and photosynthetic bacteria, beta-carotene plays an important role in photosynthesis, the process by which plants convert water and carbon dioxide into carbohydrates and oxygen. In nonphotosynthetic bacteria and fungi, beta-carotene protects the organism against the harmful effects of light and oxygen.

Animals require beta-carotene for normal growth and development, but are unable to manufacture the compound

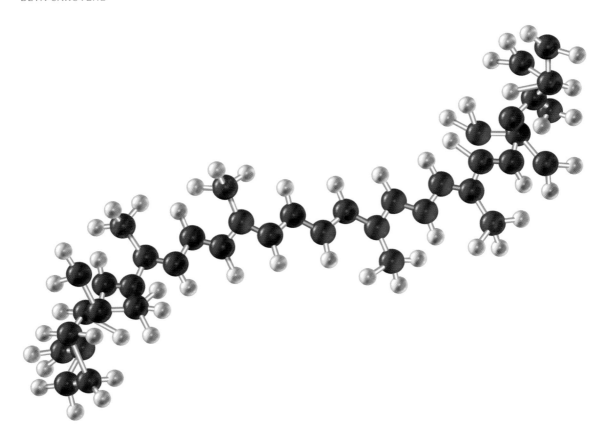

*Beta-carotene.* White atoms are hydrogen and black atoms are carbon. PUBLISHERS RESOURCE GROUP

themselves. As a result, they must ingest some beta-carotene from plant sources in order to stay healthy. The compound is a provitamin, a substance that is converted in the body to a vitamin. Beta-carotene is converted into vitamin A, whose role in the body is the maintenance of strong bones and teeth and healthy skin and hair.

Beta-carotene also acts as an antioxidant, a substance that attacks free radicals in the body that may cause cancer. It may also protect against heart disease and strengthen the body's immune system.

Beta-carotene was first isolated by the German chemist Heinrich Wilhelm Ferdinand Wackenroder (1789-1854), who extracted the compound from carrot roots in 1831. The compound was first synthesized in 1950 by the Swiss chemist Paul Karrer (1889-1971).

## Interesting Facts

- The name carotene comes from the Latin word for "carrot."

- Scientists have found a way to change the genetic structure of rice so that it contains beta-carotene. The modified rice is designed to help people in countries where vitamin A deficiency is a serious problem.

- At least eight other carotenoids are known. They include $\alpha$-carotene, $\beta,\psi$-carotene, and $\psi, \psi$-carotene.

### HOW IT IS MADE

Beta-carotene can be obtained from natural sources by crushing or pulverizing the source (such as carrots) and adding a solvent that will dissolve the organic components of the plant. These components can then be separated from each other by chromatographic techniques. A major commercial source of beta-carotene obtained by this method is the algae *Dunaliella salina*, which grows in large salt lakes in Australia. The compound can also be prepared synthetically by one of two methods, the BASF and the Roche methods, both named after the pharmaceutical firms where they were developed. Both methods of preparation begin with long-chain hydrocarbons containing about twenty carbon atoms each. These hydrocarbons are then joined to each other to form the 40-carbon beta-carotene compound.

### COMMON USES AND POTENTIAL HAZARDS

Beta-carotene has two uses: in vitamin supplements and as a food additive. Anyone who eats a healthy diet that includes foods rich in vitamin A, such as fish oil, liver, eggs, butter, and orange or yellow vegetables and fruits, will get adequate amounts of beta-carotene. However, many

## Words to Know

**ANTIOXIDANT** A chemical that attacks free radicals, chemical structures that attack cells and may be responsible for the development of cancer.

**CHROMATOGRAPHY** A process by which a mixture of substances passes through a column consisting of some material that causes the individual components in the mixture to separate from each other.

**FREE RADICAL** An atom or group of atoms with a single unpaired electron. Free radicals are very active chemically and tend to attack and destroy other compounds. They are responsible for damage in cells that may lead to a number of health problems, including cancer and ageing.

**SYNTHESIS** A chemical reaction in which some desired chemical product is made from simple beginning chemicals, or reactants.

people take vitamin supplements to ensure that they have enough beta-carotene (as well as other vitamins) in their daily diet. Although some warnings have been issued about taking too much vitamin A, there is no clinical evidence that an overdose of the vitamin does any long-term harm to a person.

Beta-carotene is used as a food additive to increase the color intensity of a product. It is used primarily with yellow and orange foods, such as butter and margarine, although it is sometimes added to ice cream and fruit juices as well. Beta-carotene is used in only very small amounts as a food additive. In these amounts, it poses no health hazard to humans or other animals. The compound has also been used in experiments to test its effectiveness against certain diseases, such as lung cancer. In such cases, it has been found to be more harmful than beneficial, increasing the risk of cancer and death among people participating in the studies.

### FOR FURTHER INFORMATION

"Beta-carotene." University of Bristol School of Chemistry. http://www.chm.bris.ac.uk/motm/carotene/beta-carotene_home.html (accessed on September 22, 2005).

"Beta-carotene." University of Maryland Medical Center. http://www.umm.edu/altmed/ConsSupplements/BetaCarotenecs. html (accessed on September 22, 2005).

Palvetz, Barry A. "A Bowl of Hope, Bucket of Hype?" *The Scientist* (April 2, 2001): 15.

"Taking Supplements of the Antioxidant." *Consumer Reports* (September 2003): 49.

*See Also* Chlorophyll

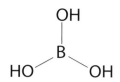

# Boric Acid

## OVERVIEW

Boric acid (BORE-ik ASS-id) is a colorless, odorless, white or colorless powder or crystalline material with a slightly oily feeling that slowly decomposes with heat, changing first to metaboric acid ($HBO_2$), then to pyroboric acid ($H_2B_4O_7$), and eventually to boric oxide ($B_2O_3$). The compound's solubility is very much a factor of temperature. In cold water, about 5 grams (0.2 ounce) of boric acid dissolve in 100 mL (3.4 ounces) of water, while at 100°C (212°F), its solubility increases to 25 grams (0.9 ounce) in 100 mL (3.4 ounces) of water.

Boric acid occurs naturally in a number of locations where it has precipitated out of hot springs. It may occur then in the form of the mineral sassolite. Given its abundance in nature, it is not surprising that the compound has been known to and used by humans for many centuries. For example, the Greeks are known to have used boric acid as an antiseptic, to preserve foods, and as a cleaning agent. The first person to prepare boric acid in Europe is thought to be

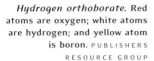

*Hydrogen orthoborate.* Red atoms are oxygen; white atoms are hydrogen; and yellow atom is boron. PUBLISHERS RESOURCE GROUP

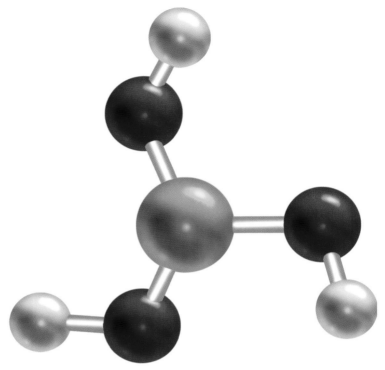

the German chemist Wilhelm Homberg (1652-1715), who in 1702 treated natural borax ($Na_2B_4O_7 \cdot 10H_2O$) with acid to obtain a product he called sedative salt, probably a form of boric acid. The chemical structure of the compound was determined in 1808 by the French researchers Louis-Joseph Gay-Lussac (1778-1850) and Louis-Jacques Thénard (1777-1857).

## HOW IT IS MADE

The most common method of producing boric acid is by treating the relatively abundant borax with hydrochloric or sulfuric acid and crystallizing out the boric acid that forms in the reaction. A less common method of preparation involves the treatment of borax brine solutions with a chelating agent that binds to the borates present in the brine, which can then be converted to boric acid.

## Interesting Facts

- The most common sources of boric acid are hot springs and volcanic sites such as the mineral springs at Vichy and Aix-la-Chapelle in France and Wiesbaden in Germany, around the volcanic regions of Tuscany in Italy, and in dry lakes of California and Nevada, such as California's Borax Lake.

- Boric acid was once used as an ingredient in talcum and diaper powders and in salves for diaper rashes because of its antiseptic properties. The compound was eventually banned for such uses, however, when regulators decided that it was too toxic if it accidentally entered the body through an open wound or by being swallowed.

### COMMON USES AND POTENTIAL HAZARDS

By far the greatest amount of boric acid is used in the production of heat-resistant (borosilicate) glass, glass fibers, porcelain enamels, crockery, laboratory glassware, and other specialized types of glass and ceramic materials. In 2004, about 80 percent of all the boric acid used in the United States was applied to these purposes. Although accounting for a much smaller amount of boric acid, another well-known use of the compound is as an antiseptic in eyewashes, ointments, and mouthwashes. It is also used as a preservative in foods and as a fungicide on citrus fruit crops. In the United States, a residue of no more than 8 parts per million is permitted on fruits treated with boric acid.

Some other important applications of boric acid include the following:

- In the production of flame retardant materials;

- As a pesticide for the treatment of cockroaches, black carpet beatles, termites, fleas, fire ants, centipedes, grasshoppers, and slugs;

- As a flux in welding and brazing;

- In the synthesis of many boron compounds;

## Words to Know

**BRINE SOLUTION** A solution that is saturated with or nearly saturated with sodium chloride or other inorganic salts.

**CHELATING AGENT** An organic compound that binds ("grabs on to") some specific compound or compounds present in a mixture.

**FLUX** A material that lowers the melting point of another substance or mixture of substances or that is used in cleaning a metal.

- To provide the finishing touches on the production of leather and fur products;
- In the manufacture of latex paints; and
- In the nickel plating of metallic products.

Boric acid is toxic if swallowed. It causes nausea, vomiting, diarrhea, and stomach cramps. In extreme cases, it can cause the collapse of the circulatory system, delirium, convulsions, coma, and death. Ingestion of no more than 5 grams (0.2 ounce) of boric acid can cause death in an infant. Ingestion of 15 to 20 grams (0.5 to 0.7 ounce) by an adult can also be fatal. Boric acid can also cause irritation of the skin, which, in extreme cases, can result in a condition known as borism. Borism is characterized by dry skin, eruptions of the skin and mucous membranes, and gastric disturbances.

### FOR FURTHER INFORMATION

"Borax; Boric Acid, and Borates." IPM of Alaska. http://www.ipmofalaska.com/files/Borates.html (accessed on October 12, 2005).

"Boric Acid: Technical Description." Manufacturas Los Andes. http://www.mandes.com.ar/technic-boric-acid.php (accessed on October 12, 2005).

Potter, Mike. "Cockroach Elimination." University of Kentucky Entomology. http://www.uky.edu/Agriculture/Entomology/entfacts/struct/ef614.htm (accessed on October 12, 2005).

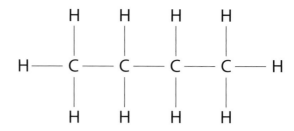

OTHER NAMES:
n-Butane

FORMULA:
$C_4H_{10}$

ELEMENTS:
Carbon, hydrogen

COMPOUND TYPE:
Alkane; saturated
hydrocarbon
(organic)

STATE:
Gas

MOLECULAR WEIGHT:
58.12 g/mol

MELTING POINT:
−138.3°C (−216.9°F)

BOILING POINT:
−0.5°C (31°F)

SOLUBILITY:
Slightly soluble in
water; soluble in
ethyl alcohol, ether,
and chloroform

KEY FACTS

# Butane

## OVERVIEW

Butane (BYOO-tane) is a colorless gas with the odor of natural gas that is highly flammable and explosive. It exists in two isomeric forms. Isomers are forms of a chemical compound with the same molecular formula (in this case, $C_4H_{10}$), but different structural arrangements. In one isomer ("normal" or "n-" butane), the four carbon atoms are arranged in a continuous chain, while in the other ("iso-butane"), three carbon atoms are arranged in a continuous chain and the fourth carbon atom is attached to the middle atom in that chain.

Butane occurs naturally in natural gas, where it is present to the extent of about 1 percent, and in petroleum, where it exists only in very small amounts. Butane is used primarily as a fuel and as a chemical intermediary, a compound used to produce other chemical substances.

## HOW IT IS MADE

Butane is obtained during the separation of natural gas into its components. Natural gas consists primarily (70 to

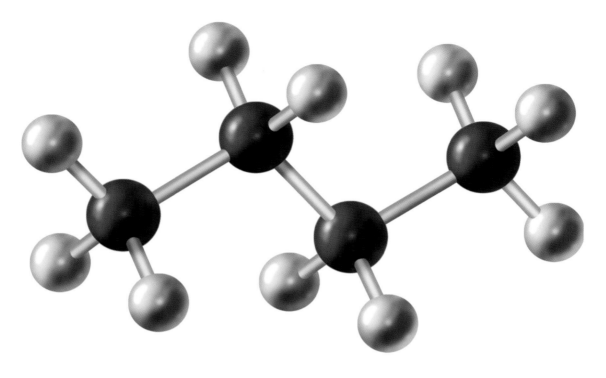

*Butane.* Black atoms are carbon; white atoms are hydrogen. All sticks are single bonds. PUBLISHERS RESOURCE GROUP

90 percent) of methane. Other components include ethane (about 9 percent), propane (about 3 percent), and butane (about 1 percent). The remaining 1 to 2 percent of natural gas is impurities, including nitrogen, carbon dioxide, compounds of sulfur, and water. The process of separating natural gas into its components begins with the removal of water. The natural gas is forced through some drying agent, such as diethylene glycol ($HO(CH_2)_2O(CH_2)_2OH$), which efficiently removes water from the gas. The dry gas is then treated with an agent to remove carbon dioxide, compounds of sulfur, and other impurities. Diethanolamine ($HO(CH_2)_2NH(CH_2)_2OH$) is an efficient "scavenger" of many of these impurities.

After dehydration and removal of impurities, the remaining gas consists almost entirely of simple hydrocarbons, primarily methane, ethane, propane, and butane. These hydrocarbons can be separated from each other by cooling them until they reach the point at which they become liquid. As each component liquefies, it can be removed from the gas and further purified. For example, butane changes from a gas to a liquid at $-0.5°C$ ($31°F$) and propane liquefies at about $-42°C$ ($-44°F$). So as the

## Interesting Facts

- Some people have used butane as a recreational drug, inhaling it to get "high." The practice is extremely dangerous, however, and has led some users to die of asphyxiation (suffocation).

- Researchers at Surrey Satellite Technology, Ltd. in the United Kingdom have built a small satellite the size of a soccer ball that is propelled by pressurized butane gas. The butane thruster was built for $15,000 and was launched aboard a Russian Cosmos spacecraft in June 2000.

- Contact with liquid butane or LPG can cause frostbite, for which first aid involves washing with cold water.

hydrocarbon mixture cools, liquid butane can be removed before any other components liquefy. In actual practice, liquid butane and propane are removed together, leaving behind only ethane and methane. The mixture of liquid butane and propane is known as liquid petroleum gas (LPG). Since propane and butane have many similar properties, there is often no commercial reason to go to the expense of separating them from each other. LPG is typically stored above or below ground in large, insulated containers and shipped in insulated trucks or rail cars.

### COMMON USES AND POTENTIAL HAZARDS

Butane, in both gaseous and liquid form, is widely used as a fuel. Because it is easily stored and transported in small containers, it is used as a fuel for backpacking stoves, small space heaters, and portable torches. Butane is also the fuel most commonly used in cigarette lighters. It may be used in its pure form or in combination with propane as liquefied petroleum gas (LPG). Butane is also used as a fuel for larger household and industrial operations.

In terms of volume, one of the major uses of butane is in the synthesis of other organic compounds, especially synthetic rubber and high-octane liquid fuels used in aviation. The gas

## Words to Know

**EUPHORIA** A state of extreme happiness and enhanced well-being.

**HALLUCINATIONS** Visions or other perceptions of things that are not really present.

is sometimes added to gasoline in cold climates to improve the rate at which the fuel evaporates and burns. A relatively new application for butane is as a propellant for spray products, such as hair spray and spray paints, and as a refrigerant. Butane is being used for these purposes as a substitute for chlorofluorocarbons (CFCs), which have been shown to have damaging effects on the Earth's ozone layer. Small amounts of butane are also used as food additives, usually in foods that are dispensed as sprays.

The primary health hazard posed by butane is its narcotic effects. When inhaled, either accidentally or intentionally, it produces a sequence of bodily changes that include, at first, a sense of euphoria and excitement. Increased doses may then produce harmful results, such as nausea, vomiting, sneezing, coughing, blurred vision, slurred speech, and increased salivation. Even higher doses result in confusion, perceptual distortion, hallucinations, and delusions. Eventually, a sequence of life-threatening conditions may develop, including depression of the central nervous system, irregular heartbeat, drowsiness, coma, and death.

### FOR FURTHER INFORMATION

"Acute Exposure Guideline Levels (AEGLs) for n-butane." National Advisory Council, U.S. Environmental Protection Agency. Washington, DC: U.S. Environmental Protection Agency, April 2004. Also available online at http://www.epa.gov/oppt/aegl/pubs/tsd102.pdf (accessed on December 29, 2005).

"Butane." International Labour Organization. http://www.ilo.org/public/english/protection/safework/cis/products/icsc/dtasht/_icsc02/icsc0232.htm (accessed on December 29, 2005).

"Butane." International Programme on Chemical Safety. http://www.inchem.org/documents/pims/chemical/ pim945.htm#SectionTitle:2.1%20%20Main%20risks%20and%20-target%20organs (accessed on December 29, 2005).

Russell, Justin. "Fuel of the Forgotten Deaths." *New Scientist* (February 6, 1993): 21-23.

*See Also* Methane; Propane

$$H_3C-C\underset{OH}{\overset{OH}{\diagdown}}\overset{H}{\underset{H}{\overset{|}{C}}}-\overset{H}{\underset{H}{\overset{|}{C}}}-\overset{H}{\underset{H}{\overset{|}{C}}}-CH_3$$

KEY FACTS

OTHER NAMES:
Three forms exist;
see Overview

FORMULA:
$C_6H_{12}O_2$; see Overview
for expanded
formulas

ELEMENTS:
Carbon, hydrogen,
oxygen

COMPOUND TYPE:
Carboxylic acids
(organic)

STATE:
Liquid

MOLECULAR WEIGHT:
116.16 g/mol

MELTING POINT:
−98.9°C (−146°F) to
−78°C (−108°F)

BOILING POINT:
95.1°C (203°F) to
126.1°C (259.0°F)

SOLUBILITY:
Insoluble or slightly
soluble in water;
soluble in alcohol and
ether

# Butyl Acetate

## OVERVIEW

Butyl acetate (BYOO-til AS-uh-tate) exists in three isomeric forms. Isomers are two or more forms of a chemical compound with the same molecular formula, but different structural formulas and different chemical and physical properties. Their names and synonyms are as follows: *n*-butyl acetate is known as butyl ester, or butyl ethanoate; *sec*-butyl acetate is called 1-methylpropyl ester and acetic acid *sec*-butyl ester; and *tert*-butyl acetate is known by 1,1,-dimethylethyl ester or acetic acid, *tert*-butyl ester. The expanded chemical formulas for the forms are slightly different: *n*-butyl acetate, $CH_3COOCH_2CH_2CH_2CH_3$; *sec*-butyl acetate, $CH_3COOCH(CH_3)(C_2H_5)$; and *tert*-butyl acetate, $CH_3COOC(CH_3)_3$.

About 100,000 kilograms (250,000 pounds) of the *n*-butyl isomer, the most popular, is produced each year in the United States. By far the most common use of the compound (and the isomers) is as an industrial solvent, with about 90 percent of total output going for this use.

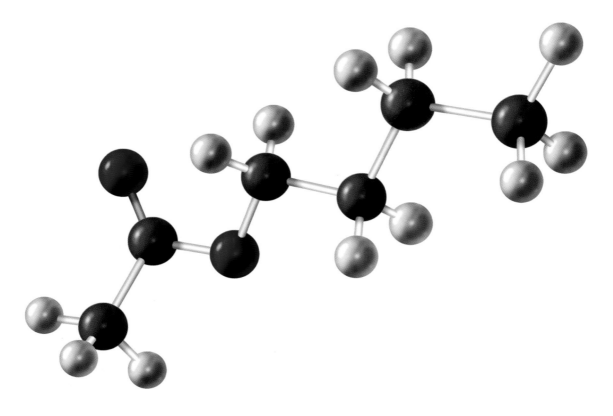

*Butyl acetate.* Red atoms are oxygen; white atoms are hydrogen; and black atoms are carbon. Gray sticks indicate double bonds. PUBLISHERS RESOURCE GROUP

## HOW IT IS MADE

All three isomers of butyl acetate are made by reacting acetic acid ($CH_3COOH$) with the appropriate butyl alcohol (*n*-butyl alcohol, *sec*-butyl alcohol, or *tert*-butyl alcohol, respectively).

## COMMON USES AND POTENTIAL HAZARDS

The primary use of all three isomers of butyl acetate is as a solvent in the production of lacquers and paints; photographic film; resins; and coatings for furniture, fixtures, containers, and automobiles. Since the 1990s, these compounds have been substituted for other solvents that are considered hazardous environmental pollutants.

Other uses of the isomers are as follows:

- *n*-butyl acetate: as an odor enhancer in perfumes; in the synthesis of synthetics flavors, pharmaceuticals, and other organic compounds;

## Interesting Facts

- Scientists have discovered that the butyl acetates are present in the so-called alarm pheromones secreted by animals, particularly insects. An alarm pheromone is a chemical secreted when an animal is under attack. It alerts other animals in the neighborhood to the attack and "tells" them to respond to the attack that has been detected.

- *sec*-butyl acetate: as a thinner for nail enamels and a solvent for leather finishes;

- *tert*-butyl acetate: as a gasoline additive.

Relatively little data are available on the health effects of exposure to the isomers of butyl acetate. The chemical is known to cause skin rash, respiratory problems, and burning of the eyes upon contact. And by comparing it with other similar organic compounds, the assumption is made that long-term exposure to high concentrations would result in damage to the nervous system. Since most people do not encounter butyl acetate in the pure form, these risks are minimal. Only workers in one of the fields in which the chemical is used need take special precautions to use care in working with the amyl acetates.

## Words to Know

**ISOMER** One of two or more forms of a chemical compound with the same molecular formula, but different structural formulas and different chemical and physical properties.

**SOLVENT** A substance that is able to dissolve one or more other substances

FOR FURTHER INFORMATION

"Global Ethyl, Butyl Acetate Demand Expected to Rebound." *The Oil and Gas Journal* (April 24, 2000): 27.

"n-butyl acetate." New Jersey Department of Health and Senior Services. http://www.state.nj.us/health/eoh/rtkweb/1329.pdf (accessed on September 22, 2005).

"Occupational Safety and Health Guideline for tert-butyl Acetate." Occupational Health and Safety Administration. http://www.osha.gov/SLTC/healthguidelines/tertbutylacetate/recognition.html (accessed on September 22, 2005).

"sec-butyl acetate." Scorecard: The Pollution Information Site. http://www.scorecard.org/chemical-profiles/summary.tcl?edf_substance_id=105%2d46%2d4 (accessed on September 22, 2005).

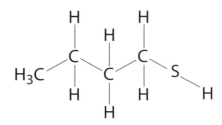

KEY FACTS

# Butyl Mercaptan

## OVERVIEW

Three isomers of butyl mercaptan (BYOO-til mer-KAP-tan) exist. Isomers are two or more forms of a chemical compound with the same molecular formula, but different structural formulas and different chemical and physical properties. The names and synonyms of the isomers are: *n*-butyl mercaptan, known as 1-butanethiol, 1-mercapto-butane, or *n*-butyl thioalcohol; *sec*-butyl mercaptan, called 2-butanethiol or 1-methyl-1-propanethiol; and *tert*-butyl mercaptan, also known as 2-methyl-2-propanethiol. The isomers have slightly different expanded chemical formulas: *n*-butyl mercaptan, $CH_3CH_2CH_2CH_2SH$; *sec*-butyl mercaptan, $CH_3CH_2CH(SH)CH_3$; and *tert*-butyl mercaptan, $CH_3C(CH_3)(SH)CH_3$. The isomers have vastly differing melting points: *n*-butyl mercaptan, −115.67°C (−176.21°F); *sec*-butyl mercaptan, −165°C (−265°F); and *tert*-butyl mercaptan, −0.5°C (31°F). Boiling points differ, but not as greatly: *n*-butyl mercaptan, 98.46°C (209.2°F); *sec*-butyl mercaptan, 85°C (180°F); and *tert*-butyl mercaptan, 64°C (150°F).

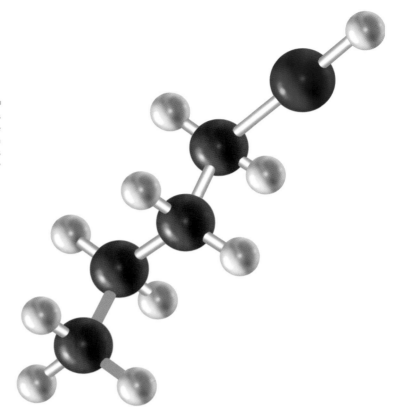

*Butyl mercaptan.* White atoms are hydrogen; black atoms are carbon; and the turquoise atom is selenium. PUBLISHERS RESOURCE GROUP

All three isomers of butyl mercaptan are mobile liquids (liquids that flow easily) with very strong skunk-like odors. At one time, chemists thought that the butyl mercaptans were responsible for the distinctive odor of skunk spray. Research has now shown that some mercaptans are found in skunk spray, but the butyl mercaptans are not among them.

## HOW IT IS MADE

A number of methods are available for the production of the butyl mercaptans. The most common method involves the reaction between an iodobutane (a butane molecule with one iodine atom, such as $CH_3CH_2CH_2CH_2I$) and a sulfhydryl compound, such as KSH. In this reaction,

## Interesting Facts

- The Israeli army reportedly developed a "skunk bomb" containing mercaptans to use as a crowd-control device against Palestinians.

- The Guinness World Records book classifies the butyl mercaptans as being among the two smelliest compounds in the world. The other chemical is ethyl mercaptan.

- The odor of the butyl mercaptans is said to be detectable at a distance of nearly a kilometer (about a half mile) from its source.

the sulfhydryl group (-SH) replaces the iodine to form the butyl mercaptan.

### COMMON USES AND POTENTIAL HAZARDS

More than 500,000 kilograms (1 million pounds) of the butyl mercaptans are produced each year in the United States. Their primary uses are as solvents and in the preparation of other organic compounds, especially insecticides and herbicides. Among their other uses are:

- Additives for natural gas, which normally has no odor, so that leaks can be easily detected;

- As an additive to enhance the flavor and aroma of certain foods;

- Nutrient in the maintenance of bacterial cultures.

All three isomers of butyl mercaptan are highly toxic. Anyone exposed to their vapors should seek medical attention immediately. The compounds are also very flammable and must be handled with care to prevent their catching fire. Since most individuals never come into contact with the butyl mercaptans, their health and safety risks are of concern primarily to workers who handle them in their everyday jobs.

## Words to Know

**ISOMER** One of two or more forms of a chemical compound with the same molecular formula, but different structural formulas and different chemical and physical properties.

**MERCAPTAN** Organic compound that contains a sulfhydryl group (-SH) attached to a carbon.

### FOR FURTHER INFORMATION

Bauman, Richard. "Getting Skunked: Understanding the Antics behind the Smell." *Backpacker* (May 1993): 30-31.

"n-Butyl Mercaptan." International Chemical Safety Cards. http://www.cdc.gov/niosh/ipcsneng/neng0018.html (accessed on September 14, 2005).

"The Stink that Stays." *Popular Mechanics* (December 2004): 26.

Wood, William F. "Chemistry of Skunk Spray." Humboldt State University. http://www.humboldt.edu/~wfw2/chemofskunkspray.html (accessed on September 14, 2005).

OTHER NAMES:
BHA and BHT

FORMULA:
BHA: $C_{11}H_{16}O_2$; BHT:
$C_{15}H_{24}O$

ELEMENTS:
Carbon, hydrogen,
oxygen

COMPOUND TYPE:
Organic

STATE:
Solid

MOLECULAR WEIGHT:
BHA: 180.24 g/mol;
BHT: 220.35 g/mol

MELTING POINT:
BHA: 51°C (124°F);
BHT: 71°C (160°F)

BOILING POINT:
BHA: 268°C (514°F);
BHT: 265°C (509°F)

SOLUBILITY:
Both are insoluble in
water and soluble in
ethyl alcohol; BHT is
also soluble in acetone
and benzene

K E Y   F A C T S

# Butylated Hydroxy-anisole and Butylated Hydroxytoluene

## OVERVIEW

Butylated hydroxyanisole (BYOO-til-ay-ted hi-DROK-see-ANN-i-sole) and butylated hydroxytoluene (BYOO-til-ay-ted hi-DROK-see-TOL-yoo-een) are very popular food additives used to preserve fats and oils. They both are antioxidants, which are compounds that prevent oxygen from reacting with substances and changing them into other materials. BHA and BHT prevent the oxidation of fats and oils that would convert them into rancid, foul-smelling, harmful products.

BHA is a white or pale yellow waxy solid with a faint pleasant odor. BHT is a white crystalline solid. Both compounds are members of the phenol family of organic compounds. The phenols are compounds containing a benzene ring of six carbon atoms to which is attached at least one hydroxyl (-OH) group.

## HOW IT IS MADE

A variety of methods are available for the preparation of BHA. The most common method involves the reaction

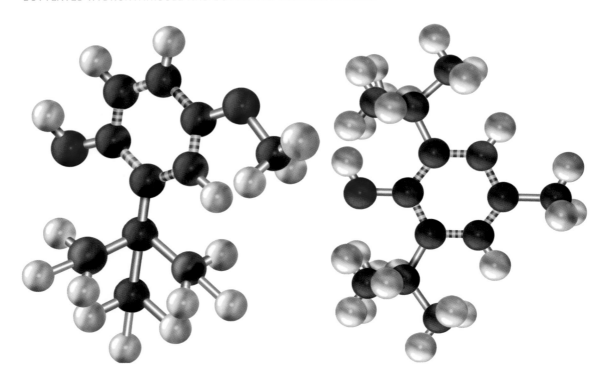

*BHA (left) and BHT (right).*
Red atoms are oxygen; white
atoms are hydrogen; and black
atoms are carbon. Gray sticks
indicate double bonds. Striped
sticks indicate a benzene ring.

PUBLISHERS RESOURCE GROUP

between *p*-methoxyphenol ($CH_3CH_2OC_6H_4OH$) and isobutene ($(CH_3)_2C=CH_2$) or *tert*,-butyl alcohol ($(CH_3)_3COH$) over a catalyst of silica (silicon dioxide; $SiO_2$) or alumina (aluminum oxide; $Al_2O_3$) at temperatures of about 150°C (302°F). BHT is usually made by reacting *p*-cresol ($CH_3C_6H_4OH$) with isobutene.

## COMMON USES AND POTENTIAL HAZARDS

The most important use of both BHA and BHT is as food preservatives. When these compounds are added to products containing fats or oils, oxygen reacts with the additive (BHA or BHT) rather than the food itself, protecting the food from spoiling. Among the vast array of food products containing either BHA or BHT or both are cereals, seasonings, frostings, dessert mixes, instant potatoes, packaged popcorn, baked goods, pie crusts, meat products, potato chips, candy, sausage, freeze-dried meats, butter, cheese, crackers, bread, vegetable oils, margarine, nuts, beer, and chewing gum.

Both compounds are also added to animal feed as preservatives. BHA and BHT are added to a number of non-food products as well. These products include paraffin wax, lipstick, eye shadow, lip-gloss, mascara, body and face lotions, diaper rash ointment, deodorant soaps, moisturizers, and shaving gels and creams.

The antioxidant properties of BHA and BHT make them suitable for other applications also. For example, they are sometimes added to paints and inks to prevent a "skin" from forming on top of these liquids. The skin is formed when the paint or ink reacts with oxygen in air to form a solid compound. The compounds are also used as additives for the preservation of drugs, rubber products, petroleum products, the plastics used in food wraps, and the petroleum wax coatings used on food boxes.

Questions have been raised about the possible health benefits and risks posed by BHA and BHT. On the one hand, these compounds may contribute to good health by destroying substances in the body that can lead to cancer. They may also destroy the herpes virus and the human immunodeficiency virus (HIV). Most nutritionists agree that antioxidants can be helpful in protecting cells and tissues from aging and damage by oxygen.

On the other hand, BHA and BHT may also be responsible for certain health problems. For example, some people appear to be allergic to these compounds, causing skin rashes, hives, or tightness in the chest, although such reactions are thought to be rare. Other people may have problems metabolizing BHA and BHT properly, resulting in a build-up of the compounds in their bodies.

Scientists are uncertain about the possible long-term health effects of BHA and BHT. Some studies suggest that these compounds may affect liver or kidney function or may be carcinogenic. Studies on this subject are inconclusive, however, and the U.S. Food and Drug Administration has decided that the two compounds can be used as food additives if the amount added is less than 0.02 percent by weight.

As with all chemicals, direct exposure to large doses of BHA or BHT can cause serious health problems. In one experiment, for example, adults who ingested four grams (0.14 ounce) of BHA experienced stomach pain, vomiting, dizziness, confusion, and temporary loss of consciousness. That amount of BHA is tens or hundreds of thousands of times the amount one would consume in foods or other products, however. Only people who work directly with the compound would ever worry about an effect such as this one.

## Words to Know

**CARCINOGEN** A chemical that causes cancer in humans or other animals.

FOR FURTHER INFORMATION

"Butylated Hydroxyanisole." CHEC's Health*e*House. http://www.checnet.org/healthehouse/chemicals/chemicals-detail2.asp?Main_ID=330 (accessed on January 9, 2006).

"Butylated Hydroxyanisole." *Gale Encyclopedia of Science.* Edited by K. Lee Lerner and Brenda Wilmoth Lerner. 3rd ed., vol. 1. Detroit: Gale, 2004.

"Butylated Hydroxyanisole." Hazardous Substances Data Bank. http://toxnet.nlm.nih.gov/ (accessed on Jnauary 9, 2006).

"Butylated Hydroxyanisole (BHA; tert-butyl-4-hydroxyanisole) and Butylated Hydroxytoluene (BHT; 2,6-di-tert-butyl-p-cresol)." In *Food Antioxidants: Technological, Toxicological, and Health Perspectives,* edited by D. L. Madhavi, S. S. Deshpande, and D. K. Salunkhe. New York: Dekker, 1996.

"Butylated Hydroxytoluene." *Gale Encyclopedia of Science.* Edited by K. Lee Lerner and Brenda Wilmoth Lerner. 3rd ed., vol. 1. Detroit: Gale, 2004.

"Butylated Hydroxytoluene." International Chemical Safety Cards. http://www.cdc.gov/niosh/ipcsneng/neng0841.html (accessed on January 9, 2006).

OTHER NAMES:
Methyltheobromine;
theine

FORMULA:
$C_8H_{10}N_4O_2$

ELEMENTS:
Carbon, hydrogen,
nitrogen, oxygen

COMPOUND TYPE:
Organic base
(alkaloid)

STATE:
Solid

MOLECULAR WEIGHT:
194.19 g/mol

MELTING POINT:
238°C (460°F)

BOILING POINT:
Not applicable;
begins to sublime at
about 90°C (190°F)

SOLUBILITY:
Slightly soluble in
water and alcohol;
soluble in chloroform

# Caffeine

## OVERVIEW

Caffeine (kaf-EEN) is an organic base that occurs naturally in a number of plant products, including coffee beans, tea leaves, and kola nuts. It occurs as a fleecy white crystalline material, often in the form of long, silky needles. It usually exists as the monohydrate, $C_8H_{10}N_4O_2 \cdot H_2O$, although it gives up its water of hydration readily when exposed to air.

Scientists believe that humans have been drinking beverages that contain caffeine for thousands of years. The first recorded reference to a caffeine drink can be found in a Chinese reference to the consumption of tea by the emperor Shen Nung in about 2700 BCE. Coffee is apparently a much more recent drink, with the earliest cultivation of the coffee tree dated at about 575 CE in Africa.

Caffeine was first studied scientifically by two French chemists, Joseph Bienaimé Caventou (1795-1877) and Pierre Joseph Pelletier (1788-1842), who were very interested in the chemical properties of the alkaloids. Between 1817

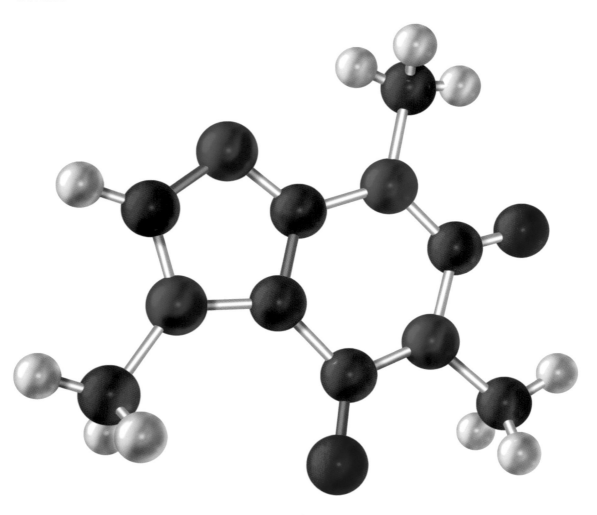

*Caffeine.* Red atoms are oxygen; white atoms are hydrogen; black atoms are carbon; and blue atoms are nitrogen. Gray sticks are double bonds. PUBLISHERS RESOURCE GROUP

and 1821, Caventou and Pelletier successfully extracted caffeine, quinine, strychnine, brucine, chinchonine, and chlorophyll (not an alkaloid) from a variety of plants. The first synthesis of caffeine was accomplished in 1895 by the German chemist Emil Hermann Fischer (1852-1919), who was awarded the 1902 Nobel Prize in chemistry for his work on the alkaloids.

Caffeine belongs to a class of alkaloids called the methylxanthines. Chocolate, from the cocoa tree *Theobroma cacao* contains another member of the class, theobromine. Both caffeine and theobromine are stimulants, that is, compounds

## Interesting Facts

- Americans drank 6.3 billion gallons of coffee, 2.4 billion gallons of tea, and 15.3 billion gallons of caffeinated soft drinks in 2003.

that act on the nervous system to produce alertness, excitement, and increased physical and mental activity.

### HOW IT IS MADE

Caffeine can be extracted from coffee, tea, and kola plants by one of three methods. These methods are used primarily to produce the decaffeinated counterparts of the products: decaffeinated coffee, decaffeinated tea, or decaffeinated soft drinks. A commercial variation of these procedures is to treat the waste products of tea or coffee processing, such as the dust and sweepings collected from factories, for the extraction of caffeine.

In the first of the three extraction methods, the natural product (coffee beans, tea leaves, or kola beans) are treated with an organic solvent that dissolves the caffeine from the plant material. The solvent is then evaporated leaving behind the pure caffeine. A second method follows essentially the same procedure, except that hot water is used as the solvent for the caffeine. A more recent procedure involves the use of supercritical carbon dioxide for the extraction process. Supercritical carbon dioxide is a form of the familiar gas that exists at high temperature and high pressure. It behaves as both a liquid and a gas. Not only is the supercritical carbon dioxide procedure an efficient method of extracting caffeine, but it has virtually none of the harmful environmental and health problems associated with each of the other two methods of extraction.

Caffeine is also made synthetically by heating a combination of the silver salt of theobromine ($C_7H_8N_4O_2Ag$) with methyl iodide ($CH_2I$), resulting in the addition of one carbon

## Words to Know

**ALKALOIDS** Organic bases that contain the element nitrogen.

**DIURETIC** A substance that increases the flow of urine.

**WATER OF HYDRATION** Water that has combined with a compound by some physical means.

and two hydrogens to the theobromine molecule and converting it to caffeine.

### COMMON USES AND POTENTIAL HAZARDS

Caffeine is used in foods and drinks and for medical purposes. Its primary action is to stimulate the central nervous system. People drink coffee, tea, or cola drinks to stay awake and alert because caffeine creates a feeling of added energy. It does this by increasing heart rate, improving blood flow to the muscles, opening airways to aid breathing, and releasing stored energy from the liver to provided added fuel for the body. In large quantities, caffeine can also cause nervousness, insomnia, and heart problems. The effects of caffeine can linger in the body for more than six hours. In medical applications, caffeine is sometimes used as a heart stimulant for patients in shock, to treat apnea (loss of breathing) in newborn babies, to counteract depressed breathing levels as a result of drug overdoses, and as a diuretic.

Caffeine stimulates the brain in two ways. First, because it has a chemical structure similar to that of adenosine, it attaches to adenosine receptors in the brain. Adenosine is a substance that normally attaches to those receptors, slowing brain activity and causing drowsiness. By blocking those receptors, caffeine increases electrical activity in the brain, creating a feeling of alertness. Caffeine also works in the brain like drugs such as heroin and cocaine, although in a much milder way. Like those drugs, caffeine increases dopamine levels. Dopamine is a chemical present in the brain that increases the body's feeling of pleasure.

Studies have shown that caffeine can become addictive. People who use the compound eventually need to take more and more of it to get the same effect. When some people try to stop using caffeine, they may suffer from headache, fatigue, and depression, though these symptoms can be controlled by gradually reducing the amount of caffeine consumed. Either way, withdrawal symptoms end after about a week.

## FOR FURTHER INFORMATION

"Caffeine." Neuroscience for Kids. http://faculty.washington.edu/chudler/caff.html (accessed on September 23, 2004).

"Caffeine Chemistry." Erowid Vault. http://www.erowid.org/chemicals/caffeine/caffeine_chemistry.shtml (accessed on September 23, 2005).

Cherniske, Stephen. *Caffeine Blues: Wake Up to the Hidden Dangers of America's #1 Drug.* New York: Warner Books, 1998.

Kluger, Jeffrey. "The Buzz on Caffeine." *Time* (December 20, 2004): 52.

Weinberg, Alan Bennet, and Bonnie K. Bealer. *The World of Caffeine: The Science and Culture of the World's Most Popular Drug.* New York: Routledge, 2002.

*See Also* Carbon Dioxide; Theobromine

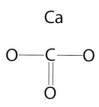

OTHER NAMES:
Limestone; chalk;
aragonite; calcite

FORMULA:
$CaCO_3$

ELEMENTS:
Calcium, carbon,
oxygen

COMPOUND TYPE:
Inorganic salt

STATE:
Solid

MOLECULAR WEIGHT:
100.09 g/mol

MELTING POINT:
Calcite: 1330°C
(2430°F); aragonite:
decomposes at about
825°C (1520°F)

BOILING POINT:
Not applicable

SOLUBILITY:
Very slightly soluble
in water; soluble in
dilute acids; insoluble
in organic solvents

KEY FACTS

# Calcium Carbonate

## OVERVIEW

Calcium carbonate (KAL-see-um CAR-bun-ate) is one of
the most common compounds on Earth, making up about
7 percent of Earth's crust. It occurs in a number of minerals
and other natural materials, including aragonite, calcite,
chalk, limestone, marble, marl, oyster shells, pearls, and tra-
vertine. Stalactites and stalagmites found in caves are made
primarily of calcium carbonate. As indicated by the melting
points of aragonite and calcite, the compound's physical
properties may differ somewhat depending on its crystal
form. It typically occurs as an odorless, tasteless white powder or colorless crystals.

## HOW IT IS MADE

Calcium carbonate is so abundant in nature that demand
for the compound can be met by mining natural sources,
such as chalk, limestone, and marble quarries. The compound can also be produced in the laboratory by reacting

*Calcium carbonate.* Red atoms are oxygen; black atom is carbon; white atom is calcium. Gray stick is a double bond.
PUBLISHERS RESOURCE GROUP

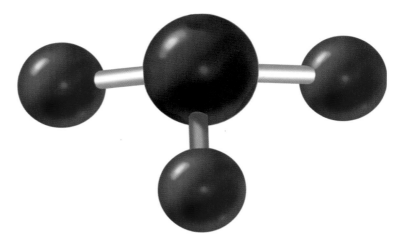

calcium chloride ($CaCl_2$) with sodium carbonate ($Na_2CO_3$). The calcium carbonate formed in this reaction precipitates out of (separates from) the solution and can be recovered by filtration.

## COMMON USES AND POTENTIAL HAZARDS

One well known use of calcium carbonate is as an antacid, a substance that neutralizes excess stomach acid (hydrochloric acid; HCl) and relieves the symptoms of acid indigestion, heartburn, upset stomach, and sour stomach. Large amounts of the chemical are also used for a variety of industrial uses, including:

• In agriculture, where it is used to maintain proper acidity of soil and supply calcium needed by growing plants;

## Interesting Facts

- It is said that Cleopatra showed her extravagance by dissolving pearls (which are made of calcium carbonate) in vinegar and drinking the resulting solution.

- Stalagmites and stalactites form in caves when calcium bicarbonate ($CaHCO_3$) dissolved in groundwater reaches the top of a cave and gives up carbon dioxide ($CO_2$) to the air. When calcium bicarbonate loses carbon dioxide, it is converted to calcium carbonate, which precipitates out on the roof of the cave as a stalactite. If the calcium bicarbonate does not lose carbon dioxide until it drips off the roof and falls on the floor of the cave, the calcium carbonate that is formed builds up a stalagmite on the floor of the cave.

- In the paper-making industry, where it is used to make strong products with a very white color, glossy finish, and firm texture for printing and dyeing;

- As a filler in the manufacture of plastics to reduce the cost of production;

- In the construction industry, where it is used in the production of concrete structures, such as paving-stones, tubes, and sewage tanks, in ready-mixed concrete, and in prefabricated elements;

- In the production of paints and other types of coating materials because of its ability to provide weather resistance, protect the coating against corrosion, reduce drying time, and maintain the proper acidity of the coating material;

- In a variety of environmental applications, such as counteracting the increased acidity of lakes and other bodies of water caused by acid precipitation, treating waste gases to remove sulfur and nitrogen oxides that pollute the air; and purifying water and waste water; and

- In the manufacture of lime (calcium oxide; $CaO$) which, itself, has a host of industrial applications.

## Words to Know

**PRECIPITATE** A solid material that settles out of a solution, often as the result of a chemical reaction.

### FOR FURTHER INFORMATION

"Calcium Carbonate." National Institute for Occupational Safety and Health.
http://www.cdc.gov/niosh/npg/npgd0090.html (accessed on September 24, 2005).

"Calcium Carbonate Powder." Reade.
http://www.reade.com/Products/Minerals_and_Ores/calcium_carbonate.html (accessed on September 24, 2005).

Tegethoff, F. Wolfgana, with Johannes Rohleder and Evelyn Kroker, eds. *Calcium carbonate: From the Cretaceous period into the 21st century.* Boston: Birkhäuser Verlag, 2001.

*See Also* Calcium Oxide

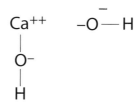

KEY FACTS

# Calcium Hydroxide

## OVERVIEW

Calcium hydroxide (KAL-see-um hye-DROK-side) is a soft, white odorless solid that occurs as granules or a powder. It has a slightly bitter, alkaline taste. Calcium hydroxide absorbs carbon dioxide readily from the air, changing to calcium carbonate (CaCO$_3$). For this reason, the compound often is contaminated with the carbonate unless it is kept in tightly sealed containers. Calcium hydroxide is a relatively inexpensive chemical and, for that reason, is used in production processes where a base is needed. Although calcium hydroxide is not very soluble in water, a suspension of the finely divided powder in water can be made, a suspension known as limewater or milk of lime.

## HOW IT IS MADE

Calcium hydroxide is produced by adding water to calcium oxide (CaO). This reaction is highly exothermic and must be carried out with some care to avoid loss of the product through spattering.

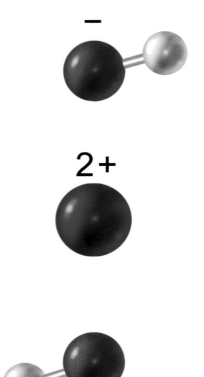

## COMMON USES AND POTENTIAL HAZARDS

Calcium hydroxide has a number of uses in building and paving materials. It is found in mortar, plasters, and cements. When used in mortar, calcium hydroxide is mixed with sand and water to make a paste. The paste is put between bricks to hold them together. When water in the paste evaporates, the remaining sand-calcium hydroxide mixture becomes a hard, strong adhesive holding the bricks together.

Calcium hydroxide is also used extensively as a neutralizing agent. As a base, it reacts with acids formed in industrial operations, in the environment, and in other situations. For example, soil that is too acidic for plants to grow properly can be treated with calcium hydroxide. The hydroxide ion ($OH^-$) in the calcium hydroxide reacts with the hydrogen ion ($H^+$) in the acidic soil to form water, resulting in a more neutral soil.

## Interesting Facts

- One of the oldest methods of coating a surface is with whitewash, a mixture made of calcium hydroxide, water, and chalk (calcium carbonate). Whitewash is used to whiten the walls of a building, a fence, or some other structure.

A similar application involves the treatment of exhaust gases from factories with calcium hydroxide. Nitrogen and sulfur oxides in the gases, which are the primary cause of acid rain, are neutralized when passed through "scrubbers" containing calcium hydroxide.

Among the many other uses of calcium hydroxide are:

- In the leather and hide tanning industry, where calcium hydroxide is used to remove hair from hides and then to neutralize tanning solutions;

- For the purification of sugar solutions, such as those used in making fruit juices;

- As a component of certain types of pesticides;

- As an additive to lubricants and oil drilling fluids, to improve the viscosity of the fluids;

- In the manufacture of paints and waterproof coatings;

- As a food additive, used for the purpose of preventing foods from becoming too acidic;

- As an accelerant (a compound that increases the rate of a chemical reaction) in processes for the production of synthetic rubber and plastics; and

- As a food additive in poultry feed, to improve the strength of egg shells.

Exposure to calcium hydroxide can cause irritation of the skin, eyes, and respiratory system. These conditions are treated satisfactorily by flushing the contaminated area with ample amounts of water. People who work directly with calcium hydroxide in the workplace are more likely to be at risk for health problems because of their exposure to larger

## Words to Know

**EXOTHERMIC REACTION** A reaction in which heat is produced.

amounts of the chemical for longer periods of time. In such cases, more serious health problems, such as burns and blistering of the skin, damage to the retina of the eye, and injury to the gastrointestinal system may develop.

### FOR FURTHER INFORMATION

"Calcium Hydroxide or Hydrated Lime." Peters Chemical Company. http://www.peterschemical.com/calcium_hydroxide_or_hydrated_li.htm (accessed on September 26, 2005).

"Material Safety Data Sheet: Calcium Hydroxide Products." Pulpdent Corporation. http://www.pulpdent.com/c_hydro/CHMSDS.pdf (accessed on September 26, 2005).

*See Also* Calcium Oxide

$$Ca = O$$

OTHER NAMES:
Lime; quicklime;
burnt lime; calx;
unslaked lime;
fluxing lime

FORMULA:
CaO

ELEMENTS:
Calcium, oxygen

COMPOUND TYPE:
Metallic oxide

STATE:
Solid

MOLECULAR WEIGHT:
56.08 g/mol

MELTING POINT:
2,898°C (5,248°F)

BOILING POINT:
Not available

SOLUBILITY:
Reacts with water
to form calcium
hydroxide; soluble in
acids; insoluble in
alcohol and most
organic solvents

KEY FACTS

# Calcium Oxide

## OVERVIEW

Calcium oxide (KAL-see-um OK-side) is an odorless crystalline or powdery solid that, in a pure form, is white to off-gray. It often appears with a yellowish or brownish tint to the presence of impurities, especially iron. Calcium oxide reacts with water to form calcium hydroxide ($Ca(OH)_2$) with the evolution of significant amounts of heat. The compound is strongly caustic.

Calcium oxide has been known since ancient times. The Roman writer Cato the Elder (234-149 BCE) described one method of producing the compound in 184 BCE. Another early Roman scholar, Pliny the Elder (23-79 CE) discussed the compound at length in his book *Historia Naturalis* (*Natural History*), published in 70 CE. By the early fifteenth century, most of Europe was using calcium oxide (widely referred to as lime) in the construction of buildings. The Scottish chemist Joseph Black (1728-1799) carried out some of the earliest scientific studies of calcium oxide. He found that when the compound is exposed to air, it combines with carbon dioxide to form calcium carbonate.

*Calcium oxide.* Red atom is oxygen and green atom is calcium. Gray stick shows a double bond. PUBLISHERS RESOURCE GROUP

## HOW IT IS MADE

The process for making calcium oxide is believed to be one of the first chemical reactions known to humans, dating back to prehistoric times. When limestone (calcium carbonate; $CaCO_3$) is heated, carbon dioxide ($CO_2$) is driven off, leaving calcium oxide behind. The reaction was probably discovered very early in human history because limestone is a common, readily available material in the form of chalk and sea shells, and the amount of heat needed to produce the reaction can easily be produced in a simple wood fire. A more efficient method for carrying out the reaction is to heat the limestone in a kiln (oven) at temperatures of 500°C to 900°C (900°F to 1,600°F), resulting in a more complete conversion of calcium carbonate to calcium oxide. This method is still used today for the commercial preparation of calcium oxide.

## COMMON USES AND POTENTIAL HAZARDS

The most important single use of calcium oxide is in metallurgy, particularly in the production of steel. When calcium oxide is added to the furnace in which steel is made, it reacts with sulfur, phosphorus, silica, and other impurities present in the mixture from which steel is produced. The complex mixture that results can be poured off the top of the molten steel in the form of a slag, a nonmetallic waste formed during the production of metals. Calcium oxide plays a comparable role in the manufacture of other metals, such as aluminum and magnesium. About 40 percent of all the calcium oxide produced in the United States goes to metallurgical applications.

The next most important use of calcium oxide is in pollution control devices. Smoke that leaves a factory's

## Interesting Facts

- Calcium oxide is often used to "lime" lake waters that have been acidified by acid rain. It reacts with and neutralizes acids in the lake formed when nitric and sulfuric acid in acid rain are carried to earth by rain, snow, sleet, and other forms of precipitation.

- When calcium oxide is heated near its melting point, it gives off a brilliant white light. In the years before electricity was available for lighting, particularly during the second half of the nineteenth century, heated lime was used to produce the bright lights needed to illuminate stage productions. From this practice came the expression "being in the limelight" to refer to anyone who was in public view of large groups of people.

- Because it was thought to accelerate the decomposition of soft tissue, quicklime has historically been used in the burial of diseased animals and humans. For example, bodies of plague victims in London in 1666 were directed to be buried in quicklime.

smokestack, for example, contains oxides of sulfur and nitrogen that, in the atmosphere, combine with water to form sulfuric acid and nitric acid. To prevent the formation of these pollutants, "scrubbers" can be installed in smokestacks. The scrubbers contain some chemical that reacts with and neutralizes the oxides of sulfur and nitrogen. One of the most common compounds used for this purpose is calcium oxide. About 15 percent of all calcium oxide used in the United States goes to this application.

Some other uses of calcium oxide include:

- In water treatment plants, to control acidity of the water being treated and to remove impurities present in the water;

- In the construction industry, where it is used to make plaster, mortar, stucco, bricks, and other building materials;

- As a filler to strengthen paper products;

## Words to Know

**CAUSTIC** Strongly basic or alkaline material that irritates or corrodes living tissue.

**METALLURGY** The science of working with metals.

- As a refractory, a heat-resistant material used to line the insides of furnaces;
- In the production of other chemical materials;
- As an additive for poultry feed;
- In insecticides and fungicides;
- In the removal of hair from hides before tanning; and
- As a food additive to maintain proper acidity and give bulk to a food product.

Exposure to calcium oxide can cause damage to the skin, eyes, nose, and respiratory system. People who use the product in their line of work or at home (for garden purposes, for example) must exercise extreme caution to avoid swallowing, breathing in, or otherwise coming into contact with the chemical. If such contact occurs, it should be washed off completely and medical assistance requested.

### FOR FURTHER INFORMATION

"Calcium Oxide or Quicklime." Peters Chemical Company. http://www.peterschemical.com/calcium_oxide_or_quicklime. htm (accessed on September 27, 2005).

"Chemical of the Week—Lime." http://scifun.chem.wisc.edu/chemweek/Lime/lime.html (accessed on September 27, 2005).

"Cheminfo." Canadian Centre for Occupational Health and Safety. http://intox.org/databank/documents/chemical/calcoxid/cie11. htm (accessed on September 27, 2005).

"Metallurgy Information Area." National Lime Association. http://www.lime.org/ENV02/Metal802.htm#IS (accessed on September 27, 2005).

*See Also* Calcium Carbonate; Calcium Hydroxide

# Calcium Phosphate

OTHER NAMES:
see Overview

FORMULA:
see Overview

ELEMENTS:
calcium, hydrogen,
phosphorus, oxygen

COMPOUND TYPE:
Inorganic salts

STATE:
Solid

MOLECULAR WEIGHT:
136.06 to 310.20 g/mol

MELTING POINT:
see Overview; tribasic
form: 1670°C
(3040°F)

BOILING POINT:
Not applicable

SOLUBILITY:
See Overview

K E Y   F A C T S

## OVERVIEW

The three forms of calcium phosphate (KAL-see-um FOSS-fate) all occur as tasteless, odorless, colorless to white crystalline or powdery solids.

Dibasic calcium phosphate, $CaHPO_4$, is also called calcium monohydrogen phosphate, dicalcium orthophosphate, or secondary calcium phosphate. It is usually found in the form of hydrate, such as $CaHPO_4 \cdot 2H_2O$. It does not melt, instead decomposing when heated to 109°C (228°F).

Monobasic calcium phosphate, $Ca(H_2PO_4)_2$, is also known as calcium hypophosphite, calcium biphosphate, acid calcium phosphate, monocalcium orthophosphate, and primary calcium phosphate. It usually exists in the form of the hydrate $Ca(H_2PO_4)_2 \cdot H_2O$. It decomposes when heated to 200°C (400°F)

Tribasic calcium phosphate, $Ca_3(PO_4)_2$, may be called calcium orthophosphate, tricalcium orthophosphate, tertiary calcium orthophosphate, or tricalcium phosphate. Unlike the other two forms, the tribasic form contains no hydrogen atoms.

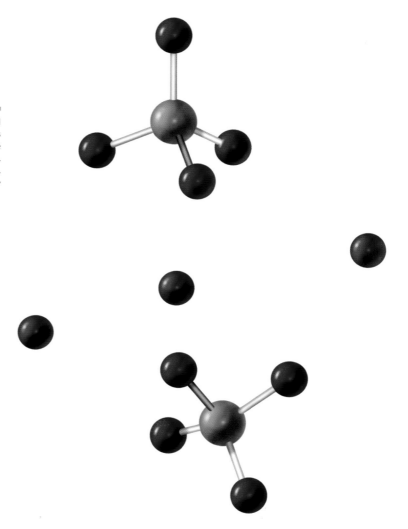

The dibasic and tribasic forms of calcium phosphate are insoluble in water and alcohol, but soluble in most acids. Monobasic calcium phosphate is soluble in water and acids, and insoluble in alcohol. All three compounds are non-flammable.

## HOW IT IS MADE

Tribasic calcium phosphate can be obtained directly from rock and minerals such as apatite, a complex and impure form of calcium phosphate, or phosphorite, a mineral that

## Interesting Facts

- The forms of calcium phosphate discussed here are only three of many ways in which calcium, phosphorus, and oxygen combine to form calcium phosphate-type compounds. Another such compound is known as hydroxyapatite ($Ca_5(PO_4)_3(OH)$), which makes up about 70 percent of an adult tooth.

- Calcium phosphate is one of the two most common compounds found in kidney stones. The second of these compounds is calcium oxalate ($CaC_2O_4$).

contains calcium phosphate mixed with other compounds. The compound can also be produced synthetically by reacting phosphoric acid ($H_3PO_4$) with solid calcium hydroxide ($Ca(OH)_2$), or in the reaction between calcium chloride ($CaCl_2$) and sodium triphosphate ($Na_5P_3O_{10}$). Dibasic calcium phosphate can also be produced in the former of these synthetic reactions by using an aqueous solution of calcium hydroxide rather than the solid compound. Monobasic calcium phosphate is produced synthetically by adding excess phosphoric acid to a solution of either dibasic or tribasic calcium phosphate and allowing the solution to evaporate.

## COMMON USES AND POTENTIAL HAZARDS

Each form of calcium phosphate has its own uses. The dibasic form is used as a nutrient and mineral supplement in animal foods and in certain processed foods, especially cereals. In addition to its nutritional value, dibasic calcium phosphate acts as a dough conditioner, stabilizer, and thickener in foods. The compound is also used in dental products to provide replacement for hydroxyapatite lost to decay or other factors.

The most common application of monocalcium phosphate is in fertilizers, where its function is to provide the phosphorus that plants need to remain healthy and grow properly.

## Words to Know

**AQUEOUS** Consisting of some material dissolved in water.

**MORDANT** A substance used in dyeing and printing that reacts chemically with both a dye and the material being dyed to help hold the dye permanently to the material.

**SYNTHESIS** a chemical reaction in which some desired chemical product is made from simple beginning chemicals, or reactants.

**WATER OF HYDRATION** Water that has combined with a compound by some physical means.

It is also used as a food additive in baking powders and wheat flours where it serves to retain the proper acidity of the food product to which it is added. It is also used, like the dibasic form, as a nutritional supplement in processed foods.

Tricalcium phosphate has the largest range of uses of the three forms of the compound, the most important of which are in the manufacture of fertilizers, the production of ceramic materials, and the preparation of other compounds of phosphorus. The compound is also used:

- As a clarifying agent in the purification of sugar solutions;
- As a mordant in the dyeing of cloth;
- In the preparation of dental products;
- As a stabilizer for plastics;
- As a food additive to prevent a powdery product from caking (becoming compacted);
- As a nutritional supplement; and
- As a means of removing radioactive strontium (strontium-90) from milk that has been contaminated by the element.

While none of the forms of calcium phosphate is flammable, they can all irritate the skin, eyes, and respiratory system. Tricalcium phosphate is the most hazardous of the family of compounds. Direct contact with the eyes may cause severe symptoms, including irritation and burning, resulting in damage to the cornea. The compound is also poisonous if taken internally. It can cause stomach pain, vomiting, and low blood pressure. These problems occur when one is exposed to relatively large amounts of the compound. In the quantities present in foods and other products with which consumers come into contact, the compound poses little risk to users.

FOR FURTHER INFORMATION

"Calcium Phosphate." Medline Plus.
http://www.nlm.nih.gov/medlineplus/ency/article/002889.htm (accessed on September 28, 2005).

"Dicalcium Phosphate." Univar USA
http://www.msdsvault.org//UNIVARUSA/332227-70621C2A2E204EBB8825668F0061E8ED-OPENDOCUMENT.PDF (accessed on September 28, 2005).

"Tricalcium Phosphate."
http://www.luminet.net/~wenonah/hydro/3capo.htm (accessed on September 28, 2005)

$$Ca^{2+} \!-\!\! Si \!\!=\!\! O$$

with $O^{2+}$ above and $O$ below the Si.

OTHER NAMES:
Calcium metasilicate

FORMULA:
CaSiO₃

ELEMENTS:
Calcium, silicon,
oxygen

COMPOUND TYPE:
Inorganic salt

STATE:
Solid

MOLECULAR WEIGHT:
116.16 g/mol

MELTING POINT:
1540°C (2800°F)

BOILING POINT:
Not applicable

SOLUBILITY:
Insoluble in water and
most other common
solvents

KEY FACTS

# Calcium Silicate

## OVERVIEW

The term calcium silicate (KAL-see-um SILL-i-kate) applies to a number of related compounds consisting of calcium, silicon, and oxygen, all of which tend to occur in a hydrated form. The most common of these forms is calcium metasilicate, for which data are given above. Calcium silicates with the formulas $Ca_2SiO_4$ and $Ca_3SiO_5$ are also well known.

Calcium silicate is a component of many minerals, including afwillite, akermanite, andradite, calcite, centrallasite, crestmoreite, diopside, eaklite, grammite, gyrolite, hillebrandite, larnite, and wollastonite. In its pure form, calcium metasilicate is a white to off-white color capable of absorbing up to two and a half times its weight of water. In this form, the hydrated powder retains its ability to flow freely. Addition of a mineral acid, such as hydrochloric acid (HCl) results in the formation of a gel.

## HOW IT IS MADE

Given its abundance in rocks and minerals, calcium metasilicate and its cousins can be extracted from a variety of

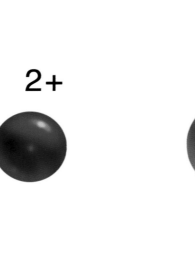
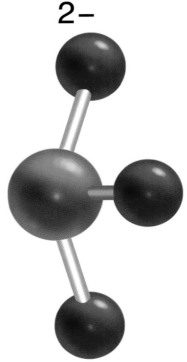

*Calcium silicate.* Red atoms are oxygen; turquoise atom is calcium; orange atom is silicon. Gray stick is a double bond.
PUBLISHERS RESOURCE GROUP

natural sources. Nonetheless, the compound is usually prepared synthetically in order to ensure that is has the purity required for most commercial applications. The usual method of preparation involves the addition of lime (calcium oxide; CaO) to diatomaceous earth, a material consisting of the fossil remains of single-celled algae known as diatoms. The lime provides the calcium and the diatomaceous earth provides the silicon dioxide ($SiO_2$) required to make calcium silicate.

## COMMON USES AND POTENTIAL HAZARDS

The calcium silicates have a number of uses in industry. Among the most important applications are their uses in building materials, such as some types of glass and cement (especially Portland cement), bricks and tiles for roofs, fireproof ceilings, and building boards. The compound is also

## Interesting Facts

- One of the most common building materials in use today is Portland cement, made from a mixture of oxides, including lime (calcium oxide), sand (silicon dioxide), and aluminum, iron, and magnesium oxides. When these components are mixed and water is added, a complex set of chemical reactions occur in which calcium silicates are among the major products formed. These calcium silicates are responsible for the great strength for which Portland cement products are known.

used as a filler in the manufacture of paper and some types of plastics, where it gives body to the final product.

Other applications of the calcium silicates include the following:

- As an absorbent for liquids and gases in industrial processes;
- As a food additive, where it absorbs moisture and prevents a product from "caking" (becoming compacted);
- In road construction;
- As a refractory material in industrial furnaces;
- For the insulation of pipes and conduits;
- In the manufacture of paints and other types of coating materials;
- In the preparation of certain types of cosmetics;
- In some fertilizers and insecticides; and
- In some pharmaceutical products, such as antacids.

There have been no reports of calcium silicate's being hazardous or harmful to humans or experimental animals. As with all chemicals, overexposure to large amounts of the compound could result in irritation of the skin, eyes, and respiratory system.

## Words to Know

**HYDRATE** Chemical compound formed when one or more molecules of water is added physically to the molecule of some other substance.

**REFRACTORY** Having a high melting point, resistant to melting. Refractory materials are often used to line the interior of industrial furnaces.

**SYNTHESIS** A chemical reaction in which some desired chemical product is made from simple beginning chemicals, or reactants.

### FOR FURTHER INFORMATION

"Occupational Safety and Health Guideline for Calcium Silicate, Synthetic." Occupational Health and Safety Administration. http://www.osha.gov/SLTC/healthguidelines/calciumsilicate/recognition.html#healthhazard (accessed on September 29, 2005).

"Scientific Principles." Materials Science and Technology Teacher's Workshop. http://matse1.mse.uiuc.edu/~tw/concrete/prin.html (accessed on September 29, 2005).

"Wollastonite." CeramicMaterials.Info. http://ceramic-materials.com/cermat/material/1705.html (accessed on September 29, 2005).

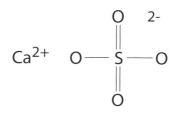

K E Y   F A C T S

# Calcium Sulfate

## OVERVIEW

Calcium sulfate (KAL-see-um SUL-fate) occurs in three forms:

- anhydrous calcium sulfate (CaSO$_4$); the anhydrous form of calcium sulfate is available in two forms, known as insoluble anhydrite and soluble anhydrite;

- calcium sulfate dihydrate (CaSO$_4$·2H$_2$O), also known as mineral white, terra alba, light spar, precipitated calcium sulfate, native calcium sulfate, and by other names;

- calcium sulfate hemihydrate (CaSO$_4$·$\frac{1}{2}$H$_2$O), also known as plaster of Paris and dried gypsum;

The physical properties of the three forms of calcium sulfate differ somewhat from each other, but their chemical properties are essentially the same. Anhydrous calcium sulfate and calcium hemihydrate are fine white odorless powders or crystalline solids, while the dihydrate may occur either as a powder or as white lumps. Both hydrates are

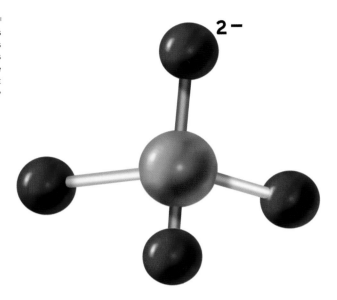

*Calcium sulfate.* Red atoms are oxygen; turquoise atom is calcium; and yellow atom is sulfur. Gray sticks show double bonds. PUBLISHERS RESOURCE GROUP

converted to the anhydrous form upon heating as, for example: $CaSO_4 \cdot 2H_2O \rightarrow CaSO_4 + 2H_2O$.

Anhydrous calcium sulfate is essentially insoluble in water. As their names suggest, the soluble form of the compound (soluble anhydrite) is somewhat more soluble in water than is the insoluble form (insoluble anhydrite). The dihydrate and hemihydrate are only slightly soluble in water. When water is added to the hemihydrate, a reaction occurs that results in the formation of a hard, solid mass (plaster of Paris) used in making casts, such as those used to hold broken bones in place. Neither the anhydrous form of calcium sulfate or the dihydrate reacts with water in this way.

Both the anhydrous and dihydrate forms of calcium sulfate occur naturally in the form of the minerals anhydrite, angelite, muriacite, and karstenite ($CaSO_4$); and gypsum ($CaSO_4 \cdot 2H_2O$). These minerals have been known to humans and used by them for thousands of years. The method for converting natural gypsum to the hemihydrate (plaster of

Paris) has also been known and used for a very long period of time. Archaeologists have learned that the Egyptians developed a method for converting gypsum to plaster of Paris, which was then used as mortars to join blocks in buildings, more than 5,000 years ago.

## HOW IT IS MADE

Gypsum is an abundant mineral providing a ready natural supply of calcium sulfate. The mineral usually consists of a mixture of the anhydrous and dihydrate forms of calcium sulfate, which can be separated into its component parts. Clay, sand, limestone, and other impurities are also present in most gypsum deposits. The process of separation and purification begins by crushing natural gypsum and heating it in an open kettle to temperatures of 100°C to 125°C (212°F to 257°F) for a few hours. Heating converts the gypsum to the hemihydrate or anhydrous calcium sulfate depending on the temperature of the reaction. The solubility of the final product can also be controlled by the temperature used in the heating container and the time during which the material is heated.

Large amounts of calcium sulfate are also produced as the by-product of other reactions or by synthetic processes. The production of phosphoric acid ($H_3PO_4$) from sulfuric acid ($H_2SO_4$) and phosphate rock, for example, results in the formation of calcium sulfate, which can be recovered and purified. Calcium sulfate can also be produced in the reaction between other calcium compounds, such as calcium hydroxide ($Ca(OH)_2$) and sulfuric acid.

## COMMON USES AND POTENTIAL HAZARDS

The most widely used form of calcium sulfate is the dihydrate, gypsum, which is an important raw material in the construction industry. It is used in the manufacture of Portland cement, in specialized plasters (known as gypsum plasters) for walls, in the production of wallboard, and in cement blocks and mortars. Gypsum is also used extensively in agriculture as a *conditioning agent* that adds both calcium ions ($Ca2+$) and sulfate ions ($SO_42-$) to the soil. The compound is also used as a raw material in the synthesis of other calcium compounds and in the production of plaster of Paris.

## Interesting Facts

- Calcium sulfate has been used in China for more than 2,000 years to thicken soy milk in the production of tofu.

- One reason that calcium sulfate hemihydrate is called plaster of Paris is that large deposits of gypsum (from which plaster of Paris is made) exist near the city of Paris, France. These deposits were long mined to obtain the hemihydrate form of calcium sulfate.

- Ancient Romans used plaster of Paris to cast copies of Greek statues.

The anhydrous form of calcium sulfate also has a number of practical applications, the most important of which are in the manufacture of cement and as a filler in the production of paper. A filler adds body to paper, making it firmer, brighter, and easier to write, draw, and print on. Soluble anhydrite is used as a desiccant, which is a material that removes water from other substances. It is usually sold under the trade name of Drierite®.

The primary use of calcium hemihydrate is, of course, in the production of plaster of Paris. Plaster of Paris has a number of important applications, such as:

- In the construction of arts and crafts projects, such as masks, ceramics, and pottery;

- For the production of plaster casts used to immobilize broken bones;

- As a building material in the manufacture of stucco, drywall, division panels, ceiling tablets, plaster board, and wall plaster.

Some other important applications of calcium sulfate include:

- As a firming agent in foods such as canned vegetables, soft-serve ice cream, regular ice cream, frostings, and gelatins;

- As an additive to animal feeds to provide the calcium and sulfate that animals need in their diets;

## Words to Know

**DESICCANT** A material that removes water from other substances.

**SYNTHESIS** A chemical reaction in which some desired chemical product is made from simple beginning chemicals, or reactants.

- In the production of polishing powders;
- As a paint pigment (white); and
- In a variety of metallurgical processes, such as the conversion of zinc minerals to zinc metal.

Although nontoxic, calcium sulfate can irritate the respiratory tract if inhaled. It may cause symptoms such as coughing, shortness of breath, and nosebleeds. The compound can also irritate the skin and eyes, causing redness and pain. Ingestion of the compound can cause stomach pains, nausea, and vomiting.

### FOR FURTHER INFORMATION

"A Brief History of Plaster and Gypsum." Association of Lifecasters International.
http://www.artmolds.com/ali/history_plaster.html (accessed on December 10, 2005).

"Calcium Sulfate." National Organic Program. Agricultural Marketing Service.
http://www.ams.usda.gov/nop/NationalList/TAPReviews/CaSO4.pdf (accessed on December 10, 2005).

"Calcium Sulfate, Anhydrous, Powder." J. T. Baker.
http://www.jtbaker.com/msds/englishhtml/c0497.htm (accessed on December 10, 2005).

Dontsova, Katerina, et al. "Gypsum for Agricultural Use in Ohio—Sources and Quality of Available Products." Ohio State University Extension Fact Sheet.
http://ohioline.osu.edu/anr-fact/0020.html (accessed on December 10, 2005).

"Gypsum Statistics and Information." U.S. Geological Survey.
http://minerals.usgs.gov/minerals/pubs/commodity/gypsum/ (accessed on December 10, 2005).

OTHER NAMES:
Gum camphor; also
see Overview.

FORMULA:
$C_{10}H_{16}O$

ELEMENTS:
Carbon, hydrogen,
oxygen

COMPOUND TYPE:
Cyclic ketone
(organic)

STATE:
Solid

MOLECULAR WEIGHT:
152.23 g/mol

MELTING POINT:
178.3°C to 178.8°C
(352.9°F to 353.4°F);
varies depending on
isomer

BOILING POINT:
207.4°C (405.3°F;
depends on isomer);
some forms sublime
before boiling

SOLUBILITY:
Insoluble in water;
soluble in alcohol,
ether, acetone,
benzene, and other
organic solvents

KEY FACTS

# Camphor

## OVERVIEW

Camphor (KAM-for) is also known as gum camphor; 2-camphanone; 1,7,7-trimethylbicyclo[2.2.1]heptan-2-one; and 1,7,7-trimethylbicyclo[2.2.1]-2-heptanone, among others. It is a volatile white waxy substance with a strong, characteristic odor and a bitter, cooling taste. Its odor has been described as fragrant, aromatic, pungent, or penetrating, similar to that of mothballs. The compound is obtained from the camphor tree, *Cinnamomum camphora*, which is native to many parts of the world, including the Indonesian islands of Java and Sumatra, as well as China, Taiwan, Japan, and Brazil.

The first mention of camphor by a Westerner occurs in the writings of the Venetian explorer Marco Polo (1254–1324) in the late thirteenth century. The Chinese had apparently been using camphor for many centuries in the embalming of their dead and the manufacture of soap, among other applications. The Japanese also had a long history of using the compound in the preparation of varnish and ink, to dilute paint, to burn for light, and to protect clothing from moths.

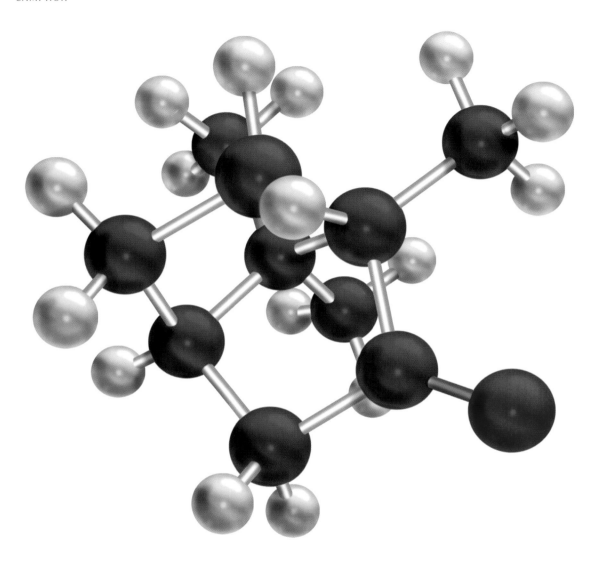

*Camphor.* Red atoms are oxygen; white atoms are hydrogen; black atoms are carbon. PUBLISHERS RESOURCE GROUP

Camphor was also used throughout Asia as a medicine to treat a wide variety of ailments, from upset stomach to rheumatism.

## HOW IT IS MADE

Camphor can be obtained from every part of the *Cinnamomum camphora* tree, including the trunk, branches, roots, and leaves. The compound is extracted from tree parts by

## Interesting Facts

Despite its name, the camphor tree, *Cinnamomum camphora*, does not produce cinnamon. That compound comes from a related member of the family, *Cinnamomum zeylanicum*.

steam distillation and crystallization of the camphor. The camphor thus obtained is one of two possible isomers, the dextrorotary (or "+") form of the compound. (The other isomer is the levorotatory or "-" form.) Since the natural sources of camphor are inadequate to meet commercial demand, camphor is also made synthetically. The process begins by converting the straight-chain hydrocarbons in turpentine oil ($C_{10}H_{16}$) to a cyclic isomer, a-pinene (c-$C_{10}H_{16}$), which is then oxidized to make camphor. Synthetic camphor differs from natural camphor in that it consists of both isomers of the compound, the dextrorotary (+) and levorotatory (-) forms. This difference has no effect on the chemical properties of camphor, although it has some modest effect on its biological properties.

## COMMON USES AND POTENTIAL HAZARDS

Camphor has a long history of medicinal use. People have used it as a liniment to treat muscle aches and arthritis; as a topical anesthetic; as a treatment for nervousness and hysteria; to treat diarrhea, bronchitis, and infectious fevers; and even as an injection to cure heart failure. Very little medical evidence exists for most of these treatments. As a result, its primary medicinal use today is in lotions and ointments for the relief of mild pain and discomfort due to arthritis, rheumatism, and sore muscles. Some common products that contain camphor are Absorbine Arthritic Pain Lotion®, Ben-Gay®, Campho-phenique®, Panalgesic®, Sloan's Liniment®, and Vicks VapoRub®. In these preparations, the compound acts as both a mild analgesic (pain-reliever) and antiseptic (an agent to prevent the growth of disease-causing microorganisms). Its pronounced odor may also help open nasal passages. Camphor is also an important ingredient in

## Words to Know

**ANALGESIC** A substance the relieves pain.

**DISTILLATION** A process of separating two or more substances by boiling the mixture of which they are composed and condensing the vapors produced at different temperatures.

**ISOMERS** Two or more forms of a chemical compound with the same molecular formula, but different structural formulas and different chemical and physical properties.

some antipruritic agents, substances used to relieve the discomfort of itching.

Although camphor is probably best known to most people because of its medicinal uses, the compound also has a number of important industrial applications. For example, it is added to cellulose nitrate as a plasticizer, a substance added to plastic to make it softer and more flexible. Other uses for camphor include:

- As a moth and mildew repellent in mothballs and moth flakes;
- In the embalming of dead bodies;
- In the manufacture of fireworks and explosives;
- As a preservative in pharmaceuticals and cosmetics;
- In the production of lacquers and varnishes; and
- As a chemical intermediary in the production of a number of organic compounds.

One of camphor's most serious disadvantages as a medicinal product is that it is poisonous. Drinking straight camphorated oil can kill a person. In smaller doses, it can cause mental confusion, irritability, jerky movements of the arms and legs, neuromuscular hyperactivity, and seizures. Symptoms can appear between five and ninety minutes after swallowing the camphor. In 1980, the United States Food and Drug Administration limited the amount of camphor allowed in consumer products to 11 percent. It also banned products that contain concentrated camphor, such as camphorated oil and camphorated liniment.

FOR FURTHER INFORMATION

"Camphor."
http://www.innvista.com/health/herbs/camphor.htm (accessed on September 29, 2005).

"Camphor." Botanical.com.
http://www.botanical.com/botanical/mgmh/c/campho13.html (accessed on September 29, 2005).

"Camphor; Gum Camphor; Laurel Camphor. Camphora Officinarum." Drugstore Museum.
http://www.drugstoremuseum.com/sections/level_info2.php?level_id=71&level=2 (accessed on September 29, 2005).

*See Also* Cellulose Nitrate

$$O\!=\!\!=\!\!C\!=\!\!=\!O$$

OTHER NAMES:
Carbonic anhydride;
carbonic acid gas

FORMULA:
$CO_2$

ELEMENTS:
Carbon, oxygen

COMPOUND TYPE:
Nonmetallic oxide

STATE:
Gas

MOLECULAR WEIGHT:
44.01 g/mol

MELTING POINT:
Not applicable;
liquefies under
pressure at $-56.56°C$
$(-69.81°F)$

BOILING POINT:
Sublimes at $-78.4°C$
$(-109°F)$

SOLUBILITY:
Soluble in water;
slightly soluble in
alcohol and some
other organic
solvents

KEY FACTS

# Carbon Dioxide

## OVERVIEW

Carbon dioxide (KAR-bun dye-OK-side) is a colorless, odorless, tasteless, non-combustible gas that can also exist under pressure as a clear, colorless, odorless, tasteless liquid and as a white, snow-like solid commonly known as dry ice. When dry ice is warmed it sublimes (passes directly from the solid to the gaseous state without first melting) at $-78.4°C$ (-109°F).

The true nature of carbon dioxide was discovered over an extended period of time beginning with the research of the Flemish physician and chemist Jan Baptista van Helmont (1580-1635?). In about 1603, van Helmont isolated a gas produced during the combustion of wood and proved that it was distinct from air. At the time, air was generally regarded as an element that could not be divided into separate components. Van Helmont called the gas *gas sylvestre* ("wood gas"), a substance we now know to be carbon dioxide. Credit for understanding the true nature of carbon dioxide also goes to the Scottish chemist Joseph Black (1728-1799) who produced

*Carbon dioxide.* Red atoms are oxygen and black atom is carbon. Gray sticks show double bonds. PUBLISHERS RESOURCE GROUP

carbon dioxide by heating calcium carbonate ($CaCO_3$). Black called the gas fixed air and conducted the first extensive studies of its properties.

The first practical use for carbon dioxide was discovered in the mid-eighteenth century by the English chemist Joseph Priestley (1733-1804). Priestley found that passing carbon dioxide into water produced a sparkling, refreshing drink that he predicted would one day become a great commercial success. He was, of course, correct, since water containing carbon dioxide is the basic component of which all soda drinks are made.

## HOW IT IS MADE

Carbon dioxide is produced in nature by a number of reactions. Among the most common is the combustion (burning) of the fossil fuels (coal, oil, and natural gas). The gas is also produced during the decay of organic material, the fermentation of carbohydrates by yeast, and the respiration of animals. In the laboratory, the simplest and most direct method of preparation is to treat a carbonate, such as calcium carbonate, with an acid, such as hydrochloric acid (HCl).

Carbon dioxide is obtained commercially as the by-product of a number of industrial reactions. For example, when calcium carbonate is heated to produce lime (CaO), carbon dioxide is released and captured as a by-product. The steam reforming (refining) of petroleum results in the production of a mixture of gases known as synthesis gas, consisting of carbon dioxide, carbon monoxide, hydrogen, and nitrogen. Carbon dioxide can be separated from the other components of synthesis gas for commercial uses. Carbon dioxide also produces as a by-product of the manufacture of ammonia ($NH_3$) by the Haber-Bosch process.

## Interesting Facts

- Carbon dioxide is the fourth most abundant gas in the atmosphere (after nitrogen, oxygen, and argon) with a concentration of about 0.036 percent. Researchers have found that the concentration of carbon dioxide in the atmosphere has been increasing at a regular rate for at least the last forty years. They believe that the reason for this increase is the escalating use of fossil fuels by humans to heat homes and offices; drive cars, trucks, trains, and airplanes; and to power industrial operations. They further suspect that an increase in the amount of carbon dioxide in the atmosphere may have significant long-term effects on the planet's climate.

- Scientists have become very interested in a form of carbon dioxide known as supercritical carbon dioxide (SCCO2 or SC-$CO_2$). Under the proper conditions of temperature and pressure, carbon dioxide (as SCCO2) behaves as both a liquid and a gas at the same time. This property has proved to be very valuable in using SCCO2 as a highly efficient solvent that has no environmental disadvantages.

## COMMON USES AND POTENTIAL HAZARDS

Carbon dioxide plays an essential role in most biological processes that take place on Earth's surface. Plants use carbon dioxide as a raw material to make the carbohydrates on which their structures are based. When animals eat plants, those carbohydrates are then used to build and maintain their body structures.

In addition to its role in natural processes, carbon dioxide has many commercial and industrial applications. One of the most important uses is in the carbonation of beverages. Although beers and sparkling wines contain carbon dioxide from natural sources (the fermentation of sugars by yeasts), nearly all carbonated beverages have their carbon dioxide added artificially. The carbon dioxide adds a zesty taste to the beverage and helps to preserve it.

## Words to Know

**SUBLIME** Changing of states from solid to gas without becoming liquid first.

**SYNTHESIS GAS** A mixture of several gases, such as carbon dioxide and hydrogen, used to produce compounds such as methanol and ammonia that can be separated out from the synthesis gas.

Carbon dioxide is also used as a fire extinguishing agent. Its use for this purpose is based on the facts that it does not burn itself and is heavier than air. Thus, when sprayed on a fire, carbon dioxide settles down on top of the flames and prevents oxygen from reaching the burning material. The carbon dioxide can be supplied in a variety of ways in a fire extinguisher. In some devices, carbon dioxide gas is produced as the result of a chemical reaction that occurs within the fire extinguisher. In other devices, liquid carbon dioxide is released from the extinguisher.

Carbon dioxide is also used in gaseous, liquid, or solid form as a refrigerant. As a gas, it is used as the "working fluid" in refrigerators, the fluid that circulates through the refrigerator changing back and forth from gas to liquid, absorbing heat in the process. In the form of dry ice, carbon dioxide is a very efficient and convenient method for cooling objects to very low temperatures (close to the sublimation point of carbon dioxide, about $-78.4°C$ ($-109°F$).

Some other uses of carbon dioxide include the following:

- As an aerosol propellant;
- To provide an oxygen-free atmosphere in which to conduct welding and other operations with flammable materials;
- In the industrial manufacture of carbonates;
- For cloud seeding to promote modifications in the weather (increases or decreases in rain fall);
- In the fumigation of rice to preserve the product for extended periods of time;
- As an artificial smoke in theater productions;

- As a moderator to slow down the speed of neutrons traveling in a nuclear power plant;
- In the frozen food industry;
- To enrich the air in a greenhouse, providing additional carbon dioxide to promote plant growth; and
- For the hardening of foundry molds and cores.

In general, carbon dioxide poses little or not threat to humans in concentrations to which one is normally exposed. Dry ice may pose a hazard if not handled carefully as its very low temperature can cause damage to the skin.

FOR FURTHER INFORMATION

"Carbon Dioxide (CO2) Applications and Uses." Universal Industrial Gases, Inc.
http://www.uigi.com/carbondioxide.html (accessed on September 29, 2005).

"Carbon Dioxide, Oxygen, and the Air." Skool.ie.
http://www.skoool.ie/skoool/examcentre_jc.asp?id=1980 (accessed on September 29, 2005).

"Chemical of the Week: Carbon Dioxide."
http://scifun.chem.wisc.edu/chemweek/CO2/CO2.html (accessed on September 29, 2005).

*See Also* Calcium Carbonate; Calcium Oxide

$$C\!\!=\!\!\!=\!\!O$$

# Carbon Monoxide

OTHER NAMES:
None

FORMULA:
CO

ELEMENTS:
Carbon, oxygen

COMPOUND TYPE:
Nonmetallic oxide

STATE:
Gas

MOLECULAR WEIGHT:
28.01 g/mol

MELTING POINT:
−205.02°C
(−337.04°F)

BOILING POINT:
−191.5°C (−312.7°F)

SOLUBILITY:
Slightly soluble in
water; soluble in
alcohol and
chloroform

KEY FACTS

## OVERVIEW

Carbon monoxide is a colorless, odorless, tasteless, toxic gas. It is one of the most common poisons in the environment and is responsible for thousands of deaths and hospital emergency room visits each year in the United States. Carbon monoxide is produced from fuel-burning appliances, such as space heaters, furnaces, stoves, and vehicles. It is also a component of cigarette smoke. Carbon monoxide is flammable and capable of forming an explosive mixture with air.

Under ideal circumstances, a carbon-containing fuel such as charcoal, natural gas, or wood burns in air to form carbon dioxide and water. Lacking an adequate supply of oxygen, at low temperatures, or under certain other conditions, incomplete combustion occurs. Incomplete combustion is a process in which a fuel is not completed oxidized. In such instances, carbon monoxide is produced along with carbon dioxide and water. An inadequate supply of oxygen can occur in enclosed, poorly vented spaces, such as the interior of houses, garages, and cars.

*Carbon monoxide.* Red atom is oxygen and black atom is carbon. Stick is a double bond.
PUBLISHERS RESOURCE GROUP

The discovery of carbon monoxide is usually credited to the English chemist Joseph Priestley (1733-1804). Between 1772 and 1799, Priestley investigated the properties of carbon monoxide and recognized the difference between carbon monoxide and carbon dioxide. The gas was first prepared synthetically by the French chemist Joseph Marie François de Lassone (1717-1788) in 1776, although he mistakenly identified it as hydrogen. The correct chemical formula for carbon monoxide was first identified by the English chemist William Cruikshank (1745-1800) in 1800.

## HOW IT IS MADE

A number of methods are available for the commercial production of carbon monoxide. In one procedure, air is passed over hot coke, graphite, or anthracite coal to make producer gas, a mixture of carbon dioxide, carbon monoxide, hydrogen, and water vapor. In a similar procedure, steam is passed over hot coke or graphite to make water gas, a mixture of carbon monoxide, carbon dioxide, hydrogen, and nitrogen. In a third procedure, steam is mixed with natural gas to form synthesis gas, consisting of carbon dioxide, carbon monoxide, and hydrogen. In all three procedures, the carbon monoxide component of the gas mixture produced in the reaction can be separated out from the other gases.

Yet a fourth method for making carbon monoxide involves the partial oxidation of hydrocarbon gases obtained from natural gas or petroleum. These gases consist of carbon-hydrogen compounds which, when oxidized, are converted to carbon monoxide, carbon dioxide, and water. By controlling

## Interesting Facts

- Some authorities believe that the American writer Edgar Allan Poe (1809-1849) owed his wild imagination and early death to chronic carbon monoxide poisoning, caused by the gas lighting used in his home.

- Public health authorities estimate that the number of suicides resulting from the inhalation of carbon monoxide fumes from automobiles has decreased by about 80 percent since the introduction of catalytic converters in cars. Catalytic converters reduce the amount of carbon monoxide released in a car's exhaust.

- Carbon monoxide bonds to hemoglobin in the blood stream 200 times as efficiently as does oxygen. This ability to exclude oxygen from the blood is responsible for the toxic effects caused by carbon monoxide in the body.

the amount of reactants used and the conditions of the reaction (temperature and pressure), the portion of carbon monoxide produced can be increased.

### COMMON USES AND POTENTIAL HAZARDS

Carbon monoxide has three major industrial uses. The first is in the synthesis of a large variety of organic compounds. For example, it takes part in a group of reactions known as the Fischer-Tropsch reactions in which carbon monoxide is first reduced with hydrogen gas and then converted to any number of organic compounds that contain oxygen. The gas is also used to make acetic acid, a major industrial chemical used in the synthesis of polymers and other organic products.

A second application of carbon monoxide, either by itself or in conjunction with other gases, is as an industrial fuel. The gas burns very efficiently with the release of large amounts of heat and relatively few undesirable by-products (the most important being carbon dioxide).

## Words to Know

**POLYMER** A compound consisting of very large molecules made of one or two small repeated units called monomers.

**REDUCTION** Chemical reaction in which oxygen is removed from a substance or electrons are added to a substance.

**SYNTHESIS** A chemical reaction in which some desired chemical product is made from simple beginning chemicals, or reactants.

**SYNTHESIS GAS** A mixture of several gases, such as carbon dioxide and hydrogen, used to produce compounds such as methanol and ammonia that can be separated out from the synthesis gas.

A third industrial use for carbon monoxide is in the refining of metals. Most metal ores exist in the form of oxides or sulfides when extracted from the earth. For example, the two most important ores of iron are magnetite ($Fe_3O_4$) and hematite ($Fe_2O_3$). After an ore has been mined, it is treated to remove the oxygen or sulfur in the ore to obtain a pure metal. Carbon monoxide is often used for this purpose with oxide ores because it combines with oxygen from the ore to form carbon dioxide, leaving the metal behind: Metal oxide + CO $\rightarrow$ Metal + $CO_2$.

Carbon monoxide is a highly toxic gas that has noticeable health effects even in relatively small concentrations. When the concentration of carbon monoxide reaches levels of about 100 ppm (parts per million), an individual is likely to experience mild headaches, fatigue, shortness of breath, and errors in judgment. As the concentration of carbon monoxide increases, these symptoms become more pronounced. Exposure to a concentration of more than 400 ppm for more than three hours is likely to put a person at serious health risk. He or she may begin to lose consciousness and experience serious disorientation. At concentrations of more than 1,500 ppm, death is likely in less than an hour. These symptoms vary somewhat depending on a person's age and overall health.

Most governmental agencies have set a recommended limit of 35 ppm for periods of up to eight hours. For purposes of comparison, the normal concentration of carbon monoxide in the atmosphere in an open area tends to be less than 1 ppm. But in urban areas or other locations with many vehicles, gas heaters, wood burning stoves, or other sources of carbon monoxide, carbon monoxide levels can be much higher. Someone traveling inside a car on a busy freeway, for example, may be exposed to carbon monoxide levels of up to 25 ppm. Concentrations of up to 100 ppm have been measured in the center of busy downtown urban areas.

### FOR FURTHER INFORMATION

"Carbon Monoxide." Chemical Fact Sheet. Plastics and Chemicals Industries Association. http://www.pacia.org.au/_uploaditems/docs/3.carbon_monoxide.pdf (accessed on October 2, 2005).

"Carbon Monoxide Questions and Answers." Consumer Product Safety Commission. CPSC Document #466. http://www.cpsc.gov/cpscpub/pubs/466.html (accessed on October 3, 2005).

Dwyer, Bob, et al. *Carbon Monoxide: A Clear and Present Danger.* Mount Prospect, Ill.: ESCO Press, 2004.

Patnaik, Pradyot. *Handbook of Inorganic Chemicals.* New York: McGraw-Hill, 2003, 1887-191.

*See Also* Acetic Acid; Carbon Dioxide

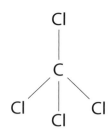

OTHER NAMES:
Tetrachloromethane;
perchloromethane

FORMULA:
$CCl_4$

ELEMENTS:
Carbon, chlorine

COMPOUND TYPE:
Halogenated
hydrocarbon; alkyl
chloride (organic)

STATE:
Liquid

MOLECULAR WEIGHT:
153.82 g/mol

MELTING POINT:
$-22.62°C$ ($-8.72°F$)

BOILING POINT:
76.8°C (170°F)

SOLUBILITY:
Insoluble in water;
miscible with ethyl
alcohol, ether,
benzene, chloroform,
and most other
organic solvents

KEY FACTS

# Carbon Tetrachloride

## OVERVIEW

Carbon tetrachloride (CAR-bun tet-ra-KLOR-ide) is a colorless, nonflammable liquid with a sweetish odor and a density 1.5 times that of water. The compound is classified as a halogenated hydrocarbon because all of the hydrogens in methane ($CH_4$), a hydrocarbon, have been replaced by halogen atoms (chlorine, in this case). Carbon tetrachloride was first prepared in 1839 by German-born French chemist Henri Victor Regnault (1810–1878). Regnault made carbon tetrachloride by reacting chloroform (trichloromethane; $CHCl_3$) with chlorine: $CHCl_3 + Cl_2 \rightarrow CCl_4 + HCl$.

Until the mid-twentieth century, carbon tetrachloride had a number of important applications, including use as a dry cleaning fluid, a refrigerant, and an industrial and chemical solvent. It was also used in fire extinguishers. By the 1950s, however, evidence of the serious health hazards posed by carbon tetrachloride began to accumulate, and its use was dramatically cut. In 1970, the U.S. Food and Drug Administration banned its use in consumer products in the United States.

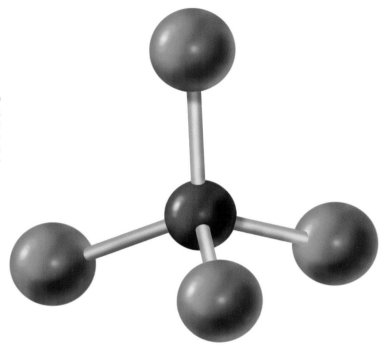

*Carbon Tetrachloride.* Black atom is carbon; green atoms are chlorine. All sticks are single bonds. PUBLISHERS RESOURCE GROUP

Production of carbon tetrachloride was not seriously affected in the long run by this ban, however, as a new use was found for the chemical: the manufacture of chlorofluorocarbons (CFCs). Between the 1930s and the 1970s, the chlorofluorocarbons were among the most successful and widely used of all synthetic organic compounds. They were used in a number of applications, including as refrigerants, blowing agents, solvents, and cleaning agents. They were also used in the production of a variety of organic compounds. In the 1950s and the 1960s, demand for carbon tetrachloride was increasing at a rate of about 10 percent a year in response to the demand for CFCs.

Eventually, that use of carbon tetrachloride was also lessened. Studies conducted by American chemists Mario Molina (1943-) and F. Sherwood Rowland (1927-) showed that CFCs were responsible for the destruction of the Earth's ozone layer, posing potentially serious health hazards to plants and animals living on the planet. In response to this discovery, the world's nations agreed to cut back on the

## Interesting Facts

- Before the ban imposed by the Montreal Protocol, more than 90 percent of the chloroform produced was used in the manufacture of chlorofluorocarbons.

- Although carbon tetrachloride was once used as a fire extinguisher, this use had its potential risks. When used on electrical fires, carbon tetrachloride can react with oxygen in the air to produce phosgene ($CCl_2O$), a poisonous gas used by Germany armies during World War I (1914-1918).

- The carcinogenic effects of carbon tetrachloride are now thought to result from the fact that the compound is converted by enzymes in the body to phosgene, which then attack cells and genes, initiating the processes by which cancer develops.

- Researchers have discovered that the bacterium *Shewanella oneidensis* is capable of degrading carbon tetrachloride, suggesting a possible simple and safe way to clean up areas contaminated with the compound.

production of CFCs and the compounds from which they are made. According to the Montreal Protocol on Substances That Deplete the Ozone Layer, adopted in 1987, the production of carbon tetrachloride for use as a raw material in the manufacture of CFCs was to be first reduced, and then banned entirely by the year 2000. As a result, the production of carbon tetrachloride and its use in modern society has diminished considerably.

### HOW IT IS MADE

Carbon tetrachloride is now made by a method invented more than a century ago. Carbon disulfide ($CS_2$) is treated with chlorine gas, producing sulfur monochloride ($S_2Cl_2$) and carbon tetrachloride: $CS_2 + 3Cl_2 \rightarrow CCl_4 + S_2Cl_2$.

This process is very efficient because the sulfur monochloride can then be treated with additional carbon disulfide to produce more carbon tetrachloride: $CS_2 + 2S_2Cl_2 \rightarrow CCl_4 + 6S$.

A relatively small amount of carbon tetrachloride is also made in the reaction between methane gas ($CH_4$) and chlorine gas at temperatures of 250°C to 400°C (500°F to 750°F): $CH_4 + 4Cl_2 \rightarrow CCl_4 + 4HCl$.

## COMMON USES AND POTENTIAL HAZARDS

The effect of bans on the production of carbon tetrachloride in recent decades has been dramatic. Production of the compound in the United States dropped from more than 50,000 metric tons (55,000 short tons) in 1989 to less than 2 metric (2.2 short tons) in 1998. The compound cannot be used in any consumer or household products and has only a limited number of industrial applications. In general, its use is restricted to those situations in which no satisfactory substitute has been found. Some of these uses include:

- Certain specific and limited types of refrigeration systems;

- Degreasing metals;

- The manufacture of certain electronic products;

- Additives for some kinds of gasoline;

- The recovery of tin from tin plating operations;

- The fumigation of limited types of grains;

- Solvents for a number of industrial operations.

The average person is likely to come into contact with carbon tetrachloride in one of three ways: by inhaling vapors of the compound, by ingesting (swallowing) the compound or any product in which it is an ingredient, and (to a lesser extent), through the skin. The primary health risks from exposure to carbon tetrachloride involve damage to the liver and kidneys and, at high doses, the central nervous system. Some symptoms associated with exposure to carbon tetrachloride include soreness of the liver or kidneys, nausea, headaches, drowsiness, and disorientation. Although strong evidence is lacking, the U.S. Environmental Protection Agency has labeled carbon tetrachloride as a probable carcinogen.

## Words to Know

**CARCINOGEN** A chemical that causes cancer in humans or other animals.

**MISCIBLE** Able to be mixed; especially applies to the mixing of one liquid with another.

**OZONE LAYER** A region of Earth's atmosphere that contains a large quantity of ozone, which absorbs some of the sun's radiation.

FOR FURTHER INFORMATION

"Carbon Tetrachloride." 11th Report on Carcinogens. National Toxicology Program.
http://ntp.niehs.nih.gov/ntp/roc/eleventh/profiles/s029carb.pdf (accessed on December 29, 2005).

"Carbon Tetrachloride." International Programme on Chemical Safety.
http://www.inchem.org/documents/ehc/ehc/ehc208.htm#SubSectionNumber:3.2.1 (accessed on December 29, 2005).

"Carbon Tetrachloride." Matheson Tri-Gas.
http://www.matheson-trigas.com/msds/MAT04310.pdf (accessed on December 29, 2005).

"Carbon Tetrachloride." National Safety Council.
http://www.nsc.org/library/chemical/carbonte.htm (accessed on December 29, 2005).

"Chemical Fact Sheet: Carbon Tetrachloride." Spectrum Laboratories.
http://www.speclab.com/compound/c56235.htm (accessed on December 29, 2005).

*See Also* Chloroform

KEY FACTS

OTHER NAMES:
None

FORMULA:
$(C_6H_{10}O_5)_n$

ELEMENTS:
Carbon, hydrogen, oxygen

COMPOUND TYPE:
Polysaccharide (carbohydrate polymer; organic)

STATE:
Solid

MOLECULAR WEIGHT:
Very large, in excess of 100,000 g/mol

MELTING POINT:
Decomposes at temperatures above 260°C (500°F)

BOILING POINT:
Not applicable

SOLUBILITY:
Insoluble in water and all common organic solvents

# Cellulose

## OVERVIEW

Cellulose (SELL-you-lohs) is a colorless to white, tasteless, odorless, polysaccharide fiber found in the cell walls of all land plants and some bacteria, seaweeds, algae, and fungi. Polysaccharides (the term means "many sugars") are polymers consisting of monosaccharide (simple sugar) monomers joined together in very large molecules. The monomer of which cellulose is made is glucose, also known as blood sugar, dextrose, or grape sugar. The subscript "n" at the end of the chemical formula indicates that a large number of these monomers combine to make the polymer. Cellulose provides the structural support for plants and other organisms in which it occurs. It is generally regarded as the most common organic compound found in nature.

Cellulose never occurs in nature in a pure form. Cotton is the purest natural form, consisting of about 90 percent cellulose. Flax (linen fiber) consists of about 70 to 75 percent cellulose, wood of about 40 to 50 percent cellulose, and seaweeds and algae of about 25 to 30 percent cellulose.

**n**

*Cellulose.* Red atoms are oxygen; white atoms are hydrogen; and black atoms are carbon. PUBLISHERS RESOURCE GROUP

Cellulose was first discovered in 1819 by the French naturalist Henri Braconnot (1781-1855). The compound was first isolated and analyzed fifteen years later by the French botanist Anselme Payen (1795-1871), who gave it its modern name of cellulose based on its origin ("cell") plus the suffix -ose. The earliest chemical studies of cellulose were conducted by a team of English chemists, Charles Frederick Cross (1855-1935), Edward John Bevan (1856-1921), and Clayton Beadle (1868-1917), who identified the compound we now know as cellulose and reported on its structure and properties in the 1890s and early 1900s.

Cellulose, in its natural forms such as wood, cotton, and linen, has countless numbers of uses as food, clothing, construction materials, and other applications. It also serves as

## Interesting Facts

- Scientists estimate that plants worldwide synthesize up to one trillion metric tons of cellulose annually.

the raw material in making derivatives such as cellulose acetate, cellulose nitrate, and cellulose xanthate with many other uses and applications.

### HOW IT IS MADE

Cellulose is synthesized in plants and some microorganisms through the process known as photosynthesis. In that process, carbon dioxide ($CO_2$) and water ($H_2O$) are combined in a complex series of reactions to produce glucose ($C_6H_{10}O_5$) and oxygen ($O_2$). Glucose molecules are then linked to each other to from successively larger and more complex molecules, eventually resulting in the formation of cellulose.

Commercially, most cellulose is extracted from wood by one of two methods, the kraft (sulfate) process or the steam explosion process. The product of these reactions is wood pulp, which consists primarily of cellulose. In the kraft process, wood chips are treated with a solution of sodium hydroxide (NaOH) and sodium sulfide ($Na_2S$) at temperatures of about 175°C (350°F) for two to six hours. This process usually results in a yield of about 40 to 45 percent wood pulp. The pulp is then treated with a bleaching agent, such as calcium or sodium hypochlorite ($Ca(OCl)_2$ or NaClO) or chlorine dioxide ($ClO_2$) to remove the color of lignin and other impurities.

In the steam explosion process, wood chips are saturated with moisture and then exposed to temperatures of 200°C to 250°C (400°F to 500°F) at pressures of one to five atmospheres. In this process, cellulose fibers are physically separated from lignin fibers, which are the other major constituent of wood. In either process, yields of up to 99 percent pure cellulose can be obtained.

## Words to Know

**POLYMER** A compound consisting of very large molecules made of one or two small repeated units called monomers.

**SYNTHESIS** A chemical reaction in which some desired chemical product is made from simple beginning chemicals, or reactants.

### COMMON USES AND POTENTIAL HAZARDS

The number of products made from pure cellulose is almost endless. The largest volume of such products include paper and paper products, including (with 2001 production numbers): newsprint (5.8 million metric tons; 6.4 million short tons), printing and writing paper (22.1 million metric tons; 24.4 million short tons), packaging and related uses (3.9 million metric tons; 4.3 million short tons), tissue paper (6.4 million metric tons; 7.0 million short tons), containerboard (26.6 million metric tons; 29.3 million short tons), and boxboard (7.7 million metric tons; 8.5 million short tons). Other uses of cellulose include:

- Manufacture of cotton products, such as items of clothing, sheeting, and industrial fabrics;

- Production of other organic products, especially ethanol (ethyl alcohol; grain alcohol) and methanol (methyl alcohol; wood alcohol);

- As insulation and soundproofing;

- As a food additive, where it is used to thicken and add bulk to food products;

- In equipment used in analytical chemistry, such as chromatographic devices used to separate the components of a mixture.

A major industrial use of cellulose is in the preparation of various cellulose derivatives, primarily cellulose acetate, cellulose nitrate, and cellulose xanthate, each of which has a number of applications.

FOR FURTHER INFORMATION

"Cellulose." Fibersource.
http://www.fibersource.com/f-tutor/cellulose.htm (accessed on September 30, 2005).

"Cellulose." London South Bank University.
http://www.lsbu.ac.uk/water/hycel.html (accessed on September 30, 2005).

"Cellulose Processing." Organic Materials Review Institute.
http://www.omri.org/cellulose_final.pdf (accessed on September 30, 2005).

Cross, Charles, Clayton Beadle, Edward Bevan. *Cellulose. An Out line of the Chemistry of the Structural Elements of Plants, with Reference to Their Natural History and Industrial Uses.* Elibron. Replica of 1895 edition by Longmans, Green, and Co., London.
http://www.elibron.com/english/other/item_detail.phtml?msg_id =10006054 (accessed on September 30, 2005).

*See Also* Cellulose Acetate; Cellulose Nitrate; Cellulose Xanthate

OTHER NAMES:
Nitrocellulose;
nitrocotton;
guncotton; pyroxylin

FORMULA:
$C_{12}H_{16}N_4O_{18}$

ELEMENTS:
Carbon, hydrogen,
nitrogen, oxygen

COMPOUND TYPE:
Carbohydrate poly-
mer (organic)

STATE:
Solid

MOLECULAR WEIGHT:
Varies, but very large

MELTING POINT:
Not applicable;
ignites at about
170°C (340°F)

BOILING POINT:
Not applicable

SOLUBILITY:
Insoluble in water,
alcohol, ether, and
most organic
solvents; also see
Overview

KEY FACTS

# Cellulose Nitrate

## OVERVIEW

Cellulose nitrate (SELL-you-lohs NYE-trate) is a derivative of cellulose made by adding nitric acid ($HNO_3$) to cellulose. Its physical properties tend to differ somewhat depending on the relative amount of nitrogen present in the compound. For example, the so-called "high nitrogen" form is soluble in both acetone but insoluble in an alcohol/ether mixture. The "low-nitrogen" form is soluble in both solvents. Cellulose nitrate is available in a variety of forms, ranging from color-less to white flakes or powder to a liquid or semi-solid gel-like material.

Cellulose nitrate was first discovered in 1845 by the Swiss-German chemist Christian Friedrich Schönbein (1799-1868). The story is told that Schönbein used his wife's cotton apron to clean up some nitric acid that he had spilled on his laboratory floor. He was amazed to discover that the cotton and nitric acid reacted to form a new compound that exploded when heated, releasing a puff of black smoke. He immediately recognized the potential application for the new

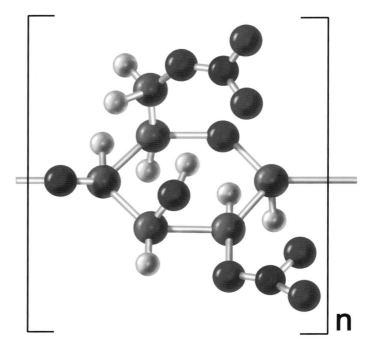

*Cellulose nitrate.* Red atoms
are oxygen; white atoms
are hydrogen; black atoms are
carbon; and blue atoms
are nitrogen. PUBLISHERS
RESOURCE GROUP

material as an explosive and suggested the name guncotton
for it. He developed a more efficient method for making the
product and, within a short period of time, guncotton had
become very popular as an explosive for both construction
and military purposes.

Researchers soon found that modifying the way in which
cellulose nitrate is prepared could significantly change its
chemical and physical properties, and, therefore, its uses. For
example, the British inventor Alexander Parkes (1813-1890)
experimented with using a variety of solutions to dissolve
cellulose nitrate, after which the material could be precipitated
in one or another form. At first he called the reformulated
cellulose nitrate "synthetic ivory," because of its similarity to
natural ivory, but later referred to the product as parkesine,
named after himself. He was unable to obtain financing
needed for the commercial manufacture of his invention,
however, and it fell to an American inventor, John Wesley
Hyatt (1837-1920) to reinvent a similar product less than a
decade later. Hyatt and his brother Isaiah developed a mixture of cellulose nitrate and camphor that was an even more

## Interesting Facts

- Cellulose nitrate was first used for the manufacture of photographic film in 1889 by the Eastman Kodak company. Films made in that era are highly unstable, with a tendency to catch fire spontaneously. Efforts are now under way to protect and preserve some classic motion pictures originally captured on cellulose nitrate film that are unlikely to survive for many more years without such treatment.

- Although the Hyatt billiard balls made out of celluloid were very popular at first, they had one serious disadvantage: They had a tendency to explode upon contact with each other.

- Items of clothing made from cellulose nitrate in the late nineteenth century were sometimes known as "mother-in-law" clothing. They were so flammable that some people thought that the item of clothing along with a cigarette lighter was the perfect gift for an unappreciated mother-in-law.

satisfactory substitute for ivory than was Parke's parkesine. The Hyatts obtained a patent for their new product, to which they gave the name celluloid. Originally developed to meet a growing demand for an ivory-like material that could be use to make billiard balls, celluloid eventually had a number of other applications, including false teeth and photographic film.

## HOW IT IS MADE

Cellulose nitrate is produced in essentially the same way as it was (albeit accidentally) by Christian Schönbein in 1845. A mixture of nitric acid and sulfuric acid are added to cellulose in one of various forms (as wood pulp, powder, flakes, or a colloidal mixture with water, for example). The properties of the product formed depend on the relative quantities of each reagent used and the conditions under which the reaction is carried out. One of the most important variables is the amount of nitrogen present in the cellulose nitrate formed. The more nitrogen present, the less stable the compound is and the more appropriate it is for use as an explosive. The less nitrogen present, the more stable the compound, and the more suitable it is for household and commercial applications.

## COMMON USES AND POTENTIAL HAZARDS

Cellulose nitrate continues to be used as an explosive, most commonly in a product known as smokeless gunpowder. The name comes from the fact that, when ignited, the compound produces less smoke than is the case with most other explosives. Smokeless gunpowder is used primarily for smaller weapons, such as artillery rockets and projectiles. A solution of cellulose nitrate dissolved in ether, known as collodion, has been used for a number of applications since its discovery independently in 1846 by the French chemist Louis-Philippe Ménard (dates not available) and the American physician Dr. J. P. Maynard (dates not available). These uses include the coating of wounds; preparation of bandages, surgical dressings, and other medical paraphernalia; the production of photographic film; and the manufacture of laboratory equipment and devices. Cellulose nitrate is also used as a coating material in fast-drying automobile lacquers, on the cloth used to cover hardbound books, and as a leather covering.

Cellulose nitrate poses two major health risks. First, old film made of cellulose nitrate has a tendency to deteriorate and decompose. That process results in the release of oxides of nitrogen, which may be toxic to a greater or lesser degree. This problem is of special concern to people who have occasion to work with old films, but not usually to the general public. Second, cellulose nitrate is a very flammable material that ignites when exposed to even minimal flames or sparks. Most products that contain cellulose nitrate today have been treated to minimize that risk. However, products that were made many years ago do not have the same protection and may pose safety risks to people who come into contact with them.

### FOR FURTHER INFORMATION

"Caring for Cellulose Nitrate Film." Conserve O Gram. http://www.cr.nps.gov/museum/publications/conserveogram/ 14-08.pdf (accessed on September 30, 2005).

"Cellulose Nitrate." Conservation and Art Material Encyclopedia Online. http://www.mfa.org/_cameo/frontend/material_description.asp?name=cellulose+nitrate&language=1 (accessed on September 30, 2005).

"DiscoverLight[TM] Membrane." Pierce Biotechnology. http://www.piercenet.com/files/5186.pdf (accessed on September 30, 2005).

Fox, Berry. "Not Fade Away." *New Scientist* (March 1, 2003); 40.

"Nitrocellulose-Applications, Characterisation, Production and Storage." Bayer Material Science. http://www.azom.com/details.asp?ArticleID=2785 (accessed on September 30, 2005).

*See Also* Cellulose; Cellulose Acetate; Cellulose Xanthate

OTHER NAMES:
Viscose rayon;
xanthate rayon

FORMULA:
$[C_6H_7O_2(OH)_2 OCS_2Na]_n$

ELEMENTS:
Carbon, hydrogen,
oxygen, sulfur,
sodium

COMPOUND TYPE:
Polymer

STATE:
Solid

MOLECULAR WEIGHT:
Very large (50,000 to
100,000 g/mol)

MELTING POINT:
Not applicable

BOILING POINT:
Not applicable

SOLUBILITY:
Soluble in aqueous
caustic solutions

KEY FACTS

# Cellulose Xanthate

## OVERVIEW

Cellulose xanthate (SELL-you-lohs ZAN-thate) is a compound produced from cellulose in the viscose process for making rayon. The subscript "n" in the chemical formula indicates that many molecules chain together to make up the polymer. In this case, between 200 and 400 $C_6H_7O_2$ $(OH)_2OCS_2Na$ molecules combine to make a molecule of cellulose xanthate.

Although rayon is made from a naturally-occurring material, cellulose, it is regarded as a synthetic product. It was the first synthetic fiber made by humans. The method for making rayon was discovered in about 1891 by three English chemists, Charles Frederick Cross (1855-1935), Edward John Bevan (1856-1921), and Clayton Beadle (1868-1917). The discovery occurred while the three chemists were looking for a way of making artificial silk. Although silk is an excellent fiber for making clothes and other materials, it had to be exported from Japan and was, therefore, very expensive.

## Interesting Facts

Rayon was first sold in the United States as "artificial silk." But manufacturers thought the word "artificial" would not appeal to consumers. So they held a contest with a $1,000 prize to choose a better name for the fabric. More than 10,000 names were suggested, but the committee appointed to choose a winner rejected all of the names. Finally, a member of the committee suggested the word *rayon*, French for "a ray of light."

The first plant for the manufacture of rayon in the United States was built in 1910 by the newly-formed Viscose Corporation of America. Sales of the new product were slow at first, but by 1925, rayon had become more popular than silk. Today, the Cross-Bevan-Beadle method of making rayon is only one of four processes used by the industry to make the fiber.

## HOW IT IS MADE

The process to make rayon begins with wood pulp or wood chips, usually from spruce or pine trees. The wood is treated with carbon disulfide ($CS_2$), which converts cellulose in the wood to cellulose xanthate. The purpose of this step is to change an insoluble material (cellulose) into a soluble material (cellulose xanthate). The cellulose xanthate is then dissolved in sodium hydroxide (NaOH), a strong alkali, forming a thick, viscous solution. The viscosity of the solution is responsible for the name given to this method of making rayon, the viscose process.

The cellulose xanthate solution is then allowed to stand for eight to ten hours in a "ripening room." During this period, the cellulose xanthate slowly gives up its carbon disulfide and reverts to cellulose. The end result of these steps is the recovery of cellulose in a form that is easier to work with and from which long fibers can be made. The fibers are produced by forcing cellulose from the viscous solution through plates called spinnerettes with many small holes in them.

## Words to Know

**ALKALI** A strong base.

**AQUEOUS SOLUTION** A solustion that consists of some material dissolved in water.

**CAUSTIC** Strongly basic or alkaline, capable of irritating or corroding living tissue.

**POLYMER** A compound consisting of very large molecules made of one or two small repeated units called monomers.

**VISCOUS** Syrupy material that flows slowly.

### COMMON USES AND POTENTIAL HAZARDS

Rayon has many properties that make it a desirable fabric. It has a soft, silky feel that is comfortable to the skin. Its fibers are strong, abrasion resistant, easy to dye, and resistant to bleaches and most chemicals. Electric charges do not collect on the fiber, allowing it to remain static-free and to hang smoothly from the body. Rayon does have some disadvantages. It tends to wrinkle easily, shrinks when it gets wet, and is very flammable. Among the many products made from rayon are the following:

- Clothing, such as suits, dresses, sports shirts, ties, lingerie, and work clothes;

- Domestic textiles, such as upholstery, curtains, drapes, bedspreads, sheets, and blankets; and

- Industrial textiles, such as reinforcing threads in rubber products, such as tires, hoses, and conveyor belts; braided cords; and tapes.

Rayon is very flammable, probably its greatest disadvantage in commercial products. During the late 1940s and early 1950s, a number of accidents were reported in which rayon clothing caught fire, resulting in injury or death to wearers. In response to this problem, the U.S. Congress passed the Flammable Fabrics Act of 1953 (FFA), banning the sale of any fabric (such as rayons) likely to catch fire. Since passage of the FFA, manufacturers who use rayon in their products must treat the fiber in some way to prevent it from catching fire.

FOR FURTHER INFORMATION

"Rayon Fiber (Viscose)." Fibersource.
http://www.fibersource.com/f-tutor/rayon.htm (accessed on September 14, 2005).

"Rayon Fibers." Raghavendra R. Hegde, Atul Dahiya, and M. G. Kamath.
http://www.engr.utk.edu/mse/pages/Textiles/Rayon%20fibers.htm (accessed on September 14, 2005).

"Rayon Viscose."
http://www.swicofil.com/viscose.html (accessed on September 14, 2005).

*See Also* Cellulose, Cellulose Nitrate

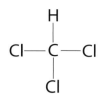

OTHER NAMES:
Trichloromethane,
trichloroform,
methane trichloride,
methenyl trichloride,
methyl trichloride

FORMULA:
CHCl$_3$

ELEMENTS:
Carbon, hydrogen,
chlorine

COMPOUND TYPE:
Halogenated
hydrocarbon, alkyl
halide (organic)

STATE:
Liquid

MOLECULAR WEIGHT:
119.38 g/mol

MELTING POINT:
−63.41°C (−82.14°F)

BOILING POINT:
61.17°C (142.1°F)

SOLUBILITY:
Slightly soluble in
water; soluble in
ethyl alcohol, ether,
acetone, benzene, and
other organic
solvents

KEY FACTS

# Chloroform

## OVERVIEW

Chloroform (KLOR-oh-form) is a clear, colorless, flammable, volatile liquid with a characteristic odor and a sweet taste. It was discovered almost simultaneously in 1831 by American chemist Samuel Guthrie (1782-1848), French chemist Eugene Soubeiran (1797-1858), and German chemist Justus von Liebig (1803-1873). The chemical structure of the compound was determined by French chemist Jean-Baptiste-André Dumas (1800-1884), who suggested its modern name of chloroform in 1834 or 1835. The compound's anesthetic effects on animals were first observed by French physiologist Marie Jean-Pierre Flourens (1794-1867) in 1847.

The potential value of chloroform as an anesthetic for humans was immediately evident. In Great Britain, Liverpool chemist David Waldie (1813-1889) suggested to a surgeon friend of his, Sir James Young Simpson (1811-1870), that he might try using chloroform instead of ether to ease the pain of childbirth with his patients. On the evening of November 4, 1847, Simpson and two physician friends experimented

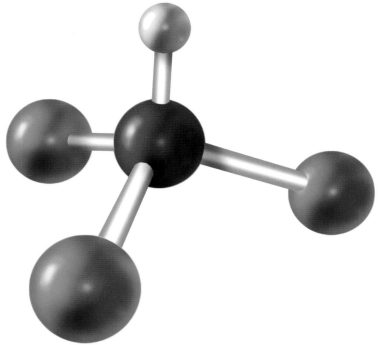

with chloroform to test its effects and all three passed out. Simpson was convinced of chloroform's value as an anesthetic and began using it in his medical practice. He did this over the objections of many clergymen of the era who believed that women should suffer the pain of childbirth because of Eve's actions in the Garden of Eden, as described in the Bible. The use of chloroform as a painkiller soon spread widely throughout Great Britain and other countries of the world.

In the twenty-first century, chloroform has been almost entirely replaced as an anesthetic by other compounds that are more effective and have fewer undesirable side effects. The compound is now used almost exclusively for the production of hydrochlorofluorocarbons (HCFCs), compounds developed to replace chlorofluorocarbons (CFCs) that have been banned because of their harmful effects on Earth's ozone layer.

## HOW IT IS MADE

Chloroform is produced commercially by the reaction between chlorine gas and methane gas. In this reaction, each

## Interesting Facts

- The debate over the use of chloroform as an anes-thetic during childbirth was largely resolved in 1853 when Queen Victoria (1819-1901) chose to have the procedure during the birth of her son Prince Leopold (1853-1884).

- Chloroform is recom-mended for the removal of lipstick stains.

- At one time, chloroform was used internally (usually in small doses) to treat a variety of medical problems, including cholera, gonorrhea, colic, cramps, spasms, and convulsions. Improper doses led to problems that were more serious that those being treated, including coma and death.

- Chloroform was once used in a number of consumer and household products, including toothpastes, cough syrups, and skin ointments. Its use for these purposes was banned in the United States in 1976.

of the four hydrogens in methane is replaced, one at a time, by chlorine atoms. The reaction must be carefully controlled, therefore, to ensure that maximum amounts of the desired product (chloroform, in this case) are obtained.

Chloroform can also be produced in the reaction between acetone and bleaching powder ($CaOCl_2$) in the presence of sulfuric acid ($H_2SO_4$): $2CH_3COCH_3 + 6CaOCl_2 \rightarrow 2CHCl_3 + (CH_3COO)_2Ca + 3CaCl_2 + 2Ca(OH)_2$.

## COMMON USES AND POTENTIAL HAZARDS

In the early twenty-first century, more than 90 percent of the chloroform produced in the United States is used in the preparation of hydrochlorofluorocarbons (HCFCs). HCFCs are compounds consisting of carbon, hydrogen, chlorine, and fluorine. They were developed in the 1980s to replace the chlorofluorocarbons (CFCs) that, at the time, were widely used for a number of industrial applications. Replacing CFCs had become necessary because they were also destroying the

## Words to Know

**ANESTHETIC** A substance that is used to temporarily deaden the feeling in a part of the body or to make a person unconscious.

**CARCINOGEN** A substance that causes cancer in humans or other animals.

**POLYMER** A compound consisting of very large molecules made of one or two small repeated units called monomers.

**VOLATILE** Able to turn to vapor easily at a relatively low temperature.

ozone layer in the stratosphere that protects plants and animals on Earth's surface from harmful ultraviolet radiation.

Chloroform is used to make one specific HCFC known as HCFC-22. HCFC-22 is also known as Freon 22, halocarbon 22, fluorocarbon 22, or R22. By 2003, an estimated 600 million metric tons (660 million short tons) of chloroform were being used in the United States for all commercial purposes. Of the HCFC-22 produced, about 70 percent was being used as a refrigerant, while the remaining 30 percent went for the synthesis of polymers.

In addition to its use in the production of HCFC-22, chloroform has a number of other minor uses, including:

- As a solvent for fats, oils, waxes, rubber, and a number of pharmaceuticals;

- In the manufacture of certain dyes and pesticides;

- As a cleansing agent in various industrial operations;

- In fire extinguishing systems;

- As a glue for methyl methacrylate products; and

- As a laboratory reagent.

Long-term prospects for chloroform are not very promising since the production of HCFCs is scheduled to be phased out over time. Although they have less serious effects on ozone than do the CFCs, they are still regarded as a threat and their use has been restricted under provisions of the Montreal Protocol on Substances that Deplete the Ozone Layer. The U.S. Environmental Protection Agency plans to ban the use of HCFC-22 under the Protocol by 2010.

Chloroform is an irritant to the skin, eyes, and respiratory system. Moderate, short-term exposure may cause redness, pain, and dryness of the skin; redness and pain in the eyes; and coughing, nausea, headache, dizziness, drowsiness, vomiting, abdominal pain, and unconsciousness. At higher doses and longer exposure, chloroform is believed to cause serious damage to the liver and kidneys. It is also thought to be a carcinogen.

### FOR FURTHER INFORMATION

"Chloroform." 11th Report on Carcinogens. National Toxicology Program.
http://ntp.niehs.nih.gov/ntp/roc/eleventh/profiles/s038chlo.pdf (accessed on December 29, 2005).

"Chloroform." International Programme on Chemical Safety.
http://www.inchem.org/documents/ehc/ehc/ehc163.htm (accessed on December 29, 2005).

"Occupational Safety and Health Guideline for Chloroform." Occupational Safety & Health Administration.
http://www.osha.gov/SLTC/healthguidelines/chloroform/recognition.html (accessed on December 29, 2005).

Stratmann, Linda. *Chloroform: The Quest for Oblivion.* Phoenix Mill, UK: Sutton Publishing Co., 2003.

"ToxFAQs™ for Chloroform." Agency for Toxic Substances and Disease Registry.
http://www.atsdr.cdc.gov/tfacts6.html (accessed on December 29, 2005).

*See Also* Carbon Tetrachloride

# Chlorophyll

## OVERVIEW

Chlorophyll (KLOR-uh-fill) is the pigment that gives plants, algae, and cyanobacteria their green color. The name comes from a combination of two Greek words, chloros, meaning "green" and phyllon, meaning "leaf." Chlorophyll is the substance that enables plants to create their own food through photosynthesis.

At least five forms of chlorophyll exist. They are:

- chlorophyll a (also known as α-chlorophyll), with a formula of $C_{55}H_{72}O_5N_4Mg$
- chlorophyll b (also known as β-chlorophyll), with a formula of $C_{55}H_{70}O_6N_4Mg$
- Chlorophyll c1, with a formula of $C_{35}H_{30}O_5N_4Mg$
- Chlorophyll c2, with a formula of $C_{35}H_{28}O_5N_4Mg$
- Chlorophyll d, with a formula of $C_{54}H_{70}O_6N_4Mg$

Chlorophyll a occurs in all types of plants and in algae. Chlorophyll b is found primarily in land plants. Chlorophyll

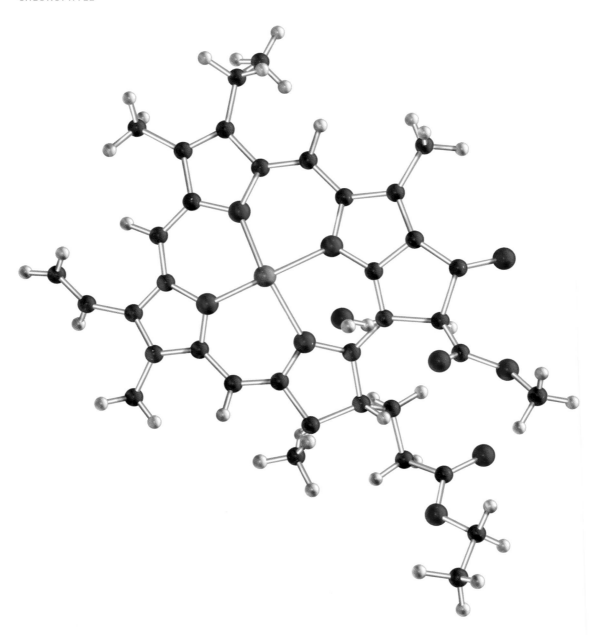

*Chlorophyll.* Red atoms are oxygen; white atoms are hydrogen; carbon atoms are black; blue atoms are nitrogen; and green atom is magnesium. PUBLISHERS RESOURCE GROUP

c1 and chlorophyll c2 are present in various types of algae. Chlorophyll d is found in red algae.

All forms of chlorophyll have a similar chemical structure. They have a complex system of rings made of carbon and nitrogen known as a chlorin ring. The five forms of

## Interesting Facts

- The chemical structure of chlorophyll is very similar to that of hemoglobin, the molecule that transports oxygen in the red blood cells of mammals. The major difference between the two is that hemoglobin contains an atom or iron at the center of a large ring compound, while chlorophyll has an atom of magnesium in the same location.

- Leaves contain compounds called carotenoids that are red, orange, and yellow in color. These colors are masked by the green color of chlorophyll. In fall, plants stop producing chlorophyll, and the red, orange, and yellow of carotenoids become visible. Carotenoids do not perform photosynthesis, although they do transmit light energy to chlorophyll, where photosynthesis takes place.

chlorophyll differ in the chemical groups attached to the chlorin ring. These differences result in slightly different colors of the five chlorophylls.

French chemists Pierre-Joseph Pelletier (1788-1842) and Joseph-Bienaimé Caventou (1795-1877) first isolated chlorophyll in 1817. In 1865, German botanist Julius von Sachs (1832-1897) demonstrated that chlorophyll is responsible for photosynthetic reactions that take place within the cells of leaves. In the early 1900s, Russian chemist Mikhail Tsvett (1872-1920) developed a technique known as chromatography to separate different forms of chlorophyll from each other. In 1929, the German chemist Hans Fischer (1881-1945) determined the complete molecular structure, making possible the first synthesis of the molecule in 1960 by the American chemist Robert Burns Woodward (1917-1979).

### HOW IT IS MADE

Plants make chlorophyll in their leaves using materials they have absorbed through their roots and leaves. The synthesis of chlorophyll requires several steps involving

## Words to Know

**CHLORIN RING** A ring of carbon and nitrogen atoms bonded to each other.

**CHROMATOGRAPHY** Process by which a mixture of substances passes through a column consisting of some material that causes the individual components in the mixture to separate from each other.

**PHOTOSYNTHESIS** The process by which green plants and some other organisms using the energy in sunlight to convert carbon dioxide and water into carbohydrates and oxygen.

**SYNTHESIS** A chemical reaction in which some desired chemical product is made from simple beginning chemicals, or reactants.

complex organic compounds. First, the plant converts a common amino acid, glutamic acid ($COOH(CH_2)_2CH(NH_2)COOH$) into an alternative form known as 5-aminolevulinic acid (ALA). Two molecules of ALA are then joined to form a ring compound called porphobilinogen. Next, four molecules of porphobilinogen are joined to form an even larger ring structure with side chains. Oxidation of the larger ring structure introduces double bonds in the molecule, giving it the ability to absorb line energy. Finally, a magnesium atom is introduced into the center of the ring and side chains are added to the ring to give it its final chlorophyll configuration.

### COMMON USES AND POTENTIAL HAZARDS

Plants store chlorophyll in their chloroplasts, organelles (small structures) that carry out the steps involved in photosynthesis. Each chloroplast contains many clusters of several hundred chlorophyll molecules called photosynthetic units. When a photosynthetic unit absorbs light energy, chlorophyll molecules move to a higher energy state, initiating the process of photosynthesis. The overall equation for the process of photosynthesis is $6CO_2 + 6H_2O \rightarrow C_6H_{12}O_6 + 6O_2$.

That simple equation does not begin to suggest the complex nature of what happens during photosynthesis. Botanists divide that process into two major series of reactions: the light reactions and the dark reactions. In the light reactions, plants use the energy obtained from sunlight to make two compounds, adenosine triphosphate (ATP) and nicotinamide adenine dinucleotide phosphate (NADPH). ATP and NADPH are not themselves components of carbohydrates, the final products of photosynthesis. Instead, they store energy that is used to make possible a series of thirteen different chemical reactions that occur during the dark stage of photosynthesis that result in the conversion of carbon dioxide and water to the simple carbohydrate glucose ($C_6H_{12}O_6$).

## FOR FURTHER INFORMATION

Attenborough, David. The Private Life of Plants. Princeton, NJ: Princeton University Press, 1995.

Buchanan, B. B., W. Gruissem, and R. L. Jones. Biochemistry and Molecular Biology of Plants. Rockville, MD: American Society of Plant Physiologists, 2000.

"Chlorophyll and Chlorophyllin." The Linus Pauling Institute Micronutrient Information Center. http://lpi.oregonstate.edu/infocenter/phytochemicals/chlorophylls/ (accessed on October 3, 2005).

May, Paul. "Chlorophyll." School of Chemistry, University of Bristol. http://www.chm.bris.ac.uk/motm/chlorophyll/chlorophyll_h.htm (accessed on October 3, 2005).

Steer, James. "Structure and Reactions of Chlorophyll." http://www.ch.ic.ac.uk/local/projects/steer/chloro.htm (accessed on October 3, 2005).

*See Also* Carbon Dioxide; Water

KEY FACTS

OTHER NAMES:
See Overview.

FORMULA:
$C_{27}H_{45}OH$

ELEMENTS:
Carbon, hydrogen,
oxygen

COMPOUND TYPE:
Sterol

STATE:
Solid

MOLECULAR WEIGHT:
386.65 g/mol

MELTING POINT:
148.5°C (299.3°F)

BOILING POINT:
Not applicable;
decomposes at about
360°C (680°F)

SOLUBILITY:
Very slightly soluble
in water; soluble in
acetone, alcohol,
ether, benzene, and
other organic
solvents.

# Cholesterol

## OVERVIEW

Cholesterol (koh-LESS-ter-ol) is also known as cholesterin; cholest-5-3n-3β-ol; 5-cholestin-3-β-ol; 3β-hydroxy-5-cholestene; and 10,13-dimethyl-17-(6-methylheptan-2-yl)-2,3,4,7,8,9,11,12,14, 15,16,17-dodecahydro-1H-cyclopenta[a]phenanthren-3-ol. It is a waxy white or pale yellow solid with virtually no taste or odor. It is present in the bodies of all higher animals, especially in the brain and spinal cord. Chemically, cholesterol is classified as a fat, a member of the lipid family. Fats are the product of the trihydric alcohol (alcohol with three -OH groups) glycerol and a fatty acid. Fatty acids are organic acids with many carbon atoms, usually eight or more.

The first description of cholesterol was written by a French scientist by the name of Poulletier de la Salle (dates not available), who isolated the compound from gallstones, a rich source of the substance. In 1816, de la Salle's compatriot Michel Eugène Chevreul (1786–1889) suggested the name of cholesterine for cholesterol, combining the French words for

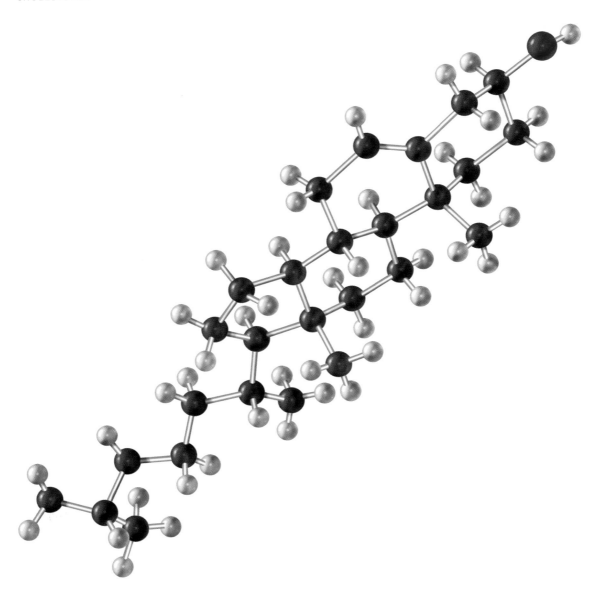

*Cholesterol.* Red atom is oxygen; white atoms are hydrogen; and black atoms are carbon. PUBLISHERS RESOURCE GROUP

bile (chole) and stone (stereos). More than a century passed before an accurate understanding of the chemical structure and behavior of cholesterol was attained. Finally, during the 1910s, research by the German chemists Heinrich Otto Wieland (1877-1957) and Adolf Winhaus (1876-1959) solved most of the fundamental problems about cholesterol, an accomplishment for which the two men were awarded the

## Interesting Facts

- The amount of cholesterol in a person's body depends essentially on two factors: genetics and diet. The ability of a person's body to produce cholesterol is determined by his or her genetic component. Some people simply make high levels of cholesterol, and other produce lower levels. Those levels can be affected to some extent by the kinds and amounts of cholesterol-containing foods (such as dairy products and organ meats) one includes in his or her daily diet.

1927 (Wieland) and the 1928 (Windhaus) Nobel Prizes in chemistry. All that remained was the determination of the structural formula for cholesterol and the first synthesis of the compound, both achieved by the American chemist Robert Burns Woodward (1917-1979) in 1955.

### HOW IT IS MADE

The primary source of cholesterol is the liver. After cholesterol is produced, the liver packages cholesterol molecules with proteins in units known as lipoproteins, which are then distributed throughout the body by way of the bloodstream. Some cholesterol is deposited in cells, where it is used as the raw material in the synthesis of a number of biologically essential compounds, such as vitamin $D_3$, steroids (such as estrogen and testosterone), and the bile acids, used by the body to digest foods. Excess cholesterol not needed by cells remains in the bloodstream until it is returned to the liver.

Commonly, the body produces more cholesterol than cells need. Or a person takes in cholesterol in his or her diet in excess of that needed by the body. In such cases, cholesterol may accumulate in the bloodstream and, at some point, be deposited on the walls of blood vessels. As these deposits grow larger, they may impeded the flow of blood, eventually leading to heart problems or stroke.

## Words to Know

**FAT** An ester formed in the reaction between glycerol ($C_3H_5(OH)_3$) and a fatty acid, an organic acid with more than eight carbon atoms.

**LIPIDS** Organic compounds that are insoluble in water, but soluble in most organic solvents, such as alcohol, ether, and acetone.

**PRECURSOR** A compound that gives rise to some other compound in a series of reactions.

**STEROL** Organic compound containing one or more ring systems and a hydroxy (-OH) group

Lipoproteins produced in the liver take one of two forms. Low-density lipoproteins (LDL) carry cholesterol directly to cells. Because this cholesterol serves a useful biological function, it is sometimes called "good" cholesterol. High-density lipoproteins (HDL), by contrast, bypass cells and remain in the blood stream. The cholesterol in HDL lipoproteins serves no useful function in the body and is often referred to as "bad" cholesterol. The role of cholesterol in the human body and dietary methods of maintaining the correct HDL:LDL ratio in the blood has been the subject of some controversy and considerable educational programs in recent decades.

A relatively small amount of cholesterol is used in making some drugs and cosmetics. The cholesterol required for these commercial purposes is obtained from natural sources, primarily spinal fluid taken from cattle who have been destroyed for meat products.

### COMMON USES AND POTENTIAL HAZARDS

Cholesterol plays three primary roles in the human body. First, it helps the body digest fatty foods. During digestion, the liver converts cholesterol into a yellowish-green liquid called bile. Bile helps break down fatty foods into a form that can be absorbed by the body. Second, cholesterol is a precursor to a number of important hormones, including androgen, estrogen, progesterone, and testosterone. Third, cholesterol is also a precursor to vitamin D, which has a number of essential functions, including the maintenance of healthy bones and nervous system, proper growth, muscle tone, production of insulin, normal reproductive functions, and proper immune system function.

FOR FURTHER INFORMATION

"Cholesterol." Chemical Land 21.
http://www.chemicalland21.com/arokorhi/lifescience/phar/CHOLESTEROL.htm (accessed on October 3, 2005).

"Cholesterol." Medline Plus.
http://www.nlm.nih.gov/medlineplus/cholesterol.html (accessed on October 3, 2005).

"Cholesterol, Other Lipids, and Lipoproteins." In *In-Depth Report*. Edited by Julia Goldrosen. Atlanta: A.D.A.M., 2004.

Goldstein, Joseph P., and Michael S. Brown. "Cholesterol: A Century of Research." *HHMI Bulletin*, 2003.
http://www.hhmi.org/bulletin/sept2003/cholesterol/century.html (accessed on October 3, 2005).

"The Nobel Prize in Physiology or Medicine 1985." Nobelprize.org.
http://nobelprize.org/medicine/laureates/1985/press.html (accessed on October 3, 2005).

"The Overall Synthesis of Cholesterol." Synthesis of Cholesterol
http://www.chm.bris.ac.uk/webprojects2000/ahester/synthchol.html (accessed on October 3, 2005).

OTHER NAMES:
See Overview.

FORMULA:
$C_6H_5CH=CHCHO$

ELEMENTS:
Carbon, hydrogen, oxygen

COMPOUND TYPE:
Aromatic aldehyde (organic)

STATE:
Liquid

MOLECULAR WEIGHT:
132.16 g/mol

MELTING POINT:
−7.5°C (18°F)

BOILING POINT:
246°C (475°F)

SOLUBILITY:
Very slightly soluble in water; soluble in alcohol, ether, and chloroform

KEY FACTS

# Cinnamaldehyde

## OVERVIEW

Cinnamaldehyde (sin-uh-MAL-duh-hide) is also known as cinnamic aldehyde; 3-phenyl-2-propenal; cinnamyl aldehyde; phenylalacrolein; cinnamal; and trans-cinnamaldehyde. It is a yellowish oily, liquid with a sweet taste and a cinnamish odor responsible for the characteristic taste and odor of cinnamon spice. It occurs naturally in the bark of the cinnamon tree, *Cinnamomum zeylanicum*, which is native to Sri Lanka and India, and has been cultivated in other parts of the world, such as Brazil, Jamaica, and Mauritius. Cinnamaldehyde is also found in other members of the the *Cinnamomum* species, including cassia and camphor.

The molecular formula for cinnamaldehyde was determined in 1834 by the French chemists Jean Baptiste André Dumas (1800-1884) and Eugène Melchior Péligot (1811-1890), although its structural formula was deciphered only in 1866 by the German chemist Emil Erlenmeyer (1825-1909).

Primary uses for Cinnamaldehyde are as a food flavoring and a medical herb. It has been used for many centuries to

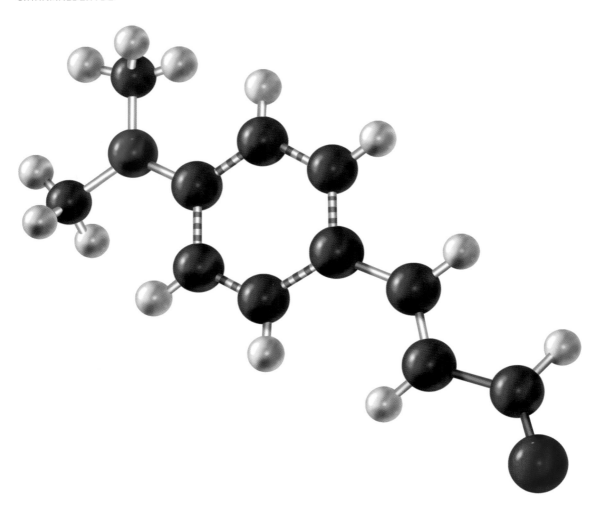

*Cinnamaldehyde.* Red atom is oxygen; white atoms are hydrogen; black atoms are carbon; and blue atom is nitrogen. Gray sticks show double bonds; Striped sticks show a benzene ring.
PUBLISHERS RESOURCE GROUP

treat a wide variety of disorders, ranging from the common cold and the flu to diarrhea to cancer. It was mentioned in Chinese medical texts as early as 2700 BCE and was described in a famous Chinese medical text, the *Tang Materia Medica*, written in 659 CE It has also been used for centuries in Ayurvedic medicine, the ancient healing art of India.

## HOW IT IS MADE

Cinnamaldehyde is prepared commercially by treating the bark of the Cinnamomum zeylanicum tree with steam. The aldehyde dissolves in the steam and can then be

## Interesting Facts

- Cinnamaldehyde is a component of sprays used as cat and dog repellents.

extracted as the steam cools and condenses to form cold water, in which the compound is much less soluble. Cinnamaldehyde can also be synthesized by reacting benzaldehyde ($C_6H_5CHO$) with acetaldehyde ($CH_3CHO$). The two compounds condense with the elimination of water to form cinnamaldhyde.

### COMMON USES AND POTENTIAL HAZARDS

In addition to its uses as a herbal remedy, the primary use of cinnamaldehyde is as a food additive to enhance the flavor and/or odor of food products. It is used most commonly in cake mixes, chewing gums, chocolate products, synthetic cinnamon oils, cola drinks, ice creams, soft drinks, and vermouth. The compound is also added to a number of cosmetics and home care products to improve their odor. Such products include deodorants, detergents, mouthwashes, perfumes, sanitary napkins, soaps, and toothpastes. Finally, cinnamaldehyde is used to some extent in agriculture as an insecticide and fungicide.

No safety concerns about the use of cinnamaldehyde as an herbal remedy, food additive, or pesticide has been expressed. The U.S. Food and Drug Administration (FDA) has classified the compound as a generally-recognized as safe (GRAS) food additive, permitting its continued use as a food additive in the United States.

## Words to Know

**AROMATIC COMPOUND** A compound whose chemical structure is based on that of benzene ($C_6H_6$).

**SYNTHESIS** A chemical reaction in which some desired chemical product is made from simple beginning chemicals, or reactants.

FOR FURTHER INFORMATION

"Cinnamaldehyde." Chemical Land 21.
    http://www.chemicalland21.com/arokorhi/specialtychem/
    perchem/CINNAMALDEHYDE.htm (accessed on October 3,
    2005).

"Cinnamaldehyde (040506) Fact Sheet." U.S. Environmental Pro-
    tection Agency.
    http://www.epa.gov/pesticides/biopesticides/ingredients/fact-
    sheets/factsheet_040506.htm (accessed on October 3, 2005).

"Oleum Cinnamomi (U. S. P.)—Oil of Cinnamon." King's American
    Dispensatory (1898).
    http://www.ibiblio.org/herbmed/eclectic/kings/cinnamomum_
    oleu.html (accessed on October 3, 2005).

# Citric Acid

## OVERVIEW

Citric acid (SIT-rik AS-id) is also known as 2-hydroxy-1,2,3-propanetricarboxylic acid and β-hydroxytricarballylic acid. It is a common constituent of plant and animal tissues. Its presence is especially noticeable in citrus fruits, such as lemons, limes, oranges, tangerines, grapefruits, and kumquat, which get their name from the acid. In pure form, citric acid is a colorless, translucent, odorless crystalline or powdery material with a pleasantly acidic taste. It frequently occurs as the monohydrate, with a single molecule of water associated with each citric acid molecule. The formula for the monohydrate is HOOCCH₂C(OH)(COOH)CH₂COOH·H₂O. The monohydrate is efflorescent, meaning that it tends to lose its water of hydration when exposed to the air.

Citric acid plays an important role in metabolism, the set of chemical reactions that occur when cells break down fats, carbohydrates, and other compounds to produce energy and compounds needed to build new cells and tissues. In fact, the series of reactions by which carbohydrates are

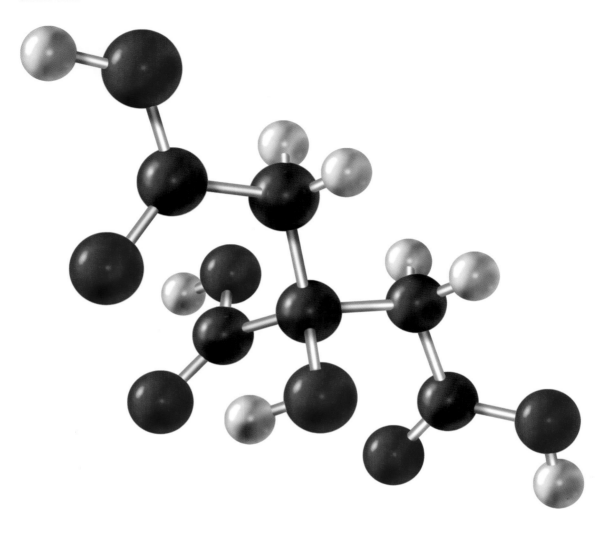

*Citric acid.* Red atoms are oxygen; white atoms are hydrogen; and black atoms are carbon. PUBLISHERS RESOURCE GROUP

converted to energy is generally known as the citric acid cycle because of the fundamental role played by the compound in those reactions. The citric acid cycle is also known as the Krebs cycle, after the German-British biochemist Sir Hans Adolf Krebs (1900-1981), who discovered the series of reactions in 1937. Citric acid also acts as an antioxidant, a substance that rid the body of molecules called free radicals that can damage healthy cells, promote cancer, and bring about ageing.

The discovery of citric acid is often credited to the Arab alchemist Jabir Ibn Hayyan (721-815), also known by his

## Interesting Facts

- The addition of citric acid to candy gives the product a "super sour" taste.

Latin name of Geber. Geber described a substance with all the properties that we equate with citric acid today, but he knew nothing about its chemical structure. The first person to isolate the compound as a pure substance was the Swedish chemist Karl Wilhelm Scheele (1742-1786), who obtained citric acid from the juice of lemons. By the mid-nineteenth century, citric acid was being produced commercially in Italy from lemons and other citrus fruits.

An important step in the commercial manufacture of citric acid occurred in 1892 when the German microbiologist Carl Wehmer (dates not available) found that citric acid could be produced by the penicillin mold. Wehmer's discovery paved the way for large-scale industrial production of citric acid. In 1917, the American chemist James Currie (dates not available) made another important breakthrough in the synthesis of citric acid. While studying the process of fermentation in cheese making, he discovered that the mold *Aspergillus niger* is able to convert sugar to citric acid. After Currie joined the pharmaceutical company Pfizerin 1917, he developed a process called SUCIAC—sugar under conversion into citric acid—by which the compound could be made in mass quantities. That process eventually became the primary method by which citric acid is produced today.

### HOW IT IS MADE

At one time, citric acid was obtained primarily from citrus fruits, such as lemons and limes. Today, it is produced synthetically using the *Aspergillus niger* mold, as described above. The citric acid produced in this reaction is purified by crystallization. The anhydrous form crystallizes from hot water, and the monohydrate form from cold water.

## Words to Know

**ALCHEMY** An ancient field of study from which the modern science of chemistry evolved.

**FERMENTATION** Chemical process by which yeasts or molds break down sugar into alcohol and carbon dioxide.

**METABOLISM** Process including all of the chemical reactions that occur in cells by which fats, carbohydrates, and other compounds are broken down to produce energy and the compounds needed to build new cells and tissues.

**MORDANT** Substance used in dyeing and printing that reacts chemically with both a dye and the material being dyed to help hold the dye permanently to the material.

**POLYMER** Compound consisting of very large molecules made of one or two small repeated units called monomers.

### COMMON USES AND POTENTIAL HAZARDS

Citric acid is added to foods, drinks, and medicines to make them more acidic. Increasing the acidity of these products not only gives them a tart taste, but also prevents the growth of bacteria. Citric acid is also used to preserve the flavors of canned fruits and vegetables and to maintain the proper acidic level of jams and jellies that will help them gel.

In addition to its use as a food additive, citric acid has a number of other commercial and industrial applications, including the following:

- As a sequestering agent to remove small amounts of metals in a solution. A sequestering agent is a substance that surrounds and captures some other substance (such as metals) and removes them from a solution;

- In the cleaning and polishing of stainless steel and other metals;

- As a mordant in the dyeing of cloth;

- In the production of certain kinds of polymers;

- For the removal of sulfur dioxide from the waste gases produced at smelters; and

- As a builder in detergents, a substance that increases the detergent's cleaning efficiency, usually by maintaining the proper acidity or softening the water in which the detergent acts.

FOR FURTHER INFORMATION

"Citric Acid." Jungbunzlauer.
    http://www.jungbunzlauer.com/products/product_1.html
    (accessed on October 3, 2005).

"Citric Acid, Anhydrous." J. T. Baker.
    http://www.jtbaker.com/msds/englishhtml/c4735.htm
    (accessed on October 3, 2005).

Kuntz, Lynn A. "Acid Basics." *Food Product Design* (May 1993).
    Also available online at
    http://www.foodproductdesign.com/toolbar_library.html
    (accessed on October 3, 2005).

OTHER NAMES:
Not applicable

FORMULA:
Not applicable

ELEMENTS:
Carbon, hydrogen,
oxygen, nitrogen

COMPOUND TYPE:
Organic

STATE:
Solid

MOLECULAR WEIGHT:
100,000 to 150,000
g/mol

MELTING POINT:
Not applicable

BOILING POINT:
Not applicable

SOLUBILITY:
Not applicable

# Collagen

## OVERVIEW

Collagen (KO-lah-jen) is the most abundant protein in the animal kingdom. Approximately one third of the protein in a mammal's body is collagen. It makes up a major portion of the connective tissue found in skin, joints, ligaments, muscles, tendons, and bones. Different types of collagen occur in different species. That is, the collagen found in humans is somewhat different from that found in cows, and both human and cow collagen differ from the collagen found in other animals, such as dogs and ats. Nonetheless, all forms of collagen have a common molecular structure that consists of three rope-like strands intertwined with each other. Each strand (called tropocollagen) is a polymer consisting of amino acids, the most common of which are glycine, proline, and hydroxyproline. Collagens differ from each other in regard to the relative amounts of each amino acid present.

## HOW IT IS MADE

Collagen is synthesized in the bodies of all higher vertebrates in a complex series of reactions that begin with the linking of amino acids with each other. Amino acids are organic compounds that contain both the carboxyl group (-COOH) and the amino group (-NH2). The amino acids are joined to each other in very long chains known as polypeptides (a word meaning "many amino acids"). After assembly, polypeptide chains intertwine with each other in groups of three to make large molecules called procollagen ("early collagen"), which is then cut into smaller pieces by enzymes designed especially for that purpose. The three strands that make up each collagen group are held together by the action of vitamin C molecules.

## COMMON USES AND POTENTIAL HAZARDS

All of the connective tissue in the body contains collagen. This collagen is flexible but not stretchy and will tear if pulled to strongly. Collagen is also a primary component of cartilage, the material that fills the gaps between bones and fills out structures that are firm but somewhat soft, such as the end of the nose and ears. There are at least a dozen types of collagen in the body, each one with a slightly different physical and chemical structure.

Type I is the most abundant kind of collagen. It forms long strands that criss-cross the spaces between cells and is found throughout the body, particularly in tendons, bones, and scars. Type II collagen is found in cartilage, and Type III collagen in granulation tissue that forms when wounds heal. Type IV collagen comprises the basal lumina, the membrane that supports skin and internal surfaces. The eight other types of collagen all have their specific functions in the body.

Plastic surgeons use collagen to fill wrinkles and lines in their patients' faces and bodies. As people age, the tissue that fills out their faces and makes the skin look smooth and tight breaks down, leaving lines and wrinkles. Injecting collagen into wrinkles fills the area under the skin with tissue that puffs out the skin, making it firm and smooth again. Doctors also use collagen to fill in scars. In most cases, collagen treatments are not permanent. The collagen breaks down or is absorbed and additional treatments are necessary to remove wrinkles.

## Interesting Facts

- When collagen is treated with boiling water, it is converted to gelatin, a widely used household product. Popular desserts such as Jell-O® are made from collagen taken from the hooves, bones, and connective tissue of cows and pigs.

- In the cooking method known as "braising", meats are heated for a long time over low heat. During braising, collagen molecules "melt" (break apart) producing a tender meaty product in a rich broth that turns to gelatin as it cools. By contrast, cooking meat over high heat causes proteins to shrink and become tougher.

Several health disorders result from inadequate or abnormal collagen in the body. Scurvy, caused by a deficiency of vitamin C, is the best known of these. When adequate amounts of vitamin C are not present in the body, collagen molecules break apart and muscles and joints are damaged. Ehlers-Danlos syndrome is a disorder that occurs when collagen molecules are weakened, causing bruising of the skin, rupture of arteries or intestines, overly flexible joints, skin and bone deformities, and hip dislocations. Osteogenesis imperfecta results in poorly formed bones and causes the sclera (the white part of the eye) to turn blue.

## Words to Know

POLYMER A compound consisting of very large molecules made of one or two small repeated units called monomers.

POLYPEPTIDE A molecule composed of many amino acids in a chain.

FOR FURTHER INFORMATION

"Collagenase and Collagen: What Is Collagen?" BioSpecifics Technologies Corporation.
http://www.biospecifics.com/collagendefined.html (accessed on December 6, 2005).

"Collagens." Kimball's Biology Pages.
http://users.rcn.com/jkimball.ma.ultranet/BiologyPages/C/Collagens.html (accessed on December 6, 2005).

Goodsell, David S. "Collagen: Your Most Plentiful Protein." Protein Data Bank.
http://www.rcsb.org/pdb/molecules/pdb4_1.html (accessed on December 6, 2005).

Cu
|
O
|
Cu

# Copper(I) Oxide

## OVERVIEW

Copper(I) oxide (KOPP-er one OK-side) is also known as cuprous oxide, red copper oxide, copper protoxide, copper hemi-oxide, and copper suboxide. It is a yellowish, red, or brown crystalline substance, depending on its method of preparation. It does not burn and is stable in dry air. In moist air, it slowly changes to copper(II) oxide (CuO). The compound has been used by humans for thousands of years, first as a pigment in glazes, and later in fungicides, electronic components, and industrial reactions.

In 1883, copper(I) oxide was the first substance found to have semiconducting properties. A semiconductor conducts an electric current, although not nearly as efficiently as a conductor like copper, gold, or silver. Semiconductor components are now widely used in computer chips, although they are now made from silicon rather than copper(I) oxide.

## HOW IT IS MADE

Copper(I) oxide occurs naturally as the mineral cuprite. It forms when native copper (copper as an element) is exposed

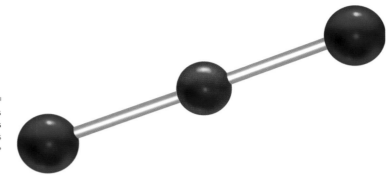

to the air, although the process occurs very slowly. Copper(I) oxide can also be made synthetically by exposing copper metal to a high concentration of oxygen at an elevated temperature. Care must be taken, however to prevent the copper from oxidizing completely to form copper(II) oxide. A number of other industrial methods are also available for the synthesis of copper(I) oxide. For example, electrolysis of a solution of sodium chloride using copper electrodes results in the formation of copper(I) oxide.

## COMMON USES AND POTENTIAL HAZARDS

Copper(I) oxide is used as a pigment in porcelain glazes and stained glass. In opaque glass, it provides a bright brick-red color if large enough crystals are used. Smaller crystals give a yellowish color. The use of copper(I) oxide as a pigment in glazes dates back to the time of ancient Egypt.

Many antifouling marine paints contain copper(I) oxide. Antifouling paints are paints that prevent the formation of barnacles and other organisms on the bottom of a boat. The compound is also used as an antifungal agent, a substance that kills mildew, rust, and other types of fungus. Fungicides based on copper(I) oxide are commonly used on a variety of crops susceptible to attack by such organisms. Copper(I) oxide acts by inhibiting the growth of fungal spores (from which new plants develop) rather than killing mature fungi.

Copper(I) oxide is used in photoelectric cells, which are cells that generate an electric current when exposed to light.

## Interesting Facts

- Copper metal is sometimes used for roofing on notable buildings, such as art museums or state capitols. Over time, the copper metal develops a patina, a thin layer of color that adds to the elegance of the roof. The patina consists primarily of copper(I) oxide.

- In 1904, the German physicist Wilhelm Hallwachs (1859-1922) discovered that a combination of copper metal and copper(I) oxide displays the photoelectric effect, in which a beam of light causes electricity to flow through a material.

Photoelectric materials are usually semiconductors. Copper(I) oxide photoelectric cells do not generate much power, but they react rapidly to changes in light levels. This property makes them useful as light detectors, which have many applications from cameras with automatic adjustment settings to automatic door openers and burglar alarms.

In the 1980s, a ceramic form of copper(I) oxide was found to have superconducting properties at temperatures higher than previously known superconductors. Superconductors have the ability to carry an electric current virtually without resistance. Once a current is initiated in a superconductor, it continues to travel through the material essentially forever. Superconductor research may lead to new technologies, from cheaper electrical power to magnetically levitated high-speed trains.

Exposure to moderate amounts of copper(I) oxide can be irritating to the skin, eyes, and respiratory system. If heated, it gives off copper fumes that can cause symptoms similar to the common cold and may discolor the skin and hair. If swallowed, copper(I) oxide has a metallic taste and may induce vomiting, nausea, and stomach pain. In the most severe cases, copper(I) oxide may cause black or tarry stools, jaundice, and bloody vomiting, with long-term damage to the liver. In the environment, copper(I) oxide is very toxic to fish and crustaceans.

## Words to know

**ELECTROLYSIS** Process in which an electric current is used to bring about chemical changes.

**OXIDIZE** To combine with oxygen.

**PHOTOELECTRIC CELL** A device that generates electricity when exposed to light.

**SEMICONDUCTOR** A substance that allows electricity to flow through it at a lesser rate than a conductor, though more than a non-conductive substance.

**SUPERCONDUCTOR** A substance that allows electricity to flow through it with very little resistance.

**SYNTHESIS** Chemical reaction in which some desired chemical product is made from simple beginning chemicals, or reactants.

FOR FURTHER INFORMATION

"Cuprite." Dale Minerals International. http://www.webmineral.com/data/Cuprite.shtml (accessed on October 3, 2005).

"Cuprous oxide." Hummel Croton, Inc. http://www.hummelcroton.com/msds/cu2o_m.html (accessed on October 3, 2005).

Patnaik, Pradyot. *Handbook of Inorganic Chemicals.* New York: McGraw-Hil, 2003, 271-273.

Richardson, H. W., ed. *Handbook of Copper Compounds and Applications.* New York: Marcel Dekker, 1997.

*See Also* Copper(II) Oxide

O
|
Cu

OTHER NAMES:
Cupric oxide; copper
monoxide; black cop-
per oxide

FORMULA:
CuO

ELEMENTS:
Copper, oxygen

COMPOUND TYPE:
Metallic oxide

STATE:
Solid

MOLECULAR WEIGHT:
79.54 g/mol

MELTING POINT:
1,446°C (2,670°F)

BOILING POINT:
Not applicable;
decomposes

SOLUBILITY:
Insoluble in water and
organic solvents;
soluble in dilute acids
and ammonium
hydroxide

KEY FACTS

# Copper(II) Oxide

## OVERVIEW

Copper(II) oxide (KOPP-er two OK-side) occurs in nature in the minerals tenorite, melaconite, and paramelaconite. In pure form, it is a black to brownish powder or crystalline material. Like copper(I) oxide, copper(II) oxide is a semiconductor, a material that conducts an electric current, although not nearly as well as conductors such as gold, silver, and aluminum.

## HOW IT IS MADE

Copper(II) oxide forms naturally in the Earth as a result of the weathering of copper sulfides ($Cu_2S$ and $CuS$). It is prepared synthetically by heating copper metal in air to about 800°C (1,500°F) or, more commonly, by heating copper(II) carbonate ($CuCO_3$) or copper(II) nitrate [$Cu(NO_3)_2$] to red heat.

## COMMON USES AND POTENTIAL HAZARDS

Throughout recorded history, copper(II) oxide has been used as a pigment to color ceramics, enamels, porcelain

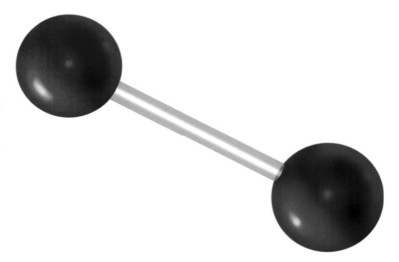

glazes, and artificial gems, applications that continue to the present day. The oxide adds a bluish to greenish tint to such materials. Copper(II) oxide also finds use as an insecticide and fumigant. It is used primarily in the treatment of potato plants and as an antifouling agent on boat hulls. An antifouling agent is a material that prevents the formation of barnacles and other organisms on the bottom of a boat. When such organisms grow on a boat's hull, they increase the friction produced when the boat rides through the water, thus reducing its speed. The compound is also used as a wood preservative, to protect fence posts, pilings, decking, roofing, shingles, sea walls, and other freshwater and marine structures from insects and fungi.

Other uses to which copper(II) oxide is put including the following:

- In the preparation of superconducting materials, materials that have essentially no resistance to the flow of an electric current;

- In the manufacture of batteries and electrodes;

- As a welding flux for use with bronze objects and materials;

- For polishing of optical glass, glass used in telescopes, microscopes, and similar instruments;

- In the preparation of phosphors, materials that glow in the dark after being exposed to light;

## Interesting Facts

- The ancient Greeks used a mixture of copper(II) oxide and copper(II) sulfate to treat wounds.

- U.S. pennies sometimes develop a black coating that is caused by copper(II) oxide. The coating can be removed by cleaning the penny in a solution of vinegar, lemon juice, and salt. Coca Cola™ can also be used because it contains phosphoric acid ($H_3PO_4$), which dissolves copper(II) oxide.

- Some fingerprinting powders contain copper(II) oxide.

- For the removal of sulfur and sulfur compounds for petroleum;

- In the manufacture of rayon; and

- As a catalyst in many industrial and commercial chemical reactions.

Inhaling copper(II) oxide fumes may result in a condition known as metal fume fever, with irritation of the throat, coughing, shortness of breath, nausea, and fever. Excessive exposure may result in chronic lung disease. Ingesting large amounts of copper(II) oxide may cause vomiting, diarrhea, nausea, excessive salivation, and intense abdominal pain. The compound is also an eye irritant.

## Words to Know

**CATALYST** A material that increases the rate of a chemical reaction without undergoing any change in its own chemical structure.

**FLUX** A material that lowers the melting point of another substance or mixture of substances or that is used in cleaning a metal.

FOR FURTHER INFORMATION

"Copper Oxide 99.99+%." Louisiana State University.
http://www.camd.lsu.edu/msds/c/copperII_oxide.htm#Synonyms
(accessed on October 5, 2005).

"Cupric Oxide." J. T. Baker.
http://www.jtbaker.com/msds/englishhtml/c5885.htm
(accessed on October 5, 2005).

Richardson, H. W., ed. *Handbook of Copper Compounds and Applications.* New York: Marcel Dekker, 1997.

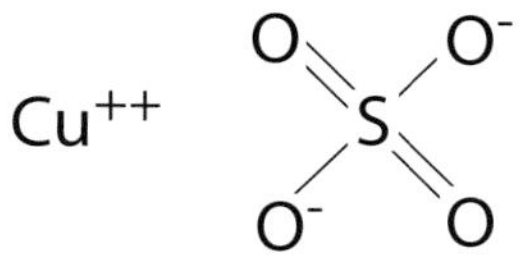

Cu++   O     O⁻
        \\   /
         S
        /   \\
      O⁻     O

# Copper(II) Sulfate

## OVERVIEW

Copper(II) sulfate (KOPP-er two SUL-fate) is a white crystalline powder in its anhydrous state, although it occurs most commonly as the pentahydrate, $CuSO_4 \cdot 5H_2O$, which is a blue granular crystalline solid. When the pentahydrate is heated, it loses its water of hydration and returns to its white, powdery anhydrous state. The transition between its white anhydrous form and its blue hydrated form is sometimes used in devices and toys that indicate the presence or absence of moisture in the air.

Copper(II) sulfate is probably the most important and most widely used of all copper compounds. It is used in agriculture, the paints and covering industry, in electrical applications, in the production of other chemicals, and in other industrial and commercial applications.

## HOW IT IS MADE

Copper(II) sulfate occurs in nature as the mineral calcanthite. Calcanthite is somewhat rare since copper(II)

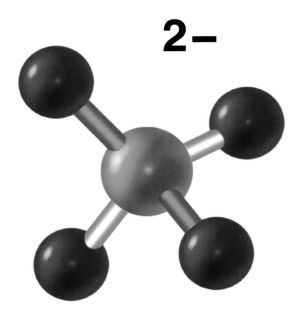

*Copper(II) sulfate pentahydrate.* Red atoms are oxygen; yellow atom is sulfur; and turquoise atom is copper. Gray sticks are double bonds.

sulfate dissolves readily in water, and therefore the mineral can leach out of rock by groundwater. The compound is made in the laboratory and commercially by treating copper metal or one of the copper oxides (CuO or $Cu_2O$) with sulfuric acid ($H_2SO_4$).

## COMMON USES AND POTENTIAL HAZARDS

Copper(II) sulfate is used extensively in agriculture as a soil additive, a fumigant for trees, a feed additive to prevent mineral deficiencies, and as a wood preservative. It is a component, along with calcium oxide (CaO; quicklime), of one of the oldest and most popular plant fumigants, a material called Bordeaux mixture. Many of copper(II) sulfate's uses depend on his highly toxic character. It is used to prevent the growth of mold and mildew; to sanitize surfaces in hospitals; to kill algae in swimming pools, reservoirs, and other bodies of water; as an herbicide to kill weeds; and as a germicide, to prevent the growth of unwanted seeds. Although very effective in such applications, copper(II) is often not the first choice because it may have toxic effects on other plants and animals in the environment and on humans.

## Interesting Facts

- Copper(II) sulfate gets the name blue vitriol from the color of the pentahydrate (blue) plus the fact that it is made from sulfuric acid, which is also called oil of vitriol.

Some additional uses of copper(II) sulfate include the following:

- As a mordant in the textile industry;

- In the production of blue pigments for paints, varnishes, glazes, dyes, inks, and other coloring materials;

- In electroplating, where it supplies the copper with which other metals are plated;

- In making lithographic prints and engravings;

- In the preservation and tanning of animal hides;

- As a catalyst in the refining of petroleum;

- As a nutritional supplement to treat copper deficiency disorders;

- In the manufacture of fireworks, where it imparts a blue color to the display; and

- In the production of water-resistant adhesives for wood.

Copper(II) sulfate is known to be toxic to humans and other animals if ingested. It may cause burning in the mouth and stomach, nausea, vomiting, abdominal pain, diarrhea, and a metallic taste in the mouth. It can cause gastrointestinal bleeding and, if not eliminated from the body, can result in kidney and liver damage, depression of the nervous system, paralysis, coma, and death from shock or kidney failure. Prolonged exposure to copper(II) sulfate dust can cause discoloration of the skin, damage to the blood and liver, and irritation of the eyes and nose. Copper(II) sulfate poses some risk to the environment, both because of its toxic nature and because it does not break down readily.

## Words to Know

**ANHYDROUS** Form of a compound that lacks water.

**CATALYST** A material that increases the rate of a chemical reaction without undergoing any change in its own chemical structure.

**FUMIGANT** A pesticide that is applied as a gas.

**MORDANT** A substance used in dyeing and printing that reacts chemically with both a dye and the material being dyed to help hold the dye permanently to the material.

### FOR FURTHER INFORMATION

"Cupric Sulfate." New Jersey Department of Health and Senior Services.
http://www.state.nj.us/health/eoh/rtkweb/0549.pdf
(accessed on October 5, 2005).

"Cupric Sulfate Anhydrous." J. T. Baker.
http://www.jtbaker.com/msds/englishhtml/c5920.htm
(accessed on October 5, 2005).

Ware, George W. *The Pesticide Book.* Batavia, Ill.: Mesiter, 1999.

Young, Jay A. "Copper (II) Sulfate Pentahydrate." *Journal of Chemical Education* (February 2002): 158.

*See Also* Copper(II) Oxide

K E Y   F A C T S

# Cumene

## OVERVIEW

Cumene (KYOO-meen) is a colorless, flammable liquid with a penetrating gasoline-like odor. Chemically, it is classified as an aromatic hydrocarbon. Aromatic hydrocarbons are compounds of carbon and hydrogen with a molecular structure based on that of benzene. Although cumene is probably not well known to the average person, it is a very important industrial chemical. In 2004, some 3.74 million metric tons (4.12 million short tons) of cumene were produced in the United States, making it the twentieth most important chemical made in that year by weight. Cumene is used primarily as a raw material in the synthesis of other organic compounds, such as phenol, acetone, acetophenone, and methyl styrene, and as a thinner for paints and lacquers.

## HOW IT IS MADE

Cumene is made in a straight-forward chemical reaction between benzene ($C_6H_6$) and propene (propylene; $CH_3CH=CH_2$).

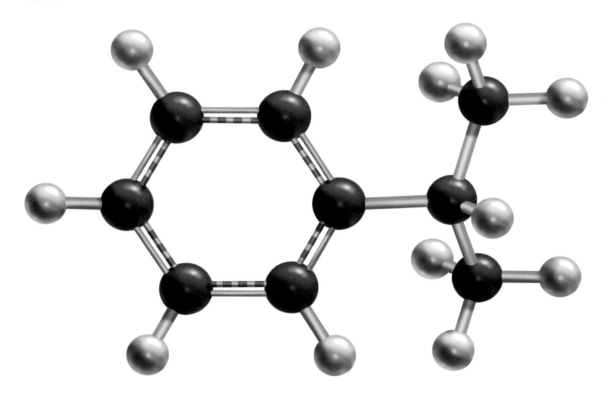

*Cumene.* Black atoms are carbon; white atoms are hydrogen. Bonds in the benzene ring are represented by the double striped sticks. White sticks show single bonds. PUBLISHERS RESOURCE GROUP

It can also be extracted from petroleum or from coal tar, the thick black material left after soft coal is converted to coke.

## COMMON USES AND POTENTIAL HAZARDS

Small amounts of cumene are used as thinners for paints, lacquers, and enamels, and as solvents in paints and other types of coatings. By far the greatest amount of cumene, however, is used as a raw material in the manufacture of phenol, acetone, and methyl styrene. These compounds, in turn, have a great many chemical and industrial uses. Some of the most important uses are the production of plastics, such as polystyrene, phenol-formaldehyde resins, and poly-carbonates.

Cumene is a skin, eye, and respiratory system irritant. If inhaled, it can cause coughing, dizziness, drowsiness,

## Interesting Facts

- Traditionally, the synthesis of cumene has involved the use of phosphoric acid ($H_3PO_4$) as a catalyst. That process results in the release of harmful by-products into the environment, and a new process that uses zeolites as a catalyst has now become more popular. Zeolites are a naturally occurring, earthy material that can be as effective as phosphoric acid in promoting the synthesis of cumene.

sore throat, headache, and loss of muscular coordination. In large doses, it has a narcotic effect, resulting in drowsiness and insensitivity to pain and other stimuli, and may lead to unconsciousness. There is no evidence that cumene is carcinogenic or that it causes hereditary damage to a person or to offspring of individuals exposed to the compound.

## Words to Know

**AROMATIC HYDROCARBON** A compound of carbon and hydrogen with a molecular structure based on that of benzene.

**CATALYST** A material that increases the rate of a chemical reaction without undergoing any change in its own chemical structure.

**MISCIBLE** Able to be mixed; especially applies to the mixing of one liquid with another.

**SOLVENT** A substance that is able to dissolve one or more other substances.

**SYNTHESIS** A chemical reaction in which some desired chemical product is made from simple beginning chemicals, or reactants.

FOR FURTHER INFORMATION

"Cumene." International Programme on Chemical Safety. http://www.inchem.org/documents/cicads/cicads/cicad18.htm#PartNumber:1 (accessed on December 22, 2005).

"Cumene." Technology Transfer Network, Air Toxics Website http://www.epa.gov/ttn/atw/hlthef/cumene.html (accessed on December 22, 2005).

"Cumene (1-methylethylbenzene)." Australian Government. Department of the Environment and Heritage. http://www.npi.gov.au/database/substance-info/profiles/28.html (accessed on December 22, 2005).

*See Also* Acetone; Phenol; Styrene

# Cyanoacrylate

## OVERVIEW

Cyanoacrylate (sye-AN-oh-ACL-ri-late) is a general term used to describe a family of esters derived in the reaction between cyanoacrylic acid and various alcohols, such as methanol (methyl-2-cyanoacrylate) and ethanol (ethyl-2-cyanoacrylate). Cyanoacrylates are all esters of cyanoacrylic acid, CH$_2$=C(CN)COOH, and include methyl-2-cyanoacrylate, ethyl-2-cyanoacrylate, and 2-octyl cyanoacrylate. The material is the primary ingredient in Super Glue$^{TM}$, Krazy Glue$^{TM}$, Duro$^{TM}$, Quick Gel$^{TM}$, and a number of other products used to glue two surfaces together with a very strong bond in a matter of seconds. The bonding activity of the cyanoacrylates occurs when the esters react with water to form polymers that bond to materials with which they come into contact. The polymerization reaction occurs very quickly, resulting in strong bonds that form almost instantaneously.

Cyanoacrylate was discovered in 1942 by American researchers Harry Coover (1919– ) and Fred Joiner, employees of the Eastman Kodak Laboratories, in Rochester, New York.

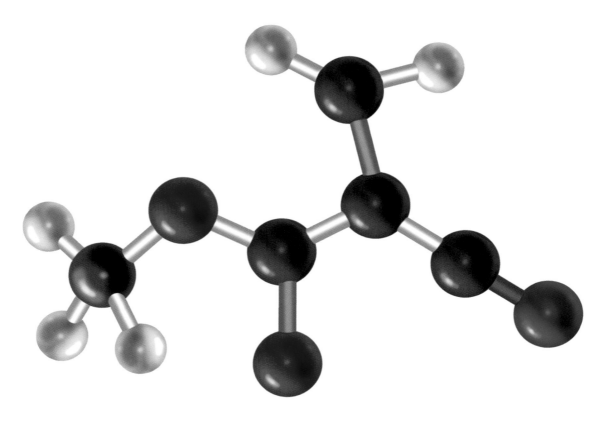

*Cyanoacrylate.* Red atoms are oxygen; white atoms are hydrogen; black atoms are carbon; and blue atom is nitrogen. Gray sticks indicate double bonds. PUBLISHERS RESOURCE GROUP

Coover and Joiner were attempting to synthesize a clear plastic material that could be used for gun sights. Instead, they obtained a liquid with a tendency to stick tightly to anything with which it came into contact. They decided that the product—then known as Eastman 910—was more of a problem than an asset and set it aside for six years before deciding to explore its adhesive properties.

At that point, Eastman Kodak began studying the possibilities of using cyanoacrylate for military applications, specifically for sealing wounds. It applied to the U.S. Food and Drug Administration (FDA) for permission to market the product for this use, an application that was approved in 1964. Shortly thereafter, military physicians tested cyanoacrylate glues in Vietnam and found them highly effective in sealing the wounds of soldiers. In a spray form, the glue stopped bleeding from chest wounds long enough to allow wounded soldiers to reach a hospital. Although the use of cyanoacrylates by the military proved to be a success, the FDA declined to approve the product for civilian use. The product had a tendency to irritate the skin when it reacted with moisture on the skin, releasing formaldehyde and cyanoacetate, both toxic substances. Eventually, research showed that the octyl ester, 2-octyl-cyanoacrylate, proved to form stronger bonds, was more flexible, and was less irritating than the methyl and ethyl esters used in the original Eastman 610 formulation. With this change, the FDA approved the use of 2-octyl-cyanoacrylate for use in closing wounds and incisions. In 2001, the FDA extended this approval to include use of the compound as an antibacterial agent.

## HOW IT IS MADE

Cyanoacrylates are made by reacting cyanoacrylic acid with an alcohol, such as methanol, ethanol, or 2-octanol, to form the corresponding ester.

## COMMON USES AND POTENTIAL HAZARDS

Cyanoacrylates are still used in a variety of medical applications to close wounds and to protect wounds from infection. The 2-octyl ester is used for this purpose because it has fewer hazardous side effects than do the methyl and ethyl esters. Cyanoacrylate is preferred to stitches for closing wounds because it is less likely to become infected and tends to leave fewer scars. For this reason, the compound is often used for cuts on the face, although it cannot be used in the nose or mouth. Consumers can buy cyanoacrylate products such as BandAid brand Liquid Bandage™ for home use.

Cyanoacrylates are sometimes used in dental procedures. Their ability to bond tightly and quickly, to seal wounds, and to prevent the development of infections make them useful for a number of surgical procedures involving teeth and gums. The primary concern is the selection of esters (such as the 2-octyl ester) that will not cause irritation or infections of the areas being treated.

Cyanoacrylates are also used widely in a number of industrial and household adhesives, perhaps the best known of which is Super Glue™. Manufacturers use cyanoacrylates in the assembly of many products, including trophies, golf

## Interesting Facts

- The commercial success of cyanoacrylates as glues was assured in 1959 when Harry Coover appeared on the television show *I've Got a Secret* and used the product to lift host Gary Moore off the floor with a single drop of Eastman Kodak's Super Glue™.

- The polymerization of cyanoacrylates with water begins as soon as the glue is spread on a material, and a strong bond is formed almost immediately. However, polymerization continues for a number of hours and is not complete for 24 to 48 hours, at which point the bonding is considerably stronger than in the first few minutes of application.

clubs and other sports equipment, tools, digital watches, optical lenses, electronic components, lampshades, plastics, scientific instruments, loudspeakers, shoes, jewelry, and videocassettes. Automobile makers use the product to attach trim to cars and trucks. The cyanoacrylates come in a great variety of formulations that make them suitable for bonding with special types of materials (such as ceramics, metals, wood, plastics, and glasses) and under a variety of specialized conditions (such as high or low temperature or very dry or damp conditions).

Cyanoacrylates are also used by forensic scientists to collect fingerprints at crime scenes. The object to be tested is suspended inside a container with at least one transparent side. A few drops of Super Glue or similar cyanoacrylate product is added to the container and the container is sealed and heated to about 100°C (212°F). That heat causes vaporization and polymerization of the cyanoacrylate, resulting in the formation of distinctive white print patterns, a process that make take two hours or more. This cyanoacrylate fuming test has now become the procedure of choice for the detection of latent prints deposited on non-porous objects, such as glass, plastic, rubber, and leather.

Cyanoacrylates bond to skin as quickly and tightly as they do to other materials, so care is required in their use.

## Words to Know

**ESTER** An organic compound formed in the reaction between an organic acid and an alcohol.

**POLYMER** A compound consisting of very large molecules made of one or two small repeated units called monomers.

**POLYMERIZATION** The process of creating a polymer; a reaction that causes a polymer to form.

**SYNTHESIS** A chemical reaction in which some desired chemical product is made from simple beginning chemicals, or reactants.

They are skin and eye irritants, and so should always be used in an area with good ventilation. Exposure to high levels of cyanoacrylate gas can cause severe respiratory problems, and in the most extreme cases can result in death.

### FOR FURTHER INFORMATION

"Cyanoacrylates." Impact Adhesives. http://www.impact-adhesives.com/pages/cyano.html (accessed on October 6, 2005).

Davidson, Elaine. "Cyanoacrylates." http://www.repairantiques.com/cyanoacrylates.html (accessed on October 6, 2005).

Fernandez, Tania, and Val Bliskovsky. "Cyanoacrylate Technology: Stay Glued." Pharmabiz.com. http://www.pharmabiz.com/article/detnews.asp?articleid=13609 &sectionid=46 (accessed on October 6, 2005).

"Methyl 2-Cyanoacrylate (MCA); Ethyl 2-Cyanoacrylate (ECA)." Occupational Safety and Health Administration. http://www.osha-slc.gov/dts/sltc/methods/organic/org055/org055.html (accessed on October 6, 2005).

"Methyl Cyanoacrylate and Ethyl Cyanoacrylate." International Programme on Chemical Safety. http://www.inchem.org/documents/cicads/cicads/cicad36.htm# 9.0 (accessed on October 6, 2005).

Schwade, Nathan D. "Wound Adhesives: 2-Octyl Cyanoacrylate." eMedicine: Instant Access to Medicine. http://www.emedicine.com/ent/topic375.htm (accessed on October 6, 2005).

*See Also* Formaldehyde

OTHER NAMES:
Cobalamin;
vitamin $B_{12}$

FORMULA:
$C_{63}H_{88}CoN_{14}O_{14}P$

ELEMENTS:
Carbon, hydrogen,
cobalt, nitrogen,
oxygen, phosphorus

COMPOUND TYPE:
Heterocyclic ring
(organic)

STATE:
Solid

MOLECULAR WEIGHT:
1355.36 g/mol

MELTING POINT:
Undetermined;
greater than 300°C
(575°F)

BOILING POINT:
Not applicable

SOLUBILITY:
Soluble in water in
alcohol; insoluble in
acetone, ether, and
chloroform

# Cyanocobalamin

## OVERVIEW

Cyanocobalamin (sye-AN-oh-koh-BAL-uh-min) is more commonly known as vitamin $B_{12}$. At least three active forms of the vitamin are known. They include hydroxocobalamin and nitrocobalamin, in addition to cyanocobalamin, all with slightly different molecular structures. Cyanocobalamin occurs as dark red crystals or a red powder that is odorless and tasteless. When heated, the compound darkens above 200°C (392°F), but does not melt when heated further.

Cyanocobalamin is required for the synthesis of DNA in cells and for the proper functioning of red blood cells and nerves. A deficiency of vitamin $B_{12}$ in the diet results in a condition known as pernicious anemia, a condition in which red blood cells are smaller in size, number, and hemoglobin content than normal red blood cells. These defects result in general weakness, nervous disorders, gastrointestinal disturbances, and, eventually and inevitably, death.

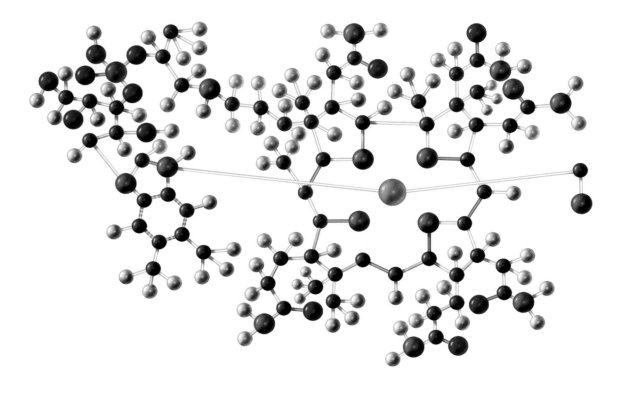

The earliest research on pernicious anemia dates to the 1920s when American physician George Hoyt Whipple (1878-1976) found that anemia in dogs could be cured by feeding them beef liver. Inspired by this work, American physicians William Murphy (1892-1987) and George Minot (1885-1950) discovered that feeding pernicious anemia patients beef liver cured the disease. These discoveries led to the suspicion that one of the B vitamins present in liver was responsible for the cure of pernicious anemia. Scientists even invented a name for the missing vitamin, vitamin $B_{12}$, long before it was actually discovered. The problem, unknown to researchers at the time, was that vitamin $B_{12}$ was such a complex molecule that its isolation and identification was a significant challenge.

In 1948, American chemist Karl Folkers (1906-1997) and his research team discovered that they could measure

## Interesting Facts

- Cyanocobalamin gets its name because it contains the metal cobalt.

- For a period of time, the only cure available for pernicious anemia was for patients to eat about a pound of liver every day. Since many patients disliked that diet, they were very happy when synthetic vitamin $B_{12}$ supplements became available.

amounts of the vitamin by measuring the growth rate of bacteria that grew on vitamin $B_{12}$. Soon the team learned how to purify the vitamin, which formed small red crystals that many scientists consider quite beautiful. It still took many years for scientists to determine exactly how the enormous molecule was structured. In 1956, however, the British chemist Dorothy Hodgkin (1910-1994) determined its chemical structure, allowing her American colleague Robert Burns Woodward (1917-1979) to actually synthesize the compound, an accomplishment of enormous complexity that took fifteen years to complete.

### HOW IT IS MADE

Vitamin $B_{12}$ is made naturally by bacteria that live in the intestines of all animals, including humans, as well as in soil. It binds to protein in food. Plants do not synthesize vitamin $B_{12}$. Manufacturers who make vitamin $B_{12}$ supplements use bacteria to grow the vitamin by a process similar to that which occurs naturally. Good food sources of vitamin $B_{12}$ include animal foods, such as fish, meat, poultry, eggs, milk, cheese, and yogurt; as well as fortified cereals. People who do not eat animal products should be sure to select foods fortified with artificially produced vitamin $B_{12}$, because the synthetic vitamin is produced by a natural process that does not involve the destruction of animals or the consumption of animal products.

## Words to Know

**DNA** Deoxyribonucleic acid, a material with a cell that carries its genetic information and is capable of reproducing itself.

**HETEROCYCLIC RING** A compound whose molecules contain at least one ring in which some element other than carbon is also present.

**SYNTHESIS** A chemical reaction in which some desired chemical product is made from simple beginning chemicals, or reactants.

### COMMON USES AND POTENTIAL HAZARDS

Cyanocobalamin is essential to human health. The body cannot make properly functioning red blood cells, white blood cells, or platelets without it. It is also essential for the production of DNA and nerve cells. People whose diet is deficient in cyanocobalamin are likely to develop pernicious anemia. The symptoms of this disorder include fatigue, weakness, numbness, blurred vision, poor memory, confusion, hallucinations, personality changes, a smooth shiny tongue, stiffness, diarrhea, poor appetite, slow growth in children, and reduced sensitivity to pain and pressure.

### FOR FURTHER INFORMATION

Brody, Tom. *Nutritional Biochemistry.* San Diego: Academic Press, 1998.

"Dietary Supplement Fact Sheet: Vitamin $B_{12}$." National Institutes of Health, Office of Dietary Supplements. http://ods.od.nih.gov/factsheets/vitaminb12.asp (accessed on October 6, 2005).

"Nascobal Gel." Nastech Pharmaceutical Company. http://www.tzamal-medical.co.il/tzamal-pharma-products-nascobal.htm (accessed on October 6, 2005).

Opt, Robert C., and David J. Brown. "Vitamin B$_{12}$ Deficiency." *American Academy of Family Physicians.* March 1, 2003. Also available online at http://www.aafp.org/afp/20030301/979.html (accessed on October 6, 2005).

KEY FACTS

# Denatonium Benzoate

## OVERVIEW

Denatonium benzoate (de-an-TOE-nee-um BEN-zoh-ate) is generally regarded as having the most bitter taste of any compound known to science. It is sold under the trade name of Bitrex®. Although denatonium benzoate has a powerful taste, it is colorless and odorless. The taste is so strong, however, that most people cannot tolerate a concentration of more than 30 parts per million of denatonium benzoate. Solutions of denatonium benzoate in alcohol or water are very stable and retain their bitter taste for many years. Exposure to light does not lessen the compound's bitter taste.

Denatonium benzoate compound was discovered in 1958 by a scientist named W. Barnes, who was working for the chemical firm of T. & H. Smith, in Edinburgh, Scotland. Barnes was interested in developing a new anesthetic, more powerful than those already available to physicians. He decided to focus his research on lidocaine, a very popular anesthetic, and compounds chemically related to it. In one line of his experiments, Barnes added a single benzoyl group

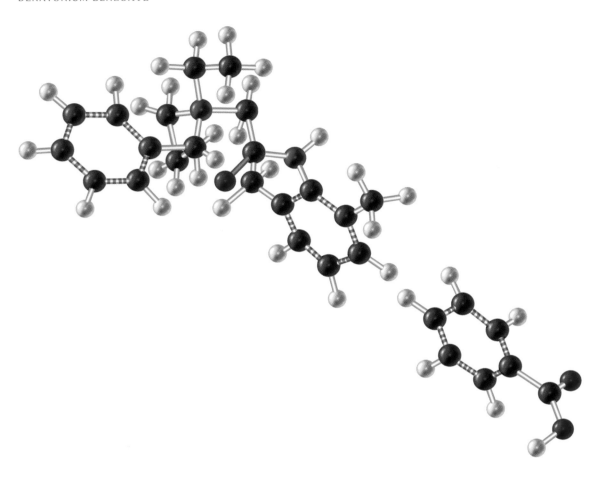

(benzoic acid with a hydrogen removed: $C_6H_5COO^-$) to a nitrogen atom in lidocaine. The resulting compound was denatonium benzoate. Although the compound had little effectiveness as an anesthetic, Barnes noted that it had a peculiar odor and taste. The Smith company decided to exploit this unusual property of denatonium benzoate, and obtained a patent for it under the name of Bitrex®. Today, the primary manufacturer of Britex® in the world is the Macfarlan Smith corporation of Edinburgh.

## HOW IT IS MADE

The process by which denatonium benzoate is made is a proprietary secret of the Macfarlan Smith corporation. A proprietary secret is a method of making a product for which

## Interesting Facts

- The claim that denatonium benzoate is the most bitter tasting chemical known is based not on scientific tests but on human taste tests alone. No automated test exists for determining the bitterness of a substance.

- Oregon was the first state in the United States to require the addition of Bitrex® to antifreeze and car windshield washer fluid. The requirement was instituted to prevent people from drinking such products accidentally or, in the case of alcoholics, intentionally.

a company holds a patent and the details of which it does not disclose to the general public.

### COMMON USES AND POTENTIAL HAZARDS

One of the first and most important uses of denatonium benzoate was as an additive to methanol (methyl alcohol; wood alcohol). Although ethanol (ethyl alcohol; grain alcohol) has some harmful effects on humans, especially if taken in excess, it is relatively safe to drink in beer, wine, and other alcoholic drinks. By contrast, methanol is highly toxic. Anyone who accidentally or intentionally consumes methanol is likely to experience serious health effects, including death. By adding a small amount of denatonium benzoate to methanol, consumers are discouraged—and usually prevented—from drinking the substance.

Denatonium benzoate has many other applications. For example, it can be used in a dilute solution to brush on the fingernails of people who are compulsive fingernail-biters. Some parents use a similar solution on the thumbs of children who suck their thumbs more than they should. Denatonium benzoate is also used as an animal repellent. Products containing denatonium benzoate can be sprayed on trees, brushes, crops, and other material to prevent deer from grazing on those products. One of the product's first applications was as a treatment on pig's tails to prevent pigs from biting each other. The coatings on electric cables are sometimes impregnated with a denatonium benzoate solution to discourage rats from chewing on them.

Some of the other applications in which denatonium benzoate has been used include the following:

- In liquid laundry detergents;
- In fabric conditioners;
- In toilet cleaners;
- In disinfectants;
- In household antiseptics;
- In kitchen, bathroom, and floor cleaners;
- In paint products and paint brush cleaners;
- In personal care products, including bath foam, soaps, perfume and after shave lotions, nail polish remover, shampoo, and shower gel;
- In pesticides, such as insecticides, rodenticides, slug bait, and ant bait;
- In herbicides; and
- In a wide variety of automotive care products, such as antifreezes, coolants, and car cleaning materials.

In all of these cases, the purpose of adding denatonium benzoate is to change the taste of the product just enough to prevent someone, especially children, from eating a substance that could cause them harm.

Despite its bitter taste, denatonium benzoate appears to pose little or no hazard to human health. Exposure to the pure compound may cause respiratory discomfort, but only people working with the substance directly are likely to encounter this problem.

## FOR FURTHER INFORMATION

"About Bitrex®." Market Actives. http://www.marketactives.com/home.html (accessed on October 7, 2005).

"Contains Bitrex." Macfarlan Smith. http://www.bitrex.com/home.htm (accessed on October 7, 2005).

"Denatonium Benzoate." C-Tech Corporation. http://www.ctechcorporation.com/benzoate.htm (accessed on October 7, 2005).

"The Most Bitter Substance." Center for the Science & Engineering of Materials. http://www.csem.caltech.edu/material_of_month/bitrex.html (accessed on October 7, 2005).

## Words to Know

**CATALYST** A material that increases the rate of a chemical reaction without undergoing any change in its own chemical structure.

**STRATOSPHERE** The layer of the Earth's atmosphere extending from about 15 kilometers (8 miles) to about 50 kilometers (30 miles) above the Earth's surface.

**TROPOSPHERE** The lowest layer of the Earth's atmosphere, reaching to about 8 miles (15 kilometers) above the Earth's surface.

ness, and death by suffocation. Sprayed on the skin, Freons® can cause frostbite, damage produced by exposure to freezing temperatures. The ignition of Freons® also poses hazards to human health because of the release of toxic gases such as hydrogen chloride (HCl), hydrogen fluoride ($H_2F_2$), and phosgene ($COCl_2$).

### FOR FURTHER INFORMATION

Baker, Linda. "The Hole in the Sky (Ozone Layer)." *E* (November 2000): 34.

Cagin, Seth, and Philip Dray. *Between Earth and Sky: How CFCs Changed Our World and Endangered the Ozone Layer.* New York: Pantheon Books, 1993.

"Dichlorodifluoromethane." NIOSH Pocket Guide to Chemical Hazards. http://www.cdc.gov/niosh/npg/npgd0192.html (accessed on October 7, 2005).

Elkins, James W. "Chlorofluorocarbons (CFCs)." National Oceanic and Atmospheric Administration (NOAA). http://www.cmdl.noaa.gov/noah/publictn/elkins/cfcs.html (accessed on October 7, 2005).

"Gas Data." Air Liquide. http://www.airliquide.com/en/business/products/gases/gasdata/index.asp?GasID=22 (accessed on October 7, 2005).

*See Also* Ammonia; Hydrogen Chloride; Sulfur Dioxide

H——

**KEY FACTS**

OTHER NAMES:
DDT; see Overview
for additional names

FORMULA:
$(ClC_6H_4)_2CHCCl_3$

ELEMENTS:
Carbon, hydrogen,
chlorine

COMPOUND TYPE:
Halogenated
hydrocarbon
(organic)

STATE:
Solid

MOLECULAR WEIGHT:
354.49 g/mol

MELTING POINT:
108.5°C (227.3°F)

BOILING POINT:
260°C (500°F)

SOLUBILITY:
Insoluble in water;
slightly soluble in
ethyl alcohol; soluble
in ether, acetone, and
benzene

# Dichlorodiphenyl-trichloroethane

## OVERVIEW

Dichlorodiphenyltrichloroethane (DI-klor-oh-DI-fee-nul-TRI-klor-oh-eth-ane) is a colorless crystalline or white powdery material with a slight aromatic odor. It is far better known by its acronym, DDT. DDT was first synthesized in 1873 by German chemist Othmar Zeidler (1859-1911) as a project for his doctoral thesis. However, the compound was essentially ignored by other chemists and remained a laboratory curiosity for more than sixty years.

Then, in 1939, Swiss chemist Paul Hermann Müller (1899-1965) discovered that DDT is very effective in killing a wide variety of insects including the common housefly, the mosquito, the louse, and the Colorado beetle. Müller's discovery gave medical workers a powerful tool in preventing a host of infectious diseases carried by these insects, including bubonic plague, dengue fever, elephantitis, encephalitis, leishmaniasis, malaria, sleeping sickness, typhus, yaws, and yellow fever. The compound was used widely during World War II (1939-1945) to control insects in both military and

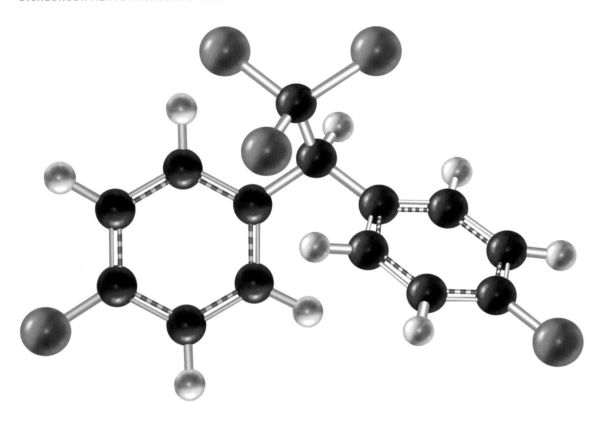

*Dichlorodiphenyltrichloroethane (DDT).* Black atoms are carbon; green atoms are chlorine; white atoms are hydrogen. Bonds in the benzene rings are represented by the double striped sticks. White sticks show single bonds.

PUBLISHERS RESOURCE GROUP

civilian facilities. It was credited for reducing the spread of what is probably the world's most common infectious disease, malaria. Once common throughout the world, malaria was essentially eliminated in Europe and North America as a result of the use of DDT.

In addition to its public health applications, DDT has long been a popular agricultural pesticide. The compound kills many of the insects and other pests that attack crops and reduce the productivity that can be achieved by farmers.

The fate of DDT took a dramatic turn in the 1960s, however, largely as the result of a single book, *Silent Spring*, written by American biologist and environmentalist Rachel Carson (1907-1964). The book described a situation in which the use of pesticides such as DDT might become so common that the chemical begins to kill off other organisms, such as birds, as well as insects. Carson's book came at a time when scientific evidence of the environmental harm done by pesticides was just becoming available. The work wa. soon adopted by the growing environmental movement as a well-documented warning of what might happen if the uncontrolled use of pesticides did not end. People began to worry about the ill effects of DDT and other pesticides not only on the environment, but also on human health.

In 1972, the U.S. Environmental Protection Agency announced that DDT could no longer be used in the United States because of the risk it posed for human health and the environment. A number of other developed nations soon followed the EPA's action. In 2001, a conference sponsored by the United Nations, called the Stockholm Convention on Persistent Organic Pollutants, adopted a statement calling for the eventual elimination of a dozen pesticides, known as "the dirty dozen," including DDT. Because of its effectiveness against malaria and other infectious diseases, DDT was given a waiver for use by public health officials in nations where the compound had not been banned.

DDT is also known by the following names: 1,1,1-trichloro-2,2-bis-(p-chlorophenyl)ethane; 1,1'-(2,2,2-trichloroethylidene)-bis (4-chlorobenzene); 1,1,1-trichloro-2,2-di(4-chlorophenyl) ethane; 1,1,1-trichloro-2,2-di($p$-chlorophenyl) ethane; 1,1-bis(4-chlorophenyl)-2,2,2-trichlorethane; 1,1-bis(p-chlorophenyl)-2,2,2-trichlorethane; 2,2,2-trichloro-1,1-bis (4-chlorophenyl) ethane; and 4,4'-dichlorodiphenyltrichloroethane.

## HOW IT IS MADE

DDT is prepared commercially in the reaction between chloral ($CCl_3CHO$) and chlorobenzene ($C_6H_5Cl$): $CCl_3CHO + 2C_6H_5Cl \rightarrow (ClC_6H_4)_2CHCCl_3$.

## COMMON USES AND POTENTIAL HAZARDS

DDT is no longer used in the United States and other nations where it has been banned. It is still used in a number of developing nations for the control of infectious diseases spread by insects that can be killed by DDT. Malaria is the most important of these diseases.

The health hazards posed by DDT are still the subject of intense debate among agricultural scientists, public health experts, and other authorities. Abundant evidence exists to show that DDT can have a variety of harmful effects on

## Interesting Facts

- Peak use of DDT in the United States occurred in 1958 when about 35 million kilograms (80 million pounds) of the compound were sprayed on U.S. farmlands.

- Extensive data exists to support the advantages of using DDT against malaria. For example, there were more than 2.8 million cases of malaria in Sir Lanka in 1948, before the introduction of DDT. Six years later, after the compound had been put into use in the country, the number of malaria cases dropped to 17. Five years later, after the use of DDT had been discontinued, the number of malaria cases rose to 2.5 million.

- Countries that have banned the use of DDT include Australia (1967), Sweden (1970), Cuba (1970), Germany (1974), Poland (1976), the United Kingdom (1984), Chile (1985), South Korea (1986), Switzerland (1986), and Canada (1989).

- DDT is still manufactured legally in only three countries: China, India, and Indonesia. It may also be produced, although illegally, in Mexico.

- DDT often occurs in combination with two other related compounds, dichlorodiphenyldichloro-ethane (DDD) and dichlorodiphenyldichloro-ethylene (DDE).

animals, ranging from marine algae to bald eagles. The compound may also have serious health effects on humans, including mild to serious damage to the liver, kidneys, and central nervous system. DDT has also been classified as a probable carcinogen by the U.S. Environmental Protection Agency although no definite evidence for that classification is yet available.

On the other hand, critics have pointed out that little scientific evidence exists for the belief that DDT is a serious health threat to humans. In one experiment, humans took capsules containing small amounts of DDT every day for 18 months and experienced no measurable health effects as a result. Some observers argue that the benefits gained from using DDT as an agricultural and public health pesticide—benefits such as the elimination of diseases like malaria—far exceed the risks posed by the chemical to human health and the environment.

FOR FURTHER INFORMATION

Carson, Rachel. *Silent Spring.* Boston: Houghton Mifflin, 1962.

"DDT." National Safety Council.
http://www.nsc.org/library/chemical/ddt.htm (accessed on December 29, 2005).

"DDT (dichlorodiphenyltrichloroethane)." Extoxnet.
http://ace.orst.edu/cgi-bin/mfs/01/pips/ddt.htm (accessed on December 29, 2005).

Dunlap, Thomas. *DDT: Scientists, Citizens, and Public Policy.* Princeton, NJ: Princeton University Press, 1983.

Edwards, J. Gordon, and Steven Milloy. "100 Things You Should Know about DDT." JunkScience.com.
http://www.junkscience.com/ddtfaq.htm (accessed on December 29, 2005).

Karaim, Reed. "Not So Fast with the DDT: Rachel Carson's Warnings Still Apply." *American Scholar* (June 2005): 53-60.

McGinn, Anne Platt. "Malaria, Mosquitoes, and DDT: The Toxic War against a Global Disease." *World Watch* (May 1, 2002): 10-17.

"ToxFAQs™ for DDT, DDE, and DDD." Agency for Toxic Substances and Disease Registry.
http://www.atsdr.cdc.gov/tfacts35.html (accessed on December 29, 2005).

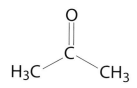

# Dimethyl Ketone

## OVERVIEW

Dimethyl ketone (DYE-meth-el KEY-tone) is a clear, colorless, highly volatile and highly flammable liquid with a characteristic sweet odor and taste. The compound is almost universally known in chemistry laboratories and industrial applications by its common name of acetone.

Acetone was apparently first prepared in 1610 by the French alchemist Jean Béguin (c. 1550-c. 1650). Béguin obtained acetone by heating lead acetate (also known as Saturn's salt) to a high temperature. He obtained a sweet-smelling, very flammable liquid that he named "burning spirit of Saturn." One of the first uses to which the substance was put was as a solvent in the extraction of the active constituents of opium. In 1833, the French chemist Antoine Bussy (1794-1882) gave the compound its modern name of acetone. The correct chemical formula for acetone was determined independently in 1832 by the French chemist Jean Baptiste André Dumas (1800-1884) and the German chemist Justus von Liebig (1803-1873).

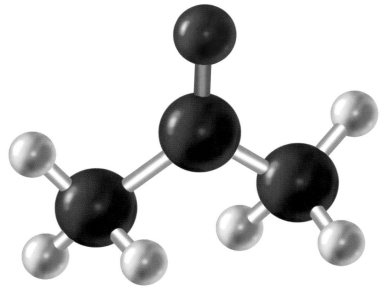

## HOW IT IS MADE

Most of the acetone produced today is made by one of four methods:

- In the Hock process, cumene [$C_6H_5CH(CH_3)_2$] is first oxidized to produce cumene hydroperoxide [$C_6H_5C(CH_3)_2COOH$], which is then reduced to produce acetone and phenol ($C_6H_5OH$); or

- Isopropyl alcohol (2-propanol; $CH_3CHOHCH_3$) is oxidized over a catalyst to obtained acetone; or

- Butane ($C_4H_{10}$) is oxidized to obtain acetone; or

- Acetone is obtained as a by-product of the manufacture of glycerol [$C_3H_5(OH)_3$].

## COMMON USES AND POTENTIAL HAZARDS

Acetone's primary applications are based on its ability to dissolve such a wide array of organic substances. It is used as a solvent for paints, varnishes, lacquers, inks, glues, rubber cements, fats, oils, waxes, and various types of rubber and plastics. It is perhaps best known to the average person as the primary ingredient in nail polish remover. The largest single use of the compound is as a raw material in the manufacture of other organic chemicals, such as chloroform,

## Words to Know

**MISCIBLE** able to be mixed; especially applies to the mixing of one liquid with another.

**VOLATILE** A term describing a liquid that can be easily changed to gas.

acetic acid, iodoform, bromoform, isoprene, rayon, and photographic film. It also finds application in storing acetylene gas (because it absorbs up to 24 times its own weight of the gas), to clean and dry chemical equipment and electronic parts, and for the extraction of components of plant and animal tissues.

The primary safety concern about acetone is its extreme flammability. Workers who handle the compound must use great care to prevent its coming into contact or even being in the vicinity of open flames. Under the proper conditions, acetone is also explosive. Exposure of the skin, eyes, and respiratory system to acetone may produce mild symptoms, such as dizziness, headaches, and disorientation and irritation of the eyes and skin. Such conditions are rare, however, and no long-term health effects of the compound have as yet been discovered.

### FOR FURTHER INFORMATION

"Acetone." International Labour Organization.
http://www.ilo.org/public/english/protection/safework/cis/products/icsc/dtasht/_icsc00/icsc0087.htm (accessed on October 7, 2005).

"Safety (MSDS) data for propanone." Physical and Theoretical Chemistry Lab Safety.
http://ptcl.chem.ox.ac.uk/MSDS/PR/propanone.html (accessed on October 7, 2005).

"Toxicological Review of Acetone." Environmental Protection Agency.
http://www.epa.gov/iris/toxreviews/0128-tr.pdf (accessed on October 7, 2005).

# Ethyl Acetate

## OVERVIEW

Ethyl acetate (ETH-uhl ASS-uh-tate) is a clear, colorless, volatile, flammable liquid with a pleasant fruity odor. Its appealing odor and fruity taste (in dilute solutions) explains one of its primary uses: as an additive in foods and drugs to improve their flavor.

## HOW IT IS MADE

Ethyl acetate occurs naturally in fruits, where it is responsible for the pleasant odor and taste of the fruit. It is also found in yeasts and sugar cane. The compound is made synthetically by reacting acetic acid ($CH_3COOH$) with ethanol (ethyl alcohol; $CH_3CH_2OH$) in the presence of a sulfuric acid catalyst.

## COMMON USES AND POTENTIAL HAZARDS

Ethyl acetate's primary use is as a solvent in a variety of commercial and industrial applications. About 65 percent

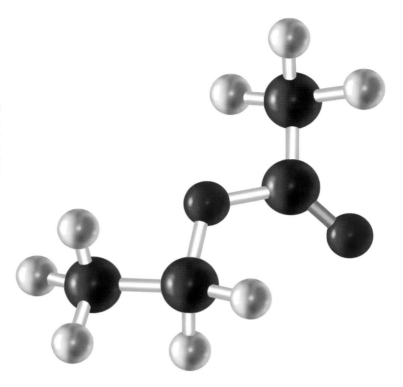

*Ethyl acetate.* Red atoms are oxygen; white atoms are hydrogen; and black atoms are carbon. Gray sticks indicate double bonds. PUBLISHERS RESOURCE GROUP

of all ethyl acetate produced is used as a solvent in lacquers, varnishes, shellacs, inks, coatings for airplanes, and other types of coatings. Another 12 percent of the ethyl acetate produced is used as a solvent for various types of plastics. The remaining amount of ethyl acetate is used in

## Interesting Facts

• Ethyl acetate is a byproduct of the fermentation of grapes in the wine-making process. The compound is also produced as wine ages in barrels and bottles. A moderate amount of ethyl acetate contributes to the pleasant fruity taste and odor of some wines. But in excess, it can give wine a slightly "off" taste and odor.

## Words to Know

**CATALYST** A material that increases the rate of a chemical reaction without undergoing any change in its own chemical structure.

**ESTER** An organic compound formed in the reaction between an organic acid and an alcohol.

**MISCIBLE** able to be mixed; especially applies to the mixing of one liquid with another.

**SYNTHESIS** A chemical reaction in which some desired chemical product is made from simple beginning chemicals, or reactants.

the preparation of other organic compounds; as a flavor-enhancing additive for foods and pharmaceuticals; in the manufacture of smokeless power, leather products, and photographic films and plates; and for the cleaning of textiles.

The primary safety concern with regard to ethyl acetate is its flammability. Both the liquid and its vapors ignite at temperatures above 200°C (392°F). Exposure to ethyl acetate vapors can also irritate the eyes, nose, and respiratory system. There is no evidence that normal amounts of ethyl acetate are carcinogenic or toxic to humans.

### FOR FURTHER INFORMATION

"Ethyl Acetate." J. T. Baker.
http://www.jtbaker.com/msds/englishhtml/e2850.htm (accessed on October 7, 2005).

"Ethyl Acetate." National Institute of Standards and Technology.
http://webbook.nist.gov/cgi/cbook.cgi?Name=ethyl+acetate& Units=SI (accessed on October 7, 2005).

"Ethyl Acetate." Spectrum Laboratories.
http://www.speclab.com/compound/c141786.htm (accessed on October 7, 2005).

*See Also* Acetic Acid; Ethyl Alcohol

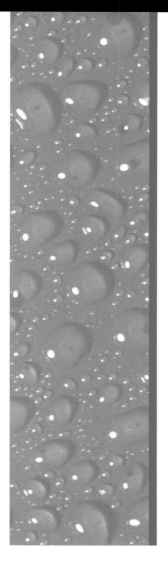

# appendices

*Lists of compounds*

Compounds by Formula . . . . . . . . . . . . . . liii

Compounds by Element . . . . . . . . . . . . . lix

Compounds by Type . . . . . . . . . . . . . . lxv

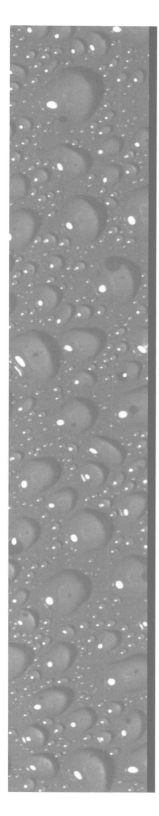

# Compounds by Formula

AgI
  Silver Iodide

AgNO$_3$
  Silver Nitrate

Ag$_2$O
  Silver(I) Oxide

Ag$_2$S
  Silver(I) Sulfide

AlF$_3$
  Aluminum Fluoride

Al(OH)$_3$
  Aluminum Hydroxide

Al$_2$O$_3$
  Aluminum Oxide

CCl$_2$F$_2$
  Dichlorodifluoromethane

CCl$_4$
  Carbon Tetrachloride

-[-CF$_2$-]-$_n$
  Polytetrafluoroethylene

CH≡CH
  Acetylene

-[-CH(CH$_3$)CH$_2$-]-$_n$
  Polypropylene

CHCl$_3$
  Chloroform

CH$_2$O
  Formaldehyde

-[-CH$_2$C(CH$_3$)(COOH)CH$_2$-]-$_n$
  Polymethyl Methacrylate

CH$_2$=C(CN)COOCH$_3$
  Cyanoacrylate

CH$_2$=CHCH=CH$_2$
  1,3-Butadiene

CH$_2$=CHCH$_3$
  Propylene

CH$_2$=CH(CH$_3$)CH=CH$_2$
  Isoprene

-[-CH$_2$-CH(COONa)-]$_n$-
  Sodium Polyacrylate

-[CH$_2$CHC$_6$H$_5$-]$_n$-
[-CH$_2$CH=CHCH$_2$-]$_n$-[CH$_2$CHC$_6$H
  Poly(Styrene-Butadiene-
  Styrene)

-[-CH$_2$CHCl-]-$_n$
  Polyvinyl Chloride

CH$_2$=CH$_2$
  Ethylene

(CH$_2$CH$_2$Cl)$_2$S
  2,2′-Dichlorodiethyl Sulfide

-[-CH$_2$-CH$_2$-]-$_n$
Polyethylene

-[-CH$_2$C$_6$H$_5$-]-$_n$
Polystyrene

CH$_2$NO$_2$CHNOCH$_2$NO$_2$
Nitroglycerin

CH$_2$OHCHOHCH$_2$OH
Glycerol

CH$_2$OHCH$_2$OH
Ethylene Glycol

(CH$_2$)$_2$O
Ethylene Oxide

CH$_3$CHOHCH$_3$
Isopropyl Alcohol

CH$_3$CHOHCOOH
Lactic Acid

CH$_3$CH$_2$OH
Ethyl Alcohol

CH$_3$COCH$_3$
Dimethyl Ketone

CH$_3$CONHC$_6$H$_4$OH
Acetaminophen

CH$_3$COOCH$_2$CH$_2$CH(CH$_3$)$_2$
Isoamyl Acetate

CH$_3$COOC$_2$H$_5$
Ethyl Acetate

CH$_3$COOC$_5$H$_{11}$
Amyl Acetate

CH$_3$COOC$_6$H$_4$COOH
Acetylsalicylic acid

CH$_3$COOH
Acetic acid

CH$_3$C$_5$HN(OH)(CH$_2$OH)$_2$
Pyridoxine

CH$_3$C$_6$H$_9$ (C$_3$H$_7$)OH
Menthol

CH$_3$OH
Methyl Alcohol

(CH$_3$O)(OH)C$_6$H$_3$CHO
Vanillin

CH$_3$SH
Methyl Mercaptan

(CH$_3$)$_2$CHCH$_2$CH$_2$NO$_2$
Amyl Nitrite

C$_5$H$_{11}$NO$_2$
Amyl Nitrite

(CH$_3$)$_2$C$_5$H$_3$NSO(COOH)NHCOR
Penicillin

(CH$_3$)$_3$COCH$_3$
Methyl-t-butyl Ether

CH$_4$
Methane

CH$_4$S
Methyl Mercaptan

CO
Carbon Monoxide

-[-CO(CH$_2$)$_4$CO-NH(CH$_2$)$_6$NH-]-$_n$
Nylon 6 and Nylon 66

-[-CO(CH$_2$)$_5$NH-]-$_n$
Nylon 6 and Nylon 66

-[-CONH-C$_6$H$_4$-NCOO-CH$_2$CH$_2$-O-]-$_n$
Polyurethane

COOH(CH$_2$)$_2$CH(NH$_2$)COONa
Monosodium Glutamate

CO$_2$
Carbon Dioxide

C$_2$H$_2$
Acetylene

C$_2$H$_2$O$_4$
Oxalic Acid

[C$_2$H$_3$Cl]$_n$
Polyvinyl Chloride

C$_2$H$_4$
Ethylene

[C$_2$H$_4$]$_n$
Polyethylene

C$_2$H$_4$O
Ethylene Oxide

C$_2$H$_4$O$_2$
Acetic acid

C$_2$H$_6$O
Ethyl Alcohol

C$_2$H$_6$O$_2$
Ethylene Glycol

[C$_3$H$_3$O$_2$Na]$_n$
Sodium Polyacrylate

C$_3$H$_5$N$_3$O$_5$
Nitroglycerin

[C$_3$H$_6$]$_n$
Polypropylene

C$_3$H$_6$O
Dimethyl Ketone

C$_3$H$_6$O$_3$
Lactic Acid

C$_3$H$_8$
Propane

C$_3$H$_8$O
Isopropyl Alcohol

C$_3$H$_8$O$_3$
Glycerol

C$_4$H$_6$
1,3-Butadiene

C$_4$H$_8$Cl$_2$S
2,2'-Dichlorodiethyl Sulfide

C$_4$H$_8$O$_2$
Ethyl Acetate

C$_4$H$_{10}$
Butane

$C_4H_{10}S$
Butyl Mercaptan

$C_5H_4NC_4H_7NCH_3$
Nicotine

$C_5H_5NO_2$
Cyanoacrylate

$C_5H_8$
Isoprene

$[C_5H_8]_n$
Polymethyl Methacrylate

$C_5H_8NNaO_4$
Monosodium Glutamate

$C_5H_{12}O$
Methyl-t-butyl Ether

$C_6H_2(CH_3)(NO_2)_3$
2,4,6-Trinitrotoluene

$C_6H_3ClOH\text{-}O\text{-}C_6H_3Cl_2$
Triclosan

$C_6H_3Cl_2NHCONHC_6H_4Cl$
Triclocarban

$C_6H_5CH{=}CHCHO$
Cinnamaldehyde

$C_6H_5CH{=}CH_2$
Styrene

$C_6H_5CH(CH_3)_2$
Cumene

$C_6H_5CH_3$
Toluene

$C_6H_5COOH$
Benzoic Acid

$C_6H_5C_2H_5$
Ethylbenzene

$C_6H_5NO_2$
Niacin

$C_6H_5OH$
Phenol

$C_6H_6$
Benzene

$C_6H_6Cl_6$
Gamma-1,2,3,4,5,6-Hexa-
chlorocyclohexane

$C_6H_6O$
Phenol

$[C_6H_7O_2(OH)_2OCS_2Na]_n$
Cellulose Xanthate

$C_6H_8O_6$
Ascorbic Acid

$C_6H_8O_7$
Citric Acid

$(C_6H_{10}O_5)_n$
Cellulose

$[C_6H_{11}NO]_n$
Nylon 6 and Nylon 66

$C_6H_{11}NHSO_3Na$
Sodium Cyclamate

$C_6H_{12}NNaSO_3$
Sodium Cyclamate

$C_6H_{12}O_2$
Butyl Acetate

$C_6H_{12}O_6$
Fructose
Glucose

$C_6H_{14}$
Hexane

$C_6H_4(CH_3)CON(C_2H_5)_2$
N,N-Diethyl-3-Methylbenza-
mide

$C_7H_5NO_3S$
Saccharin

$C_7H_5N_3O_6$
2,4,6-Trinitrotoluene

$C_7H_6O_2$
Benzoic Acid

$[C_7H_7]_n$
Polystyrene

$C_8H_7N_3O_2$
Luminol

$C_7H_8N_4O_2$
Theobromine

$[C_7H_{11}NaO_5S_2]_n$
Chloroform

$C_7H_{14}O_2$
Isoamyl Acetate
Amyl Acetate

$C_8H_8$
Styrene

$[C_8H_8]_n\text{-}[C_4H_6]_n\text{-}[C_8H_8]_n$
Poly(Styrene-Butadiene-
Styrene)

$C_8H_9NO_2$
Acetaminophen

$C_8H_{10}$
Ethylbenzene

$C_8H_{10}N_4O_2$
Caffeine

$C_8H_{11}NO_3$
Pyridoxine

$C_9H_8O$
Cinnamaldehyde

$C_9H_8O_4$
Acetylsalicylic acid

$C_9H_{12}$
Cumene

$C_{10}H_8$
Naphthalene

$C_{10}H_{14}N_2$
Nicotine

$C_{10}H_{16}O$
Camphor

$C_{10}H_{20}O$
Menthol

$C_{11}H_{16}O_2$
Butylated Hydroxyanisole
and Butylated Hydroxyto-
luene (BHA)

$C_{12}H_7Cl_3O_2$
Triclosan

$C_{12}H_{16}N_4O_{18}$
Cellulose Nitrate

$C_{12}H_{17}ClN_4OS$
Thiamine

$C_{12}H_{17}NO$
N,N-Diethyl-3-Methylbenza-
mide

$[C_{12}H_{22}N_2O_2]_n$
Nylon 6 and Nylon 66

$C_{12}H_{22}O_{11}$
Lactose
Sucrose

$C_{13}H_9Cl_3N_2O$
Triclocarban

$C_{13}H_{18}O_2$
2-(4-Isobutylphenyl)propionic
Acid

$C_{14}H_9Cl_5$
Dichlorodiphenyltrichloroethane

$C_{14}H_{14}O_3$
Naproxen

$C_{14}H_{18}N_2O_5$
L-Aspartyl-L-Phenylalanine
Methyl Ester

$C_{15}H_{24}O$
Butylated Hydroxyanisole
and Butylated Hydroxyto-
luene (BHT)

$C_{16}H_{18}N_2OS$
Penicillin

$C_{16}H_{19}N_3O_5S$
Amoxicillin

$C_{17}H_{20}N_4O_6$
Riboflavin

$C_{19}H_{19}N_7O_6$
Folic Acid

$C_{19}H_{28}O_2$
Testosterone

$C_{20}H_{30}O$
Retinol

$C_{27}H_{45}OH$
Cholesterol

$C_{28}H_{34}N_2O_3$
Denatonium Benzoate

$C_{29}H_{50}O$
Alpha-Tocopherol

$C_{35}H_{28}O_5N_4Mg$
Chlorophyll

$C_{35}H_{30}O_5N_4Mg$
Chlorophyll

$C_{40}H_{56}$
Beta-Carotene

$C_{54}H_{70}O_6N_4Mg$
Chlorophyll

$C_{55}H_{70}O_6N_4Mg$
Chlorophyll

$C_{55}H_{72}O_5N_4Mg$
Chlorophyll

$C_{63}H_{88}CoN_{14}O_{14}P$
Cyanocobalamin

$C_{76}H_{52}O_{46}$
Tannic Acid

$CaCO_3$
Calcium Carbonate

$CaHPO_4$
Calcium Phosphate

$CaO$
Calcium Oxide

$Ca(OH)_2$
Calcium Hydroxide

$CaSO_4$
Calcium Sulfate

$CaSiO_3$
Calcium Silicate

$Ca(H_2PO_4)_2$
Calcium Phosphate

$Ca_3(PO_4)_2$
Calcium Phosphate

$(ClC_6H_4)_2CHCCl_3$
Dichlorodiphenyltrichloroethane

$-ClO_4$
Perchlorates

$CuO$
Copper(II) Oxide

$CuSO_4$
Copper(II) Sulfate

$Cu_2O$
Copper(I) Oxide

$FeO$
Iron(II) Oxide

$Fe_2O_3$
Iron(III) Oxide

$HCHO$
Formaldehyde

$HCl$
Hydrogen Chloride

$HNO_3$
Nitric Acid

$HOH$
Water

HOOCCH$_2$C(OH)(COOH)CH$_2$COOH
 Citric Acid

HOOCCOOH
 Oxalic Acid

H$_2$O
 Water

H$_2$O$_2$
 Hydrogen Peroxide

H$_2$SO$_4$
 Sulfuric Acid

H$_3$BO$_3$
 Boric Acid

H$_3$PO$_4$
 Phosphoric Acid

HgS
 Mercury(II) Sulfide

KAl(SO$_4$)$_2$
 Aluminum Potassium Sulfate

KCl
 Potassium Chloride

KF
 Potassium Fluoride

KHCO$_3$
 Potassium Bicarbonate

KHC$_4$H$_4$O$_6$
 Potassium Bitartrate

KHSO$_4$
 Potassium Bisulfate

KI
 Potassium Iodide

KNO$_3$
 Potassium Nitrate

KOH
 Potassium Hydroxide

K$_2$CO$_3$ K$_{34}$NO$_{15}$
 Potassium Carbonate

K$_2$SO$_4$
 Potassium Sulfate

MgCl$_2$
 Magnesium Chloride

MgO
 Magnesium Oxide

Mg(OH)$_2$
 Magnesium Hydroxide

MgSO$_4$
 Magnesium Sulfate

Mg$_3$Si$_4$O$_{10}$(OH)$_2$
 Magnesium Silicate Hydroxide

(NH$_2$)$_2$CO
 Urea

NH$_3$
 Ammonia

(NH$_4$)$_2$SO$_4$
 Ammonium Sulfate

NH$_4$Cl
 Ammonium Chloride

NH$_4$NO$_3$
 Ammonium Nitrate

NH$_4$OH
 Ammonium Hydroxide

NO
 Nitric Oxide

NO$_2$
 Nitrogen Dioxide

N$_2$O
 Nitrous Oxide

NaBO$_3$
 Sodium Perborate

NaC$_2$H$_3$O$_2$
 Sodium Acetate

NaCl
 Sodium Chloride

NaClO
 Sodium Hypochlorite

NaF
 Sodium Fluoride

NaHCO$_3$
 Sodium Bicarbonate

NaH$_2$PO$_4$
 Sodium Phosphate

NaOH
 Sodium Hydroxide

Na$_2$B$_4$O$_7$
 Sodium Tetraborate

Na$_2$B$_4$O$_7$·10H$_2$O
 Sodium Tetraborate

Na$_2$CO$_3$
 Sodium Carbonate

Na$_2$HPO$_4$
 Sodium Phosphate

Na$_2$SO$_3$
 Sodium Sulfite

Na$_2$S$_2$O$_3$
 Sodium Thiosulfate

Na$_2$SiO$_3$
 Sodium Silicate

Na$_3$PO$_4$
 Sodium Phosphate

SO$_2$
 Sulfur Dioxide

SiO$_2$
 Silicon Dioxide

SnF$_2$
 Stannous Fluoride

ZnO
 Zinc Oxide

# Compounds by Element

## ALUMINUM

Aluminum Fluoride
Aluminum Hydroxide
Aluminum Oxide
Aluminum Potassium Sulfate

## BORON

Boric Acid
Sodium Perborate
Sodium Tetraborate

## CALCIUM

Calcium Carbonate
Calcium Hydroxide
Calcium Oxide
Calcium Phosphate
Calcium Silicate
Calcium Sulfate

## CARBON

1,3-Butadiene
2-(4-Isobutylphenyl)propionic
   Acid
2,2′-Dichlorodiethyl
   Sulfide
2,4,6-Trinitrotoluene
Acetaminophen
Acetic acid
Acetylene
Acetylsalicylic acid
Alpha-Tocopherol

Amoxicillin
Amyl Acetate
Amyl Nitrite
Ascorbic Acid
Benzene
Benzoic Acid
Beta-Carotene
Butane
Butyl Acetate
Butyl Mercaptan
Butylated Hydroxyanisole
   and Butylated
   Hydroxytoluene
Caffeine
Calcium Carbonate
Camphor
Carbon Dioxide
Carbon Monoxide
Carbon Tetrachloride
Cellulose
Cellulose Nitrate
Cellulose Xanthate
Chloroform
Chlorophyll
Cholesterol
Cinnamaldehyde
Citric Acid
Collagen
Cumene
Cyanoacrylate
Cyanocobalamin
Denatonium Benzoate
Dichlorodifluoromethane

Dichlorodiphenyltrichloro-
ethane
Dimethyl Ketone
Ethyl Acetate
Ethyl Alcohol
Ethylbenzene
Ethylene
Ethylene Glycol
Ethylene Oxide
Folic Acid
Formaldehyde
Fructose
Gamma-1,2,3,4,5,6-Hexachloro-
cyclohexane
Gelatin
Glucose
Glycerol
Hexane
Isoamyl Acetate
Isoprene
Isopropyl Alcohol
Lactic Acid
Lactose
L-Aspartyl-L-Phenylalanine
Methyl Ester
Luminol
Menthol
Methane
Methyl Alcohol
Methyl Mercaptan
Methyl-t-butyl Ether
Monosodium Glutamate
N,N-Diethyl-3-Methyl-
benzamide
Naphthalene
Naproxen
Niacin
Nicotine
Nitroglycerin
Nylon 6 and Nylon 66
Oxalic Acid
Pectin
Penicillin
Petrolatum
Petroleum
Phenol
Poly(Styrene-Butadiene-
Styrene)

Polycarbonates
Polyethylene
Polymethyl Methacrylate
Polypropylene
Polysiloxane
Polystyrene
Polytetrafluoroethylene
Polyurethane
Polyvinyl Chloride
Potassium Bicarbonate
Potassium Bitartrate
Potassium Carbonate
Propane
Propylene
Pyridoxine
Retinol
Riboflavin
Saccharin
Sodium Acetate
Sodium Bicarbonate
Sodium Carbonate
Sodium Cyclamate
Sodium Polyacrylate
Styrene
Sucrose
Sucrose Polyester
Tannic Acid
Testosterone
Theobromine
Thiamine
Toluene
Triclocarban
Triclosan
Urea
Vanillin

## CHLORINE

2,2′-Dichlorodiethyl Sulfide
Ammonium Chloride
Carbon Tetrachloride
Chloroform
Dichlorodifluoromethane
Dichlorodiphenyltrichloro-
ethane
Gamma-1,2,3,4,5,6-Hexachloro-
cyclohexane
Hydrogen Chloride

Magnesium Chloride
Perchlorates
Polyvinyl Chloride
Potassium Chloride
Sodium Chloride
Sodium Hypochlorite
Thiamine
Triclocarban
Triclosan

## COBALT

Cyanocobalamin

## COPPER

Copper(I) Oxide
Copper(II) Oxide
Copper(II) Sulfate

## FLUORINE

Aluminum Fluoride
Dichlorodifluoromethane
Polytetrafluoroethylene
Potassium Fluoride
Sodium Fluoride
Stannous Fluoride

## HYDROGEN

1,3-Butadiene
2-(4-Isobutylphenyl)propionic
Acid
2,2′-Dichlorodiethyl Sulfide
2,4,6-Trinitrotoluene
Acetaminophen
Acetic acid
Acetylene
Acetylsalicylic acid
Alpha-Tocopherol
Ammonia
Ammonium Chloride
Ammonium Hydroxide
Ammonium Nitrate
Ammonium Sulfate
Amoxicillin
Amyl Acetate
Amyl Nitrite
Ascorbic Acid

Benzene
Benzoic Acid
Beta-Carotene
Boric Acid
Butane
Butyl Acetate
Butyl Mercaptan
Butylated Hydroxyanisole and
   Butylated Hydroxytoluene
Caffeine
Calcium Hydroxide
Calcium Phosphate
Camphor
Cellulose
Cellulose Nitrate
Cellulose Xanthate
Chloroform
Chlorophyll
Cholesterol
Cinnamaldehyde
Citric Acid
Collagen
Cumene
Cyanoacrylate
Cyanocobalamin
Denatonium Benzoate
Dichlorodiphenyltrichloro-
   ethane
Dimethyl Ketone
Ethyl Acetate
Ethyl Alcohol
Ethylbenzene
Ethylene
Ethylene Glycol
Ethylene Oxide
Folic Acid
Formaldehyde
Fructose
Gamma-1,2,3,4,5,6-Hexachloro-
   cyclohexane
Gelatin
Glucose
Glycerol
Hexane
Hydrogen Chloride
Isoamyl Acetate
Isoprene
Isopropyl Alcohol

Lactic Acid
Lactose
L-Aspartyl-L-Phenylalanine
   Methyl Ester
Luminol
Magnesium Hydroxide
Magnesium Silicate
   Hydroxide
Menthol
Methane
Methyl Alcohol
Methyl Mercaptan
Methyl-t-butyl Ether
Monosodium Glutamate
N,N-Diethyl-3-Methyl-
   benzamide
Naphthalene
Naproxen
Niacin
Nicotine
Nitric Acid
Nitroglycerin
Nylon 6 and Nylon 66
Oxalic Acid
Pectin
Penicillin
Petrolatum
Petroleum
Phenol
Phosphoric Acid
Poly(Styrene-Butadiene-
   Styrene)
Polycarbonates
Polyethylene
Polymethyl
   Methacrylate
Polypropylene
Polysiloxane
Polystyrene
Polyurethane
Polyvinyl Chloride
Potassium Bicarbonate
Potassium Bisulfate
Potassium Bitartrate
Potassium Hydroxide
Propane
Propylene
Pyridoxine

Retinol
Riboflavin
Saccharin
Sodium Acetate
Sodium Bicarbonate
Sodium Cyclamate
Sodium Hydroxide
Sodium Polyacrylate
Styrene
Sucrose
Sucrose Polyester
Sulfuric Acid
Tannic Acid
Testosterone
Theobromine
Thiamine
Toluene
Triclocarban
Triclosan
Urea
Vanillin
Water

## IODINE

Potassium Iodide
Silver Iodide

## IRON

Iron(II) Oxide
Iron(III) Oxide

## MAGNESIUM

Chlorophyll
Magnesium Chloride
Magnesium Hydroxide
Magnesium Oxide
Magnesium Silicate
   Hydroxide
Magnesium Sulfate

## MERCURY

Mercury(II) Sulfide

## NITROGEN

2,4,6-Trinitrotoluene
Acetaminophen

Ammonia
Ammonium Chloride
Ammonium Hydroxide
Ammonium Nitrate
Ammonium Sulfate
Amoxicillin
Amyl Nitrite
Caffeine
Cellulose Nitrate
Chlorophyll
Collagen
Cyanoacrylate
Cyanocobalamin
Denatonium Benzoate
Folic Acid
Gelatin
L-Aspartyl-L-Phenylalanine
  Methyl Ester
Luminol
Monosodium Glutamate
N,N-Diethyl-3-Methyl-
  benzamide
Niacin
Nicotine
Nitric Acid
Nitric Oxide
Nitrogen Dioxide
Nitroglycerin
Nylon 6 and Nylon 66
Penicillin
Polyurethane
Potassium Nitrate
Pyridoxine
Riboflavin
Saccharin
Silver Nitrate
Sodium Cyclamate
Theobromine
Thiamine
Triclocarban
Urea
Nitrous Oxide

## OXYGEN

2-(4-Isobutylphenyl)propionic
  Acid
2,4,6-Trinitrotoluene
Acetaminophen

Acetic acid
Acetylsalicylic acid
Alpha-Tocopherol
Aluminum Hydroxide
Aluminum Potassium Sulfate
Aluminum Oxide
Ammonium Hydroxide
Ammonium Nitrate
Ammonium Sulfate
Amoxicillin
Amyl Acetate
Amyl Nitrite
Ascorbic Acid
Benzoic Acid
Boric Acid
Butyl Acetate
Butylated Hydroxyanisole
  and Butylated Hydro-
  xytoluene
Caffeine
Calcium Carbonate
Calcium Hydroxide
Calcium Oxide
Calcium Phosphate
Calcium Silicate
Calcium Sulfate
Camphor
Carbon Dioxide
Carbon Monoxide
Cellulose
Cellulose Nitrate
Cellulose Xanthate
Chlorophyll
Cholesterol
Cinnamaldehyde
Citric Acid
Collagen
Copper(I) Oxide
Copper(II) Oxide
Copper(II) Sulfate
Cyanoacrylate
Cyanocobalamin
Denatonium Benzoate
Dimethyl Ketone
Ethyl Acetate
Ethyl Alcohol
Ethylene Glycol
Ethylene Oxide

Folic Acid
Formaldehyde
Fructose
Gelatin
Glucose
Glycerol
Hydrogen Peroxide
Iron(II) Oxide
Iron(III) Oxide
Isoamyl Acetate
Isopropyl Alcohol
Lactic Acid
Lactose
L-Aspartyl-L-Phenylalanine
  Methyl Ester
Luminol
Magnesium Hydroxide
Magnesium Oxide
Magnesium Silicate
  Hydroxide
Magnesium Sulfate
Menthol
Methyl Alcohol
Methyl-t-butyl Ether
Monosodium Glutamate
N,N-Diethyl-3-Methyl-
  benzamide
Naproxen
Niacin
Nitric Acid
Nitric Oxide
Nitrogen Dioxide
Nitroglycerin
Nitrous Oxide
Nylon 6 and Nylon 66
Oxalic Acid
Pectin
Penicillin
Perchlorates
Petroleum
Phenol
Phosphoric Acid
Polycarbonates
Polymethyl Methacrylate
Polysiloxane
Polyurethane
Potassium Bicarbonate
Potassium Bisulfate

Potassium Bitartrate
Potassium Carbonate
Potassium Hydroxide
Potassium Nitrate
Potassium Sulfate
Pyridoxine
Retinol
Riboflavin
Saccharin
Silicon Dioxide
Silver Nitrate
Silver(I) Oxide
Sodium Acetate
Sodium Bicarbonate
Sodium Carbonate
Sodium Cyclamate
Sodium Hydroxide
Sodium Hypochlorite
Sodium Perborate
Sodium Phosphate
Sodium Polyacrylate
Sodium Silicate
Sodium Sulfite
Sodium Tetraborate
Sodium Thiosulfate
Sucrose
Sucrose Polyester
Sulfur Dioxide
Sulfuric Acid
Tannic Acid
Testosterone
Theobromine
Thiamine
Triclocarban
Triclosan
Urea
Vanillin
Water
Zinc Oxide

## PHOSPHORUS

Calcium Phosphate

Phosphoric Acid
Sodium Phosphate

## POTASSIUM

Aluminum Potassium
  Sulfate
Potassium Bicarbonate
Potassium Bisulfate
Potassium Bitartrate
Potassium Carbonate
Potassium Chloride
Potassium Fluoride
Potassium Hydroxide
Potassium Iodide
Potassium Nitrate
Potassium Sulfate

## SILICON

Calcium Silicate
Magnesium Silicate
  Hydroxide
Polysiloxane
Silicon Dioxide
Sodium Silicate

## SILVER

Silver Iodide
Silver Nitrate
Silver(I) Oxide
Silver(I) Sulfide

## SODIUM

Cellulose Xanthate
Monosodium Glutamate
Sodium Acetate
Sodium Bicarbonate
Sodium Carbonate
Sodium Chloride
Sodium Fluoride
Sodium Hydroxide

Sodium Hypochlorite
Sodium Perborate
Sodium Phosphate
Sodium Polyacrylate
Sodium Silicate
Sodium Sulfite
Sodium Tetraborate
Sodium Thiosulfate

## SULFUR

2,2'-Dichlorodiethyl
  Sulfide
Aluminum Potassium
  Sulfate
Ammonium Sulfate
Amoxicillin
Butyl Mercaptan
Calcium Sulfate
Cellulose Xanthate
Copper(II) Sulfate
Magnesium Sulfate
Mercury(II) Sulfide
Methyl Mercaptan
Penicillin
Potassium Bisulfate
Potassium Sulfate
Saccharin
Silver(I) Sulfide
Sodium Cyclamate
Sodium Sulfite
Sodium Thiosulfate
Sulfur Dioxide
Sulfuric Acid
Thiamine

## TIN

Stannous Fluoride

## ZINC

Zinc Oxide

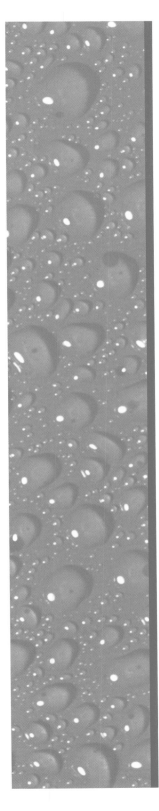

# Compounds by Type

## ACID

2-(4-Isobutylphenyl)propionic
  Acid
Acetic acid
Acetylsalicylic acid
Ascorbic Acid
Benzoic Acid
Boric Acid
Butyl Acetate
Citric Acid
Denatonium Benzoate
Folic Acid
Hydrogen Chloride
Lactic Acid
Naproxen
Niacin
Nitric Acid
Oxalic Acid
Penicillin
Phosphoric Acid
Potassium Bicarbonate
Potassium Bisulfate
Potassium Bitartrate
Sodium Bicarbonate
Sulfuric Acid
Tannic Acid

## ALCOHOL

Ethyl Alcohol
Ethylene Glycol
Glycerol
Isopropyl Alcohol
Menthol
Methyl Alcohol
Retinol

## ALDEHYDE

Cinnamaldehyde
Formaldehyde

## ALKALOID

Caffeine
Nicotine
Theobromine

## ALKANE

Butane
Hexane
Methane
Propane

## ALKENE

1,3-Butadiene
Ethylene
Propylene

## ALKYNE

Acetylene

## AMIDE

Acetaminophen

## BASE

Aluminum Hydroxide
Ammonia
Ammonium Hydroxide
Caffeine
Calcium Hydroxide
Magnesium Hydroxide
Potassium Hydroxide
Sodium Hydroxide
Theobromine

## CARBOHYDRATE

Cellulose
Cellulose Nitrate
Fructose
Glucose
Lactose
Sucrose

## CARBOXYLIC ACID

Acetic acid
Acetylsalicylic acid
Butyl Acetate
Citric Acid
Lactic Acid
Naproxen
Niacin
Oxalic Acid

## ESTER

Amyl Acetate
Amyl Nitrite
Cyanoacrylate
Ethyl Acetate
Isoamyl Acetate
L-Aspartyl-L-Phenylalanine
   Methyl Ester
Nitroglycerin

## ETHER

Ethylene Oxide
Methyl-t-butyl Ether
Vanillin

## HYDROCARBON

1,3-Butadiene
Acetylene
Benzene
Beta-Carotene
Butane
Cumene
Ethylbenzene
Ethylene
Hexane
Isoprene
Methane
Naphthalene
Propane
Propylene
Styrene
Toluene

## INORGANIC

Aluminum Fluoride
Aluminum Hydroxide
Aluminum Oxide
Aluminum Potassium Sulfate
Ammonia
Ammonium Chloride
Ammonium Hydroxide
Ammonium Nitrate
Ammonium Sulfate
Boric Acid
Calcium Carbonate
Calcium Hydroxide
Calcium Oxide
Calcium Phosphate
Calcium Silicate
Calcium Sulfate
Carbon Dioxide
Carbon Monoxide
Copper(I) Oxide
Copper(II) Oxide
Copper(II) Sulfate
Hydrogen Chloride
Iron(II) Oxide
Iron(III) Oxide
Magnesium Chloride
Magnesium Hydroxide
Magnesium Oxide
Magnesium Silicate Hydroxide
Magnesium Sulfate
Mercury(II) Sulfide
Nitric Acid
Nitric Oxide
Nitrogen Dioxide
Nitrous Oxide
Perchlorates
Phosphoric Acid
Polysiloxane
Potassium Bicarbonate
Potassium Bisulfate
Potassium Bitartrate
Potassium Carbonate
Potassium Chloride
Potassium Fluoride
Potassium Hydroxide
Potassium Iodide
Potassium Nitrate
Potassium Sulfate
Silicon Dioxide
Silver Iodide
Silver Nitrate
Silver(I) Oxide
Silver(I) Sulfide
Sodium Acetate
Sodium Bicarbonate
Sodium Carbonate
Sodium Chloride
Sodium Fluoride
Sodium Hydroxide
Sodium Hypochlorite
Sodium Perborate
Sodium Phosphate
Sodium Silicate
Sodium Sulfite
Sodium Tetraborate
Sodium Thiosulfate
Stannous Fluoride
Sulfur Dioxide
Sulfuric Acid
Water
Zinc Oxide

## KETONE

Camphor
Dimethyl Ketone

## METALLIC OXIDE

Aluminum Oxide
Calcium Oxide
Copper(I) Oxide
Copper(II) Oxide
Iron(II) Oxide
Iron(III) Oxide
Magnesium Oxide
Silver(I) Oxide
Zinc Oxide

## NONMETALLIC OXIDE

Carbon Dioxide
Carbon Monoxide
Hydrogen Peroxide
Nitric Oxide
Nitrogen Dioxide
Nitrous Oxide
Silicon Dioxide
Sulfur Dioxide

## ORGANIC

1,3-Butadiene
2-(4-Isobutylphenyl)propionic
  Acid
2,2′-Dichlorodiethyl Sulfide
2,4,6-Trinitrotoluene
Acetaminophen
Acetic acid
Acetylene
Acetylsalicylic acid
Alpha-Tocopherol
Amoxicillin
Amyl Acetate
Amyl Nitrite
Ascorbic Acid
Benzene
Benzoic Acid
Beta-Carotene
Butane
Butyl Acetate
Butyl Mercaptan
Butylated Hydroxyanisole and
  Butylated Hydroxytoluene
Caffeine
Camphor

Carbon Tetrachloride
Cellulose
Cellulose Nitrate
Cellulose Xanthate
Chloroform
Chlorophyll
Cholesterol
Cinnamaldehyde
Citric Acid
Collagen
Cumene
Cyanoacrylate
Cyanocobalamin
Denatonium
  Benzoate
Dichlorodifluoromethane
Dichlorodiphenyltrichloro-
  ethane
Dimethyl Ketone
Ethyl Acetate
Ethyl Alcohol
Ethylbenzene
Ethylene
Ethylene Glycol
Ethylene Oxide
Folic Acid
Formaldehyde
Fructose
Gamma-1,2,3,4,5,6-Hexachloro-
  cyclohexane
Glucose
Glycerol
Hexane
Hydrogen Peroxide
Isoamyl Acetate
Isoprene
Isopropyl Alcohol
Lactic Acid
Lactose
L-Aspartyl-L-Phenylalanine
  Methyl Ester
Luminol
Menthol
Methane
Methyl Alcohol
Methyl Mercaptan
Methyl-t-butyl Ether
Monosodium Glutamate

N,N-Diethyl-3-Methylbenza-
  mide
Naphthalene
Naproxen
Niacin
Nicotine
Nitroglycerin
Nylon 6 and Nylon 66
Oxalic Acid
Penicillin
Phenol
Poly(Styrene-Butadiene-
  Styrene)
Polycarbonates
Polyethylene
Polymethyl Methacrylate
Polypropylene
Polystyrene
Polytetrafluoroethylene
Polyurethane
Polyvinyl Chloride
Propane
Propylene
Pyridoxine
Retinol
Riboflavin
Saccharin
Sodium Cyclamate
Sodium Polyacrylate
Styrene
Sucrose
Sucrose Polyester
Tannic Acid
Testosterone
Theobromine
Thiamine
Toluene
Triclocarban
Triclosan
Urea
Vanillin

## PHENOL

Butylated Hydroxyanisole
  and Butylated Hydroxy-
  toluene
Phenol

## POLYMER

Cellulose
Cellulose Nitrate
Cellulose Xanthate
Nylon 6 and Nylon 66
Poly(Styrene-Butadiene-
    Styrene)
Polycarbonates
Polyethylene
Polymethyl Methacrylate
Polypropylene
Polysiloxane
Polystyrene
Polytetrafluoroethylene
Polyurethane
Polyvinyl Chloride
Sodium Polyacrylate

## SALT

Aluminum Fluoride
Aluminum Potassium Sulfate
Ammonium Chloride
Ammonium Nitrate
Ammonium Sulfate
Calcium Carbonate
Calcium Phosphate
Calcium Silicate
Calcium Sulfate
Copper(II) Sulfate
Magnesium Chloride
Magnesium Silicate
    Hydroxide
Magnesium Sulfate
Mercury(II) Sulfide
Monosodium Glutamate
Perchlorates
Potassium Bicarbonate
Potassium Bisulfate
Potassium Bitartrate
Potassium Carbonate
Potassium Chloride
Potassium Fluoride
Potassium Iodide
Potassium Nitrate
Potassium Sulfate
Silver Iodide
Silver Nitrate
Silver(I) Sulfide
Sodium Acetate
Sodium Bicarbonate
Sodium Carbonate
Sodium Chloride
Sodium Cyclamate
Sodium Fluoride
Sodium Hypochlorite
Sodium Perborate
Sodium Phosphate
Sodium Silicate
Sodium Sulfite
Sodium Tetraborate
Sodium Thiosulfate
Stannous Fluoride

## VITAMIN

Alpha-Tocopherol
Ascorbic Acid
Cyanocobalamin
Folic Acid
Niacin
Pyridoxine
Retinol
Riboflavin
Thiamine

# for further information

## BOOKS

Attenborough, David. *The Private Life of Plants.* Princeton, NJ: Princeton University Press, 1995.

Brody, Tom. *Nutritional Biochemistry.* San Diego: Academic Press, 1998.

Buchanan, B. B., W. Gruissem, and R. L. Jones. *Biochemistry and Molecular Biology of Plants.* Rockville, MD: American Society of Plant Physiologists, 2000.

Buechel, K. H., et al. *Industrial Inorganic Chemistry.* New York: VCH, 2000.

Buschmann, Helmut, et al. *Analgesics: From Chemistry and Pharmacology to Clinical Application.* New York: Wiley-VCH, 2002.

Butler, A. R., and R. Nicholson. *Life, Death and Nitric Oxide.* London: Royal Society of Chemistry, 2003.

Cagin, Seth, and Philip Dray. *Between Earth and Sky: How CFCs Changed Our World and Endangered the Ozone Layer.* New York: Pantheon Books, 1993.

Carpenter, Kenneth J. *The History of Scurvy and Vitamin C.* Cambridge, UK: Cambridge University Press, 1986.

Carson, Rachel. *Silent Spring.* Boston: Houghton Mifflin, 1962.

Cavitch, Susan Miller. *The Natural Soap Book: Making Herbal and Vegetable-Based Soaps*. Markham, Canada: Storey Publishing, 1995.

Challem, Jack, and Melissa Diane Smith. *Basic Health Publications User's Guide to Vitamin E: Don't Be a Dummy: Become an Expert on What Vitamin E Can Do for Your Health*. North Bergen, NJ: Basic Health Publications, 2002.

Chalmers, Louis. *Household and Industrial Chemical Specialties*. Vol. 1. New York: Chemical Publishing Co., Inc., 1978.

Cherniske, Stephen. *Caffeine Blues: Wake Up to the Hidden Dangers of America's #1 Drug*. New York: Warner Books, 1998.

"Cholesterol, Other Lipids, and Lipoproteins." In *In-Depth Report*. Edited by Julia Goldrosen. Atlanta: A.D.A.M., 2004.

Cooper, P. W., and S. R. Kurowski. *Introduction to the Technology of Explosives*. New York: Wiley-VCH, 1997.

Cornell, Rochelle M., and Udo Schwertmann. *The Iron Oxides: Structure, Properties, Reactions, and Uses*, 2nd ed. New York: Wiley-VCH, 2003.

*CRC Handbook of Chemistry and Physics*. David R. Lide, editor in chief. 86th ed. Boca Raton, FL: Taylor & Francis, 2005.

Dean, Carolyn. *The Miracle of Magnesium*. New York: Ballantine Books, 2003.

Dick, John S., and R. A. Annicelli, eds. *Rubber Technology: Compounding and Testing for Performance*. Cincinnati, OH: Hanser Gardner Publications, 2001.

Dunlap, Thomas. *DDT: Scientists, Citizens, and Public Policy*. Princeton, NJ: Princeton University Press, 1983.

Dwyer, Bob, et al. *Carbon Monoxide: A Clear and Present Danger*. Mount Prospect, IL: ESCO Press, 2004.

Eades, Mary Dan. *The Doctor's Complete Guide to Vitamins and Minerals*. New York: Dell, 2000.

Environment Canada, Health Canada. *Ethylene Oxide*. Ottawa: Environment Canada, 2001.

*Food Antioxidants: Technological, Toxicological, and Health Perspectives*, D. L. Madhavi, S. S. Deshpande, and D. K. Salunkhe, eds. New York: Dekker, 1996.

Gahlinger, Paul M. *Illegal Drugs: A Complete Guide to Their History*. Salt Lake City, UT: Sagebrush Press, 2001.

Genge, Ngaire E. *The Forensic Casebook: The Science of Crime Scene Investigation*. New York: Ballantine, 2002.

Grimm, Tom, and Michele Grimm. *The Basic Book of Photography*. New York: Plume Books, 2003.

Harte, John, et al. *Toxics A to Z.* Berkeley: University of California Press, 1991.

Hermes, Matthew E. *Enough for One Lifetime: Wallace Carothers, Inventor of Nylon.* Philadelphia: Chemical Heritage Foundation, 1996.

Holgate, S. T., et al. *Air Pollution and Health.* New York: Academic Press, 1999.

Hyne, Norman J. *Nontechnical Guide to Petroleum Geology, Exploration, Drilling and Production*, 2nd ed. Tulsa, OK: Pennwell Books, 2001.

Jeffreys, Diarmuid. *Aspirin: The Remarkable Story of a Wonder Drug.* New York: Bloomsbury, 2004.

Johnson, Peter S. *Rubber Processing: An Introduction.* Cincinnati, OH: Hanser Gardner Publications, 2001.

Karger-Kocsis, J. *Polypropylene—An A-Z Reference.* New York: Springer-Verlag, 1998.

*Kirk-Othmer Encyclopedia of Chemical Technology*, 4th ed. New York: John Wiley & Sons, 1991.

Knox, J. Paul, and Graham B. Seymour, eds. *Pectins and Their Manipulation.* Boca Raton, FL: CFC Press, June 2002.

Kurlansky, Mark. *Salt: A World History.* New York: Walker, 2002.

Leffler, William L. *Petroleum Refining in Nontechnical Language.* Tulsa, OK: Pennwell Books, 2000.

Mead, Clifford, and Thomas Hager, eds. *Linus Pauling: Scientist and Peacemaker.* Portland, OR: Oregon State University Press, 2001.

Mebane, Robert C., and Thomas R. Rybolt. *Plastics and Polymers.* New York: Twenty-First Century, 1995.

Meikle, Jeffrey L. *American Plastic: A Cultural History.* New Brunswick, NJ: Rutgers University Press, 1995.

Menhard, Francha Roffe. *The Facts about Inhalants.* New York: Benchmark Books, 2004.

Misra, Chanakya. *Industrial Alumina Chemicals.* Washington, DC: American Chemical Society, 1986.

*Mosby's Medical, Nursing, and Allied Health Dictionary*, 5th ed. St. Louis: Mosby, 1998.

Multhauf, Robert P., and Christine M. Roane. "Nitrates." In *Dictionary of American History.* 3rd ed., vol. 6. Stanley I. Kutler, ed. New York: Charles Scribner's Sons, 2003.

Nabors, Lyn O'Brien, ed. *Alternative Sweeteners (Food Science and Technology)*, 3rd rev. London: Marcel Dekker, 2001.

Packer, Lester, and Carol Colman. *The Antioxidant Miracle: Put Lipoic Acid, Pycogenol, and Vitamins E and C to Work for You.* New York: Wiley, 1999.

Patnaik, Pradyot. *Handbook of Inorganic Chemicals.* New York: McGraw-Hill, 2003.

Rain, Patricia. *Vanilla: A Cultural History of the World's Most Popular Flavor and Fragrance.* Edited by Jeremy P. Tarcher. New York: Penguin Group USA, 2004.

Rainsford, K. D., ed. *Ibuprofen: A Critical Bibliographic Review.* Bethesda, MD: CCR Press, 1999.

Richardson, H. W., ed. *Handbook of Copper Compounds and Applications.* New York: Marcel Dekker, 1997.

Sherman, Josepha, and Steve Brick. *Fossil Fuel Power.* Mankato, MN: Capstone Press, 2003.

Snyder, C. H. *The Extraordinary Chemistry of Ordinary Things*, 4th ed. New York: John Wiley and Sons, 2002.

Strange, Veronica. *The Meaning of Water.* Oxford, UK: Berg Publishers, 2004.

Stratmann, Linda. *Chloroform: The Quest for Oblivion.* Phoenix Mill, UK: Sutton Publishing Co., 2003.

Tegethoff, F. Wolfgana, with Johannes Rohleder and Evelyn Kroker, eds. *Calcium Carbonate: From the Cretaceous Period into the 21st Century.* Boston: Birkhäuser Verlag, 2001.

Tyman, J. H. P. *Synthetic and Natural Phenols.* Amsterdam: Elsevier, 1996.

Ware, George W. *The Pesticide Book.* Batavia, IL: Mesiter, 1999.

Weinberg, Alan Bennet, and Bonnie K. Bealer. *The World of Caffeine: The Science and Culture of the World's Most Popular Drug.* New York: Routledge, 2002.

Weissermel, Klaus, and Hans-Jürgen Arpe. *Industrial Organic Chemistry.* Weinheim, Germany: Wiley-VCH, 2003, 117-122.

Wyman, Carolyn. *JELL-O: A Biography.* Fort Washington, PA: Harvest Books, 2001.

## PERIODICALS

"Another Old-Fashioned Product Vindicates Itself." *Medical Update* (October 1992): 6.

Arnst, Catherine. "A Preemptive Strike against Cancer." *Business Week* (June 7, 2004): 48.

Baker, Linda. "The Hole in the Sky (Ozone Layer)." *E* (November 2000): 34.

Bauman, Richard. "Getting Skunked: Understanding the Antics behind the Smell." *Backpacker* (May 1993): 30-31.

Drake, Geoff. "The Lactate Shuttle—Contrary to What You've Heard, Lactic Acid Is Your Friend." *Bicycling* (August 1992): 36.

Fox, Berry. "Not Fade Away." *New Scientist* (March 1, 2003); 40.

"Global Ethyl, Butyl Acetate Demand Expected to Rebound." *The Oil and Gas Journal* (April 24, 2000): 27.

Gorman, Christine. "The Bomb Lurking in the Garden Shed." *Time* (May 1, 1995): 54.

Karaim, Reed. "Not So Fast with the DDT: Rachel Carson's Warnings Still Apply." *American Scholar* (June 2005): 53-60.

Keenan, Faith. "Blocking Liver Damage." *Business Week* (October 21, 2002): 147.

Kluger, Jeffrey. "The Buzz on Caffeine." *Time* (December 20, 2004): 52.

Lazear, N. R. "Polycarbonate: High-Performance Resin." *Advanced Materials & Processes* (February 1995): 43-45.

Legwold, Gary. "Hydration Breakthrough." *Bicycling* (July 1994): 72-73.

Liu, Guanghua. "Chinese Cinnabar." *The Mineralogical Record* (January-February 2005): 69-80.

Malakoff, David. "Public Health: Aluminum Is Put on Trial as a Vaccine Booster." *Science* (May 26, 2000): 1323.

Mardis, Anne L. "Current Knowledge of the Health Effects of Sugar Intake." *Family Economics and Nutrition Review* (Winter 2001): 88-91.

McGinn, Anne Platt. "Malaria, Mosquitoes, and DDT: The Toxic War against a Global Disease." *World Watch* (May 1, 2002): 10-17.

Metcalfe, Ed, et al. "Sweet Talking." *The Ecologist* (June 2000): 16.

Milius, Susan. "Termites Use Mothballs in Their Nests." *Science News* (May 2, 1998): 228.

Neff, Natalie. "No Laughing Matter." *Auto Week* (May 19, 2003): 30.

"Nitroglycerin: Dynamite for the Heart." *Chemistry Review* (November 1999): 28.

O'Neil, John. "And It Doesn't Taste Bad, Either." *New York Times* (November 30, 2004): F9.

Pae, Peter. "Sobering Side of Laughing Gas." *Washington Post* (September 16, 1994): B1.

Palvetz, Barry A. "A Bowl of Hope, Bucket of Hype?" *The Scientist* (April 2, 2001): 15.

Rawls, Rebecca. "Nitroglycerin Explained." *Chemical & Engineering News* (June 10, 2002): 12.

Rowley, Brian. "Fizzle or Sizzle? Potassium Bicarbonate Could Help Spare Muscle and Bone." *Muscle & Fitness* (December 2002): 72.

Russell, Justin. "Fuel of the Forgotten Deaths." *New Scientist* (February 6, 1993): 21-23.

Schramm, Daniel. "The North American USP Petrolatum Industry." *Soap & Cosmetics*, (January 2002): 60-63.

Stanley, Peter. "Nitric Oxide." *Biological Sciences Review* (April 2002): 18-20.

"The Stink that Stays." *Popular Mechanics* (December 2004): 26.

Strobel, Warren P. "Saddam's Lingering Atrocity." *U.S. News & World Report* (November 27, 2000): 52.

"Strong Muscle and Bones." *Prevention* (June 1, 1995): 70-73.

"Taking Supplements of the Antioxidant." *Consumer Reports* (September 2003): 49.

Travis, J. "Cool Discovery: Menthol Triggers Cold-Sensing Protein." *Science News* (February 16, 2002): 101-102.

U.S. Department of Health and Human Services. "Methanol Toxicity." *American Family Physician* (January 1993): 163-171.

"Unusual Thermal Defence by a Honeybee against Mass Attack by Hornets." *Nature* (September 28, 1995): 334-336.

"USDA Approves Phosphate to Reduce Salmonella in Chicken." *Environmental Nutrition* (February 1993): 3.

Vartan, Starre. "Pretty in Plastic: Pleather Is a Versatile, though Controversial, Alternative to eather." *E* (September-October 2002): 53-54.

"Vitamins: The Quest for Just the Right Amount." *Harvard Health Letter* (June 2004): 1.

Walter, Patricia A. "Dental Hypersensitivity: A Review." *The Journal of Contemporary Dental Practice* (May 15, 2005): 107-117.

Young, Jay A. "Copper (II) Sulfate Pentahydrate." *Journal of Chemical Education* (February 2002): 158.

## WEBSITES

"The A to Z of Materials." Sydney, Australia: Azom.com. http://www.azom.com/ (accessed on March 1, 2006).

"Air Toxics Website." U.S. Environmental Protection Agency Technology Transfer Network http://www.epa.gov/ttn/atw/ (accessed on March 10, 2006).

Calorie Control Council. Atlanta, GA: Calorie Control Council. http://www.caloriecontrol.org/

CHEC's Health*e*House: The Resource for Environmental Health Risks Affecting Your Children. Los Angeles, CA: Children's Health Environmental Coalition. http://www.checnet.org/ehouse (accessed on March 13, 2006).

Chemfinder.com. Cambridge, MA: CambridgeSoft Corporation. http://www.chemfinder.cambridgesoft.com (accessed on March 13, 2006).

"Chemical Backgrounders." Itasca, IL: National Safety Council. http://www.nsc.org/library/chemical/ (accessed on March 1, 2006).

"Chemical Profiles." Scorecard. The Pollution Information Site. Washington, DC: Green Media Toolshed. http://www.scorecard.org/chemical-profiles/ (accessed on March 1, 2006).

The Chemistry Store. Cayce, SC: ChemistryStore.com, Inc. http://www.chemistrystore.com/ (accessed on March 13, 2006).

Chemistry.org. Washington, DC: American Chemical Society. http://www.chemistry.org/portal/a/c/s/1/home.html (accessed on March 13, 2006).

Cheresources.com: Online Chemical Engineering Information. Midlothian, VA: The Chemical Engineers' Resource Page. http://www.cheresources.com (accessed on March 13, 2006).

"Dietary Supplement Fact Sheets." Bethesda, MD: U.S. National Institutes of Health, Office of Dietary Supplements. http://ods.od.nih.gov/Health_Information/Information_About_Individual_Dietary_Supplements.aspx (accessed on March 13, 2006).

Drugs.com. Auckland, New Zealand: Drugsite Trust. http://www.drugs.com (accessed on March 13, 2006).

EnvironmentalChemistry.com. Portland, ME: Environmental Chemistry.com. http://environmentalchemistry.com (accessed on March 13, 2006).

Exploratorium: the museum of science, art and human perception. San Francisco, CA: Exploratorium at the Palace of Fine Arts. http://www.exploratorium.edu/ (accessed on March 13, 2006).

ExToxNet: The Extension Toxicology Network. Corvallis, OR: Oregon State University. http://extoxnet.orst.edu/ (accessed on March 13, 2006).

Fibersource: The Manufactured Fibers Industry. Arlington, VA: Fiber Economics Bureau. http://www.fibersource.com (accessed on March 13, 2006).

General Chemistry Online. Frostburg, MD: Frostburg State University, Department of Chemistry. http://antoine.frostburg.edu/chem/senese/101/index.shtml (accessed on March 13, 2006).

Household Products Database. Bethesda, MD: U.S. National Library of Medicine. http://householdproducts.nlm.nih.gov/ (accessed on March 13, 2006).

Integrated Risk Information System. Washington, DC: U.S. Environmental Protection Agency. http://www.epa.gov/iris/index.html (accessed on March 13, 2006).

"International Chemical Safety Cards (ICSCs)." Geneva, Switzerland: International Labour Organization. http://www.ilo.org/public/english/protection/safework/cis/products/icsc/index.htm (accessed on March 1, 2006).

"International Chemical Safety Cards." Atlanta, GA: U.S. National Institute for Occupational Safety and Health. http://www.cdc.gov/niosh/ipcs/icstart.html (accessed on March 1, 2006).

IPCS INTOX Databank. Geneva, Switzerland: International Programme on Chemical Safety. http://www.intox.org/ (accessed on March 13, 2006).

Kimball's Biology Pages. Andover, MA: John W. Kimball. http://biology-pages.info (accessed on March 13, 2006).

Linus Pauling Institute Micronutrient Information Center. Corvallis, OR: Oregon State University, Linus Pauling Institute. http://lpi.oregonstate.edu/infocenter/ (accessed on March 13, 2006).

MadSci Network. Boston, MA: Third Sector New England. http://www.madsci.org (accessed on March 13, 2006).

Medline Plus. Bethesda, MD: U.S. National Library of Medicine. http://www.nlm.nih.gov/medlineplus (accessed on March 1, 2006).

Mineral Information Institute. Golden, CO: Mineral Information Institute. http://www.mii.org (accessed March 13, 2006).

Mineralogy Database. Spring, TX: Webmineral.com. http://webmineral.com/ (accessed on March 13, 2006).

"Molecule of the Month Page." Bristol, United Kingdom: University of Bristol School of Chemistry. http://www.chm.bris.ac.uk/motm/motm.htm (accessed on March 1, 2006).

National Historic Chemical Landmarks. Washington, DC: American Chemical Society. http://acswebcontent.acs.org/landmarks/index.html (accessed on March 13, 2006).

NIST Chemistry Webbook. Gaithersburg, MD: U.S. National Institute of Standards and Technology. http://webbook.nist.gov (accessed on March 13, 2006).

PAN Pesticides Database. San Francisco, CA: Pesticide Action Network, North America. http://www.pesticideinfo.org (accessed March 13, 2006).

"Polymer Science Learning Center." Hattiesburg, Mississippi: University of Southern Mississippi, Department of Polymer Science. http://www.pslc.ws/ (accessed on March 13, 2006).

PubChem. Bethesda, MD: U.S. National Library of Medicine. http://pubchem.ncbi.nlm.nih.gov/ (accessed on March 13, 2006).

Reciprocal.net. Bloomington, IN: Indiana University Molecular Structure Center. http://www.reciprocalnet.org/ (accessed on March 13, 2006).

The Science Center: A Teacher's Guide to Educational Resources on the Internet. Arlington, VA: Chlorine Chemistry Council. http://www.science-education.org (accessed on March 13, 2006).

Shakhashiri, Bassam Z. "Chemical of the Week." Science Is Fun. Madison, WI: University of Wisconsin. http://scifun.chem. wisc. edu/chemweek/chemweek.html (accessed on March 13, 2006).

3Dchem.com. Oxford, United Kingdom: University of Oxford, Department of Chemistry. http://www.3dchem.com (accessed on March 13, 2006).

"ToxFAQs™" Atlanta, GA: U.S. Agency for Toxic Substances and Disease Registry. http://www.atsdr.cdc.gov/toxfaq.html (accessed on March 13, 2006).

"Toxicological Profile Information Sheets." Atlanta, GA: U.S. Agency for Toxic Substances and Disease Registry. http://www.atsdr.cdc.gov/toxpro2.html (accessed on March 1, 2006).

TOXNET: Toxicology Data Network. Bethesda, MD: U.S. National Library of Medicine. http://toxnet.nlm.nih.gov (accessed on March 13, 2006).

World of Molecules Home Page. http://www.worldofmolecules.com/ (accessed on March 13, 2006).

# index

*This index is sorted word-by-word.* Italic *type indicates volume numbers;* **boldface** *indicates main entries; (ill.) indicates illustrations.*

Abbott Laboratories, *3:*742

Abrasives, *1:*50

Acetaminophen, *1:***19-22**, 20 (ill.)

Acetic acid, *1:***23-26**, 24 (ill.)

Acetone, *1:*289-291

Acetylene, *1:***27-30**, 28 (ill.)

Acetylsalicylic acid, *1:***31-35**, 32 (ill.)

Acid rain, *1:*149, 153; *2:*499; *3:*822

Activated charcoal, *2:*457

Adenosine, *1:*140

Advil, *1:*11

Alarm pheromones, *1:*127

Albrecht, H.O., *2:*407

Alcohol, *2:*297-301, 449-453

Aleve, *2:*477

Alka-Seltzer, *3:*726

Alkenes, *2:*307-311

Alpha-tocopherol, *1:***37-40**, 38 (ill.)

Aluminum fluoride, *1:***41-44**, 42 (ill.)

Aluminum hydroxide, *1:***45-48**, 46 (ill.), 50

Aluminum metal, *1:*42, 50-51

Aluminum oxide, *1:***49-52**, 50 (ill.)

Aluminum potassium sulfate, *1:***53-56**, 54 (ill.)

Amatol, *1*:18

Ammonia, *1*:**57-61**, 58 (ill.), 69-71,
   73-74; *2*:446; *3*:761-762, 868-869

Ammonia-soda process, *1*:64

Ammonium chloride, *1*:**63-67**, 64 (ill.)

Ammonium hydroxide, *1*:**69-71**, 70 (ill.)

Ammonium nitrate, *1*:**73-76**, 74 (ill.); *2*:495

Ammonium perchlorate, *2*:541-542

Ammonium sulfate, *1*:**77-80**, 78 (ill.)

Amoxicillin, *1*:**81-84**, 82 (ill.)

Amyl acetate, *1*:**85-88**, 86 (ill.)

Amyl nitrite, *1*:**89-92**, 90 (ill.)

Analgesics, *1*:9-13, 19-22, 31-34

Andrews, Edmund, *2*:514

Anesthetics, *1*:211-212; *2*:514-515

ANFO (Ammonium nitrate fuel oil), *1*:75

Angina, treatment of, *1*:90

Anhydrous calcium sulfate, *1*:165-169

Animal feeds, *3*:652, 661, 870

Antacids
   aluminum hydroxide, *1*:45-46
   calcium carbonate, *1*:144
   magnesium hydroxide, *2*:416-417
   potassium bicarbonate, *3*:621-622
   sodium bicarbonate, *3*:726

Anti-inflammatories, *1*:9

Antibiotics, *1*:81-84; *2*:535-539

Antifouling agents, *1*:248

Antifreeze, *2*:315

Antioxidants, *1*:38, 110, 135

Antiseptics, *1*:117, 261; *2*:365;
   *3*:652, 859-865

Arm & Hammer, *3*:724

Armstrong, Henry E., *1*:1

Aromatic hydrocarbons, *1*:255-258;
   *2*:303-306

Ascorbic acid, *1*:**93-97**, 94 (ill.)

Aspartame, *2*:401-405

Asphyxiants, *1*:27-30

Aspirin, *1*:31-35

Astringents, *1*:54; *3*:834

Atlantic Richfield Corp., *2*:459

Avery, Charles E., *2*:392

Azeotropic mixtures, *2*:459-461

**B**

Bad breath, *2*:457

Baekeland, Leo Hendrik, *2*:561

Baking soda, *3*:723-727

Banks, Robert, *2*:580, 582, 588

Baratol, *1*:18

Barnes, W., *1*:271

BASF Corp., *1*:28; *3*:598

Bauxite, *1*:45, 49

Bayer, Otto, *3*:610

Bayer AG Co., *1*:33; *2*:576

Beadle, Clayton, *1*:196, 207

Beecham lab, *1*:83

Bees, *2*:379

Béguin, Jean, *1*:289

Ben-Gay, *1*:173

Benzene, *1*:**99-103**, 100 (ill.); *3*:855

Benzoic acid, *1*:**105-108**, 106 (ill.)

Beriberi, *3*:847-851

Berthollet, Claude Louis, *1*:57; *3*:760

Berzelius, Jons Jakob, *3*:853

Beta-carotene, *1*:**109-113**, 110 (ill.); *3*:678-680

Bevan, Edward John, *1*:196, 207

B.F. Goodrich, *2*:384; *3*:616-617

BHA, *1*:133-136

BHT, *1*:133-136

Bishop, Katherine Scott, *1*:38

Bitrex, *1*:271-274

Black, Joseph, *1*:151, 177-178

Black Leaf 40, *2*:489

Black mercury(II) sulfide, *2*:439-442

Bleaches, *2*:365; *3*:761, 796, 820

Block copolymers, *2*:571-574

Blyth, Alexander Wynter, *3*:683

Bock, Walter, *2*:572

Bondt, N., *2*:307

Boots Co., *1*:9-11

Borax, *1*:116; *3*:789-792

Boric acid, *1*:**115-118**, 116 (ill.)

Bosch, Carl, *1*:58

Boyle, Robert, *2*:451, 513; *3*:659

Braconnot, Henri, *1*:196

Breast implants, *2*:594

Bristol-Meyers, *1*:11

Brown-Séquard, *3*:837-838

Brucite, *2:*415

Brunton, Sir Thomas Lauder, *2:*508

Büchner, Johann, *1:*32

Buffering agents, *3:*721

Building products, chemicals in
  calcium carbonate, *1:*145
  calcium hydroxide, *1:*148
  calcium silicate, *1:*162-163, 167-168
  polystyrene, *3:*599
  polyvinyl chloride, *3:*618
  silicon dioxide, *3:*698

Bussy, Antoine, *1:*289

Butane, *1:119-123,* 120 (ill.)

Butenandt, Adolf Friedrich Johann, *3:*838

Butlerov, Alexander Mikhailovich, *2:*325

Butyl acetate, *1:125-128,* 126 (ill.)

Butyl mercaptan, *1:129-132,* 130 (ill.)

Butylated hydroxyanisole (BHA), *1:133-136,* 134 (ill.)

Butylated hydroxytoluenene (BHT), *1:133-136,* 134 (ill.)


## C

Caffeine, *1:137-141,* 138 (ill.); *3:*843-846

Calcium carbonate, *1:143-146,* 144 (ill.), 151-152, 178

Calcium hydroxide, *1:147-150,* 148 (ill.)

Calcium magnesium acetate, *1:*25

Calcium oxide, *1:151-155,* 152 (ill.)

Calcium phosphate, *1:155-159,* 156 (ill.)

Calcium silicate, *1:161-164,* 162 (ill.)

Calcium sulfate, *1:165-169,* 166 (ill.)

Calcium sulfate dihydrate, *1:*165-169

Calcium sulfate hemihydrate, *1:*165-169

Campho-phenique, *1:*173

Camphor, *1:171-175,* 172 (ill.)

Carbohydrates. *See* Sugars

Carbolic acid, *2:*559-563

Carbon dioxide, *1:177-181,* 178 (ill.)

Carbon monoxide, *1:183-187,* 184 (ill.)

Carbon tetrachloride, *1:189-193,* 190 (ill.)

Carbonation of beverages, *1:*179

Carcinogens
  benzene, *1:*102
  carbon tetrachloride, *1:*192
  chloroform, *1:*214
  dichlorodiphenyltrichloroethane (DDT), *1:*283-287
  ethylene oxide, *2:*320
  formaldehyde, *2:*327
  gamma-1,2,3,4,5,6-hexachlorocyclohexane, *2:*335
  isoprene, *2:*384
  methyl-t-butyl-ether, *2:*462
  polyvinyl chloride, *3:*619
  saccharin, *3:*691
  styrene, *3:*805
  triclocarban, *3:*861
  triclosan, *3:*865
  trinitrotoluene, *1:*18

Carotenoids, *1:*109-113

Carothers, Wallace, *2:*519

Carson, Rachel, *1:*284

Cartier, Jacques, *1:*95

Cavendish, Henry, *2:*494

Caventou, Joseph Bienaimé, *1:*137, 219

Celluloid, *1:*202-203

Cellulose, *1:195-199,* 196 (ill.)

Cellulose nitrate, *1:201-205,* 202 (ill.)

Cellulose xanthate, *1:207-210*

Cement, *1:*145, 162-163, 167-168

Chain, Ernst, *2:*536

Chalk, *1:*143

Chemical intermediaries, *1:*119, 121-122, 131

Chemical manufacturing, chemicals used in
  acetylene, *1:*28
  benzene, *1:*101
  carbon monoxide, *1:*185
  cumene, *1:*255-256
  ethylene, *2:*309
  ethylene oxide, *2:*317-318
  hydrogen chloride, *2:*359
  methane, *2:*446
  methyl alcohol, *2:*451
  methyl mercaptan, *2:*456
  propylene, *3:*671
  sodium chloride, *3:*737
  sulfur dioxide, *3:*820
  toluene, *3:*855

Chemical warfare, *1:*5-7

Chemiluminescence, *2:*407

Chevreul, Eugène, *1:*223; *2:*349

Chlorine, *2:*358; *3:*795, *3:*786
Chlorofluorocarbons (CFCs), *1:*190-191, 277-281
Chloroform, *1:***211-215**, 212 (ill.)
Chlorophyll, *1:***217-221**, 218 (ill.)
Chocolate, *1:*138; *3:*843-846
Cholesterol, *1:***223-227**, 224 (ill.)
Church, Austin, *3:*724
Cinnabar, *2:*439
Cinnamaldehyde, *1:***229-232**, 240 (ill.)
*Cinnamomum camphora,* *1:*171, 173
*Cinnamomum zeylanicum,* *1:*229
Citric acid, *1:***233-237**, 234 (ill.)
Cleaning products, chemicals in
    ammonium hydroxide, *1:*70
    denatonium benzoate, *1:*274
    oxalic acid, *2:*527
    sodium bicarbonate, *3:*726
    sodium hydroxide, *3:*755
    sodium hypochlorite, *3:*761
    sodium perborate, *3:*766-767
    sodium silicate, *3:*780
    tribasic sodium phosphate, *3:*771
    *See also* Soaps and detergents, chemicals in
Clinton Corn Processing Co., *2:*330-331
Clorox, *3:*761
Cloud seeding, *3:*702-704
Coal tar, *2:*473-475
Cocoa beans, *3:*843-846
Coffee, *1:*137-141
Cola drinks, *1:*137-141
Collagen, *1:***239-242**; *2:*338
Contact process, *3:*827
Coolants, *2:*315
Coover, Harry, *1:*259-260
Copper(I) oxide, *1:***243-246**, 244 (ill.)
Copper(II) oxide, *1:***247-250**, 248 (ill.)
Copper(II) sulfate, *1:***251-254**, 252 (ill.)
Cotton, *1:*195-198
Cox enzymes, *1:*12; *2:*479-480
Cracking process, *2:*309, 382; *3:*669-670
Cream of tartar, *3:*629-631
Crede, Carl, *3:*705
Crest toothpaste, *3:*800
Cross, Charles Frederick, *1:*196, 207
Cross-Bevan-Beadle method, *1:*208
Crude oil, *2:*548, 553-557
Cruikshank, William, *1:*184

Cumene, *1:*101, **255-258**, 256 (ill.)
Currie, James, *1:*235
Cyanamide process, *1:*58
Cyanoacrylate, *1:***259-263**, 260 (ill.)
Cyanocobalamin, *1:***265-269**, 266 (ill.)
Cyclamates, *3:*741-744
Cyclohexane, *1:*101

# D

Daguerre, Louis Jacques Mandé, *3:*702
Darby, William J., *2:*322
Davy, Edmund, *1:*27
Davy, Sir Humphry, *2:*358, 513, 515
Day, Harry G., *3:*800
DDT, *1:*283-287
de la Salle, Poulletier, *1:*223
de Lassone, Joseph Marie François, *1:*184
Dead-burning, *2:*419-420
Death penalty, *3:*641
Decaffeination, *1:*139
DEET, *2:*469-471
Deicers, *1:*25; *3:*721
Deiman, J.R., *2:*307
Denatonium benzoate, *1:***271-275**, 272 (ill.)
Dentistry, chemicals used in
    cyanoacrylate, *1:*261
    dibasic calcium phosphate, *1:*157
    nitrous oxide, *2:*514-515
    sodium fluoride, *3:*748-749
    stannous fluoride, *3:*799-802
Deodorizers, room, *1:*90
Diabetes, *2:*346
Diapers, disposable, *3:*773-776
Diazonium compounds, production of, *1:*91
Dibasic calcium phosphate, *1:*155-159
Dibasic sodium phosphate, *3:*769-772
Dichlorodifluoromethane, *1:***277-281**, 278 (ill.)
Dichlorodiphenyltrichloroethane (DDT),
    *1:***283-287**, 284 (ill.)
Diesel fuel, *2:*555
Dimethyl ketone, *1:***289-291**, 290 (ill.)
Dow, Herbert Henry, *2:*412
Dow Chemical Co., *2:*584; *3:*598
Dow process, *2:*412
Drain cleaners, *3:*755

Dry cell batteries, *1:*65
Drying agents, *3:*698
Dumas, Jean Baptiste André, *1:*211, 229, 289
DuPont Chemical Corp., *1:*277-278; *2:*519; *3:*603-604, 742
Dwight, John, *3:*724
Dyes and pigments
    2,4,6-trinitrotoluene in, *1:*18
    aluminum potassium sulfate, *1:*55
    copper(I) oxide, *1:*244
    copper(II) oxide, *1:*247-248
    iron(II) oxide, *2:*367
    iron(III) oxide, *2:*373
    mercury(II) oxide, *2:*441
    *See also* Paint, chemicals in
Dynamite, *2:*508

Eastman Kodak, *1:*259-260
Eggs, preservation of, *3:*781
Ehlers-Danlos syndrome, *1:*240
Eijkman, Christiaan, *3:*849
Elvehjem, Conrad Arnold, *2:*484
Engel-Precht process, *3:*634-635
Environmental concerns
    acid rain, *1:*153, 149
    chlorofluorocarbons (CFCs), *1:*190-191, 277-281
    dichlorodiphenyltrichloroethane (DDT), *1:*283-287
    methyl-t-butyl ether, *2:*461
    nitric oxide, *2:*497-499
    nitrogen dioxide, *2:*504-505
    ozone layer depletion, *1:*190-191, 213-214, 279
    petroleum, *2:*556
    phosphates, *2:*568
    pollution control, *1:*152-153
    polystyrene, *3:*600
    polyvinyl chloride, *3:*618-619
    sulfur dioxide, *3:*822
    triclocarban, *3:*862
    triclosan, *3:*865
Epsom salts, *2:*429-433
Erlenmeyer, Emil, *1:*229; *2:*473

Esters, *1:*259-263
Ethane, *1:*120-121
Ethyl acetate, *1:***293-295**, 294 (ill.)
Ethyl alcohol, *2:***297-301**, 298 (ill.)
Ethylbenzene, *1:*101; *2:***303-306**, 304 (ill.)
Ethylene, *1:*2; *2:***307-311**, 308 (ill.), 581-582; *3:*666
Ethylene glycol, *2:***313-316**, 314 (ill.), 318
Ethylene oxide, *2:***317-320**, 318 (ill.)
Eutrophication, *2:*568
Evans, Herbert McLean, *1:*37-38
Exhaust gases, treatment of, *1:*148
Explosives
    acetylene, *1:*29
    ammonium nitrate, *1:*74-75
    cellulose nitrate, *1:*204
    nitric acid, *1:*60
    nitroglycerin, *2:*507-510
    perchlorates, *2:*542-543
    potassium nitrate, *3:*656
    styrene, *3:*805
    TNT, *1:*15-18
    toluene, *3:*855-856

Fabrics
    bleaching, *3:*760
    cotton, *1:*195-198
    dyeing of, *1:*55; *3:*720
    flax, *1:*195-198
    nylon, *2:*519-523
    polypropylene, *2:*589
    polyurethane fibers, *3:*612
    rayon, *1:*207-210
    stain and water resistance, *3:*605-606
Fahlberg, Constantine, *3:*689-690
Faraday, Michael, *1:*99
Farben, I.G., *3:*598
Fats, artificial, *3:*813-816
Fawcett, Eric, *2:*580
FDA (Food and Drug Administration, U.S.), *1:*260-261; *2:*404; *2:*404; *3:*815
Fermentation, *1:*294; *2:*298-301
Fertilizer, chemicals in
    ammonia, *1:*59-60

ammonium nitrate, *1:*74; *2:*495
ammonium sulfate, *1:*77-78
monocalcium phosphate, *1:*157
phosphoric acid, *2:*567
potassium chloride, *3:*641
potassium sulfate, *3:*660
sulfuric acid, *3:*827
tricalcium phosphate, *1:*158
urea, *3:*870
Film, photographic, *1:*203-204
Fingerprints, collection of, *1:*262
Fire extinguishers, *1:*180; *3:*622
Firestone, *2:*384
Fireworks, *1:*75; *2:*542-543; *3:*656
Fischer, Emil, *1:*138; *2:*345
Fischer, Hans, *1:*219
Fischer-Tropsch reactions, *1:*185
Fittig, Rudolf, *3:*855
Flammable Fabrics Act of 1953, *1:*209
Flavorings
    amyl acetate, *1:*85-86
    cinnamaldehyde, *1:*231
    ethyl acetate, *1:*293-295
    isoamyl acetate, *2:*377-380
    salt and salt substitutes, *2:*465-468; *3:*641,
        653, 735-739
    sugars, *2:*329-332, 343-347; *3:*807-811
    sweeteners, artificial, *2:*349-352, 401-405;
        *3:*689-693, 741-744
    vanillin, *3:*873-876
Flax, *1:*195-198
Fleming, Alexander, *1:*82; *2:*535
Florey, Howard, *2:*536
Flourens, Marie Jean-Pierre, *1:*211
Fluoridating agents, *3:*644
Fluoridation, water, *1:*43
Fluorides, dental, *3:*747-751, 799-802
Foams, *3:*611-612
Folate, *2:*321-324
Folic acid, *2:***321-324**, 322 (ill.)
Folkers, Karl, *1:*266-267; *3:*674
Food additives
    acidification agents, *1:*158; *3:*641, 771
    buffering agents, *3:*721
    colorings, *1:*112
    cream of tartar, *3:*630-631
    folic acid, *2:*321-324

isoamyl acetate, *2:*377-380
jelling agents, *2:*531-533
lactic acid, *2:*393
lactose, *2:*397-399
leavening agents, *3:*723, 726
nutritional supplements, *1:*158
potassium bicarbonate, *3:*621-622
potassium bisulfate, *3:*625-627
preservatives, *1:*107, 117, 133-135, 233-236;
    *3:*786-787
stimulants, *1:*117, 137-141
*See also* Flavorings; Vitamins
Food and Drug Administration, U.S. (FDA),
    *1:*260-261; *2:*404; *3:*815
Food packaging, *3:*775
Food production, *3:*649
Forensic science, *2:*409
Formaldehyde, *2:***325-328**, 326 (ill.)
Fox, Daniel W., *2:*577
Free radicals, *1:*38
Freon, *1:*214, 277-281
Friedel, Charles, *2:*349
Frohlich, Theodore, *1:*95
Fructose, *2:***329-332**, 330 (ill.)
Fruits, *2:*531-532
Fuels
    additives, *2:*450, 459-462, 515-516
    butane, *1:*121
    ethyl alcohol, *2:*299
    gasoline, *2:*555
    industrial, *1:*185
    methane, *2:*445
    oil, *1:*75; *2:*555
    perchlorates, *2:*542-543
    propane, *3:*663-667
Fumigants, *1:*252
Fungicides, *1:*117, 244
Funk, Casimir, *2:*483
Fusion, *2:*420-421

# G

Gamma-1,2,3,4,5,6-hexachlorocyclohexane,
    *2:***333-336**, 334 (ill.)
Gasoline, *2:*555
Gatorade, *3:*744

Gay-Lussac, Louis-Joseph, *1:*116
G.D. Searle Co., *2:*401-402, *2:*404
Geber. *See* Jabir ibn Hayyan (Geber)
Gelatin, *2:***337-341**
Gemstones, *1:*50
Gerhardt, Charles Frederic, *1:*19, 32; *2:*559
Gibson, Reginald, *2:*580
Glacial acetic acid, *1:*23-26
Glass manufacturing, chemicals used in
    boric acid, *1:*117
    potassium carbonate, *3:*636
    potassium fluoride, *3:*645
    silicon dioxide, *3:*698
    silver oxide, *3:*711-712
    sodium carbonate, *3:*731-732
    sodium tetraborate, *3:*791
Glass substitutes, *2:*584
Glauber, Johann, *1:*73, 75; *2:*358, 493, 559; *3:*659
Glazes, *1:*244; *3:*716
Glow sticks, *2:*410
Glucose, *2:***343-347**, 344 (ill.)
Glycerol, *2:***349-352**, 350 (ill.)
Goldeberger, Joseph, *2:*484
Gout, *2:*394-395
Green chemistry, *1:*11
Grignard, Victor, *2:*592
Grijins, Gerrit, *3:*849
Gum benzoin, *1:*105
Guncotton, *1:*201-205
Gunpowder, *3:*656-657
Guthrie, Frederick, *1:*5
Guthrie, Samuel, *1:*211
Gypsum, *1:*165-168

Haber, Fritz, *1:*58-59
Haber-Bosch process, *1:*58-59, 178
Hall, Charles Martin, *1:*50-51
Hallwachs, Wilhelm, *1:*245
Hard-burning, *2:*420-421
Harris, S.A., *3:*674
Haworth, Sir Walter Norman, *1:*95
HDPE (high density polyethylene), *2:*579, *2:*582
Heart attack, prevention and treatment,
    *1:*33-34; *2:*500, 510

Helmont, Jan Baptista van, *1:*177; *2:*497;
    *3:*825-826
Hematite, *2:*371-373
Hexachlorophene, *3:*860
Hexane, *2:***353-356**, 354 (ill.)
High-density lipoproteins (HDL), *1:*226
High-fructose corn syrup, *2:*330-331
Hodgkin, Dorothy, *1:*267
Hoffman, Felix, *1:*33
Hofmann, August Wilhelm von, *2:*325; *3:*853
Hogan, John, *2:*580, 582, 588
Holberg, Wilhelm, *1:*116
Holst, Alex, *1:*95
Hormones, plant, *2:*307-308
Hot springs, *1:*115-118; *2:*430-431
Hula hoops, *2:*581
Human body
    cholesterol, *1:*225-227
    collagen, *1:*239-241
    fetal development, *2:*321-323
    hormones, *3:*837-840
    lactic adid, *2:*392-393
    nicotine, effects of, *2:*489-490
    nitric oxide in, *2:*499-500
    nitroglycerin, use of, *2:*510
    salt and, *3:*738-739
    sucrose, effects of, *3:*811
    urea in, *3:*867-870
    water in, *3:*882
    *See also* Medicine and medical products;
        Vitamins
Hyatt, John Wesley, *1:*202-203
Hydrocarbons, *2:*553-554
Hydrochloric acid, *2:*357-361
Hydrochlorofluorobarbons (HCFCs), *1:*212-214
Hydrogen chloride, *2:***357-361**, 358 (ill.)
Hydrogen peroxide, *2:***363-366**, 364 (ill.); *3:*765
Hydroxyapatite, *1:*157

Ideda, Kikunae, *2:*465
Imperial Chemicals Industries (ICI), *2:*580
Industrial accidents, *1:*75
Insect repellants, *2:*469-471
Insecticides, *1:*283-287; *2:*335, 488-489

Iron(II) oxide, *2:*367-369, 368 (ill.)
Iron(III) oxide, *2:*371-375, 372 (ill.)
Isler, Otto, *3:*679
Isoamyl acetate, *2:*377-380, 378 (ill.)
Isoprene, *2:*381-385, 382 (ill.)
Isopropyl alcohol, *2:*387-389, 388 (ill.)

Jabir ibn Hayyan (Geber), *1:*23, 234-235
Jams and jellies, *2:*532-533
JELL-O, *2:*337-338
Joiner, Fred, *1:*259-260

Kaminsky, Walter, *2:*581-582
Karrer, Paul, *1:*38, 110; *3:*678, 683
Kekulé, Friedrich August, *1:*99-100, 102; *2:*326
Kerosene, *2:*555-556
Kidd, John, *2:*473
Kidney stones, *1:*157
King, Charles Glen, *1:*95
Kipping, Frederic Stanley, *2:*592
Kirchhof, Gottlieb Sigismund Constantine, *2:*343
Klate, Friedrich Heinrich August, *3:*616
Knox Gelatin, *2:*337-338
Krazy Glue, *1:*259-263
Krebs, Sir Hans Adolf, *1:*234
Krumbhaar, E.B., *1:*7
Krumbhaar, H.D., *1:*7
Kuhn, Richard, *3:*674, 679, 683

L-aspartyl-L-phenylalanine methyl ester, *2:*401-405, 402 (ill.)
Lactic acid, *2:*391-395, 392 (ill.)
Lactose, *2:*397-400, 398 (ill.)
Laughing gas, *2:*513-517
Lauwerenurgh, A., *2:*307
LDPE (low density polyethylene), *2:*579, 582

Lead chamber process, *3:*826
Leavening agents, *3:*723, 726
Lebedev, Sergei, *1:*1-2
Leblanc, Nicolas, *2:*358; *3:*730-731
Leroux, Henri, *1:*32
Lethal injections, *3:*641
Levenstein process, *1:*6
Libavius, Andreas, *1:*79
Liebig, Justus von, *1:*289
Light-burning, *2:*420-421
Lignin, *3:*874-876
Lime, *1:*151-155
Limestone, *1:*144
Lind, James, *1:*95
Liniments, *1:*173
Liquid Bandage, *1:*261
Liquid paraffin, *2:*548
Liquid petroleum gas (LPG), *1:*121
LoSalt, *3:*641
Low-density lipoproteins (LDL), *1:*226
Lucite, *2:*584
Luminol, *2:*407-410, 408 (ill.)
Lye, *3:*753-757

Macfarlan Smith Corp., *1:*272
Magnesium chloride, *2:*411-414, 412 (ill.)
Magnesium hydroxide, *2:*415-417, 416 (ill.)
Magnesium metal, production of, *2:*412
Magnesium oxide, *2:*419-422, 420 (ill.)
Magnesium silicate hydroxide, *2:*423-427, 424 (ill.)
Magnesium sulfate, *2:*429-433, 430 (ill.)
Malaria, *1:*283-286
Marggraf, Andreas Sigismund, *2:*343
Marlex, *2:*588
Mattson, Fred, *3:*813
Maumee Chemical Co., *3:*691
Maynard, J. P., *1:*204
McKay, Frederick S., *3:*801
Medicine and medical products
    analgesics, *1:*9-13, 19-22, 31-34, 173
    antacids, *1:*45-46, 144; *2:*416-417; *3:*621-622, 726
    antibiotics, *1:*81-84; *2:*535-538

antiseptics, *1:*117, 173, 261; *2:*365; *3:*652, 859-865

aspirin, *1:*31-34

astringents, *3:*834

caffeine, *1:*137-141

cough and sinus treatments, *2:*437, 562

Epsom salts, *2:*431

hormones and hormone treatments, *2:*543; *3:*837-840

laxatives, *2:*550

liniments, *1:*173

nitroglycerin, *2:*500, 510

NSAIDs, *2:*477-480

polyvinyl chloride in, *3:*618

silver nitrate, *3:*707-708

skin treatments, *2:*437-438, 548-549, 562

SSKI, *3:*652

theobromine, *3:*845-846

vasodilators, *1:*90

wound sealants, *1:*260-261

*See also* Dentistry, chemicals used in

Melsens, Louise, *2:*487

Ménard, Louis-Phillippe, *1:*204

Menthol, *2:***435-438**, 436 (ill.)

Mercury metal, *2:*441

Mercury(II) sulfide, *2:***439-442**, 440 (ill.)

Metals, refining, *1:*186

Methane, *1:*120-121; *2:***443-447**, 444 (ill.)

Methanol, *1:*272; *2:*449-453

Methyl alcohol, *2:***449-453**, 450 (ill.)

Methyl mercaptan, *2:***455-458**, 456 (ill.)

Methyl-t-butyl ether, *2:*450, **459-463**, 460 (ill.)

Methylxanthines, *1:*138

MFP (Sodium monofluorophosphate), *3:*801

Midgley, Thomas, *1:*278, 280

Military dynamite, *1:*17

Milk, *2:*397-399

Milk of Magnesia, *2:*415-417

Miller, A. K., *1:*1

Mineral oil, *2:*548

Minerals (nutritional), *1:*143-146, 155-159

Minot, George, *1:*266

Mitchell, Henry K., *2:*322

Mitscherlich, Eilhardt, *1:*99

Mohammad ibn Zakariya al-Razi, *3:*825

Mohs, Frederick, *1:*51

Molina, Mario, *1:*190, 278

Monobasic calcium phosphate, *1:*155-159

Monobasic sodium phosphate, *3:*769-772

Monosodium glutamate (MSG), *2:***465-468**, 466 (ill.)

Monsanto Corp., *1:*24

Montecatini, *2:*588

Montreal Protocol on Substances that Deplete the Ozone Layer, *1:*191, 214, 279

Morse, Harmon Northrop, *1:*19

Mortar, *1:*148

Mothballs, *2:*475

Motrin, *1:*9-10

MTBE (methyl-tert-butyl ether), *2:*450, 459-463

Muhler, Joseph C., *3:*799-800

Müller, Paul Hermann, *1:*283

Mummification, *3:*730

Murphy, William, *1:*266

Murray, Sir James, *2:*415

Muscles, *2:*392-393

Muspratt, James, *3:*853

Mustard gas, *1:*5-8

*n*-butyl acetate, *1:*125-126

*n*-butyl mercaptan, *1:*129-132

Nail polish remover, *1:*290

Napalm, *2:*475

Naphthalene, *2:***473-476**, 474 (ill.)

Naproxen, *2:***477-481**, 478 (ill.)

Nascent oxygen, *2:*365

Natta, Giulio, *2:*384, 588-589

Natural gas, *1:*119-120; *2:*443-446; *3:*663-665

Neljubow, Dmitri N., *2:*308

Neutralizing agents, *1:*148

Niacin, *2:***483-486**, 484 (ill.)

Nicot, Jean, *2:*487

Nicotine, *2:***487-491**, 488 (ill.)

Nitrating agents, *2:*505

Nitric acid, *1:*60, 73-74; *2:***493-496**, 494 (ill.)

Nitric oxide, *2:***497-501**, 498 (ill.), 504

Nitro, *2:*515-516

Nitrogen, *1:*74, 78

Nitrogen dioxide, *2:***503-506**, 504 (ill.)

Nitroglycerin, *2:*500, **507-511**, 508 (ill.)

Nitrous oxide, *2:***513-517**, 514 (ill.)

N,N-diethyl-3-methylbenzamide (DEET), *2:*469-472, 470 (ill.)
Nobel, Alfred, *2:*508-509
NSAIDs (nonsteroidal anti-inflammatory drugs), *1:*11-12, 19-22; *2:*477-481
Nuisance dust, *1:*50-51
Nuprin, *1:*11
NutraSweet, *2:*401-405
Nylon 6 and nylon 66, *2:*519-523, 520 (ill.)

Obesity, *3:*811
Odors and odorants, *1:*130-131, 173; *2:*377-380, 455-456
Oil of vitriol, *3:*825-829
Oklahoma City bombing, *1:*75
Olestra, *3:*813-816
1,3-Butadiene, *1:*1-4, 2 (ill.)
Ostwald, Wilhelm, *1:*60; *2:*494
Oxalic acid, *2:*525-529, 526 (ill.)
Oxidizing agents, *2:*505
Ozone layer, *1:*190-191, 279

Paint, chemicals in, *1:*145, 244; *3:*886
    *See also* Dyes and pigments
Paint thinners, *1:*256
Paper manufacturing, chemicals used in
    aluminum potassium sulfate, *1:*55
    calcium carbonate, *1:*145
    cellulose, *1:*198
    hydrogen peroxide, *2:*365
    sodium hydroxide, *3:*755
    sodium silicate, *3:*781
    sodium sulfite, *3:*785-786
    sodium thiosulfate, *3:*795
Parkes, Alexander, *1:*202
Pauling, Linus, *1:*96
Payen, Anselme, *1:*196
Pearl ash, *3:*633-637
Pechmann, Hans von, *2:*580
Pectin, *2:*531-534
Péligot, Eugène Melchior, *1:*229

Pellagra, *2:*483-485
Pelletier, Pierre Joseph, *1:*137-138, 219; *3:*853
Pelouze, Théophile-Jules, *2:*349
Penicillin, *1:*81-83; *2:*535-539, 536 (ill.)
Pennies, *1:*249
Pentolite, *1:*17
Peppermint, *2:*435-436
Perchlorates, *2:*541-545, 542 (ill.)
Periclase, *2:*419
Pernicious anemia, *1:*265-268
Perrin, M.W., *2:*580
PET (polyethylene terephthalate), *2:*315
Petrolatum, *2:*547-551
Petroleum, *2:*353-354, 473-475, 553-557; *3:*663-665, 671
Petroleum jelly, *2:*547-551
PFOA (perfluorooctanoic acid), *3:*606-607
Phenol, *2:*559-563, 560 (ill.)
Phenylketonuria, *2:*404
Phillips, Charles Henry, *2:*415
Phillips, Peregrine, *3:*827
Phillips Petroleum, *2:*580, 588
Phosgene, *1:*191
Phosphates, *2:*568
Phosphoric acid, *2:*565-569, 566 (ill.); *3:*827
Photoelectric cells, *1:*244-245
Photography, *3:*702, 706-707, 796
Photosynthesis, *1:*217-221; *2:*345
Pictet, A., *2:*487
Pigments. *See* Dyes and pigments
Piria, Raffaele, *1:*32
Plants, *1:*195-199, 217-221; *2:*307-308, 310; *3:*831, 833
    *See also* Photosynthesis
Plaster of Paris, *1:*165-168
Plastic surgery, *1:*240
Plastics manufacturing, chemicals used in, *1:*107
    benzoic acid, *1:*107
    ethylene, *2:*309
    ethylene glycol, *2:*325-327
    formaldehyde, *2:*325-327
    nylon, *2:*521
    1,3-butadiene, *1:*3
    petroleum, *2:*556
    poly(styrene-butadiene-styrene), *2:*572-573
    sodium hydroxide, *3:*755

styrene, *3:*804-805

Plexiglas, *2:*584, *2:*585

Plunkett, Roy J., *3:*604

PMMA (Polymethylmethacrylate), *2:*583-586

Poisoning, treatment of, *1:*90

Pollution. *See* Environmental concerns

Polycarbonates, *2:***575-578**, 576 (ill.)

Polyethylene, *2:***579-582**, 580 (ill.)

Polymethylmethacrylate (PMMA), *2:***583-586**, 584 (ill.)

Polypropylene, *2:***587-590**, 588 (ill.); *3:*669, 671

Polysiloxane, *2:***591-596**, 592 (ill.)

Polystyrene, *3:***597-601**, 598 (ill.), 804

Poly(styrene-butadiene-styrene), *2:***571-574**, 572 (ill.)

Polytetrafluoroethylene, *3:***603-607**, 604 (ill.)

Polyurethane, *3:***609-613**, 610 (ill.)

Polyvinyl acetates, *1:*107

Polyvinyl chloride, *3:***615-619**, 616 (ill.)

Poppers, *1:*91

Portland cement, *1:*162-163, 167-168

Potash, *3:*633-637

Potash, caustic, *3:*647-650

Potassium benzoate, *1:*107

Potassium bicarbonate, *3:***621-623**, 622 (ill.)

Potassium bisulfate, *3:***625-627**, 626 (ill.)

Potassium bitartrate, *3:***629-631**, 630 (ill.)

Potassium carbonate, *3:***633-637**, 634 (ill.)

Potassium chloride, *3:***639-642**, 640 (ill.)

Potassium compounds, production of, *3:*648

Potassium fluoride, *3:***643-645**, 644 (ill.)

Potassium hydroxide, *3:***647-650**, 648 (ill.)

Potassium iodide, *3:***651-654**, 652 (ill.)

Potassium nitrate, *3:***655-658**, 656 (ill.)

Potassium perchlorate, *2:*541-543

Potassium sulfate, *3:***659-662**, 660 (ill.)

Preservatives, food
    benzoic acid, role in, *1:*107
    BHA and BHT, *1:*134-135
    boric acid, *1:*117
    citric acid, *1:*233-236
    sodium sulfite, *3:*786-787

Priestley, Joseph, *1:*57, 178, 184; *2:*358, 513; *3:*821

Procter & Gamble, *3:*813-815

Propane, *1:*120-121; *3:***663-667**, 664 (ill.)

Propellants, *1:*122

Propylene, *3:*666, **669-672**, 670 (ill.)

Provitamins, *1:*110

PVAs, *1:*107

PVC (polyvinyl chloride), *3:*615-619

Pyrex glass, *3:*791

Pyridoxine, *3:***673-676**, 674 (ill.)

Quicklime, *1:*153

Radiation exposure, *3:*652-653

Raschig, Friedrich, *2:*561

Rayon, *1:*207-210

Recreational drugs
    amyl nitrite, *1:*89-82
    butane, *1:*121
    hexane, *2:*355
    nicotine, *2:*489-490
    nitrous oxide, *2:*514, *2:*516

Red mercury(II) sulfide, *2:*439-442

Refrigerants, *1:*180, 277-281

Regnault, Henri Victor, *1:*189

Reichstein, Tadeusz, *1:*95-96

Reimer-Tiemann reaction, *3:*875

Remsen, Ira, *3:*689-690

Repe, Walter, *1:*28

Retinol, *3:***677-681**, 678 (ill.)

Riboflavin, *3:***683-687**, 684 (ill.)

Ritthausen, Karl Heinrich, *2:*465

Rochow, E.G., *2:*593

Roebuck, John, *3:*826

Röhm, Otto, *2:*583

Röhm and Haas, *2:*583, *2:*585

Rotschy, A., *2:*487

Rouelle, Hilaire Marin, *3:*867

Rowland, F. Sherwood, *1:*190, 278

Rubber, synthetic
    isoprene, *2:*383-384
    1,3-butadiene, *1:*1-4
    Poly(styrene-butadiene-styrene), *2:*571-574
    polystyrene used in, *3:*598

polyurethane, *3:*609-613

Rufen, *1:*9-10

Rum, *3:*810

Runge, Friedlieb Ferdinand, *2:*559

Rust, *2:*371

## S

Saccharin, *3:***689-693**, 690 (ill.)

Sachs, Julius von, *1:*219

Sal ammoniac, *1:*63-64

Sal soda, *3:*729-733

Salt and salt substitutes, *2:*465-468; *3:*641, 653, 735-739

Saltpeter, *3:*655-658

Saponification, *2:*349-350

SBS rubber, *2:*571-574

Schaefer, Vincent, *3:*702-703

Scheele, Karl Wilhelm, *1:*235; *2:*349, 392, 525; *3:*629, 760

Schlatter, James M., *2:*401-402

Schnell, Hermann, *2:*576

Schönbein, Christian Friedrich, *1:*201

Scrubbers, *1:*153

Scurvy, *1:*93-95, 240

Sea water, *3:*639-640, 736

*sec*-butyl acetate, *1:*125-127

*sec*-butyl mercaptan, *1:*129-132

Semiconductors, *1:*247-250

Semon, Waldo Lonsbury, *3:*616-617

Silica gel, *3:*696-697

Silicon dioxide, *3:***695-700**, 696 (ill.)

Silicones, *2:*591-596

Silver iodide, *3:***701-704**, 702 (ill.)

Silver nitrate, *3:***705-709**, 706 (ill.)

Silver oxide, *3:***711-713**, 712 (ill.)

Silver(I) sulfide, *3:***715-717**, 716 (ill.)

Simon, Eduard, *3:*597

Simpson, Sir James Young, *1:*211

Sinn, Hansjörg, *2:*581, 582

Skin treatments

    petroleum jelly, *2:*548-549

    phenol, *2:*562

    sunscreens, *3:*886

    talc, *2:*425

    tretinoin, *3:*680

Skunk spray, *1:*130-131

Smokeless gunpowder, *1:*204

Soaps and detergents, chemicals in

    phosphates, *2:*568

    potassium hydroxide, *3:*648

    sodium hydroxide, *3:*756

    sodium tetraborate, *3:*791-792

    triclocarban, *3:*861

    triclosan, *3:*864

    *See also* Cleaning products, chemicals in

Soapstone, *2:*423-427

Sobrero, Ascanio, *2:*507

Soda ash, *3:*729-733

Sodium acetate, *3:***719-722**, 720 (ill.)

Sodium benzoate, *1:*107

Sodium bicarbonate, *3:***723-727**, 724 (ill.)

Sodium carbonate, *3:***729-733**, 730 (ill.)

Sodium chloride, *3:***735-739**, 736 (ill.)

Sodium cyclamate, *3:***741-745**, 742 (ill.)

Sodium fluoride, *3:***747-751**, 748 (ill.)

Sodium hydroxide, *3:*648, **753-757**, 754 (ill.)

Sodium hypochlorite, *3:***759-763**, 760 (ill.)

Sodium perborate, *3:***765-768**, 766 (ill.)

Sodium percarbonate, *3:*767

Sodium perchlorate, *2:*541-543

Sodium phosphate, *3:***769-772**, 770 (ill.)

Sodium polyacrylate, *3:***773-777**, 774 (ill.)

Sodium silicate, *3:***779-783**, 780 (ill.)

Sodium sulfite, *3:***785-787**, 786 (ill.)

Sodium tetraborate, *3:***789-792**, 790 (ill.)

Sodium thiosulfate, *3:***795-798**, 796 (ill.)

Soil additives

    calcium hydroxide, *1:*144, 148

    calcium sulfate, *1:*167

    copper(II) sulfate, *1:*252

    gamma-1,2,3,4,5,6-hexachlorocyclohexane, *2:*335

    potash, *3:*635

    *See also* Fertilizer, chemicals in

Solvay, Ernest, *1:*64; *3:*725, 731

Solvents

    butyl acetate, *1:*126

    butyl mercaptan, *1:*131

    dimethyl ketone, *1:*290

    ethyl acetate, *1:*293-294

    hexane, *2:*353-354

    isopropyl alcohol, *2:*388

Soubeiran, Eugene, *1:*211
Specht, Walter, *2:*407
Stahl, Georg Ernst, *1:*23
Stalagmites and stalactites, *1:*143, 145
Standard Oil Co., *2:*387
Stannous fluoride, *3:***799-802**, 800 (ill.)
Stannous hexafluorozirconate, *3:*801
Steam cracking, *1:*2
Steel production, *1:*152
Stockings, nylon, *2:*522
Stroke, protection against, *1:*33-34
Styrene, *2:*303-304; *3:***803-806**, 804 (ill.)
Styrofoam, *3:*599
Sucaryl, *3:*743
Sucrose, *2:*329, *2:*331; *3:***807-811**, 808 (ill.)
Sucrose polyester, *3:***813-817**, 814 (ill.)
Sugars
    fructose, *2:*329-332
    glucose, *2:*343-347
    high-fructose corn syrup, *2:*330-331
    sucrose, *2:*329, 331; *3:*807-811
Sulfur dioxide, *3:***819-823**, 820 (ill.)
Sulfuric acid, *3:***825-829**, 826 (ill.)
Sunscreens, *3:*886
Super Glue, *1:*259-263, 261-262
Supercritical carbon dioxide, *1:*139, 179
Sveda, Michael, *3:*741
Swallow, J.C., *2:*580
Sweeteners, artificial
    glycerol, *2:*349-352
    L-aspartyl-L-phenylalanine methyl ester, *2:*401-405
    saccharin, *3:*689-693
    sodium cyclamate, *3:*741-744
    sucrose, *3:*807-811
Szent-Györgi, Albert, *1:*95; *3:*673

Tachenius, Otto, *3:*659
Takaki, Kanehiro, *3:*849
Talbot, William Henry Fox, *3:*706
Talc, *2:*423-427
Tannic acid, *3:***831-835**, 832 (ill.)
Tanning (hides), *3:*831-834
Tarnish, *3:*715, 717

Tastes, bitter, *1:*271-274
Tea, *1:*137-141
Teflon, *3:*603-607
Terpenes, *2:*381-385
*tert*-butyl acetate, *1:*125-127
*tert*-butyl mercaptan, *1:*129-132
Testosterone, *3:***837-841**, 838 (ill.)
T&H Smith, *1:*271
Thénard, Louis Jacques, *1:*116; *2:*363
Theobromine, *1:*138-139; *3:***843-846**, 844 (ill.)
Thiamine, *3:***847-851**, 848 (ill.)
Thiele, Johannes, *1:*101
Thyroid gland, *3:*652-653
Tilden, Sir William Augustus, *2:*384
TNT, *1:*15-18; *3:*855-856
Tobacco, *2:*487-491
Tocopherols, *1:*37-40
Tofu, *2:*413
Tollens, B.C.G., *3:*855
Toluene, *1:*105-107; *3:***853-857**, 854 (ill.)
Tooth decay, *3:*748-749, 799-802, 811
Torches, *1:*27-29
Torpex, *1:*17
Tournefort, Joseph, *1:*64
Tribasic calcium phosphate, *1:*155-159
Tribasic sodium phosphate, *3:*769-772
Triclocarban, *3:***859-862**, 860 (ill.)
Triclosan, *3:***863-866**, 864 (ill.)
Troostwyk, A. Paets van, *2:*307
Tschunkur, Eduard, *2:*572
TSP, *3:*771
Tsvett, Mikhail, *1:*219
Twenty-Mule-Team Borax, *3:*791-792
2-(4-Isobutylphenyl)-propionic acid, *1:***9-13**, 10 (ill.)
2,4,6-Trinitrotoluene, *1:***15-18**, 16 (ill.)
2,2-Dichorodiethyl sulfide, *1:***5-8**, 6 (ill.)
Tylenol, *1:*21

Umetaro, Suzuki, *3:*847
Upjohn Co., *1:*10-11
Urea, *3:***867-871**, 868 (ill.)

Vaccines, *1:*47

Vanillin, *3:***873-877**, 874 (ill.)

Vaseline, *2:*547-549

Vasodilators, *1:*89-90

Vermillion, *2:*440

Vicks VapoRub, *1:*173; *2:*437-438

Vinegar, *1:*23-26

Viscose Corp. of America, *1:*208

Vision, *3:*679

Vitamins
    alpha-tocopherol (E), *1:*37-40
    ascorbic acid (C), *1:*93-97
    beta-carotene, *1:*109-113; *3:*678, *3:*680
    cyanocobalamin ($B_{12}$), *1:*265-268
    folic acid ($B_9$), *2:*321-324
    niacin ($B_3$), *2:*483-486
    pyridoxine ($B_6$), *3:*673-676
    retinol (A), *3:*677-681
    riboflavin ($B_2$), *3:*683-687
    thiamine ($B_1$), *3:*822, 847-851
    *See also* Minerals (nutritional)

Volpenhein, Robert, *3:*813

Vonnegut, Bernard, *3:*703

Wackenroder, Heinrich Wilhelm
    Ferdinand, *1:*110

Waldie, David, *1:*211

Warning odors, *1:*87

Washing soda, *3:*729-733

Water, *3:***879-884**, 880 (ill.)

Water treatment
    aluminum potassium sulfate, *1:*55
    ammonium sulfate, *1:*78
    fluoride, *1:*43; *3:*748-749
    sodium sulfite in, *3:*786
    softeners, *3:*737

Wedgwood, Thomas, *3:*706

Wehmer, Carl, *1:*235

Wells, Horace, *2:*514

Whipple, George Hoyt, *1:*266

Whitehall Laboratories, *1:*11

Wiegleb, Johann Christian, *2:*525

Wieland, Heinrich Otto, *1:*224-225

Wilbrand, Joseph, *1:*15

Williams, Robert R., *3:*849-850

Willow bark, *1:*31-32

Wills, Lucy, *2:*321

Winhaus, Adolf, *1:*224-225

Wislicenus, Johannes, *2:*392

Wöhler, Friedrich, *1:*27; *2:*525; *3:*867

Wood alcohol, *2:*449-453

Wood preservatives, *1:*248, 252

Woodward, Robert Burns, *1:*219, 225, 267

Wounds, sealing of, *1:*260-261

Wulff process, *1:*28

Wurtz, Charles Adolphe, *2:*313, 317

Xylene, *3:*855

Zeidler, Othmar, *1:*283

Zeolites, *1:*257

Ziegler, Karl, *2:*384, 580, *2:*582, 588-589

Zinc oxide, *3:***885-888**, 886 (ill.)